MW00893515

ISBN-13: 979-8621145972

Cover design by: MoonQuill
Printed in the United States of America

THE WHEEL OF SAMSARA

Ashes of the Abyss

Liron

CONTENTS

PROLOGUE

Before a Beginning, There is an End

On a pleasant spring night, a cool breeze softly blew against a field of grass that grew by a small lake. The clear water rippled gently, distorting the reflection of the night sky as small waves were pushed ashore. The cloudless sky made it easy to see the glistening stars floating in the darkness above.

A man and woman laid on the grass, side-by-side, looking at the stars. The man, Alexei, held a wineskin in one hand and caressed the dew-covered grass with the other. His shoulder-length, golden hair was disheveled, but his piercing green eyes still drew attention. Although he saw himself as a carefree person, his tattered blue clothing spoke more of sloppiness. His friends would laugh in his face when he brought it up, but very few dared to use any word other than the former to describe him. Despite his handsome features, his cold expression made most avert their gazes.

Alexei never took his eyes off of the full moon that hung above his head. He raised the wineskin to his lips before realizing that it was empty. Annoyed that his fourth, and last wineskin was dry, he grumbled, clearly uncomfortable. Alexei often turned to drinking when he felt tense, but tonight he was drinking far more than usual. Throwing the empty wineskin to the side, he sighed and gently tapped the crystalline ring on his finger, seemingly lost in thought. After a short moment, he glanced over at the object next to him.

A slender sword, glistening with droplets of dew, was lodged in the grass beside Alexei and the woman. The iron blade was three fingers wide and polished to a high shine. The grip was wrapped with cheap, black leather, so worn out it was almost possible to make out the shape of the man's fingers. The hilt was just as simple, but its crescent moon design gave the sword an air of finesse. The only luxury the sword had was a blood-red gem embedded into the middle of the guard, adding to its elegance.

Despite being simple, no one could find a flaw in it. It was the pride of the blacksmith that forged it, but no matter how much care was put into its making, it would never stop being a common iron sword; unfit for the one who wielded it. Nevertheless, its wielder was someone that despised things like common sense. Anyone that dared to underestimate the sword in his hands paid dearly when facing it.

The woman, Lya, gently ran her finger across the flat side of the sword, causing a thick drop of water to slide down its blade. She wore a plain, white dress that settled just above her knees, revealing her long legs. She was thin, but not starved and regardless of the darkness, Lya's face seemed to glow. Her crystal-blue eyes avoided Alexei completely. She was clearly worried about something, but held back her words through pursed lips.

Lost in their own thoughts, they hadn't noticed that the breeze had stopped blowing and the waves had stopped crashing. There was nothing but an unnerving silence, almost as if nature was holding its breath—a calm before the storm.

"At this rate you might really get drunk."

His actions didn't escape the eyes of the woman by his side. Her sarcastic, yet melodious voice broke the silence. A normal person would be way past the point of being drunk after having four whole wineskins, but that wasn't the case for him.

"I wish I could. It's been so long that I've forgotten the last time I was inebriated," Alexei said, giving a wry smile. He knew she was joking, but that was a sensitive topic for him, especially in recent years.

"Isn't that a good thing?" Lya replied, trying to raise his spirits.

"Being able to enjoy alcohol without worries is nice sometimes, but not being able to get drunk when you want to isn't worth it," he answered, still gloomy.

"Your life must've been really awful as of late," she joked, but immediately regretted it.

Bitterly replying, he said, "It isn't as if you don't know about it."

She looked down apologetically.

"I'm just trying to ease the mood a bit."

"I know, it's just..." he tried to find the right words, but they evaded him. "It doesn't matter. I'm sorry."

They both fell silent for a moment. Lya was clearly unsatisfied with the conversation, but she knew how troubled he was.

"Are you sure about this? There's still time to turn back," her voice was more concerned than before.

"I won't turn back. This is what I believe is right. Even if others don't... I *am* giving them the chance to stop me," Alexei responded firmly.

"I don't like this. Not a single bit. I know you're not one to give in, but I really think that this time you should."

If she didn't change his mind, no one would.

"My decision won't change. All that's left is to see it through. I will change things, Lya." He turned his gaze away from the moon. "I've had

7

enough of being restrained by things I don't understand. I've had enough of being controlled by things I cannot see. I've had *enough* of walking a path that was set by things I cannot grasp!"

His hands emitted a pale glow as he lightly touched her, as if he were afraid that she would scatter with the wind. He raised her chin with care, looking into her eyes.

"Look, this is all for the best. Otherwise, I'd never do something like this, and I never would've found others that think like me."

Both of them knew that it was sophistry, but he didn't really care.

Lya's dissatisfaction was evident when she softly replied, "Arthur can certainly use the same argument as you, however, we both know what his opinion is regarding this."

Alexei's brow furrowed as dark lines creased his forehead—he was starting to lose his temper.

"Arthur can have his own opinion, I don't mind it. What I *do* mind is him painting us as criminals and deciding that we were his enemies," his voice grew louder and hoarser as he spoke. It was certainly a sensitive matter for him. "He betrayed us, Lya. He abandoned us."

"Alexei..."

She tried to stop his train of thought.

"Lya, we've known each other for years; decades; centuries even. We've travelled around the world and we've seen the same things. I've always wanted to change those things when I was weak. Now that I'm strong, I can actually make it happen. Tell me, why shouldn't I try?"

His gaze made her shiver as his voice became louder. She knew this was a serious question. There was a chance he'd change his mind if she could find a proper answer.

"I... I'm not saying your concerns are wrong, or that you mustn't change things. It's just that I don't think this is the right way to do it. If you really want to do this, I can't stop you, but things have gone too far. I don't think you or anyone else should suffer the consequences of your actions that could be avoided." She looked deeply into his eyes, trying to sound as firm and secure as possible. "Isn't what you're doing the exact same thing you're fighting against? Aren't you deciding the fate of others? Controlling their lives? Making their decisions for them?"

"Lya, what I'm doing is giving them freedom. I'll destroy these shackles that bind us to death. I'll destroy this disgusting cycle that brings nothing but suffering. People might be scared at first, but soon enough, they'll realize the good in what we're about to do. Hell, even the people we fight with today will be brought back when we succeed. No one will ever have to be pained by the loss of a loved one again. No one will have to fear death anymore."

Her answer was not enough. The light in his eyes grew brighter; it was clear he was trying to reassure himself. Lya's face was flushed with disappointment—she didn't want this. It would be a bloodbath. No matter the victor, there would be no winners in this war.

Before she could answer, they heard a loud rumbling far away. The ground started to quake beneath them and clouds of dust formed in the distance. The water in the lake started rippling wildly, splattering everywhere as chaotic waves crashed against each other. The night sky grew bright with golden streaks of light that looked like shooting stars colliding in the distance. A dusty, violent wind shook the trees surrounding the lake. Annoyed, Alexei covered his mouth, coughing erratically, before jumping to his feet and waving his hands. The dust was blown away and the wind calmed down. He directed his gaze towards the clashing lights on the horizon.

"It's started," he mumbled.

A loud screech echoed in the distance and roaring, scarlet flames rose from the ground, devouring the lights. The flames incinerated everything in their path, tainting the dark sky with a hellish radiance. The heat was so intense that he could feel the temperature rising from where he stood.

"He is here, together with that annoying bird," he scowled, not hiding the despise in his voice. Alexei adjusted his messy clothes and used his fingers to try to comb his hair, before looking at Lya, who was now standing next to him—not a speck of dust could be found on her ethereal, white dress. She raised her hands and gently fixed his still messy hair. Closing his eyes, he enjoyed the relaxing feeling of the breeze moving through his hair.

Lya took her time and gave him a slight nod when she was done, confirming that his appearance was at least acceptable now. When he troubled himself to look presentable, he took the matter seriously. Unfortunately, when he did, some people would inevitably die.

With a fierce gaze, he stared at the beautiful woman beside him.

"There's no turning back anymore, do you understand?"

She looked at him without hiding her anxiousness, realizing that it was already too late.

"If you can't compromise, can you at least not kill each other?"

She was worried for their friend, but she was even more worried for the man in front of her.

Growing hesitant, he tried to find the right words. He was not doubting his decision, rather, he was afraid of what she would say, or what she would do, when he presented his answer with action.

"I'll try my best, but if we win, we can always bring him back. Can't you trust me on this, Lya?"

Alexei extended his hand to her, waiting for her answer—the final permission he needed to continue with a clear mind.

She said nothing, but the sorrow in her eyes was evident. Looking into his eyes one last time, she gently grabbed his hand and disappeared into thin air.

Pained, he sighed and tightly gripped the sword's hilt. The gem in the guard was slightly illuminated as he raised the sword. He brought the blade close to his face, looking at his reflection. He whispered gently, "Don't worry, Lya. It will all end well."

He looked at the moon for a brief moment, reminiscing about the past. He would be happier after today—no—everyone would. His life would truly begin after this battle.

He raised his foot and stepped into the air. Golden light glowed at his feet as he lurched forward, turning into another streak of light that shot into battle.

Meanwhile, Lya was crying in a black void. Its endless space gave her an ominous feeling as a crimson light constantly flickered around her. She often thought she saw walls of red crystal, inching their way towards her on every side. Each time she reached out to touch them, they would elude her fingertips. They seemed so close, yet infinitely far, causing her to feel constricted. The lack of sound and inability to put her feet on solid ground filled her with loneliness. She longed to feel free. She needed to feel someone—anyone—in the vast confinement.

Fear weighed down in the depths of her heart. Alexei had changed too much since they first met. She regretted not being able to ease the pain that set him on this path. She regretted not seeing the chaos that started to brew within him when treading through past events.

Their happy days were long gone and would never return. Maybe she had changed too. Alexei's words started echoing in her head. *Destroying the shackles that bind us to death.* The shackles, however, were life itself. Destroying them would be the same as eliminating the purpose of their existence, causing nothing but despair. In the end, people might fear death, but she couldn't think of anything more horrifying than immortality.

THE SECT OF SCRAPS

The room was dark. There were no windows or cracks in the walls through which light could enter. If not for the glowing runes on the floor, it would have been impossible to see anything.

They were world-like, alive, and twisting—a chaotic tangle of interconnecting scribbles, coiling like luminous snakes. Although they were not uniform, their varying shapes and sizes formed a wondrous circle on the floor, repeatedly breaking apart and melting back together in flux. At the center lay a boy, common in looks. His black hair was glued to his face and forehead with sweat and his black eyes quivered in fear as they filled up with tears.

A tall man with similar features stood in front of him. His ravenous eyes stared at the boy sprawled at his feet. His chiseled face was painted with a devious smirk; it wasn't concerned with the boy's emotions. He knelt down to make eye contact, his serene voice breathed calmness into the scared child.

"I need you to be brave, Amon. This is going to hurt, but you can't leave. It's okay to cry and scream if you want, but never move from this spot," the father coaxed, before walking around the golden circle.

As he placed fist-sized, black crystals on a few of the runes, he didn't look at his son. He knew that Amon was terrified. Afterwards, he ventured to a corner of the room. There, he stood next to a short man that had been silent the entire time. The golden light from the runes seemed to be absorbed by wriggling shadows as they tried to illuminate the small man's face, giving him an ominous air.

"Scholar, he's ready."

The father gave a nod and the other man approached the circle. The Scholar bent down and touched two runes on the floor with his hands; his sneaky eyes were filled with pity. He took a deep breath and a strange pulse flowed from his shoulders to the tip of his fingers before finally entering the runes before him. This caused them to glow with a blinding, golden light that travelled through the other runes on the floor.

A bizarre hum emitted from the walls and ceiling, but the area beneath the runes was unnaturally silent. As each rune lit up, the sound

11

became louder, making the room vibrate wildly. The crystals twirled, their shape was now blurred and indistinguishable. They launched into the air, floating a few meters from the high ceiling and Amon went with them.

His body contorted into unnatural positions with the sound of his young bones cracking and mending back together. Blood-curdling screams filled the room as the two men looked on. They knew Amon would never escape the hell they had thrown him into.

❊ ❊ ❊

Amon woke up abruptly—it was the same nightmare every time. His body was pained and drenched in sweat. His clothes clung to him, making him feel restrained, uncomfortable, and heavy. He felt like he hadn't slept in days.

He dejectedly pulled off the white, linen sheets and threw them to the side before slowly getting up. The warm wooden floor felt comforting beneath his feet. Upon opening his creaking windows, the sun greeted him from the bright, blue sky, lighting up every inch of his room.

Amon's room wasn't anything spectacular. Somehow, in his restless slumber, his pillow ended up in front of his small desk on the opposite side of the room. Although the desk was usually tidy, a few pieces of paper and a pen were scattered at its center. A circular black rug was positioned at the center of the room, worn down from years of use and torn around the edges. On the wall adjacent to it was a simple mirror hanging on the wall above a small table which held a basin filled with water to wash himself.

Amon stood in front of the mirror and stared at his reflection. His youthful face, framed by black hair, contrasted his peculiar golden eyes. The dark circles around them made his eyes look like lamps shining in the dark.

He ran his fingers through his black hair as he tried to comb it, but something felt off. He looked at his hand and saw a black stain on his skin. He turned around and examined his pillow; it too was stained with smeared black patches.

Amon couldn't help but sigh. He would have to buy a new batch of black nuts soon. He tried to wash the stain off in the basin before him, but was unsuccessful. He gave up and continued to wash the remainder of his body with a damp cloth. The cool water in the basin was a relief to his hot and sticky skin. He kicked open a chest next to his bed and put on a fresh set of white clothes. They were plain, but he hated standing out.

After making his way to the shabby kitchen located at the other end of the house, he noticed an old iron pot on the countertop. He carefully reheated its contents, some lumpy rice porridge, and scooped it into a small bowl. The steamy porridge gently jiggled in the bowl as he carried to a small room located off the living room.

He knocked twice on the wooden door and a weak voice called beckoned him to enter.

"Come in, Amon," his mother, Rebecca, crooned.

A sweet smile caressed her face when she saw him step into her room. It was as quaint as his; small and lightly decorated with a medium sized storage chest at the foot of the bed.

"Mom, I brought some food," Amon said, slowly walking to her bed. He steadied the bowl and spoon in his mother's shriveled hands. Her frail arms shook slightly under their weight. She looked older than she actually was. Her thin hair was a soft platinum color—a stark contrast to the thick, golden locks she once had.

"You've eaten some too, right?" she asked worriedly, her misty-green eyes staring at his tired face as he sat down next to her.

Amon nodded before changing the subject.

"I'm going to exchange some contribution points. We need more rice, vegetables, and black nuts."

Rebecca giggled at his serious tone, gently ruffling his hair. He closed his eyes and smile; the feeling was quite pleasant to him and he enjoyed her spoiling him on occasion.

"Oh my," his mother said, playfully tugging at his hair, causing him to open his eyes.

She held out her black-stained hand causing him to avoid her gaze.

"Why don't you forget about the black nuts? You could save the points and use them on other things for yourself after a few months."

"I need them, mom. I don't want anything else for myself, having them is enough for me."

He couldn't look at her loving face. He knew he'd give in to her requests if he did.

She started poking him on his arm and then again on his belly. His mother loved trying to make him laugh, even if it meant tickling him

"I'm thirteen, mom. Don't do that!" he protested with a reddened face.

"Oh, I'm sorry, mister grown-up. You are old enough to refuse my tickles, but not old enough to stop me ruffling your hair, are you?"

Amon grumbled at her comment before turning to face her.

"You know I love your hair and your eyes, don't you? I find them so beautiful. You should really stop with the black nuts, Amon."

"Not yet. Let me keep buying them for a bit longer, alright?'

His shoulders drooped and his head hung low in embarrassment.

"Fine. You've got one month. After that, you'll stop, promise?"

She knew she had to make a compromise early to avoid excuses from him later. She extended her pinky finger to him and he stared at her, slightly confused.

"It is a pinky promise," she continued, "or are you too old for that too?"

A smirk grew on her face and Amon knew he had been defeated. As much as he wanted to keep his hair black, he could never do anything to hurt or anger his mother. Interlocking his pinky with hers, he gave her a wide smile.

"I promise I'll stop," he said, ruffling her hair.

Rebecca scowled with feigned annoyance, before trying to tickle him once more. He dodged her attacks before giving her a hug. She pulled him in tight and kissed his cheek before sending him off. As he exited the room, he left the door open. His mother liked it more when her door was open. It made her feel less restrained. Even with a large bay window letting light into her room, all she could do was dream about going outside again.

Amon entered the living room, making his way to the main door. He suddenly stopped midway, directing his gaze at the strange, guardless sword hanging on the wall. Its glossy, pitch-black scabbard shone like a perfectly polished piece of glass. The thin, single-edged blade was slightly curved, making it good for slashing and chopping. Although it was hidden by the scabbard, Amon knew its color was even darker.

Amon didn't know if it would affect the handling or the balance of the weapon, but the lack of a guard made it seem menacing even when sheathed. It was a sword made only with killing in mind—focused on being swift and aggressive, forgoing defense in exchange of efficiency in murder.

Amon had never held the sword in question, but he had seen his father using it. Raven, he called it. Even though it piqued his curiosity, he had no affection towards the weapon, just hate. If his mother hadn't been so persistent on leaving it there, he would have sold it ages ago.

Feeling himself growing agitated, he quickly left the house to take care of his errands. A sea of lush and vibrant trees surrounded their home. Being on the northern outskirts of the Abyss sect had its perks. The area was quiet and fertile with plenty of streams and rivers to draw water from. The sect's headquarters was located inside of Hell Keeper's Mountain. It was massive in scale and rumored to have been a volcano at some point, though he didn't bother at all with such meaningless things. Looking at the mountain only made him feel queasy and angry.

Despite all farms and livestock belonging to the Outer Sect, Amon and the other members managed them year-round. They exchanged their work for contribution points, which they could use to buy almost anything. Food, medicine, and technique manuals were the most affordable things. Classes from specialized teachers and access to the infamous Red Quarters, located within the Inner Ring, were more expensive.

Housing and land rental also required the use of contribution points. The closer you lived to Hell Keeper's Mountain, the more expensive rent was and the higher your standing in the Outer Sect. Buying your way into the Inner Sect was also an option for those with enough points. However, buying a master to teach you the ways of cultivation was impossible.

People from the Inner Sect lived with just one worry: cultivation. They only had to pursue power and contemplate the mysteries of the world, paying back the sect's investment by doing special missions. While the sect covered all of their daily needs, the elders would handle specific requests or problems, but only if they were worth the trouble.

Amon turned south towards the mountain. He couldn't see the top due to a blanket of white clouds swirling around it. He felt intimidated by its sheer size. Even its shadow seemed as though it would crush him at any moment. His chest felt full. An uneasy feeling welled up inside of him, causing his breathing to turn raspy. Closing his eyes, he took deep breaths until the feeling subsided. The warm sun helped to ease his tense mind. He lowered his head and set off towards the monstrosity in the distance.

Amon followed a paved, stone path. His house appeared smaller and smaller the farther he walked. The irregular stones below his feet were mostly covered in grass and dirt, but he could still see some of them timidly peeking from beneath the earth.

There were small streams of clear water and large expanses of farm-land in every direction. Small children assisted adults with gathering water, taking care of the crops, and feeding the livestock. With the sounds of their hard work, chirping birds, rustling grass, and flowing water, the Outer Sect was always a lively scene.

After walking for two hours, the first few buildings of the Northern Junction came into view. The agglomerate of administrative buildings and stores was a place for people from the northern side of the Outer Sect to mingle. It served as a central hub for those that couldn't make the long trip to the headquarters. Members could spend their contribution points or apply for new jobs within the sect.

Since the Outer Sect had a radius greater than fifty kilometers, eight junctions were spaced evenly around its perimeter. There were carriages that provided transportation services from one junction to the next. The rides, of course, took hours and cost a considerable amount of points. These junctions made up the Middle Ring of the Outer Sect.

The junction itself wasn't fenced off from the rest of nature. Docile animals were often seen roaming the streets and nibbling on the shrubs. A multitude of buildings gave the junction its shape and defined its bound-aries. The main street was in a much better condition than the path Amon had taken. Smooth slabs of white stone were neatly arranged close to each other, making it easier for carriages to traverse and for people to see from a distance. A perfectly-cut carpet of grass was placed along the sides of the street and between the buildings. Lush trees were planted and flowery bushes nearly lined the entryway to the more important buildings, making the entire area visually pleasing.

At the end of the street stood the northern market. It was a three-story building made from green jade that glistened in the sun. Its thick, white doors were open and the ground floor was bustling with activity.

Wide windows welcomed the warm rays of sunlight, illuminating the inside of the building. Inside, the jade walls stood out against the white marble floors and pillars. At the far right side, a set of stairs cascaded to the next floor where more goods were being sold. The cashiers were positioned at the front of the store where a long line of patrons patiently awaited their turn. Anyone that caused a ruckus was thrown out by white-robed guards with golden spears.

Amon chose the shortest line and waited to be served.

"Have you heard? It seems like Jake managed to kill an earth dragon during his last mission. That kid is only sixteen and can already kill a class four spirit beast."

"The son of the second protector? Of course he would be able to do something like that. Even if we ignore his father, he still is the direct disciple of Sect Master Borgin."

"There he is, slaying monsters left and right while the most dangerous thing we do is face this terrifying line."

"If you want to go on a hunt you can always finish body tempering and reach elemental purification to get into the Inner Sect. Just remember to wake up on time for work afterwards."

People were gossiping everywhere in the marketplace, bored by the long lines. Amon stood in silence, mechanically walking forward whenever needed, thinking on how many contribution points he would end up spending.

When he approached the third position in queue, a familiar voice dragged him back to reality.

"Found you!"

Amon turned around to see a young man looking at him. He seemed to be in his twenties, had black hair, brown eyes and a handsome face punctuated by a sharp nose. He was a bit short and somewhat slim, but one could see his well-built muscles bulging slightly from his blue clothes.

"Hey, Daniel. What's up?" Amon asked with a smile. Daniel was one of his few friends. Maybe the only one he could really count on. Daniel, on the other hand, was clearly annoyed.

"Nothing much. I was sure you would still be sleeping when I visited your house. To my surprise, you were already up and had even left without me. I thought we had agreed to come together and discuss our plans for the Scavenging."

"Sorry about that," Amon nonchalantly replied, frustrating Daniel more.

"Forget it. We'll talk later. Look, it's your turn."

Amon saw that there was no one in front of him anymore. He walked to the counter and took a purple card from his clothes. He faced the clerk, a pretty woman wearing neat purple robes and a somewhat stiff smile.

"I'll need three bags of rice, one of onions, one of carrots and ten black nuts. Add a bottle of nourishing pills too," he said while offering the card in his hands.

The clerk nodded and took the card from him. She took a crystal ball from behind the counter and her hands glowed for a moment. The crystal ball slowly floated above her open palms and a stream of white words flowed from it, gathering in the air in front of her.

She pressed a few of the words with amazing speed, and a number popped out from the ball.

"It will be two hundred contribution points," the woman said with an indifferent voice.

"Two hundred? Are you kidding me? Last week it only cost me one hundred and seventy points!"

Amon was surprised. There is no way the price could increase so much in a mere week.

"I'm sorry sir, but this week we received fewer supplies than normal. Except for the pills that are made by the elders, everything had a slight increase in price. The sect had to cut the prices of our exports, so we have to sell more than usual. There's currently a small shortage of just about everything," the clerk replied in an apologetic tone.

Amon calmed down and thought for a while before making a decision. He gave a long sigh, subconsciously running his fingers through his hair.

"Forget about the black nuts. I guess I can do without them for now," he said, clearly disheartened.

The clerk nodded and waved her hands. The numbers disappeared and the words scattered in fragments of light before joining again. She tapped a few of the words again and a new number popped up.

"It will be one hundred and seventy contribution points."

It was the same price as last week. Things were indeed much more expensive.

"I'll take it."

The clerk touched the ball with his purple card. The words dissolved and the card lit up with a faint light before dimming again.

"Your balance is seventeen contribution points," she informed, offering the card back to Amon.

As she spoke, a tall man wearing purple robes appeared from the back, carrying the items that Amon had purchased and dropped them on the counter. Amon hid the bottle in his clothes before taking the heavy bags and thanking them before departing.

As they left, Daniel took the bags from Amon's hands and signaled him to stop by a small tree in the shade of two buildings. They sat under the tree while Daniels searched for something in a small leather pouch. It took him a long while, but he finally retrieved a tiny bottle and a bundle of cloth from the pouch before closing it and putting it back in his clothes.

"Here. Aunt Becca asked me to give you these. She said you didn't have breakfast and didn't sleep very well, so she was worried."

Amon's face sank. He couldn't fool his mother in the end. Unable to accept Daniel's things, he refused them politely. Daniel didn't waver.

"It's nothing much. Just a piece of cheese and a drink. A friend gave them to me for free."

Amon was resolute.

17

"Just take it. I don't care about what you want. I don't want auntie nagging me because I didn't take care of you properly," Daniel said, pushing the items into Amon's arms despite his protests.

Satisfied, Daniel grinned as he leaned against a tree and closed his eyes, enjoying the refreshing shade.

Amon pouted for a bit, but was completely ignored. He sighed and opened the bundle. There was a piece of strong-smelling, yellow cheese inside. Opening the bottle, a sweet and delicate smell invaded his nostrils. A clear red liquid was churning inside the bottle.

He ate the cheese in one bite and sipped the beverage to get rid of the sour taste from the cheese. The drink was sweet and left a tart aftertaste. It was cold, but seemed to turn hot as it went down his throat. Amon liked it quite a bit.

After he finished, he left the bottle and the cloth beside the bags of food and tried to relax. He was still stiff from the uncomfortable night, but he managed to get comfortable. Drowsiness overcame him, and his eyes started to droop.

"Hey! Don't fall asleep on me now," Daniel scoffed.

Amon opened his golden eyes, giving him a reproachful glance.

"Don't look at me like that, we still have plans to discuss."

Daniel took out his pouch and retrieved a tightly bound piece of parchment. He opened it on the ground, revealing a detailed map. Amon's face scrunched in annoyance.

"I told you before, I'm not going," Amon huffed.

"Is that why you were avoiding me today?"

Daniel narrowed his eyes as he spoke.

"If you really want to know, yes."

Amon didn't hide it. It was Daniel's fault if he didn't take him seriously before.

"You hurt me," Daniel said disappointedly, lowering his head.

"Oh please. You're twice my age, act like it."

Amon knew that Daniel was being dramatic.

"Aunt Becca was right. Puberty is making you grumpy."

The counterattack was swift and fierce. Amon couldn't take the blow.

"Not you too!"

Daniel cackled as he revelled in victory, his fake sad expression from a moment ago was completely gone.

"Anyway, the Scavenging is in a week and you are going with me."

"I refuse. Even if you drag me there, I won't go."

"Oh, really? Then how are you going to make it through next week?" Daniel struck a weak point. Amon was basically broke, and because of the Scavenging, it wouldn't be easy for him to find work that could pay for the weekly expenses of him and his mother.

"I'll manage somehow. If I decide to go, chances are we will return empty-handed and I would've wasted four days without getting any contribution points."

His reasoning was sound. The Scavenging was nothing short of a bet. A bet that people lost most of the time. It was never a big loss, but not many people could afford to not work without carefully planning for months, saving enough points to make up for it.

Though it only took place every five years, Amon still felt it was a waste of time and resources. Rummaging the area north of the sect for remnants of a war long gone was pointless. Even if a single fragment of a weapon could be sold for thousands of points, and even though the sect allowed people to keep their findings as long as they were reported, the place could be considered barren for decades now.

There was no way Amon and Daniel would gain anything in the Scavenging, so Amon would rather stay in the sect and work as much as possible.

"What if I have a commission to investigate a certain place?" Daniel inquired with a mischievous look.

Commissions were one of the faster ways to gather contribution points within the sect. Someone filed a request at the Commission Center and after processing it, the sect would divulge it to anyone interested. Some of them were for hunting monsters, others were for gathering materials or herbs. Even if the difficulty was low, the pay was always good.

Most of the tasks were designed for members of the Inner Sect. However, a few of the jobs managed to reach the Outer Sect, causing people to fight over them as if their lives depended on them. Commissions issued by the sect itself were exclusive to Inner Sect members and were treated as official missions.

Amon was shocked. He could tell when Daniel was lying and he knew that he was telling the truth about this mission.

"What!?"

"I'm not joking. One thousand points to search in a specific place. We'll get paid even if we find nothing. If we do find something, the client will receive seventy percent of the reward points. We'll get thirty percent plus the one thousand points he will pay anyway."

Amon was surprised. He couldn't even begin to understand who would be insane enough to spend that many points in such a crazy way. The only explanation would be that they were reasonably certain that something was there.

He cautiously tried to read Daniel's expression. He had many questions. Why Daniel? Why now? Why this absurd pay?

Amon was sure this task was not going to be easy.

There was no way that Daniel could have found such a job on his own. Amon questioned him about it but Daniel insisted that it was dumb luck.

"I was hanging out in the Commission Center when someone posted the listing right beside me. I reached for it before anyone else could read it and that was it," Daniel said, scratching his face.

Amon didn't buy it, but decided to let it go for now.

"Are you in or not?" Daniel asked with an innocent smile.

He heavily considered Daniel's proposal. The pay was good and once he split his earnings with his friend, he would have a minimum of five hundred contribution points; enough to cover expenses of almost a whole month.

"Before I make a decision, what's the plan?"

Daniel turned to the stretched map across the ground. He pointed to a mountain in the south, the largest on the map.

"Here is Hell Keeper's Mountain. To the east, we have the Red River."

He ran his finger across the map, going from the mountain to a wide river drawn next to it.

"The Red River flows to the north for kilometers on end. When it more or less surpasses the Sword Abyss, it makes a turn to the east before branching off into a series of smaller streams."

Amon studied the map carefully. The Abyss Sect was on the lower edge of the map. The Red River occupied most of the right edge. The center and a good chunk of the left edge were covered by the Broken Forest which spanned hundreds of kilometers.

There was a blank, distorted circle in the left corner of the map. Based on the map, it was at least two hundred square kilometers. This area was known as the Scorched Lands.

More impressive than the Scorched Lands was a horizontal stroke of black paint that almost divided the map in two. It was hundreds of kilometers long and at least three kilometers wide in its real scale. Everyone knew of the legendary Sword Abyss because it was the biggest mark that a war had ever left on the land. It was also the origin of the Abyss Sect's name.

East of the Scorched Lands was a mountain cut in half by another battle, but it paled in comparison to the chasm a sword strike had left in the forest. Amon had never seen it with his own eyes, but he shuddered thinking about the person that managed to create such a devastating blow. How powerful did one have to be to do that? How much pent up bloodlust did they have to unleash such a terrifying strike?

"We are interested in the northern bank of the Red River. To be more precise, the exact place it turns to the east. Can you guess why?"

Amon thought for a moment before pointing somewhere east of the Red River and somewhat close to Hell Keeper's Mountain. Long streaks of barren land were marked in that area. They looked like long, thin scars from a cat's scratch or multiple knife slashings—another mark the war had left in the forest.

"It should be the Scars, no?"

"Smart kid. Yes, it is because of the Scars. Chances are many things fell in the Red River during a past war. The river would've dragged any relics north. Chances are a few of them would've ended up in the northern bank when the river changed direction."

"So the client wants us to search there? It's not a bad plan, but he's certainly not the first one to think of this."

20

"True, but that's not our problem. Our client decided to make a bet after using his brains for a bit. He probably has the points to spare and doesn't want to go through the trouble of checking his own theory. That's why he made the commission."

"Are you sure about the details? Is it really such a simple job?" Amon asked for reassurance.

Daniel tried to put on a serious face as he nodded, but failed horribly in hiding his smile. He was one step away from victory.

"It is. There's no catch."

Amon's brow furrowed as he shook his head.

"I'll speak with my mother before I decide. Don't ask me about it again."

With a shrug, his friend replied, "Fine, do as you wish." It was fairly obvious that he was pretending not to care, as he knew his win was inevitable. This entire plan was never Daniel's idea to begin with.

As Daniel began to put the map away, a low whistling sound rapidly approached them. Without thinking, Daniel swung his right arm to block the flying object from hitting Amon in the head.

"Damn it, Daniel. Why are you always with that geezer?" A high-pitched voice called from the distance.

A group of people was walking down the street and at their lead was a thin, young boy. His luxurious, red clothes glistened in the sunlight, making him appear to be on fire. His long, brown hair was neatly tied up with a golden ribbon. Accompanying him were a few boys and girls. A husky, red-haired man walked behind them. His muscles bulged through his clothes, giving off an intimidating aura.

Daniel gave the man a cold stare as he slowly opened his hand and revealed a small, sharp stone. It had embedded itself in his palm, and blood started to flow from his injury.

Amon, on the other hand, was scared. If Daniel hadn't been by his side, he would have been hit on the head.

"I hope it wasn't you who threw this stone, Roger."

Daniel's voice was cold as he looked at the burly man. Roger shook his head.

"Young master, Erin just finished his first round of body tempering and wanted to test his strength."

Amon and Daniel stared at the young boy leading the pack.

"What of it? People say that he has some really good senses despite him being stuck at the qi gathering stage. I wanted to help him sharpen them a bit," Erin quipped.

Amon was surprised. Not at the ridiculous excuse he used for him throwing the stone, but at the fact that the boy had already reached body tempering.

"Is that true, Erin? You're already at the body tempering stage?" Amon inquired.

"Of course he is! Erin is someone that will reach the Inner Sect in a few years. You, however, will forever stay a farm b—" one of the girls chimed in.

"Let it go, Amber. Don't waste your breath on such pitiful people. It must be really hard being abandoned by your own father and having a crippled mother," Erin interrupted, waving his hands dismissively.

He had a derisive smile and his heartless words cut through Amon like a sharp sword. Amon's breath quickened and he reddened in anger. He clenched his fists and his arms trembled. His jaws were clenched so hard it hurt. A fierce light shone in his golden eyes. He started walking towards the group, but Daniel extended a hand to block his path.

"I'm sure you won't mind if I help you with your body tempering too," Daniel growled.

Daniel's eyes burned with rage, but his face was emotionless. Amon himself had never seen Daniel like that and it gave him chills. He took a few steps back when he saw Daniel prepare to attack.

Roger reacted instinctively. He dragged Erin behind him as a loud whizzing noise shrieked around them. He crossed his arms in front of his chest and braced for impact. Roger took two steps back as a grey streak cut through the air and hit his arms at a blinding speed before he lost his balance and fell backwards.

He grunted in pain and tried to get up, but he realized he couldn't raise his arms. Upon looking down, he saw that both arms were bent at awkward angles. A thick piece of bone was sticking out of his right arm as blood gushed from the wound. Roger made an incredible effort to endure the pain without screaming.

Erin's face turned a ghostly-white as shock prevented him from moving. The other kids shuddered in fear.

"Are you insane? That could have killed me!" Erin yelled, incredulous.

The object that hit Roger's arm was the same stone that Erin had thrown at Amon. The speed and strength at which it was thrown were many times greater than Erin's. At most, Amon would have suffered a minor injury or been knocked unconscious. Erin, however, would have had a hole cut clean through his chest.

Luckily for Erin, Roger was in the middle stages of body tempering and somehow managed to soften the blow, breaking his arms in the process.

"Other than these boot-lickers, I doubt anyone besides your parents would miss your ugly face," Daniel replied, his demeanor hadn't changed.

"Let's see if you can keep spouting such nonsense after I take care of you."

Erin's face turned red and he pointed his finger at Daniel as he threatened him.

"Hire as many thugs as you would like with your father's money. And please, don't forget to tell them who I am," Daniel mocked, causing Erin to grow silent.

Roger, who managed to stand up somehow, put himself between the two boys and sent Erin a cold glare of disapproval.

"Young master, that's enough. Leave it be. We already got what we wanted. Let's go home."

Erin was still enraged, but eventually gave up. He looked at Daniel begrudgingly before directing his gaze at Amon.

"You missed a spot, grandpa," he said, patting the top of his head.

Amon quickly covered his hair with his hands, turning away from them in shame.

Erin and the others laughed hysterically as they departed. Roger followed with his arms hanging awkwardly from his shoulders as he grunted from the pain.

Once they were out of sight, Daniel's aggressive behavior changed.

"Are all kids from the Inner Ring that dumb?" he questioned, shrugging off the situation.

It was mostly his fault that things developed like that. This had been going on for a while, but never to the point of a physical altercation. He never expected Erin to attack Amon like that; not without warning anyway. Daniel realized Amon was covering his hair in the same place Erin had patted his own head.

"Hey, there's nothing there. Erin was messing with you. Your hair is still black."

Amon quickly removed his hands and patted his clothes.

"Of course... I knew that."

"Where was this cockiness when that brat was here?" Daniel rolled his eyes.

Amon averted his gaze, his ears slightly red in shame.

"If you didn't stop me I would have kicked his ass," he said, almost whispering to himself.

"Well, I saw that you were finally angry enough to take action, but you can't face him head-on anymore. He's already started body tempering, you've lost your chance."

Amon was saddened, but he couldn't deny Daniel's words.

"Thank you for helping me out," Amon meekly responded.

Daniel smiled and wrapped an arm around Amon's shoulder. The wound on Daniel's hand had stopped bleeding—body tempering was really something else.

"Hey, let's go back to your house. I'm sure you still didn't meditate today and I need to speak with your mother anyway."

"Didn't you just talk to her?"

Taken by surprise at the question, Daniel scratched his face.

"I forgot to ask about something. It isn't that important, but we finished what we had to do here, so I might as well help you with your meditation and talk to her at the same time."

Amon nodded quietly. He had almost given up cultivation. He could sense the qi surrounding him, but he still couldn't manage to absorb any of it.

It didn't take long for them to return to Amon's house. The afternoon sun had peaked and the temperature was rising rapidly. Upon entering the house, Amon made his way to his mother's room, leaving Daniel to drop the food bags in the kitchen.

As Daniel made his way into the living room, he noticed Raven, the black sword, mounted on the wall. With a sad smile, he started to reminisce about a moment from five years ago. Although Erin's words had been sharp and offensive, they held some truth.

What a waste. You did something horrendously stupid, he thought. His expression turned sour when he remembered someone who was no longer in his life.

His own situation wasn't much better. Ten years ago, Rebecca could have found Daniel to be as pitiful as he found Amon now, and thus decided to take him under her wing.

He sighed. Being a scion of a powerful family and not living up to their expectations was complicated. He wondered how his little brother felt when his father deceptively told him that Daniel decided to live on his own and left the household without saying goodbye. It had been years since they last saw each other. There was news that the little brat was now a personal disciple of Sect Master Borgin. His brother's talents surpassed his father's expectations by a landslide.

Daniel wondered if they would see each other again. Maybe by that time, Jake would be old enough to share a cup of wine with him. Daniel's smile widened at the thought. He really missed his brother's contagious laughter.

* * *

Amon had quietly knocked on his mother's door.

"Come in," Rebecca said warmly.

She was still in bed, looking out through the open window beside her. Her gaze stayed locked on the trees and sky for a moment before turning to face Amon.

"What's wrong?" she asked, noticing sadness in his expression.

His eyes were growing red and his face was tense. Amon shook his head, made his way into her bed and hugged her tightly.

"I love you, mom."

Rebecca was taken aback, but she returned the hug and gently patted his back.

"I love you too."

They stayed like this until Amon finally released her from his bearhug.

"Want to tell me what happened?" she asked, but he simply shook his head again. She ruffled his hair as she studied his golden eyes.

"Somehow, Daniel got a commission and he wants me to go with him to the Scavenging. The pay is really good and the job seems to be easy."

Rebecca quietly listened to the details as he explained in a weary voice.

"Well, what do you want to do?"

Amon had a pensive look as he pondered.

"I don't want to go, but the pay is good. We could earn enough to make it through the month in just four days."

"Why don't you want to go?"

Amon frowned, perplexed by her feigning naïvety.

"I'm afraid. I don't want anything like that to happen again."

"Do you think it was your fault?" she asked.

"Of course it is, mom! I wish I had listened to you. I should've never participated in the Scavenging! If I hadn't gone against your wishes, then you wouldn't be like this today," he said with a shaky voice.

Rebecca gently rubbed his back. Amon's voice grew louder as he continued, "I have no idea what fa... that man did to me, but I haven't been myself since that day. I can hear things, mom. I can see things and sense them. My eyes, my hair..."

Poisonous words from his past echoed in his mind. The hurtful words clawed at his soul every waking second. His father's chilling voice and indifferent eyes were just as unforgettable. They left Amon's heart more scared and broken than his body had been after that day.

Tears spilled from his eyes and his breathing hastened. Rebecca's expression turned serious as she used her hands to hold his face close to hers and sent him a penetrating glance.

"Listen to me, Amon. What happened is not your fault. Sometimes coincidences happen and they change the courses of our lives, for better or for worse. People who give in to fear can never be strong. Fate tests us with these trials to see how strong we are. Without them, we would never learn or grow. It is part of life."

She gave a sad smile as she spoke, her eyes turning blurry.

"If you continually cower in fear inside this house, life will simply pass by you. You won't realize it until it's too late. Life doesn't give you second chances for everything."

Amon shuddered in his mother's arms. Feeling her heart aching as she hit a sensitive spot, Rebecca steeled herself. He had to hear the truth, even if it hurts.

"I want you to go with Daniel. I want you to do the commission and have a good time. I want you to face your fears. As a mother, there is nothing I want more than to see you grow up, but you must never let fear hold you back."

She gave him another firm, warm hug. Amon hadn't stopped crying, but he nodded his head as he silently accepted what she told him.

After a good while, they finally let each other go. Amon wiped his tears and runny nose with his sleeves, making Rebecca lightly poke his forehead.

"Alright. I'll go."

His voice was low, but it was enough for Rebecca to hear.

"Good. Listen to Daniel's instructions and don't do anything reckless."

"I'll listen. I promise."

His words made Rebecca satisfied. He stared out the window awkwardly before changing the subject.

"Are you hungry? I bought food for the week. I'll go make lunch," he said as he stood up.

"I love your food," she replied cheerfully.

Amon made his way to the kitchen, but stopped when he saw Daniel staring at Raven in a daze. Once Daniel realized this, he regrouped his thoughts and looked at his friend. Although Amon's face was still moist from tears and his eyes were red, Daniel made no comments. Slightly embarrassed by his appearance, Amon awkwardly nodded at Daniel before entering the kitchen.

Amon quickly made some rice porridge and poured it into a wooden serving bowl. Glancing around, he checked to make sure that Daniel couldn't see him. He retrieved a small, porcelain bottle of nourishing pills from his robes. He crushed a pill in his palm and brushed it into the bowl before thoroughly mixing it into the food. It faintly smelled of medicine, but he figured it wasn't noticeable.

Making his way back through the living room, Amon told Daniel to meet him in his room. Upon returning to his mother's bedroom, he passed the bowl to her on a wooden serving tray.

"I'm going to meditate. Just call if you need me," he said with a soft smile."

"Remember to focus," Rebecca called after him as he swiftly left the room.

Once in his room, Amon sat on the black mat in the middle of his room with his legs crossed. He closed his eyes, trying hard to control his breathing as Daniel carefully watched by his side.

"You are too tense. Relax your body and mind."

Amon tried his best to follow his instructions. He relaxed his limbs as he breathed rhythmically, clearing his mind.

Daniel slowly recited the mantra cultivators used when preparing their minds for meditation. In order to open his divine sense, Amon needed to give up his notions of self. Only then could he enter a state of conscious emptiness. This would enable him to feel the qi that permeated the world. It was a delicate balance to maintain. Only with years of practice and self-discipline could one enter and leave such a state at will. Sensing qi had nothing to do with the five senses. It was a special talent that only a few people ever developed—the divine sense. Those who had even a bit of talent could manipulate the qi at will and they could also absorb it into their bodies.

For the Preparatory realm, the first level was called qi gathering. It had three parts: sensing, manipulating, and absorbing. When qi was absorbed into the body, it circulated through meridians and into the person's dantian, allowing the individual to step into the body tempering stage.

"Spread your divine sense outwards. Don't try to visualize your surroundings, feel them instead," Daniel continued patiently.

As he spoke, his voice seemed to distance itself from Amon.

"There are no memories. No emotions, no thoughts... There is no one—not even you," Daniel said with a softer voice, slowly walking around Amon. He was careful not to touch him. Interrupting his training could set him back a great deal of time. "There is only nature. There is only the world. There is only qi."

His voice hypnotically flowed through Amon, further calming his chaotic emotions as he lost him himself in nothingness. As he progressed, Daniel's voice faded completely, and only darkness remained.

Suddenly Amon sensed something different. Though his eyes remained closed, the world around him presented itself through his divine sense. Everything within two meters of his body was engulfed in a mysterious smoke emanating from the earth. It waltzed around the room, dancing around Daniel exotically. The smoke was fast and nimble when floating in the air, but slow and steady when close to the ground.

Amon had been stuck at the initial stages of qi gathering for years. His affinity with qi was low, and so was his talent. These setbacks made it impossible for him to manipulate qi in any way. In meditation, the longer one could maintain the ethereal state of conscious emptiness, the bigger the benefits. Naturally, the longer they sensed the qi, the higher their understanding of it became, no matter how slow the process was.

Qi gathering was nothing more than a preparatory stage. It is said that with enough talent and affinity, one could soar through it in a single day.

Nevertheless, such a high level of talent and comprehension were only seen once every hundred years. Of one thousand mortals, only one would have the ability to develop their divine sense. Out of a thousand people with divine sense, only ten would be able to absorb qi, direct it to their dantian, and be able to start body tempering.

Satisfied that Amon had successfully entered a meditative state, Daniel quietly made his way downstairs. On his way through the living room, he picked up a chair and carried it to Rebecca's bedroom.

"Come in, Daniel."

He had barely lifted his hand to knock on her door before he heard her voice. After closing the door behind him, he sat in the chair and faced the frail woman. A faint medicinal fragrance made its way into his nose.

"I have a stubborn son. I don't know how many times I've told him to stop buying nourishing pills for me and just get something for himself."

Daniel gave a small chuckle and smiled.

"What happened today?"

Her voice was gentle, but it had a hint of authority behind it. It sounded more like an order for a report than a question.

Daniel showed her the faint mark on his palm from where the stone had pierced his skin.

"Erin. He reached the body tempering stage."

Rebecca sighed—she knew it would be troublesome.

"There were no provocations. He just threw the stone at Amon's head," Daniel continued.

A chill crept up Daniel's spine. The room's temperature dropped several degrees as an icy killing intent surged from the woman facing him. He felt like he was facing a completely different person. Rebecca's clear eyes were filled with fury. The gentleness surrounding her had been completely swallowed by pure hostility. Few cultivators in the whole Abyss sect would have been able to produce an aura like that.

"Looks like Claude is a horrible cultivator *and* father. I should have taught him a lesson a long time ago," she said, her voice cold and full of regret.

People once feared her name—the White Flame, Rebecca Skoller. However, in her current state, there was not much she could do.

"Auntie, your skin is reddening again," Daniel sheepishly pointed out.

Rebecca raised her hands and, sure enough, a reddish hue had started to spread over her shriveled skin. It didn't take long for her breathing to turn ragged and a terrible sense of heat assaulted her senses.

She hurriedly grasped something beneath the sheets, controlling her breathing and trying to calm herself. After a while her skin returned to its original sickly pale tone and her breathing stabilized. Seeing her returning to normal, Daniel gave a sigh of relief.

"Isn't it funny, Daniel? When you're strong, the people around you will show you respect and avoid getting on your bad side. If you show respect back, they will gladly sing your praises and call you a role model. If, however, you step on them, they will only cower in fear."

Rebecca's voice was monotone, and robotic. Though she stared directly at him, her eyes were distant and dull.

"If you ever fall from grace, the end result will mostly be the same. It doesn't matter if you were kind or cruel when you were strong, what was important was the fact that you had strength. The people you once relied on won't praise you when you've become one of them. They didn't mind being stepped on and they never wanted to be respected by those above them. All they wanted was someone they could rely on. As soon as they can't rely on you anymore, you disappear from their eyes. After all, they want to be carried by the strong; they don't want to carry the weak." She smoothed the covers around her and fluffed the pillows behind her back before she continued. "Sometimes I'm surprised at just how easily humans will turn against you."

The threatening aura had slowly subsided.

"I think the best decision I've ever made in my life, other than having Amon, was helping you that day. I'm really glad I became friends with one of the few decent people in this hellhole," Rebecca said with a sad smile.

"You can always count on me, auntie," Daniel reassured her without hesitation.

Rebecca laughed hearing that. It was always a bit surprising every time Daniel called her "auntie," but it always warmed her heart.

Changing the subject, she said, "I'm sure you already know this, but Amon agreed to participate in the Scavenging. You pulled off a nice trick. Even if he was suspicious it was too good a deal for him to ignore."

"Well, he would have never accepted my contribution points if I just gave them to him. Taking him along should also help resolve the fear he has of the event itself."

Rebecca agreed.

"I can't thank you enough, Daniel."

"Don't worry about it."

"Please, promise me you will take good care of him."

"Of course I will. He's like a little brother to me."

"Good luck on the Scavenging. I really hope you find something. The spear I found seventy years ago was buried right there."

Her eyes lit up. The good memories of being a rebellious, young girl swam through her mind. She still remembered the day she sneaked out of the Inner Sect to join the Scavenging. Richard Layn had almost ripped out his beard in anger after he had finally found her.

"Well, Amon is meditating in his room. I'll go take care of the preparations."

"Goodbye, Daniel."

With that, Daniel left the house. Rebecca glanced at the evening sky through her window. Her thoughts meandered around how life was unfair to good people. Maybe that was the reason this world was filled with trash.

Rebecca fished for something under her blanket. After a short moment, she revealed a necklace—the item which she had grasped earlier to calm her down. The small, scarlet jewel glistened as the sunlight bounced off of it. A strange, red light floated inside of it, flickering nonstop. It was the last gift her husband had given her, and the one thing she managed to retrieve from their old house besides Raven. Not even Amon knew about it. She knew better than to show it to him.

The jewel reminded her of her husband's broad back as he left. She could almost feel the cold night wind entering through the open door and making her shudder as tears fell from her face. *What kind of person was he?*

Despite spending a vast number of years with him, the question plagued her dearly whenever she thought about her husband. She clutched the necklace tighter, pushing those horrid thoughts from her mind.

In truth, she knew the answer. She had always known. It was just that a part of her refused to admit how blind she had been. Sometimes it was better to fool herself than to face the truth.

A week had passed and Amon still hadn't managed to control a single strand of qi. Instead of going to the Northern Junction again, he took long walks around the area in the mornings and completed a few odd jobs to earn contribution points.

As the sun rose on the day of the Scavenging, Amon was gathering some clothes for his journey. Daniel had arrived an hour earlier and had made his way to Rebeccas's room.

"Here, auntie. I've brought you enough water, bread, cheese, and dried meat to last for a week," Daniel said, taking a bottomless pouch from his robes.

She gracefully accepted the pouch, though her expression turned funny when it was fully in her hands.

"It's been a while since I've held one of these. I could never get used to putting my arm into one. It's like submerging it in water, but without getting wet. It gives me the creeps."

They both laughed merrily. The bottomless pouches weren't favored by everyone. After a short moment, Rebecca regained her serious tone.

"Daniel, be very careful in this Scavenging," she said in a low, but stern voice, her eyes fixed on his.

"Did something happen?" he asked, surprised.

"No... at least I think not. It's just a bad feeling. Though, you *are* venturing into the Broken Forest, so keep your guard up."

She seemed a bit confused as to why she felt this way.

"I promise you, auntie. I'll be careful and take good care of Amon."

His words slightly soothed the churning pit in her stomach and the worry in her heart.

"Thank you," she replied, her eyes lighting up as Amon entered the room.

Daniel stood up and said his goodbyes. Meanwhile, Amon stood at the corner of her bed with a small linen sack full of clothes on his shoulder. His black hair had a strange glint to it, almost as if it was shining. It had been more than a week since he last used the black nuts and soon the dye would lose effect.

Rebecca opened her arms and beckoned for him to give her a hug. She ruffled his hair and kissed his forehead.

She whispered into his ear, "You have to be careful, okay?"

Her voice was full of worry.

"I will, mom."

"Listen to Daniel and, if something happens, promise me you'll run to safety."

"I—"

"Promise me!"

"I promise. I'll run."

Amon was starting to feel insecure. *What is this about?*

"Good. I'll see you in a few days."

She tightened her hug and kissed his forehead once more. Amon kissed her cheek and left. Rebecca ran her hand across her neck, and twirled the scarlet gem between her fingers as she watched the two of them walking down the front path. The sun slowly peeked over the horizon, its bright rays illuminated Amon and Daniel as they laughed and joked with one another.

A strange feeling churned in her chest. Was this worry or fear? She had dismissed Amon's worries a week ago. She thought it was just him blaming himself for something that was out of his control. Yet, she felt strange whenever she remembered his words. What if it wasn't just his guilt speaking? She didn't know what Lloyd had done to her son that day. Maybe she had made a mistake. Hoping she was wrong, Rebecca lightly pressed the necklace onto her chest with her palm.

❋ ❋ ❋

After a few hours, Amon and Daniel had finally reached the Broken Forest. Black stone watchtowers were manned by heavily armed guards throughout the day and night. They were connected by a thick, black stone wall that clearly defined the sects grounds from that of the forest.

The Abyss Sect lay alone in the area. Spirit beasts, animals that cultivated by instinct, lurked at every corner. Fraught with hidden dangers, none of the nearby mortal kingdoms or smaller sects dared to venture into its maw.

Should the beasts decide to invade the sect's grounds, people in the Outer Sect had no chance of fighting them. Despite it being an extremely rare occurrence, a stampede of these formidable creatures could attack with little notice.

As Amon and Daniel approached the golden gate in the wall, they saw a multitude of people gathered at the entryway. They were divided into more than twenty lines. An elder stood at the head of each one, confirming the participants prior applications to the Scavenging.

When Amon and Daniel reached the front of their queue, Daniel presented two wooden plaques with their registration information. Glancing at the plaques, the elder instructed the two of them to stand off to the side after he confirmed their applications.

Soon after, a middle-aged man approached them. His purple robes were embroidered with silver embellishments, and his short, salt and pepper hair was neatly combed to the side. With a light kick on the ground, his body shot up, creating a gust of wind that blew into the faces of a few dozen people next to him. Once he landed atop the wall, he began to speak and his voice sounded clear in everyone's ears. His voice was calm and serene, his tone steady.

"Good morning. As you all know, today we will open the Broken Forest for the Scavenging. Twenty elders will be roaming the forest for the next four days. They will provide assistance to anyone who needs it. For the parents that brought their children, I don't recommend staying more than two kilometers away from the gates. Nevertheless, the forest is big and the elders are few. Your lives are ultimately in your hands."

"You may return anytime between now and the deadline. If you overstay the allotted time, a penalty will be applied for trespassing. Are there any questions?"

He looked around the crowd and a few people inquired about a few unimportant matters. When they were done, he raised his hands high into the air.

"Let the Scavenging begin!"

The enormous gate slowly opened. There was pushing and pulling everywhere. Daniel grabbed Amon by his collar and held on tightly. He didn't want to explain to Rebecca that her son was trampled at the entrance by their fellow cultivators.

Once they managed to step out of the center of the madness, Daniel pointed east and said, "Come on. We have to be fast!"

They ran for a few minutes without slowing down. Amon tried his best to keep up with Daniel's long legs. They had barely covered a kilometer, but Amon was already panting for breath and covered in sweat.

"Alright, this should be far enough. We can slow down a bit."

Amon couldn't speak, he needed to catch his breath. Giving a slight nod, he motioned for Daniel to continue.

"We're about thirty kilometers away from the Red River. We should get there by nightfall if we don't take too many breaks."

"I... fine. G-give me a s-second," Amon stuttered as he took several deep breaths.

He sat down on the ground and slowly regulated his breathing. They were still near the wall, but he could already see the forest from up close.

The trees were dozens of meters tall, with dark green leaves at their crowns. Their branches intertwined, blocking the sunlight. Their twisted, dark trunks had a circumference of at least three meters. The trees were hundreds of years old, if not thousands.

Amon couldn't see past a few meters inside the forest. A sharp chill ran through his body and he suddenly felt pressure within his chest. He found it difficult to breathe, and his face paled.

Daniel realized it and slapped his back, snapping him out of it.

"Are you okay?"

Amon looked delirious and his arms and legs were trembling.

"I'll be fine."

Daniel nodded and sat by his side. Amon clenched his fists hard and tensed his muscles, trying to stop his body from trembling. It took him a few minutes to collect himself. When Daniel saw that he was somewhat better, he jumped to his feet.

"Let's go, or we will never get there in time," he replied, helping Amon to his feet.

"What's the plan? I don't know if we'll be able to get there and return in four days."

Daniel scoffed. He continued walking east and Amon cautiously followed suit.

"Once we reach the river we'll build a raft. It should only take us half an hour at best. The river will take us straight to our destination and we should arrive by sunrise. If you get tired you can sleep on the raft."

Amon was impressed, but not surprised. Daniel always seemed to be thinking a few steps ahead.

As the midday sun lazily rose into the sky, the temperature rose as well. They walked closer to the edge of the forest to seek refuge in the shadows as they moved. Being that close to the forest put him on edge. Daniel tried to lighten his mood, but was unsuccessful.

They had spent over eight hours walking along the forest's edge. Their journey would have been quicker, but Amon's young and weak body demanded rest every few hours. The soft sound of water trickling gave them a boost of energy. Quickening their pace, they approached the river in the distance.

The mud-brown water of the Red River gushed loudly at their feet. Amon took several steps back, fearing he would fall in and be swept away in its current. Daniel, on the other hand, wasted no time getting started on the raft.

He pulled open his bottomless pouch and retrieved an axe and some rope before powerfully striking one of the young trees along the river. His axe whistled through the air with each swing, its impact shaking the surrounding trees. When he was done, several logs sat on the ground, each four meters in length.

"Help me out a bit," Daniel said.

Amon helped hold the ropes in place as Daniel firmly tied them around the logs. After he was satisfied, he let out a long breath, cleaning the droplets of sweat from his face. By the time they dragged the raft into the water, only a few slivers of red light still shone on the horizon. They climbed on the raft and secured their belongings. Using a long stick he made from one of the branches of a tree, Daniel pushed the raft away from the riverbank. By then, Amon was falling asleep. His face was pale and his clothes clung to his body, covered in sweat. The dropping temperature made him shiver. He retrieved a blanket from the pouch and used his own bag as a pillow. Before long, he fell soundly asleep, not acknowledging the gentle rocking of the raft.

Daniel, on the other hand, was fine. He had done most of the work, but he only felt slightly tired. He could actually go on for a few days without sleep, although he hated doing so. He seemed to enter a trance as he navigated the raft downstream. Stars slowly lit up the sky, and a full moon appeared from behind the clouds, coldly gazing at them from above.

On occasion, large waves would pass beneath the raft, briefly waking Amon from his slumber. It wouldn't take him long to fall asleep again, but these interruptions occurred quite often throughout the night. This left him feeling groggy and heavy when Daniel finally woke him.

"We're here."

The sky was still dark, but Amon could already hear the chirping of the birds alongside the screeching of cicadas.

"What time is it?" Amon asked, rubbing his golden eyes which seemed like lanterns glowing in the dark.

"There are two hours left until sunrise. Let's go. The quicker we search here, the quicker we can return," Daniel said, jumping off the raft and dragging it onto the riverbank.

Meanwhile, Amon splashed the cold river water on his face to properly wake up. Daniel began to rummage through his pouch, handing several items to Amon. The first was a slender sword with an azure scabbard and pure white handle. It was a high-grade artifact that his father had given him long ago.

The second was a palm-sized, crystalline shield. It was an expendable treasure that could create a thick barrier around the user for a limited time. The third item was a jade disc filled with runes that glowed with a green light. Daniel injected his qi into the disc and it spun madly before floating slightly above his hand.

This qi compass was designed to tilt in the direction where qi was more abundant. Artifacts had high concentrations of qi and thus the compass was a great tool to have on their journey. It was extremely rare and it cost a fortune, which was why not many used it in the Scavenging.

Daniel and Amon walked along the riverbank with the disc in hand. They had walked for over an hour, covering two kilometers east of their starting point, yet they found nothing. When they were about to give up, the disk suddenly tilted towards the river.

Daniel was surprised. He had never expected to find anything and was waiting for Amon to give up so they could return. Amon's eyes shone with excitement as they carefully inched towards the river, desperately scanning for treasure. Suddenly, the disc flew out of Daniel's hands and started floating above the ground. Using a burst of his divine sense, Daniel examined the area and detected an object shaped like a spearhead buried a few feet underground. The duo kneeled on the ground and started digging frantically.

The sun had already started to rise on the horizon, painting the river with a hellish red tint. There were no birds chirping. No cicadas screeching. There was no sound at all, almost as if time had stopped. However, the pair was far too excited to notice.

Amon felt his hair stand on end and his body started to heat up. He could feel his blood churning from what he thought was excitement. A strange numbness started to course through his body like electricity. His primal instincts kicked in as he felt something approaching from the forest at an incredibly fast speed.

Trembling and pale, a cold sweat ran down his back. This familiar feeling was not nearly as strong as the one he felt five years ago, but he wasn't going to take any risks.

"Daniel, we have to go!"

Daniel stared up at Amon's ghostly face, slightly confused.

"Daniel, we have to go now!"

Without asking questions, Daniel grabbed the disc and tossed Amon onto his left shoulder, running back from whence they came. Unfortunately, it was too late.

A black shadow jumped in front of him and blocked his path. Daniel barely managed to keep his balance as he slid to a halt. A piercing trill echoed through the forest as Daniel drew his sword with his right hand.

He heard something snap to his right. Slowly turning his head towards the sound, Daniel saw a huge shadow taking shape between the trees. With each step it took, the ground shook beneath his feet. The color drained from his face and Amon's heart skipped several beats.

A pair of crimson eyes locked onto the two young men. A paw that was as big as an adult's torso appeared from the shadows. The creature's large, dagger-like claws scratched the ground as it walked, leaving large grooves in the earth. Its black fur presented itself more like an armor made of iron needles. The beast opened its mouth revealing a row of razor-sharp fangs.

"AWOOOOOOOOOOO!"

The beast's howl made Amon's ears bleed as he was blown off of Daniel's shoulder, causing Daniel to stumble. Its eyes then focused on Amon. He tried to inch his way over to Daniel, but to his horror, he couldn't control his frail body. The beast approached him and stopped five meters away, glaring at him with hostility as the fur on its back stood up and a deep growl resonated from its throat.

Daniel snapped out of his trance. He recovered the shield talisman from his clothes and shattered it, moving closer to Amon. A thick and translucent golden light materialized from thin air and encompassed them. Daniel grabbed Amon and threw him over his shoulder once more. He used the shield covering them to smash through the wolf like a cannonball before bolting at full speed towards the raft.

Another howl echoed around them, making the surface of the shield ripple, and the beast ran towards them. Daniel was scared out of his mind. A beast like that shouldn't be here. He refused to believe what he was seeing, but the name of the beast still made its way out of his mouth.

"Dire wolf!"

THE SWORD OF THE IMMORTAL

hat are they doing here?

W Daniel was afraid and confused. Dire wolves and other strong spirit beasts shouldn't be in this area. Although dire wolves were only class four, they were still incredibly rare. They usually roamed north, dozens of kilometers away from this section of the Red River. The only exception happened five years ago, when a pack led by a silverback wolf made its way into the region near the Hell Keeper's Mountain, close to the northern walls.

The sect had wiped them all out after a dozen disciples were attacked, but a silverback wolf was still a class six spirit beast. Even though Rebecca was one of the strongest cultivators in the sect, she suffered grievous injuries and ended up crippled protecting her son and stalling until reinforcements arrived.

The dire wolf in front of them was at least six meters long and three meters high. Daniel knew they had no chance. He could only hope that the shield would protect them until they made their way back to the raft.

Amon was completely out of it. The trees were no more than brown and green blurs as Daniel ran like mad. His weighted steps cracked the ground and any tree trunk was utterly decimated when he used it as leverage.

Daniel saw a dark blur passing by his side and it came to a halt in front of them. The frightened cultivator tried to change directions but it was too late. The dire wolf brandished its claws, hitting the shield that surrounded them.

They took no damage, but they were sent flying backwards, smashing through a pair of trees before finally hitting the ground. The dust and broken wood from the impact flew everywhere, obscuring their vision. The shield lost its luster and started flickering. Daniel knew it would only last a few more seconds. He hesitated for a moment before continuing his sprint.

They shouldn't be too far from the raft; if he rushed, they could make it in time.

Amon snapped out of his stupor and tried to free himself from Daniel's grasp.

"Daniel, you have to let me go!" He screamed with his high-pitched voice, his face flushed as he struggled.

"Now is not the time to throw a tantrum, kid! Do you want to die?" Daniel rebuked in a harsh tone. He was not going to put up with this right now.

"You don't understand, that wolf is coming for me! If you don't let me go you'll die!" Amon cried out, desperate to break free.

What the hell is Amon talking about? he thought as he shook his head to clear up his thoughts. Now was not the time to worry about such things. He continued dashing through the forest while Amon shouted in desperation. He had no idea what had gotten into the young boy, but if he didn't calm down he would make things worse.

From the corner of his eye, he saw the dire wolf surpassing them again. He didn't even think before he launched himself towards the nearest tree and used it as a foothold. He shot over the wolf as it struck again, its enormous claw grazed past his leg and shattered the shield.

They heard another howl behind them, making Daniel's ears hurt and Amon's bleed even more. Amon covered his ears with a scream of pain before he started mumbling, "I'm sorry," over and over again.

The raft on the riverbank came into view.—they had finally made it. He heard another howl coming from the right, but this one was weaker than the ones from the wolf pursuing them. Daniel's blood froze as another howl echoed from the back, followed by another from the front. Three more wolves emerged from the shadows, making their way towards the two young men. They had the same burning eyes and black fur, but were half the size of the dire wolf following them. One of them was the same wolf Daniel had hit earlier; it was seemingly unhurt.

Daniel's heart filled with despair. There was no way for them to escape. Amon started crying on his shoulder, drenching Daniel's robes. As he looked over Daniel's back, he became silent. Daniel didn't need to guess why. He heard bushes rustling behind him. Slowly turning around, he prepared to face the larger monster.

Daniel gripped the sword in his hand tightly, gritting his teeth. The gigantic wolf slowly approached. Pieces of flesh were lodged between its fangs, loosely jiggling as it shook its head and stopped in front of them. Its hot breath gave off a foul odor of blood and rotten meat, making Amon sick to his stomach.

Daniel's mind raced as he tried to find something, anything to get them out of this horrible situation. His chances of survival were slim to none while fighting them alone. He didn't have to imagine what the odds would be once he factored in protecting Amon as well. Getting Amon out of harm's way was his first priority, but distracting them was imperative.

He closed his eyes for a moment before making a decision. When he opened them again, they shone with determination. He suddenly spun, turning his back to the alpha dire wolf. He held Amon up and looked past the wolves in front of them. The raft was about thirty meters away.

He took aim and mustered every ounce of his strength before throwing the crying Amon over the trees, in the direction of the river. Before he could see if his aim was on point, he spun again, sword in hand.

The sword glistened brightly while it drew a beautiful arc in the air, propelled by Daniel's momentum. The blade hit the enormous dire wolf behind him, opening a deep gash in its head, hitting an eye and partially blinding him.

The dire wolf stood in place, its eyes burning while dark blood dripped from its head. He didn't howl and he didn't growl. He simply opened its mouth and jumped at Daniel, baring its fangs. As the wolf's teeth inched towards his head, Daniel knew he wouldn't be able to dodge the attack. Suddenly, the sound of Amon landing on the raft echoed through the area, turning the wolf's attention towards the raging water. Its attention was no longer on Daniel. Instead, it ventured towards the noise.

Amon was squirming in pain atop the raft. Being thrown to safety came at a price; he was clearly injured.

Daniel used all his willpower to focus for a moment. He had no more than a second to gain control over a huge amount of qi that was far away from him. A very difficult feat even for talented people. Yet, he somehow managed to accomplish it in his desperation.

He hurriedly focused, sensing the dark strands of mist that covered the world. By his will, they started to swirl, coming together and forming into a misshapen sphere. With a blast, the air pushed the raft onto the river's surface. The violent waves quickly pushed the raft along the river's length. Unfortunately, it was heading towards them.

The dire wolf locked its eyes on Amon and bent its hind legs, preparing to jump. Daniel panicked; he would never be able to stop the beast from pursuing Amon if he didn't distract it first. Trembling in fear, he attacked the dire wolf a second time.

"Hell no!" Daniel shouted, brandishing the sword again.

He jumped up and tried to hit the dire wolf's back. Unexpectedly, the wolf turned around and swatted at him like a fly. The dire wolf only saw him as an annoyance, never as a threat. Nevertheless, its half-hearted strike could still cut Daniel in two. He desperately twisted his body midair, barely avoiding a hit to his waist. The claws slashed his right shoulder and arm, making Daniel scream in pain as the sword in his right hand escaped from his grip.

He painfully hit the ground, and barely managed to stand up. Looking at his arm, he noticed that it was nothing more than an indistinct mass of flesh and blood. Shreds of muscle peeked through the torn skin and most of his forearm was now flayed and laying on the ground. However, his hand was still intact.

The beast sent him one last glance before snarling, signaling to its pack to chase after the raft. Grimacing in pain, Daniel knew he had to do something to save Amon. His mind started fading as he began to lose consciousness. Gritting his teeth, he retrieved a small, sword-shaped piece of jade from his robes. He didn't want to use it, but he had no choice.

This jade object was a single-use, offensive artifact and the last gift his father had given him when he left. It was, for all intents and purposes, a parting gift for his disappointment of a son.

For the first time in many years, Daniel felt grateful towards his father. He was surprised by the power it held considering their relationship. It turns out that his father didn't hold back when making this for him. He sneered at the thought. It was obvious his father would never allow anything related to his name be subpar—it was a lesson he would never forget.

Daniel always saw himself as a failure. He was shunned from his family the very moment his younger brother's talents exceeded his own. Those who had called themselves his friends rejected him the moment he lost his connections to his father. Only one person extended her hand to him in that dark and lonely madness. A gentle, white flame lit up his life, destroying the darkness that was growing inside of him. He owed her his life.

He would never let her son suffer the same way he did, nor would he let her son die. Daniel refused to let Rebecca down, even if it meant dying in this place. And so, the disgraceful Daniel bravely faced his death with a savage look on his face.

"You're all dead!" Daniel shouted as if mad while he slashed at the wolves with the tiny sword from far away.

Daniel sent his qi into the tiny artifact, causing it to glow with a glacial-blue light. A terrifying aura burst from its center and the wolves turned towards him once more. This time, their eyes were full of apprehension. A deranged smile slid onto Daniel's sweaty, pale face as his heart filled with nostalgia.

The jade sword drew an arc in the air, creating a blinding flash which was immediately followed by an unbearable cold. All color in the world vanished, except for a speckled trail of blue light. A strong gust of wind exploded from the source, leaving behind a frightening wave of death and destruction.

Amon slowly opened his eyes, only to be greeted by the blinding sun. He was confused; his head felt light and his body heavy. All he could hear was a loud buzz reverberating inside his head. As he turned away from the bright rays, a sudden piercing pain in his left shoulder made him scream.

The pain properly woke him up, pulsating throughout his body. A splitting headache made him grunt and he almost passed out again. He closed his eyes hard until his head's throbbing lessened and the pain became somewhat manageable.

Then, he looked around. He saw that he was still on the raft, stranded in a riverbank. He had no idea if he was still in the Red River or in one of the streams that originated from it.

He was feeling cold despite the blazing sun and realized his robes were completely drenched, clinging to his body. Not only were they wet, but they were tattered and stained with black patches on his chest and shoulders.

Amon tried to slowly move his arm, but realized he couldn't handle the pain. His shoulder was incredibly swollen. Perhaps his collarbone was broken from Daniel slinging him onto the raft from such a distance.

Bruises covered his arms and legs. They, too, refused to function properly and the feeling of lethargy started to greatly affect him.

He turned on his right shoulder, trying to slightly move his right hand and his legs and get used to the pain. He moved his limbs around, trying to pull himself up, but raising his arm or moving his legs seemed to be a herculean task. It felt like an eternity, but Amon eventually managed to stand up. With no idea where he was, his only choice was to limp upstream.

His traveling bag was nowhere in sight. Without it, he had no food or medicine to hold him over until someone, hopefully Daniel, could find him. With his hearing damaged, he couldn't hear the sounds of the river. Only the ringing in his head kept him company as he walked. Unfortunately, this also meant that he wouldn't be able to hear anything approaching him, much less escape with his current condition. His chances of making it back alive were grim.

Hungry and delirious, Amon vacantly peered into the sky and started crying from both sorrow and relief. He had survived the ordeal, but he didn't know what price Daniel had paid because of him. It *was* his fault. It had been his fault five years ago and it was his fault today. His mother had been hurt because of him, and now Daniel was hurt too. He had no idea why, but he was sure that the strange feeling had something to do with the wolves targeting him.

"Daniel is alive. I'll find help to save him," Amon muttered, trying to convince himself while he limped as fast as he could. His dirty appearance, pale face, and endless babbling made him look more like a ghost than a person.

The young boy walked for what seemed like hours, almost in a trance. He fell more than once, but always got up. The pain was still there, but was greatly numbed by his clouded mind. He didn't know how far he walked alongside the river, but he never stopped.

"Eh?"

A shock ran through him, clearing his mind. He looked around, confused. He felt something tugging at his mind, almost calling to him.

He realized he knew this place, which should have been impossible. He gazed somewhere in the middle of the trees and had a sudden impulse to go there. As he walked he felt the headache returning, stronger than ever.

A strange, feeble voice echoed in his head, whispering. It managed to stand out from the ever-present buzz in his ears. However, it was so faint and low that he couldn't understand what it was saying. All he could feel was a soul-crushing sense of longing and sorrow. He had lost something, and he wanted to get it back at all costs. His head throbbed and he fell to his knees.

"What the hell? Stop!" he screamed into the air.

The impulse started getting stronger and he stood up. His body no longer felt like his own. He couldn't control where he wanted to go or what he wanted to do. He didn't know if he wanted to do anything at all. Amon's thoughts contradicted his actions as his brain seemed to split and sew itself back together, making for an inharmonious whole. Only sorrow and an inexplicable sense of longing stood clear in his mind.

As his body dragged him along, he suddenly felt a jolt. He looked ahead and realized he was walking directly into a tree. Amon tried to stop, but couldn't. His body lurched forward, not minding the tree one bit. Squeezing his eyes closed, he braced for impact, but it never came. A cold sensation ran through his body, making it difficult for him to move.

The feeling disappeared as quickly as it came and Amon found himself sprawled on a soft patch of green grass. Confused, he looked around and found that he was definitely somewhere new. *Have I been teleported to another world,* he thought, starting at the vast field before him.

At first glance, the area's beauty surpassed that of anything he'd ever seen and Amon was sure he was inside of a painting rather than the real world. Small trees filled with delicate, white flowers were surrounded by a lush blanket of green grass. They rustled in the gentle breeze blowing against Amon's dampened skin.

In the distance, he could see a lake, shining under the sun's golden rays. The lake was only a few hundred square meters. The silky, white clouds and dusty-blue sky were reflected on its mirror-like surface as small waves, gently pushed across the lake with the wind.

Examining his surroundings further, Amon saw that not all of it was beautiful. Long gashes crisscrossed on the ground, giving the terrain a woven look. Many of the trees were chopped in half with the remnants of their trunks withered and cracked.

Amon started feeling grief and regret as he looked at the scars. He didn't know why, but he could feel great pain hidden within them. These emotions overwhelmed him and his eyes filled with tears and he tried to collect himself. Suddenly, out of the corner of his eye, he noticed something near the lake's edge and his body tensed.

Should I approach it?

Amon stood there for a moment, waiting for the object to move, but it remained still. Walking closer to it, he noticed that it was a skeleton draped in the scraps of torn, blue robes. The bones were quite odd. They looked as though they were made of crystal as they glimmered in the sunlight.

Amon knew that this must have been a powerful cultivator in the past. Having one's body tempered countless times, would cause one's bones to physically change, giving them the appearance of crystal. The duration of this process took place over the cultivator's entire life, and it was more natural than forced tempering. Their corpses could be preserved for centuries as long as nothing destroyed them, which wasn't an easy thing to do.

Amon examined the skeleton closely. The deceased died lying down on the grass, looking up. The young boy could almost feel the wistfulness that certainly showed in his eyes as he died gazing at the sky. His arms were wrapped around a sword, holding it close to his chest in a tight embrace—he obviously held it in high regard. On one of his fingers, a crystalline ring sparkled under the sunlight.

Amon's heart grew heavy and pressure spread throughout his chest. He wanted to cry, and he had no idea why he felt like this. He hesitated before carefully moving the skeleton's arms away from the sword. Amon took it in his hand, taking a better look.

It was a beautiful, yet simple weapon. The blade was one meter long and the hilt was approximately thirty centimeters in length. The sword's sheath and handle were made from black leather, and a complex pattern of silver lines decorated the sheath's surface. Its silver, crescent moon-shaped guard was embellished with a small, red gem that accented the sword elegantly.

He found it strange for the weapon of an expert to be so simple. Powerful cultivators usually liked being recognized and thus, they would customize their artifacts to their liking; the results varied greatly. These relics became a symbol of their identities, so it was rare to see such simple items in the hands of an expert.

Amon wondered how much this sword would be worth. He speculated that its value could earn him enough contribution points to sustain him and his mother for years. At the very least, he would be able to buy medicine that could heal her completely.

Though his mother's recovery would bring him great joy, Amon's thoughts of selling the sword filled him with discontent.

With his one, working hand, he gripped the handle and unsheathed the sword with great difficulty. The blade hummed as it was revealed to the world after an unknown number of years. Although the blade was nothing fancy, it was polished to a high-shine, enough to clearly see one's reflection. Though it was seemingly perfect in appearance, its balance was not.

Its grip was heavily worn to the point that one could see the outline of the owner's fingers; Amon's were quite small in comparison. Holding the sword was uncomfortable, somehow feeling both appeasing and unnerving at the same time.

"Brightmoon," he whispered.

He was taken aback by his own words and a scorching pain suddenly burned through his palm. Surprised, he quickly dropped the sword on the ground and looked at his sore hand. It had turned bright red and was throbbing violently.

"Who dares to disturb this sacred resting place!?"

The angry, mysterious voice was directly broadcasted into Amon's head. Its loudness made Amon feel as though his brain would implode and the air around him became frigid, quickly constricting his movement. The invisible restraint tightened and he found it harder to breathe. Amon screamed as his injured shoulder was squeezed, causing the pain to flare up once more.

The sword floated up from the ground and a silhouette appeared by its side. After the shadowy figure fully materialized, a woman stood in front of him, holding the sword tightly by her side.

She was breathtaking. Her slender figure was held up by a pair of gorgeous, long legs. She wore a pearl-white dress that sat just above her knees. Its silky material glided against her porcelain skin without a hitch. Flowing, black hair framed her face, making her crystal-blue eyes appear to pierce one's soul.

The woman's eyes shone with a cold glint as she raised the sword. The pressure over Amon's body grew heavier and his vision started to fade. As he was prepared to feel the cold blade slashing through his neck, he heard a voice speak to him again. This time, however, it wasn't angry. The melodious tone of a woman's voice soothed his aching mind as it spoke.

"Alexei?"

It was gentle, yet full of surprise and incredulity.

Then, he passed out.

Richard Layn was hovering above the trees of the Broken Forest, enjoying the fresh air. It was the second day of the Scavenging and the sun hadn't risen yet. A gentle breeze blew above the trees, rustling the leaves and lightly tousling his hair as he looked at the dark sky.

He had long white hair that fell upon his shoulders and a beard that reached to his chest. His face was gentle, but filled with wrinkles. A pair of black eyes shone brightly behind his hair, making him seem really energetic despite his old age. His purple and silver robes were flawless; not a single speck of dust could be found on them.

This, of course, was expected for someone with his position. Out of the ten seats within the Elders' Council, Richard held the third. Although the ten members had equal authority, they still had to answer to the sect master and the four protectors.

With this in mind, it was quite peculiar to see someone of his status patrolling the Scavenging. Truth be told, Richard was bored out of his mind. Despite his old age, he still hated deskwork and bureaucracy. He felt he wasn't fit for such responsibilities as a member of the Elder Council, but he was forced into the job by Sect Master Borgin.

This year, the sect master demanded that security for the Scavenging be increased due to the incident at the last Scavenging. There was still great uncertainty about why the silverback wolf was so close to Hell Keeper's Mountain. Regardless, Richard was the first to offer his services. Getting away from his humdrum routine would be a well-deserved break.

Richard looked at the Red River and sighed deeply. Being near this area reminded him of the young girl from many years ago. She had almost driven him insane with her mischievous ways, sneaking out of the Inner Sect, and uncontrollable free spirit.

As he was lost in thought, a blinding light exploded from the trees a few kilometers away. A terrifying aura rose from its blazing blue light.

Its intensity forced Richard to close his eyes and turn away from its rays. A few moments later, it started to subside and everything around him shook.

Boom!

A loud sound erupted shortly after the light appeared. Its force made Richard feel as if he had been punched in the chest. A violent windstorm arose, tossing dirt and debris everywhere as it ripped trees from their roots and sent them flying in every direction.

Richard watched in surprise as the light disappeared and the wind gradually died down. Such a phenomenon would have injured him even at his power level. Curious as to what had just happened, he made his way over to the blast zone. Moving closer, his body grew cold and he shivered uncontrollably. The temperature had dipped greatly and a white mist slowly escaped from his lips as he struggled to breath in the frigid air.

Though the wind had died down a few minutes earlier, dust still floated about, leaving Richard unable to see more than a few meters in front of him. Once his hazy vision was clear again, a wide field of ice came into view.

A trail of frozen needles and dust was left near the river bank. It extended for fifty meters leaving everything covered in a thick layer of ice, and a small portion of the river had been frozen solid. The few trees that managed to survive were left with crisp, white leaves that stood erect. Their sharp, blade-like appearance didn't last long as they soon fell to the ground, shattering into countless glistening shards.

Near the beginning of the trail, an unconscious man was sprawled on the ground in a pool of blood. His robes were in tatters, slowly being covered by frost causing their blood-soaked strands to freeze. Richard could see that the cultivator's right arm was a mangled mess and his left hand was tightly holding a broken amulet.

Upon moving closer, Richard noticed that the carcasses of three black wolves were scattered at the trails end. Their bodies were unrecognizable chunks of flesh and bone that left the white frost speckled with crimson. Not far from their remains was a long, wide trail of blood that led into the forest. It was clear that something had dragged itself away, badly injured from the battle.

Shocked by the size of the bloody trail, Richard's expression grew uneasy as he cautiously stood next to the young man on the ground. He crouched to check for a pulse, keeping his eyes on his surroundings. The pulse was faint, but it was there. Richard took a pill from his pouch and gently turned the man over, preparing to feed it to him. His face grew pale —he knew this young man well.

"Daniel? What the hell happened here?" he asked more to himself than to Daniel.

Of course, no response was given. Richard cursed and administered several pills forcing them between Daniel's partially frozen lips. If Daniel died in his care, Richard would never live it down. No matter what people said about Daniel's relationship with his father, he was still the son of a highly respected man. He wrapped Daniel's arm with a few bandages, before taking a spare robe and hurriedly covering him to ward off the cold.

Careful not to injure him more, Richard slowly made Daniel float in the air using his qi. A frown of both concentration and concern was plastered on his face. Somehow, the creature that Daniel had faced was still alive and the elder hoped that it didn't return while they were still there.

This is the second time they've left their territory during the Scavenging. What's going on?

Richard shook his head and fished a flat, golden disc from his inner robe pocket. It flashed with a blue light and started floating above his palm.

"This is the third elder, reporting from the Scavenging patrol team. The second protector's son is gravely injured and needs urgent care. I'll be delivering him to the medical center in a few minutes. Please inform the staff that there is a high priority emergency incoming. We'll need to issue a sect hunt for a dire wolf—I'll be sending the coordinates soon."

Richard's voice was calm and slow as he spoke into the disc, trying to be as clear as possible. The disk flashed again and fell back onto his hand. After putting his gear away, Richard held Daniel close. He could feel the young man's body growing colder as he secured his body to Daniel's.

He steadied himself and then shot up into the sky at an amazing speed, disappearing into the distance

✳ ✳ ✳

Deep within Hell Keeper's Mountain, Lawrence Meyer sat cross-legged in his laboratory. Its walls were midnight-blue and the floor was black. Runes made of light connected to intertwined, forming words that slid across the floor. A thin layer of ice covered everything in the room, and a cold mist made it difficult to see.

Lawrence's black hair was stiff from the cold, and his straight nose was slightly red on its tip. His sharp features and oppressive aura matched perfectly with his blood-red robes and the curved sabre resting on his legs as he meditated. His eyelids appeared to be frozen shut with tiny icicles daintily hanging from his eyelashes.

Slowly opening his eyes, the ice fell into his lap as he released a long breath. He raised his left arm, looking at a thin golden thread tied around his wrist. It was decorated with numerous ornaments of varying shapes and sizes. Looking closer, he saw that a small, sword-shaped ornament had cracked. After a few moments, it finally gave in and shattered completely.

Though Lawrence didn't seem to mind, he seemed a bit surprised. He flicked the remains of the ornament off of his lap; he didn't think his son would manage to hold onto the talisman for ten whole years.

On his right wrist, three blood-red beads hung from a silver chain. They showed no signs of change, and so he felt no need to worry. He took a deep breath and returned to his meditation. Soon after, there was a light knock on his door—the constant interruptions irritated him greatly. Waving his hand, the mist and the frost on him disappeared. The layer of ice and the cold in the room, however, remained.

"Come in," he said in a voice as cold as his surroundings.

A small door hidden in a corner of the room opened, and Jake entered the room. At first, he seemed to be affected by the cold, but a burst of energy exploded from him and his body started emitting steam as his temperature rose. Every step he took made the ice melt at his feet and Lawrence gave a satisfied nod; his son's progress was satisfying as usual.

Jake, of course, heavily resembled Lawrence and Daniel. Afterall, they were related. His handsome face exuded a heroic bearing that he could not hide. He had a prideful air about him, but didn't feel unapproachable.

"Father," he greeted as he kneeled on the floor.

His father gave a slight nod and replied, "You may speak."

"Daniel is gravely injured. I heard he was attacked by a grown dire wolf during the Scavenging."

Jake's voice was steady, but his expression gave away his true feelings. He felt nothing but love, longing, and pity for his older brother.

"That must be why he used his talisman," Lawrence scoffed as he stroked his chin, his expression unwavering.

The worry on Jake's face melted and was replaced with a sad, but sour look. He felt sorry for Daniel—their father's heart was truly made of stone.

"The Elder Council has called for a hunt to take down the beast. I've accepted," he said, still trying to read some emotions from his father. "I'll be leaving with Karen and Joshua for a few days," he informed, standing up and straightening his clothes.

"What if I say no? You still haven't finished your final round of purification," Lawrence's voice was full of annoyance.

"Well, the sect master already cleared me to go, so I'll be off. I just stopped by to notify you," Jake retorted, giving a half-hearted and shallow bow.

Without another word, Jake turned to leave. Steam and puddles of water trailed behind him as he glided out of the lab. He wanted nothing more than to mutilate the dire wolf that had hurt Daniel.

Lawrence's brows scrunched in disapproval. He knew that Jake was greatly upset at his dislike of Daniel, but he refused to let it ruin his day. Returning to his meditation, he cast a new layer of frost over himself and the mist returned the room to its sinister atmosphere.

Lya held Brightmoon in her hand as she stared at the unconscious boy in front of her. Her ghostly figure floated centimeters above the ground and a silver light surrounded her.

Her face crumpled with curiosity and she could tell that he was a sorry mess. His clothes were torn and soiled with mud. The dark purple bruises covering his body were starting to swell. As she got closer, she saw that the boy's shoulder was swollen three times its normal size. It was obvious he had been through hell before arriving there. Though his face was average at best, his eyes were bright gold and his ash-grey hair was streaked black and disheveled.

"Is this dye?" Lya thought aloud. Gently waving her hands she cleaned the boy with a burst of qi. The black dye dissolved and the dirt was blown away from his clothes and face. The cleaner version of him seems more enticing and more... exotic.

Lya turned her head to the skeleton lying on the grass. Her lips trembled and her eyes glazed over with tears. No matter how many times she looked at him, the pain never diminished; it only got worse.

"I'm sorry," she whispered.

She lost count of how many times she had said that, but she always felt it wasn't enough. A few tears stained her face as she waved her hands again. The crystalline ring flew away from the skeleton's finger and fell in her hand. She lightly swiped the ring and looked dazed for a moment, as if daydreaming. When she recovered, the ring flashed with a faint light and a red pill was seen in her pale hands.

"This might be a bit too much, but I don't have anything weaker than this," she mumbled as she gently placed the pill between the boys lips.

It immediately dissolved on his tongue, making a bright, gummy liquid that churned in his mouth. She flicked a finger lightly, and a small strand of qi pushed the red liquid in his mouth down his throat.

The boy coughed hard and his body started to heat up. His skin turned red and steam started to rise from his body and clothes. The bruises rapidly faded away and the swelling on his body was greatly reduced.

"I'm sorry in advance," Lya said, as she focused and clapped her hands together, making the qi around the boy's shoulder clamp together.

A loud *crack* came from his arm and his shoulder suddenly returned to place. Still unconscious, a pained expression appeared on the boy's face as he started twitching. It took some time before he finally stopped moving and his skin returned to normal.

Lya's face had softened from when she first saw him. When she found him holding Brightmoon, immense anger welled up inside of her and she was prepared to kill him. She was worried that someone had managed to take down the barrier that protected the lake and was trying to rob the sword. To her surprise, it was still intact and the boy's aura gave her a strange, yet familiar feeling of nostalgia.

Lya focused and spread out her divine sense. She was now a lot stronger than she was in the past, so she felt confident she could sense it. A faint spark of hope lit in her heart as she concentrated.

She focused solely on the boy in front of her, trying to scrutinize every single part of him.

"It really is you," she said after a long while.

It was just a fragment that had become a small whole, but that was enough for her. She felt a mix of longing and regret rising up in her chest, and for a moment, she lost her composure.

There were no similarities between them. The boy's face didn't have his handsomeness. His hair was grey instead of blond and his eyes were golden instead of green. His hands were small and his fingers didn't have any calluses from holding a sword nonstop for days on end.

This young man didn't have an ounce of the proud and cold aura she had gotten used to. Instead, the boy felt rather passive and weak—they were complete opposites.

A sad and tired smile graced her face when she realized this. Maybe it was for the best that things were this way.

Amon slowly opened his eyes. He felt quite comfortable, almost as if he just had a great night of sleep. His pain was gone and he was full of energy. Sat up, stretching his renewed limbs. When he saw the beautiful woman in front of him, he almost screamed in terror until he realized that she was in a daze.

He slowly started sneaking away. A painful sting spread from his shoulder, but this time it was bearable. When he thought he was a safe distance away, he decided to sprint. Suddenly, his face hit something solid and he was thrown back. He looked ahead and saw nothing but air in front of him.

What happened? he asked himself.

"You know, running away without thanking the person that helped you is quite rude," a melodious voice rang out from behind him.

Amon felt a chill running through his back and turned to see the woman glancing at him from afar.

"Don't worry, I won't do anything to you," Lya said.

This time, her voice didn't echo inside his head, and Amon could properly hear her. He was confused when he realized this. Her attitude was much softer than it had been before. As he moved around, almost entirely free of pain, he wondered if she had healed him while he was unconscious.

"Look, what happened before was my fault. You caught me in a bad mood and I thought you were a thief," she said, with an amiable smile on her face.

Amon raised a brow as he took a few steps back, not taking his eyes from her.

"I'm sorry," she added, her face blushed with embarrassment at her clearly unacceptable behavior.

"Who are you? Why did you help me?"

"My name is Lya," she replied with a slight bow. "I reside in Brightmoon, the sword you touched before."

"Are you... a sword spirit?" he questioned, slightly dazed by the charming way she was presenting herself.

Spirits were things of legends. Throughout history, only a few cultivators came into possession of a weapon that contained a spirit within; they could be counted on one hand.

"Oh, please! Do not compare me to those things. I'm me," she said, as she crossed her arms.

"Again, why did you help me?" he asked.

Upon realizing that Amon had stopped backing away from her, she let out a small sigh of relief.

"Because we're fated. You wouldn't have been able to get past the barrier otherwise. You simply walked in—this is clearly fate," she said in a serious tone, brushing her hair out of her face.

Amon remembered the strange feeling he had when he first stumbled upon this space. He thought barriers were much different than what he experienced. After thinking for a bit, he thanked the woman for her kindness. Blushing, Lya dismissed his thanks as if it were her job to take care of him.

Amon finally understood Lya's words.

He thought about all the hardships he had endured in his life. He was nothing but a failure to Daniel, to his mother, his father... to everyone. If he had been stronger, his father wouldn't have left. If he was wiser, his mother wouldn't have been crippled in her bed, wasting away. If he had been more advanced with his qi, Daniel wouldn't have been mauled by wolves.

Amon tightened his fist and his gaze seemed to change. He held his head high, with an unprecedented serious expression. He turned to face Lya, staring into her eyes with determination.

Lya lightly trembled. She knew the look on his face too well. It was the kind of gaze she once fell in love with. It could easily lead someone to greatness or to death. She still remembered when a golden-haired boy looked at her with that same expression. He promised her that he would climb to the top of the world and change everything wrong in it. A futile dream. A futile path that he still treaded until the very end, only to fail. Still, he went further than anyone else had ever managed. All because he never lowered his head. All because his gaze never wavered, always focused in the distance, looking at something only he could see. It *was* fate that brought him here.

"If we're truly fated, please teach me how to be strong."

Lya thought it was a good choice of words. He wasn't asking her to lend him her strength, nor was he asking her to make him strong. Amon simply wanted guidance.

She smiled and stared into his eyes. His hard gaze was comforting, yet strange. The boy seemingly turned into a different person as soon as he realized what chance he had in front of him. However, the moment she saw those unwavering eyes she had decided on her answer.

"No."

The boy was taken aback. He didn't expect her to say no. His face flushed and his ears turned bright red in shame.

"W-Why not?" Amon asked, confused and slightly saddened.

He wasn't sure that Lya would accept his request, but going through all of the trouble of healing him and presenting herself to just deny him like that didn't make much sense to him.

"We are fated, yes. But do I know you?"

She looked at him, her blue eyes shining with a ferocious light.

"Why do you want to be strong? How would you use such power? What kind of person are you? What kind of person do you want to be?"

She stepped forward at each question, her voice full of authority. Amon's face paled as he started stepping back.

"Can you guarantee to me that you will always think as you do now? Can you guarantee that you will never throw everything away and disregard everything and everyone because you think that you're right?" Her voice grew louder and the fierceness in her eyes grew stronger. Amon was quite overwhelmed by the stream of questions.

Lya paused, her breathing quickened and her face was serious. However, she looked off to the side, staring at the remains on the ground.

"Who will you become?" she asked softly.

Her voice had changed. It was full of sorrow and regret.

Amon was dumbstruck. He was surprised at her reaction to his request, but all the questions she asked were clearly warranted. He took a deep breath and began to answer the barrage of questions.

"My name is Amon Skoller," he said calmly.

Lya's brow perked up as she heard that.

Amon spoke slowly, carefully choosing his words.

"I don't know the answer to most of these questions, nor can I give you the guarantees you want, but I can answer one thing—I want to be strong so that I can protect the ones dear to me. Nothing more, nothing less."

Lya closed her eyes. They certainly were different. A weak breeze blew past her. She always found it funny, how Alexei loved to feel the breeze by the lake, while all she could do was watch and imagine how it felt.

"What would you do if you lost everyone you hold dear? If you lost your reason for being strong? What would you do then, Amon?"

Amon had no answer. He truly didn't know what he would do if he lost Daniel. He was even less sure of what he would do if he ever lost his mother. Just the thought of it gave him a fright.

"The stronger you are, the longer you live. That means that the stronger you are, the more you will outlive the ones dear to you." Lya said, opening her eyes.

"I will not accept that reason. The answer is still no."

The breeze blew stronger, hitting Amon, making his clothes flutter and messing up his hair. He stood there, disappointed and full of regret.

"Still, we are indeed fated. We do not need to part ways," Lya continued, tossing the crystalline ring to Amon. "You can hold onto it for now, even if you cannot use it."

Amon looked at the ring attentively. It was crystal-blue and translucent. Tiny, silver runes were inscribed into its band; they were barely visible to the naked eye.

The ring was too big for his fingers. He looked at Lya, but she just gave a slight nod, telling him to go on. He quietly slipped it onto the ring finger on his left hand. The ring dimly glowed and contracted to perfectly fit his small finger.

He extended his fingers and raised his hand against the sky, appreciating how the ring sparkled in the sunlight. Lya waved her hands again, and the black sheath on the ground floated to her. She gently sheathed Brightmoon in it and offered it to Amon.

"You can take me and Brightmoon with you."

She warmly smiled as Amon carefully took the sword. He strapped it to his back, making sure it wouldn't fall.

With a gracious smile, he sincerely thanked her. Soon after, he scratched his head and became slightly flustered.

Lya cocked her head to the side and asked, "What's the problem?"

"I don't know where we are or how to return to the sect," he replied in a low voice, looking away.

His ears reddened with embarrassment.

"Is it close? Can you draw a map for me?"

Amon nodded. He picked a dried branch on the floor and slowly drew the map he remembered from what Daniel showed him. He pointed at Hell Keeper's with the branch and said, "The sect is here."

He slowly made his way to the Red River, tracing the path he took with Daniel until they reached the riverbank where they searched for artifacts.

"My raft carried me from this point for a few hours. I was unconscious, so I don't know where exactly we are."

Lya acknowledged his words, however, they were not enough for her to help. She didn't recognize much of the landscape. It had certainly changed in the years she was isolated from the world.

"Is there anything else you can show me?"

Amon thought for a while, and his face suddenly lit up. He carefully drew an irregular circle in the western part of the map, as well as a bunch of crisscrossing gashes in the southeast.

"This is the Scorched Lands," he said, pointing at the irregular circle. He ran his finger in a line towards the gashes. "These are the Scars. They're remnants of a war that happened centuries ago," he said, turning to face Lya. She had a deep frown or her face, as if she was trying to piece a few

51

things together.

Was it not enough?

"Ah, I almost forgot!" He held the branch firmly and drew a long line on the map, almost dividing it in two.

"This is the Sword Abyss. It is hundreds of kilometers long and is a really dangerous place. Our sect,the Abyss Sect, is named after it."

To his surprise, Lya's eyes widened. Her face paled and she had a strange expression.

"Have you seen it before?" he asked, confused.

Catching herself, Lya recovered a bit and tried to put on a blank face, but failed miserably.

"Yes, I have."

Her voice trembled and her eyes became misty; Lya was on the verge of tears.

Noticing the sudden change in her composure, Amon decided to keep quiet. He never expected to see her so vulnerable. Amon turned and walked closer to the lake, taking a seat a few meters from the edge. The breeze felt cooler than earlier, but was still enjoyable to his slightly aching body.

After a few minutes, Lya finally spoke again.

"We are not far from your sect. Luckily you were only dragged a few kilometers away."

Amon turned to see that she wasn't looking at him, but her sad eyes were focused on the skeleton instead.

"We need to bury him," she continued, her voice trembled more and a tear ran down her cheek.

He got up and walked over to her and stood by her side for a moment. Dropping to his knees, he moved the skeleton to the side and began to dig with his bare hands. However, Lya raised a hand to stop him. She waved her other hand and the air seemed to undulate as a huge chunk of earth rose from where Amon had been digging.

Amon gently placed the skeleton in the grave and asked Lya if she had any words for the departed. She shook her head and softly mumbled, "Anything I wanted to say was already said long ago."

She quietly approached and Amon stepped back. She leaned over and kissed the skeleton's forehead. A few tears streamed down her face and fell into it. They simply went through the bone, as if they had no substance; they left no sign of ever existing.

"What was his name?" Amon asked hesitantly.

He didn't want to overstep any boundaries or cause her more pain.

"Alexei. Alexei Vine."

Amon nodded before bowing towards the expert to express his gratitude.

Lya waved her hand again. The chunk of earth, which was still floating in the air, gently lowered over the grave, covering the remains. The lush grass smoothed and a small bunch of flowers bloomed on site—it was impossible to tell that it has ever been tampered with. Now, all that remained in the isolated space was the lake and the scarred landscape.

"Let's go," she instructed, her figure blurred before finally vanishing.

"I'll be waiting for the day you find an acceptable answer."

Her voice made its way into his mind, melodious and ethereal.

Amon knew that Lya had returned to Brightmoon. Although he had never witnessed a sword spirit personally, he was unsurprised by her disappearance. Silently touching the sword on his back, Amon turned away from the lake, and ran his fingers through his hair as he marched towards the boundary of the serene area.

After a short time, Amon had finally reached the Red River with the help of Lya's instructions. The sun had started to set and its red glow made the muddy water appear scarlet. During his walk, Amon explained to Lya what he was doing in the forest. She questioned him about the Scavenging and wondered why the cultivators bothered to search for remnants of the war as a tradition.

"How old is this tradition?" she curiously asked.

"If I'm not mistaken, it's been around since the sect's creation. The founder organized the first Scavenging a few years after the War of Falling Leaves. At the time, they were yearly from what I heard," Amon answered, trying to remember the details.

"Such a strange thing to do. Who was that founder you mentioned?"

"I think his name was... Arthur. Arthur Royce," Amon said with a pensive look. The sect's history was never a worry for those in the Outer Sect. He only knew of such things because his mother had told him.

Lya went silent. He had no way of knowing what she was thinking since she hadn't materialized and he couldn't see her face. For all intents and purposes, she was just a voice in his head.

After a long time, she asked, "This Arthur... is he still in the Abyss Sect? Is he alive?"

"I don't think so. I think he died a few decades ago."

"I see."

Lya returned to her silence. Amon could hear some disappointment in her voice. Did she know Arthur? That wasn't entirely impossible. Amon thought for a moment, before deciding not to ask; Besides asking about the Scavenging, Lya mostly avoided subjects about the past.

As darkness set in, a silvery light danced over the forest. The dim light of the moon was hardly visible through the tall trees. Amon didn't stop for a break, but instead continued to follow the sound of the river to keep on track, determined to reach the Abyss Sect as fast as possible. Thanks to the pill Lya had given him earlier, his body was still full of energy.

He suddenly stopped in his tracks, his face pale and full of fear.

"What's wrong?" Lya asked, concerned.

Amon didn't answer. His hair was standing on end and his body was heating up as his blood churned. This feeling was no stranger to him. He raised his head and looked to his right, in the direction of the trees.

"Amon?" Lya asked again, turning anxious.

She then spread her divine sense towards Amon's line of sight.

Amon stood in shock—the massive dire wolf from earlier lay hidden in the shadows. Its form was barely visible in the sliver of light that managed to peek between the trees, but the two of them could see that it was bloody and limping.

"Calm down," Lya instructed, trying to ease his anxiousness. "Don't make any sudden movements. Slowly raise your hand and try to unsheathe Brightmoon."

Her voice was slow and steady, helping to calm Amon down. He slowly managed to raise his right hand to Brightmoon's hilt, but his entire body was shaking uncontrollably.

"Wait... Are we going to fight it?" he asked, in disbelief.

"Yes."

"Lya, I am not even able to manipulate qi, yet you want me to defeat a grown dire wolf!?"

"Of course not, I just want you to face it."

"Why?"

"Because you are afraid."

Amon had no time to discuss with her. The dire wolf made its way out of the trees and faced him. Looking at the gash on its flank, Amon's heart clenched. He was certain that it was the same beast they had faced before and that Daniel had caused the wound. The fact that the animal was still alive meant that Daniel was either badly injured or dead.

His grip tightened and the shaking stopped. The dire wolf looked at him and prepared to pounce. A low growl came from its throat as the fur on its back stood erect.

Lya didn't quite believe Amon when he said he could feel the wolves coming, but something was off. This dire wolf was not hunting them—it was challenging them.

She searched her memory for the connection. *Isn't his surname Skoller?* she thought. *His ashen hair and golden eyes... Could it really be true?*

If Arthur was the one that founded the Abyss Sect it was highly possible that this was the case. She would have to speak about this with Amon later.

As she was thinking, she noticed that he had stopped trembling. His tight grip had turned his knuckles white, and his breathing had quickened. A murderous intent colored his face beet red and his eyes glowed fiercely. Amon wanted to avenge Daniel.

Amon called for her as he unsheathed Brightmoon.

"Lya?"

"Yes?" she answered with uncertainty.

"Can you help me kill it?"

Lya shook her head. She couldn't blame him for the way he was feeling, but it just confirmed her previous decision—Amon was far too naïve.

"No. Do you still want to try to kill him?"

"I can't. I would only kill myself."

His tone was harsh, but it was self-loathing. This answer satisfied Lya.

"Don't worry, you won't have to. There is someone coming."

Her voice slowly drifted away and she stopped talking. Amon was confused, but he suddenly heard a loud screech coming from somewhere above the trees. The dire wolf sensed something too, as his flaming eyes left Amon and focused on the sky.

A gust of wind came out of nowhere. Amon stumbled backwards as a black ship broke through the trees, sending bits of wood and leaves everywhere. It rammed towards the wolf with incredible speed, however the beast managed to dodge the attack as it lept to the side. The black ship struck the ground, sinking deep into the earth and three passengers jumped off, cursing that their surprise attack failed.

Amon was surprised to see a spirit vessel before his eyes. It was usually used for heavy combat which focused on speed and offense. As it crashed, its sharp, defined edges and spear-shaped prow cut through more trees as it slid to a stop.

"Karen, stay at the back and cover me. Joshua, you go to the left. I'll hide in the trees and wait for an opening," Jake, the leader of the bunch, commanded as soon as their feet hit the ground.

The red-haired lad, Joshua, sped towards the forest, never putting his back to the vicious animal.

"AWOOOOOOO!"

A brown-haired girl quickly stepped up. She hastily waved her hands and the air seemed to freeze. Thanks to the dust and dirt that were kicked up during the collision, Amon could see her defensive technique clearly.

The air around them turned completely still, as if they were inside of a bubble. The howl seemed to brush past this bubble and the sound and impact were negated.

A wind cultivator...? Amon thought, his eyes growing wide in amazement. One would only be able to gain control over the elements when they reached the Elemental Purification stage.

"Jake, now!" the girl exclaimed.

The black-haired boy jumped from the trees, unsheathing the sabre on his back.

Flames covered his sabre and his body as he shot forward like a fireball. The dire wolf couldn't react in time and Jake smashed into it, slashing away. A terrible smell of smoke and burnt fur invaded Amon's nostrils as Jake retreated, still holding his sabre.

The dire wolf's fur on his left flank was charred and the sabre had left a deep wound. The beast wouldn't be able to properly move now that both flanks were injured. The dire wolf growled in fury as he glared at Jake.

Joshua appeared from the side, his short spear in hand as he pierced the dire wolf's right side. The spearhead sank deep into its flesh, making blood spurt out as the creature turned and snapped it's jaws at Joshua. Unable to retrieve his spear in time, he let it go and kicked its exposed handle, pushing it deeper into the animal as the force propelled him away from the wolf's attack.

Jake moved again, making use of the opportunity. This time, he went for the kill. His flaming sabre plunged into the dire wolf's neck. Jake was actually surprised as he couldn't manage to make a clean cut. Jake's legs dangled in the air as he hung from the sabre lodged in the beast's neck.

The dire wolf leaned forward, preparing to crush Jake with its weight. A black blur sped through the air and punctured the wolf's left eye—Karen had struck it with a whip. The dire wolf howled and took a step back, its eye bleeding profusely.

Jake let out a breath of relief as he saw he had been saved in the nick of time. He used all his strength to raise his legs and, with all his weight, forced his sabre to slice down through dire wolf's neck. Jake was instantly covered in an ocean of blood as its neck split open.

Upon losing its fleshy support, the sabre, and Jake, fell to the ground and he gracefully landed on his feet. With a huge thud the dire wolf finally fell to the ground; its breathing was short and labored.

Jake slowly walked towards it, sabre in hand, prepared to deal the final blow.

"Wait!" a juvenile voice called out.

Jake turned and saw Amon running towards him, holding a sword in his hands.

"Let me do it," the boy said, halfway asking and halfway demanding.

"Why should I? We defeated it," Jake questioned, his voice slightly annoyed.

"It… it probably killed a friend of mine. This is personal," Amon said, downcast.

"Who was this friend of yours?" Jake couldn't help but ask. His brother was still alive. If the dire wolf had indeed killed someone else, Jake wouldn't mind letting the boy finish him off.

"Daniel. Daniel Meyer," Amon answered without hesitation.

Jake was taken aback by his answer.

"You know Daniel?" Amon asked, uncertain.

"Of course I do," Jake replied with a sigh. "That fool is my older brother."

"You are Jake? Wait, why are you here? Do you know what happened to him?" Amon was the one who was surprised this time.

"Daniel is gravely injured, but he has a good chance of making it. An elder was close when Daniel fought with the dire wolves and managed to bring him back to the sect in time. A hunt was issued to take the dire wolf down," Jake explained. "As his brother, I naturally accepted it."

Amon was relieved when he heard that. His legs gave in and he fell to the ground as all the tension in his body disappeared.

"That is great," he managed to say with a shaky voice.

Jake patted him on the back with an awkward look on his face.

"Well, I already took that thing down, I don't mind if you finish it."

Jake felt strange. He was Daniel's brother, but he ended up having to comfort this kid he just met a few minutes ago.

"Sorry about that," Amon said as he recovered.

He held Brightmoon tightly as he walked towards the dire wolf.

Its black fur was bloody and charred. A strong burnt smell exuded from it and its breaths were shallow and irregular. Amon stopped close to its head, looking straight into its eyes.

Amon said nothing as he raised Brightmoon high over his head. Its edge hovered above the wolf's neck and reflected the silver light of the moon. The sword was trembling slightly as Amon's hands started shaking.

"Why hesitate now? You've already made your choice," Lya whispered to him.

Amon took a deep breath and steeled himself.

With all of his weight, Amon brought the sword down in a quick blow. Surprisingly, it cut without much effort at all. The sword sank into the beast's flesh, leaving only the hilt exposed.

The dire wolf shivered once. Amon looked intently into the clear, limpid red eye close to him and he could faintly see his reflection. After a moment, the light in its eyes faded and the dire wolf stopped moving.

Amon stared at his reflection. His ashen hair was a mess and his golden eyes showed hesitation. He was pale and frightened. That's all he could see —a frail, scared boy.

No more. He said to himself, tightening his grip on Brightmoon.

He let out a long breath and pulled the sword out from the lifeless beast. He cleaned the blade on the dire wolf's fur before sheathing it again.

Jake nodded seeing this. He sent a glance to Joshua, who took a long rope out of his bottomless pouch and approached the wolf.

Amon slowly returned to Jake's side.

"Thank you," he said.

"No problem," Jake answered.

He found it unusual that the boy was able to pierce the dire wolf's neck so easily, but he didn't inquire further. He walked over to the spirit vessel and climbed aboard. Jake made his way to a golden circle that was embedded into the floor and sat upon it. The vessel shook and rose into the air, freeing itself from the hole it had dug, completely undamaged.

Karen offered a hand to Amon and he accepted it. She held him in her arms as she jumped on the vessel. Joshua followed suit, his hands were covered with blood, holding the end of a rope on one hand and a black crystal the size of a grown man's fist on the other.

"I figured we should retrieve its spirit core now," Joshua said as he handed the crystal to Jake and firmly tied the rope to the vessel.

They weren't proficient enough to skin the beast without damaging the leather, so he decided to only dig out the spirit core from it's chest and bring the whole corpse with them.

The vessel slowly started to rise with the dire wolf's corpse in tow.

"Let's go home," Jake said cheerfully.

The spirit vessel rose above the trees, making a sharp turn before speeding off to the distance.

A SWORD
CULTIVATOR

The sun was rising in the sky as the spirit vessel made its way to the top of Hell Keeper's Mountain. Like a shadow, it silently pierced through the clouds leaving no trace that it had been there.

When they were getting close to the peak, the vessel suddenly tilted to the left, guiding them to Sky Reach Village. It was a few times bigger than the Northern Junction, and every single building was more lavish than anything Amon had ever seen in the Outer Sect. This place only housed members of the Elder Council, the protectors, and their families.

During their journey, Amon felt uneasy around Jake due to him being Sect Master Borgin's disciple. Though he wasn't completely sure of their ranks, Karen and Joshua status most likely didn't fall far behind. He wasn't surprised at all, considering their excellent fighting techniques used on the direwolf.

As Jake looked for a spot to land, Amon was given a gorgeous view of the shiny mansions and architecture. A large, intricate golden gate separated the battle port from the rest of the city. The guards were heavily armed and alert. This ensured that no one could tamper with the spirit vessels when they weren't in use.

This village would never leave Amon's memories. Not for its beauty, but because of his past. He stared at one of the older buildings in the corner of the village. *I need you to be brave, son*—his father's cold voice played within his mind, sending a chill down his spine. His body shook slightly and he turned a bit pale. He felt something clutching at his stomach and he became nauseous. Jake was worried about him, but Amon assured him that it was just the sudden turn of the ship that had gotten to him. Truth be told, this city was Amon's home when he was younger. His father had still been a part of the sect and his mother was uninjured; they were all happy.

The gigantic carcass of the dire wolf swayed beneath the black spirit vessel as it slowed down to land on a golden platform. A few other vessels were parked there as well. Some guards and other citizens worriedly stared at them as they approached.

"Be careful with that damn wolf, Jake!" someone shouted from below.

Jake smiled wryly as he carefully landed the vehicle, which was a complete contrast to how careless he had treated it just hours ago.

"We are here. Karen, take care of Amon for a bit, Joshua and I will go give the report."

Karen nodded and motioned at the young boy.

"Come with me, Amon, I'll take you to a nice place to eat."

Karen gave a sweet smile and took him to a red and shiny building. It was two stories tall and a small board hung above the doors which read: *Sky Reach Restaurant.*

Amon's eyes lit up and his stomach growled. He hadn't eaten in over a day and he hadn't been near a restaurant in years as they weren't common in the Outer Sect. The residents from Amon's part of town were generally poor, and thus, restaurants were an unnecessary expense to them.

For the Inner Sect, restaurants were a place to relax and enjoy themselves. Select dishes were paid for by the sect for Inner Sect disciples. They were given two meals a day and the more elaborate dishes had to be paid for.

"This place has some really good food. You can order anything you want. I'll cover it," Karen said as they walked in.

Inside, there were servants wearing azure robes. Their perfect posture and kind greetings matched the restaurant's tidiness. A few tables made of expensive wood were distributed on the ground floor, their varnish was glossy and spotless.

An old servant made his way over to them wearing an amiable smile.

"Welcome back, Miss Karen. Would you like the same table as always?"

"Yes, please," Karen replied.

The servant bowed and showed them to their table, but the strange way he looked at Amon didn't escape Karen's eyes. Karen thought it was expected, considering that this was Amon's first time in the place and the servant certainly didn't know him. Plus, his clothes were a mess, and his hair and eyes were a bit bizarre.

Amon, however, thought otherwise. He had visited the restaurant quite frequently when he was younger and recognized the servant instantly. His name was Old Lu and he had been working at Sky Reach Restaurant for decades. He probably found Amon familiar but couldn't recognize him since it had been about five years since they last saw each other and even then, Amon's eyes and hair were vastly different.

Amon was feeling nostalgic as they sat at a corner table. Taking Brightmoon off of his back, he leaned it against the wall by his feet. Karen politely ordered a few pork ribs and looked at Amon, waiting for him to order. After a short moment, he said, "I'll have some rice cakes."

He wasn't in the mood to eat, but he took the rice cakes with him after he politely stalled Karen for a while.

Old Lu nodded and left them alone as he made his way to the kitchen. Amon looked at Karen wanting to say something but was hesitant to do so; it didn't go unnoticed.

"Tell me what's on your mind," Karen prodded.

"To be honest, I'm quite impressed by the way you and your friends treated me. Why would you go so far? You could have left me in the middle of the forest and I still would've been grateful."

"I understand why you feel that way, but please understand that I don't mind treating any and every member of the sect with respect. It might not be the case for others, but we all serve the same purpose," Karen said after thinking for a moment. "However, I agree that bringing you here was a bit much. If I had to guess, I would say it's because of Daniel. Jake really likes his brother and doesn't get to see him because of their father intervening. I think he was really surprised by the way you acted," she said, smiling awkwardly.

Amon's could feel his ears grow warm as they turned bright red from embarrassment.

"Daniel never told me much about his family. In fact, he's only mentioned Jake once," Amon stated. "B-but I'm sure he likes Jake too," he added hastily, thinking he was making Daniel look bad.

At that moment, Old Lu returned with their orders. Leaving the food on the table he asked if they'd like anything else, before departing again.

"Go on, dig in," Karen said, eagerly extending her hands to the food.

She took a rib and carefully nibbled it, trying not to let anything fall in her clothes. Amon sheepishly extended a hand to the rice cakes and took one. As Karen glanced at him between each bite, he decided to at least try to eat. He took a small bite, trying his best to enjoy the rich taste. It was really nostalgic. He loved when his mother brought him here to eat rice cakes every week. He started feeling warmth in his chest, and suddenly the nausea he felt was gone. He earnestly took another bite, making Karen smile.

Before he realized it , he had wolfed down half of the plate. Karen laughed seeing his desolate expression, but Amon didn't take another. Instead, he asked Old Lu to wrap up what was left so he could take them to his mother.

As they finished eating, they stood up and Amon retrieved Brightmoon, tying it to his back again. He was finding it strange that Lya had been silent ever since he got onto the spirit vessel, but he didn't want to speak with her in front of Karen.

Amon carefully held the silky cloth with the rice cakes and stashed it in his clothes. As Karen led him away, Jake and Joshua were returning from their briefing.

"How was it?" Karen asked when she saw them.

"Just fine. We got ten thousand contribution points from the bounty and the carcass, plus three thousand for the spirit core Joshua retrieved from it," he said after some quick calculations. "Adding up, it should be three thousand and a few hundred to each one."

"That doesn't add up at all! What kind of math is this?" Karen asked, confused.

"Of course it does. We are dividing it by four," Jake replied. This time, Amon was confused. Why would they do something like this?

Before he could reject their generosity, Jake cut him off.

"You faced that thing twice and even managed to distract it enough for us to attempt a surprise attack. You also dealt the finishing blow, It is only fair."

Jake was twisting the situation around so it would look like Amon had been a huge part of the battle. As Amon opened his mouth to say something, Karen subtly poked him with her elbow, hinting at him to keep silent and accept.

To be fair, even if Jake didn't tell her about this before, she didn't mind. She would never be lacking in contribution points and this mission was an unexpected benefit. The real reason they were allowed to go on this mission was to get experience fighting spirit beasts, not to get contribution points.

Despite their insistence, Amon was still reluctant to accept. Jake took a glowing ball from his robes and threw it to Amon.

"Touch your contribution card with it and the points will be added."

Amon clumsily managed to hold the ball. When he looked up and saw Jake's stern expression, he gave up declining the favor. *He's as stubborn as Daniel,* Amon thought, as he loaded the points onto his card before saying his thanks.

"Come on, I'll find someone to take you home," Jake said, taking Amon away.

Once they got a few meters away, Jake spoke again.

"I'm sorry about this, but I can't take you home myself. I can only leave the village on missions and my father is quite rigid regarding such matters," he said with a sigh.

"That's okay, I understand. Thank you for going through all this trouble for me. Do you—"

"You want to know about Daniel, right?"

Amon nodded silently and clutched the sleeve of his robes nervously.

"He's at the medical center. We can't visit him right now, so you'll have to wait until he's able to return home to see him. I'm sorry, but I think it will take some time," he apologetically said.

Amon was disheartened by the situation, but he knew it was for the best. At least Daniel was alive.

"Please tell him that I'm sorry about what happened. Let him know that I'm really thankful for what he did and I couldn't be happier to hear that he's alive."

"Heh, Daniel's lucky to have you," Jake said with a light chuckle.

"He is also a good friend. In fact, he's a great friend," Amon replied. "And you also have some good friends from what I could see."

Jake laughed again; he was starting to really like this kid.

They walked to the golden platform where the spirit vessels were stored. Jake quietly approached a white-robed man and traded a few words with him. After a while, he called Amon to join them.

"Luke will take you home. Just tell him where you want him to drop you off," Jake informed Amon, motioning towards Luke.

"Thank you for everything, Jake. Please thank Karen and Joshua again too," Amon said, genuinely grateful.

Jake slapped Amon on the back.

"You worry too much kid. You should be more carefree." He then looked Amon in the eye, unblinking. "Please continue being a good friend to my brother. I hope that one day you'll join the Inner Sect so we can see each other again."

"I'll do my best."

"I'll wait for you," Jake said with a nod before turning to leave.

Luke quietly approached Amon.

"Where should I take you, sir?"

"You can leave me at the Northern Junction, if it isn't much trouble."

Luke then guided him to a small spirit vessel. It was much smaller than the one Jake had used and was completely white. Amon got on board and Luke took off.

❋ ❋ ❋

"Are you there, Lya?" Amon asked, concerned as he walked home. Luke had dropped him off close to the Northern Junction. He didn't fly directly to it at Amon's request, as he didn't want to attract too much attention.

"Of course I am!" Lya's voice echoed in his head, excited.

"Then why didn't you speak before?" he asked, confused.

"Because I didn't want you to sound insane to your new friends, talking to yourself and all."

"You heard everything that happened, right?"

"Yes, I did. Why?"

"Just to be sure," Amon said, and turned quiet, leaving Lya confused.

Soon enough, he reached his shabby house. He made his way in, not trying to keep his silence at all. He went past the living room and stood at his mother's door and gently knocked twice.

"Come in."

Amon opened the door, seeing his mother resting in her bed, looking at him.

"You shouldn't be back until tomorrow. What happened?" she asked, her brows furrowed slightly.

She saw Amon's tattered clothes and undyed hair. She glanced at the sword on his back and the crystalline ring on his finger. When she noticed that Daniel wasn't around, she knew something was wrong.

Amon threw himself into her embrace, just like he had done a few days ago. This time, however, he didn't cry. He just hugged her tightly.

She returned the hug, slowly patting his back and ruffling his hair. Even if he wasn't crying, she could feel that her son was having a hard time controlling his emotions.

After a while, they separated. Her eyes were calm, albeit full of worry. His eyes were red, full of pain.

"Can you tell me what happened?" Rebecca asked, concerned.

She grew anxious and remembered the bad feeling she had the day Amon left. She quietly grasped the necklace under her sheets.

Amon told her about everything that had happened since they left. When she heard about the dire wolf, her face paled and she hugged Amon again, almost suffocating him. Silent tears fell from her eyes. Still being hugged, Amon continued recounting what happened. When he started to mention the isolated space, Lya's voice interrupted him.

"Don't tell anyone about that lake! Just tell her you found a corpse lying around with the sword."

Her voice was urgent. Amon hesitated for a moment, but then quietly nodded. If word ever got out about that isolated space, there might be trouble. Even more so if someone found out about Lya. It would be better if he didn't get his mother involved. He slightly altered the story and told her everything that happened afterward. How he stumbled upon the dire wolf again and how Jake and his friends saved him.

His mother hugged him with even more strength at each word he spoke, clearly worried. When he finished the story, he took the pack of rice cakes from his clothes.

"Here, I managed to save these from the restaurant in Sky Reach."

He offered her the rice cakes and she put her hands on his face and gave him a long kiss on his forehead before saying, "I love you."

"I love you too, mom."

They ate the rice cakes together and talked for a long time. Rebecca never once touched on the matter of what he would do with the ring or the sword, as she decided to let him choose. Amon stayed in her room until it was almost sunset. He quickly left to whip up some dinner using the food Daniel had given her.

He quietly brought the food to his mother, and then left to his room. Sitting on the black mat, he took Brightmoon from his back and laid it across his legs.

"You saw my mother, didn't you, Lya?" he suddenly asked.

"Yes, I did."

"It happened five years ago, in the last Scavenging. My father had just left us and a lot of things I couldn't understand were happening to us. We had to move from Sky Reach to the Outer Sect, and a lot of strange people visited our house every day," he said, his voice full of sadness.

"I really wanted to go to the Scavenging that year because I wanted to find a huge artifact and sell it for a fortune so my mother wouldn't have to worry so much anymore."

"She didn't want me to go. She was worried about me, and probably had too much on her hands already. She couldn't waste four days for nothing." He took a brief pause as if fighting hard to choose the right words to say. "I was very persistent—stubborn, even. In the end, she gave in."

"In the first three days, nothing happened, and we also found nothing. On the fourth day, a silverback wolf found us. An interesting fact about silverback wolves is that, even if they are class six spirit beasts, they are no-where near as big as dire wolves. The silverback wolf that attacked us would be able to enter this room without a problem," Amon said, looking around. "That silverback wolf had been only two meters high and four meters long. Nevertheless, their speed and strength compensate for their relatively small sizes. This is important because even if my mother was stronger than it, she wasn't faster. If she was alone, she could have made it retreat, even if she sustained some injuries."

He had a blank look as he spoke, almost as if he was trying to distance himself and present the facts.

"The problem is that my mother had to focus on protecting me that day. She couldn't show her full strength because I was close, and she couldn't outrun the wolf. All she could do was fight with a gigantic disadvantage. You already saw the end result."

Amon stopped for a moment, but Lya listened quietly.

"Five years ago, my mother was crippled because of me. Yesterday, Daniel almost died saving me," he said holding Brightmoon tightly. "That happened because I was weak, Lya. Because I couldn't protect myself."

He raised the sword, looking intently at it, almost as if he could see Lya inside.

"Please, help me become strong enough to protect myself. I don't ever want anything like this to happen again!" He pleaded, almost begging.

What answered him was only silence.

Amon could only loathe himself. What utter foolishness. He shook his head, disappointed.

At that moment, however, her voice made its way into his mind.

"This is a reason I can accept."

"Really?" Amon asked, dumbstruck.

"Yes, really," Lya said in a serious tone.

Specs of light started gathering in front of Amon and Lya's beautiful figure materialized in front of him. Lya's form seemed to glisten in the dim moonlight that filled Amon's room.

"There is a huge difference between wanting to be strong to protect others and wanting to be strong to protect yourself."

She looked at Amon intently, her blue eyes seemed to glow in the dim room. As she moved around, the light seemed to pass through her, and no shadow could be seen at her feet.

"It's related to the question you asked me, right?"

Lya's face lit up in satisfaction. Even though he didn't understand the difference in full, he had some grasp of it.

"It is okay to rely on others, but some things we must do for no one but ourselves." Her blue eyes didn't blink as she stared at Amon. "Cultivation is one of those things. Humans are fickle, Amon. You never know what one might do, because one can never completely understand another human. You might know them for years, decades, or even centuries, and they might still surprise you when you least expect it."

Her voice trembled and she looked down, seeming mildly ashamed, but still, she spoke again.

"Humans and their motives are ever-changing. When you don't know what motivates them, you don't really know what to expect from them, nor can you know how far they are willing to go. Therefore, the search for strength, longevity, and knowledge must be exclusive to oneself, because you never know how and when fate will sever the ties you have with others. The only person that will always accompany you while you are alive is yourself. That being the case, you must cultivate for you and you only."

Her wisdom threw Amon deep into thought. He didn't understand what she said in full, but he understood the important aspects of it. He immediately thought of his father and how he never truly knew him. If he did, maybe things would have turned out differently.

Lya interrupted his thoughts by snapping her fingers repeatedly as she tried to get his attention.

"Did you hear what I just said?"

"Huh?" Amon was confused, he hadn't heard her say anything at all.

"I asked you to teach me about cultivation," she said impatiently, causing Amon's face to twitch in confusion.

"What do you mean? Don't you know about cultivation?"

"I do, but I don't quite understand how you people cultivate nowadays. From what I understand, people here follow the path of elemental cultivators, yes?" Lya asked, dead serious.

"Yes, we do, but isn't that the norm? How can you not know about this?"

"I've been isolated for hundreds of years. Do you expect me to know anything at all related to recent times? From what I know, elemental cultivation was supposed to be an alternative path, and quite a weak one at that."

"What was cultivated in your time, then?" Amon asked, careful not to annoy her further.

"The soul."

Her answer surprised him; he had never heard of soul cultivators.

Seeing Amon's confusion, Lya sighed. This was to be expected given the situation, but a few doubts remained. Wasn't Arthur one of the most powerful soul cultivators that ever existed? How could Amon be a part of the sect he founded and not know about soul cultivation?

"Looks like we have a lot to explain to each other," Lya said, her brows furrowed, still thinking about what could have happened. "You can go first."

Amon nodded and said, "Well, I guess I'll explain the different realms and stages." Taking a deep breath, he said, "The Preparatory realm starts with qi gathering. In this stage, we must feel the worldly qi, manipulate it, and finally absorb it, making it flow through our meridians and gathering it in the dantian. After that is body tempering. A normal person wouldn't be able to execute the techniques that use qi, as it would ruin their bodies. To avoid this, the user must master the body tempering stage."

Lya nodded and motioned for him to continue.

"In this stage, cultivators systematically hurt themselves and channel specific techniques to heal faster and perfect their bodies in the process. There are a lot of differences in strength within this stage, as the techniques and how much a cultivator is willing to temper his body all affect the final results."

"The consensus is that once a cultivator goes through the first round of tempering, he will have reached the initial stages. His strength will then be measured and when he becomes five times as strong, he will be in the middle stages. When he becomes ten times as strong, he will be in the late stages."

"I know about body tempering too," Lya said.

"Next, we have the Refinement realm and its first stage is elemental purification. Each person has elemental affinities, and an elemental cultivator must purify the qi in their bodies to match the element of which they have the highest affinity. This way, they can quickly execute techniques with their own reserves of qi. This can be done without gathering it from the surroundings and extracting the elemental energy.

"For that, they absorb qi in special locations where it is naturally aligned with an element or absorb qi from special elemental crystals to speed up the process. The techniques also help change the cultivator's meridians, and so they also start to serve as natural filters. As the worldly qi is absorbed and circulates through the meridians, it is automatically purified according to the element cultivated.

"The stages are defined by the purity of the elemental qi. The initial stages range from zero to thirty percent. The middle range starts at thirty one to sixty percent and after that is when the late stages occur. During this stage the cultivator can purify most of the qi that they absorb by simply circulating the qi throughout their body.

"Afterwards, they use their elemental qi to condense elemental cores. The purified qi in their dantian and how much qi they can store affects the quality and size of the core. Elemental cores can automatically purify and compress the gathered qi with greater efficiency. This enables an elemental core cultivator to have a lot more power than a cultivator at a lower level.

"Next, we have the elemental shedding stage, but I know nothing of it," Amon finished, letting out a long breath.

Lya had a pensive look on her face.

"Wait, so every cultivator only uses one element?" Lya asked with a strange expression on her face.

Amon nodded in response, making her frown.

"There are special cases where someone might have a high affinity with more than one element. I've heard rumors that a small number of people have managed to cultivate more than one element at the same time, and that they were quite stronger than usual cultivators," he stated.

Her expression became more unsure every time Amon explained something.

"What about natural laws?"

"Natural laws? I think they're related to the elemental shedding stage, but I'm not sure. What of it?"

Lya gave a long sigh.

"Alright, I can kind of get the picture here."

She closed her eyes for a moment, thinking deeply. When she opened then again, her gaze was firm with resolution.

"Amon, what I'm about to teach you must never leave these walls. You must never speak of this to anyone, or you might put yourself at risk."

Amon turned serious hearing this. He gave a slight nod.

"Let's start from the beginning. What do you know about the soul?"

"The soul is us, right?" he guessed. "It's where our consciousness resides. It's our soul that goes through the cycle of reincarnation when we die."

"That is mostly correct, but also terribly lacking. What do you know about qi?"

"Qi is the origin of everything we have here. It is from qi that all matter is created and all elements are derived. All of the phenomena in this world are a manifestation of the qi that permeates it."

Amon gave a textbook answer. His face was blank as he recited what he heard from his mother years ago.

"That is a good answer. Now tell me, how can cultivators control qi?"

"We expand our divine sense to perceive it. Then we... control it." he said after pondering for a moment.

Lya smiled hearing that. The conversation was going the way she wanted.

"Then what is the divine sense?" she asked, analyzing him as he answered.

"I-I don't know. I've never thought about it," he said shamefully, lowering his eyes from her gaze.

"Then allow me to explain it to you. Both the soul and qi have similar origins resulting in them sharing a deep connection. Your soul allows you to sense qi. It's not special in any way. This divine sense is just you perceiving the world through your soul."

"If that is the case, then why can't all people develop a divine sense?

Why isn't everyone a cultivator?" Amon asked, terribly confused.

"Everyone can be a cultivator. It is just that their souls are weak. Some people are simply born with stronger souls. They have a head-start of sorts. Even so, everyone strengthens their souls during their life, even if they don't realize it."

She stared at the young boy, trying to see how much he was able to understand.

"As a soul develops, the user is able to feel and control qi more easily and understand it and it's transformations better. These are the natural laws. If you understand them, you will be able to emulate them."

She opened her hands and a small flame appeared in her palms. Its light overtook the moonlight, painting the room orange. Dark shadows started dancing in the room as the flame flickered.

"Cultivate enough and you might be able to sense the divine foundations. This is what soul cultivators do. This is what cultivation should be. Understanding what is around you and ultimately being able to influence everything. Change it, create it, destroy it... That's completely up to the cultivator."

The flame in her hand grew, flashing as it changed from orange to red and red to green before it finally turned into a blinding white.

"The world is ours, Amon. What you do is entirely up to you. This is why cultivators are so dangerous. One cultivator alone can completely ruin the balance of the world if they're strong enough."

The flame suddenly froze in place, shining, but not moving.

Amon stared at the stiff flame as it turned grey and started falling apart like shattered glass. It dispersed into specs of light that floated through the room before disappearing. Amon was impressed and speechless—he had never even imagined such phenomena. Lya's words were too overbearing and absurd, yet he knew them to be true. He had seen the strange flames in her hands and he was certain that no fire cultivator could produce the same technique.

"Any questions?" she asked, smiling widely, her eyes glowing with a strange light.

"You said the soul and qi have similar origins. What did you mean by that?"

"I'm really not certain of their origins, but they've always gone hand in hand. This has always been one of the great mysteries of this world, and spawned countless studies and theories."

"What about the divine foundations you spoke of?" he inquired, his golden eyes shining with curiosity.

"Do you know the divine language?" Lya questioned him instead of answering.

"I've seen it," Amon said, wearily.

He didn't know the divine language, but he had seen it. The day his father put him inside that golden circle filled with runes, the divine language was the basis for its array formation.

"They say it is the language of the Creator. The divine foundations are nothing more than a higher level of perception that the divine sense can reach. At that level, everything you sense is nothing more than the divine language."

"People in my time used to say that the divine language was the prose that wrote this world. When we peer into the divine foundations, we can understand it. At that point, your control over the natural laws will already be above what any elemental cultivator can accomplish. But this is a matter for another day. You are far from the level you need to reach to worry about such things. From all of that, I believe you can understand my point."

Lya noticed Amon was visibly dejected by her statement, but she completely ignored his sulking and continued, still smiling.

"While an elemental cultivator can control one element, a soul cultivator can control them all as long as he comprehends the natural laws. The only advantage elemental cultivators ever had over soul cultivators is the speed and proficiency of their attacks and control of the natural laws respective to their elements. This is why elemental cultivation has always been an alternative and nothing more." Her smile turned into one of derision. "What is the point in cultivating a single element when everyone around you can control more than one at the same time?"

She raised her hands again. The same small flame lit up in her right hand. Then, on her left, the air started swirling, forming a miniscule hurricane.

"Of course, controlling them separately is also a waste," she said, bringing her hands together. The fire spun around the hurricane, turning wilder and larger. Amon felt the room's temperature increasing and his eyes widened.

"With that, I believe the basics are covered. Again, never repeat to anyone what I just told you."

Lya dismissed the swirling fire as she looked at Amon. He nodded repeatedly, assuring her of his understanding.

"If you want, we can start now," she said in a gentle voice, slightly hesitant of Amon's understanding.

"First, I'll teach you how to cultivate the soul. After countless years of study, it was discovered that the soul is divided into two parts: the aster and the nebula. Within the aster, individuality is developed and determination is formed."

"Surrounding the aster, we have what we call the nebula. It is nothing more than the energy and vibrations produced by your thoughts and feelings."

A small, white ball appeared in her hands as she raised them. It shone with a silvery-blue light, looking like a star.

"When your soul becomes strong enough to perceive other souls, you will see the nebula as a mist swirling around the aster. That is how it got its name."

As she explained, a white mist formed around the ball, covering it. All one could see inside the mist was a blurry silvery glow.

"The nebula is the bridge between the aster and the physical world. During the cycle of reincarnation, your aster is wiped clean of all memories and desires contained within. Your nebula is also erased before the aster is sent back to the world and into a new being."

The mist vanished, revealing the glowing orb once again, but it had dimmed considerably.

"Regardless of being recycled, every aster is unique. It is hard to explain, but it's like their nebulae have a specific energy signature. If you live long enough and are very, very lucky, you might be able to see the same aster residing in completely different people."

"Soul cultivation uses the energy in the nebula to nourish the aster, making it grow. This process happens naturally over the course of one's life but is very slow. The speed at which one's aster grows is entirely dependent on how much they have loved, hated, and suffered throughout their life. Their tears and laughter are accounted for in this process too."

The mist formed again around the ball, this time much thinner than before. As it slowly grew thicker, the ball started to get brighter and seemed to be slowly growing as the mist increased.

"Although there is a limit, soul cultivation speeds this process and allows us to break said limit."

Suddenly, the ball started to absorb the mist, and its size grew considerably in a matter of seconds. There was almost no mist remaining around the ball, making Amon frown.

"The mist is almost gone. If that's the case, then..."

Lya shook her head, knowing what he meant.

"Soul cultivators naturally have near perfect control of their emotions after they reach a certain point in their cultivation. Because of that, they might seem as excessively cold and indifferent as you speak with them."

"Their beliefs are incomparably firm and their resolve is unshakeable. In other words, they are stubborn." She smiled as she let out a slight giggle. "Make no mistake, it is not that they don't feel, it's just that they use these feelings as a chance to cultivate and get stronger. The nebula is just a manifestation, not the source. Never forget that," she explained.

"When you said some people are born with a stronger soul—"

"Yes, their asters are larger. This means that they either experienced many eventful lives or that they were soul cultivators once before."

"Then I guess my past lives weren't that interesting," Amon said with a sour look on his face.

Hearing that, Lya didn't know whether to laugh or to cry. If the boy knew who he was in his past life, he would never say something like that. She made a huge effort to stay neutral during the conversation.

"Why do you say that?"

"Even if I can sense qi, I can't manipulate it. By your explanation, my master must be lacking."

After thinking for a long time, Lya said, "You are right, your master *is* lacking." She had decided to keep what she knew to herself. "We'll deal with this soon enough, don't worry."

Amon nodded and asked, "When an aster goes through reincarnation, is there a chance that past memories could be retained?"

To his surprise, Lya shook her head.

"To be honest, I don't know. In theory, it would be possible for a person to seal a small part of their aster, protecting it. But they would need to have a deep understanding of the soul and an incredible power. Even if they managed to do so, it would be a miniscule fragment, and at most, the new being would have an impulse to do something, or a broken memory—nothing more. However, this is all speculation. I've never heard of such a thing."

This made him frown slightly; it was possible, but the chances were absurdly low. If he had a weak aster, there is no way he was a soul cultivator in a past life.

Lya read his expression easily. She tried to divert his attention and raised a slender finger which started dancing in the air in a methodical way, leaving behind a golden trail of light.

"Don't mind these things. Now, pay attention here," she said as the light slowly connected, forming strange runes. When Lya was finished, she had drawn two incredibly long strings of runes. "Amon, these lines are what we call the soulrousing technique."

He stared at the runes without blinking. He had seen them before, but he wasn't entirely certain where.

"Is this the divine language?"

"Yes. The first line increases the production of nebula. In other words, it magnifies your emotions. The second line catalyzes the nebula and makes the aster grow. The effects of the first line are far more complicated and dangerous than those of the second. All you need to do is think about them. I'll engrave the lines in your mind, to make sure you remember them right. If you get one rune wrong, who knows what might happen." Lya extended a pale hand to Amon. "Do not resist."

Before Amon could react, a finger descended upon his forehead. His forehead started to itch and his body tensed as an unbelievable amount of information gushed into his memory, and a splitting headache took over Amon, making him want to scream. He shut his mouth firmly, gritting his teeth as he barely managed to endure the pain.

When it stopped, Amon was left with his head ringing as Lya took her finger away from his forehead.

"Good. Now all you have to do is picture the lines in your mind as you meditate and they should work." Lya gave a satisfied smile. "You already have an impressive nebula around your aster, so for now, skip the first line of the technique."

Amon took a deep breath, adjusting his mind as he closed his eyes. His breathing became rhythmical and the dark world lit up in monochromatic tones.

The qi covered everything and made itself known through Amon's divine sense. He carefully started thinking about the second line Lya had written in his mind. The golden runes floated in front of his eyes as he focused on what was now a memory.

The runes started to dance around his head, and he suddenly shuddered. He felt a cold sensation creeping into his body as if ice snakes started to slither under his skin. He felt unbearably cold for a moment, and then he felt extremely hot. His body broke out into a cold sweat as the sensations constantly fluctuated. His muscles started contracting and the sweat made his clothes cling to his body. His teeth clattered as his body shivered uncontrollably.

When Amon thought he couldn't endure another second, a loud sound exploded in his mind. His divine sense suddenly expanded outwards, covering the entire room. The monochromatic tone was taken over by a faint color pallet, and the qi's color changed from grey to clear. Now, everything Amon saw through his divine sense was translucent.

He was dumbstruck. Is this how his divine sense would evolve as he gained strength? Maybe that talk about sensing the divine foundations wasn't nonsense after all.

Lya's gentle voice echoed in his head "Oh? Looks like you advanced quite a bit. Why don't you try moving the qi."

Amon focused on a particular wisp of qi swirling in front of him. He extended his hands to it, imagining himself grasping it.

"Move."

He swiped his hands in the opposite direction that the qi was moving. The wisp of qi stopped before slowly moving in the direction he willed.

"It worked!"

After almost eight long years, he had finally managed to move qi. If he could absorb it, he would be able to start tempering his body and turn many times stronger.

"Of course it did. You thought I was lying to you?" Lya said with a sneer.

Amon's ears turned red in shame as he looked down.

"I would never doubt you! Do you think I'll be able to absorb qi now?"

Lya shrugged and replied, "Well, the only real hurdle is the fine control. All you need to do is absorb qi through your acupuncture points and get your meridians filled before moving it into the dantian."

In a way, acupuncture points worked as floodgates to control the stream of qi and doorways that allowed the absorption and expulsion of qi from the body. The dantian was the core of the meridian system, located a bit below the navel.

Amon took a deep breath and concentrated. He tried his best to focus on his surroundings, willing for all the qi to gather near him. It was a slow process that demanded an absurd amount of willpower and concentration. Soon enough, the grey mist in the room started swirling around his body like a whirlpool—Amon could barely be seen through the madness.

He let out a long breath and sent a bit of qi to one of the acupuncture points in his arm. However, his meridians were closed as this was his first time trying to use them. He needed to open each one individually.

Slowly, the wisp of qi burrowed in his skin, making its way into his meridian as it glowed under his skin. This process had to be repeated more than four hundred times to open every point. A cultivator needed to manage them all at once, trying to optimize the absorption of qi and the flow in the meridians.

Lya patiently floated by Amon's side, using her divine sense to supervise his efforts. He was quite clumsy and took an excessively long time, but it was a fine result for a first try. Furthermore, he was slowly getting better and better; Amon was clearly trying to end the process in one go.

She made no comments, nor did she offer any help. It was best if he experienced it all by himself, adapting to the control of qi overtime.

After what seemed like hours, Amon finally let out a long sigh. His face was pale and his whole body was drenched in a cold sweat, but also seemed to be glowing and full of energy. His meridians were all filled to the brim, and all points had been opened.

Amon had never maintained meditation for this long. He was incredibly tired, but he refused to rest. He wanted strength, and he would chase after it as fast as he could.

The glow in his body started to dim, but a shiny dot lit up in his abdomen. As his body dimmed, the radiance grew brighter. By the time his body had returned to normal, that small dot lit up the entire room. It flashed once with a blinding light, and then went out.

Amon looked at his dantian carefully. He had finally done it. He was now prepared to start body tempering and leave his frail and weak body behind. Soul cultivation seemed to be a far better path than elemental cultivation.

"Congratulations," Lya said, her bright eyes gave Amon an excited glance.

Amon gave her a tired smile as sweat dripped down his face.

"Now we can officially start your training."

Lya wanted to be sure that Amon would never repeat the same mistakes she and Alexei had made. She always wanted to prove that if she ever had a second chance, things would have a different end. Now she had the chance to do exactly that.

Alexei had been the strongest soul cultivator of his generation, but he was far from the best. He never managed to overcome his flaws, and he paid the price for that. A sad smile made its way onto her face as she thought about him.

Kneeling down next to Amon, Lya placed her hand on his shoulder. As she stared into his tired eyes, she thought, *I'll make you into the best Sword Cultivator this world has ever seen.*

"Do you know any body tempering techniques?" Amon excitedly asked, waking Lya from her daze.

"I don't know of the techniques, but I know a method to guarantee maximum efficiency when you use one," she informed, causing Amon's excitement to fizzle out.

"That guy, Jake... He gave you some contribution points, didn't he?"

"Yes, he did," Amon answered, raising his brows.

"I'll need you to buy a few things for me."

Amon got up quickly and stumbled to his desk. Grabbing a piece of paper and a pencil from his desk, he jotted down the items as she listed them off.

"The points I got will hardly be enough." Amon's brow raised even further hearing her requests.

"Doesn't matter," Lya said, extending her hand to the ring in Amon's finger. She hesitated for a moment, thinking about something. After a while she seemed to make up her mind. The ring flashed and two small daggers appeared in her hands. She promptly threw them to Amon. "You can sell these, I'm sure they'll fetch a good price," she said dismissively.

"I didn't ask this before, but this ring... is it an interspatial ring?"

He gulped looking at the ring on his finger.

"Of course it is," Lya said with an arrogant smile.

As far as he knew, only the four protectors and the sect master had one. Having an interspatial ring was the same as having a vault on your fingers, with no waste of space or unbearable weight. An interspatial ring was engraved with an array formation that acted as the key to a pocket dimension where the owner could store their belongings and retrieve them at will. Not only that, but time on that dimension was slowed to a crawl, keeping its contents perfectly preserved—the value of an interspatial ring was unimaginable.

A bottomless pouch, on the other hand, simply had an array formation that gave it expanded storage and lightened the weight of whatever was kept in it.

"I won't show it off around the sect, it'll be for the best if I leave it here."

He took the ring from his finger and started to place it in a chest with his clothes, but Lya stopped him.

"No need for that," she said, snapping her fingers.

The ring vibrated and started changing. What looked like a ring made of ice before now was a simple iron ring with a few spots of rust here and there. Amon stared in amazement and started to speak, but Lya cut him off.

"It's just a lighting trick. I can also ward off any intrusive divine senses from the inside, so no one will notice."

Amon decided to trust her judgement and he slid the ring back onto his skinny finger.

"We will go to Hell Keeper's Mountain tomorrow to sell the daggers and buy the manuals. Although the Northern Junction has some manuals in the market, the headquarters has copies of all of the manuals in the sect, so we will be able to buy more stuff there," Amon said, taking off his clothes.

He threw them in a corner of the room, washed his body with the water in the basin and passed out on his bed, exhausted.

Seeing this, Lya gave a gentle smile. As she was looking at him, her face suddenly fell and she directed her gaze to the wall, as if she was trying to see through it. She gave a sigh and floated away, traversing the wall into the hallway before eventually entering another room.

As she entered the room, Rebecca's moon-lit face came into view. Her green eyes were shining with a menacing light and a killing intent. Lya, on the other hand, seemed to glow, being perfectly visible, almost as if she was made of light.

She stared at Rebecca for a moment before greeting her with a smile which wasn't well received. Instead of receiving a response, Lya was warned with an oppressive aura that wrapped around her slowly tightening around her body.

"That's not very polite," Lya snorted and the pressure disappeared. "You know, I just showed myself here because I felt like it, not because you demanded it."

Her tone was serious, but she said it with a sneer.

"Who... what are you?" Rebecca asked with a grave voice, tightly holding the red necklace in her hands, ready to crush it at any time.

"My name is Lya, resident spirit of Brightmoon, the sword your son found."

Lya bowed respectfully as she presented herself.

"A sword spirit?" Rebecca showed no surprise, but was inwardly shaken. "What do you want with my son?"

"I recognized him as my new master." Lya looked into Rebecca's eyes to show that she was not telling a lie. "I will naturally guide him along his cultivation path."

"Why did you recognize him as your master?"

Lya hesitated for a moment, but managed to say, "He and I are fated. I have nothing but good intentions towards him. I'm sure you've noticed that he has already managed to absorb qi."

"How did you manage to do that?" Rebecca finally showed concern as she asked. "He hasn't been able to manipulate qi for years, but somehow, in only a few hours, you've prepared him for body tempering."

When Lya explained to Amon about soul cultivation, she had made sure to block all sound from escaping the room, but decided not to block Rebecca's divine sense, as it would only bring trouble to Amon. When Amon started to cultivate and move qi, attracting Rebecca's attention, she managed to see the entire process.

"It's a lost method," Lya said, shrugging her shoulders. "It will bring him no harm at all. Plus... I think we both know this is the only way he will ever manage to cultivate."

Rebecca frowned, but said nothing. She knew there was some truth to it. Her son's talent was terrible, no matter how good a person he was. In truth, Rebecca knew this was an amazing chance for her son to overcome his shortcomings. Maybe he could finally obtain the strength he wanted so much.

Rebecca had scanned Lya with her divine sense many times, and all she could feel was a bunch of qi refracting light, with no real physical form. She couldn't think of a single reason for Lya to hurt her son, and she saw herself the results of her guidance. Rebecca didn't mind one bit if Amon was a cultivator or not, but she knew her son very well. Though she didn't know what this "lost method" was, she decided to take a chance for his sake. She could only hope that neither of them would regret trusting the sword spirit.

"I'll allow this... for now," Rebecca said, and the atmosphere in the room seemed to lighten considerably. Her green eyes locked onto Lya's blue eyes as she said, "I hope you can take care of him when I'm not around."

From Rebecca's expression, Lya knew she would not be satisfied with a simple answer. She took a deep breath and proclaimed. "I swear I will guard Amon Skoller with my life, and will never bring harm to him."

Rebecca stared at her for a few seconds before nodding. "I hope you stay true to your words. From what I know, sword spirits can never betray their masters."

Lya flinched. What Rebecca said was absolutely true; sword spirits never betrayed their masters, as they were a part of them.

"If something happens to him, you can be sure I'll smash that sword into smithereens and destroy you."

Rebecca's eyes flashed with a cold light and an even stronger pressure emitted from her. Her skin started reddening, and her breathing quickened. The pressure was incredibly powerful, causing Lya's body to briefly distort. If she had a physical body, her bones would have been crushed and her lungs would have collapsed.

"What a strong soul," Lya muttered to herself as she examined Rebecca with her divine sense. Rebecca was certainly not a soul cultivator, but her aster was incredibly developed and the nebula surrounding it was thick and dense. She thought it was strange that Rebecca's skin was reddening, so she took a look at her meridians.

To her surprise, what she saw was a jumbled mess of broken pathways. Although everything above her navel was mostly undamaged, the meridians in her lower body were snapped or twisted, reflecting her terribly damaged legs. Even her dantian looked misshapen and bloated as a red star inside it was flickering randomly. Red lava seemed to leak from the dantian and course through her meridians, seeping into her muscles and skin and slowly burning them from the inside out.

Lya could tell that it was not an intentional effect. Whenever the woman in front of her lost the focus on her own qi for a moment, it would start circulating by itself, causing horrible side effects.

Her respect for Rebecca increased tremendously. Though her dantian was damaged and she couldn't cultivate through the standard means, she could still use her divine sense and manipulate qi. Most importantly, she did so for her son's benefit even if it might kill her one day.

"You can rest assured," she managed to say to Rebecca, a bit distraught.

The pressure faded and Rebecca looked away at the night sky. The red jewel in the necklace glowed brighter, and her skin started to regain its original color.

"That fire crystal won't be able to store much more qi," Lya said carefully as she stared at the necklace.

"That is none of your concern," Rebecca answered in a snappy tone.

She then put a hand out the window, and Lya could see a thin stream of hot air blowing up from her fingertips as she released the excessive fire qi from her body.

Lya knew that the conversation was over. She was sure Rebecca wouldn't mention her to anyone—for Amon's sake.

Lya bowed again and quietly disappeared. Rebecca was left alone in the room again, looking at the window, her body leaving a long shadow in her room. She clenched her chest, looking hesitant.

The next day, Amon woke up and prepared to leave for the market. As he stared at himself in the mirror, Lya's voice came into his mind.

"You know, I like your hair. It makes you seem exotic."

"Good morning."

Although he pretended not to hear her, his ears reddened slightly. Lya chuckled, but didn't point it out as she watched Amon take Brightmoon from under his bed. He was about to strap it to his back, but hesitated, unsure if he should bring it along.

"I see no reason for you to carry the sword with you," Lya informed hesitantly. "I'll be inside the ring. Just call for me, and I'll answer."

He felt the weapon's weight disappear and to his surprise, the sword was gone. Amon looked at the iron ring in awe.

"Come on, kid. Are you going to stand there in a daze?"

Amon snapped out of his stupor and went downstairs to say goodbye to his mother, informing her that he would be going to the mountain to buy some stuff. Oddly enough, Rebecca didn't ask him any questions, he simply nodded and told him to be careful.

He made his way out of the house and slowly walked to the Northern Junction, enjoying the morning sun and the cold breeze. In the distance, the farmlands glistened with droplets of dew and the small streams looked like liquid gold as the sunlight reflected on their surfaces.

"This place is beautiful," Lya commented, as she examined the area with her divine sense.

"Yes, it is."

As soon as they arrived at the Northern Junction, Amon found a carriage and paid the owner to take him to the mountain. Amon hopped into the small carriage pulled by two strong and healthy horses. When it was time, the carriage pulled off, following a stone road towards their destination.

Throughout their journey, Lya excitedly talked about the delightful scenery and how much she enjoyed the Outer Sect's beauty. At first, her reaction and commentary made Amon smile, but soon after, he became sad.

Maybe she's just excited to be away from the lake. It must have been awfully lonely spending decades all alone. How did she manage to stay sane? His thoughts were interrupted by Lya squealing as she saw a family of deer lazing around a few meters ahead. He smiled once more and gently rubbed the ring on his finger. It was nice to have someone to accompany him.

It took them almost two hours to reach the foot of Hell Keeper's Mountain. The carriage driver dropped him off at the mountain's golden-gated entrance. The gate itself was carved into the mountain and stood over twenty meters tall and ten meters wide.

As Amon approached them, he took a deep breath and proceeded towards the inside. However, a mechanical voice and a barrier of green light stopped him in his tracks.

"Entrance to Hell Keeper's City is three hundred contribution points," it announced.

He knew about the rules, but the high price was displeasing. The fee simply served as a deterrence to keep traffic to a minimum.

He took his purple card from his pocket and swiped at the kiosk at the side of the gate. The barrier opened slightly, only allowing room for one to go through. Once inside, the opening sealed itself again, leaving Amon in a dimly lit passageway to the center of the city.

A myriad of small houses occupied the majority of the space inside of the mountain. The other buildings were made of jade and gold—they were exclusive to elders and the most important buildings within the entire sect.

The inner walls were carved into houses which were mostly empty, but they existed in case the Abyss Sect found itself in a dire situation. These empty living spaces were enough to house the entire Outer Sect. The mountain itself would be more than enough for defense, equipped with combat ships and other necessary machinery.

The streets were paved with black slabs of stone, and a few trees were planted between the houses, giving a bit of color to the monotonous atmosphere. In the center of the mountain, a gigantic tree towered above everything.

The tree was thirty meters high, and its crown covered all of the jade palaces surrounding it. Its trunk was white with a few blood-red lines twisting around it, like veins. The leaves were the size of Amon and were all ashen-gray, just like his hair.

"The Ashen Heart tree..." Lya mumbled, seemingly impressed.

"You know of it?" Amon asked, raising a brow. From what he knew, the founder himself had planted this tree when the sect was founded.

"I know of its existence, nothing more," she quickly replied before returning to her silence.

Amon himself didn't know much about the tree, but no matter how much he asked Lya just kept quiet. He gave up and made his way through the streets and towards the buildings located under the tree's shade.

He stopped in front of one of the biggest buildings. Much like the marketplace in the Northern Junction, it had light-green walls, but was at least four times larger and focused solely on trading technique manuals. A black sign, affixed to a golden pillar read, "Myriad Exchange," in golden letters.

As he walked in, he could see his reflection in the floor tiles, causing him to blush with embarrassment; his shabby robes were an eyesore compared to some others he had passed on his way in. Thankfully, the building was almost empty. There were very few Inner Sect members and they spent most of their time cultivating.

Overwhelmed by all the luxury, Amon walked up to one of the counters and was greeted by a young man dressed in purple robes and an obviously trained smile.

"How can I help you, sir?" The man politely asked, giving a bowing in Amon's direction.

"I would like to sell two artifacts I found in the Scavenging," Amon said in a serious tone.

The clerk nodded and asked Amon to present the artifacts. Amon quietly retrieved the two daggers from his bottomless pouch and placed them on the counter.

The young clerk took them and analyzed them carefully with trained eyes. He checked their balance and slowly scrutinized the polished blades before letting out a deep sigh.

"Excuse me for a moment," he said, placing the daggers back on the counter and walking through a side door.

Amon stood there confused and grew anxious when the man didn't return for a long while. When he thought about leaving, the side door opened again and an old man appeared with the clerk following suit. He, too, wore purple robes with golden embroideries, and his noble demeanor was a stark contrast to the passiveness of the clerk's.

His white hair fell over his shoulders and his clear, penetrating eyes made Amon want to avert his gaze. His long beard flowed down to his chest and was adorned with small golden rings, making the old man seem quite rich.

The old man looked at Amon and introduced himself.

"I am Elder Li. I'm in charge of this business."

"I am Amon Skoller, Outer Sect member," Amon said with a nervous bow.

These must be extremely rare. Why else would he retrieve such an extraordinary appraiser to assist me? Amon pondered.

Elder Li immediately began to examine the daggers in silence, ignoring Amon's childish gawking.

"It really is Danasian steel. We'll need to test the properties of this specific combination, but they shouldn't be ordinary," the elder said sternly as he stroked his beard. "Good job, Oliver. I'll take over from here."

The clerk gave a deep bow and left. Amon was surprised that he was in possession of Danasian steel. Artifacts made of such material were incredibly rare.

"Where did you find these daggers?" Elder Li asked, raising the daggers at his eye level and carefully looking at them.

"I found them near the northern bank of the Red River, being held by a corpse," Amon replied.

"You're very, very lucky Amon. I'll offer you fifty thousand contribution points for both daggers," the elder stated, never taking his gaze off of the young boy.

Fifty... thousand?

The offer made Amon's head spin. With that many points, he could buy everything he needed and there would still be thousands left for other expenses. He made a great effort to control his excitement, and his breathing. In truth, he was almost jumping with happiness.

"I... I accept," he managed to say, his voice trembling.

Elder Li nodded and extended his hand to Amon.

With a fluid motion, he passed Amon's purple card over a glowing ball behind the counter before returning the card.

"If you ever have anything you want to sell, you are always welcome here," Elder Li said, giving Amon a slight nod and walking away with the daggers in hand. Amon bowed deeply, and quietly left.

"Lya, what the hell?" Amon exclaimed.

He was still in disbelief of the generous gift she had given him.

"How would I know these cheap daggers would be valuable?" she answered, somewhat annoyed.

Amon wasn't convinced. Even before the War of the Falling Leaves, Danasian steel was considered very rare and expensive, as only a handful of blacksmiths from the Southern Flame Sect could forge it. Nevertheless, Amon didn't voice his doubts.

"If your previous owner was so rich, why did he use an iron sword like Brightmoon?"

"Brightmoon had emotional value. That's all I can say," Lya said hesitantly, returning to her silence as she finished.

Realizing he had been insensitive, Amon didn't question her any further. He walked for a few minutes until he reached the Divine Arts Keep. Its white walls were pristine and its doors were decorated in markings he had never seen before. This was the place that held all of the sect's manuals and techniques.

As he pushed the heavy wooden doors open, Amon's nose was assaulted by the strong scent of paper, ink, and old leather.

Amon took a deep breath and savored the store's slightly musty air. Rows and rows of golden bookshelves were neatly organized on the ground floor. They were almost as tall as the ceiling, but packed with books of all sizes and colors, organized by cultivation topics.

The higher floors of the store housed manuals higher in level, quality, and price. All of the shelves were protected by a barrier of light with a wooden counter. Behind it stood a few clerks dressed in purple robes.

"I've come here to get a few manuals," Amon said to the clerk closest to him.

The clerk was slightly shocked by the rude and abrupt words of such a young boy, but working for high status sect members had brought him worse attitudes than this.

"If it's not too much of a bother, can you assist me, please?" Amon spoke again, this time softening his words out of respect.

"Very well," the clerk responded, noticing Amon's shame when he realized he had been rather brash.

The clerk nodded and placed a small ball on the counter and lightly tapped on it. The ball flashed with a blue light and started glowing.

An overwhelming number of letters started materializing in the air in front of the ball, forming countless lines of words and numbers that shone with a pale white light. Looking closely, the lines were names followed by numbers that were probably the price.

"Select a title and the manual's synopsis will appear," he explained patiently when he saw Amon's hesitation. "You can change sections by swiping the list to the side. All manuals on the first and second floors are listed here. All other floors require an Inner Sect token to be unlocked."

This technology was a bit strange to Amon, but he got used to it quickly. As he swiped, he mumbled the titles and summaries to himself.

"*Lesser Sword Art* — A manual that covers the basic use of qi when wielding a sword in combat."

"*The Art of Earth-shattering* — At completion, a cultivator would be able to shatter the earth with each strike, known for its unstoppable power."

"*The Art of Storm-breaking* — Learn a new sword art that allows a cultivator to use the wind as blades and strike from a distance. At completion, one would be able to cleave storms apart..." He continued to read just loud enough for Lya to follow along. "*Fundamentals of the Sword—*"

"That one looks good," Lya said as Amon touched it's title.

Amon raised his brow. This manual covered nothing but the fundamental uses of the sword. There were just stances, no real techniques in it.

Amon sighed and touched the *Fundamentals of the Sword* manual again. The light changed from white to green, signaling that he had selected the manual.

"Pick two more manuals," she instructed.

He spent almost an hour skimming through the rest of the list, but he couldn't use any of the manuals now. They either put a huge strain on the body or had different elemental alignments than his affinity. In the end, he chose *The Art of Storm-breaking* and the *Lesser Sword Art* manuals.

"So you have a wind affinity?" Lya asked, to which Amon nodded. His strongest affinity was with the wind, even if it was quite a weak one, making his situation quite tragic. He was deemed as being untalented because of that, and the years he took to manage to absorb qi only proved that point.

"Well, these are good choices. These will be perfect to teach you. Also, learning stormbreaker will be really useful," Lya chimed in approvingly.

"Now I need you to pick about ten more manuals. The more varied and different they are from each other, the better. This includes manuals from other elements."

"But my only affinity is wi—" Amon complained.

"It doesn't matter. I'll explain later," she interrupted, clearly showing she was starting to get annoyed.

Amon took another thirty minutes to pick the manuals Lya asked. He was sure it would all add up to at least five thousand contribution points, but Lya didn't give in.

Next, Amon began to look for some movement technique manuals, but the struggle was still the same. Eventually he settled on a few mediocre ones like *Gale Steps* and *The Essence of Movement*.

"Lya, this is a bit much," he whispered again, and the clerk raised a brow seeing him talking alone.

"It's fine. We only need one for body tempering."

He went to the body tempering section, trying to look for the more expensive manuals. While he was skimming through the list, Lya suddenly interrupted him with a shout.

"That one!" she said full of excitement. Amon looked at the name beneath his finger.

"*Skyreacher: A Body Tempering Technique?*" he mumbled, taking a sneaky glance to the clerk, but he seemed to be too bored to pay attention to Amon.

Upon looking at the cost, Amon let out an audible, "Are you kidding me?!" He caught himself, and avoided looking at the clerks as his ears reddened in frustration. "Lya, this one costs almost ten thousand points. Are you insane?" he scoffed.

"That's pretty damn cheap considering your dear founder developed it himself," she said arrogantly.

"How do you know that?"

"It doesn't matter. Just trust me and take it."

Amon continued without hesitation. He went on to choose ten cheap elemental purification manuals and signaled for the clerk that he was ready to complete his purchase.

Looking at the list, the clerk raised his brow and looked at Amon, full of doubts. Still, he said nothing.

"The thirty-seven manuals you asked add up to thirty-eight thousand contribution points," the man said, trying to maintain a neutral expression. Amon felt his chest tighten, but still gave the man his purple card. As the man swiped the card in the light ball, Amon felt the pain of losing more than half of the points he had obtained just a few hours ago.

The clerk quietly left the counter to get Amon's manuals. He walked through the light curtain as if it didn't exist, and started going from section to section. After a few minutes, he returned. His upper body was hidden behind a gigantic pile of books that shook the counter as he set them down.

"If you try to take any of those manuals out of the sect's grounds, they will immediately burn. The Skyreacher manual in particular will explode, and will for sure kill you or whomever tries to steal it." The clerk warned. "Also, as soon as you open one of them, they will cut your finger and draw a drop of blood. If anyone else tries to read them after that they will either burn or explode."

Amon's face paled, but he quickly nodded. He took his bottomless pouch and stored the books in it one by one. He then quickly left the Divine Arts Keep. He still had around fifteen thousand contribution points adding what Jake had given him, so he could cultivate in peace without worrying about his expenses.

* * *

Once he had returned home, Amon checked on his mother before sitting down to eat dinner with her. Afterwards, he went to his room and softly closed the door. Lya materialized by his side, and took the bottomless pouch from his waist. She removed the manuals and waved her hands, causing them to levitate in front of her. She read them, using small puffs of air to turn the pages.

"Guess they didn't account for that," Amon chuckled.

"There is only so much they can do. Also none of these manuals are really that valuable," Lya commented as she continued to read. "I would say the best thing they can do is keep an eye on the people that have the more valuable manuals."

"People could still make copies and smuggle them out of the sect," Amon pointed out.

"True," Lya shrugged, "but who knows. Maybe there are a few elders who hunt down and kill people who obtain illegal copies."

"You think they would go that far?" Amon asked, distraught.

"Kid, you just bought a bomb disguised as a book," Lya dismissed him.

Seeing him looking clearly bothered, she sighed.

"Don't think too much about it. We won't use them to cause harm. If anything happens, I'll be here," Lya said in a soft voice, trying to appease him.

Amon climbed into bed, leaving Lya to her reading. The crisp sound of the flipping pages were the last thing he heard as he slowly fell asleep.

When he woke up the next morning, the first thing heard was the flipping of a page. He opened his drowsy eyes and saw Lya still reading in the same position, her face calm, completely absorbed in the task at hand.

He sat on the bed and rubbed his eyes. Lya slowly closed the book she had just finished reading and added it to a huge pile by her side.

"Good morning," she said with a smile.

Amon greeted her back in a weary voice.

"Don't you need to sleep?"

"Not really. It's really hard for me to feel exhausted, but if I use too much of my divine sense, I'll need to return to Brightmoon for a rest. Nevertheless, if it is just reading or talking it would take weeks for me to start feeling tired. Although It takes a long time for me to feel tired, it also takes longer for me to recover. I don't have a body, after all. It's not like being able to stay awake for days on end is an exciting matter, it is actually quite boring sometimes."

"I see..." Amon responded, averting his eyes.

"Do you want to ask anything else?"

"Well... I mean, what exactly am I looking at?" He turned his gaze to her and stared at her blue eyes and porcelain skin. "If that's not your real body, why bother pretending to have one? Sitting down, expressing emotions and everything else? In the end this is just your divine sense making illusions."

"Would you rather speak with a voice in your head?

Amon promptly shut his mouth.

"Anyway, this is not really about you. At this point, it is like an instinct, almost like a second nature. I would rather do that and pretend to be alive and have a real body than to quietly slip into insanity," She answered emotionlessly.

Amon sat on his bed. He didn't mean to upset her, but it was quite strange for a spirit to go through such efforts.

"Give me your ring," she demanded.

Amon promptly took the ring from his finger and gave it to her, still feeling guilty.

Lya took the iron ring in her hands and retrieved a simple sword from it, offering it to Amon. The blade was thick and was a few centimeters longer than Brightmoon. It was also wider, making for a much heavier blade and the black handle, sculpted from stone, gave it an ancient feel. Needless to say, it was a simple and crude weapon.

"What will you name it?" Lya asked curiously as she watched Amon struggle to keep the sword from falling to the ground.

Using both hands, Amon managed to hoist the weapon up, letting the flat side lay against his shoulder. "Windhowler," he said, slightly out of breath. His knees buckled for a while before he finally decided to rest the sword's tip on the ground.

Lya giggled and nodded in approval. She began to search through the pile of books by her side and fished the *Lesser Sword Art* manual from it. She threw it to Amon, saying, "I've already read it. The content was concise and there were no problems with it. The explanations were also really good, so chances are you will learn more from it than from me."

Amon managed to catch the book in the air. It was very thin and the pages were all yellowed from age.

"You will read this book and use the sword to train. This will help you learn how to infuse your qi into a sword and refine your control of qi at the same time. When you reach a satisfying level on both, we can start body tempering."

Lya picked up another book and began to read it, turning away from Amon.

"Why can't we start it now?" he asked while frowning.

"Do not be too hasty," she reprimanded. "Skyreacher is a great technique, but it requires incredibly complex maneuvering of the qi in your body, and you have no chance to properly use it as you are now."

Being struck down like that, Amon couldn't retort. All he could do was grumble, making Lya chuckle a bit.

"How do you know about the Skyreacher technique?" he asked her again.

"It was a technique that was already famous in my time. It has spread everywhere and was one of the reasons your founder became famous. If your founder managed to polish it even further, then it is certainly among the best in the world."

"Sounds like an amazing technique," Amon managed to say.

He sneaked a glance at Lya, thinking. In the end, he decided to say nothing. If Lya wanted to talk about it, she would.

"It's truly incredible. So be patient and study the manual," she instructed, tossing him a stern, but teasing smile.

Amon nodded and started to read the book. Its pages were mostly occupied by large amounts of text and a few, but precise, illustrations. It went into great detail on how to properly control qi and how to imbue a sword with it.

Just as everyone had personal traces in their calligraphy, cultivators had personal traces in the way they handled qi. As such, one would have to experiment until they found what they felt more comfortable with when manipulating qi.

When a cultivator spends a lot of time using an artifact, the qi they imbued in it would not only make it evolve, but also naturally engrave the pathways the cultivator's qi used. As such, one's artifact would be best suited to them. Using another person's artifact would not have the same effects, as the qi pathways were already set and would affect the flow of the new owner's qi.

Amon was enthralled as he read the book. It didn't take too long for him to finish, and as he did he stood in silence for a long while, his eyes closed as he pondered. When he opened them again, he got up and left the room. He took a quick break to eat breakfast and talk with his mother, clearing his mind. When he returned, he read the book again, trying to memorize all of its steps.

He realized that the *Lesser Sword Art* manual was incredibly important, especially for inexperienced cultivators or those that didn't have a master.

He would certainly have trouble cultivating any of the other techniques if he didn't grasp the basics in the manual, even if he was strong enough. Sword arts were, after all, a way to channel the elemental qi a cultivator had in the sword and unleash it in different ways.

"Any questions?" Lya looked at him over a book with a smile on her face.

"Not right now."

Amon shook his head and closed his eyes, entering meditation.

As his divine sense spread, Amon extended his hands, calling forth small wisps of qi and started playing with them. It was as awkward as it had been when he first opened his acupuncture points, but he focused, trying to get as relaxed as possible.

He stretched the wisps, broke them down, and fused them together. He kneaded them into a ball and then threw the ball around. The ball turned out to be obviously misshapen, but he took his time trying to perfect it.

He dispersed it and formed it again, before making it circle around him a few times. Then he would disperse it again, and this time would make it spin as fast as he could.

These were all exercises that the book recommended for beginners. Maybe most would feel it was boring, but Amon was completely invested in the marvelous feeling of being able to control and shape qi at his will. He didn't stop until Lya told him to take a break. It was only then that he realized his clothes were drenched and his face was red from the effort.

After a short break, he returned to his studies. His control slowly grew smoother. Amon started more complex exercises, controlling greater amounts of qi and turning them in different shapes.

A week passed as he trained his control without him realizing. One night, after Amon had long gone to bed, Lya went to sit with Rebecca.

"He was training until now?" Rebecca asked with surprise.

Lya nodded at her question.

"He is more resilient than I thought." Rebecca sighed. Her son was starting to grow up. "I still can't believe he didn't tell me he managed to absorb qi and is preparing for body tempering."

She was somewhat bitter as she complained. If this had happened a few weeks ago, the first thing Amon would have done was storm into her room and tell her, jumping in happiness.

"Well, he is trying to hide my existence," Lya smiled sadly. "I'm sure he will tell you when he goes through his first round of body tempering."

Rebecca grumbled sourly.

"Well, how is he doing?"

"It's not a spectacular speed, but it is also not slow. He seems to be having fun," Lya answered, chuckling a little.

"That's a good mindset to have."

"I'll give him a slight push to tell you something." Lya thought for a while before adding, "He'll probably say he found a pill or something together with the sword that allowed him to control qi and he didn't want to make you worried."

"So you think he will lie?" Rebecca asked, growing more annoyed.

"Some people are like that. When they think lies will protect someone, they won't hesitate to lie, even if it causes greater damage than the truth. The problem is that not many realize the damage beforehand."

Rebecca could only sigh. She knew it to be true. She hated the idea, but understood why her son was lying, or at the very least withholding the truth. On the other hand, calling him out might have an adverse effect. She wanted her son to make his own choices, even if that included lying to her. Nevertheless, this was not something she would easily accept.

"I'll be sure to set him straight. Help me out, okay?"

Rebecca looked into Lya's eyes and Lya nodded.

"Do you think he's ready?" A frown could be seen in Rebecca's pale face and her green eyes were full of worry.

"He'll start training with the sword tomorrow. I believe that in two to three days he will be ready."

"Thank you for the help," Rebecca said with some difficulty, as if struggling with the words.

"You're welcome," Lya smiled, giving a bow before leaving the room through the wall.

"Again!" Lya ordered as she guided Amon.

His face was red and large beads of sweat dripped from his forehead, creating a small puddle on the floor. His breathing was labored and his wet hair was stuck to his face. In his hands was a crude sword that was obviously too heavy for him to lift.

He gave Lya a resentful glance, but closed his eyes and focused, trying to control his breathing. He tightened the grip on the sword and his hands started to glow, sending small lines of light onto the sword's surface. They started to branch out and eventually covered the entire weapon in a peculiar pattern, leaving it glowing except for a small corner on the blade.

"Again!" Lya said in an unsatisfied voice.

Her blue eyes shone with a fierce light, making Amon cower. He retracted his hand from the sword and the lines of light disappeared. He took a deep breath, but it didn't help much. His hands were pale from the excessive strength he was putting in his grip and he was trembling. His whole body was sore.

Lya made him circulate all of the qi in his body once before trying to imbue Windhowler with it. It was a way to test his control and get some practice before he started body tempering.

"Come on, stop stalling and do it again!" Lya said again, her voice louder.

Amon thought she was pitiless. He had been going through this hell for almost two days straight. On the first day, he actually passed out from his efforts.

Keeping his focus at its peak and maintaining his divine sense for this many hours took a toll on him. Furthermore, controlling the qi to make sure it passed through each and every one of his meridians was exhausting in both body and mind. After some time, terrible headaches would assault him, making it impossible for him to focus and giving Lya no choice but to allow him to rest.

Still, even if he felt somewhat resentful he couldn't deny the results. He had greatly advanced under Lya's constant pressure. Regardless of her nagging, learning about the intricacies of qi kept him interested and he was thrilled about improving.

Controlling the qi and using lines to form pathways for the qi, was a good way to optimize its use and not overcharge the sword. This would ensure that the weaker artifact wouldn't be destroyed during his training. The problem, however, was that if he missed a spot, it would turn into a weakness. The artifact could break if it was hit in that weak spot with a strong enough attack, leaving Amon unarmed and putting his life at greater risk.

He let out a long breath and held the sword again. The lines of light spread again, slowly covering the sword. This time, however, as the last line was drawn, the sword flashed with a blinding light and the lines disappeared. The blade started to glow as Amon injected qi into it.

"I did it!" He shouted, dropping the sword to the ground as he raised his hands in victory. A satisfied smile danced across his face. As soon as the sword left his hands, the glow disappeared, revealing the lines of light before they slowly faded again.

"Good job. You even managed to be a bit faster than what I expected."

Amon gave her a cheesy grin as he fell on the bed, looking at the ceiling.

"I think you're ready to start body tempering."

Lya fished the Skyreacher manual from the pile of books beside his bed and passed it to him.

"Read this very carefully and be sure to memorize everything properly. When you do, we'll practice it for a bit before properly using the technique," Lya said with a serious tone.

Amon frowned, causing Lya to chuckle.

"Did you think it would be easy to just read it and use the technique?"

Amon diverted his eyes, confirming her suspicions. She shook her head and scoffed, "Things are never easy, Amon. You must always be sure to be perfectly ready before using a technique. You don't want to try it without proper preparations and ruin your body, do you?"

Amon shook his head; he obviously did not want that. He promptly took the thick manual and opened it.

"Ah!" He was caught off guard as something cut his finger, smearing the book in blood. It soon disappeared, as if it had been absorbed by the pages.

"Damn, I forgot about that," he grumbled for a bit before starting to read.

Amon raised his brow as he read. The first lines of the book were a long string of runes, probably written in the divine language. He would have to memorize all of the runes perfectly in order to mentally recite them as he used the technique.

Following that, the first few chapters were an introduction to the human body. There were detailed explanations and drawings of human anatomy, as well as the meridians. It also explained what body tempering really was. Amon's eyes grew wider as he read, surprised by the contents.

"So this is what goes on in our body during tempering?"

He glanced at Lya, who just gave an uninterested nod.

Amon knew the basics about the human body. He knew about the acu-puncture points and meridians. He also knew about organs, bones and a bit about cells, but just from the explanations of the manual alone he suddenly understood that knowing anatomy was essential for proper training.

Body tempering wasn't simply breaking down one's body and channel-ing a technique to increase the healing speed and perfect one's cells. Much like imbuing an artifact with qi, there was a proper method to imbue one's cells with it and increase their efficiency.

The disparity of strength in the body tempering stage came from the limits a cultivator would go through to temper their bodies and the differ-ent methods used to imbue the qi.

Human bodies were incredibly feeble when compared to spirit beasts. Their cells had a low capacity to handle qi, so one had to find a proper way to compress and distribute it to maximize the efficiency as they saturated quickly.

A great body tempering technique would allow one to heal their injur-ies faster, compress the qi better, and infuse more qi in the new cells pro-duced during the healing process.

Not only that, but a proper body tempering technique would enhance a cell's functions rather than simply strengthen it. If someone managed to temper their nervous system, for instance, they would have greater reaction speeds. If one were crazy enough to temper their eyes, their vision would be enhanced. Of course, this was all in theory, as a single mistake could cause irreparable damage.

A cultivator could also extend their lifespan in the body tempering stage. A cultivator who properly tempered their body with a strong technique would live from three hundred to four hundred years. They would age slower, gaining the ability to retain their youth for decades. The Skyreacher technique, when properly cultivated, would allow one to live at least five hundred years. This was the greatest proof that this manual was leagues above the others.

"This is mind-blowing," Amon exclaimed as he flipped through the pages, unable to look away from the manual.

Lya chuckled with a wistful look in her eyes. *Arthur had truly been a cultivation genius, after all of that,* she thought.

"I told you it was a great technique," Lya reminded.

Amon didn't answer her as he was too focused on reading the book. He was also using this time to give his body a full rest. Despite all of that, He ended up skipping lunch without realizing it, and only closed the book when it was time for bed. He had a headache from reading so much. He rubbed his temples with his eyes closed, trying to absorb what he had just read.

"Lya, how can qi have such miraculous effects?" he asked as he opened his eyes and put the book away. "I understand the logic behind elemental cultivation, but this is just so much more than I thought."

"Well... the answer isn't a simple one. Since qi could be considered the prime matter of the universe, imbuing your body and using the right technique will bring it closer to perfection, or at the very least, closer to the origins of nature."

"I suppose that another way of thinking would be that you are slowly shedding away your mortal body as each round of body tempering has cells with a greater saturation of qi. At some point your body might even become qi itself." Lya shrugged her shoulders before saying, "The soul is immortal anyway. If you somehow manage to bind it to a coil that is immortal too, you could achieve complete immortality."

Seeing Amon's eyes widening, Lya gave a small smile.

"Don't be too surprised. Something like that had been discussed for centuries even before I was born. Of course, discussing theory and putting it to practice are different matters altogether. If it were that easy, people would have done it ages ago.

"As far as I know, the last step of that theoretical possibility is impossible," she continued. "Your soul is bound to your flesh and blood. One thing is to enhance them using qi, another one is to completely discard them. From what I remember, everyone that tried immediately died. They lost their bodies and their souls, having lost their coils, returned to the cycle of reincarnation."

"That's... terrible." Amon managed to say.

"Well, it's the price of trying to push forward the limits of knowledge. Experiments with cultivation are always dangerous."

Lya was unphased by the carelessness of others, but when she saw Amon grow anxious, she signed.

"You don't have to worry about it. Did you know that living in an area with thick qi enables people to temper their bodies passively?"

Amon was taken aback.

"Yes. Just by breathing people can absorb qi, although the quantity is negligible and it is not a conscious process," Lya explained. "You can picture your body as a cold cup, and qi as water. Just by staying in an area with great humidity, the cup will slowly be filled, although it would be something like a single drop of water every decade."

Amon stared at her, curious, but confused; he beckoned for her to continue.

Lya brushed her long, black hair out of her face before saying, "Body tempering would be like using that water to make small pieces of ice, and then putting them into the cup. Of course there would be a limit to how many pieces of ice you could put there, and even at the limit there would still be empty spaces left since the pieces of ice are not a perfect fit for the cup. The different body tempering techniques basically tell the size and shape of the pieces of ice. A great technique would be the one that, at the end, will minimize the empty space. In order to completely fill the cup without any imperfection, you would still need centuries for the qi to naturally fill in the blanks."

Amon seemed hesitant. He didn't know how, or when, he would achieve such results.

"You have no need to worry. You still haven't taken your first step in a thousand-mile journey. If someday you get close to the end, only then can you worry about what follows. Otherwise, you're just wasting your time and creating mental obstacles before you've begun.

"Go eat something and rest. Tomorrow we will start practicing," Lya finished.

Amon nodded and did as he was told. When he returned an hour later, he threw himself into his bed, heavily exhausted from the day's activities. His head was spinning with information, and he found himself too agitated to sleep properly.

Lya quietly observed him, but made no comments, letting him alone with his own thoughts.

After breakfast the next day, he sat down and read the manual again. He closed his eyes and entered a meditative state, slowly gathering the qi surrounding him. He absorbed it until all of the qi reserves in his body were full again.

When he was brimming with energy, he started practicing the movement of qi within his body according to the manual. To complete a single revolution of the technique took a few minutes of intricate and complex maneuvering of the qi in his meridians that spanned the entirety of his body.

As he wasn't using the divine language runes described in the manual, moving his qi that way was inconsequential and served only as training. At the same time, he took a blank piece of paper and a pen and started writing the runes of the technique as he circulated his qi.

At first, it was incredibly hard. He made many mistakes and had to start over from scratch as Lya carefully observed his training. The effects of making a mistake in such a technique were unknown; it might even lead to deformities in his body, so Amon took the task very seriously.

It took him a few hours to finally complete the first revolution of the technique perfectly. He didn't stop after the first success. Instead, he tried again, and again, each time trying to complete it faster than before. Although he failed repeatedly, Amon slowly started to grasp the intricacies involved and eventually started succeeding more than failing.

Soon, he was training mindlessly and it became instinct instead of active attempts. When Lya noticed, she became a bit worried, but she didn't dare to interrupt him.

The pile of used papers slowly started growing as Amon trained repeatedly. Eventually, his body shivered and he snapped out of the trance. He was ghostly pale and his limbs were trembling.

"I... think.... I'm ready," he said with great difficulty as he gasped for air. His chest was burning, and he felt as if he had been holding his breath. He had rehearsed dozens of times and succeeded in his last twenty tries in a row.

"I think so too, but take a break and recompose yourself," Lya said gently.

Amon closed his eyes and did his best to control his breathing. He was feeling very confident about his chances.

"Are you ever going to tell your mother about your training?" Lya asked as she sneaked him a glance.

Amon shuddered. What would he tell his mother?

"I know I have to tell her something, but I can't talk about you. It would only bring trouble," he replied, pondering what to do. "I think I'll tell her that I found a treasure that increased my talent, but I didn't tell her before so that she wouldn't worry about me."

As he nodded to himself, satisfied with the answer he would give, Lya rolled her eyes.

"Maybe lying isn't a good idea."

"I have no real choice, Lya. I'd do anything to save my mother from trouble... Even if it means lying to her," he declared.

Amon's golden eyes showed no hesitation as they stared at her intently.

She didn't press the issue any further, however, she informed Amon that it was time to start training.

"What I will do now will hurt. You mustn't give in, no matter what."

She silently approached Amon, making goosebumps appear on his skin.

"We will use body tempering to boost your soul cultivation too," she said as she glanced at him.

Amon gulped and his voice quivered as he stuttered.

"Y-you don't m-mean—"

"I'm sorry, but you will have to use the first line of the soulrousing technique. It will boost the pain even further, but it will be the fastest way for you to produce more nebula and further develop your soul," she explained, her voice was full of worry.

"What will you do?" he asked with a low voice.

"I will send my qi into your meridians. I will make sure the qi spreads through your whole body. Then I will use the qi to slowly grind away your body from the inside out."

"I will leave no organ untouched, except for the brain. I will make sure to slightly damage every inch of your body, but I'll be very careful. It will be just enough for the technique to work, but not enough to compromise anything. It will also be very demanding for me, since you can imagine that each part of your body will need individualized attention, but this is the only way to guarantee a uniform tempering in all of your body to attain the best results."

"I don't think this is a good idea."

Amon retreated, but his back was soon pressed against the wall. He cowered as Lya towered over him.

"You want to become strong, don't you?"

Her question made Amon's resistance disappear.

"You can start using the first line of the soulrousing technique," she said with a gentle voice.

Amon prayed that things would go as planned as he started focusing. The runes of the divine language appeared in his mind, spinning chaotically.

"I'll try to be as gentle as possible," Lya said hesitantly.

Amon was too worried to notice the hint of hesitation in her voice.

She extended her hands and reached for him. Amon closed his eyes, focusing solely on the runes. Still, a little part of him was screaming, saying that he had made a grave mistake.

Then, for the second time in his life, he felt as if he had been thrown into Hell.

I need you to be brave, son. This is going to hurt, but you can't leave. It is okay to cry and scream if you want, but never move from where you are.

His father's word played on repeat inside of Amon's head. He vividly remembered the burning sensation that spread through his body, making him feel like his blood had turned to acid. Whatever his father had done to him gave him a splitting headache that numbed his consciousness. His muscles tore, his skin ruptured, and blood seeped from every pore. Amon always thought that he would never feel so much pain again in his life, but he was terribly wrong.

As Lya channeled her qi into his meridians, he felt even more pain, but he still held on. He felt as though he had no choice. He needed strength. No, he *wanted* it. The moment he plunged Brightmoon into the dying dire wolf he decided he would do everything possible to attain that.

He knew this pain was necessary. He would not run away from it; he would face it and grow stronger.

Amon screamed in agony. He felt as if fire was crawling under his skin, eating away at his flesh and burning what remained. His eyes were completely closed, but he still felt them aching. He couldn't think clearly, as he felt like someone was stirring the insides of his head with an iron spike. All he had was pain, and in that pain he steeled his resolve.

His temperature started to rise, and his skin reddened considerably. Lya continued to focus, trying hard to ignore his screams as her qi spread further inside him. Time turned into an indistinct blur. It might have been an hour, or it might have been seconds; he didn't know.

He felt his whole body numb as the burning stopped, and all he could hear was a buzz in his head as he started feeling dizzy.

"Don't pass out!" Lya's urgent voice shouted. "Start channeling the technique so you can recover!"

Amon pulled himself together, circulating the qi in his body. The runes of the divine language naturally came to mind, and the qi slowly started moving according to his will.

He managed to complete the first revolution, though it was clumsily done. The effects were immediate; the pain subsided and his thoughts became more clear. Every successful revolution made the next one easier.

After a while, all he felt was numbness. He couldn't lift a finger and all he managed to do was open his sore eyes. What greeted him was a Lya that looked pale as a ghost, her face full of worry and anxiety.

"You will be unable to move for a few hours, maybe a day. I recommend you use the chance to properly rest," she said with a frown. "Even after that, it will take awhile to fully recover and you will need to continue channeling the Skyreacher technique every time you wake up."

Amon closed his eyes. The numbness made his body feel incredibly light and soon he was fast asleep.

As Lya watched him sleep, she wanted to punch herself.

I overdid it. I should have done it the normal way and slowly temper each part of his body instead of forcing it all at once, she thought to herself in regret.

Lya had never gone through body tempering, and when she met Alexei he had been way past that level. All that she knew had been theoretical. The method she chose to use on Amon was a method Alexei and Arthur devised together, but she had only seen it being used on a single person, and didn't quite feel the need to ask Alexei details about it when she had the chance.

She spread her divine sense and checked his body. To her surprise, he was healing at a much faster rate than she imagined. Additionally, his cells were overflowing with energy and his body emitted a pale glow under her divine sense.

The effects of the first round were stronger than she expected. This made her even more suspicious of Amon's identity. She thought about how she would confirm her hypothesis, but decided not to act on it. She shook her head to clear her mind and left for Rebecca's room.

As she expected, Rebecca had been waiting for her. She was gripping the edge of the quilt so tightly that her knuckles were white.

"How did it go?" she asked with a glint in her eyes.

To spare her from worrying too much, Lya had blocked all the sound in Amon's room, as well as Rebecca's divine sense.

"It went well. He's resting now," Lya said with a comforting smile.

Rebecca let out a sigh of relief and loosened her grip on the blanket. She questioned Lya about the process and they discussed the specifications of Amon's process. Lya informed her that he would reach the middle stages in a few months. Amon's mother was shocked, yet happy about this news. It had taken her over two years to reach the middle stages, even though she had been born with a high affinity.

The way Rebecca cared deeply for her son and her intelligence made Lya have a deep respect for her. It was one of the reasons Lya revealed her presence and relieved Rebecca's worries by giving reports from time to time.

More than that, the sheer willpower she showed moved Lya. It was naturally hard for Rebecca to do anything more than give him advice from time to time, but Lya could see how much his mother regretted being able to do only that much. Nevertheless, the fact that she got herself into this state by defending her son was worthy of Lya's admiration.

Lya had decided she would do her best to help Rebecca. It was also a good way to get to know Amon and help him to make up for his flaws. Even though some of these flaws were glaring, the real danger was the ones he hid. He never spoke of his father, and Lya could see that there was something more to it than what he and Rebecca showed. She would do everything she could to make sure Amon would not stray from the correct path. She would prove to herself that she could do it. Even if it was just a mere fragment, a shadow of him, Alexei had returned to her, and she would never let him make the same mistakes again.

* * *

When Amon woke up, his body was still numb. He managed to make small movements, but his limbs felt heavy and lethargic.

"You should use the second line of the soulrousing technique to absorb all of the nebula you generated the other day."

Lya materialized by his side and gave him a careful look.

Confused by her statement, Amon asked, "Wasn't it yesterday?"

"You slept for a whole day," Lya said lightly.

Amon closed his eyes and focused. As the runes of the divine language started spinning in his mind, his weary body was, once again, overtaken by the alternating feelings of heat and cold, making him shiver and sweat. Thankfully, the process was much faster this time.

"Start using the Skyreacher technique again; it will help you recover faster," she advised.

He didn't waste time as he closed his eyes. Slowly, the numbness in his body subsided and his weariness disappeared. After a few hours, he managed to sit on the bed, despite feeling mentally exhausted. His body felt light and somewhat clumsy, as if it didn't belong to him. Amon started feeling sore all over, but it was manageable.

He found it very hard to move as he wished. He couldn't apply the right amount of force in any of his limbs and his balance was off, making him barely able to sit straight. After a few attempts, he expressed his concern to Lya.

"This is all very common. You have to get used to your new strength. The first time is the worst by far. You'll realize every new round of tempering will have a smaller impact on your body and you won't need to go through this every time," the pale-skinned woman explained.

"Lya, this is strange but… I feel amazing."

His voice sounded strange as his tone changed with every word. He never thought that controlling his voice would be a part of the side effects.

Though his body was hard to control, his senses were not. Amon felt as if he was seeing the world for the first time. He could feel the weakest current of air grazing his skin. He could see the smallest imperfections in the walls of his room, and he could clearly hear and pinpoint the locations of the chirping of birds coming from trees dozens of meters away from his house. Most of all, his mind was clear, but he was slowly starting to feel inebriated in this strange feeling of discovery.

"About that… Let's not do it again. Maybe we should use the normal way and temper each part of your body at a time," she said full of regret.

"No," he said sternly as he looked her dead in the eyes.

His eyes seemed to be blazing, a gaze so intense Lya actually looked away for a moment. This surprised her. What had gotten into him?

"I think the pain is too much for you to handle," she declared, returning her gaze onto the young boy.

"The pain is something I can take. I know the results will be far less impressive if we do it any other way." Amon didn't avert his gaze from hers. His eyes were as hard as steel and his suddenly assertive attitude made Lya feel strangely uncomfortable.

"I want to keep doing it this way," he said, softening his tone and facial expression. "Please help me with that."

"Fine, we can do it that way." She thought for a moment before adding, "However, you must speak to your mother immediately."

It was a test to see what Amon would truly say to her. He was sure Rebecca would corner him with a ton of questions. She wanted to see how far he would go to hide the truth in his attempt to protect her.

"This... fine, I'll talk to her."

He managed to stand up from the bed, but quickly fell to the floor. He tried to stand up again, but his balance was terrible. Lya couldn't hide her laugh as she saw Amon struggling to stand up.

"A little help, please?" he asked with a red-faced frown.

"Sorry, but you need to adapt to the changes."

Lya was trying to keep a straight face, but the corners of her mouth were twitching.

"There's no way I'd spoil the fun," she added, disappearing into thin air.

Amon cursed at her and continued to fight his body for control. It took him a few minutes before he barely managed to stand up and take a few steps. Supporting his upper body in the wall, he slowly walked to his mother's room.

BAM, BAM!

As he tried knocking, the sound he produced was way louder than what he intended. The door shook and seemed to be about to crack. His face paled, but his mother's voice showed no surprise as she asked him to enter.

"Hi, mom," he managed to say before he fell to the floor again.

His mother raised a brow and asked, "Is this... body tempering?" Her face was full of shock as she looked at Amon.

"Yes, it is," he said in his uneven tone.

"How?"

From the ring, Lya quietly complimented her acting skills. However, Rebecca was truly shocked. She was probing her son with her divine sense and saw that every inch of his body was glowing with densely-packed qi. She had never seen a tempering as uniform and complete as his.

"Mom..." Amon started, "I've been hiding a few things from you. I found more than just a sword in the Scavenging"

"What do you mean by that?" she replied, feigning anger.

"Well, I... also found a pair of daggers," he said sheepishly, averting his eyes from his mother's gaze.

"Continue," she demanded.

"There was a bottle of medicine with it."

She rolled her eyes and said, "Let me guess, you just took the medicine?"

Rebecca was no longer faking anger. She was hurt and annoyed that he chose to lie to her.

"Well, in the bottomless pouch there was a brief explanation on how the medicine worked and—"

"What kind of person wouldn't know how to use the medicine they're carrying on them?"

Rebecca was ruthless with her rebuttal, making Amon flinch.

"I thought it was a trap, but something told me it was a chance. So I decided to risk it."

He still didn't look at her. It was like the feet of her bed were incredibly interesting as he simply focused his gaze there.

Rebecca sighed. At the very least her son was a terrible liar. She put her hand on her forehead, unsure if she should laugh or cry.

"Well, it obviously worked," she scoffed.

Amon nodded and described the effects of his first use of the soul-rousing technique in an attempt to hide the lie with some truth. Rebecca, continued to question him, wondering how much of the truth he would withhold.

He went on to explain that he sold the daggers and used the money to buy the best body tempering manual in the sect and that there was still enough to sustain them for years.

"Why didn't you tell me? Body tempering is incredibly dangerous! You could have ruined your body!"

"I'm sorry. I wanted to surprise you."

He looked at her pitifully.

Rebecca beckoned him to sit with her. Her green eyes were full of conflict as she looked at him. When he was close enough, she grabbed him and hugged him tightly, almost suffocating him. Her thin arms were surprisingly strong.

"Never do anything like that again!"

"I promise I won't. I know it was a risk," he tried to reassure her.

"I truly hope you do," she had a sad smile that Amon couldn't see. "Is there anything else you've been keeping from me?"she asked in a cold tone.

"No. That was all," he lied again.

Rebecca sighed and released him from her arms.

"Don't lie to me like that again," she reprimanded him in a harsh tone.

"I promise," Amon said looking at her seriously.

"Promises are meant to be kept, Amon." She looked at him with a bit of resentment. "Can you truly keep this one?"

Amon felt his chest tighten. There was something different in her tone as she said that. It was a seriousness he hadn't felt in the conversation before. Guilt was starting to take over him. All of the happiness he had from completing his first tempering was gone. He looked at his mother, gazing intently into her green eyes.

"I can," he said with his golden eyes full of resolve.

Rebecca nodded hearing that. Amon quickly hobbled out of the room, still struggling to control his legs.

As she watched her young son leave, she thought about Lloyd. The thought made her heart ache.

"Don't be like him," she pleaded in a low voice as tears started spilling from her eyes.

Amon left with a sour expression on his face. His lips were tightly pursed and somewhat pale from the pressure, but his golden eyes were glowing with decisiveness. He needed to get some fresh air. Walking out of his house, Amon made his way to the Northern Junction, but the trip was taking longer than usual due to his restricted movement.

The real problem was his five senses. He wouldn't be able to adapt to them so easily, and the heightened sounds and perception were starting to really get under his skin. Every small noise that he heard sounded like an explosion. He wanted to cover his ears and scream, but managed to refrain from doing so. His mood was getting worse by the second and he felt there was nothing he could do to improve it.

He made his way to the Northern Junction and went behind the market to a small plaza. The plaza was covered with grass while small trees provided shade for those that wanted to enjoy the breeze and scenery. Due to Amon's heightened senses, he was heavily affected by the outside stimulants. He shuddered in discomfort, but continued on his way. The sooner he finished this, the sooner he could return home.

"What a great idea," he grunted to himself.

Lya became suspicious of what was truly happening to him, but didn't say a word. She took a peek at his soul, checking his nebula before confirming her suspicion. Nevertheless, she decided to let things play out before interrupting. He would see for himself what ignoring her warning about soul cultivation would lead to.

The biggest building in the plaza was the administration building. It had lustrous golden walls which blinded Amon as the sun bounced off of the exterior. Even while squinting, he was barely able to see the path in front of him.

Once inside, the usual counters and clerks dressed in purple were at the entrance. The strange looks and stares that the guards gave made him feel uneasy. He grew increasingly annoyed by their bright white robes and sneering looks.

Amon made his way to one of the shorter lines. He knew there would be quite a bit of a wait and this caused him to tap his foot impatiently. The *tap tap tap*, grew louder the longer he had to wait, and thus frustrated him more, yet Amon didn't stop.

When it was finally his turn, the clerk assisting him rolled his eyes, clearly unhappy, and the previous person in line gave Amon a reproachful look as he left the store. Amon huffed and his brows furrowed like two furry and angry caterpillars.

"What can I help you with?" the clerk asked after giving an almost unperceivable bow.

"I want to measure my strength and update my records, as I've reached body tempering," Amon said with his voice still uneven.

The clerk raised his brow, but nodded and called someone from a side door. A burly with a shaved head appeared. His purple robes were torn at the shoulders, blatantly showcasing his muscular arms and tanned skin—it was clear he demanded attention.

"So, little boy, I heard you just went through your first round of tempering?" he said with a smile, ignoring Amon's hostile expression.

"Yes, I did," he managed to say while gritting his teeth, from the man's thunderous voice.

"My name is Brandon. Please, follow me. We'll properly gauge your strength with a measuring pillar."

Amon nodded and together they went through the side door and up a set of black, spiraling stairs until they reached the third floor.

The room on that floor was a simple, wide open space with a large pillar made of obsidian. The pillar was covered in gold runes of the divine language. Floating next to the pillar was a small, glowing ball sitting on an altar. A line of patiently waited their turn. One was a middle aged man with grey hair and common robes. The other was a fairly stylish girl, younger than Amon. It was clear her family had poured a lot of resources into her training.

Brandon pointed to the end of the line, instructing Amon to wait his turn. As he made his way to the back, he heard a high-pitched voice that deeply annoyed him and made him squirm.

"What is Old Grandpa doing here?" a girl asked with surprise.

Amon stopped in his tracks and turned to see Amber, one of Erin's followers. Her oval face was perfectly framed by her short brown hair with bangs that fell onto her face, slightly covering one eye. Although she was plain, she was pretty nonetheless, but none of that could make up for her annoying attitude.

Amon's face turned red and his breathing grew heavy. He wanted to toss her across the room, but decided against it. He took a deep breath and ignored her childish comments before taking his place in line.

"Everyone, you know the drill! Just punch the pillar with all you have and I'll oversee the results. This will be the basis we will use to measure your stages of body tempering in the future, so don't hold back!" Brandon said as he stepped next to the pillar. "When you're called, swipe your identification cards on the ball in front of you and punch away!"

The first on the line was a teen that seemed to be about sixteen years of age with a highly confident attitude. He took a purple card from his pocket and swiped it over the ball. When it began to spin, the young man positioned himself in front of the pillar.

Bam!

The pillar trembled as his fist struck the golden light surrounding it. Amon felt as if someone had shouted right in his ears. His head buzzed as the runes moving on the pillar seemed to be in disarray for a moment before they stopped in place and a huge number was displayed on the pillar.

"Two hundred and fifty. Not a bad punch," Brandon nodded in approval before calling the next person.

The youth smiled in satisfaction and quietly left as a small girl made her way forward. She wore a blue skirt made of silk and was somewhat chubby. She was without a doubt from a rich family. Once she was in position, she had some difficulty reaching the glowing ball. She had to tiptoe and stretch her arms in order to swipe her card, making for a cute scene. However, when she punched the pillar, everyone's smiles disappeared.

Bam!

The pillar shook violently, just slightly less than the youth before her. Amon had already covered his ears, but it wasn't of much help. He still felt as if he was going to go deaf at any moment.

"Two hundred! Amazing! When you go through puberty you can easily increase this number!" Brandon smiled widely. "Next!"

As people stepped forward to punch the pillar, the floor started emptying. The numbers varied greatly, from one hundred and fifty to three hundred units. The best results were amongst the wealthier participants.

Bam!

The pillar shook and the ground quaked weakly. Even Brandon had a surprised expression as he looked at the numbers shown.

"Three hundred and twenty! Incredible!"

He couldn't stop praising Amber as he looked at the numbers. The first hundred units were more or less the same strength an average adult had. This meant that one of Amber's punches were three times stronger than that of an average adult. It was more than enough to instantly kill anyone that had not tempered their body if she hit the right place.

Amber looked extremely satisfied with herself. She looked at Amon with a mocking grin and stuck out her tongue.

"I think I'll wait a bit. I want to tell Erin how much you've embarrassed yourself," she said, stepping off to the side. "And you certainly should dye your hair again, that ashen color hurts my eyes."

Amon was still covering his ears, but he heard every word. He looked at Amber with a burning gaze filled with rage. He wanted to kick her teeth in and ruin her perfect smile and bloody her robes.

Thankfully, Brandon called him forward. Amon got into position and swiped his card, waiting for the ball to spin. Once it did, a terrible screeching sound pierced his ears, leaving him gazing intently at the pillar.

"Just so you know, Erin got four hundred units!" Amber shouted from the sidelines. Don't get too demotivated."

Amon ignored her taunts. He was too busy picturing Amber's face on the pillar in front of him. Stepping back, he took a deep breath and shouted as he struck the object with all his might.

BAM!

The pillar shook and the ground quaked. Faint cracking sounds could be heard coming from the floor beneath the pillar. Amon shivered at the sound made by his own punch. He quickly covered his ears and retreated with a pitiful look on his face.

Brandon's mouth was gaping with surprise as he looked at the numbers the pillar displayed. "Five hundred units... We only see results like this within the Inner Sect..."

Amon started walking away, not caring at all. His ears were ringing and his head was starting to spin. He just wanted to get home as soon as possible.

"What did you do!?" Amber's annoying voice pierced his ears. He was starting to feel a strong headache. He ignored her as he made his way to the door leading to the stairs.

"Don't ignore me!" Amber screamed as she grabbed his arm and tried to pull him back.

Amon whipped around and gave her a deathly cold glare.

"Get your dirty hands away from me."

He shook his arms and freed himself from her, still trying to make his way to the door.

"Don't ignore me you filthy son of a..."

Before Amber could finish, Amon's fist was already on its way to her face.

He knew what she was about to say, and it was the last straw. He wouldn't be taking any more of her stupidity. He did not hold back at all in the punch, putting all of his strength into it.

Amber's face paled and Brandon shouted, but he was too far from them to do anything.

As Amon was about to hit her, his fist suddenly stopped, as if it had hit a wall. Amber fell to the ground as her legs gave in. Her face was deathly pale, her lips were trembling and her eyes were misty. She had clearly not expected such aggressiveness from the always passive Amon.

"Amon!" Lya shouted in his mind. "What the hell do you think you're doing?"

Amon didn't answer, he just silently glared at Amber, who was paralyzed on the ground. He raised a foot, about to stomp on her legs, but something grabbed it and pulled him away, carrying him through the open door.

Amon was dragged down the stairs all the way to the ground floor. He felt as if there was a rope tied around his body, keeping him immobile. He was floating slightly above the ground, as if an invisible force was carrying him.

"Lya—"

"Shut up and go home!"

The ties binding him disappeared and he was able to move again. He stormed out of the building and was soon out of the Northern Junctions's boundaries. He remained silent the entire way back as he knew he had made a terrible mistake.

When he finally got home, it was already dark. A sea of twinkling stars covered the night sky, and a crescent moon smiled at them. Amon didn't pay attention to the beautiful scene one bit. He entered the house and went straight to his room, closing the door behind him.

Lya materialized by his side. Her face was full of anger and her hands were trembling in fury. Her black hair waved around as she floated from side to side in the room, trying to calm herself.

"Did I ever tell you to use the soulrousing technique after you left the house!?" she shouted into his mind.

He could feel how upset she was but couldn't find an answer. Ever since he had spoken with his mother, he had been channeling the first part of the soulrousing technique.

"What is wrong with you?"

Her blue eyes were cold and ruthless—Amon could see no forgiveness in them. Dark lines creased her forehead as she contemplated what to do.

"I just wanted to train," he said in a low voice, looking away from her eyes.

"You could have gravely injured or killed that stupid girl!"

Lya was still shocked by what had happened. She never thought he would go to such lengths after he lost his nerve.

"Is this what you wanted to do with the strength I helped you obtain?"

That was the final nail on the coffin.

Amon fell to his knees, in a daze. What had he done? He knew he hadn't been acting like himself, but he just couldn't stop.

"It's not," he said full of regret. "I am sorry."

"Good." Lya nodded, but was still angry. "Do you know why I said nothing to you, even if I realized what you were doing?"

"I suppose it was a test. A test that I clearly failed."

He dropped his head and buried his face into his palms.

Lya shook her head and scowled, "No. This was a warning." She looked directly into his eyes, demanding his undivided attention.

"As I told you before, cultivation takes time. There are no shortcuts. You just started using the soulrousing technique. Do you really think you are ready to keep your emotions in check if they are as strong as they were today?" she asked with a serious expression.

The cold starlight made her face feel menacing in the dark room.

"No..."

"Then why did you do it? Just because you felt upset? Just because you wanted to get stronger faster? To punish yourself for lying?"

Amon tried to look away in shame, but she held his face in place with two walls of qi. This made him even more embarrassed and regretful, as he had no choice but to face her.

"Do you take such things as a joke? Cultivation is not something you do on a whim, nor is it something you do when you are mentally unstable, especially in soul cultivation!" Lya was slowly getting closer to him as she spoke.

"Mess up with your cultivation and it will ruin you. If I weren't there to stop you, you would have killed that girl, Amon. Do you realize that? Are you ready to take the burden for something like that?"

Amon's face was alternating between red and pale as Lya's words hit him.

"You would have killed her just because she offended you! A few words!

Damn vibrations in the air!" She looked at him, outraged by his immaturity. "Is this the type of cultivator you want to be?"

Lya's outburst was merciless and he knew she had reason in all of her arguments.

"Killing people is not a walk in the park. If the day comes when you feel it is easy, then I will cut you down myself."

She had her eyes closed as she spoke, but Amon could feel the coldness in her voice. A coldness that wrote her statement in stone.

"I'm terribly sorry, Lya. I promise I'll never do it again," he said, staring into her eyes.

"Promises are to be kept, Amon." Lya was looking at him coldly as she said the same words Rebecca said. "Can you truly keep this one? For soul cultivators, promises are of the utmost importance."

"I want you to make that promise to me and to yourself," she said with a weary voice.

"Promise... to myself?" Amon didn't understand the meaning behind that.

"You know, breaking a promise is not uncommon. Things change... *People* change. Sometimes you cannot help but break a promise made long ago. That is forgivable."

Her eyes turned hazy and tears spilled from her eyes, looking like pearls under the dim moonlight. continued, "It becomes a problem if you break a promise you made to yourself. That means you're no longer the same. If you were decisive enough to the point of making a promise in the first place, then maybe the changes that you've been through are not good ones." She closed her fists tightly, and they started to tremble. "If you live for centuries on end, how many of the promises you made to yourself will you end up breaking?"

Amon was silent for a long time. His eyes were blank, lost in shame. He was blaming himself for acting rashly and made a series of awful mistakes. The tears she wore were proof that he had caused painful memories to surface. It was no different than the day she said her goodbyes to Alexei. Seeing her crying hurt Amon much more than words. At that moment, he made a decision—he didn't want to see her like that ever again.

"Lya, I don't know how long I'll live. I also can't even fathom what kind of man I'll be if I live for centuries." His golden eyes were limpid and pure as he spoke. "But what I can say is that I don't like the person I've been today.

As such, I promise to you, and myself, that I will become a cultivator you can be proud of. No matter what happens, I want to make sure your memories of me bring smiles and not tears."

Lya raised her head, looking at him with those glowing blue eyes.

"Do you really understand what this promise means? Are you ready to bear the responsibility behind it?" she asked in a weary voice.

"I am."

"You have no idea what you're talking about," she snapped.

"If I ever break that promise, I give you permission to punish me as you see fit. If that ever happens, it would mean that I've become a person that my current self would not like. I don't want that to happen."

Lya looked at him for a long time before closing her eyes and recomposing herself. Only then did she speak again.

"Never forget that promise, Amon. If you truly meant what you said, then you're ready to learn about swords."

Lya had regained her composure, but stared at Amon with an unwavering and serious expression. The last signs of her tears had disappeared from her face as she asked Amon, "What do you know about swords?"

"Do you mean sword art?" Amon asked, cocking his head in confusion. Lya shook her head.

"I've read all the manuals that you purchased from the bookstore. They were nothing like the true sword arts of the past. What you understand as sword art is nothing more than channeling elemental qi into the sword and using it as a medium to concentrate an element and attack. The sword is just a catalyst. A true sword art should be based on the sword, not on the element being channeled."

Amon looked at her, clueless to her statement. Lya sighed and raised a hand, beckoning for the crude sword lying on the floor. The sword trembled once and shot through the air, stopping near Lya's hand.

"This is the earth-shattering technique," she said as the sword hovered in the air. Its blade started humming before it floated through the window. Lya lowered her hand, making the sword swing once. The air seemed to be split by the sword as a deafening howl sounded within the room. The ground quaked, causing Amon to stumble. As the blade lightly touched the ground, a cloud of dust rose, and the ground shook even more.

"It's a relatively powerful strike, but it is not fitting for a sword," Lya said emotionlessly within Amon's mind as the dust settled.

Amon was stunned that the house was still standing and his room was perfectly intact.

"W-why is the house unscathed?" he questioned.

"I protected it, of course. Though... the ground outside might need a bit of landscaping," Lya said with a smile.

Outside the window, illuminated by the moonlight, Amon could see a gigantic hole in the ground, surrounded by a web of cracks. The hole was so big it could probably swallow his whole house.

"Such a crude technique. It looks more like someone smashed the ground than used a sword to strike at it."

Lya waved her finger and the sword vibrated before returning to her side. With another wag of her finger, droplets of water appeared on the sword like morning dew.

"This is the waking rivers technique."

As she wiggled her fingers, the sword performed a beautiful, complex dance. Each movement sent a wave that left shallow gashes on the ground.

When the dance had ended, all that was left was a series of gashes. They twisted around each other and looked like a web of small riverbeds more than anything else.

"This technique is all about controlling the flow. It might be shallow and somewhat weak, but once perfected, it will be hard for someone to stop your attacks. This is a real sword strike." Lya said with conviction.

As she returned the sword to her side once more, Amon's hair stood on end; Lya had started to concentrate on the next technique. Thin lines of light started glowing on the blade. The longer she focused, the more they appeared, connecting to each other in an elaborate pattern. Brightmoon flashed and vibrated violently with a low buzzing noise.

This was the imbuing of qi that Amon had learned early, but it was clearly on a different level. He watched in awe as Lya raised an arm and the vibrations ceased. It slowly rotated, pointing its edge to the sky, standing parallel to Lya's arm.

"Pay attention."

Lya glanced at Amon as she cut the air with her hand in a swift, chopping motion. The blade swung downwards. A bright beam of condensed qi shot from the sword at an incredible speed, whistling like an arrow as it cut through the ground.

Its crescent moon shape shot to the distance, hitting the trees behind his house and cutting them down. A storm of leaves fluttered around the area as they fell to the ground, leaving Amon speechless.

"Can you tell me the difference between this strike and the others?" Lya questioned, raising her left eyebrow with a slight smirk.

"This one was far more powerful," Amon said with muddled excitement.

"Yes, but it's not what you think. I used the same amount of qi all three times."

"Was it wind, instead of earth or water?" he pondered aloud.

"There was no elemental qi involved in that strike." Her eyes glistened as she spoke. "What I used was what we call sword qi. We use the qi as a sword to increase the power of a strike to an overwhelming degree." Lya raised a hand and extended her forefinger and her middle finger. "If you manage to condense the qi enough, you can even launch it just like I did."

Qi swirled around her fingers, so condensed it seemed solid. It shone with a bright light as it took the shape of a small blade that surrounded her extended fingers. Lya waved her hand, and the qi shot out, assuming a similar form to her previous strike.

"How is it so powerful?" Amon was dumbstruck. "If it's simply condensed qi in the form of a blade, at most it should be sharp. That strength is absurd!"

"The secret is not in the qi itself. It is in the blade," Lya said dismissively. "I told you, the soul can affect the material world through your determination and emotions. The nebula is a manifestation of that."

Amon listened to her words attentively, eager to understand.

"The strength of your determination defines your power limit, as it's determination that moves the qi and makes it do your bidding. Now, tell me, what is the purpose of a sword?" Lya glanced at him as she asked.

Amon didn't have to think for too long. Even if he wanted to deny it, the sword had only a single purpose. It was a weapon made for battles. A weapon made for wars.

"To kill," he answered in a serious tone.

"Yes." Lya nodded, highly satisfied. "Now, if you give the qi the properties of a sword, what would it entail?"

"A blow used to kill an opponent," Amon said as he stroked his chin.

"True sword qi is not simply manipulating the qi and making it sharp. True sword qi is formed when you have an unbearable will to kill. That is when your sword qi will be the strongest, and that is where you must draw a line. Those that can kill on a whim are the ones that must value life the most.

"Soul cultivation was mostly the same for every soul cultivator, but the weapons they chose told a lot about who they were. The soul cultivators that used swords were called sword cultivators for obvious reasons." Lya paused for a moment before continuing. "We had a saying back then, 'You know the values of a sword cultivator by seeing what it takes to make them draw their sword.'"

Amon became red-faced as he thought about his earlier outburst.

"Nevertheless, every single sword cultivator had one thing in common: they would never draw their swords to make threats. A sword would only leave its sheath to draw blood. Never forget this, for this is the path of the sword. If you walk this path, death and destruction will forever follow you."

She closed her eyes for a brief moment as she focused. When she opened them again, they burned with a fierce and merciless light.

"You must understand and embrace them. If you ever reject them, no matter how strong you are, you will certainly fall. Still, you must never enjoy them. I'll say it again. Those that can kill on a whim are the ones that must value life the most. If you act any different from this, then you are nothing but a rabid animal, and such animals were put down without hesitation by true sword cultivators."

Amon stood in silence, trying to understand everything. He closed his eyes, calming his mind. After the outbursts of qi that Lya dispersed, the area around the house was silent. Not a single owl hoot could be heard—it was clear anything that was awake at this hour had fled.

Amon now understood why Lya had gotten so mad. If she was going to teach him such a powerful technique, she had to be certain that he understood that killing is only a last resort.

"Do you know why I had you buy all of those sword art manuals?"

Amon shook his head. In all honesty, he thought it was a waste of contribution points.

"You will learn them all," she said with a mischievous smile.

"But I just have a weak affinity to wind…"

"The point isn't to use them. The point is to grasp their essence. All renowned soul cultivators have a degree of mastery over all elements." She approached and tapped his forehead, sending a light breeze over his body as she continued. "Combat requires all elements, even if it's a passive requirement," Lya stated.

She turned away and held her hands behind her back as she started talking. Amon stood quietly, paying close attention.

"Your attacks must flow like water, so you can understand and control the battle's rhythm. They must remain unpredictable like fire, so you can catch your opponent off guard. Attacks must be as swift as the wind, so you can attack before he can defend. Lastly, your attacks must be stable like the earth, so they may never waver. You must be able to be adaptable, fierce, precise, and powerful. Most of all, you must learn to understand. You need to know where you are, so you know where you will be in the next move. Observe what is around you, so you can use it to your favor. Learn your weaknesses and how to make up for them. Understand your opponent, so you can predict his decisions and know where, when and how to strike him. If you understand everything, then you can defeat anything."

Amon was finally starting to understand and joy filled his heart. Sensing his zealous spirit, Lya turned and stared into Amon's eyes.

"Never be too arrogant. One misstep, one small mistake in your judgment and something you may lose everything. Be prepared for failures and be suspicious of those around you. Someone might do something that even they didn't expect, and that will bring disaster."

Her voice was stern and heavy; it seemed hard for her to say those words. For whatever reason, Amon could faintly feel guilt coming from Lya as she spoke.

"The closer you are to someone, the easier it is for them to hurt you. Do you understand?"

She turned around, facing him with a sad smile.

Amon nodded sincerely.

"So, what do you think?" Lya looked away, gazing at the stars. "Can you walk through such a path?" she asked almost in a whisper.

Amon approached her, staring towards the stars as well.

"I can," he declared, his voice firm and assertive.

"Then prepare yourself, boy. I promise I will make you the best sword cultivator this world has ever seen."

She had already promised this to herself. This time, she was promising it to Amon.

SIBLINGS

Daniel could faintly hear the chirping of birds. He slowly opened his eyes and was greeted by a pure white that surrounded him. His sight was hazy due to the gauze over his face, and he felt incredibly drowsy.

His body was heavy and numb, but he still tried to move. When his body didn't respond, he attempted to call for help, but only a low mumble escaped his parched lips. He suddenly felt a sour taste in his mouth, as well as an unquenchable thirst. It was an uncomfortable sensation, and his body seemed to respond to his commands as he continued to try to move.

He squirmed on a fluffy surface and muttered to himself. After a long while, Daniel finally heard a door opening next to him. Soft footsteps scuffed across the floor, getting closer to where he was.

A gentle voice said, "I see that you're awake now."

Daniel, frustrated by his failed attempts to regain control of his body, stopped wriggling and tried to nod.

"You must be thirsty. Let me get you a drink," the voice sounded again.

A careful, yet firm hand slowly lifted his head and a cold substance touched his lips. The person instructed him to drink slowly so that he wouldn't choke. The sour taste in his mouth was washed away and the thirst was quenched. Daniel felt his body heating up as a sweet aftertaste was left on his tongue and the hand supporting him gently placed his head back on the pillow. He relaxed and the warm sensation spread comforted him, and he soon fell asleep.

Once he was awake again, he felt fairly energetic and his vision was clear. There was a big window not far from him and he could hear a faint and gentle pelting. A cold breeze blowing from the cracks of the window, carrying the humid scent of rain rushed into his nose. Daniel grew excited by these simple things.

I'm alive...? I'm alive!

He wiggled his toes which he saw moving under the warm quilt and white sheets covering him. He carefully sat up to sit on his bed, tossing the linen to the side. His left hand moved clumsily, but he somehow managed to support his weight on it. Then, he tried moving his right hand, and his face froze—he couldn't feel it.

Daniel turned his head, fearful of what he might see. From his shoulder to the tip of his fingers, his right arm was wrapped in bandages. Worst of all, it was clear that big chunks of flesh were missing, as some parts were eerily thin compared to others.

He wanted to laugh, but cried instead. Silent teardrops fell from his face as he looked at his crippled arm. He knew there was no chance he could ever recover from that injury. Even if his body tempering had been impeccable, he wouldn't be able to regenerate the parts of his body that were lost.

He remembered the hellish eyes of the dire wolf that did this to him, and couldn't help but shudder.

"Amon!" he shouted.

Upon remembering that Amon was with him, Daniel began to panic. *Where is he? I must find him!*

He mustered all of his strength and managed to pull himself to his feet. The door swung open and a tall woman, dressed in white clothes entered. She was carrying a bundle of clothes and a basin filled with water. Her raven hair was neatly wrapped into a bun at the back of her head, and her face was gentle.

Shocked that Daniel was standing on his own, she quickly placed the items on a small table, and rushed over to him.

"What are you doing?" she asked in a concerned voice.

"Where is Amon?" he asked frantically.

"Who?" The nurse raised a brow, looking at him as if he was a madman.

"The kid that was with me when the dire wolves attacked, where is he?" Daniel asked hurriedly.

"I'm sorry sir, but the third elder only rescued you."

"The third elder? Does that mean I'm in Sky Reach?"

"Yes," the nurse replied, averting her eyes from his mauled body.

"How long was I unconscious?"

"It's been a month," she responded calmly. "The fifth elder decided that it would be best if we kept you sedated until you were fully healed."

Dazed, Daniel stared out the window, watching the rain fall. If the fifth elder—the elder with the highest medical skills—had given such instructions, then things were much more serious than he thought, regardless of how close he came to death.

"Can you try to find someone for me?" he asked without looking at the nurse.

The nurse nodded, and informed him that she'd have to get someone else to do it for her, since she had to tend to others within the medical center.

Daniel started describing Amon the best he could as he gesticulated with his left hand. "He is about this tall, has golden eyes and his hair will be

111

either black or gray. His name is Amon Kr..."

Thankfully, Daniel caught himself. Chances were that no one in Sky Reach would help if they knew who he was.

"His name is Amon."

"Just Amon?" the nurse asked as she cocked her head.

"Yes, just Amon. His house is in the northern reaches of the Outer Ring. Not too far away from the Northern Junction."

The nurse reassured him that she would do her best to find his friend. She ushered Daniel back into bed and demanded that he rest until the fifth elder came to examine him. He thanked her kindly as she turned to leave.

"Wait!" he called after her, causing the nurse to stop in her tracks. "I'm sorry for not asking before, but what's your name?"

She brushed her black hair behind her right ear and said, "Call me Delia."

He smiled and thanked her again. She returned his smile and adjusted his pillow again before hurrying out of the room.

The rest of the night was uneventful. Since it was already late, the nurse didn't return to check on Daniel again. He was truly alone with his own thoughts. He looked at his right arm with a sad smile as the rain hammered the window in his room.

Between his disabled arm and thinking about Amon, Daniel had a lot of trouble falling asleep. He was growing incredibly anxious when the sound of the rain suddenly increased and a splash of water hit his face. His eyes darted over to the window and, to his surprise, it was ajar and a slim silhouette was standing in front of it.

Daniel was about to shout when the figure slowly raised its right hand, and a small flame lit up the culprits face.

"It's been a while, hasn't it?"

Daniel's mouth fell open in shock as he saw Jake approaching him. He was not as chubby as he remembered him to be, nor did he have that glint of curiosity in his eyes. Daniel simply couldn't believe what he was seeing as he looked at the person his younger brother became over the years. He was slimmer, more muscular, and definitely a lot taller than when they last spoke.

"It's good to see you."

"Too bad you had to almost die for this to be possible," Jake retorted with a chuckle.

"How are you doing?" Daniel asked, feeling awkward.

"Just fine. Master treats me really well and father, well, as long as I improve he doesn't care," Jake had a sad smile as he said that.

There was an awkward silence again. Daniel felt that the longer it took for any of them to speak, the harder it would become.

"How is mom?"

"I don't remember how she was before, but she's been really quiet over the years. Mom is very lonely and depressed. She told me to tell you that no matter what father says, you'll always be her son. She will always love you,"

Jake looked down, depressed. "Too bad she never managed to stand up to father," Jake lamented.

"It is not her fault. You know how father is. He'll get rid of her the moment she causes trouble for him. She already gave him all that he wanted from her anyway."

Another awkward silence filled the room. They avoided looking at each other for a while before Jake spoke up again.

"We killed that dire wolf that attacked you and Amon. The—"

"Amon? Amon is alive?" Daniel started laughing out loud in relief and happiness.

"Want to hear the story?" Jake asked as he quietly took a chair and sat by Daniel's bed and told him what had happened.

"He said he is thankful for what you did and he's glad that you are alive. He is a good kid."

"Yes, he is," Daniel said, in deep thought. *So Amon asked to kill the dire wolf himself... Maybe he really is growing up*, he thought before raising his eyes to look at Jake. "I'm glad that both of you are fine."

"It was nothing much."

Jake immediately regretted his words. Luckily, Daniel didn't seem to take them in a bad way. Jake's face stiffened with seriousness.

"Father has a message too," he said, clearly annoyed.

Daniel knew it wasn't going to be anything good.

"A promotion competition, Season of Rigor, will be held towards the end of the year. Everyone in the Outer Sect is eligible. The ones that reach the top ten will be promoted to the Inner Sect, regardless of talent or cultivation. Additionally, the elders will be able to pick any others, if they see fit."

"That's a good opportunity for many people," Daniel said, slightly relieved.

"Father said that it was about time you stopped messing around with business that's not yours." Jake took a deep breath as he tried to control his anger. "Since you're his son, he demands that you participate *and* crush everyone else, even with one hand."

Jake's voice trembled for a moment, and Daniel wanted to laugh. His father was truly heartless. Not only did he make fun of his lost arm, he even gave Daniel a warning to stay away from Rebecca and Amon.

"If you can't do that, father said there is no reason to keep you in the sect."

Although it hurt to do so, Daniel laughed hysterically.

"I'm sorry, Daniel. It's my fault. If I hadn't defied him when I went to kill the dire wolf..."

Jake's face was painted with regret. This was the first time he had seen his brother in ten years, and it was only to give him a heartless message. To make it worse, their father knew that Daniel would never win. He might have had a shot before the Scavenging, but with one arm crippled there was no hope at all.

113

"It is not your fault. This isn't about you," Daniel said with a grin. "He's just mad that I got hurt by a simple class four spirit beast, showing weakness and giving him trouble with the medical expenses. Worst of all, I did so saving the son of the person he hates the most."

Daniel had a hard time speaking as he laughed like a madman.

"Wait, Amon is…"

Jake's eyes bulged hearing that. Why didn't he realize this sooner?

"Yes. Amon is the son of the White Flame, Rebecca Skoller and also the son of our former fifth protector, Lloyd Kressler."

Daniel's laughter slowly died down, turning into a self-deprecating smile.

"I am really glad that he wrecked our father as he stole from the sect and got away unscathed."

Daniel smiled widely thinking about how bad his father had been beaten for the rumors to spread all the way to the Outer Sect and no one was able to suppress them.

"Maybe if I speak with—"

"It will only make things worse. The moment he realizes how far you are willing to go for me, the more he'll want to get rid of me." He gave a wry smile, "I am just dead weight in your life."

"Daniel…"

Jake's voice trembled and tears started spilling from his face. How long ago had it been that he had cried? He didn't remember. Looking at his brother and what his father was doing to him was breaking his heart. Seeing his younger brother crying made Daniel feel emotions he hadn't felt in years. All of the awkwardness between them was cast aside.

"You're my brother, Jake," Daniel said standing up and pulling Jake into a tight embrace. "We are family and that's all that matters.

THE KEEPER
OF HELL

In the throne room, located a few hundred meters underground, a group of men sat around a large wooden table. The ashen-grey floor was shined to perfection and the transparent walls only served as a barrier between them and the magma encompassing the room. Despite its unique location, the chamber was at a comfortable temperature.

"We've announced the promotion competition as requested," Lawrence said in a grave voice as he respectfully knelt before the throne.

His blood-red robes were covered in frost as usual, and a bone-chilling coldness made the area around him unreasonably cold. Though his usual demeanor was full of arrogance and sharp words, he was different here.

A few feet from him was a sword sheathed in a crimson scabbard hanging from the throne. Its glossy casing resembled colored glass and its black guard was formed into a cross, adorned with an alluring red gem. This was the legendary Crimsonroar, the companion sword of the founder himself. It was made with Danasian steel, and was the strongest artifact in the sect. Only sect masters could wield this sword, which was the greatest symbol of their position.

Lawrence gave the weapon a wistful look, but managed to correct his behavior before anyone noticed. He lowered his eyes to the leg of the throne before him. It was made from a thick wood that was beautifully charred. It twisted around itself and seemed to grow into the small, golden platform underneath it.

Sitting on the throne was a man with short brown hair and crystal-blue eyes. He wore red silk robes perfectly fitting for him, decorated with intricate designs made with golden thread. His face was chiseled, but his expression was cordial. He was shorter than average, even in comparison to Lawrence, who was only a few centimeters above average. Regardless of this fact, no one dared to look down on him. His terrifying aura demanded respect—a demand that was never denied.

He seemed somewhat distracted as a shiny dagger pivoted between his fingers. It's blade was one that would shine in even the dimmest light.

"Excellent. Our sect has been in decline for a few decades now. We need to invest in the future, even if the winners are lackluster," Sect Master Lars Borgin said.

He nodded as he looked at the oddly submissive elder kneeling in front of him; the dagger never stopped moving all the while.

Lawrence made a great effort to hide his displeasure with the decision, but the corners of his mouth still twitched.

"It'll also allow the elders to scout hidden talents in the Outer Sect. I understand that the requirements are low, but we have too few disciples in the Inner Sect. We must choose quantity over quality in order for our sect to survive. Who knows, we might find someone exceptional born from the ordinary," Borgin pondered as he stroked his chin with his free hand.

"I still believe we should have stricter requirements," Lawrence retorted. He couldn't stand the thought of trash entering the Inner Sect.

Borgin raised a brow and replied, "We can't afford that. The Olen Kingdom is forging an alliance with the Rising Sun Sect. The Crown Prince Cedric is engaged to Emma Lowe, the sect's inheriting disciple."

Lawrence froze and his face turned sour as he started to piece the whole picture together. The Olen Kingdom had no real cultivation history. They were a mortal kingdom that sat a few hundred kilometers north of the Broken Forest. The distance was enough to hinder their ability to gather resources and make use of their somewhat privileged location. The Rising Sun Sect, however, was located even farther north, almost on the edge of the Central Continent.

"Rising Sun is helping them with incursions on the Scorched Lands and the Broken Forest." Borgin's brows creased as he explained. "The Olen Kingdom is already exporting spirit beast byproducts and expanding their farmland southward, coming closer to our usual hunting grounds. Soon enough, we'll have to consider them real competitors. We've already taken a hit from having to export at lower prices, so don't tell me we can be picky with talent."

"How is Rising Sun able to provide any assistance? They shouldn't have anyone above the elemental core stage," Lawrence spat in disbelief.

"Obviously they've been hiding a few wild cards," Borgin answered with a savage smile. "That being said, we can no longer take the old battlefield for granted. We need to quickly increase our power and remind them who rules the Central Continent."

"Just one word, a single word from you and I can wipe them both out of the map," Lawrence proposed, a dangerous glint flashed in his eyes.

"I appreciate the thought, but we can't afford that. We're in a delicate position with the other cardinal sects—doing something like this would be rather troublesome."

Lawrence clenched his fists, his face darkening with malice. This was all Lloyd Kressler's fault.

"We should have taken care of loose ends while they were in reach!" Lawrence yelled.

Displeased, Borgin tapped the throne's armrest once, and the room started to tremble. A silent pressure fell over Lawrence, forcing his head to lower in submission—any and all words lost in his throat. Such transgressions would no longer be tolerated.

"I heard something happened to Daniel a few weeks ago…"

The sect master gave Lawrence a cold glance as he forcefully changed the subject, rubbing salt on his wound.

Through a mask of humiliation and a set of gritted teeth, Lawrence replied, "It's been taken care of."

"Forget it, you should know by now what I expect from you. I trust you handled it appropriately. You may now take your leave."

With the pressure lifting off of him, Lawrence stood, indignation hidden in his floor-bound gaze. With a small bow, he turned away.

"Oh yes, tell Old Lu he may enter," Borgin ordered.

Moments later, an old man shuffled into the room. His white hair scantily fell over his wrinkled face causing him to take careful steps. He stopped a few meters away from the throne and gave a deep bow before kneeling with some difficulty.

"Sect Master Borgin," Old Lu greeted as he looked down.

"Tell me about this child Jake brought to Sky Reach Village," Borgin demanded with a deep voice.

As Old Lu felt a chill run down his spine, he lowered his head further and started shivering as he spoke.

"It was Amon Kressler, sir. Miss Karen brought him to the Sky Reach restaurant. I recognized him with a glance, but decided to keep quiet. When he left, young master Jake paid Luke to return him to the Outer Sect."

Borgin closed his eyes as he heard Old Lu's report. The dagger danced between his fingers, reflecting the light on his face.

"Was there anything noteworthy about him?"

Old Lu thought for a moment.

"Y-yes… His hair was ashen-grey and his eyes were golden. I might be wrong, but he had black hair and eyes before."

"You've quite the memory, Old Lu. Something in him changed the day Lloyd betrayed us," Borgin said with a frown.

He remembered the reports, but he had no idea what Lloyd had done to his son. Regardless, the effects didn't seem to have much of an effect.

"You mentioned he was returning from the Scavenging, did he have any treasure on him? A token? A pair of daggers?" Borgin questioned.

Old Lu was surprised at the question and seemed to be in a daze for a moment. His face paled as he grew nervous. Suddenly, he jumped up from his position.

"He had a sword strapped to his back," Old Lu said eagerly. Feeling Bor-

117

gin's stare, he began spilling details regarding the weapon. "I've never seen Lloyd or Rebecca use anything like that, so I found it a bit strange, but didn't think much of it."

"Is that all?" Borgin asked with a milder tone.

"Yes, sir. This is all I remember."

"Very well. You may leave."

Old Lu gave a deep bow and departed from the throne room.

Left alone with his thoughts, the sect master raised his eyes trying to make sense of what was happening. Something was bothering him about the whole situation, but he couldn't quite put his finger on it. Subconsciously, he caressed the charred armrest of the throne again, looking at the words engraved on the wall opposing the throne.

Engraved on the wall was a quote from Arthur Royce, the sect's founder. It read, "You all know the price we paid for this. We must not be captivated by the beauty of power; we must be disgusted by it." It served as a reminder for those who were strong enough to hold the throne.

"Nemeus," Borgin bellowed with a frown. "What do you think?"

The scarlet gem in the sword hanging from the throne flashed and Nemeus materialized in front of him.

He was an incredibly tall man with a disheveled, flaming-red mane that reached the waist of his muscular frame. His features were crude, and a savage glint rested in his wisdom filled eyes.

"I was right," Nemeus said with a deep, booming voice. "I'll have to keep an eye on Amon Kressler."

"Are you sure about this?"

"I am," Nemeus answered, looking at the dagger. "Send Jake to oversee the promotion competition," Nemeus ordered. "I'll accompany him. It's about time we started teaching him what it truly means to be the inheritor of a master's legacy."

Borgin couldn't disagree. Jake Meyer was the best candidate to be his successor. He had dazzling talent and a cool head, but his compassionate personality would have to be reformed over the next few years.

"Are these daggers that important?" Borgin asked, still unsure. "They're nothing more than Danasian steel."

Nemeus shook his head and replied, "The daggers are not important. It's who they belonged to that is paramount."

He was convinced that Amon had stumbled upon Alexei's missing corpse. The Scavenging had finally paid off—the sword Old Lu described was awfully similar to the Brightmoon Nemeus knew of. However, Nemeus couldn't be sure without seeing it for himself.

"Who was it?"

"It does not concern you."

Nemeus' response made Borgin scrunch his face.

"I'm the sect master."

Borgin tried to use his position as a bargaining chip, but it was clearly a poor move. Sadly, there wasn't much else he could try. The muscular figure before him wouldn't give in. His scarlet eyes seemed to be ablaze as he faced Borgin coldly.

"One thought from me and you'll be crippled of your cultivation and banished. The only person that had the right to know about this was my master. Now that he's gone the matter doesn't concern any of the living."

His ruthless response kept Borgin quiet; he knew this was the only warning Nemeus would give. The truth was that no one knew about the secrets of the Abyss Sect as well as Nemeus did, and most likely, no one ever would.

"The Season of Rigor will be held in six months. Make sure the news reaches the boy," Nemeus commanded.

How Borgin would make it happen was not his problem. It should be time enough for Amon to develop further and confirm his suspicions.

Nemeus returned to the sword. It put Borgin at ease, but only slightly. He sat on the charred throne for a moment, thinking deeply about the war from a few centuries ago. He needed to know what was really going on, but there was no one to turn to. The only ones that could have known what Nemeus was thinking were all dead, and they made sure to bury the past with them.

Lya's voice echoed in Amon's head as he held the crude sword with his right hand. The sword was covered by a layer of light that exuded a dangerous aura.

"You've managed to properly control the shape of the qi you've injected into the weapon in only three days; it is not a bad result at all," Lya praised.

A wide grin slid onto Amon's face, though he tried to hide it. He had been training under Lya for more than a month, and his progress was very satisfying. He had also been reading the manuals on sword art. Every time he finished one, Lya would test him to measure his comprehension. If he failed even one question, he was forced to read the manual again.

"Now, do it again. This time, I want you to execute the stances from *Fundamentals of the Sword*," Lya ordered as she floated next to him.

Amon nodded and hoisted Windhowler into the air. It had been difficult for him to lift just weeks prior, but now, he could manage it without struggling. Lines of light reappeared on the blade causing it to shine immensely. He slightly bent his knees and straightened his back before raising his right hand and pointing the sword downwards, covering his upper body. Finally, with his left forearm, he supported the flat side of the blade.

This was one of the basic stances described in the *Fundamentals of the Sword*. Amon could defend against blows from most directions in this stance while retaining the ability to attack quickly.

Lya approached him and moved her hand, making a stick fly to her side. Lines of light moved across its surface, and soon the stick was glowing. This made Amon sweat feverishly.

With a gentle smile, Lya told Amon to use the soulrousing technique. He recited the first part of the technique in his mind, shivering in fear.

"I'll give you a second to adjust if you need to," Lya said in a sweet voice.

Damn! Amon thought to himself, trying his best to reposition his body in what he felt was a more accurate representation of the descriptions and illustrations of the manual.

"Time's up!" Lya shouted, circling Amon like a vulture; her eyes scrutinizing every inch of his body.

"Your right knee is pointing outwards—you fail."

The stick cut through the air, whacking his knee.

Amon shouted in pain, but still held the stance. He sent Lya a resentful gaze as he corrected his knee.

"Your left arm is too relaxed. One strong strike and you'll hit yourself with your sword if your arm gives in. Also, your elbow was flexed too much. Your stance is a failure."

The stick hit him in his left elbow, making it sting with pain. Amon focused and corrected his stance again before Lya examined him again.

"Your stance is good," Lya paused and Amon let out a sigh of relief. "But your grip is too loose."

The stick hit his right wrist and the sword flew from his hand, falling heavily on the floor with a *clang*.

"Your grip is a failure."

"You old hag!" Amon shouted as he held his wrist which had begun to swell. "That hurt!"

The soulrousing technique enhanced both his pain and his impulse of cursing. Amon was still far from managing his emotions; the result was a terrible slip of the tongue.

Lya's face fell and a vein protruded from her forehead.

"Old... hag?" she asked as a menacing aura started emanating from her.

Amon's face paled as he realized he made a grave mistake. His eyes widened with fear as he shook at the knees.

He tried to run, but an invisible binding tightened around his body, immobilizing him as the stick whacked him repeatedly. Unable to defend himself, he fell to the ground, squirming in pain.

"Your manners are a failure," Lya scoffed and tossed her hair over her shoulder. "How dare you call me an old hag? I am merely a few cen—" She caught herself and cleared her throat loudly. "You can't say such things to a lady!"

"I'm sorry, I'm sorry!" he cried pitifully as the stick kept hitting him.

"Hmph. Start again!" Lya snorted as the stick flew back to her. Her blue eyes shimmered with displeasure.

Shaking his head, he recovered the sword from the floor, reassuming the stance.

"Your grip is too tight." Lya said as the stick flew again, hitting his wrist a second time. Amon grunted and loosened his grip a bit. This time, he managed to endure in silence. Amon took a deep breath and returned to his initial stance. This had been his life lately, reading manuals and training nonstop.

"You need to engrave the basics in your memory. Your stance must always be perfect, or your opponents will strike at your glaring openings."

Their training continued for quite some time. To Lya, Amon was nothing more than a beginner. He had never properly used a sword before, and his foundations were nonexistent. She had to help him build them from the ground up.

Still, this was a good thing. He had no bad habits and no set idea on what his style should be. Amon was a blank slate that she could paint however she wanted. Additionally, his soul cultivation was also going well. He listened to every word she said and followed her instructions with precision. His body was now ready for his third round of tempering.

Overall, Lya thought that things were going well. Soon enough it would be time for him to put what he was learning into practice, and completely absorb the knowledge he knew only in theory so far.

As she was thinking of this, a rare knock could be heard from the front door.

Amon had a confused look on his face as he heard the sound. For years, Daniel had been the only one to knock on that door—could it be?

Amon's eyes lit up as he hurriedly dropped his sword on the bed and rushed to the door, almost ripping it off the hinges as he swung it open. The warm sunlight spilled into the living room and Amon parted his lips to shout, "Daniel!"

However, his excitement was all for naught. It wasn't Daniel who stood in the doorway, but a complete stranger instead. She was a short woman in purple silks with blond hair like molten gold and violet eyes to contrast.

She gave Amon a strange glance, but her expression soon turned gentle.

"Pardon my sudden visit, but is this the Skoller residence?" she asked politely.

"That depends. Why do you ask?" Amon asked, his tone cautious and even.

The woman's purple robes signified her employment with the sect—a fact which immediately put Amon on guard.

"I am here to deliver your invitation to the sect competition that will be held in six months," the woman giggled as she handed a small silver token to Amon. "Present this token with your identification card at the registration desk near the Ashen Heart tree, and you'll be qualified to participate in the promotion competition."

Amon tilted his head in confusion. *What promotion competition?*

"You don't know?" the woman was taken aback. The news had already spread like wildfire over the past few days.

121

"Unfortunately, I've been out of the loop as of late," he said apologetically.

"No worries!" The woman remained professional as she patiently explained. "In six months time, a competition, the Season of Rigor, will be held in Hell Keeper's City. All Outer Sect disciples are allowed to participate, so long as they present their token."

"Is that it?"

"Certainly not!" the woman leaned in close, her voice an excited whisper as she continued. "The top ten competitors will be elevated to the Inner Sect. Furthermore, the sect elders are looking to recruit some hidden talents and will be keeping an eye out for potential candidates."

Amon could hardly contain his surprise—great boons such as these were few and far between, and he would not let the opportunity slip away. However, tasty morsels often came with hook and line attached, and Amon was skeptical the sect would honestly be generous for generosity's sake.

"Remember to use your time wisely," she said. "The matches will be one-on-one eliminations, so be sure to practice diligently!"

"Hold on, what about the qi gathering cultivators? What are they supposed to do?" Amon felt it was a peculiar way to select disciples when it was guaranteed that most of them could hardly put up a decent fight against an opponent with superior cultivation.

"Honestly, they can only rely on themselves," she shrugged. "And perhaps, an elder will take their best efforts into consideration and take them under wing."

"That seems unfair."

He was not convinced.

"Is it really? They've been given the opportunity to enter the Inner Sect before fulfilling the requirements. Remember, that luxury is usually reserved for the families of elders and sect protectors."

Amon pondered for a time. Perhaps a small chance was better than none, especially if the rewards far outweighed the risks. Inner Sect disciples receive superior resources and nourishment from the sect—along with access to the higher floors of the Divine Arts Keep and other essential facilities. They were also allowed to take up residence in Hell Keeper's City.

"Alright. I'll join," he declared excitedly.

This was the lucky break Amon needed: a chance to proceed unhindered by his father's name and ill repute.

"That's the spirit!" she cheered with much enthusiasm. "Lastly, I have an invitation for the remaining person in your household. Shall I leave it with you?"

"There's no need," Amon's face soured. "She can't take part."

"My apologies. In that case I will take my leave," she said, awkwardly storing the additional token.

Amon watched her retreating silhouette before returning to his room. Lya was waiting for him; her playful grin on full display.

"A tournament!" she chirped. "It'll be a great opportunity. You'll finally experience actual combat."

"Six months... Twenty-four weeks... 168 days..." Lya mused to herself. "Not an ideal time frame to be sure, certainly a fixer-upper job, but with some elbow grease and the stick, we can whip you into shape."

The mention of a certain beating apparatus caused Amon's hair to stand on end—the future certainly looked bleak.

"W-well, the best part is the chance to join the Inner Sect..."

"Is there a facility where you can practice in private?"

"The Warrior Hall had something like that," Amon said, trying to recall. "If I am not wrong, there should be an arena where we can challenge other cultivators. It also has a few sparring puppets controlled by an array."

"That's perfect!"

Lya spun around a few times and started rambling on about how exciting it would be to watch Amon compete. Her giddiness passed on to Amon and he felt slightly more at ease. He watched as she imitated a few positions, insisting that he learn them well. The last time he had seen her this excited was when she had accompanied him to Hell Keeper's City.

"A tournament! It has been an eternity," she said as she floated in the air. "We have much to do! If we speed things up, you can reach the middle stages of body tempering with a bit of time to spare. You must also properly learn a few movement techniques after you grasp the basics of the sword. I think I'll be a bit more rigid from now on. We need to optimize our time," she continued to ramble, causing Amon's head to spin.

"Lya, it's just a tournament. There's no reason to—"

Lya's actions ceased abruptly. She turned around with a devious look in her eye and said, "You don't know what you're talking about. Amon, you know very well you'll need to train longer and harder than anyone else. That girl you nearly killed clearly has a wealthy family to back her and she's been training for years. But you? You've barely made it through a month without dying," she scoffed, suddenly appearing directly in front of him. "I refuse to go easy on you."

Lya's face was flushed and her hands were curled into fists. She was absolutely right, but he was unable to suppress his apprehension.

"This will be a great chance for you Amon! You could learn endless things during the competition. But first..."

Lya paused, turning away from Amon and resting her chin on the forefinger of her left hand. She had been silent for quite some time before he finally worked up the nerve to speak, his tongue tripped over his words.

"W-what is it?"

Lya rotated her body to the right, slowly facing Amon. Her icy-blue eyes had turned a sinister violet, and a sweet, but wicked smile slid onto her face. Unbeknownst to him, the wooden stick had inched closer, steadying at his nape.

"You must learn how to take a beating."

WARRIOR HALL

It was a few hours before the stick finally dropped to the ground. A bruised, yet unbloodied Amon staggered to his feet. With his heart drumming away at his chest cavity, he glared at the slender beauty before him, but before he could speak, Lya stopped him.

"Go back to your room and study the first stance from *Fundamentals of the Sword*."

Amon scowled and trudged off towards the house. Once there, he ventured to his mother's room, straightening his robes and dusting himself off before entering. If Rebecca were to see any of the bruises hidden under his clothes, she would unleash an inescapable wrath.

As usual, Rebecca was sitting on her bed, staring out the open window. He greeted her and sat at the end of her bed.

"Good morning," she said, almost in a whisper.

He realized her tone was a bit dry, but he ignored it. The last few weeks had been awkward between them and he chose not to let it bother him today.

"I received an invitation to a promotion competition," Amon announced. "I want to participate."

She stared at him in silence. Despite her neutral expression, he knew she was carefully choosing her words.

"Participating would be good, but do you think you can win?"

"I have six months to prepare. I think I have a chance if I don't procrastinate," Amon replied confidently.

"You certainly have a lot of confidence all of a sudden. I suppose you've developed a good method for training alone."

Rebecca tried to keep her voice steady, regardless of the anger she felt from the lies he would spin.

Amon's spirits fell and a long sigh fluttered from his mouth. It was clear his heart was twisted in two as Lya's speech about promises came to mind.

"Please don't ask about my training. I don't want to lie to you. The details of my training are... complicated. I know I've disappointed you before, but I hope that you can trust me this time. I promise I won't lie to you again."

His mother brushed her thinning hair from her face and a cold look sat in her eyes. She wanted to believe him, but with his ongoing shenanigans, she couldn't risk being hurt again.

"If you think you can honestly keep that promise, I'll trust you."

Amon placed his hand on hers. Looking into her eyes, he solidified his promise and hugged her tightly. Rebecca's warm embrace felt comforting to his aching body. After a long moment, they separated.

"I'll be off then."

Making his way to the door, he turned around and gave his mother one last look before heading up to his room.

✳ ✳ ✳

Natasha Barnes was a middle-aged woman with a gentle face. Her brown hair was pulled back into a bun and not a strand had fallen out of place. Despite her perpetually furrowed brow, she was a beautiful woman and had a scholarly bearing to her. Many imagined the fifth elder as an old woman that spent her life studying the ways of healing. The truth, however, was that she was surprisingly young for her position as the fifth elder and the knowledge she possessed.

"Well, the muscles and skin are healing nicely, and the fractured bones are mostly mended," she said as she examined Daniel's right arm.

Although the wounds had closed, thick scars covered the remaining flesh that clung to the fragile bones and tender muscles.

"There's nothing we could do about the severed meridians," she stated in a soft voice. "I'm sorry that we couldn't heal your arm fully. There's no medicine that can regenerate tissue, nor repair broken meridians."

"Being alive is enough for me. I'm eternally grateful for everything you've done." Daniel flashed her a bright smile. "Do you know when I'll be able to leave?"

"It'll take one more week for the bones to be fully healed. However, since you've been bed-ridden for over a month, you'll need to undergo physiotherapy. I've scheduled daily sessions for you over the next two months."

"That long?"

"My job is to guarantee that you are fully healed and in tip-top shape before I let you leave," she replied, giving Daniel a quick wink.

Daniel cringed at her words.

"I imagine my father asked you to be very cautious regarding that."

"Indeed, it is as you say."

Daniel's face twisted hearing that. He would lose two months of prep time for the event. His father wasn't even giving him a chance. He couldn't help but send a resentful glance to the fifth elder.

Her smile grew and she spoke again.

"Well, to be honest, I feel that your injuries need extra care. I believe that six months will be enough."

"Seriously? Lawrence has outdone himself this time," Daniel said bitterly.

"While your father is heartless, he wasn't the one who gave me these instructions. It was someone I have a higher regard for. Let's just say the agreement was more of an investment," she answered as she checked her nails as carefully as she did Daniel's arm.

Daniel was still confused as he looked at her. She gave him a slight smile, as if cheering him on into discovering what she meant.

Daniel started thinking. It was someone other than Lawrence Meyer that had made this absurd request, and the fifth elder held this person in even higher regard. This meant that the person had to have at least the same status as Lawrence, or higher.

The problem was that none of the remaining three protectors would waste their time being petty. The remaining option was Sect Master Borgin, but he didn't care about anything other than the sect; such schemes were beneath him.

The fifth elder called it an investment. What if that person was still not in such a position of power? Then the only one that would fit the descriptions would be...

"No way!" Daniel had a surprised expression as the pieces fell into place.

"Have you figured it out?"

"It makes no sense. How would staying here help me?"

"As I told you before, my job is to make sure that you leave here fully healed. I'll settle for nothing less."

The meaning of her words had changed. These words were like a beacon of hope to Daniel. He looked at his useless right arm with a frown. What could they do for him?

"We will find a way to get around this problem," she said, fidgeting with her robes.

"Is he insane? This would bring him a great deal of trouble if Lawrence ever found out."

"He knew you would say that, so he wanted me to give you a message." Natasha straightened her posture and looked Daniel dead in the eye. A strong aura of respect filled the space around them. "He said, 'We're family, and that's all that matters.'"

A few days later, Natasha entered his room with her assistant, Delia, in tow. The young nurse had a large package in her hands, wrapped in a thick cloth. Placing it on the table, she bowed deeply to Natasha and left.

"What's this?" Daniel asked, surprised that anyone would give him anything.

The fifth elder said nothing, but instead, she unwrapped the bundle revealing a prosthetic arm. She motioned for him to take it. As he studied it, the arm began to twitch and suddenly, the wooden hand grabbed his wrist. Spooked, Daniel fell from his bed, hitting his elbow on the hard floor. As he lay there cursing, Natasha cackled in delight.

"Spread your divine sense and probe it," she said, wiping a tear from her eye.

Using his divine sense, he examined the object. He found that the artifact had qi pathways that matched perfectly with the meridians in a real arm. This meant that Daniel would be able to use qi in the meridians to execute movements instead of the muscles and tendons. He'd become a puppeteer of the arm, by using it to train his qi control.

"I want you to be able to execute a series of complex tasks with it," Natasha. "Furthermore, you can't have any physical contact with the arm as you train. All will be done through qi control. After that, you'll start training using your own arm."

"It will be far from perfect, especially in a fight where your focus will be divided into many other tasks, but it will be usable. I recommend you use this arm for simple tasks, nothing more," Natasha said, holding her arms behind her back.

"This... How did you think of this?" Daniel questioned. "I don't think you just had this idea."

"You are right," Natasha looked up as if reminiscing about something. "I had this idea five years ago, when a friend was hurt."

"Did it work?" Daniel couldn't help but ask.

"I wouldn't know," Natasha sighed gently. "All I managed to do was tell her about the theory."

"Borgin and your father made sure to get in my way after that," a rare trace of emotion was shown in her face as it distorted into a mask of anger and her eyes turned cold. "You better make that bastard suffer a loss."

Talking about such matters had made Natasha lose her calm for a moment, but it was enough for Daniel to see how deep her hatred for Lawrence ran.

Daniel nodded firmly and with a devious smile he said, "You can be sure that I won't let him feel the least bit of satisfaction from this," Daniel smiled darkly.

Natasha sent him another piercing glance before turning her back and neatly pinning her hair up.

"You can train on your own. How you use the knowledge that you gain from this experience is up to you," she responded, slowly making her way to the door. "Delia will help you with anything you need. I'll visit every day to guide you through physiotherapy and check on your progress. It might be a good idea to start training your left arm to be your dominant one. I expect nothing but total dedication on your part."

"You can rest assured about that," Daniel declared.

"Thank you for saving Amon Skoller," she added in an unusual gentle tone before turning her back away and leaving.

"I'm off!" Amon's voice sounded from his mother's room.

"Don't overdo it!" Rebecca said flashing her son an encouraging smile.

Amon gave her a quick squeeze; a parting embrace for the road. The bottomless pouch he had left by her bedside, well within arms reach. Food and drink were contained within, enough for two weeks and some days.

Amon left the house and made his way towards Warrior Hall. He would occasionally throw a glance back over his shoulder—out of worry perhaps, or the onset of homesickness. Only Amon knew what longing burdened his every step.

Since the Abyss Sect had a restriction in place for non-Inner Sect disciples, Amon was only allotted thirty days total. Heeding Lya's advice, Amon would exchange a few thousand contribution points to reserve a private room. He would use half of the allotted days now, and keep the rest for later. This way, his training would be most efficient and he would be going into the competition at peak performance.

The distance from the Skoller residence to Warrior Hall was long and tedious by foot. He had covered the starting distance at a brisk pace, but would soon come to regret it. The all-black attire he had chosen was waterlogged from perspiration and clung to his body like a zealous lover. Furthermore, each step caused Windhowler to knock against the small of his back, leaving it sore. The blade was *just* a middle-grade artifact, but still, he had grown fond of it.

It had been three months since his training sessions with Lya began. As Amon approached his fourteenth birthday he started growing taller, and his thin, sickly frame became nothing more than an unpleasant memory. Alongside his natural growth, the effort he put in with Lya bore fruit as toned muscles replaced skin and bone.

Every three weeks, Lya subjected him to a round of body tempering. The agony he endured during each session was no less than masochistic torture, but the end results were clear. He had undergone his fourth tempering which left his body feeling weightless and bursting with vitality. Along with the physical benefits, Amon's senses had become increasingly developed, and his soul grew in strength by the day.

Somewhere along the way, Lya demanded Amon travel while practicing in tandem.

"I already explained how this will work," Lya's voice echoed in his mind. "So be ready—or *else*."

An all too familiar stick hovered by Amon's side; its surface infused with a layer of light. The youth shuddered upon catching a glimpse of it. Motivated by his fear of pain, he regulated his breathing and focused intently.

He mentally recited the first part of the soulrousing technique, preparing himself for what was to come.

"Begin!" Lya said as the stick split the air, aiming for Amon's head. The stroke was lightning fast, bordering on impossibility, but the stick ended up hitting nothing but the ground.

Twisting his body to the side, Amon barely avoided the attack. As the stick missed its mark,, he started running southward with a faint light enveloping his feet enhancing his speed. His steps were light and agile, covering a great distance every time they pushed off the earth.

"Excellent, keep it up," Lya said to him with a satisfied tone.

Amon was utilizing the most basic of the movement techniques described in *The Essence of Movement* manual he had purchased long ago. These techniques would help him accomplish two things: moving faster and covering greater distances. How a cultivator used them was limited only by their imagination.

Amon would need to learn how to make incredibly difficult decisions in a split-second and have his body move as faster than thought. More importantly, he would have to learn to commit to each of his strikes, for hesitation would result in openings—*fatal* openings.

"First stance!" Lya shouted as the stick blindsided Amon in a horizontal slash.

He promptly drew Windhowler and assumed the first stance. The blade produced lines of light which covered its surface.

Clang!

Amon warded off the blow, but didn't stick around to celebrate. He had already dashed off into the surroundings, resuming their absurd game of tag.

Using a movement technique was similar to infusing qi into a sword, the difference being the cultivator reinforced his feet and legs, and the pathways for the qi to flow through were already defined.

Having trained to imbue Windholer with qi, Amon made great progress in the basics of movement techniques. The most troublesome part was keeping his body under control and maintaining balance as he moved at such speeds. Luckily for Amon, his body tempering was perfect. The strength of his limbs and his heightened senses and quick reactions allowed him to maintain maximum speed with little risk.

"Second stance!" Lya shouted again as the stick came from below.

Amon promptly blocked the strike using the proper stance.

Lya had decided that the trip to Hell Keeper's City was a good opportunity for him to train. This impromptu session would also test the upper limits of his body. It would be a good warm-up before the real training—Warrior Hall.

As such, Amon would have to run, dodge, block and strike his way to Hell Keeper's City instead of taking a carriage. Lya had her divine sense spread to not only control the stick but to check the surroundings and avoid prying eyes.

It was a long and exhausting trip. Amon left in the morning and arrived at nightfall. The silvery moonlight was barely enough to illuminate his sorry figure. His robes were drenched in sweat and dirt was smudged on his face from the few times he had lost his balance. His disheveled appearance made him look like a thief running from the law in the night.

"Entrance to Hell Keeper's City is—"

"Yeah, yeah, yeah," he said in annoyance as he swiped his identification card and entered the pitch-black tunnel.

He had a terrible headache and was naturally annoyed. Thanks to the soulrousing technique, he was feeling even worse than his real state. He couldn't help but give a resentful glance to the stick still following him.

Halfway through the trip, Lya had decided to stop giving him a heads up for her strikes and telling him how he should block. This, of course, resulted in Amon being hit over and over again and having to keep his divine sense spread to the maximum to ward off her attacks.

"It really is beautiful," Lya said in a daze as Amon walked into the city.

Amon couldn't help but agree with Lya. It was truly beautiful. He walked in a daze as he looked all around him. The city felt completely different during the night. The Ashen Heart tree was illuminated by the moon, making its leaves glow and the trunk's luster resembled slightly polished steel. A few crystals stood atop the buildings where people resided, shedding a cold-blue light in the darker corners of the town.

After a fairly short walk, Amon stood under the Ashen Heart tree. It was only a few meters from the entrance to the Warrior Hall. Silver doors accented its black exterior, giving the building a simple, but classy ambiance. Being one of the most important buildings in the sect, Amon was surprised that it didn't have more extravagant features.

Amon slowly entered the building as a feeling of oppression burst from its sheer magnificence. The ground floor was brightly illuminated with the same crystals used outside. There was one long counter to the right of the entrance, and a single clerk stood there, wearing the usual purple robes.

His hair was a mess and dark circles surrounded his eyes. He gave a long yawn as Amon approached him.

"How can I help you, kid?" he asked in a drowsy voice as his eyelids trembled.

"I want to rent a room for fifteen days," Amon replied.

Yawning again, the clerk retrieved a glowing ball from the counter and put it in front of Amon.

"That will be six thousand contribution points for the room and access to the facilities. Meals will be brought to your room at set times during the day. The times are listed on a piece of parchment in your room."

Amon swiped his card on the ball and it flashed once, annoying the clerk with its sudden brightness.

"Room thirty-three. It is on the third floor," the man said, rubbing his eyes sleepily.

Amon thanked him and hurriedly climbed the stairs next to the counter, reaching the third floor. The hallway was just as black as the exterior. Not a single light fixture was present and the rooms were only identifiable by the lit crystals above their silver doors.

He felt strange since he couldn't see where the floor ended and the walls started. He felt like he was in an open space, even if the doors re-affirmed him it was just a hallway.

"What an interesting array," Lya's voice echoed in his mind. "A very cunning use of light."

"Is this shadow thing just an illusion?" Amon was troubled as he tried to find his room.

"Yes; a weak illusion to make you feel disoriented. It's often used in certain training sessions. This is a good way for you to rely less on your sight and more on your other senses."

Amon nodded as he took in her words. It didn't take too long for him to find his room. He swiped his card at the door and it creaked open, revealing a simple room. It had a comfortable bed, a mirror, a small desk, and another silver door that led to a bathroom.

"Even here they put this damn illusion!" he said outraged.

"Every time is time to train," Lya commented to his outburst.

Amon undressed and bathed himself. The hot water felt nice against his sore body, and soothed his chaotic emotions. Despite this, he still felt a bit nauseated and dizzy—his sense of balance was completely off.

"This will be a great place to train movement techniques," Lya said with a sneer, making Amon's heart clench.

He threw himself on the bed, curled up at its center, and closed his eyes. His heart felt heavy as he mentally prepared himself for what was to come.

The construct gave Amon chills every time he looked at it head on. Its rigid movements, all white body, and lack of a face were shocking to be sure, but there were more important things to worry about. Like the long spear and its razor point piercing toward him like a storm of arrows.

The Warrior Hall loaned them out for a price. *Sparring puppets,* the clerk had called them while briefly explaining their operation. A cultivator just needed to select a weapon type and difficulty and the puppet's array would do the rest. Even elemental affinities could be selected to maximize training efficiency.

Lya was less than impressed by their shoddy construction, but Amon paid the fee and brought one to the training room regardless. Afterall, one could only improve so little from self practice.

Under Lya's meticulous observation, the pair had been going at it for several hours without pause. Amon had set the puppet's power level to the initial levels of body tempering, making it weaker and slower than himself. He believed it to be a good warm up before upping the difficulty, though this proved more challenging than expected.

Though it was true the puppet was set to a lower cultivation level, the way it wielded its spear and weaved in and out of combat gave the youth a run for his money. Amon found himself struggling to gain the upper hand in their numerous exchanges, as he soon learned technique and experience could often win over a gap in cultivation levels.

Despite suffering some small losses, the youth enjoyed the intimate dance of combat. His muscles burned and his breathing grew laboured, though this would soon give way to a feeling of weightlessness. It was a pleasant sensation, and a thrill the golden-eyed teen had never felt before.

Clang!

Amon blocked another stab aimed at his chest with the flat of the blade, and pushed the spear down. This broke the puppet's stance, denying it of balance and creating a window of attack. Stepping forward, he thrust toward the puppet's head, putting the full force of both arms behind Windhowler's handle. To his surprise, he hit nothing but air. The puppet lightly twisted his body, and as Amon's strike went past him, he grabbed Amon's arm and pulled him. Amon lost his balance and fell to the ground, still holding his sword.

Pak!

He felt a blunt strike on his back as the puppet hit it with the spear. Amon felt pain, but there was no real damage. The weapons there were using had no real edges or tips, they were all blunt weapons.

"You lose."

Lya's voice penetrated his concentration as the darkness melted away and revealed a wide room with white walls and a solid floor. The puppet retracted his spear, took a step back and assumed a neutral stance, holding the spear by his side. The light on the spear subsided and the puppet stood still, as if it was nothing but a statue. A stark contrast to the nimble and precise movements it had displayed until now.

"You managed to withstand him for about a minute."

Amon heard Lya speaking and his ears started reddening. This was his tenth fight, as well as his tenth loss.

"What was your mistake in this fight?" Lya asked.

Amon thought for a while, trying to remember every movement and decision he made in the fight since it began. To his luck and shame, it was quite easy to do that, as it was an incredibly short fight.

"I was late by a split-second to use the opening I created, and the step I took was too long. My sword arrived late and my stance was wrong, resulting in a weak strike. My stance also caused me to lose my balance when he pulled me."

"I see that you're learning," Lya agreed with him. "As I said before, don't trust your eyes. Rely on your divine sense instead."

"I know that, it is just..." Amon was somewhat ashamed as he spoke. "Maintaining the state of conscious emptiness while fighting is incredibly hard, I can't do much else besides controlling qi to use the movement techniques."

Amon hadn't shown great difficulty in using his divine sense as he moved ever since he first used the soulrousing technique. He even managed to use it in his training with Lya, although the mental strain was high.

However, a real fight was a completely different matter. Amon had to maintain the qi in his sword, properly control and circulate the qi in his legs, observe the enemy's movements, and always know what was surrounding him.

"So now you understand why experience is important, right?" Lya questioned in a harsh tone.

Ashamed, Amon nodded slowly. He had to admit that he thought he would have an easier time training in combat. One part of him secretly thought that it was going to be easy and he would surprise Lya with his performance.

The truth was that he was overconfident. Now all he could do was gather the pieces of his shattered pride and move on with his head lowered as he learned from his mistakes.

Lya, of course, knew all of that. She was actually surprised at how cool-headed Amon was regarding his constant failures after the confidence he had built up during three months of training.

It's good that he can keep focused," she thought to herself.

"What can I do, Lya?" he asked, looking at the ring on his hand.

"Keep training. Eventually you'll get used to doing everything at once," she responded without hesitation.

Amon nodded. He took a deep breath and relaxed his body as he closed his eyes. Lya was right, as always. He had to be patient and keep practicing.

"Again!" he shouted as he gripped his sword firmly.

His face was full of determination as he smiled, welcoming the blank faced puppet to another battle.

A shiny ball grazed past Amon's temple, ruffling his hair and giving him a chill. If he fell victim to a single distraction, he would be pummeled with metallic balls the size of grapefruits. The deadly objects darted across the room from every which way, causing the young cultivator to dodge left and right to escape them.

Although his feet glowed with qi, they weren't bright enough to illuminate the lightless space. The movement technique had made his steps light and nimble as he contorted his body. With his divine sense, he was able to avoid the majority of the metal spheres. Unfortunately, his practice was not enough to keep him from being smacked by the flying objects; he already had multiple bruises of various colors.

Keeping track of the balls was only the first part of passing this test. He needed to successfully evade multiple waves and find a pattern to take advantage of. If he managed to do so, he'd be able to prove to Lya that he had greatly improved since he first picked up Windhowler.

According to Lya, this was supposed to be an incredibly useful exercise and he didn't disagree. He'd eventually learn to "dance" and focus on several things at once. It made sense to Amon since all combats had their particular rhythm depending on who their opponents were. Lya was surprised he had lasted this long. She had seen his attempt at dancing shortly after he found out that Daniel was alive, and it was rather horrifying to say the least.

"It is better this way. The array doesn't stop when you are hit, so you're forced to move to a safe spot instead of taking a break," Lya chimed from the sidelines.

Like the room prior, the Protean Projectile Room gave the user the option to make adjustments catered to their training style. Lya had changed them herself to make sure the session would give Amon a vigorous workout.

Amon let out an exhausted groan as he barely dodged a ball to his shin. He had activated the soulrousing technique to generate more nebula and boost his soul's growth. If he was going to get mowed down by inanimate objects, he wanted to make the most of it. He was forced to find a way to properly use his divine sense, otherwise he would be hit. The pain from impact would cause him to get anxious, and his body would produce nebula. With the soulrousing technique boosting it, this would allow his soul to grow faster and his divine sense to get stronger, making the practice beneficial to him, even in failure.

After six days of failing in both rooms, he managed to defeat the sparring puppet after a dragged out match during his last fight of the day. He spent a good part of that night excitedly reliving the entire battle with Lya, failing to forget she had been watching over him the entire time. Amon boasted that he surely wouldn't lose to the puppet again. She nodded with a strange smile, but he failed to notice.

On the seventh day, Amon finally beat the Protean Projectile Room and confidently strutted into the Sparring Room after lunch. To his surprise, the puppet now held a sabre and his physical ability was the same as Amon's. The other adjustments had changed on the puppet as well. The sabre had a shorter reach compared to the spear, but it excelled in close-quarters with wide sweeping attacks and ferocious blows.

Needless to say, Amon lost miserably. On a good round, he managed to last forty seconds. When all was said and done, he glanced resentfully at the ring on his finger—he knew this was a warning from Lya. He could hear her saying, "Don't get too cocky," in the back of his mind, though she never spoke a word.

Days had passed and Amon was continuously failing to pass either test. He knew that his efforts weren't being wasted, but he couldn't help but wonder if he was cut out for the promotion competition.

On the twelfth day, Lya had arranged for him to face a sword-wielding puppet. Its strength was set to that of an average cultivator in the middle stages of body tempering. This meant that the puppet was fairly stronger than him.

"It will be good for you. You won't be the strongest cultivator in the promotion competition," Lya reminded. "You'll need to rely on your skills and wits to close the gap between you and your opponent. I recommend that you look closely at their actions."

Amon nodded and started to analyze his opponent.

Hmm... Its sword is the same length as mine, but the puppet is taller. It'll have a greater range than I. It appears that its main hand is his right hand, so I'll have to be careful of powerful blows aiming for my left side. I hope I can keep focus on my defense while looking for an opening, he thought, nodding his head to reassure himself.

The puppet positioned himself in the third stance of *Fundamentals of the Sword*.

Maybe he'll use moves from that manual... No, this is nothing but a front to throw me off like before.

He took a deep breath as he himself assumed the first stance.

"Start!" he shouted, looking closely at the shiny sword in the puppet's hand. Shadows started to swallow the white walls and the floor, immersing the room in seamless darkness.

As the puppet had no expression, Amon had no way to tell where he was aiming. He could only try to focus on the puppet's body as a whole, analyzing his movements and trying to deduce where and how he would strike. Seasoned warriors could feint with nothing but their eyes, tricking their opponents into believing they would strike where they were looking.

The puppet held the sword with both hands, raising it horizontally next to its head while its body was at an angle, with its left foot to the front. It was a classic stance for a diagonal, downward sweep, aiming for Amon's left shoulder.

Upon further examination, Amon noticed that the left foot was at a 45 degree angle indicating that its stance and possible attack would cause the puppet to be slow and weak, or lose balance. For such a strike, the puppet's left foot would have to be pointing straight at Amon. The puppet would spin counterclockwise using the left foot as a support as he took a step forward with his right foot. It was the only way to maximize the range and power of such an attack.

Amon hurriedly raised his sword to block an attack aimed at his right side—he was spot on. The puppet spun using his left foot, but it moved clockwise. It almost did a complete spin as his sword cut the air. The sword came at Amon in an upward diagonal slash aiming at his right leg.

Clang!

The swords collided and Amon felt a numbing pain in his right hand as he stared at the puppet's eerily illuminated face.

The swords started trembling as the puppet forced the strike in. Amon gazed in terror as it approached him forcing Windhowler to be pushed back with terrifying force.

Amon hurriedly stepped back to escape this entanglement, but the puppet accompanied him with a step forward, their swords still clashing against one another.

"Damn!" Amon shouted in frustration.

He swung his sword outwards, trying to break the puppet's stance. As he did so, the puppet took a step back. Amon's sword whistled through the air as he violently swung at nothing, causing him to become completely exposed. In the blink of an eye, the puppet stepped forward and stabbed Amon's chest.

Pak!

Amon was completely defenseless. A look of resignation plagued his young face when the blunt sword hit his ribcage, sending him tumbling back.

He had lost the fight. The room lit up as the shadows dissolved and the puppet returned to his starting position before turning immobile again.

"To be honest, you surpassed my expectations," Lya's voice echoed in his mind. "I was surprised at how you saw through his feint. It was an incredible move on your part. However, you managed to dance right into the puppet's hands" she added, not letting the compliment swell his head. "There is still much work to be done."

FOUR MONTHS

The warm sunlight shone upon the expanses of the Outer Sect as a carriage slowly made its way to the north. Inside the carriage, a young boy rested his head on the wooden wall with his eyes closed. His breathing was slow, and the rocking of the carriage didn't seem to bother him one bit as he enjoyed a deep sleep.

Amon had forced himself to stay awake over his last few days at Warrior Hall. As a body tempering cultivator he could forfeit sleep for a few days without it affecting him much, so Lya allowed it. It was also a good way for him to test the limits of his stamina and mental resistance as he dealt with one failure after another without rest. Lya realized that he was becoming more irritable by the hour, but he managed to vent his frustrations through training.

This was a lesson for him, because Amon started losing his cool and making more mistakes than usual. He had to learn to clear his mind during combat or it would make him perform at a lower level than usual.

On the fourteenth day, Amon failed the fourth level of the Protean Projectile Room, but almost managed to win. During combat with the puppet, his strikes became increasingly aggressive, lacking the cunning and coolheadedness of the previous day. As such, his results worsened very swiftly. This only added to him getting more and more frustrated as he felt he was taking a step back instead of a step forward. His eyes were bloodshot as he left the room in defeat without a word. Looking at his expression, Lya knew that his exhaustion and frustrations were piling up and he wasn't able to deal with them anymore. It was at that moment that Lya decided to act.

"Amon, you can't let yourself be influenced by emotions this way."

"I know that, Lya. But what else can I do?" he asked, annoyed. "At most I'll learn how to suppress my feelings."

"It is not about holding them back, it is about dealing with them," Lya's tone was grave. "Sit down and close your eyes."

Amon had a weary look on his face and dark circles surrounded his eyes as he hesitated for a moment before sitting down and crossing his legs.

"You must never hold back. If you do, you'll eventually become numb and your cultivation will suffer greatly. What you must do is face these emotions head on. You have to accept them, but not let them influence your thoughts or your decisions.

"When you're feeling overwhelmed, you must balance your feelings, otherwise you'll always be a slave to your emotions. Use your frustration and anger to power your strike instead of using it to determine how you will act in a fight.

"Your emotions power your sword; your reason controls your body," she recited what she had learned from heart.

Amon took deep breaths as he listened to her. He knew he was being overwhelmed by his emotions, but getting back in control was incredibly hard.

"Try again," Lya said when Amon seemed to have calmed down.

Her words had been like a cold stream of water extinguishing a raging flame. Amon slowly got up, still taking deep breaths. He opened his eyes and faced the blank puppet.

"Start!"

The room went dark and the puppet moved closer. This time, the fight lasted longer. Amon had gotten a better hold of himself, but it still resulted in a loss. This continued on the fifteenth day as well. Regardless, Lya was impressed at his rapid progression in only half a month.

On the sixteenth day, Amon packed his things at sunrise and left Hell Keeper's City. His ashen hair was a mess and his eyelids were drooping. Nevertheless, there was a faint and cold confidence in his golden eyes that had not been there before—he now had a well-rounded understanding of what he could do.

The bright sun peeped over the clouds as the carriage got closer to the Northern Junction. The scenery was oddly calming to Lya as she sat within Brightmoon.

Arthur really built something nice, Lya thought to herself. *Still, a volcano in the middle of the continent, surrounded by streams and a forest... He must have really enjoyed the nonsense of it all.*

Arthur Royce had been a strange man. He fought for his ideals with everything that he had, just like Alexei. Even though he did his best to avoid killing, Lya knew that Arthur had no real regard for life. Alexei, however, was the complete opposite. He cherished life like no other, yet he wouldn't hesitate to kill if needed. They had been the strongest cultivators of their generation, and they were most likely the most flawed of them all.

As she walked the road of nostalgia, tears streamed down her face. *Maybe if they accepted their flaws they would have been able to deal with them. I won't let Amon go down that path. I refuse to let his pride stand in the way of his growth.*

"So, how was it?" Rebecca asked Amon in a tender voice.

The sunlight coming from the window made her blond hair shine like gold as she looked at Amon with a warm gaze.

"It was incredible," Amon answered with a wide yawn.

He had slept for a few hours in the carriage, but he was still feeling exhausted.

"Tell me about it later. Go rest, I can see how tired you are," Rebecca gave him a firm hug and a light kiss on his cheek. "I missed you."

"I missed you too, mom," Amon said before slowly making his way to his own room, where he fell on the bed and immediately entered a deep sleep.

Shortly afterwards, Lya materialized by her side looking fresh-faced and bright eyed.

"It's been a while," Rebecca greeted her, raising one eyebrow. "I hope things went well."

Her green eyes were twitching with anxiety as she looked at Lya with a somewhat eager expression.

"Yes, it went better than I could have hoped. His progress was far above what I expected," Lya replied with a proud grin. "He has talent. He might not be a genius, but he has talent."

Rebecca laughed aloud as she heard that. Her laugh reverberated through the room like the chimes of a bell. Her perfectly-white teeth were clenched as she tried to muffle herself. Tears filled her eyes as she clutched her sides. She tried to catch her breath, but the more she thought about Lya's words, the harder it became. It wasn't out of sadness or disbelief, but more so out of pride and relief that Amon wasn't a lost cause. When she finally calmed herself, she said, "This is the first time someone said my son was talented."

Lya stood silent for a long time as she heard Rebecca's words. She couldn't help but feel touched. She looked intently at Rebecca's eyes.

"We'll spend the next three months further developing his skills. Afterwards, we'll spend the last two weeks training in the Warrior Hall. It's important to get him as much experience as possible prior to the competition. By the end of the Season of Rigor, more people will say that your son has talent," she said boldly, straightening her posture. "That's the very least they'll say about him, I assure you.

This was a promise, and Lya would make sure to follow through with it.

Rebecca was eternally grateful that a complete stranger would help Amon.

"Thank you, Lya. I will never be able to repay you."

"There is no need to repay me, Rebecca," Lya's tone was gentle. Her body started to disperse as her words echoed in the room. "Just be sure to keep being a great mother."

"This is also the first time someone said I was doing a good job," Rebecca whispered, staring at the spot Lya had been.

Rebecca Skoller needed no recognition from others. She spent her whole life doing her best and she slowly reached out for the peak with nothing but her own efforts. Still, the moment Amon was born, cultivation gained a new meaning for her.

It wasn't about proving to herself that she was as good as everyone else anymore. She now sought strength to protect him and nothing more. She did not hesitate to put his life above hers when Lloyd betrayed the sect and left them alone to deal with the aftermath.

She didn't hesitate to use her power to fight for her rights against the backlash her husband's betrayal brought them. Her rampage had been so violent that even Sect Master Borgin had to give in, even if he was the one enraged the most with the situation. She was sent to the Outer Sect to be "observed" as they judged if she was involved in Lloyd's betrayal.

She also didn't hesitate to put her life on the line to protect her son when the silverback wolf attacked. The result was her losing most of the strength she once had, but she did so with a smile on her face.

Regardless of all of this, she wasn't kicked out of the sect. Not because people respected her and what she did, but because she was not a threat anymore. Even if they were still under superficial surveillance, they held no importance. She doubted her name even passed by the minds of the higher-ups of the sect on a regular basis.

She had to raise her son alone, dealing with the trauma of abandonment and not even being able to properly move out of the bed. She still had delusions of Lloyd Kressler one day returning to take them away, but she knew deep down that it would never happen.

She gripped the necklace tightly, looking at its beautiful glow.

She was doing all that she could, but she always felt it wasn't enough. She felt that she would break down at any time, but somehow her son managed to help her to hold it together. Now all she could do was stare out the window and reminisce about the good times. Rebecca longed to take Amon for a walk around the sect again. Closing her eyes, she imagined how it felt to walk outside and feel the elements brush against her skin. But now, she was bedridden and unable to progress. When Lya proclaimed that Amon had talent, it filled Rebecca with joy and hope. She knew that Amon finally had a chance to move forward and escape the past that plagued him.

* * *

Clang!
Clang! Clang! Clang!
Sparks flew everywhere, causing the dark training room to look like a night sky squeezing fireworks until they burst. Once again, Amon was at Warrior Hall to train for the competition. This time, he clashed with two puppets: one with a spear and one holding a sabre.

His golden eyes were cold as an arctic breeze as he carefully dodged and blocked their strikes. Amon charged at the spear puppet with his left shoulder, sending it tumbling back. He made use of his momentum to spin clockwise, blocking a stab aimed at his back. The spear puppet took a step back as soon as his strike failed, but instead of advancing, Amon stood still for a moment.

A feint; he could see that. Even though the puppet stood back, its body leaned forward, preparing to charge at Amon once more. Amon took a step back and twisted his body to the right. The stab he was expecting came a heartbeat later, grazing his garb. As the puppet moved past Amon, his sword came crashing down on its head.

Pak!

The blunt sword hit the spear puppet, knocking it to the ground like a ragdoll. Amon had no time to enjoy the short victory, as he sensed a sabre was slashing at his neck from behind.

These guys are fast, Amon thought, trying to catch his breath.

His sword was still in a low position thanks to his last strike and he would have no time to raise it and block the strike. Amon decided to take a step back, colliding with the sabre puppet. He managed to get out of range and the puppet's upper arm hit his neck. It hurt a lot, but it did not count as a lethal blow. Amon swung his left elbow backwards, striking the puppet's abdomen.

The puppet lost its balance and created some space as it retreated. Amon spun counter-clockwise, using his left foot as a pivot. His blunt sword made a whistling sound as it cut through the air, chopping at the puppet's left shoulder in a diagonal slash.

Pak!

Windhowler hit the puppet, which fell to the floor, becoming motionless. The shadows in the room dissolved and the two puppets got up and stood side-by-side. Amon let out a long breath as his tension subsided and he sat on the ground. His body was shivering and he was finding it hard to properly breathe. He felt hot and he couldn't stop trembling.

"Not bad, not bad at all!" Lya applauded as she complimented him. "It took you five whole days to obtain a victory, but you still managed to do it!"

"The middle stages of body tempering are amazing," he stated through labored breaths.

He could feel his body coursing with explosive power. He had managed to reach the middle stages of body tempering just a few days before. He had needed more than ten rounds of tempering to advance to the middle stages. His soul also benefited greatly. His divine sense was stable and he could grasp his surroundings better than ever.

"Don't get overconfident," Lya warned. "This puts you above average at best. What are your expectations for this tournament?"

"At the very least, I hope to catch the attention of an elder and earn a spot in the Inner Sect as a disciple."

"It's good to have reasonable expectations to avoid disappointment. I'm proud of you for being humble. Nevertheless, that doesn't mean that you shouldn't aim higher."

Wiping sweat from his brow, he nodded and made his way to his room.

He was barely able to control his excitement. He was feeling reasonably confident and he couldn't wait to use Windhowler in combat.

Amon lay in bed staring at the ceiling. Sleeping was proving to be difficult due to the anxiousness building up inside of him. The Season of Rigor would start the next day, and he wanted nothing more than to prove to himself, and the sect that he had surpassed their expectations.

SEASON OF RIGOR

Amon exited the Warrior Hall wearing specially made combat attire. He had purchased it from a shop near the bookstore when he arrived a few days prior. The material was light in weight and although it clung tightly to his body, it didn't restrict his movement in the slightest.

It was still dark, as the sun had yet to rise over the city, but a few dozen clerks in purple garb were stationed at a circular black counter surrounding the Ashen Heart tree. Only a handful of cultivators were present as most participants decided to travel from their homes the morning of instead of spending extra money renting a room in the city.

Amon approached a girl in her late teens. Her black hair was neatly pulled back into a ponytail and her long nails were perfectly filed and painted a jade-green with gold tips. As he got closer, she looked at him from head to toe, trying to hide her curiosity. Amon, being too anxious and oblivious, didn't notice the young woman's blushing cheeks.

"Good morning, sir," she smiled at him. "Do you have your registration token?"

"Y-yes," he stammered nervously.

Amon searched his person and retrieved the silver token from an inner pocket and handed it to her with his identification card.

"Thank you very much, sir," she said with a wink before swiping the two objects over a glowing ball by her side.

Once the registration process was completed, she handed the items back to Amon along with a wooden card engraved with a number.

"Your identification number is 42," she said politely. "The competition will be held in Royce Paradigm Arena, located in the west zone of the city."

Amon thanked the clerk and discreetly stored his I.D and token in his ring.

"Good luck!" she called after him, waving her right hand in the air.

The other clerks looked at her strangely, but she didn't seem to mind. Amon waved back and turned to leave.

She's awfully friendly, he thought, examining the card she had given him. When he flipped it over, he noticed she had etched a small heart in one of the corners. Stopping in his tracks, he spun around and looked at her once more; her flirtatious smile caused Amon's face to grow hot and flushed. The young woman quickly returned to attending other cultivators, leaving him slack-jawed and confused. He stuffed the card in his pocket and swiftly headed west towards the arena.

It was somewhat cold inside the mountain, but he didn't mind. The chilly air helped him stay alert and he enjoyed the light prickling sensation from goosebumps forming on his skin.

"There will be a lot of people participating," Lya pointed out.

"I think it will be a number around three thousand or so," Amon predicted.

Even if it was an open tournament, everyone knew that the crushing majority would be of cultivators in their teens and twenties. Those that were too weak, too old, or too young would definitely avoid the competition altogether.

Amon felt that it was a heartless setup, as it was giving hope to those that could never really achieve it. He was sure that the final competitors in the top ten would be from the Inner Ring, as they had the resources to grow strong.

For him, it was nothing but a ruse to shake things up in the Outer Sect. Giving people the impression that the higher-ups cared about them when in reality, it was just an excuse to promote more Inner Ring members without them having to meet the requirements. It was essential that those members were accepted sooner rather than later. They'd have access to better cultivation material and could excel quicker than an underprivileged member from the Outer Sect. Nevertheless, Amon was excited.

The closer he got to the arena, buildings became more sparse and the street widened, making for a grand entrance path to the behemoth edifice before him. Royce Paradigm Arena was round and stood forty meters high, with glossy white walls that looked like porcelain. It had to have at least a half a kilometer in diameter.

Its large, golden doors were five meters tall and three meters wide. They lead into the spacious receiving hall that was decorated with a highly-polished, pastel-pink marble floor. On the other side of the hall stood another set of doors which led to the fighting areas.

The hall, which could hold a thousand people at once, was protected with numerous, spear-wielding guards dressed in white uniforms similar to Amon's. The welcome counters stretched along both sides of the foyer and were manned by over fifty attendants donning purple uniforms with long, silk pants and sleeveless tunics.

Amon approached one of the helpers and registered as a participant. The attendant instructed that he'd have to wait in another area, and signaled for a guard to let him pass.

"The competition will start in the afternoon, so you will have to be patient."

Amon thanked him and entered the hall, not minding the wait. After finding a quiet corner, he sat down and closed his eyes to rest with Windhowler being tightly held in his arms. There was no reason for him to stay on alert as Lya would certainly wake him up if something were to happen.

Soon, more cultivators began to flood in. The quality of their clothing spoke volumes about where they came from and Amon could hear a lot of them gossiping about members from other parts of the sect.

The Inner Ring was notorious for such behavior. The families would spread rumors about the deeds of their scions, trying their best to make them reach as far as possible. They wanted to have their names to be praised throughout the Outer Sect. This not only gave them a fanbase, but it also encouraged people to bet on them as well.

Time slowly passed, and the foyer and participant area filled rather quickly. Spectators eagerly waited for the competition to start, many of them wore the numbers of the cultivator they came to support. The noise level was at a well-managed roar, but it was still enough to hurt one's ears. As Amon stood to stretch his legs and get some water, a serene voice washed over the sea of noise, silencing the excited crowd.

"We'll be starting the competition in a few minutes," the voice announced directly into their ears. "Please enter the arena respective of your numbers."

The inner doors shuddered, opening with a deafening howl. A blinding light emitted from the fighting area as the crowd flooded in to take their seats. Amon held Windhowler tightly, caressing the leather sheath as he was pushed along with them.

"Oh, I forgot to mention," Lya started. "I forbid you from using a sword until further notice."

Her voice tapered off with a sneer. Amon was baffled why she was just now telling him this, especially after multiple months of training with a sword. Windhowler sneakily slipped from his hands and made its way into his bottomless pouch and was quickly replaced with something else.

"You'll have to use this instead."

He stared down at the object in his palms with bloodshot eyes.

Is she insane? This must be a joke. This woman is truly heartless.

"If you imbue it with qi properly, it won't lose to any other weapon," she replied, muffling a giggle.

Angered, Amon said, "I thought you were trying to lay low."

"As far as I know you are just showing off your mastery over qi to the few that would pay attention to that," she sneered.

"Why make my life harder?" he cried inwardly.

"Every fight is a struggle. I won't let you have an unfair advantage over others in the first few stages of the competition. A middle-grade artifact is too much—a stick is just fine."

Amon walked through the golden gates, fuming with disbelief. His grasp on the stick made his knuckles turn white and his face was painted with fury. After he stepped out of the blinding light, it took awhile for his eyes to adjust to the interior of the Royce Paradigm Arena.

There were thirty-two platforms distributed in a wide area covered with grass. Bleachers, which were being supported by the walls, were filled with thousands of spectators, cheering and scanning the participants for their loved ones. The roar of the people was deafening, and Amon felt his chest rumbling within.

As expected, there was an exclusive cabin for important guests, perfectly positioned to see the entire area. Its thick, purple walls were enough to drown out the sound of the arena, making it perfect for elders to discuss amongst themselves at a civil volume.

Special platforms were constructed for competitors. They were pure white and a barrier of blue light covered each one like a curtain. Glistening numbers floated in the light, like leaves in a puddle; they served as an indication for where participants were assigned to go. It took awhile, but Amon managed to find his designated area. It was positioned near the purple cabin. It was an ideal location for participants to get recognized by a higher official.

He approached the platform, and with a small jump, he made it past the curtain of light. As he entered the area, he felt as if he had taken a dive in a cool lake. The wooden card in his pocket heated up, causing him to shiver with the contrasting feeling of the cold light.

There were already a dozen cultivators inside and most of them were older and bulkier than Amon. Seeing the stick in Amon's hands, they gave him a smug look, but didn't bother to approach him. They were too busy focusing on what was to come.

One person stood out to him in an instant. A handsome youth with golden hair and blue eyes stood at the far side of the room with his eyes closed. His blue robes were made of silk and a long black spear rested in his hands.

"The rules are simple," the female announcer's voice started again. "The last one standing on each platform at the end of the round will advance to the next battle. Weapons are allowed, but there's no need to worry about injuries. If a lethal blow is dealt to you, the wooden card on your person will instantly generate a shield. Once the shield is activated, it will count as your loss, and you will be escorted from the platform. Stepping out of bounds will also count as a loss, even if it's only a hair's width."

The voice became silent, almost as if waiting for questions from participants, though none came.

"Now, I humbly invite our special guest, Jake Meyer to do the honors."

The purple cabin trembled and partially dismantled itself, revealing Jake in formal robes and a golden lapel pin. Across his back, hung a sword in a blood-red scabbard. There was something different about him, a coldness in his eyes that wasn't there before. Raising his right hand he announced, "The Season of Rigor starts now." His voice was firm and authoritative, a stark contrast to when Amon first met him.

A loud buzz rang through the Royce Paradigm Arena, and the platforms lit up in a red light. The participants started at each other hesitantly. No one wanted to make the first move and have chaos break out. Everyone was tense; it was painted on their faces. Not long after, the blond-haired boy from before opened his eyes and took a step forward. Seconds later, a brawny man with deeply-tanned skin assaulted him from behind, throwing a punch at the back of his head. He had considered the youth as a threat, and wanted him taken care of as soon as possible.

Swoosh!

His fist tunneled through the air, hitting nothing. As he spun around in surprise, he only caught a glimpse of gold. The young boy had ducked and swung his body around to face the man before quickly thrusting his spear towards the man's skull.

A loud scream escaped the man's lips as he watched the speak lunging towards his eye socket. Within the blink of an eye, his wooden card activated, encasing the man in a black shield. He was immediately lifted off the ground and thrown backwards, into a darkened area of the arena. His number, which had been floating at the entrance to the platform, burst into a red light and disappeared.

The blond youth recovered his spear, hitting the floor with its shaft. Cracks spread around it like a web as he held it alongside his body.

"You better come at me as a group, otherwise I'll be in one hell of a mood if I have to defeat you one by one," he scoffed as he picked up his spear and twirled it until it was only a blur.

An excited smile danced across Amon's face as he backed away and sat on the ground. There was no way he was going to step up to be defeated. Instead, he wanted to observe his opponent. The other cultivators stood in shock, uncertain if they should interrupt the intimidating spear twirling.

The blond boy grew impatient; even more so after he saw an ashen-haired brat blatantly disrespecting him.

"I'll be sure to take my time with you after I deal with the trash," he said, stopping his spear and thrusting it into the ground. "Whoever dares to touch that brat will pay."

He cracked his knuckles and launched forward, savagely punching another young man in the chest.

Crack!

A layer of light covered the man and sent him out of the platform. Another number in the curtain of light burst and faded.

"Even his punches are that dangerous?!" a teenage girl shouted in shock.

Her face paled as she did her utmost to retreat to the edge of the platform.

Crack! Crack! Crack!

One beam of light after another lit up in the crowd of competitors as the youth came for them. The numbers on the light curtain were disappearing by the second. Amon looked at him closely, almost unblinkingly as he analyzed his movements.

He's right-handed. His strikes are straightforward and he prefers to use sheer force to suppress rather than use smart movements to conserve his strength. This guy isn't cunning. His movement techniques are effective, but basic just like mine. That's expected, as neither of us are in the elemental purification stage. Amon thought as he calmly watched. *He also seems to have a good grasp of his surroundings. He exposing himself in the beginning was a bait to try to frighten the competition.*

Hmm... He left his spear on the ground. Maybe he is cunning after all. He's deliberately hiding his moves with his spear under the guise of arrogance and he still hasn't let me out of his sight. Amon stroked his chin.

He wants me to watch this and he is also wary of me deciding to attack. He could also be trying to bait me into sneaking on him, only to counter as I approach. This whole show is nothing but a feint. Amon concluded as he watched the youth. *He sees me as an opponent.*

Why would that arrogant youth see Amon as an opponent if they hadn't even exchanged blows? It was simply because Amon showed no fear after his first move and because Amon even dared to sit down and wait after the youth told everyone to come at him.

This meant that either Amon was stupid or he had strength; at the very least more strength than the other competitors in the platform. The blond youth might be arrogant, but he wouldn't underestimate a foe and leave his back open for a potential threat. As such, he gave himself the trouble to divide his attention between Amon and his targets as he fought.

"He has some nice moves, doesn't he?" A sweet voice rang by Amon's side, almost making him jump.

Amon did his best not to show any reaction as he slowly nodded as he looked to his left. A young girl approached him as she stretched her arms. Her chocolate brown hair and hazel eyes were a nice complement to her delicate skin. Her robes were made of white silk, just like the youth fighting before them. A thin sword hung from her waist in a black scabbard, decorated with a silk ribbon. She took a seat next to Amon and a soft *thud* sounded as her weapon hit the floor.

"I hope John doesn't take too long. It's been a while since we've had the chance to play," she pouted. "I'm upset that he hasn't realized that I'm here." She turned and looked at Amon with a wickedly sweet smile. "What's your name?"

He hesitated. All of his instincts were yelling at him to run away from the beautiful girl with a dangerous aura.

"I think you should introduce yourself first if you want to ask my name."

The girl giggled at Amon's cocky attitude.

"Fair enough," she shrugged with a wink. "My name is Cecilia."

"Amon," he answered, keeping his responses short and neutral.

She tried to make small talk with him, but he certainly wasn't having it. They sat there in silence as they watched John defeat several more people in one blow. With each passing moment, Cecilia's became more bored and antsy.

Crack! Crack! Crack!

More and more competitors were eliminated as John continued his rampage. It took about five minutes for him to clear the platform. Unfortunately, a similar scene played out on the other platforms. Members of the Outer Sect were being overthrown by those from the wealthy families of the Inner Ring.

Crack!

Only three numbers left on the platform. John's expression hadn't changed—not until he saw Amon still sitting on the ground. Cecilia clapped her hands loudly and stood up.

"What an amazing performance, John!" she chirped, dusting the back of her robes off with her hands. "You took a lot longer than I expected, however your time was still within an acceptable range."

John's face froze with apprehension as he looked at Cecilia.

"You talk too much," he said coldly, slowly retreating to the center of the platform, taking care not to leave any openings.

He had only seen her when she sat by Amon's side, and his heart had almost stopped at the time. Luckily for him, Cecilia liked to show off, so she would never use a sneak attack. At least not while he was busy cleaning the arena for them to fight properly.

"No need to be scared, Johnny. I won't bite you while you're unarmed," Cecilia with her seemingly permanent and nefarious smile.

Her smile sent chills down Amon's spine. It was less forgiving than before, so Amon decided to create some distance between them. His actions made Cecilia burst into a fit of giggles.

"At least someone knows their place," she stated, wiping a single tear from her eye and lightly fingering the weapon at her waist.

John grasped the spear with his right hand and ripped it out of the floor, never taking his eyes from the stoic beauty.

"Are you sure this stick of yours will be enough to stop me?" John retorted, his voice was firm, yet uncertain.

"Well, if you are talking about sticks, you should be asking our new friend."

Cecilia tossed her hair to the side and squinted at Amon. A piercing trill echoed through the platform as she drew her sword. It's highly polished surface reflected the platform lights, making it glow a frosty blue.

John assumed stance, pointing his spear tip at Cecilia. To Amon's surprise, the tip was shaking.

Amon took a deep breath, trying to not be drawn into John's reaction. If Cecilia was that much stronger he would soon witness it himself. He mentally cursed Lya with all that he had as he assumed the first stance of the *Fundamentals of the Sword*.

Thin lines of light slithered through the stick in his hand, covering it in a split second. When they finished spreading, the stick flashed as a pale light covered it.

Cecilia glared at Amon, but seemed unconcerned. She carefully pulled a few threads that were neatly hidden within her robes. Its sleeves and flowy bottom fell to the ground, revealing a leotard made from extremely pliable material. She kicked the discarded material to the side, removed the ribbon from her scabbard and used it to tie her hair into a messy bun. Assuming her battle stance, she shouted, "Come on, boys! It's about time we started a real fight!"

THREE-WAY

Neither Amon nor John moved after Cecilia's taunt. It was imperative that they keep an eye on her at all times. Amon wanted the two of them to duke it out without him interfering. It would be beneficial for him to learn more about John, and even a smidge about Cecilia.

He took a step back and his two opponents shot towards his direction at the same time. The ground beneath their feet cracked from their initial steps.

Damn! Amon thought, mentally panicking about the predicament he'd just walked into.

Cecilia was closer, but she was probably stronger than John. Facing her would not be a good idea as he would probably be too busy with her to avoid any strike John dealt to his blind side. On the other hand, if he faced John he would leave an opening for Cecilia, and he wasn't sure if he would be able to handle it.

Amon would have to keep them close together to be sure his back wouldn't be exposed. The only way to do that would be to have the two of them attack one another. With a quick, deep breath, calmed himself and planned his move. Time seemed to slow down as he kicked the ground and sped in John's direction. John seemed surprised for a moment, and Cecilia sneered in amusement.

I'm not letting you get away from me.

She jetted after him, almost completely ignoring John in the chase. Completely focused on the task at hand, Amon continued towards the blond-haired cultivator. John raised his black spear and prepared to attack. Analyzing his stance, Amon calculated where and how John would move, along with the speed and distance. With each step, the calculations reset, making for the optimal prediction.

One... Two... Now!

Amon hurriedly stomped his right foot on the floor, making it crack as he forcefully stopped. Lowering his upper body, he tossed himself to the left just in time to hear a deafening whistle blaze past his ear. The shiny edge of the spearhead cut off a few strands of his hair as he barely managed to dodge the attack.

The air howled as the spear moved forward and the missed attack was now aiming directly for Cecilia's chest, taking her by surprise. Within a second, Amon managed to recover his balance and swung the glowing stick at Cecilia's exposed back as she ran past him.

Being attacked at the front and the back, Cecilia was in a tough spot. She growled in frustration and with a firm flick of her wrist, the sword collided with the spear, changing its trajectory. Amon cursed her internally as he was forced to change his own strike due to the spear now aiming at him once more. He swung his stick at the spear, sending it to his left and creating an opening in John's stance.

Amon felt his hand going numb as the stick forcefully sent the spear away. John had immense strength! For Cecilia to change that stab with a flick of her wrist meant she was even stronger.

Cecilia raised her sword and stabbed at John's exposed chest, aiming straight for his heart. With his stance broken and no time to retrieve his spear to block, John was doomed to be eliminated. However, John let go of his spear and jumped backward, letting his body fall to the ground, landing on his back. As Cecilia moved past him, he supported his hands behind his head and raised his knees, kicking out.

Both his feet hit Cecilia's abdomen, sending her flying back into Amon's direction. Cecilia hit Amon and they both fell to the ground, entangled in a mess as John clambered back to his feet. As Amon and Cecilia tried to get away from each other, John jumped up high.

Cecilia's eyes turned serious as she kicked Amon and slid away from her original position just as John started falling. Amon rolled away in the nick of time as John landed exactly where he and Cecilia had been, punching the floor.

CRACK!

The floor quaked and a dust cloud rose where John landed. He walked away from it moments after, allowing the spectators to see the massive hole on the floor surrounded by a network of cracks.

Amon had managed to recover, but his ribs were throbbing in pain. Cecilia's kick had been strong and precise.

"Is that how you treat a lady, John?" Cecilia whined as she feigned injury to her mid-section.

Her breaths had quickened and her hair had partially fallen out of its style. Her eyes glowed with fury and she raised her sword and assumed a fighting stance once more.

"What lady? All I see is a snake!" John replied as he kicked his fallen spear, launching it into the air before catching it.

Yet again, the three of them stared at each other, not wanting to make the first move—Amon had to make a decision. He could either attack John together with Cecilia, as he was the only one that hadn't been hurt yet, or he could attack Cecilia together with John, as she was the strongest of them and it was a good chance to take her out.

After debating with himself for a moment, Amon decided that John had to go first. Even though Cecilia was stronger, John wasn't hurt and he showed that he could have a proper exchange with her and come out on top. At the moment, he held the advantage.

Amon locked eyes with Cecilia for a moment, and they both seemed to reach an agreement. Amon grasped his stick tightly as he shot forward to John again, with Cecilia closing on him from the other side.

John didn't seem surprised. He took a step back as he swung his spear in a wide sweeping attack. Amon had to stop immediately as the spear nearly hit his head. That single moment was enough to break his pace and give John a split-second of time to deal with Cecilia.

The spear was still swinging in her direction as she smiled at John. That strike was too high. It was just a little bit, a few centimeters, but that was enough. Cecilia lowered her head and continued running.

The spear whistled through the air as it hit nothing, leaving John exposed again. Cecilia bolted at him like lightning, her sword ready to kill. John's expression sunk as he slid his left hand along the spear's shaft.

It was a move that demanded incredible reflexes and incredible strength and with a bit of maneuvering, he shifted the spear. What had been a sweeping strike with the tip pointed outwards was now turned into another sweeping strike, but with the blunt end end of the shaft whistling through the air, aiming for Cecilia's waist.

Cecilia was forced to heavily stomp the floor, coming to a halt as she raised her sword to parry the strike. John's brows furrowed as he was left with no time to react. She spun her body and kicked the end of the shaft, making the spear stab at John. The tip was pointing at his chest, and he cursed out loud as he was forced to yet again let go of his spear or he would be eliminated by his own weapon.

The few seconds that it took for Cecilia to distract him were sufficient enough for Amon to get an opening. He swung his stick at the back of John's head at a breakneck speed but John somehow managed to turn and block the strike with his left arm.

Crack!

Gritting his teeth through the pain, John let out an aggressive growl and attempted to punch Amon with his uninjured arm. Fortunately for Amon, Cecilia heavily struck their competitor, sending him flying to the other side of the platform.

He managed to roll and stopped just a bit away from the edge. His body was in a ton of pain and it was difficult for him to breathe. Rage was burning in his eyes as he looked at Cecilia, whose grin sadistically beamed at him. As John got up, one could see a set of footprints imprinted on his back.

Grabbing his black spear with her left hand, Cecilia threw it off of the platform. It flew in an arc and landed a few feet behind the curtain of light.

"You've gotten a lot better, Johnny." Although she was pouting, her eyes were brimming with happiness. "I can't play around with you anymore."

John gritted his teeth as he forced himself to hold back his words. An unwilling expression appeared on his face as he looked at his broken arm. He then raised his eyes to Amon, with nothing but hate on them.

Cecilia turned to Amon, that same vicious smile remained, but this time he knew he was in trouble. Placing her hand on her hip, she said, "Who'd have thought that you'd be able to break his arm... Looks like you are stronger than I expected. Why don't we have some fun, just the two of us, eh?

Amon shivered as he raised his guard and kept his weary eyes permanently glued to her figure and odd stance. Her feet shoulder width apart and chest straight on with a blade held in both hands, tip pointing forward. Such a wide stance invited many openings, but Amon stayed his weapon— observing and keeping a cautious vigil.

On the other side of the platform, John grunted in pain while supporting his broken arm. Tearing off his sleeve, he hurriedly fashioned a makeshift sling with the fabric, securing the broken appendage to his chest.

Down a limb and weaponless, John took deep, steady breaths to calm his nerves and dull the ache. He observed his competitors every move, patiently waiting for the perfect opportunity to strike. He was well aware of Cecilia's craftiness, but Amon's hidden tenacity took him by surprise.

Cecilia was the first to make a move. She approached him while maintaining her stance. Just by looking at it, Amon could tell the sword was made for swift and precise stabs. Stabs that Amon didn't have the confidence to block faster than she could unleash them. His best choice was to stay out of her range. Amon and Cecilia were almost the same height, so their natural attacking range was more or less the same.

The only option left for him was to strike and retreat before she could retaliate. Otherwise, he would need to force her into a defensive position, to prevent her from overpowering him. Even though Cecilia held the advantage, she was injured and Amon had managed to keep up with them for two exchanges despite being the weakest—his injuries were minimal at best. The only way she'd be able to win was to eliminate Amon as quickly as possible so she could fight against John alone.

The three of them took a deep breath at the same time as they prepared for the next exchange.

Crack!

The tiles on the floor fractured as Cecilia stomped on them and shot towards Amon at breakneck speed. Amon narrowed his eyes and focused on her movements; her upper body was leaning forward, and her grip on the sword was tight. It was clear she would unleash a flurry of stabs the moment he entered her range.

When she got close enough, Amon also bolted towards her and with his glowing stick in hand, Amon swung at Cecilia's left temple. She sneered as she blocked his strike with ease. The sword and stick collided, making

Amon shudder in pain as he felt the bones in his hand start to break.

As she slashed at his neck, he lowered his head to dodge it, but a knee was already homing in on his face. Jumping to the right, he slid a few meters across the floor and jumped up again. This time, he was close to the platform's edge.

Cecilia raised her sword and charged at him again. With his back to the edge of the platform, Amon did his best to hold on against Cecilia as she attacked. Her stabs were like raindrops in a storm, mercilessly raining over Amon as he did his best to defend. They seemed to follow a pattern as the sword in her hands twisted and turned mid-strike, becoming unpredictable and increasingly deadly.

He was forced closer to the edge of the platform with each strike. John cursed and threw a cold stare at Amon; he had no choice but to rejoin the fight. He dashed towards Cecilia and punched her in the back, forcing her to reposition herself to avoid his attack. Amon decided to take advantage of the distraction and kicked John's ribcage with his right foot.

John grunted in pain as he was thrown off course, nearly hitting Cecilia and falling from the platform. Cecilia raised her sword to cut his neck, but Amon was already upon her once more. He was determined to prevent her from eliminating John.

"You're one troublesome brat!" she scoffed; her eyes had lost all playfulness and she exuded an aura of pure loathing.

Amon ignored her banter as he eyed John in his peripherals. The golden-haired boy was still on the ground, but he appeared to be reaching for something with his right hand. His qi was moving rapidly enough for Amon to feel it.

Good, it was close enough for him, Amon thought as he retreated once again.

With a look that could kill, Cecilia raised her sword and entered her stance again. This time, she wasn't going to hold back. Amon blinked, and the world seemed to stop for a moment. In the nanoseconds in which his eyes were closed, Cecilia had made her way upon him; her sword was only centimeters from piercing his heart.

Amon gritted his teeth and forcefully twisted his body, swinging his stick at her head. To his surprise, she showed no reaction at all, doubling down on her own strike.

Puchi!

He screamed as the sword pierced his left shoulder and a burning sensation and sharp pain took over his senses. His strike was still moving towards her head, but she simply raised her hand and held his arm.

"No more playing around," she growled, knocking the stick away from him, sending it spinning towards the end of the battle stage.

Cecilia twisted her sword, pushing it into his arm even more. He screamed in pain, almost wishing that the shield would activate, but it never did. Despite being on the verge of passing out, he was in no danger of dying, and thus the shield remained inactive.

As she pulled her sword away, Amon grabbed her wrist with an iron grip. A dumb smile was plastered on his sweat-drenched face.

What is this idiot doing? He's not strong enough to hold me here. I doubt he could... Wait!

Upon realizing what was happening, Cecilia's face paled and she kicked Amon in the chest, sending him sliding across the floor. She spun around to defend herself, but it was too late.

John's spear howled as it whipped through the air at an unstoppable speed. Its target—Cecilia.

Crack!

The spearhead stopped millimeters away from her spinal cord, instantly activating her protection shield.

"You shouldn't play so much, Cecilia," John teased, dismissively wiggling his spear in her face.

As she was pulled away from the platform, her number shattered in the curtain of light, leaving two remaining on its surface.

"I didn't think you'd escape her fury," John said as he pointed his spear at Amon. "The Middle and Outer Rings really have some interesting people."

Striking the floor with the shaft of the spear, the battered boy introduced himself as John Lucan. For someone of the Inner Sect to present themselves in such a manner was a sign of respect. Surprised at the gesture, Amon introduced himself as well, never moving his focus off of John.

The two of them readied their weapons again. Lunging at one another with their respective limbs tired and dysfunctional, they resumed battle. Their weapons clashed, and the sound of their performance echoed around them.

Raising his stick, Amon swung for his opponent. John dropped his spear, extending his right hand to catch Amon's arm and immediately followed up with a vicious kick to Amon's ribs that would certainly eliminate Amon once and for all.

Amon's mind was racing. He needed to act fast or he'd surely never get noticed by the elders.

Now's the time. I must endure this pain to win!

He gritted his teeth and struck John's incoming arm with a last-ditch effort palm strike, destroying his own hand in the process. The devastation from the impact shot excruciating pain up his arm into his mangled shoulder. John's arm was forced away as Amon descended his weapons strike with unbridled wrath.

Crack!

A layer of light formed, preventing John's skull from caving in. John's face went blank with confusion. The look in his eyes changed from determination to rage as he was pulled from the arena.

TO THE SECOND ROUND

I won... I won!

Amon stared at the curtain of light in disbelief. He could feel his arm going numb, but he didn't care. The cheering crowd erupted into a roar sending adrenaline pulsing through him. Tears filled his eyes and a temporary deafness silenced the thunderous applause.

"Congratulations number forty-two! You may return to the waiting hall to recover," the announcer's voice chimed, breaking Amon's stupor.

He made his way back to the waiting area, where a purple-clad young woman was waiting for him. She gave him a congratulatory round of applause and a cheerful smile before taking the lead.

"Follow me to the medical center, young challenger."

Amon lightly nodded, holding his shoulder tightly he followed her. She brought Amon through a side door, taking him down a long hallway full of rooms. The lighting was dim, hardly bright enough to reveal the silhouette of the doors lining either side. Most of them were closed; no doubt occupied. Amon could only guess how many injured the staff had to deal with.

The woman ushered Amon into a compact room. A single bed was tucked away into a corner and it smelled of dampness, but he cared little for luxury and comforts for the time being.

"An elder from our medical center will be with you posthaste. We'll have you up and about in no time!" the attendant cheerfully reassured him as she closed the door with a soft thump.

Amon waited until her receding footsteps grew faint and spread his divine sense. Except for the recovering patients a few doors down, his divine sense didn't pick up any other presences. He rested his back against the cold walls, holding the stick tightly.

"Lya!" he shouted through gritted teeth, his voice hoarse and harsh to the ear.

"You called?" a mockingly gentle and faux sweetness answered.

157

"Are you insane?" Amon's eyes were bloodshot and brimming with fury as he roared at the metal ring. "A freaking stick!?"

"You are correct! That is indeed a stick, a damn fine one at that. What of it?"

"You saw what happened If I had a sword—"

"If you had a sword, your opponents would have jumped you like rabid dogs! You only managed to make it to the end partly because of luck and skill, but more so because they saw you as little more than a fool and not a threat," she stated nonchalantly. "Just consider it training for those moments when you are forced to defend yourself without a proper weapon. In the heat of battle, anything can happen. Your weapon could break or your opponent could disarm you. What will you do then? Will you mope about and offer your helpless head on a silver platter? Or will you pick up whatever tool is available to you and seize the day?"

"But still—"

"No buts. You're lucky I even gave you a stick in the first place. I should have sent you in with naught but what your mother gave you—bare hands and nothing more. Besides, the pressure of fighting without your accustomed weapon forced you to hone your survival instincts. All I see are positives from this whole ordeal. Am I wrong?" she snapped at him.

"No," he answered honestly, his ears reddened slightly. "I don't know what happened. Things just started clicking in my head as I thought about what to do."

"It is becoming almost instinctual to you, which is definitely an improvement," Lya said. "Regardless, you impressed me with how you handled that fight. You should keep it up and I'm sure making the quarterfinals is of little issue to you now."

Amon nodded happily, savouring the compliment.

"But this was just a one off thing right? Please tell me I can use my sword in the next round."

A wicked grin curling up her lips.

"Not a chance in the world."

The sound of approaching footsteps prevented Amon from complaining. He promptly swallowed his grievances and sat on the bed as a middle-aged man entered the room. Behind him, the attendant gave a cheerful wave before respectfully closing the door, ensuring their privacy.

"Luckily, it stopped before the bone," the man said, examining Amon's shoulder.

He signaled to the attendant as she searched inside a medical box for a moment before recovering a red pill.

"Take this and rest. It won't fully heal you in time, but at least you'll be able to move your arm to a degree," the man said before hurriedly leaving the room.

"You can use this room for tonight, sir challenger. The second round will begin tomorrow. Hopefully, we won't have to see you here again!" the woman said rushing off to catch up with the elder.

Exhausted, he looked at the pill and ate it without much concern, closing his eyes as he fell asleep.

❋ ❋ ❋

A deep, cold voice sounded in Jake's mind, making him shudder. It had been only a few months since Jake had been told of the existence of Nemeus, but he still couldn't get used to the feeling of someone directly injecting their words into his brain.

"What is it?" Jake asked in a low voice, keeping his eyes on the platforms.

"What did you think of that boy?" Nemeus questioned.

"What boy?" Jake asked, distracted.

He had been focusing most of his attention on a single platform, where a fierce fight was taking place. Jake was tense as he watched and his black eyes couldn't hide his worry.

"The grey-haired one that won a few minutes ago," Nemeus answered.

Jake pondered for a moment, before carefully choosing his words.

"His performance was decent. Both of his opponents were stronger than him, but his victory was accomplished using only his wits and basic skills," Jake calmly recalled. "He has a very good foundation."

"When you met him before, did he look so well-trained to you?" Nemeus asked.

"Actually... no. He hadn't even reached body tempering, and he seemed rather frail." Jake knitted his brows as he thought. "In regards to his bearing, he was a completely different person."

"Certainly it's not possible to go from a weakling to a warrior in only seven months, is it?

"Not unless you are abnormally talented, or means unknown to me," Jake said with a thoughtful expression. "I really don't know how he managed to do it; his talent back then was horrible."

Jake waited for Nemeus to continue his interrogation, but only silence came. Nemeus already knew everything he needed to know about Amon. He should have had an extremely thick nebula surrounding his aster. Yet, when Nemeus probed him with his divine sense, he saw no nebula at all. At that moment, all of his doubts had been cast away—Amon Kressler was using a forbidden technique that had been banished four centuries ago.

A light knocking on the door awoke Amon the next morning.

He felt strangely energetic and refreshed—likely a side effect of the red pill. The wound on his shoulder had closed, but a deep pain prevented him from using full range of motion or abrupt movements.

At least I can use it at all, he thought to himself before asking his visitor to hold a moment.

He washed his face thoroughly and changed into a fresh set of robes. At last presentable, Amon opened the door to see the same attendant from yesterday. They exchanged pleasantries as the young woman explained the reason for her early-morning visit.

"I'm here to escort you to the waiting hall. Whenever you are ready, please follow me," she said cheerfully. "Make sure you do not leave anything valuable behind. The medical center is not responsible for any lost or stolen possessions."

Amon smiled wryly and exited the room; stick in hand and nothing else. He followed her closely, observing the now mostly vacant rooms in the hallway.

"How generous your sect is, wasting all these resources on canon fodder," Lya said. Her voice sounded in his head, mockery dripping from every syllable. "Such a waste, and this was just the first day of the competition. I imagine the elders will be mourning the dent in their finances for some time."

He remained silent. In his mind, Amon agreed with Lya's opinion but the short walk to the waiting hall was coming to an end. The attendant held the door open and gestured for him to enter with a curt nod. He thanked her and entered, taking in the interior.

The spacious waiting hall was eerily quiet, a complete contrast to the absurdity of yesterday. There weren't many individuals inside; thirty to be exact. However, tensions were high and he could feel it like a tingling on his skin. They kept their distance, eyeing the competition and trying to get a read.

The current competitors were well equipped and eager to perform. Colorful and exotic garb worn beneath armor worth their weight in gold was, if nothing else, a clear indication that personal wealth was an absolute requirement for cultivation. Compared to himself—especially his "weapon" of choice—the disparity was blatantly embarrassing.

There were however two exceptions that stood out from the Inner Ring members. One was a tall woman sporting a slender frame with essentially tatters hanging from her shoulders. Tucked away in the far corner, her sea-green gaze was locked to the ceiling, glazed over with boredom. Her legs bounced to the tune of an imaginary song, causing her flowing golden hair to shift with each beat. Amon watched her for a moment, entranced by her quirkiness, but shifted his attention to the man blending into the shadows closeby.

His features were concealed by the darkness, except for a pair of unnerving pupils that flicked about the hall. A black cloak lined with raven feathers completed the rest of his ensemble, obscuring even the shape of his body. The other contestants kept their distance, likely due to the frigid aura he emitted and the air of mystery about him.

"Keep your eye on him, Amon. There's something familiar about his aura. It reeks of danger."

Amon agreed. An uneasy feeling took hold of him when he moved anywhere near the man, so he steered clear. He continued on, but felt a chill run down his spine. As he walked past, the man had set his cold gaze upon the youth.

While Amon was contemplating the familiarity of how he felt, someone slammed into his shoulder with their own. He winced in pain before turning to see Erin's ridiculous smile.

"It really is you, old man," Erin snorted.

"Nice seeing you, Erin."

"It's a pity you stopped dying your hair. It hurts my eyes seeing that awful hair."

"One more reason to keep it that way," Amon retorted, not hesitating in the slightest.

Erin narrowed his eyes, carefully looking at Amon from head to toe. There was something strange. Erin couldn't believe when he first heard that an ashen-haired boy with golden eyes had beaten both Cecilia Faye and John Lucan in a three-way battle.

Erin remembered a day a few months ago when Amber came crying to him, insisting that Amon had tried to kill her. After calming her down, she explained that Amon has scored five hundred units and that he has reached the body tempering stage. Of course, at the time, Erin didn't believe that someone as useless as Amon could cause even a scratch. Nevertheless, he vowed to avenge Amber, but first he trained for the tournament.

"I'll be sure to make you pay for what you did to Amber," Erin said with a voice as chilling as his gaze.

"You're welcome to try," he said firmly, showing no fear at all.

Erin's eyes turned even colder for a moment.

Erin turned his head away and moved to a corner. He sat with his legs crossed and started breathing deeply, trying to calm himself. He had beaten people stronger than him to get to the second round. He had proved that, despite his young age, he did not lose in talent to anyone in the Inner Ring. Losing his mind to the rage he felt would only drag him down during his next fight.

Nevertheless, behind all of the blazing rage he felt, there was surprise and some apprehension. Whatever Amon had done was certainly unorthodox. This meant that he was dangerous. Erin would not let his pride blind him in a fight with an opponent of unknown strength. He would take Amon out with all he had.

"Congratulations to all of you for advancing to the second round!" a serene voice echoed through the hall.

It was the same voice from the previous day, but this time it was accompanied by its owner, Richard Layn. He was greeted by the crowd with a bow as they let out a cultish chime, "We greet the third elder."

"The second round will be a standard duel. The thirty-two of you will draw lots to decide the matchings. You'll only have one opponent this round,

161

so every move counts."

Richard dismissed them and the participants quickly formed a line and crossed the golden gates, being cheered on by the crowd. Richard's eyes narrowed, focusing on a man in a black, hooded robe at the end of the line. Using his divine sense, he was able to identify the young man. As the man walked by, Richard spoke to him in a low voice.

"It's good to see that you're okay."

The man stopped for a moment, turning to look at Richard. He then gave a deep bow and turned away without saying a word.

Pity was all that showed in the eyes of Richard Layn as he watched the man walk away.

"Truly a stubborn family. All of them," he sighed, shaking his head.

Amon squinted at the strong light. As his pupils adjusted to the brightness, he saw that there were fewer platforms in the interior of the arena than in the first round. From the original thirty-two, only eight remained and they were positioned perfectly in front of a long black table decorated with a golden box. The participants were instructed to approach the box and touch it to obtain a number.

First in line was a young man with scarlet hair. As he got closer to the object, his hair was brightly illuminated, resembling a still, roaring flame. The moment his fingers touched it, a click sounded, and a huge number "6" was projected above it. The youth was then directed to sit in one of the luxuriously cushioned seats as the next in line approached the table.

Soon after it was Amon's turn. Showing no hesitation, he firmly grasped the box causing it to shudder as a wave of heat spread through his fingers. The golden cube went still and projected a number "6" into the air.

Seems like I'll be facing that red-haired guy.

Amon turned to look at his opponent. His red silk uniform was embroidered with golden threads. They were seemingly under a bit of pressure from his tightly packed muscles bulging beneath their construction. An unwavering glint of pride coddled the young man's energetic eyes; the air about him was definitely filled with overbearing confidence and unrestricted arrogance. Using his divine sense, Amon was able to determine that his opponent was in the late stages of body tempering, teetering on the cusp of the Refinement realm. His power level seemed to exceed Cecilia's without a doubt. Amon would have to rely on his wits and bolster his resolve to survive this next fight.

The hooded man followed the same procedure as the others, obtaining the number "1" before taking a seat near the other contestants.

"As you might have guessed, the duels will be between the competitors that drew the same number. The sixteen competitors that drew numbers one through eight, please proceed to their respective platforms," Richard announced.

As they made their way to the platform, Amon spotted the man in a hooded, black robe. He eyed him for a moment as he climbed onto his assigned platform and waited for his opponent.

Huh? Why is he dressed that way? Does he really not want anyone to know who he is or is it an intimidation tactic?

As the man in black clambered awkwardly onto the platform, he slapped his bottomless pouch. Retrieving a golden buckler and and a silver sword, he lightly tapped them together, making a higher pitched *clang* echoed around him. Both objects were polished to the point where their surfaces reflected even the smallest amount of light that hit them, blinding the competitors as well as the crowd. Fascinated by his mysterious presentation, Amon decided to refer to him as "One" and the scarlet-haired man in front of him he would name "Blaze" for obvious reasons.

Facing One was a beautiful girl in her late teens. Her silky black hair fell over her shoulders like a waterfall, and her charming dark eyes were leagues above mesmerizing. Her delicate brows were deeply furrowed as she looked at the man in front of her with apprehension. Like many others, she had special clothing for the competition. Her white robe stopped just above her knees and was tapered at her waist as if bound by a corset. Its sleeves hung only a few inches above her wrists and flared out like a half-bloomed lotus flower.

Oddly enough, she lacked a weapon. Amon found it fascinating that she had high confidence in her fighting skills. One had to be an incredible expert in hand-to-hand combat to win such a competition with no weapon; he knew that she shouldn't be underestimated.

"Clara White," the girl declared with a polite bow.

To some, her politeness was unwarranted, but she knew better. The remaining cultivators were quite powerful. If they did not come from the Inner Ring, it meant that their talent surpassed that of their highly privileged peers. She would give respect where respect was due, and the underprivileged fighters had definitely earned her respect.

One didn't utter a word. Instead, he returned her bow and prepared his stance. Clara pouted a bit, but took no offense; not everyone's actions were as good-willed as her own.

"Let the second round begin!" the third elder shouted, causing some to wake from their analyzing trances.

Clara kicked the ground and rushed to One's position. She wouldn't let him force her into a passive position. She raised a fist and threw a punch at his face.

Clang!

The buckler rang like a bell as it intercepted the punch. Raising her other fist, she tried to punch him again, but his stance was incredibly solid. Forced to give up, she twisted her body and hastily dodged as the sword violently whistled through the air, barely missing her.

Using the momentum she gained, she did a quick spin and kicked at the side of his head, but he simply ducked to avoid her attack. His hood fluttered lightly from the near hit as he stabilized his stance and swung at her again.

Annoyed at his simple moves, Clara aimed her fist at his wrist lightning speed. With immaculate precision, her fist smashed into One's wrist, deflecting his strike. Bones cracked upon impact, causing a satisfying grin to grace her face.

Clink!

The sword fell to the floor with a heavy *thud*. Before Clara could enjoy the small victory, a knee hit her chest, and she lost her balance. One didn't give Clara a chance to correct her stance. He advanced with a shield bash forcing a pig-like grunt to escape her mouth as she was hit in the stomach and tossed across the platform.

As Amon watched on, he noticed that he could feel a slight movement of qi every time One moved the shield. It seemed as though the qi itself was sustaining the shield, not his arm.

Clara fell back even further, trying to retrieve her balance. She narrowed her eyes as she gazed at One, trying to find a way to deal with him. That short exchange was enough for her to determine how tough of an opponent he was. He had a strong defense and good movements. He also knew how to use her openings to his advantage without giving any openings of his own.

The only way Clara would be able to deal with such a fighter would be to force him into a situation where he couldn't help but give her an opening. She would have to overwhelm him or bait him into attacking her, as she had done just now. Thankfully, she now held the upper hand in the fight.

To her surprise, however, One retrieved his fallen sword with the very hand that she had smashed.

W-what's going on? He shouldn't even be able to wiggle his fingers, let alone pick up a sword, she thought, thoroughly confused.

Her thoughts were cut short when the floor cracked beneath One's feet as he shot towards her like a cannonball, curling up behind his shield.

Clara quickly jumped to her left. If she jumped right, One might strike at her with his sword. A fierce wind hit her face as he flew past her. When he stomped the floor to bring himself to a halt, Clara rushed to his direction, trying to attack his exposed back.

She came crashing down on him, sending a flurry of punches and kicks. As she stepped forward, he stepped back, keeping the distance between them the same while skillfully parrying her attacks. Clara narrowed her eyes as she punched slightly to her left on purpose. One promptly moved his shield to his right to block the strike. Clara smiled as she raised her right knee, kicking his shield even more to his right. One's stance was broken as his arm forcefully moved, exposing his body. As Clara was about to give him a punch that would ensure her victory, her smile disappeared.

No way, she thought as she saw why he had been defending this entire time—his left arm was grasping nothing.

Crack!

A layer of light surged from her suddenly. Clara looked in shock as she turned her head to see a shiny sword hovering on the air, that incredibly sharp blade mere millimeters away from her neck. She was dumbstruck as the sword slowly hovered back to the man, circling around him slowly.

"What insane control," she muttered. "Did you drop it while you were rushing to me?"

As she expected, One said nothing, but only gave a nod before climbing down from the platform. Amon kept his eyes glued on him the whole time. A peculiar feeling washed over him, but he brushed it off.

Once the matches were done, competitors with numbers five through eight were instructed to take place on the platforms. Amon stared at Blaze, ready to battle. In silence, both jumped into a platform, never taking their eyes away from each other. Amon firmly grasped the stick in his hands as Blaze took a sabre from his bottomless pouch.

"You may start!"

As Blaze rushed to him, Amon waved his stick, imbuing it with qi. Blaze's eyes ignited with a thirst, as his arm and sabre extended out to his side. He gave a savage smile as he swung at Amon.

Leaping directly in front of Amon, Blaze rotated his shoulder arcing the sabre into an overhead slash. The blade howled, cutting through the air at blinding speed. Amon's pupils constricted as he looked at the incoming attack. It certainly contained absurd power and speed, but it was also a simple downward slash, nothing more.

Amon slightly bent his knee to stabilize his stance. He held the glowing stick with both hands and positioned it above his head, slightly tilted down over his right shoulder. Amon took a deep breath preparing himself for the impact that was to come.

Bak!

The sabre hit the stick with terrifying strength. Amon felt his hands numbing and bones creaking as he forcefully tilted the stick even more to the right. The sabre slid down the stick and the strike hit the floor by his side.

Crack!

The sabre sunk deeply on the floor, creating a web of cracks around it. Blaze seemed somewhat surprised at how his attack had been deflected, but he had no chance to dwell on the thought as a glowing stick was coming at his head.

He forcefully pulled the sabre out of the floor, ripping out huge chunks of stone with it as he vaulted backwards into the air. The power of his landing crushed the platform and a cloud of dust emitted into the air, construing the cold stare that Blaze gave Amon.

Despite deflecting the attack, the damage was done. Amon's body was already feeling the repercussions from attempting to block an all out attack from this offensive behemoth. Amon stared at his opponent holding the resolve to not show his current state of wellbeing. The wound on his left shoulder was flaring up, but he could still move without difficulty regard-

165

less of the pain.

"I expected more," Amon sneered.

Amon began to understand how his foe operated in battle. When Amon fought Cecilia, she was also overconfident in her combat prowess, but her fighting style relied on using cunning and precise moves. Her downfall was imminent the second she lost her temper and dropped her guard.

Blaze, on the other hand, was used to crushing all opposition with brute strength, ending his battles swiftly. He would never allow his foes the time or space needed to formulate a strategy to overtake him. Amon's best chance of surviving this fight was to break Blaze's confidence for a split second, using his indomitable track record against him.

His straightforward style was predictable, but also incredibly efficient. A simple style meant faster training. As a result, his form and offense were unparalleled. Blaze's speed and power would make up for any deficiencies in it.

Blaze knitted his brows at Amon's mocking, but said nothing. He assumed his power stance again before slowly approaching Amon. When he was two meters away from Amon, he abruptly started running circles around him, his bloodshot eyes lusting for the first sign of an opening in Amon's guard. He didn't know how much pain Amon was in just from deflecting his strike. If he knew, he would be sending a barrage of attacks that would certainly eliminate Amon. He had bought Amon's bluff, giving Amon valuable time to recover and plan his next move.

If Amon did not take control of this battle, he would miss his one window of opportunity. Victory hung in the balance entirely on whether or not Blaze would fall for Amon's final gambit.

Two more exchanges, he thought, thinking of a plan.

Amon took a step forward with his right foot, and Blaze's eyes rekindled their desire to obliterate Amon. He sprung into striking range of Amon, sending a horizontal strike honing in on his exposed left side. Predicting his opponent's assault on the first opening given, Amon quickly took a small step back. The sabre hit the air millimeters away from his nose, sending a huge blast of wind to Amon's face, causing his ashen hair to whip about.

The sabre did not stop after it missed Amon, leaving Blaze vulnerable. Blaze's face fell as Amon's stick came whistling through the air at his head. He hurriedly twisted his body and retreated, avoiding the attack.

Blaze bit his lip, pissed off that this kid was toying with him. Amon recognized that his impatience and frustrations had already begun to influence his actions. He shot towards Blaze with a ferocious look on his golden eyes. Amon jumped as he aimed his stick at the Blaze's head, putting his all into the strike.

Pak!

Blaze blocked the strike with his sabre, using his free hand to reinforce the back of the blade. The floor started cracking at his feet. Amon might be weaker than he was, but that didn't mean he was not incredibly strong.

Amon's feet touched the ground and he brought his face closer to Blaze's, leaning all of his weight into his weapon.

"What a waste of my time," Amon taunted.

Blaze's eyes flashed with rage as the muscles in his arms bulged. Then, he forcefully pushed his sabre to the side, trying to break Amon's stance. That was the emotionally charged mistake that Amon was looking for. He couldn't help but give a wry smile as he took a step back. He had been on the receiving end of such a cheap move before and knew how frustrating it was. The sabre screamed through the air as it swung violently, missing its target once again. Amon took a step forward with his weapon in hand.

Blaze looked dumbstruck as he realized his mistake. In that final fit of rage, he stepped forward with the wrong leg for his stance. Unable to block or avoid the incoming attack, he accepted his fate as Amon's strike descended from the heavens.

Crack!

Amon gave a long sigh as Blaze was dragged away by the light. He had won, but he didn't feel satisfied. This fight was lackluster at best and he longed for a challenge similar to his previous battle. His opponent was far above him in terms of strength, but he also had a fatal weakness in his pride.

He wasn't sure what use experiencing the same repeating outcomes actually gave him going forward, if any at all. He was winning, but his opponents weren't capable of giving him a challenge to prove himself.

He slowly descended from the platform in deep contemplation, before heading back to the waiting hall, his body still numb.

"Real fights are to the death, Amon," Lya declared. "You should learn to enjoy every victory, no matter how dull they might have been. Remember, every fight you win is another day you get to live."

LINES THAT CAN'T BE CROSSED

In the medical center of the arena, Daniel sat on a bed, slowly recovering from his wounds. He had already taken a recovery pill earlier in the day, so his broken wrist was mending nicely. He took the hood off of his head, showing an abnormally pale face and sunken eyes. He glanced at the sword on the floor, lying at his feet. Its blade hummed before it rose up and hovered around him as if answering a call.

Looking uninterested, he sent it flying through the room. While controlling the flying blade, he tracked the movements of its numerous strings of light invoked by his qi. Daniel was able to alternate the direction of his qi infused blade into a flurry of slashes. This form of offense lacked strength but was more than enough to draw blood in a sneak attack, allowing him to catch his foe off guard.

Natasha had been right. Using the qi to forcefully move his right arm made it lack strength and finesse. Still, just as she said, it was enough for simple movements. Because of this, Daniel had decided to use a shield to compensate for his weakness. He could also use the qi to directly move the shield in dire situations instead of using his arm. It was a good way to hide the deficiencies he had.

He looked at his left arm, trying to close his fingers. A stinging pain led him to give up on the idea, but he couldn't help but smile. He had bluffed when Clara broke his wrist. He had used qi to control his sword and pretend he had grabbed it with his injured hand. It had been enough to confuse her and give him an opening.

Daniel closed his eyes, but he couldn't rest yet. Soon enough, the final phase of the second round would start. He needed to win this promotion no matter what, but, as he thought of that, a youthful face made its way into his mind.

What happened to you, Amon?

When he saw him in the waiting hall, he had to make an incredible effort to hide his agitation. Amon was far too different from what he remembered.

He didn't dye his hair anymore, and he walked with his head held high, carefully analyzing everything around him, similar to that of a seasoned warrior. There was an air of confidence that exuded from his being; one that Daniel had never seen in all the years they had known each other.

Additionally, he somehow managed to get into body tempering and, considering his opponents in the competition, it had not been a trivial tempering.

How could he have changed so much in less than a year?

Daniel's mind was racing. He was happy that Amon was growing up, but he knew it had come at a cost.

Unfortunately, Daniel had no desire to talk to him until the competition was over. Daniel had to send his father a message, and he would. He would win the competition and get to the Inner Sect, but he was going to be sure that he did it without elevating his family's name in the process. He refused to play his father's game and let him profit from it. It would be an empty victory, but Daniel didn't mind. Pissing off his father would be worth it.

It would be an empty victory; nothing but a dull, childish move, but Daniel didn't mind. A victory over his father was a victory nonetheless. If this ruse could make his father knit his brows for even a second, it would have been worth it, because Daniel had grown to hate his father.

For the first time since he was born, he wished nothing but misery to one person.

Nemeus used his divine sense to probe Amon Kressler as he slowly left the platform. In the boundless void of red, his scarlet eyes shone as he focused on the ring the boy wore on his finger.

Nemeus was long past the point of simply sensing qi with his divine sense. Whatever the towering man sought to know, the world presented itself to him in gold and black. There was no matter, there was only the divine language.

Arthur had told Nemeus that if one went deep enough, it would be possible to read the inner thoughts of any individual; this could possibly include reading the markings of their soul. As such, Nemeus was easily able to look past Lya's illusion, seeing the true form of the ring in Amon's finger. He narrowed his eyes and his fiery mane stood on end as he sent an enraged bellow.

"Lya!" he called, transmitting his voice to the ring.

His deep voice seemed more like the howling of a beast than of a human. Still, what answered Nemeus was silence. His scarlet eyes were bloodshot as he started to growl and the muscles in his body bulged.

"LYA!"

The dark-red void started trembling as if it was going to shatter when Nemeus howled her name again. His deep voice echoed through space for a long time, becoming more distorted as it slowly faded away into silence yet again.

Inside Alexei's ring, Lya shuddered. This was not a good time nor place for Nemeus to finally find her. She couldn't blame Nemeus for acting that way. A pensive look showed on her face before she waved her hands, forming an invisible air ripple.

When Nemeus sensed the ripple, he took a deep breath, calming himself. His rage was mostly gone, but the savage look in his eyes remained. A wickedly blank expression fell upon him and he softly spoke once more.

"Ignore me if you want. Let's see how this ends up for you."

With his eyes closed, he focused on sending her a message that only she would receive. He opened his eyes as his gaze fell on the shiny box lying on the table and a bloodthirsty smile curled onto his face, revealing a sharp row of fangs. Nemeus was a beast enjoying the thrill of the hunt.

"Eh?" Amon suddenly shuddered as his ashen hair stood on end.

He stopped in his tracks as he walked to the waiting hall. He had a bad feeling. He turned his eyes to the purple cabin where the important guests were watching the competition, but the feeling soon faded away. Seconds later, his finger started to itch and the ring seemed somewhat hot, but it only lasted for a moment. Amon was confused as he started walking again, picking up his pace.

"Lya?" he asked in a low voice as he passed through the gates

When Lya failed to answer, a slight panic ran through his veins.

"Is everything okay?" Amon asked worriedly.

"Yes, don't worry," Lya's voice echoed in his mind, calming him down a bit. "Just... be careful in the next fight."

With a slight nod, Amon made his way into the waiting hall where he was greeted by the same nurse from the day before. She escorted him to a room and told him to rest until the next phase. Amon jumped on the bed and closed his eyes, trying to relax his aching body. He replayed his previous battles in his mind, trying to find something he could have improved. After a short moment, his hands started trembling without him noticing. He somehow felt excited as he remembered the look in Erin's eyes when he threatened him.

"I sure hope we face each other," Amon mumbled through an enormous grin.

Knock! Knock!

The nurse came to escort Amon to the arena. It had only been a couple of hours since his fight had ended. Since none of the winners had any serious injuries, the break was rather short.

When he got to the hall, there were fifteen competitors already waiting; Erin included. The two boys locked eyes, staring each other down in both displeasure and eagerness. The only thing that broke their concentration was the voice of the third elder, announcing that they would begin the pairing shortly.

"The eight winners in the next fights will be guaranteed entrance to the Inner Sect. Tomorrow they will compete for extra prizes from the sect. The losing eight will also compete tomorrow for the remaining two slots of promotion," the third elder sent them a long and piercing glance.

"Best of luck to the lot of you," he said with a gentle smile.

A few spots ahead of him, One stood in the line, still disguised in his usual dark, hooded attire. Amon was almost sure it was Daniel, even if he hadn't seen his face. Insecurities surged through him.

Why hasn't he contacted me? Is he mad because I almost got us killed? Does he think I'm just a weak kid who doesn't deserve his attention? Maybe it's because I didn't visit him...

Sadness overtook him, nagging him to call out to Daniel. At that moment, the man turned to him, but only darkness showed its face. The chilling aura he emitted caused Amon more uncertainty, but he steeled himself.

As he was about to call Daniel, the man put a finger in front of his face, signaling Amon to keep quiet. Amon was dumbstruck, and in his moment of confusion, the line started moving. Amon's curiosity turned into a mindless stupor. He followed the line as it moved without noticing he wasn't moving at all.

The feeling from before resurfaced. Something bad was about to happen. He looked at the purple cabin again, and the feeling intensified. He took a deep breath, trying to calm himself with his eyes closed.

Shaking his head, he regained control over his feelings. He had to focus —he had to win. He closed his fist tightly as the competitors started to touch the box and their numbers started to shine.

Erin was one of the first in line. When it was his turn, he walked with firm steps to the box and grabbed it firmly. The golden light shone on him like a beacon, and his red clothes seemed to be set ablaze as a huge number "4" was projected above him.

After Erin, was One. Like a few hours before, he seemed to slide to the box, touching it with his left hand. He got number 1, so he would be the first to fight. As he saw that Amon's senses seemed to explode.

"What the hell is happening?" he thought, lost in confusion. Why was he having such a bad premonition?

"I need to get number four," he started mumbling to himself nonstop as he approached the box.

Time seemed to slow down as Amon looked at that golden box. He extended his fingers to it, during what seemed like an eternity. He felt the coldness of the box as he grabbed it, looking at how the light shone through his fingers, falling on his face.

Then, the box flashed once, and Amon looked in shock to the number above him.

"BASTARD!" he heard Lya screaming with all her might inside his mind.

She realized she had made a mistake. Amon seemed to pay it no mind.

In fact, her words came hardly at a whisper. Though, nothing else seemed to phase him either—Amon had lost the capacity to think as he looked at the number floating above his head.

Daniel was dumbstruck as he saw the number floating above Amon's head. Like Amon, he had lost all sense of his surroundings, frozen in time as the world went on around them.

"Ha.. haha... hahahahaha!"

Daniel's maniacal laugh startled a few and others looked on pity, fearing that he had lost his mind due to the stress of the competition. It was a strange filled with regret and anger. Though they couldn't see his face, everyone was certain he was nearly in tears. Not from joy, but from undeniable misery.

Amon, however, remained silent. He stared at his lifelong friend, hoping it was a sick illusion created by Lya. Despite their intentions to win, they both knew that neither of them could go on with this fight.

Daniel jumped to a platform. His black robes and cloak fluttered in the wind, flapping behind his back like dark wings. He landed heavily on the platform, raising a cloud of dust that hid him.

"Let's end this already," he said with a hoarse voice.

Amon didn't show reaction at first, still looking at Daniel with sadness. Then, he lowered his head and slowly walked to the platform. His body moped and drooped, disheartened by the tragedy about to unfold.

Seeing him like this made Daniel even more upset. Couldn't he have just lost a fight to a strong opponent? Couldn't he have given it his all, climbing as high as he could before he fell?

He had a sour taste in his mouth as he looked at the boy in front of him. He had grown taller since they last saw each other. His muscles were well defined under his clothes, even if not fully developed. His features were refined and developed and it was clear that puberty had been kind to him. However, at this moment, Amon resembled the pitiful kid Daniel threw on the raft during the Scavenging.

"You may begin," the third elder's voice echoed in their ears, but none of them moved.

This was it. His journey to redemption would end here. Even if he won the next fight and got in the top ten, it would be meaningless. Being the champion was all that mattered. He looked into Amon's eyes as he pulled his hood away from his face. His black hair was a mess, and his dark eyes were sunken deep into his colorless face. It was clear he hadn't slept in days.

"We had a good time," he said with a weary smile.

I was right... One was Daniel afterall.

Amon's eyes welled up with tears. This was the first time he had cried in a long time.

Amon was family to Daniel, and Daniel would rather be kicked out of the sect than get in the way of his growth. He refused to be like Lawrence, who cared about nothing but strength. This was a line he couldn't cross.

He'd rather be a decent person than a decent cultivator.

Daniel gave a sigh as he raised his left hand in the air. He gave Amon a sincere smile as he said with a low voice, "Sorry I didn't speak with you before; I had a lot going on. It's good to see you're okay," his smile widened before he turned to face the third elder. He opened his mouth, uttering words he would never regret, "I conc—"

Pak!

Something hit his wrist with unbelievable strength. Daniel could feel his bones creaking, almost breaking again. He couldn't hide his surprise as he looked at the floor beneath his feet. The glowing stick that had been thrown at his hand was lying there; its light dimming before it turned back to normal.

Incredulous, Daniel turned to look at Amon. The young boy's face was red with anger, his breathing was rapid and he was prepared to fight.

"Don't you dare!" Amon shouted, extending his right hand, and the stick on the floor trembled before returning to him. "I'll never forgive you if you go easy on me!" Amon shouted.

He refused to let Daniel sacrifice himself for his sake again. He owed Daniel his life. Yet, even in his tired stupor, Daniel continued to throw himself to the wolves for Amon's sake.

I can't, no, I won't take it anymore, Amon vowed to himself. *I can't continue to let everyone give up their lives for me. I won't be weak, not even against Daniel.*

"Amon, I—"

"Take out your sword and shield," the young cultivator demanded through pursed lips.

Daniel didn't react. Tears fell from his eyes in sadness, yet a smile lazily appeared.

This kid... he's truly something special, Daniel chuckled as the thought crossed his mind.

"Take out your sword and shield!"

Daniel was shocked that Amon would get so heated, but he understood. Amon wanted to prove himself worthy. He wanted to belong and be accepted. He knew Amon needed this fight as much as Daniel wanted revenge on his father. With an energetic smirk, Daniel scoffed at Amon's newfound arrogance.

"Alright, kid. Show me what you've got."

Amon kicked off the ground, shooting towards Daniel. His ashen hair was like a puff of smoke zipping about as he covered the distance between them in a heartbeat. Daniel was surprised when he saw those golden eyes so close to his face after a split-second. He instinctively raised his shield to cover his body.

Clang!

The glowing stick hit the golden shield with tremendous force. Daniel rebalanced himself as Amon forced down his strike. Then, as quickly as he had come, he retreated.

How the hell did he manage to get to this level in less than a year? Daniel pondered, examining Amon carefully. He knew his junior brother had gotten stronger, but he never imagined it was to such a degree.

Amon's eyes glinted as he approached again. His stick whooshed through the air like an airborne baseball bat. This time, Daniel was ready. He stomped the floor and held his stance as the strike hit his shield.

CLANG!

This strike was even stronger. Daniel could actually feel the shield trembling for a moment and he was forced to take a step back, but this time he didn't have the excuse of not being ready. The shock in his eyes grew stronger as Amon unleashed a flurry of attacks, making Daniel retreat to the edge of the platform.

In this fight, Amon didn't care about strategies. He didn't care about giving or creating openings. He didn't care about being witty and cunning. He didn't care about victory. He pushed Daniel back step by step because he wanted to make a point. This was what he cared about the most in this fight. As long as that point came across, he didn't mind the results.

Daniel gritted his teeth as he held his ground. Keeping his eyes on Amon, he took a step forward instead of retreating. With a shield bash, he pushed Amon away, but as soon as Amon's feet touched the ground, he jumped forward again, not giving Daniel a chance to breathe. Amon was in a frenzy as his face reddened. He didn't hold back at all in his strikes, and it seemed like Daniel had no chance to counter.

In truth, Daniel had many chances to strike back, but when he saw Amon's attitude he understood what he wanted. Daniel welcomed his intentions with open arms as he never once looked away from Amon's eyes.

He wanted to understand him better. He wanted to see how much he had changed. Daniel wanted to give Amon a chance to prove himself. Having made up his mind, Daniel faced Amon's attacks head-on.

Daniel took a deep breath, and Amon seemed to understand. He stopped his attacks and took a step back, breathing heavily. His chest heaved up and down as he tried to recover and beads of sweat cascaded from his forehead.

Resuming his stance, Daniel stomped the floor, causing it to crack under his feet. He bent his knees to stabilize his balance, as he prepared his shield to nullify whatever this *new* Amon had in store for him.

Amon looked at him calmly, waiting. When Daniel was ready, he gave Amon a slight nod. Amon closed his eyes for a moment, focusing. Awakening from his state of zen, he threw his stick to the side and closed his right hand into a fist. Launching off the platform, he bolted towards Daniel, his eyes shining with resolve. Amon threw a punch with all the strength he could muster.

BANG!

The shield resonated a deafening ring throughout the arena, as

Amon's fist collided with it. Blanketed from the thunderous clash, Amon heard a grotesque *crack*. He hid the pain in his eyes as he forcefully pulled apart his balled up fist. His fingers were trembling, bent in awkward angles, and the skin on his knuckles had been torn away. Blood started seeping out from the injury, flowing down his arm.

Slightly in shock, Amon's eyes slowly raised to look at his friend. He was in the exact same position as he was prior to Amon launching his attack. Daniel had effortlessly negated his strongest blow, without even moving a single muscle. Disappointed, Amon looked down at his injured hand with an ironic smile.

Releasing his stance, Daniel straightened his posture, but avoided Amon's eyes. He looked down to see a faint scuff mark on the floor. Even though his stance hadn't been broken, Amon had moved him. As he glanced over to Amon, a brotherly smile spread across his face.

"You're stronger than I thought," Daniel praised, wiping sweat from his brow.

Voice trembling, Amon replied, "I worked really, really hard."

Daniel took a step forward and ruffled his hair playfully before giving Amon a pat on the back.

"I can see that."

Amon threw himself onto Daniel, hugging him tightly. He didn't care what everyone around them thought. He didn't know them, and their opinions meant nothing to him. Daniel was more important than those gossiping buffoons. As Lya had said, their words were nothing more than vibrations in the air.

"I missed you," Amon mumbled, holding back tears. "I'm really glad that you're alive and well."

"I missed you too, brat."

"Thank you," Amon said with a smile as he walked away.

He was thanking Daniel for what he did in the Scavenging. He was thanking Daniel for how he helped Amon take care of his mother. He was thanking Daniel for being Daniel.

Amon silently glanced at Richard Layn who was watching the scene in silence. A look of utter confusion was plastered on his wrinkly face. Seeing the third elder baffled by the lackluster fight gave Amon a strange satisfaction. Without hesitation, he raised his left hand and uttered, "I concede this match."

THE FALLEN FOE, THE LOST LOVE

"**Y**ou are more stupid than I thought," Erin sneered as Amon jumped from the platform, making his way past the other competitors.

"To me, some things are more important than this competition and the inner sect," Amon retorted without stopping or turning around to face his foe.

From the purple cabin, Jake watched the scene in sadness. On one hand, he felt incredibly happy for Daniel. He was on the top eight and had a real shot to become the ultimate champion. On the other hand, he felt bad for Amon. He had shown potential and Jake liked him, but seeing Amon concede the match eased Jake's worry.

"What terrible luck for both of them to end up fighting each other," Jake sighed.

He found it somewhat strange that Nemeus had been quiet all day, but he didn't mind it. Jake didn't like when Nemeus spoke directly to his mind, he actually preferred the silence. A weary voice made its way into Jake's room, coming from the other side of one of the walls.

"Such a pity, he had so much potential."

Jake closed his eyes and silently focused on hearing. It was a somewhat old and tired voice, belonging to one of the elders close by.

"They seemed to know each other. Still, to willingly give up such a chance... Even if he made it to the top ten tomorrow, the risks are too high," A younger and more energetic voice answered. "How far can such a person go in the path of cultivation?"

"Not very far. Cultivation is a selfish concept. We fight for treasures, we fight for knowledge, and we fight for power," the old voice echoed again, seeming more and more tired at each word. "There is no room for mercy in this path. There is no room for personal feelings. That kid might be a good person, but he will be a terrible cultivator."

Jake knew that the elders weren't wrong. The world was cruel, and cultivation was for no one but one's self. Developing such thoughts was necessary to survive in such a world. Nevertheless, it was exactly because of that mentality that the situation would perpetuate. It was nothing but an endless cycle of misery and selfishness.

Amon's chances of being accepted as an elder's disciple were now incredibly low. Giving up on a fight because of his emotions and feelings of gratefulness might not have been a truly bad thing, but openly admitting that for him such things were more important than the Inner Sect revealed a lack of ambition.

Even if he was talented, even if he showed incredible adaptability and insight in combat, even if he reached this far having come from the Outer Ring, it wouldn't matter. Lacking ambition, lacking an objective to pursue and lacking a resolve to do whatever it was needed to make such things come true meant one would not walk very far in the path to immortality.

No elder would waste precious time and resources on such a person. As they had said, Amon Skoller might be a good person, but he would be a terrible cultivator.

❋ ❋ ❋

Amon sat in a medical room with his right hand wrapped in bandages. The recovery pill was slowly mending his broken bones and so he would need to stay put for a bit longer. Absentmindedly looking up at the ceiling, Amon zoned out, thinking about what had just transpired.

He had been like this for the last hour or so, but Lya didn't want to interrupt him. She thought it best that he sort out his feelings on his own. She didn't voice it, but she felt really proud of what he had done. She was certain that Amon would become a dazzling cultivator, a star shining in the bright sky above the blood-soaked earth where the other cultivators walked.

She hoped he would become a beacon of light, an example that the world did not need to be the way it was. An example that decent people could reach the top and do more than simply survive the harsh reality thrown at them.

It didn't take too long for Amon to fall asleep. Despite being incredibly tired and emotionally worn out, Amon's breathing was light and regular. He was resting peacefully for a few hours before a knock came at the door.

Rubbing his eyes sleepily, he made his way to the door only to be surprised to see Daniel standing before him.

"Sorry to disturb you," he said as he scratched his face, feeling somewhat awkward. "Want to take a stroll outside?"

"Sure," Amon smiled as he heard Daniel.

He washed his face with the cold water in a basin in the room, getting rid of the drowsiness.

"Amon, leave the interspatial ring here," Lya called him in a low voice, a bit hesitant, "Don't ask why, just do it."

Amon was confused at her request, but took off the ring and left it by the basin. He gently tapped it once before he left with Daniel.

They walked in silence, leaving the Royce Paradigm Arena. It was nighttime, and the blue crystals shone above the city. Above the mountain, a full moon shone with a bright light, surrounded by countless stars. Even though Amon could only see a tiny piece of the sky through the mountain's opening, it was enough for him. He liked watching the night sky, especially when it was a night of full moon.

They stopped at a small building near the Ashen Heart tree. Jumping on the roof, Daniel gestured for Amon to follow him. Once there, he saw two chairs and a small table. Daniel took his bottomless pouch from his waist and started taking out food, placing it on the table. He then sat on a chair, gazing at the Ashen Heart tree.

Amon joined him, enjoying the view. He could never get enough of how the tree seemed to shine under the moonlight, and its grey leaves seemed to glow with a pale light.

They both looked at it in silence. The city was deathly quiet, leaving them to their own thoughts. After a while, Daniel retrieved a wineskin and two wooden cups from his pouch.

"Here," he said, offering a half-filled cup to Amon.

Amon looked at the liquid churning in the cup and sent Daniel a doubtful glance.

"I thought you and my mother agreed to never let me drink any alcohol," he said as his golden eyes shone with a faint mockery.

"Well, as long as you don't tell Aunt Becca, we'll both live to see another day," Daniel rebuked, giving a hearty laugh.

He then turned to Amon, with a serious look. "Kids can't have wine, but I don't think you are a kid anymore. You might still be a whiny brat, but you're certainly not a kid. Cheers," he said with a smile as he raised his cup.

Amon raised his cup with an awkward smile on his face.

Cluck!

The cups lightly hit each other, and Amon took a sip of the wine. A bitter taste made its way into his mouth, making him almost spit it out. Daniel started laughing as he watched.

"Horrible, right?" he asked playfully with a cunning smile. "Only adults are entitled to good wine. You're still far from it."

"Shameless!" Amon complained, taking another sip.

He discovered that if he drank it slowly it wasn't so bad, even if it still was incredibly bitter.

"You'll get used to it," Daniel chimed as he chewed on some jerky.

He paused for a moment, staring at the tree before speaking again.

"So, tell me what happened to you," Daniel asked, still looking at the glowing leaves of the tree.

"Well..." Amon took another sip. He slowly started retelling the story he told his mother.

* * *

Somewhere in Hell Keeper's City, there was a room completely shrouded in darkness. It was hard to say if it was underground or if it was simply isolated from all light. All that could be seen in the room was a towering man that seemed to emit light from his body.

His long and wild scarlet hair reached his waist, and a pair of blazing eyes shone with impatience as he glanced somewhere in the darkness. His bulging muscles seemed to be made of steel as he unhurriedly extended his arms.

The air in front of him seemed to distort and specs of light lit up one by one in the dark room. They slowly bundled together, materializing the figure of a beautiful woman with silky black, hair and icy blue eyes. The man opened his arms even wider and gave a savage smile to the woman, revealing a row of sharp fangs in his mouth.

"Hello, Lya," he said in a deep voice that seemed more like the growling of a beast. "It has been what, a bit more than four hundred years?"

Lya didn't bother with Nemeus as she faced him, expressionless.

Her voice was as cold as her gaze when she asked him, "Why did you do it?"

"You decided to ignore me," Nemeus said as his distorted smile grew wider, making him seem quite frightening. "Even after you basically called out to me when you sold the Elysiam Daggers."

"It was not the time and you know it," he retorted. "Still, I did try to get your attention before. I have many questions for you, and you *will* answer them."

"Why would I?" Nemeus asked as his smile disappeared.

The fire in his eyes blazed even wilder as he looked at Lya.

She stood quiet for a moment before answering. When she finally spoke, she tried to make her voice sound cold and indifferent, but she couldn't hide the regret and pain in it. Her voice ended up being feeble and sad.

"Because you owe me."

Nemeus looked at her for a long while, his expression a mix of unwillingness and rage. However, in the end, he didn't deny it.

"You know, we call it the Sword Abyss nowadays," Nemeus said in his deep voice, looking away from Lya.

It was almost as if his eyes could pierce through space and time and reach that gaping chasm carved in the Broken Forest.

He remembered the expression on Alexei's face as he dealt that strike. The sheer killing intent he exuded, the coldness in his eyes, the blazing rage

179

in his heart. Alexei had poured his all into that sword strike.

It was, without a doubt, the strongest sword qi Nemeus had ever seen. Arthur would have certainly been decimated by such a strike with no chance to resist at all. Unfortunately, for Alexei, the strike was a miss.

It was nothing but a few centimeters, a distance so small that would be negligible in almost all situations. Nevertheless, it was what decided life and death in that fight. Alexei missed, and Arthur countered immediately.

"You know, Master never knew for sure, but he always felt it had been you."

Nemeus' voice was serious, and most of his animalistic features had been somewhat smoothed out. He looked at Lya with a complex gaze.

"Sometimes we do things that even we did not expect," Lya said in a trembling voice.

Tears started streaming down her face as her expression turned sorrowful. Lya had been impulsive. The moment she felt how much Alexei wanted to kill Arthur she was horrified. She didn't want to see the man she loved fall to such a level, where he would even kill his best friend. She didn't think, she just acted on instinct. Her feelings took control of her. She moved Brightmoon ever so slightly the moment Alexei unleashed that astounding blow.

"Even I was caught by surprise at what I had done," she gave a pitiful smile. "But what surprised me even more was the blow that Arthur dealt."

"To try to erase Alexei's soul like that..."

A cold rage and indignity filled her eyes as she faced Nemeus. "It seems even I underestimated Arthur's despise for other lives."

Nemeus looked at her blankly, but ended up just shrugging his shoulders, making Lya mad.

"I guess the moment he created you was a sign, but neither I nor Alexei realized it at the time," she said with her eyes still glued on him, with a self-loathing smile on her face.

"How cruel was it, to shatter the soul of the proud Hellblaze Lion he defeated and combine a fragment of it with a piece of his own soul to make a monstrosity such as you," she shook her head, making her black hair gently wave behind her back. "Arthur made that incredibly strong godbeast into nothing more than a slave."

"All spirits are slaves. All spirits are a part of their masters."

Nemeus seemed unaffected by her words.

He had no memories of anything before he was created. For him, Arthur Royce was the one that gifted him existence and meaning, nothing more. How his own existence came to be was not of his concern.

"Don't compare me with your kind. I am me," Lya's blue eyes shone with a fierce light as she looked at Nemeus, as if he had offended her.

"And how did that turn out?" Nemeus sneered.

He knew he had no need to say anything more. Lya was taken aback by his retort, but soon enough her face changed.

180

"I've dealt with it for more than four hundred years, Nemeus," she looked at his eyes with a somewhat crazed look. "For four hundred years I was stuck with nothing but the consequences of my actions. For four hundred years I saw his body slowly decay until only the bones remained," she said in a desperate voice.

Her face was distorted in pain and sorrow as she finally took a huge weight out of her chest.

"For four hundred years I stood on the edge of madness, crossing the line and returning innumerable times. For four hundred years I either had to endure the hell that is the Soulstone or face his corpse."

A strange light flickered in her eyes as she spoke, and for a moment Nemeus felt a nerve-wracking sense of dread assault him. He could feel it. He could feel, seethed deep into her, a strange distortion, an almost twisted obsession that was slowly creeping at her very being.

However, that feeling was gone as suddenly as it arrived, as if it had never existed. It showed itself for such a short time that even Nemeus doubted if he had truly sensed it. He slightly furrowed his brows as he continued listening to her.

"For four hundred years I thought about my life. I thought where things had gone wrong," her voice was trembling as she shuddered. "What mistake had I made? When? How could I have changed it?"

"I could have left anytime. All I had to do was get away from the array formation Alexei had set up," she shook her head with a wry smile, her tears never ending. "But I would never do that. I couldn't run from what I did. I owed Alexei that much. He broke many promises in his lifetime. By the time he died, he was a completely different person than the man I had fallen for centuries before," Lya cried.

She didn't expect Nemeus to even have an understanding of what love was, or what kinds of pain and joy it could bring. She was simply venting her feelings, not expecting any reaction from him.

"Nevertheless, he managed to accomplish the one promise he made on his dying breath. It took more than four hundred years, but he did return to me." Lya said as her expression eased.

She was still crying, but a gentle smile appeared on her face, showing all the appreciation she had for the boy that had found her by the lake. Amon would never know how much that moment meant to her.

"Amon Kressler is not Alexei Vine," Nemeus said in a grave tone.

It was an obvious thing to say, but it also wasn't. For them, that lived for centuries and had knowledge far beyond the humans of this time, things were not as simple.

"Yes, he's not," Lya shook her head, still smiling. "But I think it is better that way."

"I'm not sure if you really understand that," Nemeus sighed.

He closed his eyes, trying to weigh the possibilities on his mind.

"He seems to be a decent person, and for him to reach that level in seven months, you did a good job."

He let out a long breath and slowly opened his eyes. Almost all of his ferocity was gone. Looking at Lya, with blazing eyes and scarlet hair, was nothing more than a weary person.

"However, we have a grave problem here."

Nemeus sent her a piercing glance.

"I figured," Lya responded with a nod. "What happened to soul cultivators?"

She found it strange that the sect Arthur Royce founded would follow the weak path of elemental cultivation. It made absolutely no sense, unless something had happened to soul cultivation as a whole.

"Virtually extinct, even if a handful still remain," Nemeus answered. "Most of them died in the war, but the survivors didn't pass on the method."

"Why not?"

Lya's face fell and she furrowed her brows.

"Master decided it would be best to follow other paths," Nemeus looked uninterested as he spoke. "Soul cultivation was an inherently flawed concept in his view. It brought nothing but the worst in people while also giving them power."

"What utter hypocrisy for him to spew," Lya's face distorted into a mask of despise. "What is the real reason?"

"To hide the World Rift and the Starry River..." Nemeus looked up as he pondered his words. "He wanted to be sure that there would never be a second Alexei Vine."

"Hahahahaha!" Lya couldn't hold it in anymore. "That is so like him! Such arrogance! Just like Alexei."

She laughed a tragic, sad laugh.

"The four of the cardinal sects agreed with his decision. Master founded the Abyss Sect to become the fifth and to stand guard over the spatial array locking the World Rift."

"I bet he was really satisfied with people holding him in such high regard. He must have really liked being considered a hero."

Lya still had a derisive smile on her face as she spoke about Arthur. She might have liked the view of the sect he had built, and she admitted that he was a cultivation genius, but she would never forgive him.

"You're misunderstanding something," Nemeus looked at her, and for the first time since they met, Lya saw something more than rage in his eyes.

"For my master, this place was nothing more than his personal hell," Nemeus had a sad look as he spoke, shaking his head. "A dark abyss from which he would suffer for his mistakes until the end of his days, while he followed through with the choice he made."

Lya turned quiet. She gave Nemeus a look of disbelief.

"The Scavenging?" she asked after some hesitation.

"Trying to find and bury the corpses of the ones who fell in battle," Nemeus answered looking straight in Lya's eyes. "More specifically, trying to

182

find his only friend. The only man that truly understood him and that he killed with his own hands."

Lya said nothing. She only looked at Nemeus with a complex glance. She couldn't sort out her feelings after hearing that.

"What happened to him?" she asked with a low voice, almost a whisper.

"Master is dead, Lya," Nemeus' expression turned even sadder. He looked somewhat unwilling as he faced Lya.

"Who?" Lya asked, feeling a chill.

Arthur Royce still had many centuries ahead of him after he survived the War of Falling Leaves. This meant his death was not natural. Arthur had been killed. However, who would be able to kill Arthur Royce if Alexei Vine was already dead?

For some reason, Lya felt incredibly anxious. Nemeus' scarlet eyes lit up again as they blazed with immense hatred. With nothing but despise in his voice, he uttered a name that made Lya reel in shock.

"Dale Loray."

What do you know about swords?

That question echoed in Lya's mind. It was asked by a voice she never wished to forget, to someone that lay dying in a pool of his own blood.

"How... Why..." Lya couldn't properly form the words she wanted to say.

She couldn't piece her thoughts together, and an unknown fear started assaulting her.

"Even gravely injured, he managed to kill Geralt Borgin and Lara Riven," Nemeus said with an enraged voice. "He slipped through our fingers and disappeared. We searched for him for decades as we hunted rogue soul cultivators, but not a trace was found. He was supposedly dead, as Master himself dealt the blow that almost killed him on the spot."

Lya shivered hearing that. Turbid emotions rose in her heart. Anger, rage, regret, longing and relief all fought inside of her as she tried to think. What came out on top, however, was soul-chilling dread.

"How did he kill Arthur?"

Even if Nemeus was personally telling Lya all of that, she couldn't quite believe it. She knew it most likely true, but a part of her refused to accept it.

"I am not sure." Nemeus shook his head. "One day, Master received a message. He said nothing about it, but I never saw him so pale in my life. Master was scared, Lya."

Nemeus was frustrated—he never had to help Arthur Royce in a situation that was grave enough to scare him.

What could make Arthur Royce scared? He didn't even flinch when he faced a war. He didn't run away from a fight to the death with Alexei Vine. Yet, Nemeus had no idea of what Arthur would be afraid of.

"He looked at me and said that he would leave the control of the

Abyss Sect to me. He appointed his personal disciple as new Sect Master and left without a word." Nemeus could barely speak, as his voice turned more and more like a growl. "The very next day... I could feel his soul being extinguished."

Nemeus and Arthur Royce shared an unbreakable bond. Nemeus was born from a piece of Arthur's soul, so they could feel each other to a certain extent.

"How do you know it was him?" Lya couldn't help but ask.

"I have no proof at all," Nemeus smiled bitterly. "But I don't think anyone else had the potential to surpass Arthur in strength, nor the wit to apparently get hold of a weakness of his. The only person that had a reason to kill Arthur and wasn't confirmed dead was him."

Lya stood in silence as she heard his words. She had a deep frown on her face as she pondered deeply. If Dale was indeed alive... she couldn't fathom what would happen. Either way, it was an incredibly dangerous situation. Lya couldn't help but shudder. She shook her head, trying to clear her thoughts.

"Are the Guardian Beasts aware?" she asked.

"Yes, although they all agreed it was highly unlikely," Nemeus squinted his eyes. "They helped in the search over those years, so more than anyone else they were convinced he was dead. The Vermilion Queen even descended to the Chaos, but returned empty-handed."

Lya calmed down a bit. If the four Guardian Beasts didn't find a trace of him, even after looking in the Chaos, then the odds were that he was dead.

"Don't be too hopeful," Nemeus saw through her.

"The Guardian Beasts have been acting strange, especially the Azure Monarch. I have no idea what is on their minds. They have been slowly drifting apart after Master's death and even reaching them is almost impossible. The only one I can still properly reach is the White Emperor." Nemeus sighed. "It is very possible that there is something going on with them, so I wouldn't take their word for it."

Lya felt her head spinning. It was too much to take in.

Nemeus gave her the time she needed to calm down. He had shared his worries with her, and that was enough proof that he saw her as someone on his side, at least regarding Dale Loray. If he was indeed alive, she would have no choice but to stand against him. In the end, though, speculating would get them nowhere.

"I have something else to ask." She looked at Nemeus after a while. "Is Amon a descendant of Grant Skoller?"

"Yes." Nemeus nodded, giving a sneer. "Ironic don't you think?"

Grant Skoller, a legendary cultivator that had sided with Arthur Royce in the War of Falling Leaves. Unfortunately, he had fallen in battle. Alexei himself had finished him off.

Lya ignored his comment and asked another question, "Did his father try to awaken his bloodline?"

Grant Skoller had been nothing but an orphaned vagrant cultivator in his youth. He was untalented and had no prospects for life, but had a good heart. No one knows how or why, but somehow he received the blessing of the Suneater Wolf, Skoll. Grant's eyes turned golden, his hair turned silver and his body became incredibly strong. He also received an almost innate understanding of the natural laws of Fire. From an unknown cultivator, he became a dazzling figure. As a gesture of gratitude to Skoll, Grant adopted the Skoller surname, leaving his old one behind.

"Apparently so," Nemeus nodded but soon sighed. "However, the effects seem to be no more than aesthetic."

The only explanation for the physical changes Amon had experienced five years ago was that Lloyd Kressler had, through unknown means, managed to partially awaken his son's bloodline. However, his son's talent didn't increase, and the only effects were changes in his hair and eyes.

"No, his body has changed considerably." Lya shook her head as she heard Nemeus' words. She had an inkling of suspicion when Amon completed his first round of tempering and, as time passed, her suspicions grew into certainty.

"Oh?" Nemeus raised a brow, showing some interest.

"That boy is in what could be considered the middle stages of body tempering, as his physical strength is five times greater than after his first round of tempering," Lya said with a wry smile on her face. "The problem is, his cells aren't reaching the point of saturation at all."

She refrained from mentioning that his aura was also the reason why so many wolf spirit beasts had been leaving their territory to wander close to the Outer Sect. For them, Amon's aura was like a beacon of light in a dark night. It made most of them feel threatened, but the stronger spirit beasts would see him as an opportunity. His bloodline, that had the blessing of the Suneater Wolf, a godbeast, would probably help them grow stronger if he was consumed.

"So his limit is above that of a normal human..."

Nemeus' interest seemed to fade away as he thought. He eventually shook his massive shoulders. "That will give him a powerful body, but nothing more."

Then, he looked at Lya as his eyes blazed with a savage light. He smiled like a beast again, and his aura turned cold. "I doubt you came to meet me just for that."

Lya could have gotten mad at how he manipulated the lots of the promotion competition, and she might have wanted some answers, but Nemeus knew this was far from enough to convince her to finally talk to him. Not only that, she had already brought up that Nemeus owed her.

"I need a favor from you," Lya said as her brows furrowed and her expression hardened.

"What do you want?" Nemeus asked as he squinted his eyes.

"I want Amon Skoller to be allowed into the Hellblaze Secret World."

LINES THAT SHOULDN'T BE CROSSED

"**I**'m sorry, father," a somewhat high-pitched voice echoed in a spacious room of a mansion.

Everything one could lay their eyes on this mansion was either gold or covered in it. The only exceptions would be curtains, sheets and clothes that were all silk of the most exotic colors.

A young boy dressed in red clothes was kneeling on the floor, looking at the shiny tiles below him with a regretful look. His long brown hair was neatly tied to the back of his head with a golden thread, and his eyes were misty.

In front of him, a middle-aged man sat in a maroon-colored cushioned seat. His brown hair had streaks of grey, and a few wrinkles were on his face. Even if he looked to be in his forties, the man was actually reaching his third century of life.

Age was coming for Claude Drey, whether he liked it or not. He never went past the late stages of body tempering, but with his keen mind and business sense, he managed to fight his way into the Inner Ring, eventually securing his spot as the richest man in the Outer Sect.

He was used to the ruthlessness of the Inner Ring. He accepted it and he used it. If he didn't, he would still be nothing more than another face in the Outer Ring, slowly waiting to die as life went past him without accomplishing anything. Claude Drey knew what kind of world he lived in, and he was not afraid to play by its rules.

He looked at his son while lightly tapping the golden armrest of his seat. Erin Drey was his pride. The heavens had blessed his son with good affinity to fire and a strong will to improve. Not only that, his son was born with an ambition even greater than his own.

While Claude Drey didn't want to stay in the Outer Ring during his youth, Erin Drey didn't want to stay in the Outer Sect, and his father provided him a solid foundation through which he could soar to the skies. Unfortunately, Erin Drey was not only ambitious, he was also very arrogant.

Claude closed his eyes for a moment, thinking. Maybe having had a setback now was not a bad thing.

"Do you know why I had you return home?" Claude asked as he raised a brow.

Erin shook his head, not daring to raise it.

He glanced at his son, but his gaze was gentle, "Do you know why you lost?"

Erin seemed to freeze for a moment before taking a deep breath. He raised his head to look at his father with a look of regret in his eyes.

"I overestimated myself," he admitted.

"It is good that you know," Claude nodded hearing these words. "You grew too arrogant, son."

Erin looked down again, ashamed. His father was right, he had been arrogant. He let his streak of victories get over his head, and faced an enemy stronger than him head-on. Naturally, he lost. Still, it was hard to accept.

"If I were at the late stages—"

"But you're not at the late stages," his father interrupted him. "You should never count on things you don't have. You work with everything you have at your disposal, nothing more. How many times have I told you this?"

Erin didn't answer, just lowered his head further. Claude sighed. His son wasn't even fourteen years old yet. Making mistakes like this was natural.

"Don't lower your head. You still have a chance to reach the top ten tomorrow."

Erin silently nodded. Hope was not lost, he still could get one of the remaining two slots for a direct promotion to the Inner Sect.

"You'll have to keep your head in place and never look down on your enemy," Claude spoke seriously. "Arrogance will bring us nothing but hate. Look at what happened to that Amon kid."

Erin flinched.

His father had a cold look in his eyes as he continued, "What did picking on that kid bring to you, Erin? He always minded his own business, but you had to show off. Now you have an enemy, and a powerful one at that, from what I heard." His father shook his head in disappointment. "No teacher. No guidance. No easy path. He is now on the same level as you, relying on nothing but his own efforts and has nothing but hate towards you. He is now someone that can block your path to the Inner Sect. Your arrogance brought you trouble yet again."

"I will strike him down," Erin said, not hiding the rage in his eyes. "When he attacked Amber he made it personal."

"You made it personal! She made it personal!" Claude hit the armrest of the seat in anger, making Erin flinch. "Don't waste time flaunting! This is not what I taught you!"

"I'll deal with it," Erin said, averting his eyes.

"I hope you do. I'll tell you this, do not look down on the son of Rebecca Skoller. Anyone that ever underestimated that woman or anything related to her paid dearly. Not to mention his father... We don't know what he was taught."

"His father is a traitor and his mother is nothing but a cripple," Erin tried to argue, bringing his father's rage to a boil.

"That is now! Before that, his father was the damn fifth protector and his mother was a vote away from becoming a high elder!" Claude shouted as he got up, towering above a cowering Erin. "Time changes everything. We must understand these changes and follow the flow. This way we will never have a loss in business or in life."

"Yesterday he was an ant, but today he can stand up to you. We have no idea what he will be tomorrow!" he said with an exasperated look on his face.

If his son did not learn the lesson now, he would only suffer when he left Claude's protection.

"I'll say this again—do not look down on your opponents," Claude said with a weary voice as he sat down again, looking incredibly tired. "I expect to see a performance worthy of the Drey name tomorrow."

"Yes, father," Erin said, clenching his fists.

"I mean it, son," Claude looked at Erin with a loving gaze. "You won't always be the strongest, and the world does not lack wolves in sheep's clothing. I am afraid one day you might really offend someone you can't afford to.

"It pains me to say this, but we bear the Drey surname. We are the richest family in the Outer Sect, nothing more. In the grand scheme of things, we are not even pawns. Your arrogance has no ground to stand on," Claude sent his son a deep, meaningful glance. "If you ever want to change that fact, you need to accept it first."

Erin looked at his father's eyes and said without hesitation, "One day, the Drey name will be the greatest name in the Central Continent, nothing less."

"For that to happen, you must first stop acting the way you have been," Claude said with a sigh.

Nevertheless, he almost couldn't hide the smile that was starting to curl his lips.

He gave his son a nod and allowed him to leave. Erin still had to rest for the third round, and he was looking forward to it.

* * *

Amon woke up the next day with a smile on his face. He was feeling really happy. He and Daniel had exchanged stories and laughed all night. They were both different from a few months ago, but they also weren't. It was a strange feeling, knowing that even though they had been apart, they were still close.

Amon jumped out of bed and stretched. He washed his face with the water in the basin and looked at the interspatial ring beside it. He put it back on his finger, and looked at it intently.

"Good morning, Lya!" he greeted happily.

He felt light, as if a weight had been lifted from his shoulders.

"Morning," Lya greeted back. "Are you ready for today?"

"Yes, I am!" Amon nodded as he recovered his stick from the floor, swinging it in the air.

"Good." Lya's voice sounded cheerful as she said, "Here's a gift."

The ring flashed and the stick disappeared from Amon's hands. The bottomless pouch at his waist shook, and Windhowler appeared in its leather sheath.

"Really?" Amon asked, sounding even happier.

Maybe Lya was in a good mood today, just like him.

"You need to take the next matches seriously," Lya declared. "Plus, I think you are ready."

Amon silently nodded, holding the sword in his hands. If he lost one more match, he would be done for. From now on, there was no room for mistakes.

He left the room and walked to the waiting hall. It was still early, so no clerk had to come call for him. The white hall was mostly empty, but to Amon's surprise, the third elder was already there, staring nostalgically at the platforms.

Amon walked silently, trying to not disturb him as he sat in a corner. He held Windhowler in his arms, almost hugging the sword as he also looked at the platforms. He didn't know who amongst the competitors had lost their fights, so he also did not know who he could face, nor how they fought.

I shouldn't have left like that, he thought to himself.

He had been a little too impulsive after he conceded his fight with Daniel. He lost a precious chance to gather information. As he was thinking, Richard came up behind him.

"You know, most people would take this chance to try and get on my good side," Richard spoke as he looked at Amon.

"Well... I just didn't want to disturb you, third elder, sir," Amon said, averting his eyes as his ears reddened in embarrassment.

"What a polite kid. Just call me Richard," the third elder laughed. "May I ask you something?"

Amon nodded quietly, still feeling somewhat embarrassed.

"What happened to your stick?" Richard wanted to ease the mood a bit, but only made Amon feel awkward.

"Well, I managed to obtain a good sword. I don't have use for that old stick anymore," Amon mumbled. "Also, I can't lose again."

"Then why did you concede that fight yesterday?" Richard asked curiously.

"I wanted to," Amon said as his ears flushed red.

He didn't want to speak about his relationship with Daniel or how he owed him. He didn't feel it was right.

"You just made your path to the Inner Sect harder," Richard pointed out, looking at Amon with increased interest in his energetic eyes.

"As I said yesterday, some things are more important to me than the Inner Sect." Amon declared again, looking directly into Richard's eyes.

"A strong mentality. Not a bad way to think, I suppose," Richard spoke while stroking his beard. "Nevertheless, you should know that those words certainly cut off all possibilities of an elder taking you in as a disciple."

"If such words disturbed them in the first place... then I don't think I'll regret not becoming their disciple." Amon didn't know why, but he felt he could be honest around Richard.

He didn't measure his words as he uttered what was certainly to be an offense to the elders of the Abyss Sect. To his surprise, Richard laughed heartily at his statement.

Richard felt Amon had a point. If he really thought like that, sooner or later he would have a fallout with whoever took him in as a disciple.

"An interesting kid indeed." His gaze turned sharp as he looked at Amon. "What will you do if you lose the chance to get in the top ten?"

Without hesitation, Amon responded, "Keep working hard."

"Rebecca raised a good son."

Richard smiled, tripling the number of wrinkles on his aged face.

"You know my mother?"

Amon was taken aback as he looked at the third elder. He was not surprised at the fact that Richard knew his mother, rather, he was surprised that Richard recognized who he was.

"I do. A pity what happened to both of you. I know that neither of you had anything to do with your father's drama." Richard gave a deep sigh as he shook his head. "I can only wish you the best."

"If you feel that way you could have come and said that to her instead," Amon replied coldly.

Richard found no way to rebuke him. For a moment, the third elder looked down, and the youthfulness in his eyes gave way to a weariness that matched his age and appearance.

"I wish you good luck."

There was sorrow and unwillingness in his eyes as he turned away and walked to the platforms.

This was all Richard could do. He hated politics and had no wish to get involved in them. He also had no heart to tell Amon the truth of his situation. No matter what happened, there was only a harsh path ahead of Amon.

As Richard left, Amon closed his eyes, trying to focus. The other fifteen competitors also walked into the hall one by one, in silence. The eight that had secured their spots in the top ten were relaxed, knowing that only bonus prizes were at stake. Their main objective had been accomplished, so they could have an easy mind.

Inversely, the other eight were tense. There were only two remaining slots, and a loss would inevitably mean failure. No one was willing to fail after getting this close to changing their lives.

"We will now draw lots for the first phase of the third round!"

The crowd cheered and the arena trembled. Naturally, the losers would fight first. It would be a warm-up for the main event of the day when the ranks of the top eight would be decided.

Amon slowly got up and dusted off his battle garb. Strapping Wind-howler to his back as he made his way to the golden gates, and soon after, a line formed behind him. To his surprise, Erin was also in it, standing a few spots behind Amon.

He lost his match too...

Excitement filled his heart. He really wanted to face Erin and take him down with his new strength. Clenching his fists, he took a deep breath. He was two fights away from the Inner Sect. Two more fights and he would change his and his mother's life. Amon didn't realize this, but his fists were trembling slightly—he was getting nervous.

"Calm down," Lya's gentle voice echoed in his head. "Remember, your emotions will power your strikes, nothing more. Don't let yourself be over-whelmed by them."

Amon gave a discreet nod as he walked towards the two remaining platforms. Amon gave a polite nod to the third elder and the women wait-ing by the table. Richard gestured for him to move on, and Amon walked to the shiny box, feeling incredibly excited.

The golden light reflected in his eyes, making them shine like the sun as he extended his fingers to the box. The box flashed as he touched its ice-cold walls and a gigantic number "1" appeared above it.

Amon smiled as he immediately jumped to one of the platforms, not bothering with the seats by the table at all. He sat with his legs crossed as he observed the other seven competitors drawing lots.

Number three...

Number four...

One by one, the pairings were being decided, until it was Erin's turn. Amon didn't know why, but he was sure what number Erin would pick. Erin seemed to feel it too, as he turned his head to look at Amon in disgust.

Amon's expression was serious as he stood up and Erin touched the box. The light flashed over him and the number "1" floated above the box.

Instead of jumping on the platform, Erin slowly walked to it instead, using a set of stairs on the side. His smile was wild, but his eyes were incred-ibly cold.

"By the looks of it, we're both looking forward to this," Erin said in an indifferent voice as he took a white sword from his bag.

Amon spread his divine sense, immediately recognizing it as a middle-grade artifact. Like Windhowler, however, it wasn't properly developed. It looked like Erin had only started using it somewhat recently, or at least never imbued his qi on it.

"You have no idea," Amon answered as he drew Windhowler with a piercing trill.

His golden eyes were blazing with excitement, and his blood seemed to be boiling as he looked at Erin. Neither of them moved, they simply stood there, sword in hand.

Thin lines of light flashed across Windhowler's blade, making Erin narrow his eyes as the coldness in his gaze grew.

"You may begin!" The third elder's voice echoed through the Royce Paradigm Arena, making the crowd cheer even louder.

Crack!

Amon and Erin stomped the floor at the same time, making the tiles crack as they shot forward in a violent collision. Both swords whistled through the air, before hitting each other, making sparks fly in all directions.

Amon raised his foot and stomped the floor again, forcing himself to stop and not bump into Erin with the sharp swords between them. Erin also seemed to have thought of this, as he also forcefully stopped his advance. Amon's arms were numb due to the impact, but he was feeling more and more excited. Both swords started trembling and creating sparks as Amon and Erin tried to force each other back, measuring strengths.

Erin's brows started furrowing as his sword was slowly pushed back, coming closer and closer to his chest. Amon's eyes looked like molten gold as his face also slowly approached Erin. With a sneer, Erin took a step back, but Amon followed suit, keeping their distance the same. Their swords were still locked, and their arms were trembling due to the strength both were using. Erin didn't want to admit it, but he was weaker than Amon. He would not make the same mistake twice. He would have to avoid a direct contest of strength.

Erin took a deep breath, calming himself. His eyes shone coldly as he broke his stance, raising a knee and hitting Amon in the chest.

Amon felt the air being expelled from his lungs as he was sent tumbling backwards, giving Erin some space to retreat and time to think. Erin didn't take his eyes off of Amon as he tried to calm his breath.

It was true that he was physically weaker, but it was also true that Amon was behind him in terms of skills. He might have amassed a great deal of experience in the past few months, but it could not compare to the years Erin spent training before body tempering.

They both maintained their distance and analyzed the information they acquired in the clash to come up with a plan.

Suddenly, Amon took a step a bit too slow. Like lighting, Erin shot towards him with his sword raised, stabbing at Amon's head. Amon's eyes narrowed as he focused. Erin was attacking, but his balance was perfect and he showed no openings.

Amon raised Windhowler in front of him and with a flick of his wrist he used the flat side of its blade to deflect Erin's strike to the left. His eyes widened as Erin took a small step to his right and twisted his wrist, changing the angle of attack.

Erin's white sword seemed to slide past Amon's guard, piercing the air as it came towards Amon's head yet again. Amon was forced to take a step back to avoid it, but Erin didn't give him space. Like a storm, Erin unleashed a series of quick stabs at Amon, forcing him to block in one direction, immediately stabbing at the opening created.

Amon was forced to retreat. Erin looked carefully at Amon's movements, making sure to follow up on them. When Amon extended his leg to take a step diagonally to the right, Erin moved to not grant him any space.

Amon's eyes suddenly seemed to shine. Instead of shifting his weight to his right foot and retreating, he stood his ground and, holding Windhowler with both hands, made it spin clockwise in front of him. The blade collided with Erin's sword, sending it to Amon's right and breaking Erin's stance.

Amon jumped forward as he made use of the opening and unleashed a slash at Erin's throat. Erin's face paled as he hastily jumped away, barely dodging the strike. This time, Amon took the lead as he followed suit and sent a flurry of slashes into Erin's directions.

Clang! Clang! Clang!

Sparks flew everywhere as Erin blocked each and every one of the strikes, making the swords vibrate and the steel sing. To Amon's surprise, Erin stood his ground. As Amon was about to unleash a downward slash, Erin smiled. He twisted his body as he locked swords with Amon.

Amon's hair stood on end as Erin's smile grew. Erin flicked his wrist and forcefully pushed both swords to the left. To Amon's surprise, Erin let his sword go. He formed a fist and sent it smashing into Amon's face.

Crunch.

Amon was blown away, landing on the floor heavily and sliding across the tiles before he finally managed to stop. He slowly got up, feeling the left side of his face burning in pain. He was certain something was broken. He felt a bitter taste in his mouth and he spat blood onto the floor. The insides of his mouth had been torn open, causing his face to throb and swell.

"That was for Amber," Erin said with a chilling voice as he recovered his sword from the floor. "Don't think that it will be over with just that."

Erin looked at Amon's state. The left side of his face was already turning purple, and his lips were injured, making blood seep down his chin. Seeing Amon like this brought Erin great satisfaction. Still, he knew the fight was not over. Amon had been surprisingly skillful and Erin was not completely assured of his victory.

194

"I will make sure to destroy you today," Erin squinted his eyes as he taunted. "After that, I will make sure to pay your mother a visit, maybe teach her a lesson too."

Amon's face went blank. The rage and excitement in his eyes dispersed in the air, and the air around him seemed to change. Erin's brows furrowed as he saw that, making him unconformable.

"Are you threatening my mother?" He asked in an uncharacteristically hoarse voice.

Erin did not answer. He felt something was wrong. He swiftly raised his guard as he looked at Amon with apprehension.

Amon's grip on Windhowler tightened and the sword seemed to change. The light covering it started to twist around itself and the sword vibrated madly, humming.

The light condensed around the sword, forming a sharp edge. Erin felt a chill run down his spine as he looked at Amon dumbstruck.

CRACK!

The tiles under Amon's feet flew into the air, launching him forward. Erin's face paled as he hurriedly raised his sword to block the incoming attack.

CLANG!

The swords hit each other and the floor beneath Erin started to cave in.

Erin was confused as he started to hear a faint cracking sound coming from the blades. He looked in shock as a small chip appeared at the edge of his blade, where the sharp qi was colliding with it.

Erin's hands trembled due to the effort he was making in holding his ground as he stared at Amon. To Erin's surprise, there was no rage in his eyes, no frustration and no fury.

All Erin could perceive was a chilling coldness that made him shiver.

Erin narrowed his eyes, keeping calm as he twisted his body and deflected Amon's strike to the floor. Amon's sword cut through the floor of the arena effortlessly. Erin was astonished that there was no deafening sound or excessive force used.

Erin quickly retreated, asserting the situation. He had no idea what Amon had done with his new sword, but it was certainly dangerous. He felt a chill running down his back when he saw that sharp qi covering the sword as Amon retrieved it.

Erin was already on the losing side of a contest of strength, and now even his weapon would be on the line if he locked swords with Amon. He could only dodge and make use of an opening.

Amon's eyes were still cold and his expression was blank. He was like a completely different person from their last fight. Shooting at him again, Erin jumped to his right, feeling the wind hitting his face as the shiny blade in Amon's hand whistled through the air centimeters away from his head.

Erin promptly countered, taking a step forward and stabbing the sword at Amon's back.

Clang!

Amon spun on his feet and blocked Erin's strike. Erin felt his sword trembling as another chip formed. He took a step back and slashed forward. His eyes were cold as he tried to think of a plan to deal with Amon.

"Tsk," Erin spat, with an unwilling look as he looked at his sword.

It had been a gift from his mother. Erin would feel regret if it broke, but he had no choice. He was weaker than Amon and his weapon couldn't handle the clashes.

Erin gave a sigh as his face steeled. He raised his sword, pointing it at Amon and shot forward like a lightning bolt.

Clang!

The swords collided, sparks flew and another chip appeared on his sword. Erin gritted his teeth as he sent a flurry of attacks in Amon's direction.

Amon narrowed his eyes as he saw Erin coming for him. He twisted his body to dodge the stabs and used Windhowler to block the slashes and swipes that Erin sent his way. He never looked away from Erin's eyes, trying to figure out what he was thinking.

Suddenly, Erin took a step forward, raising his sword to send a downward slash to Amon's head. The timing of the attack was wrong, Erin was exposed.

A feint! Amon realized.

He took a step back, but Erin smiled as he saw that.

Thud!

Something hit Amon's ankles, making him fall heavily on his back. The air was expelled from his lungs and he was confused. Before he could think, Erin's sword was coming down at him, in the same attack Amon took as a feint.

Amon hastily rolled away as the white sword struck the floor.

Bang!

The tiles under the sword turned to dust as a huge crater appeared in the arena. Amon managed to stand on his feet, but a whistling sound made his hair stand on end. He lowered his head and felt something grazing his hair.

He looked back and saw a piece of the platform's tiles flying through the air at an amazing speed. He raised his golden eyes to look at Erin. Erin was playfully throwing a piece of the tile up and down on his hands as he looked at Amon with cold eyes.

Amon realized that what had hit his ankles before was probably one such piece that Erin moved with his qi. His eyes turned even colder as he gripped Windhowler tightly. The condensed light around it seemed to turn even denser, and the edge even sharper.

You work with everything you have at your disposal, nothing more. Erin thought, throwing the rock at Amon's head.

The moment Erin had threatened his mother was the first time Amon really wanted to hurt someone. It was not an unbridled rage, nor was it a simple impulse. His hate for Erin ran deep from long ago, but there was a limit.

Even if Erin was taunting him, Amon refused to let that slide. Windhowler started humming as Amon took a step forward and swung the sword, turning the stone into dust.

Time seemed to slow down as he ran to Erin, and saw him sigh. Erin's eyes flashed with a strange glint as he readied his sword, clashing with Amon head-on.

Clang!

The swords collided again. This time, Amon let go of the sword with his left hand and threw a punch at Erin's stomach.

Erin coughed loudly as his body bent forward and Amon sent a knee to his face. He felt something giving in under his strike, and Erin was sent tumbling back.

When Erin raised his head, his nose was bent in an awkward angle and blood flowed freely from it.

"That makes us even," Amon said, shooting at him again.

He focused all of his qi in Windhowler and smashed with the sword at Erin's head.

Not only did Erin not dodge, he blocked the strike with a slightly regretful expression. Amon felt something was wrong, but it was too late.

Clang!

The swords collided yet again, and Erin's arms started trembling. His sword made a screeching sound as it vibrated and scraped against Windhowler's edge.

Crack! Crack! Crack!

The white sword in Erin's hands started cracking. However, Erin did not retreat. Instead, he put even more strength in his arms. Amon didn't understand why he would do so, but he forced the strike in. He would win in a head-on confrontation. Victory was in his grasp.

Crack! Crack!

Cracks ran all over Erin's sword. He was holding it horizontally over his head, with the edge pointing to his left. He took a deep breath and stepped forward with his right foot, not hiding the pain in his eyes.

CRACK!

His sword shattered. Under Windhowler's sword qi, Erin's middlegrade artifact finally gave in, exploding in what seemed to be countless shards. Amon looked in a daze at the glistening fragments of metal that reflected the light of the arena like mirrors as his body moved forward.

With the sword broken, Amon had nowhere to put his weight into. He was forced to take a step forward to not fall, passing by Erin, who had taken a step forward before.

Amon looked with surprise as Erin still held the handle of his broken sword. There was still a few centimeters of blade attached to it, cracked and about to fall apart, but as sharp as ever.

Amon's golden eyes reflected the cold glint of the broken sword as it came in his direction. Time seemed to have stopped, and he saw the scene in horror as he realized his mistake. He looked at Erin unwillingly, but all he saw on his opponent's face was pain and regret.

Ever so slowly, taking what seemed to be years, the broken sword tunneled through the air arriving with a lethal blow at Amon's exposed neck.

Crack!

A layer of light covered Amon, making the broken blade stop millimeters away from his skin.

Erin looked at Amon strangely.

"You work with everything you have at your disposal, nothing more," he muttered with a heavy voice. "And, should the need arise, we must not be afraid to make sacrifices if the victory is worth it."

This was the second part of his father's lesson. He had always taken it to heart and his father never had to repeat it.

Amon's eyes widened as he looked at Erin, but he realized that Erin was talking to himself. The boy dressed in red carefully put the broken sword pieces into his bag.

"You cost me my sword, Amon Kressler," Erin looked at him with a cold stare and piercing eyes, but somehow, Amon could see no disdain in them, only unwillingness "You should be proud of this," Erin looked away, gazing somewhere in the sky. "You made this victory worthy of a big sacrifice. From your surprised face, you don't seem to understand. In that case, I'll spell it out for you: you lost because of your arrogance," Erin said bitterly, with a somewhat wry smile.

These were the last words Amon could hear before he was pulled away by the light and thrown outside the platform.

WHAT REMAINS

Amon landed heavily on his back as he hit the ground. His ashen hair was a mess, and his golden eyes were still widened in shock. He couldn't believe what had happened. It was a fair fight, so there was nothing he could complain about. The truth was he had been inferior. He had the upper hand, but he didn't manage to turn it into a victory.

He stood there, laying on the ground for what seemed to be an eternity. Had he really been arrogant? If he had been more careful, would he have won the fight?

Victory had slipped through his fingers, and, worst of all, he had lost to Erin Drey. He couldn't get rid of the bitter taste in his mouth as he looked at the boy dressed in red standing on the platform above him.

The blood running from Erin's broken nose soaked into his clothes, but he didn't seem to mind. He had a victorious smile as he slowly descended from the platform, walking to the waiting hall. He was limping a little but still managed to walk with confidence.

Amon forced himself to stand up, feeling his body turning numb. The left side of his face was throbbing in pain, and he realized walking was hard. His legs weren't moving well, and he suddenly felt incredibly exhausted.

As the adrenaline rush from the fight faded, Amon felt a headache and dizziness made his vision somewhat distorted. Everything around him was a blur by the time he arrived at the waiting hall.

He could faintly hear someone calling for him and barely managed to see Daniel rushing over to him.

"I lost," he said, passing out in Daniel's arms.

✽ ✽ ✽

Daniel was feeling sorry as he carried Amon to the medical center of Royce Paradigm Arena, guided by a woman dressed in purple.

It was a pity that Amon had lost his chance to get into the Inner Sect, especially since Erin was the one that defeated him. Daniel let out a sigh as he placed Amon on the bed and waited for the physician to arrive.

It didn't take long for the middle-aged man dressed in white to enter the room. He held Amon's wrist for a few seconds while he had his eyes closed, frowning slightly.

"He just overexerted himself," the doctor said as he looked at Daniel. "He used too much qi in the fight, nothing more. A day of rest and he will be fine."

Daniel gave a sigh of relief as he heard these words. The doctor gave Amon a recovery pill before politely leaving.

Daniel sat by Amon's side with a blank look on his face for a long time. His thoughts were a mystery, but he was slowly turning tense and his expression was darkening.

"Sir, it would be best if we go too," the woman reminded Daniel after a couple of hours. "The second phase should be starting soon."

Daniel gave her a nod, looking at Amon one last time before leaving the room. He was a bit downcast and somewhat regretful. He had no idea how Amon would react after he woke up.

Daniel made his way to the waiting hall just in time to see the last fight.

Erin was fighting the blonde woman from the Outer Ring, and neither of the two seemed to be having a good time. Erin's nose had been put back into place, but he didn't have enough time for it to heal. He was also using a new sword, even if he seemed a bit unfamiliar with it.

There was still some blood trickling down from his nose, falling on his lips and on his clothes, contrasting with his pale face. Nevertheless, it didn't seem to affect him. He was stronger than the woman, and even if she seemed to be more agile, Erin's skill in combat was higher than hers.

It was a one-sided match from the start. Erin cornered the woman as his blows rained over her, not giving her a chance to counter. Surprisingly, she managed to hold on for a few minutes, before being struck on the chest and eliminated.

At this point, Erin was deathly pale. He had spent too much energy in his fight against Amon and didn't have the time to rest properly. The time given to rest between matches had been shortened considerably, most likely as a last test of endurance. Nevertheless, he seemed very satisfied as he slowly made his way to the medical center, completely exhausted.

Daniel stared at him resentfully, but there was nothing he could do. Amon had lost in a fair fight, it was as simple as that. Now Amon would be stuck in the Outer Sect, while Erin would go to the Inner Sect and his strength would soar.

Daniel was extremely proud of Amon. He had done his best and had gone incredibly far in the competition. He was sure Rebecca would be proud too, even if Amon didn't manage to obtain any reward other than his experience gained from the competition.

As the first phase came to an end, it was time to decide the rankings for the top eight. Whoever managed to get into the top five would get increasingly precious rewards according to their positions. Daniel wasn't particularly excited for the rewards, given that the sect hadn't even announced what they would entail.

He absent-mindedly walked to the golden box when the second phase started, not worrying at all on who he would draw as his opponent. Feeling tired, and feeling anxious, Daniel just wanted this to end already. More than anything, Daniel was feeling guilty.

He didn't want to think about it. In his heart he knew that if he had conceded the match against Amon, even if Amon really never forgave him and Daniel was banished from the sect, it would have been worth it. Amon would have guaranteed his entrance to the Inner Sect and his life would have taken a turn for the better.

Daniel jumped to a platform as soon as his fight was decided. He had an apologetic look on his face. The young man facing him, however, seemed really excited.

"I hope we have a good fight," Daniel's opponent said, drawing a sabre from his bottomless pouch as his brown hair waved about.

He couldn't hide the eagerness in his eyes. From just a glance, Daniel knew that he was the type of fighter that loved combat, no matter the opponent or the situation.

Daniel gave a wry smile as he himself patted his pouch, retrieving the sword and the golden shield that he promptly wielded.

"I'm sorry, but I don't think this will be an entertaining fight," Daniel said in an apologetic voice, making the young man furrow his brows.

Before he could say anything, Daniel patted his bottomless pouch again.

Clang! Clang!

Two more swords appeared from it, falling on the ground with a clear sound. The young man had a confused expression as he looked at Daniel, not understanding the situation.

Swoosh!

The two swords cut through the air at a blinding speed, shooting towards the young man's head with a piercing sound. The man twisted his body and barely managed to dodge the swords. Horrified of Daniel, he hurriedly retreated with his face deathly pale.

The swords returned to Daniel, hovering around him in circles as his aura turned incredibly cold.

The young man shuddered as he saw the swords floating around Daniel in a deadly dance.

"You know, I feel it is about time we ended this competition," Daniel said while shaking his head. "I don't have time to play around anymore."

He raised his head, looking at the frightened man in front of him as he sent the swords whistling in his direction in an unending stream of complex attacks. He knew the fight would be over in seconds. He knew no one here truly had a chance against him.

He only held back before to keep his ace hidden until the final round. Since Amon was out of the competition, he had nothing more to look forward to, nor did he have a reason to lose.

It was about time he went all out and slapped the taste out of his father's mouth.

"Congratulations!" Lars Borgin shouted, breaking the silence that had taken over the room ever since Lawrence Meyer arrived.

The light still seemed to dance upon the red walls of the room, and the golden words still shone above the doorway.

The only difference in the room compared to a few months ago was that Crimsonroar was nowhere to be seen. Borgin was sitting comfortably on the charred throne, looking with an amused expression at Lawrence's cold face.

"To acquire such fine control over qi in body tempering, your son really is something else." Borgin poured more salt on Lawrence's wound. Even if there was mockery in his words, they still held a stinging truth.

The way that Daniel had fought in the final round of the promotion competition had attracted quite a bit of attention. His style of manipulating multiple swords with qi while using them for ranged attacks was something unseen in the sect.

On further thought, it was something natural. Most people disregarded proper training in qi control until they reached the elemental purification stage. By then, those techniques weren't of much use to them.

It was incredibly hard for a standard cultivator to channel elemental qi into objects that they had no direct contact with as the elemental qi was stored in their dantian. Even for cultivators in the elemental purification stage, adapting such a technique to their necessities would be incredibly difficult.

For body tempering cultivators, it was a completely different story. The strikes would not be as strong as if they were dealt while holding the weapon, but the flexibility, speed and agility of the weapons made up for such a disadvantage. Whomever mastered such fighting style would be able to take on multiple opponents at a time from a safe distance.

Borgin was in deep thought about conversing with Daniel in an effort to develop a training routine and a manual for such a rare technique. The body tempering cultivators of the Abyss Sect would have an extraordinary leap in strength. Not to mention opening up the doors to learn how to properly control qi earlier than previously, while smoothing out their elemental purification.

It was not something he had paid much attention to before, as the Inner Sect disciples usually had masters that guided them through the process and taught them qi control. Maybe spreading the knowledge outside the Inner Sect would be a good idea in the end.

As Borgin was pondering over what to do, Lawrence still had the same cold face as always. He ignored Borgin's comments, but he still felt somewhat dissatisfied inwardly.

"He gained fame in the Outer Sect, nothing more. Nevertheless, he is now a member of the Inner Sect," Lawrence snapped, "I will expect and demand nothing less than perfection from him going forward."

Borgin sent Lawrence a wary glance. The red light coming from the walls gave Borgin's face a hellish glow as he stared at Lawrence for a long period of time. In the end, Borgin directed his gaze to the cold area Lawrence always surrounded himself in.

"Still punishing yourself?" Borgin asked, truly concerned.

"I'm not punishing myself," Lawrence said with a voice filled with hate. "I am simply pushing forward with all that I have."

For the first time in a long while, Lawrence showed emotion. His face distorted in a mask of hate and loathing as he remembered the moment that made him who he is today.

It had been more than five years, yet Lawrence Meyer had continuously surrounded himself with frost qi. When he lost soundly to Lloyd Kressler, he decided that he'd use every moment of his existence to cultivate. He channeled his animosity into his qi, no matter how much of a burden it became on his mind. To this day all that Lawrence could feel was his own coldness.

His black eyes were pools of viscous darkness as hatred emanated from within them.

"But I will be sure to repay this debt one day," he spat spitefully.

Borgin started tapping the armrest of the charred throne with a pensive look on his face. He closed his clear eyes, trying to focus. Nemeus had surely thrown a bomb at him the previous morning.

"I have some news for you," Borgin said as he sighed.

Dark lines creased his forehead as his gaze became sharp. Lawrence raised a brow in reaction.

"It concerns Lloyd," Borgin added, sending Lawrence a meaningful look.

Lawrence narrowed his eyes, failing to hide the cruel glint in them.

"The Hellblaze Secret World will open in a few months," he explained.

"What!?" Lawrence shouted, unable to hide his surprise.

His cold eyes widened for a split-second before he managed to control his expression, but he couldn't hide it from Borgin.

"This will be a good opportunity to train the Inner Sect members," Borgin said ignoring Lawrence as he continued explaining, "As always, five members of the elemental purification stage and five of the body tempering stage will gain entrance to the trials."

"Are you sure about this?" Lawrence's tone was indifferent, but he couldn't fool Borgin. "Lloyd stole a Hellblaze Gateway. He will surely know when the Secret World is open and he will be able to create a backdoor to it."

"I know. That is exactly why we are doing this," Borgin said, closing his eyes. "It is about time we smoke out the rats that have infiltrated our sect."

"But the members we send in…" Lawrence tried to argue.

He was sure this would be a great opportunity to harm the future generation of the Abyss Sect.

"As you know, all of the Five Cardinal Sects will send representatives," Borgin said as he tapped the armrest with more strength, making the crisp sound of his knuckles hitting the wood echoed through the room. "But yes, our members will be at risk."

"The other cardinal sects most likely have spies infiltrated on them, too," he continued, hitting the armrest harder and harder. "This will be a good opportunity to try and make whoever is acting from the shadows to show himself."

"I suppose you have the members in mind," Lawrence commented, returning to his cold expression.

"I do," Borgin nodded, making shadows dance over his face as the red light shone on it. "Jake, Karen, Joshua, Evan and Skylar will comprise our elemental purification members."

"Daniel, Abraham, Malia, and Orson," he continued, closing his eyes and letting out a long and weary sigh. "As well as Amon Kressler will comprise our body tempering members."

"Are you planning on sending that traitor's son in there?" Lawrence asked in a chilling voice as his aura rose.

A sudden cold crept into the room, and the lights darkened, their movement turning sluggish and their light dying down. The walls slowly started to solidify, becoming hot rock as the temperature continued to drop.

"That is the best way to confirm if he and Rebecca are truly unrelated to the actions of Lloyd," Borgin answered, straightening his back and unleashing his own aura with an annoyed look on his face.

The whole room shook, and an unbearable pressure weighed down on Lawrence, pushing him against the floor. He shuddered once before an unwilling look showed in his face as he retracted his aura. Borgin snorted coldly but didn't make any more comments.

"If anything at all happens to my son…" Lawrence's voice was poisonous as he glared directly at Borgin with a savage expression. "I'll make sure both Rebecca Skoller and Amon Kressler don't live another day."

Borgin's eyes flashed with a strange light, and the pressure on Lawrence increased, pushing him even closer to the floor. At this point, he was almost laying down. Completely humiliated, he gasped for air, but even breathing was turning difficult.

"You will do nothing without my permission," Borgin warned before lifting his aura.

The room calmed down, and Lawrence found himself free to move again. He spitefully looked at Borgin, who didn't seem to mind one bit.

"If something happens and any of them are related to it, I will kill both, no matter what you say." Lawrence didn't back down. "Or are you saying we should protect traitors? Would you truly protect them again after another betrayal?"

"If it turns out they are traitors I'll kill them myself," Borgin said as he sent another piercing look to Lawrence Meyer.

Lawrence ignored his words and gave Borgin a slight bow. Borgin sighed and waved his hands dismissively, excusing his third second protector.

In absolute silence, Lawrence stood up and left the room, always enveloped by the cold mist he produced.

Borgin's face darkened. There was only so much he was willing to do for Rebecca and her son.

Truth be told, Rebecca and Amon were a problem for him. Even if he personally felt pity towards Rebecca, and even some guilt, he couldn't let those feelings cloud his judgment.

In truth, as the Abyss Sect's Sect Master, he was actually glad that Rebecca got herself crippled and stopped being a threat five years ago. This calmed down most of the high elders opposing her, especially after she rampaged when people threatened to kill her son as a traitor.

The exception would be Natasha Barnes, but there was no way Lars Borgin would let her find a way to cure Rebecca and create a ticking time bomb inside his sect yet again. He got in Natasha's way to protect the newly found internal peace, while Lawrence got in her way out of spite towards Lloyd.

That being the case, he couldn't bother with Rebecca nor Amon more than he already did. He would rather have Lawrence calm down than protect them. If anything did come to happen to Jake in the Hellblaze Trials, sacrificing them to salvage the situation to a certain extent would be a price he had to be willing to pay.

Not only would it calm Lawrence to some extent, it would be an indirect attack to Lloyd. Borgin doubted that the man had no concern for his family, no matter how much Lloyd's actions contradicted Borgin's intuition.

Therefore, he would not be afraid to turn over Rebecca and Amon to Lawrence if push comes to shove. If something happened to Jake, he would make a move himself, because Jake was not only Lawrence's son. Jake Meyer was also his disciple.

Amon opened his eyes. As he stared at the white ceiling above him, he blinked, stuck in a daze. The realization of his loss hit him hard and it seemed as though all of his efforts had been for naught. It didn't help that he had lost to Erin Drey, even when he had the upper hand in the fight.

He had a bitter look in his eyes as he carefully touched the left side of his face. His skin was smooth and somewhat cool. There was no pain and all of his injuries had healed thanks to a heap of recovery pills and rest. Despite there being no physical marks to show that he lost, the memories and the bitterness remained.

"Lya," Amon called meekly.

"Yes?" Lya responded gently.

"Was I arrogant?" he asked her, still in a daze.

He couldn't accept Erin's words. He refused to be called arrogant by someone as disrespectful as him.

"You were."

Lya's answer cut through Amon.

"It was for nothing more than a moment, but you were arrogant. You started counting on victory before it was certain, and that made you lower your guard, and you lost because of it."

There was no need to point out when that had happened. Amon knew it was in that final clash, when he realized that Erin's sword would break. Indeed, he had been counting on his victory. He couldn't change what had happened. That single mistake, that single moment, had cost him everything he had fought for over the months.

As he was sulking, the air in front of his bed distorted, slowly condensing into Lya's figure. She had a gentle expression as she approached Amon. He was surprised that she revealed herself like this. She usually avoided leaving the interspatial ring when Amon was not in his own home.

Lya extended a pale hand to him, lightly caressing his chin with the tips of her slender fingers. Amon felt as if a soft breeze was blowing there, making him feel a bit awkward, but comfortable at the same time.

"You're still alive, aren't you?" she asked softly.

Amon nodded, still feeling bitter inside. Even if he was alive, he lost his chance to make life easier to his mother. He lost his chance to make her feel proud of him. All because he had been arrogant.

"As long as you learn from your mistakes, it will be worth it," she said with a sad smile. "You just have to make sure to never repeat them again."

They had a similar conversation before. Nevertheless, speaking of what could happen and experiencing it were completely different situations. Amon needed to make as many mistakes as possible now that his life was not in danger so he would not repeat them when the stakes were real. In the end, he was still a thirteen-year-old boy. Expecting him to do exactly as he was told and not committing mistakes was a ridiculous idea—there was no such thing as a perfect person.

"Even if I learn from it, the mistake was still made and the consequences are still there."

Lya's eyes shone as her expression turned grave. "Then you deal with them. You take responsibility for what you did. Own your actions, for who you are now was defined by them."

"You must never feel guilt." Lya slowly shook her head, making her black hair wave behind her back.

"Learning from your mistakes and letting guilt take over you are completely different matters."

"You might recognize a mistake you made, but you should not let it weigh you down. That is especially true for soul cultivators."

Guilt was a dangerous feeling. It leads to remorse and having remorse was no different than shackling yourself to the past. A cultivator that was stuck in the past would never be able to reach the future. Their growth would be stranded, and their minds would be tormented by the demons of their own making.

This world was ruled by strength. A person could do anything as long as they were strong enough, but they must never betray their beliefs, for this would be their own undoing. One should walk steadfast, never taking their eyes from what lies ahead, and never losing faith in the path of their choosing.

"I understand."

Lya sighed before vanishing again; it was obvious that Amon needed time to sulk and overcome his feelings..

Amon slowly got up and washed his face on the water basin of the medical center one last time. He quietly left the room, walking to the waiting hall. To his surprise, it was not empty. The third elder Richard Layn was there, looking at the platforms on the other side of the golden gates.

"I see you've recovered well," Richard commented.

He turned to face Amon with his dark eyes, sparkling with both interest and pity.

"I did," Amon answered as he gave a polite, but cold bow.

"I believe the results of the Season of Rigor may interest you," Richard stated slightly raising a brow.

"Erin Drey managed to get one of the slots for the Inner Sect promotion." Richard looked back at the platforms, turning his back to Amon. "And, even if people don't know his name, Daniel Meyer became the ultimate champion."

A sincere smile graced Amon's face as he replied, "That's great."

He didn't even mind knowing that Erin had been promoted to the Inner Sect. For a moment, all his worries and regrets were gone. He felt really happy for Daniel.

"Daniel will be busy in the coming days, so he asked me to tell you not to wait for him," Richard informed, trying to sound as amiable as possible.

Amon's smile disappeared. He would miss Daniel's company, but he knew it was for the best. Richard, noticing the young boy's dismay, placed a wrinkled hand on Amon's shoulder and congratulated him on a job well done. Amon thanked him as Richard turned to leave without another word.

Amon left the arena, walking at a leisurely pace. On occasion he would stop and start at the building where he and Daniel had drunk wine and chatted for an entire night.

"What do we do now, Lya?" Amon asked absent-mindedly as he looked at the distant Ashen Heart tree.

"You said it yourself before, didn't you?" Lya spoke with an almost scornful voice, as if his question had been incredibly foolish. "We keep working."

SWORD ABYSS

A mon was calm when he finally returned to his home after almost three weeks. He carefully closed the door behind him as he entered, and ignored Raven hanging on the wall as he made his way to his mother's room.

As always, he gently knocked twice on the door and waited patiently for his mother to invite him in with her warm voice. As soon as Rebecca called him, he came in with quiet steps.

Rebecca couldn't help but smile seeing her son. He looked healthy, and she even felt he had grown a tiny bit in the weeks they had been apart. She gladly spread her arms, receiving him in a firm hug.

"I missed you," she said tenderly, putting a warm hand on his pale face.

Amon closed his eyes, enjoying the comfortable feeling.

"I missed you too," Amon said.

Rebecca could see the regret in his eyes, making her sigh. She could guess how things went in the competition. Nevertheless, she thought it was better if Amon decided to talk about it himself, instead of her asking.

They didn't talk for a long while, rather, they stood still. It was almost a routine now, to stand hugging each other after some time apart and not utter a word, simply enjoying the proximity between each other.

"I messed up," Amon said after a while with a low voice. He was looking down with a very downcast expression. "I'm sorry."

"You are sorry for what?" Rebecca asked with a gentle smile.

"We won't be able to move to the Inner Sect because of me," Amon shook his head regretfully.

"Why are you blaming yourself?" Rebecca cocked her head as she fixed her green eyes on Amon.

"I had a real shot at making it to the top ten." Amon closed his fist tightly. "But I made a mistake that cost me everything I had fought for in that competition."

"Want to talk about it?" Rebecca asked, ruffling his hair, as she loved to do.

Amon looked at her deeply before nodding quietly.

He took his time, telling her what happened during training and the event. He couldn't hide the pain in his voice as he spoke of his defeat to Erin.

"That moment... I thought I was going to win. I lowered my guard, and that made me lose the chance I had."

"Amon, look at me," Rebecca said, gently lifting his chin and looking at his eyes with a gaze full of love.

"I'm proud of you," she said without a shred of hesitation in her voice.

"You barely trained for seven months and you had a real chance of beating the likes of Erin Drey." Rebecca smiled widely, making Amon somewhat surprised. "So what if you lost in the end? Erin himself said you made his victory worthy of a great sacrifice," Rebecca shook her head as she thought of her son's silliness. "He acknowledged you, Amon."

Rebecca pointed to the window and continued, "Look outside."

It was still afternoon, and the sun was high up in the sky. The grass swayed to the wind and the trees rustled in the distance.

"The sky is still bright," she said with a wistful look on her face as she gazed through the window. Then, with a smile as bright as the sun shining outside, she said, "As long as you raise your head and look, you can always find a way."

She raised her hand and gave Amon a light flick on the nose, making his ears redden as he looked at her with puppy eyes. Rebecca gave a small chuckle seeing him acting like that.

"Stop sulking over such matters."

He said nothing more, simply agreeing with his mother's words with a nod of his head.

"What are you going to do now?" Rebecca asked.

"I'll continue my training. When I reach the late stages of body tempering I will worry about elemental purification and the Inner Sect."

"Very good," Rebecca nodded in satisfaction hearing his answer.

Amon stood up, preparing to leave the room when Rebecca extended a thin hand to hold his arm. Confused, Amon looked at her questionably.

"You know what made me the proudest?" Rebecca asked with a happy look on her face. "What really made me proud wasn't how you defeated members of the Inner Ring, or how far you made it in the competition. What made me really proud was that you conceded that fight to Daniel."

❊ ❊ ❊

"What is the plan?" Amon asked, sitting on his bed as he faced Lya. His eyes shone like lanterns and he seemed earnest, unlike his sour mood from before.

"We'll do our best to get you to the late stages of body tempering in a few months," Lya said with a serious face. "In the meantime, we will also train your use of sword qi."

209

Amon didn't know what to say. He didn't lose control when Erin threatened his mother, but it had been enough to trigger killing intent within Amon.

"You are a sword cultivator," Lya said, sending him a supercilious look. "You need to find no excuse or apologize. The fact that you kept your calm actually makes me happy."

"From now on, your training will consist of trying to trigger sword qi at your will," Lya explained with a calm voice. "When you manage to do so, we will advance to the next step."

Amon was still disturbed by it. He felt he had done something wrong when he triggered sword qi in his fight against Erin. Lya naturally knew what he was feeling.

"I said before, didn't I?" Lya raised a brow as she spoke. The room seemed to turn cold as she gazed at Amon. "A sword cultivator only draws his sword to kill."

"That being the case, your skills using a sword should be overwhelmingly strong," her voice was indifferent as she spoke naturally. "Controlling sword qi is a part of it, and of course we will train it."

"How do we do that?" Amon asked with his brows furrowed. Dealing with sword qi wouldn't be easy.

"First, you will learn how to deal with your impulses." Lya looked up as if struggling with something. Her eyes were somewhat strange as she looked back at Amon. "Then, I will show you how sword qi should be," Lya gave a long sigh as a complex array of emotions flashed in her eyes.

"What do you mean?" Amon asked, somewhat worried by her reaction.

"We will be going to the Sword Abyss."

"I want Amon Skoller to be allowed into the Hellblaze Secret World."

"How do you know of it?" Nemeus questioned, raising a brow.

"I saw the Ashen Heart tree," Lya answered simply.

That was enough. The Ashen Heart tree was no common tree, after all. Its purpose was to serve as an anchor and a gateway. The Ashen Heart tree was the bridge that connected this world to the Hellblaze Secret World. Without it, finding the spatial coordinates of the Hellblaze Secret World would be nigh impossible.

"There are rules I must follow, Lya," Nemeus sent her a sharp glance as his scarlet eyes burned with a ferocious light. "Some of them regard the Hellblaze Secret World. Others are even more important and have no relations to it at all."

"One of these rules is to not allow any to partake in the practice of soul cultivation," Nemeus said in a clearly threatening tone as he bared his fangs.

"Are you going to ruin that child because of something that happened four hundred years ago?" Lya asked as her face became cold.

The air around her seemed to freeze as she faced Nemeus.

"I will ruin Amon Kressler because of the threat that he is to the peace we've achieved!" Nemeus roared, baring his fangs as his hair stood on end.

210

"You said so yourself, he's not Alexei!" Lya retorted coldly. Her blue eyes glowed with a dangerous shimmer.

"Yes, and I'll be sure that he never even comes close to resembling him!" Nemeus didn't back down, roaring so loud that the dark room quaked violently; Lya was unfazed at his display.

"That is my responsibility to take, not yours!" she shouted back, her cold face distorting into a mask of rage.

"How can I trust you?" Nemeus growled.

"How can you not trust me?" Lya asked indignantly.

Nemeus stood in silence for a long time as he looked at Lya carefully. Like a predator sizing up an invader in his territory, he gazed at her. More than anything, however, Nemeus seemed conflicted. He closed his scarlet eyes and his beastly expression eased somewhat. He pondered for a long time, before eventually looking at Lya again.

"This will even out our debt," he said in his deep voice.

For him, the trouble he would be going through to overlook Amon Kressler's cultivation was a price equal to what Lya had paid four hundred years ago. Naturally, Lya disagreed.

"A life can only be paid with a life. This has no relation to the debt," she said with an emotionless voice.

Nemeus owed her because she had saved Arthur's life. Overlooking Amon Kressler's cultivation had no relation to it. This was a clash of the past, present, and Arthur Royce's arrogance. Furthermore, Lya herself would deal with her mistake if Amon ever walked the same path that Alexei had.

"I'll make sure he meets the requirements," she continued, not giving Nemeus time to think too deeply. "I'm not asking you to give everything inside of it to him, just to let him in."

"Even if I allowed it, there's a grave problem," Nemeus shook his head, his face filled with concern.

"The moment I open it, his father will know," he said as he raised his eyes to look at Lya. "The only reason he wasn't able to enter the Hellblaze Secret World yet was because I completely sealed it from our side. If I open that world for the Hellblaze Trials, I cannot guarantee that Amon Kressler will leave that place safely."

"I will be with him," Lya declared sternly.

Nemeus pondered how to act. Lloyd had stolen a Hellblaze Gateway, a tool that could create a secondary passage to the Hellblaze Secret World. It was made for emergencies only, and it was intimately connected to the Ashen Heart tree.

The moment Nemeus found out what Lloyd had stolen, he sealed the Secret World from this dimension. He sealed the object that acted as the dimensional anchor and the primary gateway, the Ashen Heart tree. Thus, seal would have to be lifted for the Hellblaze Gateway to function properly again.

Lifting the seal would mean that Lloyd Kressler would be enticed to act. This would both be a risk and an opportunity. Doing so, Nemeus would have a chance to find out exactly what Lloyd wanted from the relics Arthur had left behind, and possibly deduce his intentions from that. Adding to that, the timing was in his own hands, allowing Nemeus enough time to make the proper preparations. Having reached a conclusion, he looked at Lya again.

"I'll give Amon Kressler six months," he said as his eyes blazed. "He must reach the late stages of body tempering by then."

"I'll make it happen."

"Also, there will be a total of fifty cultivators entering the Hellblaze Secret World: ten from each of the Five Cardinal sects," Nemeus' look intensified as he sent Lya a meaningful glance. "Those were the rules that Master set. Even if Amon Kressler goes inside, I don't know if he'll be able to net any rewards."

"We both know that the trials are not decided by strength," Lya argued.

Arthur Royce had envisioned the Hellblaze Trials long ago. It would be a series of challenges directed at young cultivators, trying to measure their willpower, intelligence and heart. Appropriate rewards would be given according to their accolades, depending on Arthur's ideal for cultivators. This was especially true in the Trial of Heart, which was an in-depth analysis of one's psyche.

"That's exactly why I'm saying this," Nemeus sighed and shook his head, making his mane-like hair seem even messier. "I don't know if he has the right mindset to partake in the trials."

"I can't deny that," Lya confessed, deep in thought. "In that case, I'll need another favor."

Nemeus furrowed his brows, but didn't deny her.

"Allow him to leave the Outer Sect for some time," she asked.

There was only one reason he could think of as to why Lya would want to take Amon Kressler beyond the Outer Sect.

"Are you sure about this, Lya?"

His gaze could pierce through stone as he confronted her.

"I am."

Lya nodded without hesitation, and Nemeus could only sigh as he looked upon her with his weary gaze.

"So be it," he said as his figure started fading. "Remember, Lya—six months."

❊ ❊ ❊

"Ha!" Amon shouted as he swung Windhowler.

A bright layer of light covered its blade, condensed in the form of an incredibly sharp edge. It glowed with a pale light that reflected in his golden eyes and made his ashen hair look like silver.

The sword cut through the air barely producing any sound with each swing. This was a stark contrast to the first time he properly wielded it. As he performed the stances and moves from the *Fundamentals of the Sword*, Windhowler left a trail of light in its wake, surrounding Amon with its faint radiance.

Seeing this, Lya couldn't help but remember her talk with Nemeus. The way she looked at Amon now was different. In less than a month, he had already managed to control sword qi to such a degree. It was still an embryonic form of sword qi, and the control in itself was also incredibly rustic, but Amon was able to do so at will.

"He's picking up on this much faster than I've ever expected," she mumbled to herself.

This shouldn't be surprising, given that Amon was a soul cultivator, but even the rate at which his soul was growing was unexpected.

She finally saw beyond the shroud of his fledgling age, unstable emotions, tormented past, and his passiveness. Amon Skoller had true talent for soul cultivation.

"You are ready, Amon," she managed to say, absent-mindedly.

His resolve was shallow and he needed something to strive for. He needed to see the wonders and dangers of what true sword qi could bring.

It was time to take him to the Sword Abyss.

It was a very dark night. The stars were dim and the moon was nowhere to be seen. Even so, a bit of starlight managed to get past the leaves of the trees covering the Broken Forest and tainting the ground in a pale white color. On such a night, the forest had an eerie atmosphere, and any kind of sound would make the boy traversing the forest shudder in fear.

The air was cold, and white mist shot out of Amon's mouth while he took shallow breaths. He had a black cloak tightly wrapped around his body in a vain struggle against the biting chill of the night.

As he walked in silence, the trees became sparse, allowing him more space to walk as he ventured deeper into the forest. The turf under his feet slippery and brown as the plush, green grass turned into thick mud caked with dead leaves. At some point, the trees around him abruptly disappeared, and he saw himself facing barren land.

The cold at this point was almost unbearable, and Amon the cold pricked at his skin in an invisible layer of countless needles. The cracked ground was littered with cracks and a fine soot blew into his face as the frigid wind whipped about. Other than his thoughts, Amon was left alone with the rustling of trees and the howling wind around him.

The area was void of life. The dead lands and extreme weather made it impossible for plants to grow. Spirit beasts didn't dare to roam near, for the sharp energy emanating from the chasm ahead would pierce through their skin, causing them to bleed out in a matter of hours—this was the highly avoided Sword Abyss.

"You won't be able to walk closer without getting injured, so I'll give you a hand," Lya chimed in a soft voice.

A translucent sphere of light formed from thin air and covered him. Looking at his surroundings, he couldn't help but shudder. More than once, weak disciples that had more bravery than intelligence ventured alone into such lands only to be found dead, their skin ruptured and their insides shredded.

As he continued to walk, the cold wind grew stronger, carrying an inherent sharpness, which scratched at the shield in an attempt to destroy it. Each step he took was heavier than the last one, and exhaustion crept through him. Deep footprints were imprinted in the dust as he faced the opposing wind. Beads of sweat started rolling down Amon's face. The effort was too much for him, and he would soon reach his limit.

"Lya," Amon called, clearly worried as he saw the shield starting to distort.

"It will hold on, don't worry," Lya said in a serene voice, trying to calm Amon down.

The wind brought dust that violently clashed against the shield before being dispersed and blown away. When he felt he couldn't go further, he caught a glimpse of a gigantic pair of wooden poles.

The poles were side by side, being at least thirty meters high and six meters wide. Attached to them were ropes as thick as tree trunks that disappeared in the distance, hanging above a terrifying darkness that devoured from the chasm below.

The ground simply ended out of nowhere, carved into an enormous rift. The Sword Abyss stretched as far as the eye could see, ready to devour anything that fell into it.

As he slowly got closer to the Abyss and the poles, the pressure disappeared. Amon sighed in relief when Lya dispersed the shield around him. His tired body fell to the ground, panting heavily. His clothes were drenched in sweat and his legs were trembling. Some parts of his tattered clothes couldn't resist the pressure and were ripped, while his black cloak managed to go unscathed. None of this mattered; he was happy that he had managed to get to the Bridge of Lamenting. While he recovered, he gazed in fear at the legendary Sword Abyss in front of him.

The Bridge of Lamenting had a formation inscribed on it, negating the effects of the sword qi from the Abyss and protecting it and everyone within the range of the formation. Regardless, he could still feel a chill deep within his heart as he peered into the void.

Amon took a long while catching his breath before he managed to sit with his legs crossed and closed his eyes in meditation to try to recover a bit. The air surrounding him became blurry, and a faint halo emanated from him. He slowly stopped trembling from the cold and exhaustion, and his breathing regulated.

"You should pay attention to your surroundings," Lya advised him from the interspatial ring.

Amon gave her a slight nod as he focused. Probing the surrounding with his divine sense, he felt the qi that came from the Abyss. It felt unnatural. It was sharp, cold and unforgiving. The misty qi would gather into thin, web-like strands that would cut through the air, shredding everything in their path.

When they got close enough to the bridge, however, they would suddenly disperse, as if they had never existed.

"Is this... sword qi?" he asked in awe.

His golden eyes shone with expectation as he felt the blades of qi shuttling around him.

"This is only remnant qi," Lya explained to him. "It is not even close to what you would have in the depths of the Abyss. It's just a weak echo and a mere fraction of the original strike," she said in a serious voice, making Amon even more impressed.

He was sure that if he wasn't being protected by the array formation in the bridge, just a single wisp of this sword qi would be able to split him in down the middle.

After he had recovered, he walked towards the bridge. Although it was a simple rope bridge, its scale was incredibly large. It crossed the whole width of the Sword Abyss, just shy of two kilometers. The boards placed horizontally on in it were solid, being a full ten meters long and three meters wide.

The wooden poles that supported structure were covered with strange inscriptions made with intricate runes that moved and twisted much like others he had seen before. Their movement was a bit erratic, often connecting and breaking apart at random intervals. It was hard to discern what could've been words or sentences.

"To do a formation on such a scale..." Amon mumbled.

Though he had no fear of falling into the chasm, he felt uneasy venturing across it.

"This should be enough," Lya said as Amon got halfway through the bridge.

The strands of sword qi in the middle of the bridge were exponentially larger and more aggressive than on the extremities. Amon's felt nauseous looking at the blade-like pieces of qi. He sat down on the bridge, closing his eyes to focus. The moonlight fell over his lonely figure as the bridge slightly swayed with the wind.

"Focus on each strand of sword qi that you see," Lya guided him, her voice seemingly echoing from afar. "Feel it closely. Don't try to analyze the shape, try to see behind its behavior. Feel the will contained within it."

The most important part behind the concept of sword qi wasn't simply the sharpness, but also the murderous intentions it hid. A strong soul would have a strong will. Naturally, the strongest soul cultivator would have the strongest will. The strongest sword qi he ever produced would also contain the strongest murderous intent.

Now he had to learn from it. Amon Skoller needed to learn what trying to kill a person really felt like. This would be a part of his life that he wouldn't be able to run from.

He was a sword cultivator, after all.

The moonlight shone over a lonely figure sitting cross-legged on the middle of the Bridge of Lamenting. The silvery light made Amon's face suffuse a pale glow, looking unnaturally chilling. His eyes were closed, and beads of sweat were slowly rolling down his face, glistening in the faint light like morning dew.

He observed closely how the sword qi emitting from the Abyss acted. It moved through the air, unstoppable, until it reached the array. It zipped and zoomed through any ounce of life it could find, making Amon feel incredibly nervous.

It's not enough, he thought, retracting his divine sense as his body shuddered.

He felt as though he was being stalked by a beast and that would tear him apart at any moment. Amon was unable to shake off the anxiousness, making focusing difficult for the inexperienced cultivator.

"Don't be afraid of it," Lya's instructed. "You must lower your guard and let it reach you."

"Open yourself, invite it in," she whispered. "It's the only way you'll be able to deal with these feelings. And when it finally reaches you, you may be able to reach out to it as well," she continued. "At that moment you'll be able to understand sword qi."

Amon furrowed his brows for a moment, but eventually took a deep breath, trying to calm himself. He adjusted his position, trying to get more comfortable as he slowly spread his divine sense outward again.

The murderous intent of the sword qi took over his sense again, and he froze in place. He made an incredible effort to accept it. He felt increasingly anxious as the sensation of being pointed at grew stronger, but he managed to hold on.

His clothes became drenched in sweat and he started shivering as he started to feel the sword qi slashing at him. It was as if the air surrounding Amon had suddenly became unbearably cold and started to press down on him. He felt as if he was going to be crushed by the cold aura he was feeling, and breathing became difficult.

The cold sensation invaded his body as if thousands of sharp blades were crawling under his skin, splitting his flesh apart, making him feel maddening pain. His organs seemed to twist and rupture and his muscles were useless, having been torn to shreds.

Amon tried to scream, but he found no voice coming from his throat as he tasted the blood seeping from his destroyed organs leaking through his mouth. His thoughts started to scatter, and his vision started fading. As the coldness took over his senses, Amon realized he could feel nothing.

He woke up screaming, finding himself still on the Bridge of Lamenting. He was panting heavily, making a dense white mist shoot from his mouth as he gasped for breath. He felt his body numb, and he couldn't move properly. He was so tense that his muscles had locked him in place.

He looked around, confused about what had happened. There was no pain afflicting his body and no pressure around him. The sword qi was still shooting in his direction, but it was all being blocked by the array formation, making it harmless.

"An illusion?" he asked himself as he recovered his breath. Having calmed down, he could analyze the situation.

"I guess you could call it that," Lya answered. "What you experienced was pure killing intent. What you felt was nothing more than what the striker had wanted cause to his target."

"But... how?" Amon asked in confusion. "I understand that having a strong will affects the qi, but how can something as abstract as killing intent remain behind like this?"

"The nebula," Lya's answer was very simple.

"What?" Amon was taken aback.

Wasn't the nebula the energy and vibrations generated by the will and emotions in the aster?

"If a soul is strong enough, the will can leave behind an impression in the qi. It is like an echo of the emotions the person had," Lya explained slowly, making sure Amon would understand. "This echo is a kind of nebula."

The nebula was the bridge between the soul and the material plane. As everything in this physical world was a form of qi, it could be said that the nebula was the connection between the soul and the qi. For a strong soul to leave an impression in the qi wasn't surprising, considering that the will contained in it could manipulate the qi in the first place.

"Sword qi is naturally filled with murderous intentions. Sword cultivators could use the sword qi not only in physical attacks but in psychological attacks too," Lya continued her explanation patiently.

"Such attacks could affect the minds of the targets and the surrounding spectators. It is a good way to create openings," Lya had to be sure Amon understood this. The psychological aspect of such an attack was as important as the physical one.

"What you felt just now was what the person on the receiving end of such a strike would feel," she said, waiting patiently for Amon to ponder over her words.

Amon was in awe as he thought of Lya's words. It truly made sense. He now understood why Lya wanted him to come to the Sword Abyss. It wasn't only for him to get a better sense of sword qi, it was also for him to understand this facet of its use.

"I have one question, Lya," Amon had his brows furrowed as he thought of something.

His gaze was incredibly serious, and the matter he wanted to bring up seemed very important.

"You can ask," Lya assured him. His expression had made her curious.

"The first line of the soulrousing technique…" Amon's brows furrowed even further. "It is not simply to aid in cultivation at all, is it?"

For the first time, Lya was caught off-guard by one of Amon's questions. If she had projected a body in front of him, her mouth would be open and her eyes would be widened in surprise. She never expected him to bring this matter up.

"Why did you think of this?" she asked suspiciously, trying to understand his train of thought.

"I thought that because sword cultivation makes such an ingenious use of the makings of the soul and the qi," Amon explained hurriedly as his ears reddened. He thought he had spoken something absurd and was starting to feel ashamed. "Then maybe the cultivation technique would be related to it too."

All that answered him was a long silence. Amon got even more nervous at Lya's lack of reaction. It took what seemed to be an eternity for Lya to finally say something.

"You are right," she said in a somewhat hesitant voice.

"The primary use of the first part of the soulrousing technique is indeed to boost the speed of cultivation," She spoke slowly, trying to ponder her words carefully. "Nevertheless, its second use is as important as the first."

In truth, Amon wasn't ready for this knowledge, but if he had managed to catch on, it would be better to explain properly to him.

"The soulrousing technique can greatly boost the strength of the sword qi a sword cultivator produces," she said, confirming Amon's suspicions.

It was only natural. If the sword qi's strength was heavily dependent on its imbuement and the user could boost said will, the sword qi would be stronger. Of course, such use had its risk. The stronger the killing intent was, the harder it would be to control it. Using the soulrousing technique as a means to boost an attack shouldn't be done lightly under any circumstances.

"I believe I have no need to explain to you why you should leave this matter to rest, right?" Lya asked in a serious voice. Amon could almost feel her blue eyes glaring at him.

"No. I understand," he said, not showing disappointment in his voice. He knew very well he wasn't ready for it.

"Good." Lya seemed satisfied with his answer. "Now go on, try to produce sword qi."

Amon nodded heavily as he slowly drew Windhowler from the sheath on his back. He slowly stood up, shivering from the cold as a violent wind blew in the Bridge of Lamenting.

As he assumed a stance, the air in front of him distorted, and Lya materialized out of the ring. Amon was dumbstruck as he saw her, not understanding the situation. To further his confusion, the interspatial ring on his finger flashed, and Brightmoon appeared by Lya's side, hovering around her.

"Why do you look so confused?" Lya asked with a charming smile.

"Come on, attack me," she said with a strange glint in her eyes. Amon felt a chill run down his back as he faced her, and he had a bad feeling.

Lya ignored his reaction as her smile widened. Brightmoon flew to her hands as she also assumed a stance. Under the moonlight, her figure seemed to be immersed in flowing mercury, and her white dress had a silver sheen. Her smile suddenly scared Amon as she looked at him with a piercing glance.

"I'll judge your progress."

A dazzling layer of light covered Windhowler as Amon swung downwards, drawing an arc towards Lya, who only scoffed as Brightmoon rose to block the strike.

Clang!

The swords collided with a deafening sound. Amon tried to force the strike in as the muscles in his arms bulged. The layer of light covering Windhowler flashed as the light grew even stronger, forming a sharp edge.

However, it wasn't enough. Brightmoon didn't budge an inch under Amon's strength, and the layer of sword qi covering Windhowler had no effect. With a sneer, Lya flicked her fingers, and Brightmoon moved forward, pushing Amon back.

"Too weak." Lya shook her head, making her luxurious black hair wave behind her back. "Also, your sword qi formed too late."

She waved her slender hand, making Brightmoon return to her side, giving Amon a break

"It's still hard to trigger sword qi," Amon said with eyes full of hopelessness.

Lya gently nodded her head. It was understandable. Asking a kid to have a killing intent strong enough to trigger sword qi at will wasn't easy.

"I'll demonstrate it once," she said, as Brightmoon flew to her hand and she assumed a stance.

Under the moonlight, Lya seemed like a goddess as her body was covered in a silver glow and Brightmoon shone in her hands.

Her beauty suddenly became extremely cold, and Amon felt his hair stand on end as he looked at Lya. Her blue eyes shone like stars, but all Amon could see in them was a blazing hostility. Like a beacon, beams of light shone from the blade of Brightmoon, until it flashed once.

Lya held Brightmoon with both hands, and the light condensed around the blade, in a luminous edge. The light faded as the layer surrounding the blade grew thinner, almost disappearing. However, Amon only felt more danger as the light retracted. He realized that all the qi was being compressed within the sword itself, hardening and sharpening it further.

He looked at Lya hesitantly, and when he locked eyes with her, he knew. He was going to die. There was nothing but thick desire to kill him in those bright blue eyes, and Amon couldn't even move as Lya waved Brightmoon in his direction.

"See?" she asked with a gentle smile, as the hostility dissipated as if it had never been there in the first place. Amon looked hesitant at the shiny blade floating millimeters away from his neck, almost feeling it's cold kiss.

"You shouldn't hold back any hostility when you use sword qi," Lya stated in a clear and gentle voice. It was a stark contrast to her previous murderous coldness. "You must have the desire to kill your opponent. The remnant sword qi coming from the Sword Abyss is a good guide for you."

She looked at the darkness below them and an array of complex emotions showed in her face.

"You must be willing to utterly annihilate the opposing party with your strike. I know it's hard, but I spoke of it before, didn't I?" She looked at Amon, not hiding the bitterness that slowly took over her voice. "Sword cultivators draw their swords to kill."

"I know that, it's just..." Amon remembered her words. There was no way he would ever forget them. "I can't see myself trying to kill you."

"Well, you should." Lya looked at Amon sorrowfully. "Don't you remember what I told you before? The people close to you are the ones that can hurt you the most." She shook her head, giving a bitter smile. "You must be ready to protect yourself in moments like these, even if such moments never come."

"This seems too ruthless," Amon whined, his eyes welling up with tears.

"Life is ruthless," Lya retorted bluntly. "You'll die if you don't adapt. So get used to it."

Amon understood it, but he didn't want to follow such a path.

"I'm not saying for you to kill your loved ones," Lya said with a tired yawn. "I'm saying that you should be ready to kill them if needed. There is nothing more precious than your life. It's something worth protecting at all costs."

"I disagree," he retorted immediately, with a strange light shining deeply in his golden eyes.

Lya was taken aback. Her expression was blank for a moment as she faced Amon, not knowing what to say.

"People would not sacrifice themselves if such a thing was really true." He shook his head with a bitter smile on his face. "I believe some things are more important than my life."

"Like what?" she asked, her voice coldly snapping at him.

"My family," he answered bluntly.

He clearly remembered the way his mother's red clothes fluttered behind her as she stood between him and that terrifying silverback wolf. The way her golden hair glistened in the sun and the wolf's silver fur glistened as they advanced at the same time. The look in his mother's eyes as she pushed him behind her back was filled with savagery and resolve. She was willing to lose everything as long as she could protect him.

Amon knew his mother would happily die if this meant he could live. It weighed on his mind, but also further fueled his love. He knew it was a reciprocated feeling. It was something that he felt towards Daniel too. He knew that they were the most precious things in his life. Without them, life would be pointless. He would rather have them live without him than him having to live without them.

"A great ideal," Lya looked at him with a gaze as cold as the night. "I hope you'll never have to prove it."

Amon didn't know why she was suddenly so heartless, but he refused to give in to her banter. They stood in silence for a long time, before Lya sighed and closed her eyes in annoyance.

"This should be enough for now," she said, undoubtedly dissatisfied. "You won't advance in sword qi until you truly wish to kill someone." She looked to the night sky, pondering deeply. Her blue eyes were desolate as she stood alone. "I believe you'll understand it then."

Even though Lya said these words, she was uncertain. She looked at Amon meaningfully, at those clear and innocent eyes. She was sure life would break him if he didn't listen to her advice. He was young, but he lacked flexibility.

She didn't think it was something bad, but such an unmoving stance was dangerous. His stubbornness made him brittle and in their heartless world, Amon would either die, or break, if he didn't adapt.

She wanted him to be a decent person, an example that could bring change for such a twisted world, but for that, he would need to survive until he was strong enough. It wasn't an easy balance to find, as it was borderline hypocritical. She suddenly found herself worried.

If Amon ever broke, if he ever lost everything meaningful in his life, she wasn't sure what would happen. She could only do her best and make sure he would be able to gather his pieces.

ASHEN HEART

In the heart of Hell Keeper's Mountain, on the center of Hell Keeper's City, lay a gigantic tree. Its height spammed hundreds of meters, and its crown overshadowed everything beneath it. In a place that was either in the dark or in the gloom, it was almost a miracle for such a tree to appear.

Its white and twisted trunk looked very beautiful, almost ethereal, as it seemed to glow under the faint starlight that managed to get past the gray leaves above it. Under the night sky, it seemed to be a tree made of light and silver.

The scenery was almost ruined by a lonely figure standing beside it. It was a towering silhouette that gave an oppressive feeling just by looking at it. Seeing it from behind, a wild fiery-red mane seemed to cover all of the back of its upper body, but it couldn't hide the figure's wide shoulders.

One would feel that such a being would be able to crush rocks with a wave of its arms, and the aura it emitted gave nothing but the impression of overwhelming strength. However, the silhouette's shoulders drooped, and its back was somewhat arched as if the figure was carrying an unbearable weight. The pale glow the figure suffused made it seem sickly but also gave it an eerie feeling.

Nemeus had a rare look of weariness on his face as he reached for the Ashen Heart tree. His hands could cover a grown man's head and crush it without difficulty, but there was nothing but tenderness in his touch as he extended his thick fingers to the tree.

"I'm sorry," he said in a low voice, with nothing but regret showing in his scarlet eyes.

It was an expression Lya had never seen him make. A rare moment of vulnerability for one that had to handle the matters his master had left to him. A moment of vulnerability for one that should never show weakness, lest his master's work could fall apart.

In truth, Nemeus was tired. He felt he would not be able to handle his responsibilities for much longer. Something told him that an unstoppable change was coming. It didn't start with Amon Skoller or Lya, but they certainly had a big part to play in it.

He looked up, feeling incredibly thick qi descending from the skies, being absorbed by the gray leaves and making them glow weakly. Beyond the crown of the tree, beyond the grey mass of qi that was always moving towards it, was the night sky. The sky Nemeus saw was one that only Lya and the remaining soul cultivators had the privilege to experience.

In this ominous sky was a river. It was comprised of countless specks of light, shining with varying intensities and sizes. A beautiful river that seemed to be made of stars and moonlight. It was wide and shone over the sky like a beacon of light.

It was a river that never stopped flowing. A river that twisted and turned around the whole world they lived in, covering it all. A river that didn't end nor began in the place they called home. If anything, this small world of theirs was nothing but another of the countless places in its never-ending journey through the universe.

In the distance, Nemeus could faintly sense countless light specks falling from the river like shooting stars, as well as many others rising from the earth and joining the stars in the river.

Despite it being called the Starry River, it was made up of souls.

"Dale Loray," he mumbled to himself, thinking.

Dale wasn't one to move in the open. Unlike Alexei, he would never give his opponents a chance to win. He would slowly build up strength, and even more slowly set his pieces on the board, in such a subtle way that no one would notice.

By the time he finally revealed himself, the board would be in his hands. It was how he lived, and it was how he fought. Nemeus knew that even though he wasn't as strong as Alexei Vine was, he was a much more dangerous enemy.

Just the fact that Nemeus was unsure if he was indeed alive made him worry. It was possible that whoever was moving in the shadows wasn't him. However, if it was indeed Dale, then he had the power to hide from Arthur and even kill him. Worst of all, he had not revealed himself. This meant that he was still placing his pieces on the board, still scheming, and still gaining strength.

Regardless, this could be a good thing. Dale was still not assured of his victory. He knew he could still be stopped and, if Dale felt that way, Nemeus could only agree. If his enemy wasn't Dale, Nemeus was sure he could deal with him.

His eyes suddenly became sharp as his hand seemed to melt and pass through the glowing trunk of the Ashen Heart tree.

"I'll need your help, brother," he spoke in his usual deep voice, but a surprising tenderness could be felt in it.

Nemeus was still looking tired, his shoulders were still drooped, but a fire had been lit in the depths of his eyes.

The sun was rising, tainting the farmlands and streams of the Outer Sect in a reddish light. The stones in the crude path that Daniel followed were slippery with the morning dew, still darkened by the humidity.

Even though the sun was rising, the temperature was still very cold. White mist shot out of Daniel's mouth as he breathed lightly while walking to an unsuspecting and shabby house in the Outer Ring.

Daniel's face was pale, and his eyes were still surrounded by dark circles, but his complexion was better than it had been during the Season of Rigor. Two days had passed since Amon had been eliminated and Daniel had won, but he felt it had been weeks.

Jake had been very happy about his success, but the elders presiding the competition were clearly not excited. They had cold faces as they gave a half-hearted applause to his victory, before turning silent again.

Daniel didn't expect anything else but that. Anyone that showed the smallest trace of happiness would, without a doubt, be seeking trouble from Lawrence Meyer.

Daniel had been promoted to the Inner Sect, receiving the rights to live in a residence of his choice in Hell Keeper's City, as long as it wasn't above the ground. As a bonus reward for being the champion, his smiling brother gave him ten water crystals.

Elemental crystals were incredibly rare. They were a form of crystalized qi, naturally formed in areas where the elemental qi was thick and some kind of phenomena made it condense in a single place. The grade of such crystals varied greatly according to where they were formed and their size, but even a crystal of the lowest grade would be insanely helpful for one to undergo their elemental purification.

Daniel had received nothing more than ten low-grade water crystals. It was a very valuable prize, but it would not be of much use to him. His father had used dozens of high-grade crystals with Daniel before Jake was born, and Daniel had failed to enter elemental purification.

Daniel's low affinity meant he would waste the vast majority of the elemental qi in the crystals, and the small quantity he managed to absorb would be lost in his body, mixed with the regular qi flowing in his meridians.

He would need an overwhelming number of high-grade crystals to get himself into elemental purification. Ten low-grade crystals would not make the cut. That being the case, he decided to put them to better use.

He stood before the wooden door of the small house in a daze. He felt a bit awkward as he knocked on it a few times. It took a couple of minutes for him to hear light steps coming from the other side of the door, and with a faint *creak* it opened, revealing Amon.

He had a deathly pale face and beads of sweat rolled down his face, making his clothes damp. He walked with some difficulty as if his legs were weak and couldn't sustain his body. His ashen hair was a mess and his golden eyes had a pained look in them.

"What happened to you?" Daniel couldn't help but ask instead of greeting Amon. He raised his brow as an inquiring gaze showed in his dark eyes.

"Another round of body tempering," Amon said with a wry smile.

Daniel gave him a pat on the back, showing support and making Amon freeze in pain for a moment. With a disgruntled look on his face, he invited Daniel in, ignoring the wide grin he had on his face.

"Is your mother up?" Daniel asked with some hesitation as he sneaked a glance at Amon.

Amon raised a brow seeing him acting like this, but shrugged it off.

"She is," he answered bluntly.

"Good. I need to speak with her," Daniel said with a smile, but Amon could see the deep hesitation he showed in his eyes. It was almost as if Daniel was afraid.

Amon could understand if he felt awkward or ashamed of speaking with his mother after seven months of absence. However, the way Daniel was acting was too strange. He decided he would not think too hard on it as he made his way to his room to continue his recovery.

As Amon walked away, Daniel furrowed his brows deeply. He walked to Rebecca's room with a complex look on his face, a look that bordered unwillingness.

Taking a deep breath, Daniel lightly knocked on the door.

"Come in," Rebecca's familiar voice welcomed Daniel.

He clutched his chest; his heart felt heavier than it ever had before. He gave the door in front of him a weary look before he gave a long sigh and managed to put a smile on his face.

He raised his left hand, holding the doorknob. Daniel felt he was holding a block of ice as he gripped it tightly and slowly opened the door. Through the crack, golden rays of sunlight appeared, giving his face a healthier glow and gently caressing his cheeks with their warmth.

As always, Rebecca sat by the open window next to her bed. Her green eyes were full of energy as she gave Daniel a smile as bright as the sun rising outside.

"It's been a while, Daniel," she said warmly.

Looking at her eyes, Daniel knew she was genuinely happy. This made him feel even worse.

"It is good to see you again," Daniel said with a forced smile, but he couldn't hide the pain in his eyes as he looked at her.

Rebecca's expression changed slightly. Her eyes showed worry as she gazed at him, and she gestured for him to come closer. Daniel was taken aback, but when he saw the worry in her eyes, he slowly approached her bed.

"Come here," Rebecca said as she pulled him into a hug, making Daniel freeze in surprise. His eyes widened and his mouth opened as he tried to say something, but no sound came from it.

"Thank you for what you did," Rebecca said tenderly, hugging Daniel even tighter.

"No need to thank me," he managed to say after he recollected himself. "There was no way I would let him get hurt."

As Daniel spoke, Rebecca gazed at his right arm. A black gauze covered it from the shoulder to the tip of the fingers, and Daniel wore long-sleeved clothes to hide the deformities in his arm.

"Show me," she suddenly demanded with a deadly seriousness.

He hesitated as Rebecca asked him to show his arm, but seeing her unwavering gaze he could only obey.

He rolled up his sleeve and slowly unraveled the gauze protecting his fingers, eventually revealing all the skin he had up to his upper arm. Rebecca's green eyes seemed to dim greatly as she looked at the scarred and deformed skin, as well as the missing chunks of flesh that made his arm uneven.

"Oh, Daniel," she lamented with a trembling voice.

Daniel silently covered his arm again and replied, "It's not so bad. The fifth elder helped me a great deal."

As he spoke, he focused his divine sense, controlling the qi in the broken meridians of his right arm to move it and move his fingers, making sure Rebecca saw it all.

"Natasha always had some very novel ideas," Rebecca said, trying to smile.

However, as she looked at Daniel's right arm her smile faded away, and her expression showed nothing but sadness.

"I owe you too much," she said as she lowered her head, making her blonde hair seem to be set ablaze under the sun.

"I'm sorry," she said in a heavy voice. "Going to the Scavenging was my idea."

"Forget it, auntie. We decided on it together. I haphazardly lowered my guard, so the fault is on me. If you talk like that again I'll be mad."

He rebuked her and wanted to put an end to the topic. He had to speak about a matter of greater importance. His expression turned solemn as he gazed at Rebecca, and she saw the unwillingness in his eyes.

"The Hellblaze Secret World will open again in six months," Daniel said with a stern gaze. "Amon and I were selected to go."

Daniel didn't know a better way to say it. He knew this was a sensitive matter for Rebecca. As he expected, her face was cold, and her aura seemed to change. A deep frown showed in her face as she pondered.

"Why?" she asked after a long while, looking at Daniel with a serious gaze.

"All I know is that something big is about to happen."

His brother had warned Daniel to be very careful. Daniel asked why, but it seemed that even Jake didn't know the real reason behind the danger or the opening of the Secret World. No matter how Daniel looked at it, it was strang

He knew from Rebecca that the Hellblaze Secret World had been sealed because of Lloyd, but he wasn't sure about the specifics. The Hellblaze Trials were an event organized with the cooperation of the Five Cardinal sects. For the Abyss Sect alone to simply decide to open it and just notify the other sects was suspicious. This situation was abnormal for sure.

Even stranger than that was the choice of members of the body tempering stage. More precisely, Amon. He was still not in the late stages of body tempering and, considering his identity, he would usually be the last person to be chosen for such an event.

It was almost as if the Abyss Sect wanted trouble. Such a train of thought made Daniel worried. He spoke with Rebecca because she knew more about the situation than he did. If she reached a similar conclusion, Daniel didn't know what he would do.

Rebecca had her green eyes closed as she pondered for a long time. When she looked at Daniel again, there was nothing but a chilling coldness in them.

"They most likely want to force my husband to act," she said in an indifferent voice. "The fact that Amon will be involved is to verify if we're spies or if Lloyd still has any attachment to us."

"We will be traitors or hostages by the end of this, depending on what happens," Rebecca spoke as if the matter had nothing to do with her as if what she analyzing wasn't her own situation. "Because something will happen for sure, and Lloyd will be responsible. As such, we will not be left alone."

Rebecca Skoller might have been abandoned and might have been betrayed, but she knew what she needed to know about Lloyd Kressler. When he wanted something, he would take it. When he stole the Hellblaze Gateway, it was obvious that something he needed was in the Hellblaze Secret World, and that he would not be able to take it through conventional means, nor relying on his own strength to simply steal it.

There was a catch, and the only way to get past it was using the Hellblaze Gateway. Not only that, what Lloyd wanted was important enough for him to throw away his position in the Abyss Sect and his family.

If he wanted something so much, he would certainly take it as soon as possible. He had five years to prepare for this moment, while Borgin just now decided to make a move—Rebecca was sure Lloyd would come out on top.

"Maybe we should leave."

Her voice was low, almost a whisper, as if she didn't really wish to utter the words that were coming out of her mouth.

Yes, maybe it was time to leave. Staying in the Abyss Sect would only put them at risk. Rebecca didn't have the power to protect her and her son anymore. Given their history, neither Daniel nor Amon would ever have a firm enough standing in the sect to guarantee their own safety.

Daniel's face fell as he heard her words. He knew what she meant, and he knew why she was thinking this. Nevertheless, it wasn't a simple matter to discuss. The real problem, however, was different.

"It's too late," Daniel crooned awkwardly.

Rebecca didn't deny him. She knew it was most likely true. If this event was indeed a bait to attract Lloyd, then there was no way the sect would lose the chance to have Amon involved. Lawrence Meyer and Lars Borgin had probably already put them under surveillance to make sure they would not get away and ruin their plans.

Rebecca sighed. She closed her eyes as a tired expression showed in her face. Daniel felt that Rebecca had suddenly aged decades as she gave that sigh. He could feel her situation weighing on her, and the burden that it truly was.

"I'll do my best to protect Amon, and my brother will help. He will also do his best after the Hellblaze Trials are over."

"Thank you," Rebecca said warmly.

Still, the weariness in it didn't go unnoticed by Daniel. He clenched his fist tightly, as his nails dug deeply into the palms of his hands.

In a tired and regretful voice, he said, "I'm sorry."

"The Hellblaze Trials are divided into three parts," Rebecca stated, raising three fingers.

She had called him not long after Daniel left and told him the news. Her son would need to prepare for the trials and the problems that would come with it.

"The Trial of Will, which will test the limits of your will power."

"The Trial of Mind, which will test your creativity and wit."

"The Trial of Heart, which will peer into your psyche and mindset."

"Those are the qualities our founder wanted young cultivators to excel at," Rebecca explained with a calm and gentle voice.

Rebecca recalled some things an elder had said to her years ago, when she was preparing for the trials herself.

"Cultivators need a strong will, to make sure they never stop striving for their objectives."

"Cultivators need a sharp mind, to guarantee a good use of this will and deal with all obstacles they will face in life."

"Cultivators need a good heart, to make sure their will and mind are set in the right direction."

"As such, you will have to rely on yourself," Rebecca warned.

This wasn't a test of strength, and there was no way to get around it. Whether they liked it or not, the greatest opponent the participants would have to face would be themselves. The only fact the participants could count on was that they would leave with complete knowledge of who they were, be it a blessing or a curse.

"If these trials are hosted in the Abyss Sect and the founder was the one that created them, why are the other four cardinal sects involved?"

Amon inquired.

He felt that it wasn't in the best interest of the Abyss Sect to share its resources since all of the rewards from the Hellblaze Trials were provided by the founder.

"The Hellblaze Trials were made for the younger generation of cultivators as a whole. The main purpose of these trials isn't the rewards; it's guiding the young cultivators in the right direction. It's not something our founder wanted to restrict to his own sect. It's also a way to strengthen the relationships between the cardinal sects."

Hearing this, Lya silently sneered from inside of the ring. The real purpose was to make sure the young cultivators would follow the path that Arthur Royce deemed worthy. If they had a mindset similar to what he deemed acceptable, they would be rewarded. If not, they would leave empty-handed, knowing that the way they thought was wrong.

"There is something else," Rebecca said as she looked at Amon with a pained expression. Her hesitation was clear as she tried to find the right words to speak to him. "The Hellblaze Trials will be dangerous."

"How so?" Amon raised a brow, clearly confused.

Killing was strictly forbidden in the Hellblaze Secret World. Even though only the participants could enter, the elders and representatives still had means to know what was happening inside.

"Your father will be involved."

Her face was full of regret as she said this to him, especially when she saw the anguish shoot across his face. Amon's eyes widened and he felt queasy. His face distorted into a hate-filled scowl. Seeing her son like this was hard for Rebecca, but she was powerless to do anything.

"Excuse me," Amon said in a low voice as he stood up and silently left the room.

He couldn't think straight, and he didn't know exactly what he was feeling in the raging volcano that his emotions had turned into. What he knew was that it certainly wasn't something good.

Rebecca sighed loudly as if trying to push away the matters weighing on her chest. She had a very tired look on her face as she stared at the door. She knew her son wanted to be alone to sort out his feelings. She too had a lot to deal with regarding such matters.

While Amon and Rebecca were left alone with their troubles, Lya was also going through complex emotions. The Hellblaze Secret World was something that had been achieved after the War of Falling Leaves, as Nemeus called it. All that Lya knew about it were things that Arthur had planned alongside Alexei, the Ashen Heart tree included.

Hearing Rebecca's explanation on how the Hellblaze Trials worked, Lya felt a deep contempt for all that Arthur Royce had done.

Truly arrogant, Lya thought to herself.

She understood Arthur's choice, but for him to do things that way was the same as admitting he thought he could dictate how people needed to think.

Despite that, she couldn't deny the usefulness of the trials, especially for Amon. He would be able to confront all of his flaws and weaknesses, and that was a major step he needed to take in his path as a proper soul cultivator. Amon would have nowhere to hide from himself. He would be forced to understand himself, and growth would follow.

"A pity that neither Arthur nor Alexei had this chance."

Lya shook her head as a wry smile appeared on her face. If long ago something like the Hellblaze Trials had existed, maybe things would have been different. Lya found it very ironic that Arthur was the one that made them, considering that he also decided to sever the path of soul cultivation.

Her expression slowly became cold and ruthlessness appeared deep in her eyes. She wasn't Nemeus. She didn't have to understand Arthur Royce, much less forgive him. The mess he was as a person wasn't her problem. Her responsibility was to properly raise Amon and lead him down a different path than what the others had taken.

Arthur Royce and Alexei Vine were very similar and very different. They both had an unbearable arrogance that came with power. They could bend the world itself to their will, and they were not afraid to do so with people too.

They had the strength to rule the world, and they never hesitated to do so. They felt it was only natural. In that regard, they were very similar. The point where they differed was in which direction to take the world, and that was what split them apart and eventually led to war.

They never once considered that maybe they shouldn't impose their will over those of others. However, while Alexei did what he wanted without a care, Arthur Royce hid his intentions behind his ideals, always trying to be in the moral high ground.

Lya gave a long sigh as she resentfully remembered the past. As her thoughts drifted, her expression became solemn, and the ruthlessness in her eyes gave way to an unbreakable resolve. She would not let Amon fail where Alexei and Arthur did.

What she had to do, what she decided to take upon herself, was to prove that a strong soul cultivator could be a decent human being.

THE GATES OF HELL

Six months went by in the blink of an eye without much ruckus. Amon and spent his fifteenth birthday hanging out with Daniel and his mother. He didn't mind the quaint date at all.

He became strangely silent after his mother told him about the Hellblaze Trials. His face was in a constant state of dismay and his eyes glinted with a strange light, as if he was constantly fighting something inside him.

He started training nonstop and even asked Lya to cut the time they gave his body a rest between rounds of tempering. He wanted to get as strong as possible for the Hellblaze Trials, and he would not mind the pain or the constant exhaustion.

He successfully stepped in the late stages of body tempering at the four-month mark, but Lya was surprised to see that his cells were not even close to being saturated yet. He could go on tempering his body for many years at the current rate of improvement.

Lya, however, didn't tell him any of this. Amon's psychological state was somewhat delicate, and telling him about his body would possibly worsen things. She didn't tell him that he had entered the late stages of body tempering, and they continued with his training routine.

The strength of his soul also increased greatly. His divine sense seemed to grow by the day and turned out to be much more stable and powerful than before. Amon felt that he would be able to sense beyond walls and objects soon

Nevertheless, he didn't feel joy at all in his newfound strength. He had a sour taste in his mouth whenever he thought about the trials. His father's voice continuously invaded his thoughts.

I need you to be brave, son.

That serene, indifferent voice. That cold, ruthless expression. Those cruel, dark eyes. That hateful man.

Amon gritted his teeth with enough strength to make them creak. He felt anger bubbling inside his chest, like a simmering volcano ready to explode. However, he soon realized he was losing his temper.

He took a deep breath, calming himself, and recited the second part of the soulrousing technique. It was a habit he had been developing, almost like a ritual to help him keep his emotions in check. As he felt the familiar sensation of his body's temperature alternating between hot and cold, he felt his anger dissipate.

He let out a sigh before jumping down from his bed. He washed his face with the water in the basin beneath the mirror, put on a clean set of clothes, and he carefully tied Windhowler to his back.

He silently left his room, leaving everything clean and organized. As soon as he crossed the door, however, he looked back. He didn't know why he did it, nor did he think about it for more than a moment. Still, it was the first time he had done so ever since he started living in this house six years ago.

He looked at his simple bed, where he had cried for many sleepless nights, and where he had undergone his first round of body tempering.

He looked at the mirror hanging on the wall, which he used when he dyed his hair almost every week. Now, it served for not much else besides tidying his ashen hair when he woke up.

He looked at the black mat on the floor, which he had used for years on end as he fruitlessly tried to manipulate qi. Now, he made it soar over the room during his training of qi control.

He looked at his open window, through which the sun shone. In the past, he enjoyed looking at the grass and the trees outside. Now, however, what he could see was mostly the destruction Lya had left when she first taught him about swords.

He suddenly realized what was wrong. He had left the window open. He made his way back to the room and slowly closed it. The warm sunlight shining on his face gave his way to a monotone gloom as the window finally closed. Amon was going to leave for a long time; there was no reason to leave the window open.

Unknowingly, Amon was somewhat sentimental. There was longing in his eyes as he left the room. He had no idea why he felt that way, but he couldn't get rid of the feeling.

He gently knocked on his mother's door, and carefully opened it as she invited him in.

Rebecca was looking through her window as always, but this time there was a deep frown on her face. Her green eyes were full of concern. She also seemed to be gripping something tightly under her bedsheets, as Amon could see her hand slightly trembling under the sheets from all the strength Rebecca was putting in her grip.

She turned her look away from the window, glancing at Amon's golden eyes with tenderness. She gestured for him to approach, and she gave him a hug. They didn't speak a word to each other; the bear hug she gave him held more value than anything she could ever say.

Rebecca seemed very concerned as she held Amon in her arms. She had a bad feeling, just like when he left for the Scavenging. It was as if a dark cloud had started gathering above Amon, following him wherever he was, a

232

terrible omen.

She looked at him, not hiding the worry she had at all. She felt there was something tearing at her chest as she looked at him, making her feel incredibly sad. She extended a hand and tenderly held his face, looking at him deeply.

"Amon..."

She had trouble finding the words she wanted to say. It was as if something was clutching her throat, not letting her speak or even breathe properly.

Amon became worried. Naturally, he had no idea of what was going in his mother's mind besides the potential trouble he would have during his journey. Seeing his mother like this made him uneasy.

Rebecca took a deep breath, closing her eyes for a moment. When she opened them, it was as if all the negative feelings weighing down on her had disappeared for a fleeting moment.

"No matter what, remember that I'll always love you," she said as she ruffled his hair, bringing him closer to her chest. "I want you to be happy. It's all I've ever wanted."

Amon hugged her tighter. He felt his chest tightening and his feelings were in turmoil. He was suddenly very anxious. He could feel there was something wrong in his mother's words.

"Look at me," she said seriously, gently pushing him away from her chest.

She had a complex look on her face, a mix of unwillingness, longing, and serenity. It was a gaze that pierced straight into Amon's heart. He opened his mouth to speak, but he found no words.

"Promise me that no matter what happens, no matter how bad things get, you will always try to be happy," she demanded, her voice trembling as her eyes filled with tears. "Promise me that you'll never give up on yourself, Amon."

She didn't explain her request, nor did she elaborate on it. She felt she didn't have to. She knew her son very well; she knew his flaws more than anyone else did.

Amon was growing up and he was dealing with his defects. He had experienced much more than most kids his age, but Rebecca knew things could always get worse. She knew that a single push was all it took to make someone walking on the edge to fall from the cliff and be swallowed by the darkness below.

Amon looked at his mother unwavering. The way she was acting greatly alarmed him, but he knew better than to question her. The last time he saw his mother this serious was when his father had betrayed the sect.

He did his best to hide the fear that was starting to creep up in the depths of his mind as he faced his mother. His gaze was solemn as he spoke to her.

"I promise."

There was no need to say anything else. Even though this seemed to be a simple promise, he knew it was not. He would follow through with it, for his mother's sake.

It wasn't a half-hearted promise in any way. He now knew the weight a promise should have. He promised it as a soul cultivator, and he would do his best to accomplish it.

The tension within her greatly reduced and she hugged him tightly one last time before they parted.

"I love you."

"I love you too, mom," he said from the bottom of his heart.

His voice was somewhat heavy, somewhat weary as he spoke.

"Take care," she said as she tried to put on a smile. Her green eyes seemed to glow, and the sunlight gave her golden hair a bright luster, but it also made her face seem ghostly.

"I will."

As he was leaving, he heard steps coming from the other side of the door. It was Daniel, packed and ready to go.

"We will be late," he said in a hurried tone. "I'm sorry aunt Becca, but we have to go now," he continued in an apologetic manner.

There was a serious glint in his eyes as he looked at Rebecca, and they seemed to have a whole exchange in the split second their eyes met.

"You take care too," Rebecca said to Daniel in a gentle tone.

"Thank you. Hopefully, we will see each other soon."

He gave her a deep, meaningful glance as he spoke.

There was some hesitation in his voice, as if he hadn't found the right way to express himself.

Still, Rebecca understood his meaning. He would do his best, but he was also very worried about the trials.

"We will," Rebecca spoke with a soft voice, almost as if she was whispering to herself.

Daniel gave her a slight nod, before turning back and hurriedly leaving the house with Amon.

Rebecca was left alone, looking at the sky through her window. A gorgeous azure color was painted across the sky, and the sun appeared brighter than it ever had, yet Rebecca couldn't find a single ounce of joy in the scene.

Even so, a small, weary smile made its way into her lips. For a moment, her worries were gone as she remembered the look in Amon's eyes as he his promise to her.

He didn't lie.

She seemed incredibly tired, but she couldn't hide the happiness in her voice as she spoke.

Amon and Daniel rushed towards the Northern Station at full speed, trying to make up for lost time. Their surroundings were nothing more than a blur as the wind whipped at their faces making their eyes sting.

Daniel felt somewhat awkward as he saw Amon running by his side.

The last time they traveled together was during the Scavenging. At the time, Daniel had to hold back and take several breaks, but now Amon was following his pace with ease. He most likely could go even faster without a problem.

While Daniel was thinking about how much things had changed, Amon was absent-minded. He was thinking about the way his mother had acted, and the anxiousness he couldn't get rid of in the depths of his mind. He had a deep frown on his face as he lightly stepped on the grass, propelling himself forward.

BANG! BANG! BANG!

A deafening sound echoed behind them, and Amon turned back to see rays of light flashing in the far distance. Soon enough, bells started to toll, and he was restless.

"Beasts trying to come onto the sect's ground?" Amon asked, somewhat confused.

"Seems like it." Daniel shrugged. "Some idiot must have pissed off a strong spirit beast during a sect mission."

It wasn't that rare for something like this to occur, but the walls of the Abyss Sect had an array formation that repelled weaker beasts. As such, only those of class five and above would manage to get close to the walls. The problem was that those beasts usually lived in the depths of the Broken Forest, dozens of miles away from the sect.

Amon narrowed his eyes. He knew that spirit beasts of higher classes had intelligence in no way inferior to humans, but this was strange. The beast was strong enough to resist the array formation on the walls, but not intelligent enough to know what would happen next?

"The elders will take care of it. Come on!" Daniel was restless and they were already late.

Amon nodded and together they continued to sprint.

It took no more than a few minutes for the Northern Station to appear on the horizon. As they rushed into the main plaza, dozens of Outer Sect members were already waiting. Their eyes were turned to the sky, struck with awe. A few children couldn't stop waving to whatever they were looking at in the sky as they jumped with red faces, full of excitement.

A few meters above the plaza, hovering in the air, was a massive spirit vessel. The cherry-black vessel was similar to the spirit vessel Amon had seen Jake using before, but it was much larger than the other. This combat vessel could easily accommodate more than thirty passengers.

Regardless, there were only six passengers there, and Amon could see them clearly. Standing with a clearly annoyed expression was the third elder, Richard Layn. He glared at them impatiently, motioning for them to hurry up.

The two young men jumped up, surprising the people around them. They heavily landed on the prow of the spirit vessel, but it remained steady.

"You're late," the third elder snorted.

"We're very sorry," Daniel huffed, taking a step forward and lowering his head.

He made no excuses for their delay as he was out of breath, and he knew it would only displease Richard even more.

Richard raised his eyes, looking at the barely visible light flashing far north and hearing the weak chime of the bells. He raised a brow, but said nothing.

"Do not let such things happen again." Richard dismissed their worries as he turned the spirit vessel toward Hell Keeper's Mountain. The golden circle around him flashed once and the spirit vessel sped forward suddenly, causing Amon to briefly lose his balance.

After he found his footing, he looked around and caught a glimpse of Joshua, Karen, and Jake sitting on the back of the spirit vessel, meditating in preparation for the journey. He knew they'd need all the time they could get, so he decided not to disturb them.

Accompanying them was a young, blonde-haired girl and a black-haired boy. Daniel leaned closer to Amon and signaled for him to not draw attention to themselves.

"Those two are Evan Wylde and Skylar Burton," he explained. "They're disciples of the fourth and seventh elders."

Amon gave him a slight nod. It seems all of the elemental purification members came from Sky Reach Village, which wasn't surprising in the least.

"What about the body tempering disciples in Sky Reach?" Amon asked as he raised a brow.

"They are too young. They don't have the maturity to make proper use of the trials. The best choice is to use common members of the Inner Sect at an appropriate age and close to elemental purification."

There were no body tempering cultivators in Sky Reach Village above twelve years old. They were far too talented to be at that level in what would be an appropriate age for the Hellblaze Trials. As such, the common Inner Sect members that had more maturity and experience, even if they were a bit less talented, would be a better choice.

Daniel didn't mention that the only reason he was going was because of his fighting style. If something dangerous did happen, as Jake had warned him, Daniel would be a valuable asset in the fight. He was the least talented member of the Abyss Sect in the Hellblaze Trials, but somehow he ended up being some sort of ace in the body tempering level.

The air around the spirit vessel seemed to twist and distort as it flew at such an absurd speed that Amon couldn't even locate himself. All he could see clearly was Hell Keeper's Mountain growing larger and larger in front of him by the second. There seemed to be some sort of ward in the spirit vessel, as Amon felt no wind at all, even when the spirit vessel traveled at such speeds.

Without stopping, the spirit vessel suddenly dove and traversed the golden gates to Hell Keeper's City as if the curtain of light blocking it didn't exist at all, reaching their destination in no time.

The spirit vessel finally slowed down as Richard looked at the Ashen Heart tree. He breathed a sigh of relief, and directed the spirit vessel to it in a gentle flight, unlike his previous rush. Amon looked carefully at the tree as they approached, and he saw a few figures standing beside it.

The spirit vessel took a sharp turn as Richard made it fly at a low height, barely above the buildings. It was necessary, given that otherwise they would hit the tree's crown.

They came to a halt as soon as they reached the major plaza, and Richard carefully landed the spirit vessel near Warrior Hall. As soon as it touched the ground, Jake, Karen and the others opened their eyes and stood up.

"Good to see you again," Jake greeted Amon politely while Karen waved her hands and Joshua shrugged.

Evan and Skylar simply ignored him as they jumped off of the spirit vessel.

"Nice to see you too," Amon greeted him back as he jumped down the spirit vessel with Daniel and approached the people gathered near the Ashen Heart tree.

There were a handful of cold-faced elders looking at Richard with mild annoyance, but they dared not voice their objections. Richard was a high elder, and they were below him. Seeing this, Richard rolled his eyes.

"My apologies for the delay," he said half-heartedly.

Next to the elders, two youths and a girl awaited with anxious faces. The girl, Malia, couldn't stop moving about, she wrung her hands, twisting her fingers nonstop. Her brown hair was neatly arranged into a ponytail, and her yellow clothes seemed to be fluttering due to her incessant movements. Meanwhile, Orson, her brother, seemed very annoyed.

"Calm down," Orson said gritting his teeth.

His sister didn't seem to mind as she kept darting her eyes around like a scared kitten.

Amon heard a snort by his side, and he saw Karen glancing at Malia coldly.

"Come on, Malia. Show some composure," Karen warned.

The girl suddenly froze in place as she heard that indifferent voice. She slowly turned her head and saw Karen glaring at her. Malia shuddered, but ultimately tried to control her nervousness.

"Also, Orson, you should treat her better. She's your sister and she's clearly anxious," Karen turned to the boy and admonished him.

Orson's face flushed red and he averted his gaze, but he clearly made an effort to look a bit less annoyed as he stepped in front of his sister.

"Youngsters..." Amon heard someone say in a low and weary voice.

He looked around, but the only person he saw from the direction he heard the voice was the Third elder. He was walking with a cold and authoritative expression, not at all looking as if he said something like that.

Amon looked at him suspiciously, but Richard seemed to not notice his gaze at all.

As they approached the Ashen Heart tree, the ten chosen members stood together in absolute silence. Amon closed his eyes, trying to focus.

"Our guests should be arriving soon," Richard said in his serene voice.

Not long after, a low, piercing sound trilled in the far away distance. Amon opened his eyes and saw three bright blurs shooting in their direction.

Amon squinted his eyes as the piercing sound became louder to the point of hurting his ears. The bright blurs approached them at a high speed before suddenly slowing down and revealing three gigantic spirit vessels, even bigger than the one Richard was controlling moments ago.

The first spirit vessel to land seemed to be carved out of ice, with a translucent hull that made the light ripple around it. A faint mist surrounded it, blurring the view of the prow and the passengers. It had an elegant and sleek design, full of curves rather than the aggressive edges and corners the combat vessels of the Abyss Sect had.

It landed without a sound and didn't raise even a speck of dust. Twelve silhouettes jumped from the spirit vessel, still hidden in the mist. Richard took a step forward and gave a polite bow.

"The Abyss Sect welcomes members of the Noan River Sect," he said in a monotone, almost robotic voice.

"Still annoyed by formalities, Richard?" an aged, but sweet voice echoed from the mist as a figure stepped forward.

It was an elderly woman clad in elegant, deep-blue robes. Her silver hair was tied in a bun at the back of her head, and the wrinkles on her face were more prominent as she smiled.

Richard snorted as he heard her comment, but his expression was somewhat strange as he faced her. The woman's smile grew wider, but before she could say anything, another spirit vessel arrived, raising a gust of wind and a cloud of dust.

"As rude as ever," the elderly woman complained as she waved a shriveled hand. The wind calmed down and the dust settled, revealing the spirit vessels behind it.

Unlike the other, this one looked crude in comparison. It had a wide deck and a stout design, giving it a solid look. What drew attention to it, however, was its material. It glowed with a deep, purple light that seemed to flicker nonstop.

"My apologies for that, Sarah."

A middle-aged man jumped from the spirit vessel with an apologetic expression on his face. His golden clothes fluttered in the air as he gracefully landed on the ground.

"The Abyss Sect welcomes the members of the Roaring Mountain Sect."

The man gave him a polite bow before gesturing for the passengers in the spirit vessel to come down too.

The ten young cultivators of the Roaring Mountain Sect and a woman dressed in the same golden clothes as the man jumped down from the spirit vessel.

A young man took a step forward as he looked up. He had dark-brown hair that reached his shoulders and a pair of dark eyes. His brows were furrowed as he looked at the incoming spirit vessel.

Jake's eyes shined with a ferocious light as he saw the young man. His aura rose unconsciously as his face was solemn.

"The Southern Flame Sect is here, but I don't see the spirit vessel of the Storm Peak Sect," the youth commented, not looking concerned at all.

The man dressed in golden robes gave him a sharp glance, but the youth ignored it completely, never taking his eyes away from the spirit vessel that was landing.

The Southern Flame Sect's spirit vessel was of a bright red color, covered in motes of pale light that seemed to flutter on its surface, much like ashes. It landed a bit further than the other two spirit vessels, and the passenger didn't waste any time to jump out from it.

"The Abyss Sect welcomes the members of the Southern Flame Sect," Richard greeted again, in an even more robotic voice than before. It was as if he was struggling to not show annoyance.

A bald, elderly man in red robes glared at Richard, certainly not amused. His clothes could barely contain his bulging muscles as he walked with his back straightened, full of authority.

"Is this the way your sect welcomes visitors, Richard?" he asked in a biting tone. Richard, on the other hand, showed no further reaction, making the man knit his brows as he pressed further. "You can't even take the Hellblaze Trials seriously, maybe your sect master should have sent someone else."

"Come on, Baldwin, don't be so stuck up," Sarah said with a naughty smile.

"Grow up, Sarah. You are acting a few hundred years younger than you should," Baldwin said with a displeased expression.

Sarah seemed to shrug it off and didn't mind him anymore.

Richard changed the subject as he frowned deeply. "The Storm Peak Sect is indeed late. Eustace isn't one to be late."

"I'm sure they will be arriving soon," said Leonard, the high elder from the Roaring Mountain Sect.

"You might not know this, Leonard, but Eustace is even more stuck up than our dear Baldwin here," Sarah said with a sneer. "He would rather kill himself than run late in a gathering for the Hellblaze Trials."

"Something happened in the Storm Peak Sect," Baldwin said with surprising certainty, as if it was the logical conclusion. "I believe we should try to contact them."

The four high elders looked at each other, thinking. At that moment, a weary voice echoed from the middle of the plaza. "There is no need for that."

The four of them froze for a moment as they looked at the small man that seemed to have appeared out of thin air, without any one of them noticing. Richard immediately fell to one knee, as did all the other Abyss Sect's elders and Jake. The other disciples were a heartbeat late, but they also fell to one knee.

Seeing this, Amon followed suit, even though he had no idea who the man was.

"We greet the sect master," Jake proclaimed for all of the disciples present.

Is he... Lars Borgin? Amon asked himself.

His brown hair was tidied and his clear eyes had an indifferent gaze, but just looking at him made Amon feel a horrifying pressure as if he could be killed with the snap of a finger.

A blood-red sword was hanging from his back, and Amon found it quite familiar. He frowned deeply as he looked intently at the red jewel embedded in the guard of the sword. His golden eyes had a strange glint as his suspicions grew.

Sarah, Baldwin, and Leonard, as well as the common elders from their sect and the disciples all bowed politely as they saw the sect master of the Abyss Sect.

Borgin didn't seem to care about the greetings as he waved his hands dismissively.

"There were unforeseen circumstances in the Storm Peak Sect," Borgin spoke with a calm, but cold voice. "They will be late, but should be arriving soon."

The expressions of the high elders eased somewhat, but Sarah still had a deep frown on her face. She felt something was very wrong. As she was pondering, however, a new piercing sound started to echo through the interior of Hell Keeper's Mountain.

Amon looked up and saw a new blur speeding in their direction. This one, however, was much faster than the previous three spirit vessels. In the blink of an eye, the blur was already upon them.

It suddenly stopped, revealing a spirit vessel that looked more like a needle than a boat. It seemed to be made of silver but had a strong metallic luster that made one want to avert their eyes from it.

A slender and graceful figure jumped down from it, dressed in lustrous green robes. It was a very beautiful woman with silky, black hair and brown eyes. She bowed deeply at Borgin and spoke in a polite tone.

"My apologies for the delay, Sect Master Borgin," she said with an apologetic expression.

"No problem, Veronica. Your sect master told me about it," Borgin answered in his indifferent tone.

Veronica gestured to the spirit vessel and all the passengers descended. As they approached, the high elder's expressions turned serious and they all frowned.

"Where the hell is Derek?" a youthful voice came from the side of the disciples of the Southern Flame Sect. A young, tall man had a displeased look on his face as he looked at the Storm Peak representatives. "I also don't see Thomas, Clarice, and Helen."

Baldwin sent the young man a piercing glance as his aura shot up. A gust of wind formed around him and the ground cracked. The air itself became heavy as the young man felt an almost unbearable pressure crushing him, pressing him to the ground.

"Mind your manners, Alden!" Baldwin said in a cold voice. "I wonder what the sect master would think of his disciple if he saw this pathetic display."

The pressure suddenly disappeared, and Baldwin turned to Borgin. He gave a polite bow as he spoke in a soft voice. "My apologies."

Borgin gave him a slight nod, not minding at all. Jake had a strange look in his eyes and the young man of the Roaring Mountain Sect was barely holding back his laughter.

"Enough of this," Borgin said authoritatively. "Now that everyone is here, it's time to start."

Everyone present became silent as Borgin pointed a finger to the Ashen Heart tree.

To Amon's surprise, the tree started shuddering, making its gray leaves rustle. One by one, its branches moved, pointing to the skies as the twisted white trunk started moving. The sound of breaking wood filled the air, as the white trunk began to slowly untwine.

The process took several seconds to complete, and when it was done, Amon gasped. The Ashen Heart tree's twisted trunk untwined in two thinner trunks, which arched in what looked like a gateway.

A curtain of light shone between the trunks, glowing with a hellish sheen. In the gloom of Hell Keeper's City, that ominous light was like a beacon in the dark.

Amon felt an intense heatwave coming from the gateway, making him start sweating even before crossing it. The air around the gateway seemed to distort, giving it an oppressive feeling.

As he gawked at the Ashen Heart tree and the gateway it formed, his anxiety returned at full force. He felt like his chest would explode due to the anxiety and the fear he had when he looked at that curtain of light.

All Amon could feel beyond that hellish light was a sinister void.

You all know the rules," Borgin said with a cold voice as he looked at each one of the young cultivators present. "Break any of them and you'll be disqualified. We'll all be watching."

He leered over Amon for a long time.

"Whatever you obtain from the Hellblaze Trials will belong to you alone," Borgin held his hands behind his back as he spoke, taking sluggish steps as he walked to the Ashen Heart tree. He looked at the curtain of light in the gateway with cold eyes before he turned around, facing the young cultivators again.

With a wave of his hands, fifty golden tokens appeared and flew to each one of the participants

"If you find yourselves in danger, crush this token and the guardian will come to your rescue," Borgin's face was indifferent as ever as he looked at their dumbfounded faces.

Amon looked at the golden token hovering in front of him with hesitation as he extended his hands to it. The triangle-shaped token was the size of a fist and had a smooth surface, where red runes of the divine language seemed to float. It felt cold to the touch when Amon grasped it firmly and put it in his clothes.

Jake quietly listened to his master as he put the golden token away. He felt an almost palpable tension in the air. On the surface, everything seemed normal, but he could feel that underneath that superficial calm there was something hiding.

The ten participants of the Noan River Sect, led by Anna Hale, were all dressed in blue, looking somewhat bored as they bundled together. Anna, however, looked like a sculpture. She stood there, unmoving, as Lars Borgin spoke, hiding her face behind a veil of swirling mist, showing only her long, black hair falling behind her back.

Those of the Southern Flame Sect, however, were more restrained. Being watched closely by Baldwin, they didn't dare show the slightest disrespect towards Lars Borgin, especially Alden Bren, that had already been publicly admonished.

The Roaring Mountain Sect participants were also reigned in, looking like statues as Reynard Stark stood in front of them, completely still and with a perfect posture. to Jake's displeasure, however, he saw Reynard sneer as he grabbed his token—the idea of getting hurt was ridiculous to him.

Jake tried to ignore Reynard as he looked away, watching closely the Storm Peak Sect members, all clad in green. He found out why he was feeling so uneasy. Each one of them were strangers to him, and they all looked pale. As Alden had pointed out, Derek, Thomas, Helen and Clarice, the elemental purification members they were familiar with, were nowhere to be seen.

Jake had the feeling that the Storm Peak people were unusually tense, especially Veronica. He caught himself sneaking a glance at Sarah and Baldwin, and saw that they too were looking strangely at the Storm Peak Sect's members.

In complete contrast to Jake, Amon didn't pay attention to his surroundings at all. He had never seen any of these people, and even if he did, he wouldn't be able to sense anything wrong with them, as he couldn't even think properly at the moment.

It was as if a shroud had been clouding his thoughts. He stared at that red curtain of light in the Ashen Heart tree with a dazed look on his face, as if he couldn't take his eyes away.

Amon was jolted awake by a pat on his back. He looked around and saw Daniel looking at him with a worried face.

"Are you okay?" he asked while not hiding his concern at all.

"I... I'm fine," Amon said after hesitating. "I just have a bad feeling."

Daniel gave him an understanding nod. Amon suddenly looked very tired. Even though Rebecca hadn't told him how the situation would turn out after the trials, telling Amon about Lloyd was enough to shake him to his core.

"I'm sure it'll be fine," Daniel said with a forced smile. Amon, however, wasn't fooled. He could see the hesitation in Daniel's eyes

"Thank you," Amon said in a heartfelt manner. He knew Daniel was trying to cheer him up, and he was truly grateful for it.

"You may begin," Borgin announced. The red light shining on his face gave him a sinister appearance as he scrutinized every one of the fifty participants with his cold gaze.

The members of the Five Cardinal sects formed five lines, standing side by side as they approached the gateway together. Every step closer to the gateway made Amon sweat more as the heat intensified. A loud rumbling sound came from the gateway and the ground started quaking as the curtain of light rippled like water.

Taking a deep breath, Jake stepped forward. The light suddenly became viscous and started twisting around itself. Jake launched himself into the gateway, being swallowed by the rippling red light and disappearing.

The remaining cultivators followed suit, being devoured by the hellish light as they crossed the gateway. When Amon's turn came, he couldn't help but tremble.

As he approached the red light, he looked back once. Unsure what force pulled him to do so, he locked eyes with Lars Borgin. They stared at each other for a heartbeat, but it felt like an eternity.

All Amon could see in those clear eyes was a deep, cold indifference that made his hair stand on end. Before either of them could say anything, the red light enveloped Amon.

It was a bizarre sensation. Amon felt as if he had been immersed in a pool of a viscous liquid. He had nothing supporting him, but he didn't feel as if he was falling.

The red light shifted into terrifying darkness, and Amon felt an unbearable pressure crushing on him. When he was sure his bones would break, his whole body was stretched in all directions, as if space was trying to rip him apart.

There was a brief respite, and motes of light floated around Amon, contrasting with the empty void that surrounded him. Before he could even process what he was seeing, the motes of light started spinning madly around each other, forming bright, concentric circles in front of him.

Amon tried to scream, but he couldn't open his mouth as he suddenly felt something pulling him toward the circles. He felt as if his skin was being pulled apart as he accelerated. He felt dizzy as the circles of light distorted and started overlapping and twisting around each other, as if someone was kneading them in a messy bundle. Nausea overtook him as he lost all sense of direction. He wasn't sure if it were the circles of light or him that were being distorted anymore as he tunneled through space.

When he felt he wouldn't be able to hold on anymore, the messy lights seemed to untwine, returning to their original appearances of neat circles. The circles then broke up in motes of light again, and the darkness gave way to a red gloom.

❊ ❊ ❊

"Sir, are you sure this is alright?" Richard asked in a low voice as he approached Lars Borgin in a respectful manner. His expression was full of worry, making his wrinkles stand out even more.

Instead of answering, Borgin gave Richard a cold look. Richard quietly closed his mouth, bowed respectfully and took a few steps back, not making another sound.

"His question isn't out of place, Nemeus," Borgin transmitted his voice as he lightly tapped the crimson sword he was carrying.

"It's a strange occurrence indeed, but it shouldn't change our plans too much," Nemeus answered with his hoarse voice. "The third and fourth protectors should be more than enough to handle a spirit beast outbreak and a class seven blackhorn serpent."

"Still... the timing is too coincidental," Borgin commented, showing uneasiness in his voice.

"It is. But delaying the Hellblaze Trials for an unknown amount of time right after the participants arrived would not fare well with the other cardinal sects, especially after we canceled the previous trials without further notice and didn't give them a proper explanation," Nemeus said, frowning slightly. "It will be even worse if we disclose the reason and our intentions to wait for the protectors to return. They will suspect we expect something to happen, and that would also not be acceptable."

"Maybe it would be safer to accept those consequences and delay—"

"No," Nemeus didn't let him finish. "We will go ahead as planned."

"I don't understand. Why are you making such a senseless choice?" Borgin protested. "Is it truly worth it to risk everything for a single piece of information?"

"Yes," Nemeus gave a simple answer and ended the conversation. Borgin would never understand, and Nemeus didn't trust him enough to tell him the truth.

Any and all sacrifices were worth it if it meant they would have anything to use against Dale Loray.

✱ ✱ ✱

Suddenly, Amon felt solid ground beneath his feet. His senses were a mess, and he fell to the ground, unable to balance himself. He was, however, able to fight against the urge to puke. Finally managing to recover, he stood up and looked around. The dark ground beneath his feet seemed to be made of rock, but it had a glossy sheen to it. It was incredibly smooth but uneven.

"Is this vitrified rock?" he asked looking at the ground dumbstruck.

A terrifying heat was being emitted from it, and all Amon could do was to make the qi around him spin, moving the air and artificially creating a wind. It didn't help much, though, as even the air itself seemed to be scalding hot. In a matter of seconds, Amon's clothes were already drenched in sweat.

His breath was rough as he looked around. The sky was dark, but there were no stars nor a moon in it. The only source of light Amon could see coming from it were ominous red clouds that glowed with a sinister light. The faint light wasn't enough to properly illuminate Amon's surroundings, immersing them in a reddish gloom.

No matter where he looked at, all he could see was a vast expanse of the vitrified ground below and red clouds above. The visage made him shiver. He had no idea which direction to follow, and he was completely alone.

"Where are the others?" he asked aloud.

His nervousness and anxiousness only got worse as time passed.

"Lya, are you there?"

His face was pale, and the gloom made him sick.

To his surprise and despair, there was no answer. He closed his eyes, thinking. Windhowler was still strapped to his back. The interspatial ring was still on his finger. His senses were still disoriented, but they were working.

There were three reasons for his call to go unanswered by Lya: She couldn't hear him; She couldn't answer him; She didn't want to answer him.

No matter the reason, Amon knew the cause. Whether he liked it or not, the trials had started.

Amon chose a direction and started moving forward. He had no guide nor anyone to talk to. He didn't know which direction to follow and he didn't know where he wanted to go.

In the Hellblaze Trials, he would not be able to count on anyone but himself.

A WILL GROWS THROUGH STRUGGLES

A mon's steps were uneven and hesitant as he walked forward. His face was deathly pale and his dry lips were cracked. He found it hard to open his mouth, as the dried saliva was gluing his lips together. His throat was sore and every breath he took was an agony in and of itself, as the searing hot air caused his eyes, nose, and throat to sting with dryness.

He didn't know how long he had walked. He didn't know if he was walking in circles or not. The only certainty he had was that no matter where he looked at, the ground would be that black vitrified rock and red clouds would light up the dark sky above his head.

Amon's eyes were misty as he moved forward in a daze. The uneven ground made him fall over more than once. His arms and legs were full of bruises and the temperature was so hot that he couldn't even sweat anymore.

His feet were covered in blisters, and they only made walking worse. For some reason, he couldn't open his bottomless pouch to retrieve his canteen. It was as if some force was holding the pouch shut and Amon wasn't strong enough to open it.

He was dragging his feet along the ground rather than taking proper steps. He felt too weak to lift his feet. He had never felt so exhausted before; not even during training. It was as if the atmosphere of the place was draining his energy. To top it off, his divine sense was also on the fritz. He could manipulate the qi around him, but he couldn't absorb it to recover his stamina.

The golden token weighing down on his clothes was turning more attractive each time Amon took a breath. Some time ago, Amon had started gripping the token underneath his clothes. It felt cool as Amon touched it, the only thing that seemed unaffected by the heat.

The thoughts of breaking it weren't strong, but they seemed to linger in his mind without ever going away. The temptation grew stronger the weaker Amon became. He had no idea of when that voice first appeared. It could've been mere minutes. It could've been hours. It could've been days.

Either way, it would eventually overwhelm him if he didn't find his way out.

Thud!

Amon's feet got stuck in a depression in the ground and he fell down powerlessly. He landed on his shoulder, and a sharp pain spread through it. Amon didn't mind it, though. He felt his whole body numb. If anything, this pain was somewhat refreshing.

Forcing himself to turn over, he gazed at the sky. The red clouds were still, frozen in time, quietly staring down at him. Looking closely, Amon realized all of them seemed to have the same size and the same shape. It was impossible to use the clouds to try to guide himself.

He tried to laugh in his despair, but he found no voice nor the energy for it. He could only look up with a regretful expression.

This was a place with no life, no disparity, and no movement.

A place where the only thing that seemed to try to struggle against the stillness was himself.

The heat coming from his back didn't bother Amon in the least. He thought it was very comfortable.

He stood still just like the clouds, looking up mindlessly.

Unknowingly, his vision darkened, and all he could see was nothingness.

❊ ❊ ❊

"What an unlucky kid," Sarah said with a sigh. She couldn't hide the pity in her eyes as she looked down.

All of the elders and Borgin were in a dark, spacious room with walls made of white granite. From the ceiling, innumerable white roots cascaded down in a spear-like shape. The twisted roots glowed with a beautiful light, a stark contrast to their ominous appearance.

From them, droplets of a sticky substance fell on a wide, but shallow pool at the center of the room. The pool filled with the viscous liquid glowed like the roots, shedding its pale light on the overseers and making shadows dance through their faces.

Strangely enough, the liquid was completely still, looking more like a bright mirror than a pool of sap. Even the dripping of the glowing droplets didn't make the surface ripple.

What was reflected in that bizarre mirror, however, wasn't the roots hanging from the ceiling. The wide pool seemed to be divided into fifty sections, with the sap dripping from the roots falling in each one of them. Every section showed a different image, and each section had only one person reflected on it. This pool of sap lied under the Ashen Heart tree, and it was through it that the representatives of each sect could supervise the ongoing Hellblaze Trials.

"For the guardian to throw him in Purgatory..." Sarah shook her head with a desolate look.

"The guardian decides what a fitting trial is for each one of the contestants," Borgin said with his cold, indifferent voice. "If he was thrown in Purgatory, it's because it's where he needs to be."

Sarah sighed again, but said no more. The guardian was known for being impartial and precise in his judgement. Furthermore, from her previous experience overseeing the trials, Borgin's words were right. If the boy was there, it was because he needed to be there. Sarah couldn't imagine for what other reason the guardian would put the boy through such suffering. She moved her gaze away from him, looking at a section of the pool closeby.

A graceful, but lonely figure walked through a field of fire and ice. The ground at her feet changed at each step she took, either being covered in chilling snow or turning into smoldering rock. Snow fell from the endless white sky above her, being thrown with violence at her by searing winds.

Her light blue robes were torn and wrinkled under the effects of the opposing elements, and they were clinging tightly to her body. Her silky, black hair whipped about as the hot winds and snow hit her, but she moved on stubbornly.

Sarah could imagine the fearless expression the girl had, even though she had covered her face with a dense white mist that not even the wind could blow away.

Even though she was moving forward, the raging elements were certainly taking a toll on her. Her shoulders were drooped and her steps were slow. Sarah could feel the young woman's burning desire as the girl forcefully proceeded forward, leaving small, but deep footprints on snow and smoldering rock alike.

Sarah pitied Amon for his bad luck, but she also pitied the girl she was looking at. Maybe she had even worse luck.

"Oh, Anna... when will you change?" Sarah asked herself in a whisper, feeling heartbroken as she saw the unyielding figure struggling alone in the tempestuous conflict of fire and ice.

Anna Hale was taking uneasy steps forward, but it was getting harder to move with each step she took. The ice would turn colder, and the fire would burn hotter. The wind would blow harder, and she would get weaker.

Anna would usually not have a problem with the ice at all. Ice was nothing but a form of water, and she was a water cultivator. If anything, she would use this opportunity to cultivate. The problem, however, was the fire. It intermingled with the ice, denying Anna any control.

She couldn't even protect her body from it. The strange combination of fire and ice wore down on her body slowly, and when her body was barely able to take it anymore, it started wearing down her mind.

Anna knew exactly why she was in this place. She had lived her life in such conditions, after all. Looking at it, Anna could only sneer inwardly. That guardian was surely a very cruel being. In truth, her scorn was just a nonacceptance of the defeated. She couldn't deny that she was surprised at how the guardian had seen through her.

The mist covering her face became fainter as she let out a sigh. Her shoulders drooped more and her steps almost came to a halt. She was moving forward at a pace so slow it was unbearably frustrating.

She raised her head, looking at that infinite expanse of white that was the sky above her head. The searing winds made her black hair whip violently behind her back, and the fluttering snowflakes were thrown onto her face, disappearing from view as they penetrated the shroud of mist.

She looked ahead, gazing intently at the intermingling fire and ice. As they collided, the snow would melt, turning into water and the smoldering rock would cool down, hardening. The water would evaporate, turning into a faint mist of steam and the flames would disappear, dispersing in the air.

Anna stopped walking. She stood still, looking ahead in a daze.

Even though the elements collided and neutralized each other, there was a balance. It lasted for no more than a split-second; a moment so fleeting it would seem like an illusion. Nevertheless, she saw it.

For but a moment, in the middle of that tempestuous and mutual destruction, there was a point of equilibrium. A moment where there was a stillness where fire and ice coexisted in harmony.

Moving forward without knowing where you're going was nothing but foolishness. Moving forward while ignoring your surroundings was nothing but foolishness. There was a point where moving forward would bring nothing but suffering. One had to know when to stop, or they might lose all they had achieved.

If you moved back or moved forward at that point, the balance would be ruined, and everything would disperse in the air. Like the heat of the dying flames. Like the water turning into steam.

For the first time in her life, she stopped moving. For the first time in her life, she understood that she was a fool. Because if you never stopped moving, you would never be able to properly look around.

Sometimes, standing still was the best way to move on.

❈ ❈ ❈

Amon slowly opened his eyes. His eyelids were heavy, and he felt it would be easier to simply keep his eyes closed and let his consciousness fade away than to try and wake up. Still, he couldn't give up.

A simple act, which should have taken no more than the fraction of a second, seemed to take a few minutes. When he finally managed to completely open his eyes, Amon was greeted by the same sight he had seen before he passed out.

The red clouds were still above his head, glowing ominously in the sky. All of the same size. All of the same shape. All unmoving.

Amon looked at the sky in despair. His body was completely numb and it felt heavy as if invisible chains bound him to the glossy ground beneath him. His throat and mouth were so dry that his tongue stuck to the inside of his mouth.

His head throbbed in pain, in sync with his heartbeat. It clouded his thoughts and made him even more uncomfortable. He couldn't even move his head to look at his body properly. Just the thought made his head nearly explode. Maybe waking up had been the wrong choice, after all.

Amon had lost track of time long ago. He could've been stuck there for ages, or maybe moments. His senses seemed as confused as his thoughts, and he had trouble discerning what was real or not.

In a daze, he looked at the equal red clouds in the sky. He did his best to focus on them, but no matter what he did, they were all the same. Unmovable and identical in all ways. He could see every deformity in their shape, every depression, every imperfection.

His thoughts started scattering again, and his mind was turning more and more sluggish. Just like him walking before, it was as if his mind was dragging its feet, about to fall down from exhaustion.

Even though his body was numb and heavy, Amon could still feel the cold golden token gripped tightly in his right hand. He couldn't move to look at it, but he knew it was there. However, he wasn't sure if he would be able to break it.

The scalding heat coming from the ground filled his back, legs, and arms with blisters long ago, but Amon felt none of it. As he looked up, his sense of time blurred. He didn't know if time was slowing down or speeding up.

There was an incongruity. It was as if he didn't fit in at all. There was no sync between him and his surroundings, almost as if they were experiencing different times. A change occurred. Along with that even greater uncertainty, the clouds above him seemed to turn blurrier too.

The clouds seemed blurry, even though the sky was clear. Amon tried to focus his gaze and realized the clouds seemed to be vibrating. It was a very subtle movement, very hard to see. Amon wasn't even sure if he was truly seeing it or he was hallucinating.

Maybe it was true. Maybe the only way for him to get out of this predicament was for him to understand what was different between him and his surroundings.

✱ ✱ ✱

Sarah and the other elders were looking with attention to the pool made of the Ashen Heart tree's sap. All of the cultivators showed on it were struggling against conditions tailored by themselves.

They didn't know it, but the place they were sent to was nothing but a basis for their predicament. What they realized and what they gained from it was all shaped by themselves.

A will was a resolution. A drive that moved them forward. Only a strong will would propel them along their path to cultivation. The Trial of Will was nothing but a way to show them what they already knew but never understood.

What they had to do now was to understand what their drive was. What they wanted. They had to find a path they wanted to tread. Those who failed to find their wills or those that didn't have willpower strong enough would never overcome this trial. Even if they did well in the others, this meant that at least right now, they were not truly fit for cultivation.

As Sarah was lost in thought, a faint rumbling sound started echoing through the dark room, and the ground quaked lightly.

She looked in surprise at the pool, as five of the sections started rippling wildly, distorting the images of the cultivators within it.

The red clouds were a blur, almost as if they were surrounded by a faint mist of blood. Under their sinister glow, they looked even more bizarre and ominous. Amon, however, wasn't concerned about it.

He tried his best to overcome the overwhelming feeling of exhaustion and numbness so that he could properly focus. He had the impression that the clouds were vibrating, so he wanted to study them further.

The sense of incongruity he felt eased somewhat as he looked above intently. That bloody light reflected on his eyes as he gazed at them, and for the first time, he was sure there was movement. The red clouds were indeed vibrating.

The speed of their vibrations was absurd. It was too fast for him to properly see, even with his heightened senses thanks to his body tempering.

He spread his divine sense, trying to reach for the clouds. If he managed to reach one of them, maybe he could slow them down. Yes, if he could adapt the clouds to his own pace, then maybe he could solve the problem.

The moment he thought of this, his divine sense shot up, expanding way farther than usual. It easily covered the clouds, the ground and everything around him in a radius that spammed miles.

It was a strange, but addictive feeling. Even though everything was the same, Amon felt that the whole area was under his control. He could feel every depression, every nook and cranny of the vitrified ground.

He could also feel every wisp of red steam and the billowing parts of the clouds. In this area, Amon was in absolute control. With a mere thought, the vibrations became unstable, and Amon was able to see it more clearly. It became slower, and Amon felt the discomfort going away.

A loud rumble echoed from far away, but Amon paid no attention to it. He wanted to discover what was behind the clouds. He felt there was something there that he needed to understand. The vibrations he saw were not vibrations at all. The clouds were actually dispersing and reforming in an endless cycle. Just like that, there was so much happening that he couldn't see.

He focused again, trying to make the clouds slow down even further. The cycles that were repeated a few times every second started almost coming to a halt. The rumbling became louder, and the ground shook.

Amon was surprised, but still forced the clouds to slow down. For the first time, he saw it clearly. In an incredibly slow pace, a cloud gradually faded out of existence. Amon was able to feel every detail about it; he knew its shape with a precision of millimeters.

When it disappeared, a new one took its place. However, there was a very subtle difference in their shape—there was no way Amon would be able to see it looking at it from afar. As he looked at the clouds and an idea formed in his head, the rumbling intensified causing the ground to crack under the intense quaking.

Amon felt it all, but even though he tried to calm it down, he failed. His will was supreme under his divine sense, but the world was fighting back. Being forced like this was tearing it apart. Amon looked on in dismay as the cracks on the ground grew wider and deeper, and the rumbling got wilder and louder as if the sky itself would fall over his head.

With a regretful look on his face, he let go of his surroundings, retracting his divine sense. The clouds returned to their vibrations and eventually became completely still again. The ground quaked no more.

Everything was still again. A place with no life. A place with no disparity. A place with no movement.

A place where the only thing that seemed to struggle against the stillness was himself.

However, was that really the case?

No.

The clouds were going through countless cycles of being dispersed and reformed. Even though the difference was minimal, there was a disparity between them. It was simply that Amon couldn't see it because the cycle was too fast.

Or maybe Amon was too fast.

Was his notion of time slower, making it almost come to a halt or was he experiencing millennia in what seemed to be the blink of an eye?

What Amon realized as he looked at the clouds was that it was relative. Maybe what needed to change was him, not his surroundings. This time, he spread his divine sense and focused on himself. This time, he didn't move the clouds, but he moved himself instead.

Yet again, the clouds blurred, and slowly Amon could see them vibrating.

A rumbling sound echoed again in the distance, and the ground quaked as he continued to focus.

As he and the clouds got closer to synchronization, the rumbling increased, and the quaking became more violent.

However, Amon felt a sharp pain spreading through his body. It was only then that he realized his state. Something was weighing heavily on him, obstructing his breathing and rupturing his skin. There was no rumbling coming from the skies, rather it was coming from his muscles tensing up and tearing apart, as well as his bones creaking and fracturing. His own body couldn't resist the pressure. If the world couldn't endure as Amon forced it to adapt to his time, Amon also couldn't endure when he tried to adapt to the world. He wondered if this was what immortality would feel like.

An immortal would live in a different dimension. His time would be completely different from that of a mortal's. He wouldn't be able to bring them to his own pace. It would break them, or it would break the world.

If he adjusted to their pacing, it would only bring harm to him. He would end up destroying himself as he tried to live in the world from which he had ascended. As an immortal, he had discarded his own mortality. Trying to return to it was the same as denying all that he was. There would be no balance when different times collided like this. All that would happen was the destruction of one or the other. The immortal and mortal would never be able to coexist.

Cultivators were at the boundary between both worlds. They would either die as any other mortal or leave that realm behind forever. This was what cultivation was about. Cultivators were nothing but mortals struggling alone. They died alone if they failed, and they forever lived alone if they succeeded. Cultivators were truly pitiful.

It was a very sad matter when one thought about it carefully. Of all mortals, the cultivators that failed lived the most, but alas it was all for naught. Their struggles would mean nothing at all.

Worst of all, Amon couldn't recall a single person that managed to achieve immortality. As far as he was concerned, it was nothing but a myth.

Supposing it was possible, would it be worth it? Was immortality a blessing given after countless struggles or was it a curse placed upon those that went against the natural order?

As Amon looked at the red clouds, he couldn't help but ponder deeply. Cultivation brought one power. Cultivation brought one knowledge. Most important of all, it brought one longevity.

Only with an extended lifespan would one be able to make the most of knowledge and power they obtained. Thinking that way, it was reasonable to assume that, to some extent, living more was the goal of every cultivator, or at the very least a necessary step to achieve or enjoy said goal.

One who has cultivated couldn't escape the pursuit of immortality, even if they wanted to tread that path. Every cultivator that denied this was bound to be mediocre at best because their lifespan would grow alongside their strength. For them, there would always be a downside to every breakthrough. At some point, they would stop moving forward.

Real cultivators wanted to live more than anyone else, so they fought for it nonstop throughout their lives and the stronger they became, the longer that fight would be. This made their deaths even more tragic. After all, cultivators were the ones that wanted to avoid death the most.

Cultivation was a struggle in and of itself. Maybe it was a foolish one, maybe it was a struggle impossible to overcome.

Why would Amon cultivate, then?

Why did he start cultivating in the first place?

What did he want for the long, long life that lay ahead of him if he followed this path?

Amon was in a daze as he pondered. He remembered the day he met Lya and their discussion that day.

He remembered how he was denied, and how he later found an answer that she found acceptable. He thought about the answer she gave her at that time.

He remembered the reason he gave her to pursue strength and to cultivate.

Was immortality his desire?

No. It never had truly been. It wasn't something he could comprehend or seriously consider. He had barely started his cultivation, and he had barely lived. He knew, however, that for him, a greater lifespan would be nothing but a side effect of his true pursuit.

Was knowledge his desire?

No. He didn't really mind how the world worked, and even though its mysteries were interesting and elusive, for him, cracking them open would be nothing but entertainment, not what drove him forward.

Was strength his desire?

Yes and no. Strength was a necessary step to achieve what he wanted, but it wasn't his objective. Rather than that, he was forced to become strong given his situation.

What he wanted...

He closed his eyes, and a clear image made its way into his head. He saw a pair of clear and bright green eyes looking at him tenderly. He saw flowing golden hair glistening in the sunlight that came from a window. He saw a pure smile, filled with warmth.

A smile full of happiness.

A promise was echoing in the depths of his mind.

Amon knew he would be an awful cultivator because cultivation was merely a necessary step for him. He would never cultivate whole-heartedly.

Amon also knew that he would be an amazing cultivator because cultivation was a necessary step for him. He would always cultivate doing his best.

Amon knew what he wanted. It was very simple, almost unbearably so.

What he wanted was no different from what anyone else wanted. When one pursued a wish, the result when it was fulfilled was the same, no matter what wish it was.

He was no different from any other cultivator, but he was also not nearly the same as them.

He didn't realize it, but, ever so slowly, the clouds above him started to move. There was a wind that had started blowing, pushing them forward. Slowly, but surely, they moved on without stopping.

He could hear a faint vibration coming from somewhere, and his body became light. He felt that feeling very disconcerting, but in his exhaustion he couldn't fight back. He let himself be overcome by that feeling.

When Amon finally opened his eyes, the sky above him had changed. The clouds were now pure white, and the sky was a bright azure. He was lying on a vast expanse of grass, and on the horizon, he could see mountains and trees.

Amon felt strangely full of energy as if everything that he had experienced had been nothing but a dream, a faint thought in the back of his head. His body, however, was still filled with bruises and the crippling thirst feverishly assaulted his senses.

He jumped up and took out his water canteen. He turned the whole jar upside down, taking large gulps before pouring the remainder over his head.

What happened wasn't something he would forget so soon. No, it was something he couldn't forget in his life. In that unbearable suffering, at the point where he was about to give up, he found the answer he always knew but never understood.

He didn't know if the answer was something acceptable to the guardian or whoever it was that judged him in the trials. He also didn't mind it one bit. His answer was his, and no one else's. Nothing mattered more than that. As Lya had said, cultivation was something that he had to do for himself.

For the first time in forever, he felt fulfilled.

Anna was breathing heavily as she sat on the ground with her legs crossed. A dense mist clouded her surroundings in pure white. Everywhere around her, fire and ice were colliding violently and turning into steam.

The searing winds pierced through the mist, blowing at her face, but quickly faded away. The snow they carried melted before reaching her, swallowed by the monotone whiteness that surrounded her.

Anna's blue robes were drenched and clung tightly to her body, making her movements clumsy and sluggish. Her wet hair was sticking to her face and her back. She didn't mind these conditions; she was a water cultivator after all. This was a state so natural to her that she barely even realized it anymore. Her true concern was the task at hand. She still hadn't grasped the elusive balance of fire and ice..

She never managed to combine the two elements of fire and ice without mutual destruction. She knew from the beginning it would be hard, but failing repeatedly still made her increasingly frustrated and somewhat irritated.

She knew better than anyone else what this trial meant for her. The steps she would take after the trials would depend on the answers she found now. Anna Hale was truly lost, and she realized that she would never be able to move forward while ignoring the conflict inside of her. If she didn't resolve this, it would consume her.

Looking at her surroundings in a daze. What she wanted was a perfect balance between fire and ice where neither of them would change. There was no middle ground in such a balance, there was just a perfect coexistence. Such a balance, however, lasted for no more than a fraction of a second. A window of time so small that she couldn't recall when her mistake had transpired. Maybe her pursuit was futile. Fire and ice couldn't coexist, at least not without change.

The billowing mist surrounding Anna soured her mood. She didn't want that. The endless mist surrounding her blocked her view, and all she saw was pure whiteness whenever she looked around. All she saw was emptiness.

The mist was the true balance between fire and ice, the remnant of their mutual destruction. A middle ground that Anna knew would never satisfy her because she didn't want her fire to die. She didn't want to waste the burning passion inside her melting that coldness, that stillness. That fire was all that kept her from being frozen in place. That fire was what made her feel alive. If balance wasn't possible, then she would have to choose a side.

She lowered her gaze, looking at the blue clothes clinging to her body. Wearing these colors, she felt that she was bound by heavy chains rather than wearing comfortable silk. Over time, she even came to hate the color of her eyes whenever she looked at the mirror.

She reached for the silver necklace around her neck. A silver ring embedded with a small sapphire sparkled brightly under the light that passed through the mist. It looked like a small star under that tiresome sky. A glistening star that shone with a beautiful light, but one that she would never be able to reach. No more than an idea, a dream shattered long ago.

Anna gently caressed the ring with a wistful look in her eyes as she reminisced. The ring became unbearably heavy as she held it, making her hands tremble. She closed her eyes as she put the ring away, and her expression was solemn, yet mournful.

The answer was an easy one. She had known it all along, but she always avoided it. Making that choice would be the same as inviting a change she would never be able to control. It would send her down a path that she'd never be able to return from.

Anna was hesitant because, no matter what had happened, she couldn't help but hold some things dear to her. This decision would cost her heavily. Nevertheless, a choice was made. She knew of her duties, but she also knew what her bottom line was.

She silently stood up, waving her hands and blowing all the mist surrounding her away. Her wet clothes released steam as the temperature rose, and soon started to flutter under the assault of the hot winds.

Her black hair whipped behind her back as a sea of fire rose from the ground and the ground quaked. The white sky started distorting and twisting around itself, being torn apart as the flames devoured all the ice in that world. The balance had been broken. Even though the ice weakened the flames, it wasn't enough to extinguish them.

Soon, all of the whiteness gave way to a hellish red, and the coldness was overtaken by unbearable heat. As the flames rose to the skies and the ground cracked under her feet, Anna straightened her back. The mist was still covering her face, somehow unaffected by the overwhelming heat that had spread throughout the world. That mist was enough to hide her satisfied smile as the fire reached her.

Seconds later, her figure disappeared under the flames, right before the world broke apart.

❄ ❄ ❄

As a particular section of the pool made of the Ashen Heart tree's sap rippled wildly, blurring Anna's image, Sarah gave a very long sigh.

Her wrinkles suddenly seemed to be even more prominent, and her back slightly arched as her shoulders drooped. There was no trace of a smile on her face as she looked at Anna being engulfed by the flames she spread through the world. Her worried expression and tired eyes temporarily made her age decades as she watched on.

"If you made your choice, you can only follow it to the bitter end," Sarah whispered to herself bitterly, but also trying to reach Anna somehow.

Anna was the daughter of the Noan River Sect's sect master and the inheritor, she was also herself. She had given almost everything she had to the sect without ever complaining, but she would never give up the only thing that remained.

Sarah shifted her eyes to Leonard. He was watching Reynard Stark, the likely successor to the Roaring Mountain Sect. He was walking through a vast field, moving towards the mountains that could be faintly seen in the distance. He was already at the Trial of Mind. As Sarah watched him, she sighed, her still tired eyes knew that trouble would certainly come.

The Noan River Sect had pushed Anna into making a decision that she obviously didn't agree with, despite the benefits it might bring to the sect.

Sarah knew that the sect master would certainly come to regret this. All because Anna Hale was the kind of person that would rather die than regret her choices. She would rather set the world ablaze than give up on herself.

A SHARP MIND CUTS THROUGH ALL OBSTACLES

T he azure sky above Amon's head was bright, and a refreshing breeze blew behind his back, ruffling his ashen hair. The white clouds floating up high all moved toward the same direction, no matter where Amon looked at. They were converging to a specific place as if something was attracting them all.

On the dark horizon, a stalwart and solid mountain range rose high into the sky, hiding their peaks in the clouds. They twisted and twirled; the sun was blocked, leaving the mountains in a perennial shade. Amon knew this was the direction he had to follow. There was no real mystery, nor did he need another hint.

The grass beneath Amon's feet rustled lightly as he stepped on it. Not far away from him, a wall of gigantic trees stretched tall and wide, obscuring his view, making only the mountains and the terrain in front of him visible.

Their wide crowns cast deep shadows underneath them, and their green leaves glistened underneath the sunlight. Their branches swayed with the wind, throwing their leaves in the air, where they were caught and carried away by the breeze.

Their trunks were as wide as Amon was tall, and they stood meters tall. Because of their size, they weren't densely packed, but there wasn't an ounce of uncovered area between their branches. Amon couldn't hear anything that wasn't the swishing of leaves which sounded like rushing water. There were no birds, insects or any other kind of animal in sight.

Light and shadow intermingled on Amon's face as he walked beneath the trees. His brows were slightly furrowed, and he was clearly tense. He could spread his divine sense and could even absorb qi this time, but something was still giving him a bad feeling. He knew he was in the Trial of Mind, but the way the world changed was suspicious.

As he walked while pondering, the trees around him became even sparser, gradually opening up to a wide clearing in the forest. Warm sunlight shone over a mostly empty space. The clearing would have nothing at all if it were not for a bizarre door stuck at its center. The door was at least five meters tall and two meters wide, and it absorbed all of the light that shone in it. It looked more like a window to a world made of pure darkness than a passageway.

Amon approached it hesitantly, taking slow and uneasy steps. His divine sense was completely focused on it, probing for even the smallest of changes. When Amon was a few meters away, something churned inside of his clothes and made him jump in surprise.

Cursing aloud, Amon searched inside his clothes and retrieved the golden token he had received before entering the Hellblaze Secret World. It was emitting a bright and vivid light while vibrating wildly in his hands.

Amon raised a brow and held the token tightly. Approaching the door with caution, he stayed alert, the token vibrating more with each step. When he got close enough, the door buzzed violently, and the darkness inside it started to churn, distorting and twisting until a blinding light burst from its opening.

In front of him, a was trove filled with every kind of treasure he could imagine. The walls of the trove were made of rose gold, and the floor was crafted from white jade. There were rows of swords, spears, bows, and other weapons Amon didn't recognize, all varying in shape and size. Their mirror-like blades reflected light as they rested on silver racks.

Looking further into the trove, Amon could see bookshelves filled with heavy tomes bound in leather riveted with gold and silver. They gave off an ancient aura, making Amon incredibly curious about their contents.

Even further were glossy stands filled with porcelain jars and bottles, covered in a faint, colorful mist. Amon could tell from a glance that they most likely contained pills, ointments, and other medicines. Wherever he looked, he could see a new section of the trove filled with amazing trinkets, scrolls, and weapons. He looked on in a daze, enchanted by the mystical treasures the trove held.

What the hell is this place? he asked himself, waking up from his trance.

His face was grave and fear showed in his eyes. That had been dangerous. He shook his head, trying to clear his mind. This trove was most likely a trap, one for which he almost fell for. Fear showed in his eyes as he slowly backed away. The token in his hands started shaking and vibrating in protest, but Amon didn't mind.

The viscous darkness soon spread again from the edges of the doorway, covering the view of the trove in endless shadows. His hair stood on end as he took a deep breath and sent the door one last glance before looking away.

He looked up, seeing the wind carrying the leaves it had ripped from the trees, and soon found the direction to follow again. As fast as he could, he left the clearing behind him. He tried to calm himself, remembering his mother's words. However, there was something wrong. Something was tugging at his mind, making his thoughts return to that ominous door no matter what he was thinking.

Amon had no time to worry about it. He soon found himself in another clearing, almost identical to the first one. Amon froze in place as he looked to the clearing, and his face was drained of all color.

Lying down in the middle of the clearing was a horrendous creature. It had thick, snow-white fur that resembled sharp needles. Its paws were big enough to crush Amon with a single step. They ended in curved, sharp claws so massive they looked like sabers. Its hind legs were somewhat short, while its front legs were far too long. If it stood up on its hind legs, Amon was sure the claws on its front legs would scrape against the ground. Its long, narrow head, a strange mix between a wolf and a bear, complemented the creature's bizarre appearance.

Amon stood completely still, hearing only a heavy breathing sound coming from the creature at regular intervals. It was clearly in a deep sleep. A cold sweat rolled down his back and all of the muscles in his body were tense as he backed out of the clearing. Breathing heavily, he walked to his right for a great distance before following the winds again.

His breathing had stabilized as he entered another clearing with another door made of pure darkness standing in the center of it. All of his senses screamed at him to run. Without a second thought, he bolted from the clearing. This time, instead of following the winds, he ran against them, trying to leave the woods.

After a while, the trees surrounding him were not as sparse as before.

I've made it, he thought, gasping for breath as his run slowed to a walk.

Amon turned to look from whence he came; it was dark and unwelcoming. When he turned back around, his heart clenched. Another clearing had formed in front of him. The first thing he realized, however, was the sound. A heavy, regular breathing sound. Amon couldn't hide his fear and confusion as he looked ahead, seeing the sleeping white beast in the middle of the clearing.

H-how is this possible? I went against the wind! I shouldn't be anywhere near this beast!

"It's useless," a crisp, chilling voice echoed in his mind in a tone that made his head hurt, sounding more like scraping metal.

Amon raised his golden eyes, and his gaze was met by a pair of translucent, blue eyes that seemed more like ice—the beast had woken up.

The white beast gazed at Amon with curious eyes. Its head slowly rose, revealing a giraffe-like neck, giving the beast an even creepier appearance as it approached Amon.

"You will never be able to leave unless you manage to get past me," the beast stated, opening its mouth and revealing a white tongue and a sharp row of black fangs.

Its piercing voice disoriented the young cultivator. In a daze, he looked up, and saw its eyes right in front of him. There was disdain deeply ingrained in them, and its mouth twisted into a look of silent laughter. Amon could smell putrid flesh coming from the beast's mouth, making him even more disgusted. Amon jumped back, tightly gripping Windhowler's hilt over his right shoulder.

"I suppose that is one way to go about it."

Amon heard the beast's voice in his head again, in a tone full of scorn. He was surprised that it was speaking to him. The only kind of spirit beasts he knew that could talk were the legendary godbeasts, but he had never heard of a godbeast that had an appearance as grotesque as this monstrosity.

This feels... wrong, Amon thought to himself. *This isn't the right way to approach the situation.*

As his mother had told him, the Hellblaze Trials were not about strength, at least not physical strength, nor were they about combat. They were trials made to mold the next generation into worthy cultivators and help them find their own path.

Amon lowered his sword. Neither he nor the beast spoke anything. The incessant rustling of the leaves and the swaying of the branches coming from the trees surrounding them was all Amon could hear. A light breeze made Amon's clothes flutter, and the animal's fur whipped about.

Thinking about it, he realized that the large creature's behavior was strange. It showed no hostility, nor did it make any sudden movements. It was also taking its time to speak with Amon.

The boy looked at the beast for a long while, before slowly sheathing Windhowler. His golden eyes were full of hesitation and curiosity as he faced the beast.

"How can I get past you?" he asked, raising a brow.

The beast's expression froze for a moment, full of surprise. When its surprise faded away, the disdain in its eyes grew even greater. It opened its mouth, making a strange, rhythmic gurgling sound. Amon, however, could hear an unabated and displeasing laughter echoing inside his head.

Amon's face fell, and he started getting irritated. The beast's laughter grew even louder as it saw his reaction, making the gurgling sounds echoing from his throat almost surpass the sound Amon heard in his head. It took a good while for the beast to stop, making Amon even more frustrated. When it finally stopped, it looked at Amon with eyes full of scorn.

"There are many ways to get past me," the beast said with a sneer. "You just have to find one."

"I suppose I need to find it out by myself," Amon said, not even asking a question. He already knew what the answer would be, after all.

"What I can say is that you already have everything you need," the beast said as he looked at Amon with a strange glance. "However, don't think you won't pay a price to move on."

Amon sank in silence again after hearing this. He had what he needed? His interspatial ring wasn't working, and he doubted that the beast knew about it. What was left was Windhowler, the items in his bottomless pouch that were basically food and water, his clothes and...

The token! Amon suddenly realized it.

The token opened the trove. If the trove was part of the trial, it would probably be safe. Not only that, it certainly held the answer to his predicament. What made him frown, however, were the words of the beast.

Amon would have to pay a price to move on.

"Would you be willing to trade?" Amon asked as he looked at the beast again.

Its sharp ears perked up, and it looked at Amon with interest shining in the depths of its blue eyes.

"Of course I'm willing to trade," the beast said as it opened its mouth again, showing that twisted, dangerous smile. "As long as the price paid is enough, I will allow you to pass."

"In that case, what would be a fair price?" Amon asked, showing hesitation.

"That is up to you to find out," the beast answered in an indifferent tone.

"How do I do that? How would I know what is fair?" Amon asked again, somewhat irritated, somewhat frustrated.

"Have you ever heard of the tale of the old emperor and the dragon?"

"Never heard of it," Amon said, looking suspiciously at the beast.

"It's quite a simple tale," the beast said, closing its icy eyes as if focusing for a moment.

Soon, its chilling voice started echoing in Amon's head in an indifferent, robotic tone, as if the beast was emotionlessly reading a book.

"Once upon a time, there was an emperor that ruled the world of mortals. He was the richest man in the world, and no matter what he wanted, he could get it. Except for one thing: time. His life was ending and he didn't want to die. He used his influence to search far and wide, and, after a long time, he came across rumors about a medicine that could grant immortality. The problem, however, was that this medicine was in a treasure trove owned by a black dragon.

"The emperor knew of such a dragon living in his kingdom. He took his royal carriage and traveled far away, coming across a deep cave inside of a mountain to meet the dragon. The emperor asked about the medicine, being careful not to show the slightest bit of disrespect. The creature indeed knew of the medicine, but he would only give it to the emperor if he traded his most precious asset for it."

What would be the most important thing for an emperor like him? His people? His treasure? His land?

"The emperor arrived at the conclusion that his lineage was more important, because the lineage ruled the people, owned the treasures and governed the lands. And so, with a pained heart, the emperor chose his youngest granddaughter and, as tears streamed down his face, took her with him to see the dragon again.

"When they arrived, the emperor took his granddaughter's hand and proclaimed, 'I offer you my most precious belonging.'

"The dragon nodded, took the frightened girl in his scaly embrace and allowed the emperor inside the trove. Soon after, the emperor found the concoction and promptly gulped it down. Time seemed to reverse as he regained his youth, strength and vigor.

"Very satisfied, he prepared to leave but was blocked by the dragon. His granddaughter was nowhere to be seen, and the dragon's eyes were cold and full of scorn.

'What are you doing?' the emperor asked, frightened. 'Where is my granddaughter?'

'I sent her home. Our trade didn't involve her.'

"The emperor was confused, and the dragon started laughing. Then, the dragon said the words that sealed the fate of the emperor forever

'If you were willing to sacrifice your lineage to save your life, obviously your life is what is the most precious thing for you. The trade was completed. Your life is now mine,' the beast declared as his laughter echoed throughout the trove.

"Color drained from the emperor's face, leaving him deathly pale once he realized his mistake.

"For an eternity, the dragon has guarded over the trove, and for an eternity, the emperor was imprisoned in it, as he was now one of the many treasures owned by the dragon."

The beast finished its tale, opening its eyes and sending Amon a piercing glance.

"You know nothing, kid," the beast's voice was indifferent, as if stating a fact. "Life is nothing but a constant stream of trades. You take and give all the time. This is how the world maintains its balance without ever stagnating. You breathe in and out. You consume throughout your life, and, in the end, you are consumed. Even if things are balanced in the end, this does not mean it's all equal. There is an inherent disparity in this cycle." His eyes started glinting with resentment as he spoke. "Some might have a blissful life, while others live in misery. Some die young, others die old.

"Each living being is unique, so there is no way for there to be no disparity. It is all relative.

"All that matters, in the end, is that you're born with nothing, and you die with nothing. No matter what you do during your life, the cycle will be completed and everything will start over.

"All that happened in-between the beginning and the end is meaningless because Nature will balance it all out," the light in his eyes were unbearably cold as he looked at Amon, and a silent pressure started to weigh down on him, restricting him. "No living being can escape from this. Everything will be balanced by death."

"Thinking that way, fairness is also relative," the beast said in an irritated tone. "That being the case, you must never underestimate a trade, because while you might think you're coming out on top, the other party might actually be the one winning the most."

"We might even consider a fight as a trade," the beast continued as those icy eyes came closer and closer to the restrained Amon. "We can trade blows and see who hits harder. It is one way to solve your predicament."

The pressure weighing down on Amon disappeared, and he was left alone on the edge of the clearing.

Amon stood alone at the edge of the clearing, looking at that strange beast returning to its deep sleep, not bothering with him at all. He was still trying to wrap his head around what was said. In silence, he slowly walked away, leaving the clearing and the beast behind. The direction he followed didn't matter anymore. He was stuck in a cycle until he managed to get past the beast. He would always find the treasure trove and then find the beast. There was no way to get around it.

What would be a fair price for him to obtain passage? The trove had innumerable treasures, and Amon had no idea of what would catch the beast's eye.

He doubted a cultivation manual would be worth anything for the beast. Weapons would also be useless to it, following this logic. What was left to consider was... a lot. That trove was way too vast. Going there and picking something blindly would be simply ridiculous.

How am I going to deal with this? Amon thought, finally reaching another clearing.

As he expected, the dark door stood in the center of it, as if waiting for him. The golden token started vibrating again as he approached the door, but this time it didn't bother him. He walked with confident steps as the darkness in front of him started to wriggle and collapse on itself, retreating towards the boundaries of the door and revealing the treasure trove again.

He took a deep breath as he stood in front of the doorway, and finally took a step forward. A feeling of dizziness took over Amon as he lost all sense of direction for a moment. It was a very similar feeling to when he stepped through the gateway to the Hellblaze Secret World and when he passed the Trial of Will. Before he realized it, he was standing in the treasure trove, and through the doorway behind him, he could see the grass and trees that covered the forest. As he was looking back, a mechanical voice sounded in his ears.

"You can only choose one treasure in this trove," it groaned, dispassionately. "Choose wisely."

Amon looked at the countless treasures in front of him. Since he could only take one item, his choice was going to be something of major importance. He carefully looked and saw stands of medicine. The tale the beast told him came to mind. Was there a deeper meaning in it? Was the tale actually a hint?

Amon ventured forward to examine them, but none of them were labeled and the fragrances were all mixed in the air. He couldn't identify any of them. Somewhat unsure, he looked around a bit embarrassed as his ears reddened a little.

"Excuse me," he called in a low voice. "Is there a way to identify the medicine?"

"There is," the mechanical voice answered, and soon bright letters condensed out of thin air in front of every bottle, box and jar of medicine in the stand.

He wasn't sure what he was looking for. If the tale had been a hint, then there was a chance the characters and situations were references to Amon's predicament.

"Is there a medicine for immortality here?" Amon asked again, his tone firmer as he knew the voice would answer and he wasn't talking alone.

"We do not have such medicine here," the voice answered again.

Of course such a thing as a medicine for immortality would not exist, but maybe there was a substitute, a symbol to show the beast that Amon had found the right answer. Amon looked around again, completely overwhelmed. He couldn't see the end of the trove and could have spent days walking around and not see all of it. Every step he took revealed a whole new section filled with wonderful objects for him to analyze.

There is no way I'll find the answer like this, he thought.

He didn't know what the beast could want to let him pass, nor did he know the limits of what the trove could offer. He closed his eyes, sinking into a deep silence as he contemplated. He tried to carefully remember everything the beast had told him in their conversation. Amon was sure that there was a hint there somewhere.

"Fairness... is relative?" Amon opened his eyes after a long time; a glint of excitement showed in their golden color, giving them a brightness that seemed to set them ablaze.

The beast had also said that there were many ways to get past it. For Amon, this meant that there had been no right answer from the start. A fair price was still important, but there was no way for him to know what the beast would consider fair.

The story of the emperor was the key. Even though the emperor had not realized himself what he held most dear, the way he found his answer gave Amon an idea. What the beast asked, after all, wasn't what Amon held most dear to him.

"Is there any limit for what this trove holds?" Amon asked suddenly, raising his voice as he stood up.

"As long as it exists, it can be found here," the mechanical voice chimed.

"In that case, I need you to go find something for me."

* * *

Amon walked out of the treasure trove with firm steps, not losing time at all as he returned to the forest and walked forward. Soon enough, he saw himself facing the beast.

"You're finally back," the crisp, chilling voice of the beast entered Amon's ears again as it opened its icy eyes and looked at him with no interest at all.

"I have something to trade for my passage through this forest," Amon said as he looked at the beast intently with his golden eyes.

"What do you have to offer?" the beast asked, approaching Amon.

Amon retrieved a small, golden token from his robes and raised it for the beast to see.

"I offer this," he said, keeping a straight face and a neutral voice.

A strange light flashed in the beast's eyes as it looked at the golden token Amon was showing. It opened its mouth, letting its warm and putrid breath over Amon's face as its dagger-like teeth came dangerously close to him.

"Are you sure?" the beast asked him. "You might need to use it later."

Hearing this, Amon smiled. With his other hand, he reached again to his clothes, fishing a second golden token. "Not a problem, I still have mine."

The beast's eyes widened for a moment as it showed surprise. It raised its head, and, like in their first conversation, gurgling sounds started echoing from its throat as it laughed nonstop. The flesh of its neck undulated in a strange rhythm as the beast laughed, making Amon feel somewhat strange.

"That is a good deal," the beast finally said after it calmed down.

It moved its head even closer to Amon, looking at him with nothing but interest. All of the disdain and scorn in its eyes were gone as he spoke.

"I accept."

With surprising care, the beast lowered its head and bit at the token gently, raising it from Amon's hand. The beast then retracted its neck, dropping the token by its massive body.

"In this edition of the trials, this was the best trade so far," the beast spoke with its chilling voice, but Amon somehow managed to feel a tinge of satisfaction in it.

Neither he nor Amon needed to talk about what this trade implied. In the end, Amon had thoroughly understood all of the beast's hints. Like the emperor, Amon's offering encompassed all of the things that he could give up. The token was a key to the treasure trove, where the beast could choose any of the treasures it wanted. Amon had offered the beast a treasure while also not having to make the choice. The token was also a second life, as Amon could use it to be rescued by the guardian if he found himself in a dangerous situation or if he decided to give up. For the beast, however, the

267

token had a potential third use. Maybe it could call the guardian and leave the Hellblaze Secret World, obtaining freedom.

Because as the beast regretfully spoke about trades and fairness, especially after talking about the emperor of the tale, Amon found it quite pitiful. He doubted it could leave this world on its own. It was most likely bound to it, and, as far as Amon had guessed, it probably involved a trade where he got what he wanted, but paid an unbearable price for, just like the emperor.

Amon had given to the beast everything he guessed the beast could want. At the same time, he was also getting what he wanted and not really losing anything. He still had his token and his belongings. He would leave this trial the same way he arrived. The cycle would be complete, and balance would have been met.

"You know, so far I was hacked to pieces by a rude guy that got a sword from the treasure trove and used it to 'kill' me, as well as trapped by an array formation by a girl that seemed really annoyed," the beast said, not hiding the annoyance in his eyes.

"The guy, in particular, was very aggressive. The first time we met, he already had the sword. He wasn't scared at all the first time he found the treasure trove. The moment I saw the sword I knew what kind of trade he would want to make," the beast spat. "Shows you the kind of cultivators we have nowadays.

"The girl... well, we spoke a little, but she didn't seem like the kind to want to think things through too much. I'm actually surprised she showed the consideration to simply restrain me rather than kill me," it grumbled.

"They were all valid ways to overcome the trial," the beast sighed, making Amon shudder under the effects of the piercing noise in his mind. "They used what they had in hand, and defeated me in their own ways. The world we live in is like that anyway, so it's not like I can't see where they're coming from. Maybe there is some hope for you, after all," it finally said as the look in its eyes eased somewhat. The next moment, however, its eyes were full of disdain again. "Still, don't get cocky. This wasn't the best approach I have witnessed."

Amon was surprised at first as he heard these words but soon came to understand them. The Hellblaze Trials had been happening for centuries. It was bound to receive a myriad of dazzling figures and geniuses.

"In that case... what was the best approach someone tried to use to get past you?" Looking at the beast, he couldn't help but ask.

"Many decades back... there was a girl," the beast started speaking while reminiscing. Amon could faintly discern a warm smile in the beast's bizarre face. "She showed no fear at all and approached me with a smile. We had a long and pleasant conversation, and we got to know each other somewhat after a while."

"She was a really polite girl, and obviously smarter than all the other cultivators so far," the beast said, looking up as if pondering. It then looked at Amon, with that twisted smile on its face. "That includes you, by the way."

"What did she do?" Amon didn't hide his curiosity as he heard the beast speaking with such an expression.

"She looked at me and said, 'Mister, could you please allow me to pass?'" the beast said with wistful eyes. It was certainly a precious memory.

"What?" Amon was taken aback. "Just that?"

"Yes," the beast's answer was simple, as had been the girl's approach.

"Did you accept it?" Amon raised a brow as he looked at the beast. His curiosity was turning too great for him to restrain.

"As if I'd answer that," the beast sneered.

Amon squinted his eyes, but didn't insist. He was sure the beast would continue to mess with him if he did so.

"Well, kid, it's a pass. Our trade pleased me, so I'll give you one final piece of advice: There might come a time in your life when you realize that the worst obstacles you've ever faced were no obstacles at all. All you needed to do was to look at it another way and see the truth."

The beast sent Amon a piercing glance, making him gulp.

"In the end, it's all relative. If you look at it again, you might realize there was nothing there in the first place."

The beast disappeared, scattering with the breeze blowing towards the mountain range in the distance.

Reynard Stark was a very confident person. He's been standing out within the sect since he was a child, and after his master took him in, he soared to new heights. The moment they met, the two of them knew that they'd be able to rely on one another to propel their ambitions. They formed a bond that couldn't be broken until one of them accomplished their goal.

Reynard looked at the vast mountain range in front of him with an annoyed look on his face. The breeze blowing on his back messed up his dark-brown hair and made his yellow robes flutter. Moments ago, he had held an incredibly powerful sword in his hands, though it was nowhere to be seen now. The moment he saw it in the treasure trove, he knew he had to take it. It was something his master had taught him to do.

Reynard used his sword to draw a line. It was meant to divide and cut. Under a line, everything would be split. Thinking about it, the word itself was divided and his master taught him to seek those divisions. Drawing lines was a way to expose disparity, be it in someone's stance or personality. For that matter, sometimes words were as useful as swords.

If anything was truly whole, it could never be divisible, as it would be perfect. Therefore, when Reynard saw the beast in front of him, he saw an obstacle. And like all obstacles, he could use his sword to get past it. It was a simple way to look at the world, but such an approach had its nuances and complexities. There was a single requirement to live that way: strength.

Reynard Stark was much stronger than any of his sect peers, and rumored to be deadlier than all of the inheriting disciples. He had defeated Alden Bren from the Southern Flame Sect when challenged to a duel. He had also defeated Jake Meyer in an all out battle, showcasing his physical prowess. Though… Reynard never had the opportunity to fight with Anna Hale and, no matter how much he tried, Derek Tyrell always avoided his challenges. Therefore, he couldn't say that he had defeated all of the inheriting disciples. Regardless, they didn't matter to him. There was only one person that Reynard was focused on defeating, and he wouldn't stop until he did so.

Reynard walked for hours until he was close enough to get a proper look at the mountains. Their peaks were hidden in the white vortex formed by a convergence of the clouds and wind. Combined, they paled in comparison to the sheer size of Hell Keeper's Mountain and the Roaring Mountain that served as headquarters to the cardinal sects of the west, but seeing so many of them so close to each other in the mountain range gave a feeling that no lone mountain could give.

He smiled lightly as he continued moving forward. He emptied his mind as he walked, silently meditating. He always did his best to maintain his peak state, no matter the occasion. It was a good way to make use of the time he had to spend traveling to the mountain range.

Allowing himself a break would be unforgivable. It meant that even if he wanted to continue, his body or at least part of his mind wanted to stop. There would be a division, a line between those parts of him. There would be a weakness.

As such, Reynard always moved forward, never looking back. He walked with his head held high, always gazing at the peak. He couldn't accept anything else. It didn't matter how many years it took to reach it, or how many more times he would need to defeat himself to stay on it. The peak was his, and no one else's.

He retrieved a sword from his pouch. Its single-edged blade was slightly curved and gave a cold, metallic luster as the light reflected on it. Reynard only knew of one other that used a sword like this, and he was certainly ready to strike him down when necessary.

As he got closer to the mountain, Reynard saw a building in the distance. Its red walls glowed, contrasting with the darkness of the mountains under the perennial shadow of the clouds; Reynard knew that he had to go there.

As he approached the building, he noticed it had a single floor and was bland compared to its surroundings. Reynard would have missed it entirely if the light hadn't been there. It's perfectly crafted wooden door was seamlessly aligned with the frame, melded into the red walls of the palace. It was a simple design, but the artisanship used was certainly not ordinary at all.

Stepping inside the building, he was greeted by a spacious, empty hall, and an endless sea of black tiles. Snorting loudly, Reynard walked to the center of the hall with an annoyed face.

"Do you mind explaining?" he asked impatiently.

Surprisingly, a voice answered. It was a crisp, chilling response that pierced his ears.

"You'll have to wait for the others," the voice said in a cold tone. "The third trial will start when everyone gathers."

The hall fell silent once again, but he didn't complain. Instead, he sat in the center, meditating until the sound of the door opening broke his concentration. A slender, yet elegant figure entered. Her silky black hair fell behind her shoulders, swaying gently against her blue robes and her face was shrouded in a white mist, shielded from prying eyes.

A single sweep of his divine sense would probably be enough to pierce through it, but Reynard wouldn't do that. He wanted to look at her face with his own eyes when the time came, and he would make sure she was the one to allow it.

He stood up, and dusted off his clothes with his hands.

"How have you been, dear?" Reynard asked with a smile as he faced Anna Hale.

Anna frowned in disgust. He couldn't see it, but the way her body suddenly tensed and her silence were enough for him to understand her feelings. Nevertheless, he wasn't bothered at all, his smile stretching to each ear.

"As cold as always, I see," Reynard said, never taking his eyes off her. "Well, I suppose it's fair for you to act like this while you still have the chance."

Anna didn't answer, but the air around her turned colder. A faint mist spread through the hall and Reynard's breath started condensing in the air. He raised a brow as he faced Anna, before he simply shook his head and retreated.

"Have it your way, then," he said, shrugging.

"Believe me, I will," Anna's voice echoed through the hall.

Reynard's smile faded away and a frown appeared on his face as he looked at her. There was something different about her, but he couldn't quite figure out what it was. He scratched his head, confused and uncomfortable. He opened his mouth to say something, but changed his mind and closed it again. He shrugged his shoulders and returned to his place of meditation.

Anna wouldn't be able to change anything. She was the inheriting disciple of the Noan River Sect, and as such, there were some matters she'd never be able to avoid. Their situation was one of those matters. Inheriting disciples had to consider the sect's circumstances before their own and, if the Roaring Mountain Sect and the Noan River Sect wanted to strengthen their relationship, Anna and Reynard had to abide by their sect masters' wills.

Reynard emptied his mind, forgetting about such matters. The agreement between the sects meant nothing to him, it was but another necessary burden he would have to bear during his climb.

Anna's attitude, however, made something churn inside of him. Her coldness and her strong opposition towards him... he saw it as a challenge.

The fingers on his right hand twitched, somewhat yearning for the sword hanging from his back. The line that divided Anna was clear as day, and he really wanted to draw it.

However, he knew it was nothing but personal interest. He liked to defeat strong people, with or without a sword. Anna was aware of this line, and she knew that Reynard could see how it was slowly eating away at her. It was different now. It was just a feeling, but Reynard thought that the line had blurred and one side of her was slowly being consumed by the other.

Anna glanced at the cocky cultivator once more before walking to a corner to meditate. Once she was properly situated, a third person made their way inside. His clothes were pitch black, and his messy hair was a bizarre ashen color. His golden eyes shone like lanterns under the red glow of the walls, and they quickly moved about as the figure scouted the hall.

A young man and woman... Amon thought, noticing Reynard and Anna meditating silently in the hall. They were most likely the two that the beast had spoken about. He looked Anna over carefully, noticing the mist covering her face.

He stood there, as if hypnotized, when he felt the air suddenly become frigid. His hair stood on end and he saw the girl moving her head. Somehow, he was sure she was glaring at him. His ears reddened as he shifted his gaze away.

Making his way into an empty corner, somewhat distraught, Amon took a few breaths to calm himself and soon started to meditate. If both of them were waiting silently, then it made sense that he should too.

What confused Amon, however, was why they were all gathering in the same place. Up to this point the Hellblaze Trials had the cultivators challenged individually, and he had not met anyone else in the Hellblaze Secret World until now. *Why would the Trial of Heart be different?* he pondered as Jake entered the hall.

When Jake saw Reynard, his eyes blazed with competitiveness, but he didn't utter a word. He gave Anna a glance before turning his head and seeing Amon. Jake was surprised to see that Amon had made it this far and had arrived before him. Even so, Jake's surprise was a pleasant one. He put on a genuine smile as he quietly approached Amon, sitting not far from him and entering meditation as well.

The door swung open violently, and the four irritated cultivators glared at the newcomer. The fifth person to enter was the tall youth from the Southern Flame Sect. He had dark-red hair that reminded Amon of the wine he shared with Daniel, and a solid body barely hidden by his robes. His features were sharp and defined, giving him a very stout look.

"God damn it, I can't believe I was the last of us four to arrive," he said disappointedly.

He seemed somewhat angry as he looked around, but it seemed like it was self directed. When his eyes landed on Amon, his brows perked up.

"And who the hell are you?" he asked in a surprised tone.

His words were disrespectful, but he looked genuinely surprised. At a glance, Amon could see that he wasn't a bad person, but he surely spoke before thinking.

"Amon, from the Abyss Sect," Amon answered simply, sustaining the youth's gaze.

"Great! I'm Alden Bren, from the Southern Flame Sect!" Alden proclaimed, almost shouting as he opened his arms. Anna rolled her eyes behind the misty veil and Jake gave a wry smile. Reynard, however, wasn't very enthusiastic.

"We get it, Alden. It's you. Now be quiet for once in your life, would you?" Reynard spoke coldly, not trying to hide his annoyance.

Alden's shoulders drooped and he grumbled to himself as he dejectedly walked towards an empty corner to sit in.

Time slowly passed as more cultivators arrived. Joshua, Karen, Skylar, and Evan all managed to reach the third trial. Daniel was the twentieth to pass the second trial. He quietly sat down close to Amon and Jake as they waited for the remaining participants to arrive.

Amon, didn't see any additional body tempering disciples of the Abyss Sect, but it was still a great result. The Southern Flame Sect had five disciples reach the Trial of Heart, and the Storm Peak Sect had only three. As expected, the Noan River Sect had eight, and the Roaring Mountain Sect had nine. In total, thirty-one participants had made it through.

As for the others, they were probably being kept away in another place until the trials were over. The moment the last of the qualified cultivator arrived, the walls shone brightly and the same voice that answered Reynard before echoed throughout the hall.

"Since all of the remaining participants are gathered together, the Trial of Heart shall commence."

THOSE AT THE PEAK

Amon felt that the cold and crisp voice was very familiar. If it was the guardian's, then the things Amon the last trial was even more important than what he had thought.

The red walls began to tremble and crack fiercely. The floor tiles shook and broke apart and the ceiling was blown away. The participants bundled together closely to those of their own sect, soon being completely divided into five groups as the building collapsed—it was quite a surprise for them.

"Your task is simple," the voice echoed again, jolting them awake. "All you have to do is reach the highest peak of this mountain range. As long as you don't break any trial rules, you can use all means available to you to complete this task." It spoke slowly, as if trying to make sure the thirty-one participants understood what it was saying. "What matters is only reaching the peak, nothing more and nothing less."

As soon as the voice dissipated, an uncomfortable silence took over the cultivators gathered. Only the sound of the wind blowing could be heard near the remains of the collapsed building.

Jake looked upwards, as did the other inheriting disciples. They had to reach the highest peak, but they couldn't see anything beyond the white vortex that overshadowed the mountain range. Nonetheless, it wasn't hard to guess which would be the correct mountain to climb.

The four of them seemed to reach the same conclusion as the set their gazes on the mountain at the center of the vortex; the mountain that sat at the center of that world. The highest peak had always been the center of their world. Everything else depended on it and moved towards it.

Everyone stood completely still, barely able to breathe as an increasing pressure fell upon them. Reynard's right hand reached over his shoulder, gripping the hilt of his curved sword. Anna and Alden's arms were relaxed at their sides, but the air around them distorted as they silently gathered qi.

Jake had a deep frown on his face as he held the grip of the red saber hanging from his waist. Very slowly, he sent a meaningful glance to Karen, Joshua, Evan, and Skylar that stood on guard by his side. Extending a finger, he lightly tapped the hilt twice. The other four gave an imperceptible nod as they heard Jake's instructions. Even though it was a very subtle tap, the sound exploded like a thunderclap disrupting the silence that had fallen over them.

Hearing the taps, Anna slowly dragged her feet across the ground, adjusting her posture. The Noan River Sect's disciples were visibly shaken, unable to hide their anxiousness.

Reynard smiled with disdain as he gripped his sword tighter, and each of the Roaring Mountain Sect's disciples took a deep breath before raising their weapons.

Surprisingly, Alden was completely motionless and his eyes remained shut. The disciples of the Southern Flame Sect all looked extremely relaxed compared to the others.

The three disciples of the Storm Peak Sect stood back to back, looking very nervous as the wind made their green robes flutter restlessly.

Amon remained motionless with the members of the Abyss Sect, adorning a displeased look on his face as he remembered the guardian's words. However, before he could think properly, one of the Noan River Sect's disciples took a sudden step forward. He was incredibly nervous and wasn't able to deal with the tension.

It all happened in a moment. Reynard's smile widened as he stomped heavily on the ground, shooting forward like a cannonball. Unsheathing his sword in a fluid motion, it glinted ominously under the sunlight, making Amon shiver.

"Now!" Jake shouted as he unsheathed his saber and a wall of raging fire sprang to life, unleashing a wave of hot air in every direction, raising a cloud of dust that blocked everyone's vision.

Karen took a step forward and waved her hands. A piercing howl echoed through the air as a blast of wind hit the wall of flames, propelling them towards Reynard. Amon could only see a smile of disdain on Reynard's face before he was engulfed in the fire.

BOOM!

With a deafening sound, the ground quaked violently.

Losing his balance, Amon almost fell to the ground. Rather than stopping, however, the quaking was increasing in magnitude. Gritting his teeth, Amon managed to stay on his feet as he drew Windhowler with a piercing trill.

"Come on, don't stand there!" someone called out to him, and Amon recognized Daniel, Evan and Skylar running towards him.

"What about the others?" Amon asked in a hurry.

"They're just buying time!" Skylar answered, grabbing Amon by the collar before he managed to properly turn and run with them.

"We were lucky that we were standing on that side of the building," Evan murmured, stomping at the ground, before increasing his pace. "Our group was the closest to the mountain range; we had a good advantage there."

This was because no one stood between them and the mountain range, while the other four groups had to get past them to utilize the shortest path. Jake had decided to stay behind with Joshua and Karen, so that he could hold the others back as much as possible to buy them valuable time.

Amon looked back and saw flashes of fire raging wildly as the wind howled and the ground rumbled. Streams of water pierced the air, some traveling upwards, showering the area.

A faint mist spread through what was now a crater amongst the remains of the building. The mist was being blown away by the wind and the fire, before forming again as the humidity in the air increased.

"I don't mean to sound ignorant, but why is all of this happening?" Amon asked hesitantly.

"You don't understand the situation?" Daniel responded while raising a brow. The fierce winds made his black hair whip wildly as he turned to look at Amon. "This is a race, Amon," Daniel said in a serious tone.

The Hellblaze Secret World was, after all, a world of cultivators. In one way or another, cultivators were all racing to some sort of peak, a place where they could stand above all else. For them, nothing was more important than the climb.

When Amon heard Daniel's explanation, his eyes dimmed somewhat, and he couldn't hide his disappointment.If all of the present had arrived at the same conclusion then maybe that white beast was right. This was the type of cultivators that existed nowadays.

Amon wanted to laugh. The guardian of the Hellblaze Secret World was surely a very cunning and cruel being. To lead them all into this fight was a very twisted thing to do.

No, this was wrong.

Maybe cultivators were cunning and cruel beings. The guardian had only chosen the precise words that would lead people with a certain mindset to the same conclusion.

Amon shook his head. The guardian himself had said it. All that mattered was to reach the peak, nothing more and nothing less.

This race, this fight, was nothing but an illusion the participants had created themselves. They were standing in their own way.

He could only sigh. This wasn't a race he would be taking part in. If he needed to reach the peak in order to move on, he would do so in his own terms, at his own pace.

Amon remembered the words the beast said as it looked at him with a serious gaze on its icy eyes. Every time he thought about them, he felt he understood it a bit more.

In the end, it was all relative.

The Hellblaze Trials didn't require strength. It had never been about combat, and that was a well-known fact since centuries ago. There were some slight changes to the trials from time to time, but their purpose had always been the same.

The trials were deeply personal, so telling someone how to act in common situations within the trials would be counter-productive. Most of the elders and high elders of the Five Cardinal sects even went out of their way to avoid giving information to the participants of their sect.

Even if someone obtained detailed information, however, it would not be of great help. The guardian wasn't easily fooled. He would know when people were following a script rather than thinking on their own. Their rewards would decrease and the participant wouldn't gain any personal benefit at all. It would be a waste.

Getting rewards was good, but knowing yourself was far better. With this mindset, it was rare for any information about the trials to be passed on, except what the purpose of the trials was. This was a consensus of sorts.

That being the case, it was expected that the wise participants would know that this was a trap set up by the guardian. It was a deliberate choice of words on his part that gave space to an interpretation of the Trial of Heart, that would lead to unnecessary competition.

The Trial of Heart was made to peer into the psyche and mindset of the participants. In truth, it was fair to say it had started from the moment they set their foot on the gateway to the Hellblaze Secret World.

Jake Meyer knew all of this, as did Anna Hale, Alden Bren, and Reynard Stark.

This fight was pointless. Or at least, it should have been.In the world of cultivators, however, such things were the norm. As long as one person chose a path of conflict, others would inevitably be dragged into it.

Their world was all about strength, after all. The weak had no place in such a world, so, when someone decided that a situation was worth fighting over, others would have to fight too and be sure to not fall behind. A single spark could light a wildfire.

The Trial of Heart should not have been a race, all things considered, but it was open to interpretation. That opening was enough for it to become a race. All because a single person chose the path of conflict, as the other three knew he would. Worst of all, neither of the three were confident in stopping him.

Reynard Stark had been the first to attack, and he had not stopped attacking since his first charge towards Jake and the members of the Abyss Sect.

The earth quaked with each step that Reynard Stark took. His steps seemed to be incredibly heavy but were also fluid and nimble. He slid through the battlefield as if the earth itself was aiding him, giving him a dangerous combination of strength and agility.

With a sinister smile, Reynard dodged an incoming wisp of fire thrown at him and slammed into the cultivator. He turned around and saw Alden and the Southern Flame Sect disciples as they were before, simply defending themselves and not striking back—surprisingly cool-headed decision made by Alden.

Reynard frowned; of all people, he didn't expect Alden to keep his calm in such a situation.

"Stop wasting time!" Anna shouted waving her hands.

The air became increasingly colder, and the mist that was taking over the crater condensed, forming a viscous barrier.

"Disperse and go to the mountain!" she instructed with authority.

The clashing sounds diminished somewhat, and the mist slowly started to fade away. The Noan River Sect's disciples were nowhere to be seen.

Jake clicked his tongue before turning around and leaving, followed closely by Joshua and Karen. Their task had been achieved. They were somewhat haggard and their clothes were a mess, but they were unscathed. They rushed to the mountain at full speed, not wasting time looking back.

"I'll give a special prize to the first person to reach the top!" Alden shouted to the members of his sect as they left the fight before speeding towards the mountain.

If Reynard wanted competition, Alden would gladly give it to him. The three disciples of the Storm Peak Sect were long gone, disappearing with the wind as soon as Anna made her move.

"You all know what to do," Reynard said in an indifferent voice. The remaining eight disciples gave him a slight nod before speeding off into the distance.

Reynard Stark knew very well that his actions were not considered 'ideal' by the guardian or Arthur Royce. Nevertheless, it didn't matter, as he never cared about the Hellblaze Trials in the first place.

Remembering the burning rage in the eyes of the Southern Flame Sect's disciples as they left, he couldn't help but smile. He couldn't see the expressions of the others, but he knew his task was done, even if Anna had ended his fun earlier than he thought.

Reynard Stark had a few things to take care of in the Hellblaze Trials, one of them being to disrupt the competition. This show he started had been nothing but a way to disturb all of the present participants. A way to affect their mood, their mindset.

Even if Alden had made a good decision in sparing the strength of his group during the fight before by simply defending, he still gladly took up the challenge Reynard had set, and his companions were surely enraged at Reynard for it.

Jake Meyer had taken up the challenge too. All of the decisions he made, considering the context, had been right, but Jake taking his bait was a mistake. He was still too green, too prideful.

Alden had been this way his whole life, and would hardly change. In fact, his mindset was most likely not affected at all, simply stimulated. Jake, on the other hand, had lost his cool and let his emotions make the call for him. He didn't want to lose to Reynard again, so he accepted the challenge, even if he knew it was wrong.

Anna had most likely taken the bait because of her pride. Reynard had taunted her before, and given their own circumstances. There was no way she'd let him act superior towards her in any way ever again, no matter how meaningless it might be. Pride was one of the strongest sparks one could use to start a wildfire in the world of cultivators.

The Storm Peak Sect's members were simply irrelevant. If Derek Tyrell wasn't involved, Reynard had no interest at all in them. He was, however, interested in the reason he and the other three didn't show up. Something about Derek didn't click. Reynard never managed to understand him the same way he did the others. He couldn't see the lines that divided him.

Such thoughts, however, had no importance right now. All that Reynard was concerned about was if the stance of the Roaring Mountain Sect would affect the others. His companions constantly pressuring the others would surely help the effects last, but it all depended on the inheriting disciples, and how much they were affected.

Even if it only disrupted their mindset slightly, it was worth it in the long run. Reynard was planting a seed, nothing more. What was lacking, however, was the event that would make the seed germinate.

Reynard looked up at the gigantic vortex of clouds that overshadowed the mountain range. That vast expanse of pure white reflected in his dark iris, and he gave a savage smile. He set his gaze at the position where he imagined the peak would be. Even if it was meaningless, he'd get there first.

Daniel, Amon, Evan, and Skylar were running towards the mountains at full speed. Their steps were light, and they were already under the shade of the clouds. The mountain in front of them seemed to grow with each step they took, standing stout and unsurmountable.

Rushing ahead in complete silence, Amon had a deep frown on his face. He had been like this ever since he heard Daniel's explanation. Everything he said, however, fell on deaf ears. Jake had made a call, and they'd follow through with it.

Amon understood their logic, as well as Jake's, but it still bothered him deeply. He couldn't accept such a thing. He knew the world was like this, but as long as there was another way other than conflict, he would take it.

This single-minded pursuit of strength and the pride of cultivators was what had twisted this world in the first place. It turned into a vicious cycle that few could escape from; as the weak had no choice but to be trampled upon, or to trample others to obtain the strength they needed to survive. Either way, this world would consume them. A world like this would eventually fall apart unless a balance of some sort was met.

Amon wasn't sure what this balance would require. His reason for cultivation was very simple, so he kept his methods and objectives simple. He didn't worry about anything else.

The moment Amon stared into the red clouds of the dead world, he had decided to tread a different path from the other cultivators. His conviction was later reinforced by his conversation with the white beast in the forest.

This was a world he couldn't accept. It was also a world he couldn't change.

As Amon was reflecting, they finally arrived at the foot of the mountain. He snapped out of his train of thought and looked ahead. The mountain had no vegetation on it, nor snow, as far as Amon could see. It was simply a horrendous mass of gravel, gargantuan rocks, and gigantic crevices, forming together into an abhorrent whole that stirred one's mind. It was surprising that a grey abomination like that could reach for the heavens above, piercing the pure white clouds in the sky.

The four exchanged glances, and, as they were about to rush again, Amon stopped in his tracks. He looked at Evan, Skylar, and Daniel and took a deep breath.

"I'm sorry, but I won't follow you on this rush," he said, shaking his head.

"Are you kidding me?" Evan asked, not hiding the anger that started to distort his expression.

Skylar said nothing, simply giving Evan a light tap on the shoulder as she looked at Amon with a piercing glance. He sustained her gaze, not showing hesitation or regret at all. Skylar shook her shoulders and turned away.

"Amon, why?" Daniel was dumbstruck.

He looked at Amon with his mouth agape, but when he saw the resilient look in those golden eyes, he sighed.

"Are you sure about this?" Daniel asked with concern in his voice.

"I am," Amon answered with no hesitation at all as he looked at Daniel with an apologetic smile. "I think it would be better for me to deal with this my way."

Daniel looked at Amon for a long while, as if trying to see through him. In the end, he simply patted Amon's shoulder as his expression eased.

"If you're sure then it's fine," he said with a smile.

Daniel would not question Amon's decision. He had decided not to do so since long ago, when he had offered Amon wine during the Season of Rigor. He would not be able to take care of him all the time, and the Hellblaze Trials were personal, after all.

"Come on, Daniel," Skylar called, anxiously. They could hear a faint rumble in the distance, as well as almost imperceptible clashing sounds and shouts. "They are getting close."

"As long as you believe this is the right decision, I'll support you." Daniel sent Amon one last glance as he tightened the grip over his shoulder. It was a warm grip and a gesture of affection. Amon looked up and saw the genuine smile on Daniel's face.

"Good luck, Amon. I'll see you at the peak." With one last smile, he turned away, rushing forward with Evan and Skylar.

Amon looked at Daniel leaving, and, for some reason, his chest felt heavy. The anxiousness he felt when he first saw the gateway to the Hellblaze Secret World seemed to be stirring again, churning in the depths of his mind.

The sounds of fights coming from the distance were turning louder and louder as time passed. Amon shook his head vigorously, trying to clear his mind. He looked at the white vortex that devoured the peaks of the mountains, and he couldn't sort out his emotions.

He looked back and saw a few tiny dots rushing in his direction. Other challengers were approaching the mountain.

He frowned for a moment, before turning away and rushing off. He, however, wasn't running towards the mountain. Rather, he was moving to the side, trying to avoid other cultivators and their conflicts. It would be the only way to get some peace on his climb.

He didn't know how long he had walked. The breeze that never seemed to stop ruffled his ashen hair and the green grass was tousled as Amon stepped on its blades. He had no set destination; he only wanted to avoid trouble.

At some point, he stopped. He closed his eyes and focused. He could feel the cold touch of the air on his skin. He could feel a faint tingling on his scalp as the breeze messed up his hair. He could hear the faint rustling of grass. There was nothing else. No one was in view, and no sound of conflict could reach him. Now, there was only him and the mountain. As it should have been from the start. Cultivation was, after all, deeply personal.

He doubted that one day the mountain would turn any less horrendous in his eyes. The world around it was so beautiful, but the mountain was so disconnected from it, so disjointed, that Amon couldn't find any way to appreciate it.

Amon looked up again, having to bend his body backward just to properly see the white vortex that cast a shade over him and blocked his view of the peak. Unknowingly, his body became tense. He gently shook his limbs to loosen them.

Climbing this mountain would bring no joy at all.

Maybe at the peak he'd be able to properly appreciate the vast expanses of beauty this world offered him, and it would be worth it.

Maybe the peak would be so high that he would not be able to see any of it, and it would be worthless.

Regardless, there was only one way to find out.

Amon took a deep breath and started his long climb.

Amon was panting heavily as he climbed the mountain. His absorption of qi was suppressed like it had been during the Trial of Will. He could only rely on his body, and even so, it didn't seem to be enough. His body tempering didn't seem to matter one bit, as exhaustion crept upon him after just a few minutes. Sweat covered his red face and his clothes were clinging to his body.

The steep mountain made it hard to find a path where he could rely on his legs alone. He had to use his arms to pull himself up, and all that he could hold onto was a sharp rock peeking out of the mountain, or a narrow crack where he could stick his fingers into.

His fingers and hands were covered in deep cuts and his blood flowed out profusely, sticking to his arms and falling upon his face. More than anything, it hurt a lot. Every inch Amon climbed meant gripping a dagger's blade, rather than a proper support for his hands.

Climbing the mountain was suffering. It was a very slow and painful process, and the higher he climbed, the harder it became. When Amon couldn't go on any longer, he would find a place where he could properly stand and carefully hug the mountain, taking a deep breath to recover his stamina.

It was, however, incredibly hard to find such places, and they became more rare the higher he ventured. Amon was sure that at some point there would be no return. He would either reach the peak in a rush or fall off and die.

Amon was no longer sure how high he had climbed, nor how much more was left to climb. All he could do was look up and search for the next sharp protrusion that he needed to climb further. His fingers and hands were incredibly pale due to his blood loss, and all of his limbs trembled non-stop due to the exhaustion.

Ever so slowly, the white vortex of clouds was drawing near. Like a solid wall, it blocked his view from what lay beyond. Amon wasn't sure what he'd find there, but he could only hope for the best.

The speed at which he climbed was steadily decreasing. He was no longer sure of how much longer he'd be able to keep this up. His arms and legs were burning in pain, and he couldn't feel his fingers anymore.

Some of the blood flowing through his arms had dried, gluing his clothes to his skin, making it increasingly difficult for Amon to move his weakened limbs. He had no idea how he was still managing to continue his climb, even if his pacing almost came to a halt.

His neck was hurting too much for him to move it in a way that would allow him to look directly up. Stretching his arms, Amon blindly searched for a place to hold onto. He, however, realized that a faint mist covered his surroundings, and the temperature was dropping. He surely was close to the white wall of clouds.

Like that, he raised an arm again, barely managing to bear its weight. The moment he moved it to where the wall was, however, he felt nothing but a refreshingly cold sensation.

Surprised, Amon looked up, gritting his teeth and bearing the piercing pain that came from his neck. Directly above him, there was only an endless, almost solid expanse of white. Amon spotted the elbow of the arm he had extended. His hand and forearm had been swallowed by the white wall.

He reached out again and felt nothing above him. His eyes shone with sudden relief as Amon realized what was happening. He slowly descended his arm as he moved it forward, searching for something.

A weak spark flashed across his already dull eyes, as his hands finally reached an edge. Amon had been right, there was leveled ground above him.

Mustering all of his strength, he gave a hoarse shout as he dragged his weary body upwards. As he dragged his head over the edge, his vision was overtaken by a dense white mist. Nevertheless, he still had some sense of touch in his numbed body.

With his lower body dangling dangerously from the edge, Amon wriggled his body ignoring the pain as he pulled himself further into the safe haven he finally found.

When his knees were finally in contact with the ground, he let his body loose, barely managing to turn on his back. He laughed like a lunatic with a weak voice that became fainter as he closed his eyes and started taking deep breaths.

His body relaxed as he finally managed to rest. The exhaustion he barely managed to resist all this time started taking its toll. There might've been hidden dangers around, but Amon couldn't even lift a finger anymore. All he could do was fight back the urge to sleep as he slowly managed to catch his breath and recover some strength.

* * *

"How interesting," Richard mumbled as he looked at the pool made of the Ashen Heart tree's sap. "To think that the kid would get the lead."

He shook his head slightly, making his white beard wave in front of his chest. He had a wry smile on his wrinkled face and his brow was raised. He cast a sidelong glance at the other sections of the pool. The thirty-one sections that were still glowing showed each and every ongoing conflict within the trial.

The Roaring Mountain Sect disciples were constantly pressuring the others, throwing blasts of elemental qi at their opponents ahead of them. It was very clear that most of the thirty-one would burn out before reaching the peak. They were forcing themselves to keep a pace they couldn't maintain due to the pressure, and this would come with a price.

The inheriting disciples were not far behind Amon, but they were holding each other back constantly. Now, however, they seemed to be too exhausted to do anything other than silently climb as they clenched their teeth.

Reynard had the lead and seemed to be slightly less exhausted than the others. Richard found it amazing, considering that he had a late start. The four of them pushed each other to their limits, making their pace much faster than the other disciples. Despite that, it didn't look like any of them would tire out.

The elders from all sects other than the Roaring Mountain Sect had deep frowns on their faces. They found the situation very displeasing, but couldn't say a word about it. It was, after all, the decision the disciples of their sect had made on their own. Even if the Roaring Mountain Sect had pressured them, they still could ignore the rush and follow their own pace.

Richard gave Lars a sneaky glance. The sect master had a cold and indifferent expression as he looked at the pool, but Richard could see the slightest of frowns showing on his face. What caught his attention, however, was that he wasn't looking at Jake's performance.

Lars had his eyes fixed in Amon, and his frown deepened exponentially as time passed.

✳ ✳ ✳

Amon didn't know how long he had been resting for, but, eventually, he forced himself to move. His body seemed to weigh a ton, and his movements were naturally sluggish, but he still managed to stand up.

Even if the misty clouds surrounding him were thick, he could still faintly see his surroundings. His clothes were dampened due to the humidity. His breath condensed in front of him, dispersing in his white surroundings, barely visible.

Dragging his feet, Amon moved in the direction where he believed the center of the mountain would be. The eye of the vortex.

Suddenly, his steps came to a halt, his hair stood on end, and his limbs trembled uncontrollably.

He felt his blood churning wildly inside him, and he felt a strange excitement. Unknowingly, his face reddened, and his breath became rough.

Amon knew this feeling too well, but he couldn't understand how it was possible. This feeling, however, was even stronger than what he felt the last time. It was as strong as he remembered it six years ago.

His face distorted into a mask of hate and anger as he looked ahead.

As he expected, a pair of golden eyes that glowed with ferocious hostility appeared amidst the mist in front of him. The ground rumbled and a loud sound echoed as the beast stomped the ground and took a step forward.

Its head emerged from the mist just like it had emerged from the trees of the Broken Forest that day.

The beast's head alone was almost as big as Amon, but he didn't need to see the rest to know its exact size—he still remembered it very clearly.

Amon saw the bright silver fur that covered the beast seemingly glowing with a pale light. It covered the beast's body in what looked like a beautiful moonlight, which only accentuated the bright gold of its eyes, making them seem like a pair of blazing suns.

The beast took another step forward and growled as it gazed at Amon. The fur on its back stood on end, and it lowered its upper body slightly as if preparing to charge ahead.

Amon extended his right hand to his shoulder and drew Windhowler with a piercing trill. His body was still numb, but his exhaustion seemed to fade away as adrenaline rushed through his body.

He met the beast's gaze, refusing to step back. There was no way he could outrun it anyway. This class six beast was known for its speed and agility, being able to overtake even cultivators at the Divine Foundation realm.

In front of Amon, surging from the mist, was a silverback wolf.

Amon looked at the animal with mixed emotions. He was trying very hard to keep his calm, but it was difficult to be rational in a situation such as this. Not because he felt his life was in danger, but because this was a trauma of his.

He was feeling anger, regret and fear, as well as a strong sense of foreboding. In his eyes, the wolf seemed to grow even more, and weight in his hands disappeared. He looked down and saw that Windhowler had disappeared.

His hands and fingers were smaller. It wasn't the wolf that had grown; he had returned to the poor physical shape that he was in over a year ago—a powerless, weak being that brought trouble for everyone around him.

Amon's face paled as he realized what was about to happen.

"No!" he screamed at the top of his lungs as all of his others emotions were swept away by pure fright.

"Stop this! NOW!" he screamed again, his voice high-pitched and juvenile as he pleaded desperately. Suddenly, he heard hurried footsteps on his left, and his face paled even further.

From the mist, she appeared. Donning stunning, red robes contrasted by her flowing golden hair and piercing, green eyes. She stood tall, beautiful and full of pride as she rushed towards Amon. She had a sleek sword in her hand, as white as the clouds in the sky. The flames it emitted were so hot that Amon could feel its heat from dozens of meters away.

When he saw Rebecca's delicate face, her deeply worried expression, and her graciously hurried steps, Amon's heart quivered. He lost the last shred of reason he had in him, and was overtaken by pure emotions. He didn't want to live through this again, no matter what. He would gladly use his life to stop what was about to happen if he could.

He clenched his teeth, looking at the silverback wolf with a furious light shining in his golden eyes. Amon shouted as he threw himself at the beast. His ashen hair whipped about as he lunged forward. His desperate expression and his savage shout made him look more like a beast than a human.

In an instant, Amon reached the wolf. The only way to save his mother was to remove himself from the battle that was about to happen. He would never be able to outrun the wolf, nor would his mother be able to do so holding him.

That being the case, the only option he found was throwing himself to the wolf. This would surely break his mother's heart, but for Amon, it would be better than her being crippled. She would eventually move on, become a high elder, and maybe start a new family. One with which she could be truly happy.

It was all his fault. Deep down, Amon knew it. He was better off dying right at this moment.

He closed his eyes as he approached the beast's open mouth, and the dagger-like fangs rapidly came closer to him. He was ready to feel the piercing pain that would put his suffering to an end, and then... he fell to the ground.

When he heard a roar behind him, he turned back and his face contorted into confusion. His mother had her back facing the place where he had been standing, holding the sword with one hand and extending the other one behind her, as if pushing back someone that wasn't there.

Amon rushed to the wolf again, trying to punch it and draw its attention. As if Amon was hitting nothing but the mist surrounding him, his hands went through the wolf. His confusion gave way to despair when he realized he couldn't do anything.

"Please stop!" he demanded again, almost giving up hope.

Young Rebecca's movements were fluid and precise, but they were limited to a circle around the place Amon had been. Rebecca only moved to defend, not to attack.

The world flashed as wisps of white flame covered Rebecca's surroundings, trying to keep the silverback wolf at bay, but it was useless. The flames that Rebecca conjured were not strong enough to hurt the wolf, as they would also have hurt Amon otherwise.

It was a drawn-out battle. Rebecca had crushed a jade token as soon as it started, but no one appeared in her rescue. She fought alone against a spirit beast that was close to her in strength, all while defending a child.

The simple fact that she managed to hold on for so long was proof of her proficiency as a cultivator and a warrior. Nevertheless, help didn't arrive on time, and the end became inevitable.

Large beads of sweat glistened on Rebecca's face before evaporating due to the heat. Her breath was rough and her limbs were trembling. The area surrounding her and Amon was a wasteland; everything within a hundred meters was charred, unrecognizable chunks or turned into grey ash that drifted in the air like snow.

The silverback wolf had parts of his fur charred, and his front paw had a deep gash in it, making him limp. Still, it never stopped its crazed attacks, making Rebecca even more cornered as her strength faded.

There was no way she would be able to win a fight of attrition with a spirit beast while protecting someone. The sword in her hands trembled and the flames started fading as Rebecca started running out of qi.

With an expression full of savagery and unwillingness, she slashed with her sword once more, sending a burst of raging flames in front of her. This time, she didn't hold back at all. She focused all of her power into the strike. The flames left the sword and exploded in the air, consuming everything in front of her in a blazing inferno.

It was a strike filled with hostility; a desperate attack with the intent to kill its target and burn the world, leaving nothing more than cinders if it was what it took to kill the enemy in front of it.

As soon as the strike was unleashed, Rebecca fell to her knees. She had been stalling for help that never came.

The wolf whined as the strike hit, opening a deep wound in its flank before charring it into a mess of burnt flesh as it was sent tumbling back.

It wasn't enough.

The wolf stood up, limping even more emphatically than before. Seeing this, Rebecca's already pale face turned deathly white. She somehow managed to stand up, supporting her weight on the sword that was stuck in the ground.

Amon forced himself up again. His eyes were wide as he shouted and rushed to Rebecca. He managed to stand in front of her, facing the wolf. He opened his arms wide, trying to cover her with his body.

It wasn't enough.

The wolf growled again, and jumped at the defenseless Rebecca, as if Amon had not been there at all. Amon felt a light wind hitting his body as the wolf passed through him, as incorporeal as ever.

He closed his eyes tightly as tears streamed down his face. He fell to the ground, curling himself in a ball as he desperately tried to cover his ears.

It wasn't enough.

He still heard it. He heard the blood-curdling scream his mother gave, he heard his own desperate screams, in the same juvenile voice he had that day. He heard the growling of the wolf, and he heard the horrifying sounds that came after.

Crunch, crunch!

It was the sound of bones breaking. The sound that the wolf made as it bit her legs, piercing the flesh with its fangs, ripping muscles apart and grinding bones into powder.

"I'm sorry," Amon cried desperately as he refused to look at the scene.

It wasn't enough.

Amon didn't know for how long he stood there, desperately trying to shut down his senses and hopefully pass out. Eventually, all sound had disappeared, but he could still hear it, echoing in the depths of his mind.

Why? What did I do to deserve this?

What had his mother done to deserve this?

Why did help take so long to arrive?

Amon knew the answer. He knew it very well. They were paying for the actions of someone else.

Suddenly, he heard heavy, confident footsteps that seemed to echo through the mist as if it was an empty room. Amon hesitantly opened his eyes. He saw a pair of black boots a few centimeters in front of him. He suddenly felt drowsy, and his body was aching miserably all over. He couldn't move at all, nor could he scream. Just like he had felt in his first body tempering. Just like he felt the night his black hair and eyes turned ashen and golden.

His expression was a mask of anger and pain as he managed to keep his eyes open and raise his head.

What he saw was a pair of ravenous black eyes, as cold as a winter night. Hair darker than shadows reached the man's shoulders as he squatted down to look at Amon.

He mustered all of his strength to utter the only question he had on his mind.

"Why?"

"Because you're weak," Lloyd Kressler said to his son before standing up and leaving.

The black cloak that covered his body fluttered as he took unhurried steps outside. It was like he was leaving an empty room rather than abandoning his son and his wife.

On that night, Amon realized that he and his mother had stopped existing to him.

Because you're weak.

These words echoed inside Amon's head as he dejectedly watched his father's broad back moving away. His father never once looked back before he disappeared into the endless expanse of white that surrounded him, dispersing into the mist.

The pain Amon felt in his body disappeared as Lloyd's phantom left, fading along that horrible memory. Amon stood there, lying down on the ground with a blank look on his face.

He realized he was his old self again, not the child of six years ago anymore. He looked up, trying to gaze at the sky. What he saw, however, was only a monochromatic white, a monochromatic emptiness.

Yes, he was weak. It was something he had known all along, but deep down refused to accept. Even though he knew it was pointless, he still fought hard. He had never given up.

When he saw that beautiful woman floating in front of him by the small lake, he knew he had a chance to turn his life around. He didn't hesitate in asking Lya for help, no matter how bizarre or suspicious the circumstances were.

At that point, he didn't know what to do anymore. In truth, Amon had fallen to his despair long ago, even if he didn't show it to anyone else. That was the reason why he followed Lya's directions and advice without hesitation. He felt this was his only option, his only chance. As such, he held onto it tightly, never letting it go.

He was willing to risk everything to prove his father's words wrong and to prove that he had worth; he wanted to make his mother smile as she did in the past.

No matter how much he convinced himself that this world was unfair, that it was twisted beyond repair, the fact would not change that he needed to be strong enough to pursue his objectives.

As such, Amon decided to cultivate, because only cultivation would give him the strength he needed.

Because you're weak.

His father's words echoed from the mist again, reverberating in his thoughts, taking them over. Amon shook his head and tried to clear his mind, but the voice would not go away.

He wasn't weak. Not anymore. He had met Lya, he had undergone his body tempering, and he was a soul cultivator. He was pursuing it already. He was pursuing the strength he needed. He was walking towards his goal. He wasn't stranded anymore, stuck with his despair in a limbo, a purgatory of mediocrity from which he would never escape.

Crunch, crunch!

That horrifying sound took over his father's voice, alongside the screams that both he and his mother had given that day as the silverback wolf reached a defenseless Rebecca.

"I'm not weak!" he shouted as a blazing fury burned in his golden eyes and his expression distorted into one of pure anger and denial.

He started moving again, walking towards where he believed was the center of the vortex of clouds. The place where the peak was.

"You're weak! You're weak! You're weak!" the voices said nonstop, coming from all directions. Mocking him. Looking down on him.

"ENOUGH!"

He extended his hand to his shoulder, drawing Windhowler. The blade hummed wildly, fighting back against the voices.

It wasn't enough.

Eventually, the humming stopped, and Amon had to hear it all again.

Crunch, crunch!

The sword in his hand trembled. His jaws were clenched so hard that they were starting to hurt, and his lips were turning pale from the excessive strength he used as he pursed them.

Because you're weak.

This time, Amon clearly identified the origin of the voice. He raised his eyes and saw a familiar silhouette standing ahead, covered in mist. He couldn't see it clearly, but he still could feel the cold indifference it exuded.

His gaze turned sharp, and his grip on the sword tightened even more. Like slithering snakes, thin lines of light started spreading through the blade. With a blinding flash, a pale layer of light covered the sword.

He was a sword cultivator. He refused to be weak, and he would do anything to prove his strength if it meant accomplishing what he wanted.

"Because you're weak," the figure spoke again, but before it could finish Amon was already upon it and Windhowler was whistling through the air in a wild, violent slash.

"SHUT UP!"

Lloyd looked at him with the same cold eyes, the same indifferent expression as ever. Windhowler descended with a dazzling light, hitting Lloyd's shoulder and splitting him in half.

Lloyd didn't show any emotion as his figure exploded, forming wisps of red mist that blew into Amon's face. He felt something viscous on his skin, making his hair turn wet and cling to his face, staining his clothes and making them sticky and warm. However, he didn't mind. Something else had caught his attention.

In front of him, silhouettes started to silently form from the mist. Like statues, they stood in place, and like his father, they spoke the words that tore at his heart.

"Because you're weak," they spoke as they stood on his way, blocking his path.

Amon's face distorted even more, the fire in his eyes turned even fiercer, and the trembling of his hands stopped.

Swish!

He slashed out with Windhowler, cutting a silhouette in half. More red mist exploded, tainting him even more. He took a step forward, facing another Lloyd.

He was still the same, still looking at him with cold eyes and an indifferent expression, clad in black like a shadow.

Why wouldn't they stop?

"Because you're weak," Lloyd said.

Swish! Windhowler answered for Amon as he took yet another step forward.

When was this going to end?

Crunch, crunch! The mist provoked, as if mocking Amon.

Swish! Windhowler repeated, unyielding and unforgiving. However, it hit nothing, and the mist simply billowed away as the sword cut through it.

"Why don't you stop!?" Amon shouted in a desperate and confused voice.

"Because you're weak," Lloyd said again, scorn appearing in his eyes this time as a mocking smile appeared on his lips.

Swooosh!

The qi enveloping Windhowler seemed to change, turning more corporeal as it condensed into an edge over the sword.

More red mist exploded, and Amon moved again. He felt he was stuck in an endless loop, an unending conversation that always went the same way.

"*Crunch, crunch!*" the mist would say, and the screams of the young Amon and Rebecca would reverberate Amon's ears.

"Why?" Amon would ask, more and more desperate.

"Because you're weak," Lloyd would answer.

"*Swoosh!*" Windhowler would respond, making red mist explode and Amon take a step forward.

Again and again, the same conversation would happen. Amon was stuck in a cycle he didn't know how to avoid, and slowly he started to lose himself even further.

He didn't realize that, after some time, the voices had completely stopped, and the silhouettes forming from the mist were not even similar to Lloyd. They were not speaking to Amon, nor were they standing on his way.

Nevertheless, the conversation never stopped for Amon. He could still hear his mother's screams. He could still see his father's cold face in every silhouette he put his eyes on.

As long as the conversation continued, he would answer the same way he had been answering since the start. Red mist would explode, and he would move closer to the peak.

For anyone else, however, this wasn't a conversation, but a monologue.

"Swoosh!" the sword would say.

A person would be cut down, and red mist would explode, tainting Amon even more. He had long since gotten used to whatever the red mist was and never gave it any importance.

Because of that, he never looked down to see the red droplets falling from his dirty clothes into the ground, forming a horrifying scarlet trail.

Drenched in blood from head to toe, Amon continued walking.

With no mercy nor distinction, his sword spoke to all that stood close to him in his path to the peak.

Anna was looking up with a dejected expression as she climbed the mountain. This race, this mad rhythm they were following... it wasn't what she wanted.

Her hands and arms were covered in scratches, cuts, and bruises. Her limbs were burning with pain and her body felt heavy. Her breathing was rough and she was exhausted. Still, she never stopped climbing, doing her best to not be left behind.

She looked at Reynard in the lead, soon disappearing in the vortex of clouds that was right above them. She felt mixed emotions as she saw it.

On one hand, she really wanted to defeat Reynard and prove to him and herself that she was above him. She wanted to prove that she was more than an asset to be used by their sects in a political maneuver.

On the other hand, she was pushing herself to her limits, and she wasn't sure if she would be able to keep up with the mad pace Reynard had set. Either way, she would not give up. Even if she lost, she'd fight until the bitter end and she'd make sure the fire inside her had burned the fiercest. She would scorch into the earth the path she had trod, making sure people never forgot her struggle.

She looked down to see Jake and Alden were beneath her, but not by much. Her gaze, however, was set on the tiny dots far below her. She was looking at the companions she had left behind in the climb. The people she abandoned in her prideful decision.

"I'm sorry," she said in a remorseful voice, before looking up again, to the barrier of white clouds that blocked her vision of the peak.

She'd never go down silently. Even if it was meaningless, she would always affirm herself.

She raised a hand, tightly holding the silver ring hanging from her neck. Behind the perennial mist that masked her face, Anna's blue eyes shone with fierce passion as she resumed her climb.

She was done playing by other people's rules.

At once, she finally reached the clouds and she almost collapsed on the leveled ground that gave her a chance to rest. Her chest heaved up and down as she closed her eyes and forcefully tried to control her rough breathing.

Her limbs were trembling and her clothes were drenched in sweat. Her skin was flushed and her body was hot due to the effort. The cool mist that surrounded her was very refreshing, very comfortable as it helped to cool her down and recover somewhat.

After a few moments, Anna forced herself to move again. She had no time to waste. She gritted her teeth as she hurried her steps. Her muscles were tense and her legs were rigid, about to cramp at any moment. Because of this, her movements were very awkward, but she never stopped.

She tightly held the ring close to her chest, and her eyes grew fiercer as she moved forward.

At that moment, however, the ground quaked. The mountain rumbled and the earth cracked, causing Anna to lose her balance.

Tumbling back as she desperately tried to regain her footing, she saw a gigantic shadow looming over her. From the mist, a gargantuan figure was forming.

It was at least one hundred meters high and two hundred meters wide. It was hard to make its precise shape due to its massive size, but Anna froze in place—she already knew what she was facing.

The air chilled unbearably and the muddy, cracked ground, hardened as a layer of ice formed, smoothing the broken surface.

She looked ahead with an unyielding expression, as the horrifying cold penetrated her skin, chilling her to the bone, making her movements sluggish. There was no room for warmth in such a place.

The fire inside Anna started flickering.

A freezing wind blew in her direction as the figure moved. From the mist, a head surged. What seemed to be a pitch-black beak took form from the mist, adorning a mouth so big that it could swallow a hill. Full of cracks and scratches, that sharp beak had a dangerous luster and seemed to be able to easily snap a small mountain in half.

A pair of enormous, frosty-blue eyes looked at Anna, surrounded by black scales. As it focused on Anna, the temperature fell even further, and a thin layer of frost covered her.

Her expression turned incredibly solemn, but her unyielding eyes were still the same.

The flame was flickering in front of the cold, but Anna would never let it go out.

She quietly sustained the gaze of the godbeast that served as the guardian of the Northern Continent—the Black Sovereign.

* * *

Reynard was walking through the white mist on top of the mountain with confident steps. His yellow clothes were turning damp due to the humidity, but he didn't pay it any mind. With his sword in hand, he walked forward, not caring in the slightest to his surroundings.

He was certain that he would be the first to reach the peak. All of the other three inheriting disciples had been left behind in his crazy rush to the top. In truth, he felt somewhat disheartened. He had even given them a head start, but he still ended up easily taking the lead not long after.

It was way too easy. There had been no real challenge. He played around with them for a bit, as if he was struggling as much as they were and attacking each other, but the situation never got out of his control. It was disappointingly boring.

Reynard loved winning and challenging worthy opponents. Playing with the weak would never help him grow stronger and, as such, he refused to do so.

Even Anna Hale, who was clearly doing her best, was left behind. She was faster than Jake and Alden, but it was still not enough. More than anything, this had left Reynard with a bitter taste in his mouth.

He knew the race was meaningless. He knew he had baited the others into it, but he still wanted it to be more interesting. There were some hard truths that he had to deal with, and one of those was that achieving strength was both a struggle against one's surroundings and one's self.

What was the point of reaching the peak if everything would be so simple?

What was the point of reaching the peak if he wasn't as strong as he believed he could become?

It would be all meaningless, a waste. An empty victory that he would never be able to relish.

Reaching the peak like this would never make him feel fulfilled. Reynard liked the struggle he had to go through to turn stronger. He loved it. This was probably the reason he was so strong in the first place. Thankfully, this world was filled with strong people who had yet to be defeated.

The thought alone made him tremble with excitement. He couldn't waste time with the other inheriting disciples. He was far above them now. This race just proved his point.

His mission was partially complete and he confirmed his superiority. There wasn't much worth his attention in the Hellblaze Trials anymore, at least not until he reached the peak.

Nevertheless, he still hoped that Anna would give him a pleasant surprise. The clear line that divided her thinned every time Reynard tried to probe her. She had found an interesting resolution in the Trial of Will. He hoped it could bloom into something great someday, something that would give him the excitement he wished for.

He gave a faint smile as he walked forward. No matter how many victories he had, very few of them remained in his memories. His defeats, however, he remembered in detail. There had been only two, and they were exceedingly strong, proving to Reynard just how weak he really was.

That weakness, however, made him both bitter and glad.

Being weak in front of others meant that he could grow stronger. There were more people he could pursue, more milestones in his journey.

Being weak in front of others also meant just that. He was still weak; he was still far away from the peak.

These different ideas might seem conflicting at first, but in truth, they complemented each other very well. Both of these feelings pushed Reynard in the same direction, both of them gave him the drive he needed to become stronger.

As Reynard moved, he heard light footsteps ahead of him. He stopped in place and raised a brow as a silhouette formed in front of him.

It took the shape of a tall man, fully clad in black and holding a dark, curved sword in his right hand. The sword had no guard, as if attacking was the only concern of the wielder. You would never have to defend if you were strong enough to obliterate your opponents before they could strike back, after all.

"It's not enough," the man said in a cold voice as he looked at Reynard with an indifferent expression. "I truly don't see why Master values you so much."

When he realized who was staring him down, Reynard's smile grew wider and a savage light lit within his dark eyes.

In front of him was one of the two who had defeated him. The one Reynard wanted to draw a line upon so much that his hands started trembling with excitement.

"What is this?" Reynard asked, mockingly.

Reynard had heard the words the figure spewed before. The man had said them right after he defeated Reynard years ago.

It had not been a fair fight. It was never intended to be. Reynard had been utterly humiliated that day, and in front of his master, nonetheless. It had been a pure display of strength that put Reynard in his place; a moment of shame that branded him.

"You're not qualified to be my trauma," Reynard said with a sneer as he waved the curved sword in his hands.

A thin layer of light enveloped the sword forming a bright edge. Reynard took a step forward and somehow started to slide through the ground as that single step made him move several meters. He appeared in front of the black-robed man as he slashed with his sword, splitting him in half in a fluid, calculated motion.

The man exploded in a cloud of red mist that Reynard promptly dispersed with a wave of his sword, not letting it touch him at all.

"At most you're a stepping stone, not something that will ever hold me back," Reynard scoffed and started walking forward again as if nothing had happened in the first place.

He might still be weak, but he would crush that weakness by himself. He refused to have regrets; he refused to be held back by things of the past. At most, they would push him forward.

The only person he had to prove something to was himself.

Anna looked at the humongous godbeast staring at her with no shred of hesitation in her eyes. The chilling winds that hit her made her damp clothes freeze, holding her in place. A thin layer of frost covered her black hair, creating fragments of ice that glistened like stars under the faint light that managed to get through the mist.

It made her unimaginably enchanting, but also unimaginably pitiful. Her breath condensed in front of her, and even with her control over water qi, she was unable to do a single thing to free herself.

The layer of mist masking her face started to slowly fade away, as if being peeled off. Anna hurriedly revolved the qi in her dantian, trying to reform the mask. Even though she couldn't control the surrounding qi, she could still use her own.

She was under the influence of the Black Sovereign's domain. All of the qi in a radius of miles were under the Black Sovereign's direct control, unreachable for anyone weaker than it. A pair of majestic eyes slowly descended as the beast lowered its head, slowly approaching Anna.

There was a single spark of interest in those frosty eyes. Amidst the cold, however, that spark might as well have been nothing. Anna moved her gaze upwards, passing through that strange pitch-black head that seemed to be covered in both thick scales and wrinkled leather, and looking through the mist, faintly discerning the shape of a carapace covered in spikes that seemed more like mountains to her.

Light footsteps echoed from her side, slowly approaching her direction. The mist on her side started spiraling and billowing as a middle-aged woman appeared, walking with firm steps, but a respectful expression as she stood in front of the Black Sovereign.

Her black hair was tied in a neat bundle in the back of her head, and her ocean-blue clothes were a perfect match for her sparkling blue eyes. Her pale face was starting to show signs of aging, as a few wrinkles could be seen in the corner of her vivid eyes. She could be called a beautiful woman, even if not breathtaking. She gave a deep bow to the titanic godbeast in front of her, not daring to say a word until she received permission.

"Speak, Mara."

The Black Sovereign's voice injected itself into Anna and Mara's minds, in a tone so grave and serene that its words were almost indistinguishable.

"I'd like to apologize for my daughter's behavior," Mara Hale, the sect master of the Noan River Sect declared.

She gave another deep bow as she tossed Anna a reproachful glance from the corner of her eyes. Anna had rushed into the Black Sovereign's lair ahead of her mother, not caring about etiquette at all. The fact that she had been frozen in place was proof of the slight annoyance the Black Sovereign felt.

"Young ones like their freedom," the Black Sovereign said while giving Anna an unblinking gaze, lowering its head even further and making the mist surrounding it billow away in thick wisps.

"Nevertheless, it doesn't mean they should abuse it."

Its powerful voice made Anna's mind quake, forcing her to tightly close her eyes to try to endure the headache that assaulted her.

"But this is not important. What do you need, Mara?"

"I've come in search of your permission for a marriage."

Mara bent a knee and respectfully lowered herself in front of the Black Sovereign.

"Oh? What do you have in mind?" the Black Sovereign asked, the spark of interest in its cold eyes growing brighter as it directed those enormous eyes to Mara.

"We have received news that the Abyss Sect just lost its fifth protector," Mara said with an alarmed expression, not hiding her concern. "The circumstances are unknown, but it seems to have been a betrayal."

Anna looked at the scene with mixed feelings. The first time she witnessed it, she was just a twelve-year-old girl. She had no real awareness of the situation of the Five Cardinal sects nor of the subtleties in the conversation between her mother and the Black Sovereign.

Now she could see the hidden nuances. As she grew, her mother taught her more and had let her know of the matters concerning their sect as well as the other four cardinal sects. With this information, Anna could more or less guess the thoughts of the Black Sovereign and her mother.

As Mara finished her words, she knew she didn't need to explain the situation. The Black Sovereign knew very well that something strange was happening. Throughout the last few decades, the forces of the Five Cardinal sects started declining. Powerful elders started being killed on simple missions or disappearing without a trace. Treasures and artifacts were vanishing from the vaults and external resources were slowly dwindling due to a myriad of reasons that involved from bankruptcy to the retirement or death of the providers.

For the Noan River Sect, in particular, food was a problem. They had to rely on the rare farmland at the southern end of the Northern Continent and the qi-rich food that the Abyss Sect exported to them. They had no blacksmiths of their own, so they had to rely on the experts of the Southern

Continent and the Southern Flame Sect.

The only thing the Noan River Sect wasn't lacking was water crystals—they even used them as currency. Still, the other cardinal sects didn't offer cheap services, so the secondary providers were as important as them to the Noan River Sect. The rare, smaller sects sprinkled throughout the five continents were also slowly gathering more power and influence, raising the competition for resources.

As such, losing those secondary providers was a big problem, especially since the substitutes would always ask for a somewhat higher price than before, and so, the reserves of the Five Cardinal sects were slowly being chipped away as time passed. They were paying more and receiving less. In a few years it might not make a difference but in decades, or even centuries, the effects would be devastating.

The Abyss Sect had it worse. Its sphere of influence had been restrained to a fraction of what it once was, and the sect had lost innumerable elders and promising youths in recent times. Even the smaller sects of the Central Continent were starting to close the gap between them.

Something was happening behind the scenes. Someone was moving. The problem was that the Black Sovereign didn't seem to know who or why. At the very least, he wasn't sure. The communication between the sects had also been reduced, and so did the communication between the four guardian clans. It was a process so slow, so subtle that it felt only natural.

The long-term peace that Arthur Royce had achieved would naturally bring changes to the discipline and proximity of the sects after the conflict had been resolved. Still...

"Continue," the Black Sovereign demanded, its cold gaze turned incomparably serious as he gazed at Mara.

"The Roaring Mountain Sect has shown interest in a marriage between both inheriting disciples." Mara spoke with a voice as cold as the surroundings, not showing a trace of emotion as she spoke of this. She had come to the Frozen Ravines as the sect master of the Noan River Sect, not Anna Hale's mother.

"What of the White Emperor?" the Black Sovereign asked, showing a hint of impatience.

"It is a recent matter. The other side might also be seeking permission as we speak," Mara said, lowering her head and her posture even further.

It was true that this matter had not been defined, but it was necessary to speak with the Black Sovereign nonetheless. It was a show of respect and obedience. The final answer on their side would come from it.

The gigantic head moved again, returning its gaze to Anna. In its frosty eyes, there was only a chilling void—all traces of emotion had disappeared completely.

"You will come to understand that your position is much more taxing than rewarding." It said as it looked at Anna with a gaze that seemed to pierce straight into her soul. "It is the price you pay to rule over others. Freedom is but a fleeting dream in front of the responsibilities you must bear, little girl."

"This fire you have burning inside you… If you're to inherit the Noan River Sect, you better put it out. Otherwise, it will consume you or the sect under your guidance."

Its gaze softened somewhat as it blew lightly in Anna's direction. That light blowing turned into a gale that shattered the ice covering Anna, freeing her.

"I have no problems with it. The Five Cardinal sects must tighten their bonds again if we're to revert the situation," the Black Sovereign spoke in an unhurried tone as it gave Mara its answer.

"Do you have a problem with it?"

It looked at Anna and asked, raising its head slightly. Mara too turned her head to glare at her daughter. She had been hinting this matter at her for months. It was a price she had to pay in order to do what was best for the sect that would one day be hers.

Six years ago, she had grasped the ring hanging from her neck tightly, obviously torn by the decision. In the end, however, she said nothing. She simply shook her head, silently accepting the burden she would have to bear, even if she didn't truly want it.

That had been the greatest mistake she had made in her life and, if she saw it through to the end, it would be a mistake she would have to deal with for centuries. It would be the same as shackling herself to misery in the name of the Noan River Sect.

Anna decided she would have none of that. The flames inside her stopped flickering and started burning even brighter, expelling the cold invading her.

The present Anna also stood in silence as she was faced with the Black Sovereign's question. She looked as torn as the little girl of six years ago, but the reasons were entirely different. She too, tightly held the ring hanging from her neck.

"You were right. This place is indeed too cold," Anna spoke softly in a sorrowful voice, her expression full of reminiscence as she spoke with a person that wasn't there.

She turned her gaze to the Black Sovereign. She now knew why it had spoken to her about such responsibilities and putting the sect at risk. At that moment, Anna had been presented with a choice that she couldn't recognize, one that wasn't about the marriage.

The Black Sovereign had seen through her, even if at the time she had never managed to look at herself.

"I refuse such responsibilities," she announced with a genuine smile on her face.

Because you're weak.

Lloyd's voice never stopped echoing inside Amon's head.

The words his father said as he left. The words his father said as he abandoned Amon and Rebecca. The words his father said as he destroyed their lives.

Crunch, crunch! The horrifying sound of bones breaking and flesh being torn apart, the blood-curdling screams of the past Rebecca and Amon, they also never stopped.

Again and again, Amon was forced to hear them.

Again and again, he struck with his sword.

He discovered that it was surprisingly easy. A swing of his sword and a silhouette would explode. A swing of his sword and the mist would billow away. A swing of his sword and, for but a moment, the voice would stop, the screams would cease.

Windhowler gave an ominous light as the edge of qi covering it glowed. Not a spec of blood could be found on the sword, but the same couldn't be said about its wielder.

Amon's clothes were completely covered in blood that made his ashen hair stick to his face. The scarlet color that had covered the paleness of his face made his golden eyes even more prominent as they shone with a cold light.

The gravel under his feet crunched as he walked forward, and the ground was slowly turning steep. Amon realized he had started another climb. The white mist still covered everything, but he knew he was in the right direction.

He would reach the peak, and he would prove that he wasn't weak. He would prove it to anyone that doubted him. He would prove it to everyone.

He didn't know how long he had been walking. He didn't know how many times he had swung his sword. He had never started counting in the first place. It wasn't important.

"Because you're weak."

What was important was to prove that his father was wrong.

Crunch, crunch!

What was important was to prove that he was strong enough so no one would be harmed because of his weakness.

Swoosh!

What was important was to silence the voice, to prove his strength.

One step at a time, one swing of his sword at a time, he moved forward, walking on the ever steeper ground.

At that moment, the mist in front of him started churning madly, its wisps billowing back and forth as another silhouette slowly formed, blocking his path. Amon raised his sword, prepared to strike again, but as soon as he saw who stood in front of him, his eyes widened in surprise, and his pulse shot up, so fast and powerful that he could actually feel his heart beating.

The figure was very slender and seemed to be very delicate. She was wearing a white dress that contrasted with her silky black hair that flowed down her back like a waterfall. In front of Amon stood a breathtakingly beautiful woman.

In the woman's hands was a beautiful sword, with a guard in the shape of a crescent moon with a red jewel embedded in it. Even though it was made of common iron, it was an extremely refined piece of craftsmanship, a very elegant blade.

"Why?" he asked with a sorrowful expression as he faced that pair of piercing blue eyes, full of sadness and regret.

"Because you're weak," the voice that echoed wasn't cold and indifferent, nor was it oppressive. It was a melodious, graceful voice, tainted by a depressive disappointment.

"How?" he asked, dumbstruck.

Deep in his eyes, a hint of fear was appearing. He hadn't been able to speak to her ever since he had traversed the gateway to the Hellblaze Secret World. Lya should not be appearing in front of him right now.

"Does it matter?" she asked back.

Lya stood in Amon's way and, even if her eyes showed her true feelings, her expression was incredibly solemn and resolute.

Amon didn't answer her words. He didn't speak, nor did Windhowler. Lya's gaze slowly turned into one of sheer anger and outrage. The gaze of someone that had been betrayed.

Amon looked at her in silence. A cold, overwhelming silence that turned the atmosphere tense.

"What are you, Amon?" Lya asked in an emotionless voice, and her eyes turned sharp. Her expression too changed into one of sheer indifference.

It was a strange question, a very vague one. Nevertheless, Amon understood her meaning. He knew what she wanted to hear.

"A sword cultivator," Amon said, sustaining her gaze with a careful, hesitant expression.

"What do sword cultivators do when they draw their sword?" Lya asked with her voice turning louder, her eyes even fiercer.

"They kill," Amon answered.

"What is your reason to draw the sword, then?" Lya asked again, her tone and expression still lacking any emotions.

Amon returned to his silence but was still sustaining her gaze.

"You don't know?" Lya cocked her head slightly, making her black hair wave lightly. "I see that you have your sword in your hands. I'll change my question, then."

"For what reason did you draw your sword?

Amon was a sword cultivator and he knew for what purpose a sword cultivator drew his sword. Then, if Amon had his sword in his hands, he had killed, or he was about to kill.

Amon still didn't answer her, for he knew there was no need. He knew why he had drawn his sword. She also knew why he had done so. Amon could see it in her eyes, in the disappointment she showed before.

"You're weak," Lya said again, raising a pale arm. Her white dress seemed to flutter under the effects of a nonexistent breeze.

Yes, he was weak. He might be physically stronger than he once was, his soul might have grown and his skill with a sword might be better, but he was still weak.

Those that needed to prove their strength to others were not confident in such strength themselves.

Lya gave Amon a sidelong glance before turning away. She waved her left hand in a dismissive movement, looking annoyed. Amon felt she actually looked very sad.

The mist started to revolve again, as if agitated. It billowed away from the direction Lya had waved her hands to. The direction of the peak.

"Come with me," she said, not bothering to look back at him.

Lya moved forward, climbing a few meters before the steep path ended up in flat land. It was a very narrow space, only five meters wide or so. It was almost claustrophobic.

The ground in that space was covered with gravel and sharp rocks. It was of a disgusting gray, tinged with black.

The sky above was of a deep azure, incredibly bright and beautiful. Everything else, however, was simply white. The mist formed a barrier around that small piece of flat land, blocking all vision.

In the center of that narrow space, was an elegant, yet simple throne made of pure-white wood. The wood suffused a pale light, visible even under the bright sun that shone above the mountain. The throne had a strangely magnetic aura to it, and Amon couldn't avert his eyes from its beauty.

It was a strange contrast with the dark and ugly ground the throne stood on.

"Congratulations," Lya said with scorn as she looked at Amon that had been silently following her. "You reached the peak."

"What?" Amon was caught off guard. His golden eyes shone with surprise as he looked at Lya with an open mouth.

"So, how is it?" Lya faced him suddenly with a distorted expression, a mix of frustration and pain.

"How do you feel?" she asked in a low voice, looking deep into his eyes.

"Does it feel good?" She cocked her head as she looked at him with twisted interest. "Do you feel fulfilled?"

"I..." Amon tried to speak, but he found no words.

In truth, there were no words to be said. He could only hear.

"Was it worth it?"

Amon kept his silence, slowly clenching his fists as his expression changed.

"Look at yourself," Lya said, with nothing but a profound disgust in her face. "Look at what you did."

She raised her hands, and a layer of light formed in front of Amon. It had a flat surface that seemed to be made of a viscous fluid rather than light and rippled with the breeze. Standing in front of it, Amon saw himself as if he was in front of a mirror.

He saw the blood-covered youth looking back at him with a blank expression. He saw a complete stranger.

"I wonder how high the pile of corpses you left behind would reach," Lya pondered with a sad gaze and her voice started to tremble. "Maybe it would be higher than where we stand right now."

Amon was still silent, not daring to interrupt her.

"Is this the cultivator you wanted to be?"

The question that Amon knew she would ask. The question he feared hearing the most. That question being asked meant he had failed her.

He had failed his promise.

The promise he had made her when she decided to teach him about swords. He had promised that he would become a cultivator Lya would be proud of. He promised that she would be able to smile when she thought of him.

Now, however, she was crying.

"Well, it doesn't matter, right?" She said with a horribly forced smile as a tear streamed down her face. "You are at the peak. You are strong. This should be enough, no?"

"Was this what you wanted?" she asked, trying to recompose herself, the corner of her eyes still wet from her tears.

"No," Amon said with a mortified expression.

Guilt started creeping on him as he looked at the mirror of light. His chest felt heavy, and a swirl of emotions started to overwhelm him.

He remembered now. The faces of the silhouettes he so easily cut. The innocent people he killed just to silence the voices for a moment. The people he had project Lloyd into.

What had he done?

"Why did you start to cultivate?" Lya asked with a still trembling voice, showing nothing but disappointment. "What was your reason to start this climb?"

Amon didn't answer; he was afraid to.

"Where are the people important to you?" Lya asked as if Amon had answered the question, despite him keeping his silence.

Brightmoon glinted with a dangerous light as Lya raised it above her head. The force pressing down on Amon turned even stronger, so much so that he could barely breathe.

"Killing people to prove that you're strong, killing people that you think are in your way..." Lya looked at him with a hint of disgust. "You are no different than an animal trying to carve his own territory as it takes down its opponents."

"I told you before, didn't I?" Lya looked down, slowly shaking her head. "Sword cultivators that act like animals are put down like animals. You're an animal that's better off dead."

She shed one last tear as she looked at Amon with nothing but sorrow in her blue eyes.

Then, she changed.

Her gaze turned murderous. He felt his scalp turning numb and his hair stood on end as his instincts told him to run. Still, it was all useless. He was being held in place by that crushing pressure.

No matter how much he struggled or how much he tried to push away all the qi weighing down on him, it would not budge. The qi was being held firmly in place, but somehow beyond his reach.

"Is this really all that I am to you? Are you really going to do this?" Amon asked dejectedly.

Lya's aura started to rise in response, and Amon looked at her in a daze. Her eyes seemed to glow with pure savagery, and a bright light started emanating from the blade of Brightmoon. Like a beacon, it flashed with a blinding light.

The light then started to retract back into the sword, eventually condensing in an almost solid form around the blade, in an edge so sharp that it seemed to cut the very space it touched. It was the same move Lya had shown Amon at the Bridge of Lamenting when he was learning about sword qi.

His thoughts seemed to stop as if his mind was shutting down. He was about to die, but he couldn't utter a word, nor change his dazed expression. He couldn't accept it. He didn't want to. He knew that he would never be able to knowingly hurt her, and he was sure she felt the same way.

No, deep down, he just wanted to believe so. The truth had been there all along, he just refused to look at it.

Lya waved her arm, and Brighmoon descended. The earth rumbled and was torn asunder. The skies howled in pain and were cleaved apart. All light in the world seemed to fade away, and the only thing in Amon's eyes was the enormous wave of bright qi coming in his direction.

For that fleeting moment, all that existed was that divine light reaching for him, carrying judgment and cutting anything on its way, destroying everything it touched.

Amon's vision was overwhelmed by that wave of light. All that he saw was whiteness. The same whiteness he had been surrounded by this whole time. The earth calmed down. The skies turned quiet. The world became silent, as if time had stopped.

Then, everything became white.

* * *

After an unknown amount of time, Amon opened his eyes again. It felt like an eternity, but it also felt like mere moments.

He said nothing. Somehow, he found himself lying on the ground. A dense mist covered his surroundings, and the air was cold and humid. Still,

Amon felt warm, comfortable. His body was light, and his mind was clear as if a great weight had been lifted from his shoulders.

Something was different.

He slowly stood up, looking around. As expected, he saw nothing but the mist. He felt a familiar weight over his shoulder, and he found Windhowler sheathed to his back, as if it had never left.

He looked down at his feet. He could faintly see a deep scarlet color tainting the ground below him. A red and viscous liquid was covering the gravel and rocks in the ground, forming an ominous trail.

A trail that Amon himself had created. A trail of blood.

He took a deep breath, trying to put his thoughts and emotions in order. He couldn't believe what he had done. How he had been so easily pushed over the edge. And the way Lya acted...

Why had that happened?

"Because you're weak," a voice echoed from the mist as a silhouette formed in front of Amon.

With ravenous black eyes, a hair as dark as the night and a cloak that covered him like a shadow, Lloyd Kressler stood in front of him, with an emotionless expression.

"Yes," Amon said, lightly nodding his head to his father's words. He was weak. Unbearably weak.

His will had proven to be weak. His mind had proven to be weak. His heart had proven to be weak.

All of the resolutions he had, all of the objectives he would pursue, all of his ideals. All of that had been scattered with the wind the moment Amon was faced with his weakness, when he so desperately tried to deny the truth.

What came from it was nothing but pain and sorrow.

Amon passed by Lloyd, ignoring him completely, never taking his eyes away from the trail beneath his feet.

He had caused it. He had made this. Lya was right, he had been no more than an animal.

More than anything, Amon felt deeply ashamed.

Crunch, crunch!

The horrifying sound echoed from the mist, and Rebecca's screams reverberated in Amon's mind.

Amon stopped for a moment, closing his eyes. He couldn't change what happened. He had been weak and his mother had paid for that.

He, however, could change what would happen. He was still weak, but he would not be so anymore. He would truly become strong.

And so Amon walked, stepping on the blood he had spilled on the floor as the voices echoed nonstop through the mist.

"Because you're weak," Lloyd would say.

Silence would answer him.

Crunch, crunch! The mist would say.

Silence would answer it.

Amon walked and walked, never stopping, never talking. He eventually reached the slope again, getting close to the peak.

The voices never stopped, and Amon never answered. The mist in front of him started churning again, just like it did when Lya first appeared. This time, however, it was Lloyd that appeared again.

His cloak fluttered behind his back as if it were a pair of dark wings. He held a pitch-black curved sword in his right hand. A sword with no guard, and a single edge. A sword with only attacking in mind.

Amon looked at him still maintaining his silence.

Lloyd, however, said nothing this time. He simply stood there, sword in hand, looking at Amon with those cold eyes. His posture, the arrogance he couldn't hide, were as if he was inviting Amon for a fight.

Amon sneered as he looked at Lloyd standing in front of him. He somehow forgot how tall his father truly was. Even though Amon had grown a lot, the difference still felt abysmal.

"They say that children always feel less love for their parents than the other way around," Amon stated, breaking his silence, looking deeply at Lloyd. "I think that, at least in our case, this is right. While you loathe me, I can't say I feel anything other than sheer hatred for you. The way you abandoned us, the pain you caused to mom... this is not something I will ever forgive. Not that you care about it anyway." Amon smiled wryly. "That being said, I would never kill you that way. I don't think mom would be happy. Not because of you, but because of me. You may not be at the level of an animal, but you're certainly close to it in my eyes. In truth, I find you worthy of pity."

With that, Amon ignored Lloyd again, passing through him just like that. Suddenly, however, he stopped. He slowly turned around and saw the indifferent Lloyd still looking at him with a deadpan expression.

Bam!

A fist landed heavily on Lloyd's face, making him tumble back. Amon retracted his hand with a satisfied expression and turned away from his father.

"Much better," he mumbled before resuming his climb.

He broke through the mist and reached the flat ground of the peak again.

It was truly rather simple, but also rather complicated.

As the white beast had said in what now felt like ages ago, it was all relative. Amon just needed to look at the obstacles in front of him in another way and see the truth.

He took heavy steps as he approached the throne in the center of that narrow space, leaving deep footprints on the ground.

Lya's voice echoed from the mist again, asking many of the questions she had made before.

"So, how is it?"

It was strange. Somewhat lackluster.

"How do you feel?"

Amon felt disappointed; torn.

"Do you feel fulfilled?"

How could he? He naturally was feeling empty, rather than fulfilled.

"Was it worth it?"

In the peak, he could look down and see that ugly ground that sustained the throne. He could also look around and see nothing but the white mist formed by the clouds that blocked both the view of the peak for those below and the view of what was below from those at the peak.

In truth, he could only look up, and try to peer into that cloudless sky. He couldn't see the beautiful scenery of the world below him if he stood at the peak.

He didn't feel it had been worth it.

"You're at the peak. You're strong. This should be enough, no?"

No. This wasn't enough. Strength had never been his objective.

"Was this what you wanted?"

No. This was far from what he wanted.

"Why did you start to cultivate? What was your reason to start this climb?"

He had found his answer long ago. It was all about him, but it was also about the people important to him.

"Where are the people important to you?"

They were down below. Amon couldn't see them, nor could he speak with them. He had left them behind in his climb. He had abandoned them.

At the peak, he stood alone, only being able to look up at an unreachable sky. The peak was a rather horrible place to be. A good match for the pitiful cultivators that chased after it.

Amon looked at the throne in front of him. That beautiful throne that had never stopped charming him.

Then, he looked again.

At the peak, there was nothing. There were only the clouds, the gravel, and the rocks. The throne was gone. It disappeared as if it had never been there.

In the end, it was all relative.

Amon gave a wry smile as he turned his back to the peak and slowly started walking back.

The mist around him slowly faded away, as if it had never been anything but an illusion.

The voices that always echoed from it went completely silent. There were no more conversations to be had.

In truth, there had never been a true conversation.

Ever since he had started the climb, he had been the only one speaking.

Reynard looked one last time at the man at his feet. The white mist billowed around him, in an enchanting, almost hypnotic dance. Reynard's breathing was rough, his dark-brown hair was in disarray and his clothes were a mess. Nevertheless, he had a satisfied smile on his face as he looked down.

The man's curved black sword was a few meters away, stuck on the ground. His black cloak was in tatters, full of holes and tears. A sword was firmly embedded in his chest, and blood slowly seeped from the wound, forming a scarlet pool beneath him.

The man's black eyes were already dim, and his black hair was sticky with his own blood. His face was as pale as candle wax, and his mouth was slightly opened as if he was about to say something. Words that he would never be able to utter, because he was already dead.

Reynard, however, didn't take his eyes away from him for even a moment, as if trying to engrave on his mind the dying expression of his opponent. The man's corpse exploded into a red mist that Reynard promptly dispersed.

Yes, it had to be like this. It was the only result Reynard would accept. Every time he defeated the man, he would soon be reformed from the mist, even stronger. Reynard's pace climbing the mountain had slowly fallen, almost coming to a halt. He, however, was immensely satisfied.

He looked up, trying to peer through the never-ending mist that blocked his vision. It had already been some time since the ground under his feet had turned slanted. He could only move on patiently until he reached the end of the climb.

This was a challenge worth his time. His fights were turning more and more into a struggle, and more and more Reynard felt he turned stronger. What was the point of having an easy win over the other participants? This was what he lived for, this was why he cultivated. As long as there was a chance of growth, he would fight.

A climb like this was worthy of his efforts. Reaching the peak like this was worth his time.

He took firm steps ahead, crushing the gravel under his feet as he moved up. After a moment, however, he stopped. The mist in front of him was restless, excited. A silhouette was forming again, but this one was different.

The figure formed wasn't as tall, his shoulders were not as broad, and his expression wasn't as cold as the man clad in black. This new man's clothes were of a light green instead of dark, a color easy on the eyes, like grass under the morning light. He had his arms behind his back, and he was looking up.

Even though what existed above them was nothing but a dense, white mist, looking at the figure it felt as though his gaze could pierce the skies and peer into the mysteries that were beyond a mortal's reach.

The man's brown hair was cut short, and very neat. His sharp features were framing a very pale face that bore a calm expression. If one looked at him with a glance, he would seem like a scholar. His solemn demeanor and his serene aura might fool those that didn't give him a second look.

Reynard, however, knew better. The man might have seemed composed and calm, but his bright brown eyes were anything but. If one managed to look at them for long enough, they would see a sight quite opposite to their first impression.

Seeing the man looking up like this made Reynard feel more threatened than pleased. This was the first person that had ever defeated him, the only one that truly deserved his respect. If the man he had been defeating so far was nothing but a stepping-stone in his view, the figure in front of him right now was the insurmountable mountain Reynard wanted to climb.

A mountain he would inevitably have to climb if he wanted to reach the peak of the world.

Reynard took one careful step forward, and the man in front of him seemed to finally notice his presence. The man slowly lowered his head, turning his gaze to Reynard. It was a simple movement, done with naturality. For Reynard, a fraction of a second lasted ages.

He felt his hair standing on end, and all of his instincts screamed at him to run. He, however, was stuck in place, as if frozen in place. As the man slowly gazed at him, Reynard felt nothing but fright, as if a primordial beast was glaring at him, ready to tear him to pieces. It was a gaze that shook the very foundations of Reynard's being, a gaze that almost destroyed him.

The only man Reynard ever feared in his life looked at him in a deep, profound glance that shattered the peaceful aura he exuded at first.

It was a scene Reynard had lived once before, a scene deeply engraved in his mind. At the time, he was still fully devoted to the Roaring Mountain Sect, trying to keep his ambitions at bay.

Those eyes, however, changed everything.

A savage fire burned in those eyes, a restless fire that made one feel threatened. A fire full of madness, full of resolve and full of hatred. A fire that blazed the hellish path that the man followed to the peak. A fire that would consume the world before being put out.

Behind that serene demeanor, calm expression, and bright eyes lied Hell.

"Oh?"

The man looked at Reynard with a raised brow. The fire in his eyes seemed to burn even stronger as his interest in Reynard grew. It was a gaze that Reynard felt that could burn its way into his very soul.

"A very talented child. No wonder you turned into the inheriting disciple of the Roaring Mountain Sect," the man said in a calm voice.

His tone seemed casual, but there was something in it, a certain charm, a hypnotic attraction that drew Reynard in.

Reynard was stuck in place, still frozen after that first glance the man gave him. His thoughts were a blank, his emotions a mess. The same as he had been more than seven years ago when they first met. When his life changed forever.

"What do you want for your life, child?" the man asked with a smile.

It was an amiable smile, complemented with a very magnetic voice.

It was a strange question to ask an eleven-year-old child. Even stranger, however, was that Reynard somehow felt he could speak what truly lay in his heart. Something was telling him that there was no need to lie, that he should be himself.

"Everything," Reynard said without hesitation.

He had talent, and he was taught from a young age that the world was at his reach. Why not take it, then?

It was a very simple, very vague answer. An answer that would usually be dismissed as a childish way of thinking. It, however, would turn into a very frightful answer if it were to be taken seriously and if someone made that mindset grow.

The man's smile grew even wider, and his expression turned even gentler. His satisfaction at the answer was clear. Hell turned even brighter, its flames even fiercer as the man's gaze turned sharper.

"How do you intend to acquire everything?"

The man cocked his head slightly, never blinking as he looked at Reynard.

"By becoming strong. By standing at the peak of this world," Reynard answered immediately, not hesitating in telling his true feelings again.

This world was ruled by the strong. It was a fact that even the eleven-year-old Reynard knew. If he wanted everything, naturally he would have to be stronger than all that would fight with him for it.

"Just that?"

His brows furrowed a bit as he looked at Reynard. His smile narrowed a little, as if the answer wasn't to his liking.

Reynard stood in silence as he looked at the man, not knowing what to say. How had his answer not been satisfactory?

"Your vision is too narrow. Why stop at the peak?" the man questioned, looking up again. As soon as Hell stopped staring at Reynard, the man's aura seemed to turn serene again. He didn't look at Reynard again as he spoke. "Do you know what comes after the climb?"

Reynard shook his head. He didn't voice his answer, but the man somehow knew, as if he had seen it.

"What comes after the climb... is a leap," the man answered simply.

He was still gazing at the sky, as if the stars of that night were still shining brightly beyond the mist that surrounded them.

Reynard didn't speak, as he didn't understand. He had a confused look on his face, and his brows were furrowed deeply. This was both true for the Reynard of seven years ago, and the Reynard of the present.

After all those years, he still didn't understand.

What he did understand, however, was what the man's words implied. A truth he somehow had forgotten. A truth he now remembered.

"Do you want me to teach you?" the man asked in a mild voice, its charm somehow even stronger.

Hell descended upon Reynard again. This time, however, those flames seemed very inviting, very attractive. He wanted the knowledge that rested within them. He wanted the strength they hid.

"Please," Reynard spoke respectfully, kneeling on the floor and bowing deeply.

He didn't hesitate to do so. No matter the consequences, he felt it was worth it. Deep down, he knew that this man held true strength. Something he wanted to pursue at all costs.

"Let's start from the beginning, shall we?"

The man took a step closer to the bowing Reynard. Reynard couldn't help but be consumed by the flames of his eyes, as he looked at the man in a daze.

"What do you know about swords?" With a smile, the man asked him the first question as his master.

✳ ✳ ✳

Reynard took a step forward, breaking away from the mist. His gaze was even sharper, his steps even firmer as he stepped in the leveled ground. Somehow, he felt that he was even stronger.

He gazed ahead, not showing a hint of surprise in his eyes at the scene that presented itself to him. A narrow space covered in gravel and sharp rocks. A narrow space surrounded by a wall of clouds that blocked the view of everything around him.

A narrow space with only a white throne in it.

Reynard looked at the throne with interest, not hesitating to walk to it. His dark eyes glinted with a strange light as he had his eyes fixed on it, as if savoring the view.

He approached it and closed his eyes as he extended his hands. He felt the crisp texture of the wood with his fingers, as well as a faint warmth. It was a strangely satisfying feeling.

Without hesitation, he slowly sat on the throne, enjoying the light breeze blowing on his hair. Even though the throne was made of nothing but wood, it was very comfortable. Reynard felt he would never get tired of sitting on it. He deserved it, after all.

He had been the first to get there, and the only one to stay there.

He was alone at the peak, above everyone else. The whole world was at his feet.

With his eyes still closed, he lightly supported his head on the tall backrest of the throne, getting even more comfortable. Then, he finally opened his eyes, and he saw it. He saw the only thing there was to see at the peak.

The endless expanse of azure above him; the unending sky that supervised their world; the unreachable heavens that lay above everyone, including the peak.

What comes after the climb… is a leap. The words of his master echoed in his ears.

Then, Reynard finally understood. His climb might end at some point, but he would still have something to strive for. He would still be able to pursue strength; he would still be able to move on.

On his face, a smile slowly showed itself. A very satisfied smile. A very savage smile.

In his eyes, a fire started burning, more fiercely than before.

He would take the leap. Certainly not now. More than likely not in a few decades, or even centuries.

One day, however, he would certainly take it.

Still smiling, Reynard looked down. He wasn't sure why, but he did it anyway and his smile faded.

Not far from the throne, the gravel had been subtly moved and the rocks had been kicked away, forming faint forms of feet.

On the peak, there were footprints that were not his.

HELL BECKONS

Amon stood quietly on the edge of the mountain. He simply sat there in silence, letting his legs hang above the enormous emptiness that lay below. His arms supported his body as he leaned back. The endless billowing mist that covered his vision reflected in his golden eyes as he absent-mindedly looked up in a daze.

He had no idea how long it had been since he left the peak of the mountain. He had no idea if he would ever regret that decision. Nevertheless, he felt it was the right choice.

He raised his arms and let himself fall on his back, never taking his eyes from the mist. He unconsciously rubbed the old iron ring on his finger, his gaze turning even more unfocused. The cold sensation it gave him was somewhat refreshing, but also a bit unnerving.

What would Lya have said about his decision?

He felt it had been ages since he first entered the Hellblaze Secret World, and he hadn't been able to speak to her ever since. Amon suddenly realized that he missed her. Ever since he first met that strange sword spirit, there was never a day that passed when they didn't speak to each other.

There had never been a day that he didn't receive her guidance, one way or another.

"Having second thoughts?" A cold, crisp voice suddenly echoed from the mist, making Amon's hair stand on end.

Still, he somehow managed to keep his calm as he recognized the voice. Nevertheless, his heart was still racing from the sudden visitor appearing.

"I was wondering when we would meet, sir guardian," Amon said as he slowly stood up, turning his eyes to the blurry figure forming in front of him. A tall man walked out from the mist, covered in white from head to toe.

"Or should I say it's nice seeing you again?" Amon chided with a smile.

The man's pure white hair fluttered unnaturally, seamlessly mixing with the billowing mist surrounding him. The sharp features on his pale face were further pronounced by a pair of icy eyes that seemed to peer into one's soul, making him seem more like a beast than a man. His thin lips were stretched in a cocky smile as he gazed at Amon with a rare interest.

"Heh, look who is being all cocky," the guardian said with a sneer, not hiding the scorn in his icy eyes. He smiled savagely, showing a row of black fangs protruding from his mouth.

"I have to admit, though, I didn't think you would realize it so soon." Although he said words that could be taken as a compliment, his eyes showed nothing but derision, making Amon somewhat embarrassed.

"To be fair, your voice does leave a lasting impression," Amon answered.

He had some suspicion on the identity of the guardian when it disclosed the objectives of the Trial of Heart for all disciples. That crisp, cold voice and that tone full of scorn were certainly unforgettable.

The guardian threw his head back as he started to laugh. That unnerving gurgling sound was still there, even if less pronounced than before. Amon felt it gave the man in front of him a rather eccentric feel rather than the previous sense of abhorrence that his beast form gave.

Somehow, Amon didn't feel the pressure that the guardian exuded in their first meeting. His human form was certainly more approachable, even if Amon knew it was nothing but a fake front. His instincts were screaming at him the same way they did when he first met the beast in the Trial of Mind.

Amon could only imagine why the guardian would give himself the trouble to personally preside over the Trial of Mind. Maybe he was simply bored, or maybe he wanted to keep a close eye on the next generation of cultivators. Unfortunately, Amon knew the guardian would never seriously answer his question, so he didn't bother asking.

Eventually, the guardian stopped laughing, and his gaze turned serious. He perked up his brows as he looked at Amon, a strange light shining the depths of his eyes. In truth, he found the youth in front of him very strange.

"Can you tell me something?" Amon asked as his expression turned serious.

"Only if you answer my question later," the guardian replied with a scornful smile.

"Were you the one that made those apparitions on the Trial of Heart?" Amon turned restless, almost hostile as he looked at the guardian.

"No. As you might have guessed, you made those apparitions yourself. It is a special property of the mist. The whole mountain peak is surrounded by an illusory array formation. All I do is analyze the nebula forming around the asters of the competitors to understand what they're feeling, and pair that with their actions in the mist to make an evaluation of sorts," the guardian explained.

Hearing his words, Amon gave a slight nod in acknowledgment. He had already faintly guessed most of what the guardian explained, but he still had to be sure. Even though his fist would simply pass through the guardian's projection, he still wanted to punch him if he had been responsible for the illusions.

"Now is my turn, brat. The one thing that the array shows for everyone is the throne. Why didn't you sit on it? Why did you walk away from the peak?" the guardian asked slowly, glaring at Amon with a rare serious expression. The sudden change in attitude made Amon rather taken aback.

"Well, if I have to say why, it would be because it wasn't worth it," Amon said as he looked the guardian in the eye.

"You said before that everything was relative. You said that if you took the time to look at an obstacle a second time, you might realize that there was nothing there in the first place," he pondered, "I simply thought that rather than an obstacle, that logic applied to everything. It should be especially so for the things we desire."

"So, when I gave that throne a second look, I realized that for me it was the same as nothing. The peak is nothing but a barren, lonely place."

Seeing the guardian's eyes turning even more serious, Amon was somewhat flustered. He tried to keep calm as he continued to explain.

"The price I would pay to stay there is not something I could afford. It would be a trade where I would lose rather than win."

The guardian closed his eyes for a moment after he heard Amon's words. A grave silence took over them as neither spoke a word. The world seemed to turn still as both of them stood there, surrounded by the endless expanse of white.

"You know, kid, you're quite wise for someone your age," the guardian finally broke the silence after some time. There was no longer any disdain in his eyes, nor any semblance of scorn in his expression. "Sometimes we only realize we've walked the wrong path when it's too late to turn back. I would be rather interested in seeing where this path might take you. If you truly choose to walk it, I can only hope that there never comes a day when you look back and regret the choice you made."

Amon looked at the guardian, not knowing what to say.

"Now then, I believe it's about time you and I had a talk, isn't that right, Lya?" the guardian spoke, directing his gaze to the ring in Amon's hand.

The iron ring flashed with a blinding light, making Amon reflexively close his eyes and turn his head away. The light seemed to break apart in countless ephemeral specs of brilliance that slowly gathered, turning into the figure of a beautiful white-dressed woman.

"How rude of you, keeping a lady locked away like that without even a word," Lya scoffed in her melodious voice as she faced the guardian with unfriendly eyes. "I guess some people never change, Hati."

"Oh, I'm honored to be remembered by you, my lady," the guardian said with disdain, returning to his scornful tone. "Either way, I doubt you would have interceded during the trials anyway. It is just that Nemeus asked me to go the extra mile to be sure the kid would make his own decisions."

Amon looked in surprise at the duo in front of him. Did they know each other? How? Who was Nemeus?

"Enough with this," Lya said in an abnormally cold voice. "What do you want?"

"I would like to ask you to take good care of that kid," the guardian said while furrowing his white brows, showing concern in his otherwise indifferent expression. "I know you have your own reasons to do so already, but I still feel obliged to do this. He is a descendant of Grant, after all, and he has Skoll's Blessing."

Amon opened his eyes wide as he heard the guardian's words.

"What? Who is Grant? What is Skoll's Blessing?"

Amon couldn't help but ask with surprise, his curiosity finally beating him.

The guardian sent Lya a judgmental glare.

"You didn't tell him?"

"That is for me to decide when to do," Lya said while averting her eyes from the guardian. Amon looked at her with inquisitive eyes, but she didn't spare him a glance.

The guardian didn't speak further. He looked at Amon, thinking about something for a while before he silently shook his head.

"The Hellblaze Trials are over for you, kid. Come, I will send you to get your rewards," he said, waving his hand in Amon's direction.

The space surrounding Amon started to distort, making him feel dizzy and nauseous. The world around him started to spin as an indistinct roar echoed in his ears. He tightly closed his eyes to try to fight back against the uncomfortable feeling, unable to pay attention to anything else, clinging to conscience with all he could.

As Amon's figure started to turn blurry in an unnervingly slow pace, the guardian turned to the figure of the woman that was still quietly floating in front of him, ethereal as moonlight.

"Hiding things from him is not wise, Lya," the guardian said, looking at her with a piercing glance. "He is entitled to know about himself and about you. How much did you truly tell him?"

"That's none of your concern," Lya spoke in a cold voice, her gaze turning hostile.

"Such stupidity," the guardian shook his head, clearly disappointed. "You're not raising a cultivator, you're raising a puppet. Don't spoil that kid's potential with your selfish decisions. If you truly want to make things right, turning him blind and guiding him by the hand will never work," the guardian said. "You saw the things he did and the choices he made by himself. He has a peculiar way of thinking, but he clearly lacks the proper mindset or the emotional maturity to face the hardships that are coming for him."

"Are you done?" Lya hissed.

The air around her turned unbearably cold, and a crushing pressure started weighing down on everything around her as she looked at the guardian with burning eyes.

"Those four hundred years alone certainly made your soul stronger," the guardian said, not shaken at all by her display. "Still, you lived too little, and know too little about how humans work."

He dismissively waved his hands, and Lya froze in place, as if time had come to a halt. She was completely helpless as cracks slowly spread through her body.

"It doesn't matter how much you try to convince yourself that this is for his sake. In the end, it's all because you feel guilty about the past," he said in a sorrowful voice as Lya's fragments slowly dissipated in the air. "If you keep holding back the truth from him and making his decisions in his place, he will certainly point his finger at you when things inevitably go awry. Worst of all, he will have every right to do so."

"I don't want to hear that coming from someone that willingly turned into Arthur's watchdog," Lya snorted as the cracks in her body continued to spread.

She couldn't hide the derision in her eyes for the guardian, nor the aversion she felt at speaking Arthur's name.

"Oh, yes, Arthur. That incredibly arrogant man that decided the direction the world and cultivation should take after someone almost destroyed both. That awful, horrible man that didn't allow the Natural Laws break apart and a second Cataclysm to happen. Yes, that Arthur," the guardian raised a brow, sending Lya a piercing glance with his blue eyes. "What was the adage of the sword cultivators, Lya?" the guardian asked, looking at her intently.

"I—"

"Say it," the guardian demanded.

"*Only life can raise a sword cultivator,*" Lya recited sourly, meeting his gaze with challenging eyes.

"Good, you remember it. Now tell me, why aren't you staying true to those words? Why bother raising a sword cultivator if you won't do it properly? As far as I know, what you're doing with that kid is no different than what Arthur did."

Lya shook hearing his words, and her face paled. Her mouth was open, but no words came out.

"We all make mistakes, Lya. I was afraid of death, terrified of it as I saw it coming my way. Skoll had been taken first, but I wasn't as brave as him. Arthur knew this and gave me a choice. One last act as a soul cultivator before he severed that path forever," the guardian shook his head and answered with a surprisingly dispirited voice.

"Here I am, stuck in this hellish limbo, caged to this existence by my own flesh and blood, having to accept a piece of the soul of a man that is already dead churning inside of mine. Still, I can sense the world around me, even if I can't touch it," the guardian looked up, pondering. "The days pass and I'm still here, still myself, despite not being able to say that I'm alive, nor that this is pleasant. But can you, of all people, criticize Arthur, or me, for it?"

The truth was that she couldn't. She had no right to criticize any of them, as she was the same.

"Do you regret it?" Lya suddenly asked, restless. It was almost as if she had been wanting to ask him this question all this time.

"It doesn't matter, does it?" The guardian's tone was surprisingly soft. "Not for you, at least. I won't give you the affirmation you want so desperately. I can't. I don't know if we made a horrible mistake, or if this was a blessing. For me, at least, the answer is not clear. But that is not what you want to hear, is it?"

"Do *you* regret it?" the guardian asked, looking at Lya in the eye.

Only silence answered him. Lya's body finally shattered, and motes of starlight scattered in all directions.

Hati, the Moonchaser Wolf couldn't hide the pain in his eyes as he looked at Lya's broken figure. He was seemingly talking to himself, reminiscing about his incredibly long life as he finished muttering what was on his mind before Lya's figure finally vanished alongside Amon. He couldn't help but remember Alexei.

His last words echoed in Lya's mind, making her heart clench.

"Can you bear another failure in your hands, little girl?"

In truth, the possibility scared her more than she would ever be willing to admit, because she already knew the answer to both questions.

A fierce wind howled as it blew at Daniel's back, pushing his body dangerously close to the razor-sharp rocks of the mountainside. Daniel gave an exasperated sigh as he tried his best to fight against it.

His body was trembling uncontrollably, and burning pain had taken over his limbs long ago due to his overexertion. Blood flowed from his mangled fingers and palms, covering the thick scabs that were forming and cracking on his hand nonstop.

His right arm was hanging uselessly by his side, dangerous hovering over the ground that lied hundreds of meters away. Without being able to properly replenish his qi, Daniel had lost the capacity to manipulate his crippled arm not long after he had started the climb.

He had been climbing with only his left arm and his legs ever since. To his desperation, he felt that if he didn't finish the climb soon, he would also permanently damage his left hand. After that, only the cold embrace of the soft grass far below would catch him.

Daniel grunted in pain, not hiding the frustration and despair he felt. Even if the guardian protected his life, it would be meaningless. Everyone else had surpassed him long ago, even if Daniel had had a head start. That was to be expected, but what bothered him the most was his uselessness.

When he saw the four inheriting disciples fighting their way up with one another right below him, Daniel couldn't even help his brother by trying to hold the others back. The swords he sent flying in their direction were simply ignored, being thrown away in the middle of the volatile elements and their chaotic attacks. He almost shared the fate of his swords as the impact of their attacks made their way up to where he was.

His brother tried to reach for him, but he decidedly shook his head. Now wasn't the time to have pity, nor to try to help those that would hold him back. Now was the time for his brother to worry only about himself.

He could only watch in dismay as, one by one, all competitors surpassed him, even the youngest and weakest of them. The sour taste in his mouth would not go away, even if he already knew that this would be the most likely outcome.

Daniel stopped struggling against the wind and let himself hit the mountainside. He held back a grunt as the sharp rocks pressed against his chest. Even though they punctured his skin, they gave him the support he needed to move on.

He sluggishly reached upwards with a trembling arm, fighting back against the pain and exhaustion as he firmly grasped another sharp rock. He listlessly raised his head, watching the vortex of clouds that hid the peak of the mountain.

It was completely out of reach.

He felt something weighing down on his chest, and he suddenly had the urge to throw up. He almost let go of the rock he was holding with his left hand as his body suddenly convulsed, forcing him to stay in place, barely holding on.

A dry, weary laugh escaped from his lips. His throat was already sore from dehydration, and his voice was hoarse. It brought him even more pain, but he couldn't stop. In truth, it was quite a sad sight.

When he finally got a hold of himself and looked at the rock he was holding, he realized he couldn't feel his left arm anymore. He didn't even know how he was still holding on to the rock.

"God damn it," he whispered to himself, giving a wry smile.

He stopped any and all attempts of continuing his climb, staying still in that exact same position. He had no idea how long he would manage to hold on.

He slowly looked down, gazing at the towering trees of the forest that now looked like nothing but dots in the distance. He was very sure that they were swaying with the wind, waving at him, inviting him to join them.

For a moment, Daniel considered accepting their call.

"Are you done?" A strange voice suddenly echoed in Daniel's ears, giving him a scare and almost making him lose his footing.

He quickly turned his head to the source of the voice, seeing a tall man dressed in white hovering next to him, as if the air itself was propping him up. His indifferent expression made him seem extremely arrogant, and his strange white hair and his piercing blue eyes gave Daniel chills as he faced the unexpected newcomer.

"As much as I don't want to admit, I know the truth already," Daniel answered in an incredibly tired voice, looking like he would pass out at any moment. The moment the man appeared and asked that question, Daniel already knew who he was.

The guardian continued to look at him with indifference but slowly cocked his head, as if watching a mildly interesting ant. He didn't speak, so Daniel took it as a sign to continue talking.

"I suppose you already know the answer too, don't you?" Daniel asked dispiritedly.

"Of course I do. It is my responsibility to be able to properly assess such things," the guardian spoke with his crisp, grating voice that greatly unnerved Daniel. "Still, it doesn't mean I don't have to ask you why."

"Why bother with such meaningless questions? We both know that I already am at my limit. It is not as if I'm giving up, or not giving my best. This is simply as far as I can go," Daniel said in an exasperated voice, shaking his head.

"Even though you say that, a moment ago you were still trying to push forward. Why stop now?" the guardian asked as he faced Daniel with a blank expression.

"Why are you so curious about that?" Daniel asked in a harsh tone. He was already in a terrible mood, and the guardian was only pouring salt on his wounds.

"Because you made the best deal of all the people that passed by me in these Hellblaze Trials," the guardian answered, still not showing an inkling of emotion in his face. His eyes, however, turned a bit less cold. Daniel could see a glimmer of pity in them, which made him even angrier.

"I see. I did think you sounded somewhat familiar," Daniel said dismissively, making the guardian give a rare sight.

"Pride is not something people like you should hold on to," the guardian said as his expression finally turned serious.

Daniel was taken aback by his words. His face darkened as his mind raced to give him an answer, but the words he desperately tried to look for never came to him. He couldn't help but admit the guardian was right.

Even though Daniel had been shunned by his father, and struggled to attain the miserly achievements he had, he was still proud of himself. He knew that anyone else that faced the hardships he did would most likely have fallen short to what he managed to do.

Nevertheless, it was all for naught. Facing the harsh reality would have never been easy on him, it could never have been.

Lars Borgin might have taken a liking to the technique he developed to control swords with qi, and Daniel might have managed to fight his way to the Inner Sect to slap his father's face, but that was it.

Daniel had reached his peak long ago, and it was simply not high enough.

In the grand scheme of things, he still meant nothing. He never would.

He would never be able to leave the mountainside, being stuck far from the ground and far from the peak. Inevitably, he would fall someday, joining all the others that never even tried the climb before.

The simple mortals that could only watch from afar as countless cultivators tried the climb, and countless more fell back to the ground. Daniel would never be anything but one of those people that they watched with fervor but ultimately meant nothing in their simple lives.

"The climb might give you power, but it also brings you pain. Those that are not fated to reach the peak will get nothing but suffering out of it," the guardian spoke lightly, but emotionlessly, as if he had said those words many times before. It was clear he was already numb to their meaning, numb to their effect on the people they were directed to.

"Maybe you should consider if the climb is truly worth it," the guardian added, sighing yet again. "There is nothing wrong in seeking happiness instead of power and living a fulfilling life."

Daniel gazed at the guardian with a strange look in his eyes. He didn't utter a word as he pondered for some time.

"Am I the only one left?" Daniel broke the silence after some time, furrowing his brows tightly.

"Yes," the guardian answered simply. "All the others either fell or reached the peak. You are the only one left."

"I see," Daniel sighed with a pained look.

In truth, he had been so absorbed in his own climb that he didn't even notice that other people fell from the mountain. Maybe they had been so far above him that he couldn't even see them before the guardian saved their lives.

"Well, I can't climb further, and I can't safely return to the ground," Daniel spoke in a soft voice. "What now?"

"You still haven't told me your answer," the guardian pointed out. For whatever reason, it wanted to hear a clear answer from Daniel.

"My answer is mine alone," Daniel dismissed him without hesitating.

The guardian shook his head at such stubbornness. He snapped his fingers, and the space around Daniel started to distort. It looked like Daniel had somehow changed his mind during the course of their conversation. Or rather, he wasn't willing to admit what he felt to anyone else.

In truth, this conversation had shaken Daniel greatly. Deep down, he knew the guardian was right. Still, how could he truly find happiness?

If he joined the common mortals, he would outlive many generations of his own family. This wasn't something he would ever be willing to experience. He would rather die than outlive his descendants.

In the world of cultivators, he amounted to nothing, cursed to never be able to achieve a higher level. Even Amon, who was supposedly less suited to cultivation than he, had been slowly surpassing him.

All Daniel could truly do was try his best to keep up with them. No matter how much pain it brought to him, no matter if it ended up destroying him, he couldn't stop. It was only thanks to the guardian's words that he finally understood the terrifying thought that had been creeping on his mind ever since he gained some understanding of the world.

His happiness lied with the people he loved, and they were all slowly leaving him behind.

Reynard's face soured as the space surrounding him finally calmed down. The place the guardian had sent him to was a wide hall. Walls of a blazing scarlet, embroidered with swirling and twisted patterns made with gold surrounded him. Such gold, however, had a glow of its own, serving as the source of lighting in the hall. It gave off a warm, gentle light that reflected on the white tiles of the floor, making them look like golden flames.

Reynard, however, couldn't care less. The moment he felt that he was in a stable environment again, he looked around abruptly, searching for someone that wasn't there.

Who stepped on the peak before me?

His foot unconsciously started tapping the floor restlessly as his eyes darted around. When he realized he was getting agitated, Reynard closed his eyes and took a few deep breaths. When he opened his eyes again, his lips contorted in a strange, ominous smile. The golden light mixed with the red of the walls as it shone ominously on Reynard's face, giving him a sinister look.

Just like that, the fierce rage he showed before was gone, giving place to something simpler; something purer; something darker.

How long had it been since he felt like that? How long had it been that he had tasted defeat?

Ever since he met his master, Reynard's strength had soared. His innate talent, coupled with his ambitions, made him grow at a rate that sometimes astounded even his master. His greatest strength, however, was his ability to read his enemies and use their information to his advantage.

It was a talent he had since young and was something his master greatly treasured in him. Thanks to that Reynard had only been defeated twice throughout his life, both times by people far above his own level. No one in his generation had ever been his match.

If an exception existed, it had to be Derek Tyrell. Reynard had never managed to see through him, not even once. This made him deeply uncomfortable, almost restless. He couldn't help but hold deep apprehension towards Derek, even if the latter somehow managed to avoid all situations that would lead to a fight between them.

Reynard didn't understand his reasons to lay low, but he didn't believe Derek to be a coward. If anything, he was extremely dangerous. Derek might be able to fool most people, but not Reynard.

Even though Reynard was confident in defeating him, he knew it would be no easy task. The price he would have to pay would be enormous. Just the thought alone was enough to put a smile on his face. He really wanted to punch that sly guy in the face and fight once and for all.

Nevertheless, pondering about such things was meaningless. Derek wasn't taking part in the Hellblaze Trials. This fact alone was something that worried him. Thomas, Clarice and Helen hadn't appeared either. Some-

321

thing had certainly gone awry.

Still, even if things on Storm Peak Sect were not looking so good, Reynard had the confidence to deal alone with the mission. The problem was that an undetermined variable had just appeared.

Reynard frowned again. All of the inheriting disciples had been far behind him when he managed to reach the misty peak of the mountain. He didn't believe any one of them could've surpassed him while facing their own demons.

Reynard shook his head. None of them could have done it.

Alden Bren was a simple-minded fool, but the ghosts that haunted him were not so easily dismissed. He would certainly have some trouble.

Anna Hale was a stubborn woman. Reynard knew very well what bothered her, and he couldn't help but smile lightly. However, something in the Trial of Will changed her. The lines that once clearly divided her were starting to blur. She was getting rid of her weaknesses and she would probably have an easier time than what he first expected. Still, Reynard didn't believe she was ready to simply storm through the mist and into the peak like he did.

Jake Meyer had potential, but he was a foolish youth that had been raised with a golden spoon. It didn't matter if all he had was a complicated family since he lacked the maturity to deal with it. His hardships could've been easily solved if he used his position as inheriting disciple and the attention his father gave him in a proper way, but he couldn't bring himself to do it. He was too keen on avoiding conflict, and too hesitant to make a proper decision and follow through with it.

Being overly flexible and caring too much about others was the kind of weakness that made Reynard roll his eyes. Such lines were so clear he couldn't be bothered to draw them.

His companions had also been specifically instructed to not stand out, and Reynard knew them as well as he knew the inheriting disciples, so it couldn't have been them either.

All that was left was the trash, so who did it?

Suddenly, Reynard's expression faltered. He remembered when he finished the Trial of Mind, when all remaining competitors gathered. The first to arrive had been himself, followed suit by Anna. The third one, however, had not been Alden, nor had it been Jake.

A figure came to his mind. Strange ashen hair and those insufferably bright golden eyes. Reynard slowly squinted his eyes, as his mind worked.

His name was Amon.

Reynard started remembering their conversation. The boy never stated his surname, but Reynard still knew who he was. He had all the information he needed about most of the participants of the Hellblaze Trials, the exception being the substitutes of the Storm Peak Sect.

"Amon Kressler, but always presents himself as Amon Skoller," Reynard muttered. "A failure that somehow managed to get good results in the competition. The reason behind his presence in the Hellblaze Trials is a mystery to all but a few. It certainly involves the inner politics of the sect, as well as his father.

"Of course, the more important information is his surname," Reynard said, a savage smile contorting onto his face.

Whoever was faster than him wasn't important anymore. This was a chance. Like a beast stalking a prey, his expression turned ferocious and his eyes showed expectancy.

His smile widened and the fire in his eyes burned fiercely. He would have to take a risk and change the plans slightly, but he would do so in a heartbeat. As long as the end result was satisfactory, his master had given Reynard permission to act as he saw fit if anything unexpected happened. On his path in the pursuit of strength, defeating that insufferable man was unavoidable.

It would all be worth the risk if he managed to see a line that he could draw on that person. No matter how faint, thin or small it was, as long as it was there Reynard would eventually be able to draw it, no matter how long it took.

A blinding flash of light interrupted Reynard's thoughts as a deafening roar started echoing inside the scarlet hall. The space distorting wildly, causing the golden lights to flicker and giving Reynard an unpleasant sensation.

One by one, figures of all sizes and ages started to materialize. From those that couldn't even make it past the Trial of Will to those that managed to reach the peak in the Trial of Heart, all of them were sent to the hall.

"Well, things will certainly become more interesting now," Reynard muttered to himself.

Hati coldly watched as the competitors appeared in the hall. All fifty competitors were present; it didn't matter if they had failed the first trial or made it all the way to the peak; they were all due a suitable reward, even if it was nothing but broken expectations and shattered hopes. This was the kind of world they lived in, after all.

Hati sneered when he saw the members congregate to their respective sects. When he transmitted his voice, some jumped in fright due to the sudden unpleasant sound.

"The rewards will be given out now. Step away from each other," he said, watching closely as they all promptly obeyed him.

With a thought, the space between each of the participants seemed to solidify, as if a glass wall had appeared between them. Billowing tendrils of shadow started squirming in the frozen space, slowly tainting it black and blocking the view of all the participants and closing an area of a few meters square around each one of them.

Trying to not get annoyed at their obnoxious reactions, Hati silently focused. In front of each of the competitors, a faint light escaped from the shadows, blurring and flickering, making some feel dizzy. When the light finally returned to normal, a tall man with white hair stood facing each of them.

Hati stretched and pondered a moment. Nothing unexpected had happened in the trials, so he decided to separate all of the competitors as he gave out the rewards, closely observing all of them in search of abnormalities.

Nemeus didn't know what Lloyd wanted to take away from the Hellblaze Secret World, and neither did Hati. There were far too many treasures originating from all of the cardinal sects. Most of them could be considered average, but a few could certainly spark the greed of a protector of the Abyss Sect. If they didn't know what he was aiming for, they wouldn't know his final goal. Information was vital, and they lacked it.

Lloyd Kressler wasn't a trivial enemy, but risks had to be taken in order to have a grasp of the big picture. Considering the strange occurrences that had been happening in the last few decades and how they were slowly being divided, Hati couldn't help but shudder.

Since he couldn't leave the area, Hati was only able to hear the details from Nemeus. He knew very well that the Five Cardinal sects were suffering on all possible fronts, losing disciples, money and resources at an acceptable, but still ever growing rate.

Although Hati couldn't witness these changes for himself, every ten years he could personally watch the current state of the relationships between the sects. However, a few decades ago, he also started noticing gradual changes.

The eventual fights that broke out were always more violent than the last, and he could clearly see the disciples bundling together with members of their own sects and no one else. This supported Nemeus news that disputes over territory and resources were resulting in more skirmishes between the cardinal sects and the smaller ones.

The best example would be the Abyss Sect. At face value, it seemed to be on par with the others, but in truth it had fallen behind long ago. It had suffered the most and its reputation had plummeted due to the Scavenging. Behind the scenes, the Abyss Sect's name brought nothing but disdain from the others due to its fall from grace. In a few short decades, it would certainly lose its position as the strongest sect of the central continent if the situation didn't change. Not only that, the four guardian beasts and their respective clans became more reclusive.

Oddly enough, the gaps started after Arthur Royce died and the force binding everything together disappeared. The world had fractured and its pieces were slowly drifting away. This could also have been considered natural.

Regardless, Arthur's death was quite mysterious. Neither Nemeus nor Hati could rule out the possibility of someone moving in the shadows. The thought alone gave Hati shivers. Such an opponent had the power, the resources and the information to carry this out. Worst of all, the person responsible for all of this had the patience to do so over decades or even centuries.

Such a possibility also frightened Nemeus greatly, so there was no room to wait and see how things played out, especially if Dale Loray turned out to be the one behind it all. They could either start playing the game with a disadvantage or risk being pawns on the board. For that reason, any and all sacrifices were worth the price.

❊ ❊ ❊

In the enclosed space, Amon quietly observed the humanoid form of the guardian. In the midst of shadows and dim light, the tall man was illuminated in a white brilliance. To Amon's surprise, his piercing, icy eyes were hazy, as if the guardian was in a daze.

The light by his side started chaotically distorted as Lya's figure materialized in the enclosed space. Amon's brows furrowed and he didn't hide his dissatisfaction as he opened his mouth to talk.

He wanted to ask Lya about how she knew the guardian and Nemeus. He wanted to know what Skoll's Blessing was. Before he could talk, however, Lya slightly raised a hand to interrupt him, not once taking her eyes away from the guardian.

There were dark lines creasing her brows—she was clearly in an awful mood, but she didn't speak. She simply waited as the guardian returned his attention to them.

"Well kid, it's about time we ended this," the guardian suddenly said in its crisp, cold voice. "I already have a suitable reward for you. I hope you use it well."

"Our talk is not over," Lya snapped.

Amon taken aback. He felt that Lya was acting in a very unnatural way.

Without hesitation, the guardian dismissively replied, "If you don't have a talk with the boy, there is no reason for us to continue ours."

Lya's expression sank, but when she glanced at Amon, she kept quiet, though not without hesitation.

The guardian didn't spare her a second glance as he waved his hands. A tumultuous wind rose between him and Amon, slowly forming a blob of red light. It shone with a hellish color, sending terrifying ripples and distorting its surroundings. An astounding wave of heat took over the enclosed space, causing Amon to sweat profusely.

When it was finished, Amon saw that it was actually an incredibly long feather. Its shaft was golden and its translucent barbs were a deep scarlet. Circular patterns of gold and silver appeared on it; it heavily resembled a peacock's tail feather.

Its aura alone was menacing enough, but when it was coupled with its beauty and the heat it exuded, Amon was enthralled by it. His golden eyes were glued to the feather as he started at it unwaveringly.

"Arthur still had that stored away?!" Lya asked in shock.

Her previous sour expression quickly melted into genuine surprise.

"He left it behind for a suitable candidate," the guardian declared. "The only reason I'm entrusting this to you is because of the deal we made in the Trial of Mind. I hope you keep that in mind when you decide how you want to use this."

Amon's eyes shone with surprise as he gave the feather another look.

"What is it used for?" Amon questioned.

The guardian gave a disdainful smile as he answered.

"Whatever you want, as long as you give it to the right person."

* * *

"Is that it?" Reynard asked the guardian, clearly unhappy. In his hands was a very strange sword. Its blade was about the size of Reynard's arm and had a very ordinary shape, unlike his curved sword. The guard and pommel were made from something that resembled amber, and the sky-blue grip was covered with silver threads interwoven in a delicate pattern.

What drew attention was the sky-blue, crystal-like blade. It reflected all light that touched it and the beautiful rays twinkled over Reynard's skin. Ghostly afterimages danced around as he moved the blade. Even the simplest of movements were surprisingly elegant.

"This is a legacy artifact left behind by one of the strongest masters of your sect," the guardian scoffed at Reynard's disappointment. "You can always return empty-handed if Mirage doesn't suit you."

Reynard was about to answer the guardian when his face suddenly fell. There was a very light, almost imperceptible rustle coming from the inside of his right sleeve. His brows furrowed deeply as he quickly waved his hands, shaking his sleeves.

"Well, I suppose this sword should suffice if that is the case," Reynard spoke, controlling his expression as quickly as it had changed before.

The guardian closed its eyes as the space surrounding the disciples started to ripple, and the hall soon returned to normal and the illusions dispersed as well.

"The rewards are given. Do not forget the greatest benefits you've all reaped from this place. The Hellblaze Trials aren't about the treasures in your hands, they're about the path beneath your feet."

All of the competitors gathered according to their sects again. Some looked incredibly happy, while others couldn't hide the disappointment on their faces. Reynard shook his head.

Such simple-minded fools.

He glanced at the members of the Abyss Sect. Jake and Daniel Meyer were two of the few who were incredibly happy with their rewards. Amon, on the other hand, was in a daze. Reynard furrowed his brows as he saw the boy's expression. He looked as though he was recovering from shock.

A strange light flashed in Reynard's eyes as he directed his gaze to the other members of their sect and all of them looked satisfied. He discreetly waved his left hand, making his sleeve sway lightly. Someone amidst the Abyss Sect members locked eyes with him. Those eyes had defiance and questioning in them, a look that displeased Reynard greatly. Reynard gave a sneer, arrogantly shook his sleeve again and glared back until the person averted the gaze. He then looked over at the Noan River Sect members. He saw Anna Hale slowly turning her head to face him. He gave her a gentle smile. She quietly looked away, without showing much of a reaction.

The guardian quietly observed Reynard. This seemed to be his usual arrogance and disposition. The only thing that drew his attention was the occasional swaying of Reynard's left sleeve. Focusing his gigantic divine sense on Reynard, he searched, but couldn't find anything suspicious at all. His aster was large for his age, but not much larger than the rest of the inheriting disciples. A surprising amount of nebula also covered his aster, indicating he had never cultivated soul arts before.

The guardian pondered alone in silence then diverted his attention to the outer bounds of the Hellblaze Secret World. There were no signs of the gateway being activated. Lloyd hadn't even tried to make a move. Had he not taken the bait?

As Hati scanned the boundaries, Reynard joined the members of the Roaring Mountain Sect. He had a subtle smile on his face as he held onto Mirage, but he couldn't hide the disdain in his eyes. He looked back at the Abyss Sect members again. Jake had an arm wrapped around Daniel's shoulder, and the others were jabbering on about their experiences. They were all patting each other on the shoulders, and Amon Kressler seemed to have recovered from his shock, as he looked to be having a pleasant conversation with Daniel Meyer.

Reynard's smile widened at the joyous scene. The look in his eyes turned savage, but he quickly repressed his emotions. He could feel faint ripples of divine sense constantly washing over him as an absurdly powerful soul peered into every inch this tainted world.

Reynard tried hard not to scoff. Eventually, the waves of divine sense died down, and the guardian's voice echoed in their minds again.

"I will now send you out, be prepared for the spatial transference."

He hadn't found anything. Nevertheless, his instincts were telling him that there was danger. Something wasn't right, and he couldn't figure out what it was.

"Hey," Reynard suddenly called in a low voice and swayed his left sleeve again. "I have a question."

Hati was taken aback. He directed a part of his senses at Reynard, while still carefully scanning the world again.

"Speak."

At that moment, however, Hati felt something. A weak wave rippled through space from somewhere in the hall. It was so weak that Hati almost couldn't feel it. His instincts started screaming at him as he desperately tried to trace its origin.

Another spatial wave rippled, stronger than the last one. It distorted light in a discreet way, getting the attention of the inheriting disciples. Even though it was a weak ripple, it astounded Hati greatly. The scope and complexity of the ripple were far above his own, terrifying Hati immensely —this wasn't something Lloyd Kressler could do.

He managed to trace the origins of the ripple to the surroundings of the Abyss Sect disciples. He focused his divine sense in a hurry, prepared to crush space itself if he needed to when Reynard finally asked his question.

"Who did you give the Vermilion Token to?" Reynard asked as a cold killing intent flashed in his eyes.

Hati hesitated for a split second.

How does he know about the Vermilion Token?

It took Hati a moment to realize that his hesitation and surprise had cost him his chance.

A third wave rippled through space, making the hall rumble loudly. The walls began to crack and the ground quaked disastrously. A terrifying shadow spread throughout the hall, ripping Hati's divine sense away and forcing the area into lockdown. Hati struggled in vain against the shadow as it spread, tearing the control of the area away away from him.

The cultivators stood in a frightful shock as they braced themselves for the fourth spatial ripple that was forming. Amon couldn't hide the confusion and fear in his golden eyes as the fourth spatial wave rippled from him, completely encasing the hall in darkness.

"What is happening?" Sarah, asked in a surprised panic.

Her arms were trembling as she watched the scene playing out in the shallow pool made of the sap of the Ashen Heart tree.

The boy with ashen hair had done something. The moment the guardian was about to return all of the competitors to the Abyss Sect, terrifying ripples started spreading from the Amon's body. The roots in the ceiling started to twist, as if contorting in pain. The pool of sap turned black and all the connection to the Hellblaze Secret World was lost.

"Borgin, what is the meaning of this?"

Leonard, the young high elder of the Roaring Mountain Sect stood trembling. His lips quivered and his face reddened as he held onto the hilt of the saber that hung from his waist.

A commotion broke out amidst the elders and high elders present. Sarah directed a cold glance to Richard Layn, who wasn't far from her. He had a surprised look on his face as he stared blankly at the black pool of sap in the center of the room.

Sarah frowned deeply. She had known Richard for a very long time and she could tell that his surprise was genuine. She then looked at Lars Borgin, that strangely showed no expression at all on his face. He had his eyes closed, as if pondering something.

"Leonard, stand down! I'm sure Sect Master Borgin has an explanation for this," Baldwid declared.

Leonard, refused. He gripped the hilt tighter as a fierce anger blazed in his eyes.

Boom!

A terrifying pressure suddenly fell on the room, forcing them all to their knees. The ground beneath their feet cracked as they tried to fight against it, but it grew increasingly stronger.

The weaker elders all had pale faces as they completely gave in to the terrifying strength, lying motionless on the ground while blood trickled down their lips. The high elder didn't have it much better, as they all were trembling due to the sheer strength they were exerting to fight back.

Sarah made an incredible effort to raise her head, looking straight at Lars Borgin. He had finally opened his eyes, and a savage light shone on them. A piercing trill echoed in the room as he violently drew the crimson sword on his back. He didn't spare a glance to any of the elders and high elders on the ground before shooting out of the room like a hurricane.

Even though he had left, the overwhelming pressure was still weighing down on them, making any movement excruciatingly slow and painful. The pressure finally disappeared after a few minutes, allowing them all to move again. The high elders all slowly stood up. Sarah looked incredibly feeble. Her silver hair was a mess, her blue robes were torn and her breathing was rough.

The other high elders didn't look much better. Veronica, the high elder of the Storm Peak Sect cut out a rather sorry figure. Baldwin seemed to have suffered the least, given that other than his disorderly clothes it looked like only his face was slightly paler.

Leonard looked utterly miserable. Blood trickled down the corner of his lips and his eyes were bloodshot. His clothes were damp with sweat and covered in dirt. His rage had increased significantly as he struggled to stand.

This was an unprecedented matter to most of them. They had never been so thoroughly helpless against someone before. They might not compare to the strength of the protectors and sect masters of their own sects, but they all were strong enough to stand above everyone else. Suffering such humiliation wasn't an easy thing for them to accept. Not even the ones above them dared to do such a thing, much less people from other sects. This could certainly lead to trouble between the sects. Lars Borgin, however, didn't seem to mind it one bit.

"Richard, what is going on?" Sarah asked in a weak voice as she slowly recovered from the shock.

"I truly have no idea. This is as much of a surprise to us as it is to you," Richard croaked helplessly.

He too had suffered from Borgin's outburst of power, as did all the other members of the Abyss Sect. Borgin hadn't spared even his own subordinates. It was as if at that moment all that mattered to him was to raise his aura to the limits before he shot out of the room. Sarah could only guess that he went into the Hellblaze Secret World to intervene.

"I don't think you're lying, Richard," she said lightly shaking her head before sending him a cold, penetrating glance. "But is this a surprise to all of the members Abyss Sect or just for you?"

Richard couldn't answer that question. Even though he didn't speak, his silence was all the answer Sarah needed.

The elders distributed medicinal pills to one another to aid in their recovery. They stood in silence for a moment, unable to think; such matters were very delicate, and solving them would certainly be complicated.

"Do you think this is good enough of an excuse?" Leonard asked in a harsh tone. "First, one of your young cultivators somehow managed to isolate himself and all competitors from our eyes. Then, without any explanation, your sect master jetted off without a word!"

A few of the elders of the other sects nodded, though a few high elders didn't show an explicit approval of his words. However, Richard didn't retort, for he couldn't speak.

"Six years ago, your sect suddenly announced that it would cancel the trials until further notice, without giving the other cardinal sects a proper explanation. Then, a few months ago, an announcement was made that the trials will be held again, also without an explanation. Now this happens. Although I don't know the goals of such actions, I can't help but think that this had been planned." He slowly walked over to Richard in an imposing manner, not minding his tone at all. "Does the Abyss Sect think nothing of us? Does it take us for idiots that can be used for its own interests?"

Richard stood his ground and calmly replied, "If that were the case, would Borgin harm the members of his own sect too? I don't know what is happening, but from the sect master's reaction you can clearly see that this wasn't within his expectations."

Sarah's expression eased a little. Even though his argument wasn't exactly solid, it stood to reason. She glanced at Baldwin and Veronica who were quietly watching the high elders argue. Sarah couldn't figure out why, but Veronica's horrid expression was so exaggerated that it made her shiver.

Leonard didn't say another word, but he slowly walked away from Richard, never taking his hands off of his saber's hilt.

Without warning, a blinding light flashed within the room and a crisp sound echoed as if something had shattered. Leonard looked utterly baffled as he slowly raised his right hand, making his sleeve slide down and reveal his wrist. A thin silver chain was wrapped around his wrist, adorned with ten blood-red beads that looked like marbles.

One of the beads started cracking, slowly falling apart. The room was dead silent. Like the soft sounds of windchimes, the fragments fell to the floor, leaving only nine beads hanging from the chain in Leonard's wrist.

"Drace..." Leonard said in a stupefied voice as he powerlessly stared at the beads remains.

Richard's face paled, as did the faces of the other members of the Abyss Sect. Everyone knew what those blood-red beads signified. All of the high elders present had a chain identical to the one Leonard had wrapped around their wrists, all of them with ten beads. The moment the bead shattered, they knew that a disciple had died.

No one spoke a word. Baldwin's expression turned incredibly grave, as he turned his head to face Richard. His muscles were clearly tensing as if he was preparing to fight. Sarah too, slowly backed away, silently placing her aged fingers over a ring on her left hand, ready to take action.

Veronica's eyes darted around the room, carefully examining her fellow cultivators. She and the elder from Storm Peak slowly backed away, side by side. Veronica's expression turned even uglier, and Sarah could see a hint of suspicion in it.

Leonard slowly turned to face Richard again. The crisp sound of scraping metal echoed through the room as he drew his saber in an unbearable and almost deliberate slow pace, as if trying to engrave the sound in the minds of each one of them. His eyes showed no anger anymore, and his expression was blank. All that one would feel from him was a freezing intent to kill.

Shing!

The saber was finally released from its sheath, covering the room in an ominous purple glow as the blade glowed with a flickering light.

Sarah felt cold sweat running down her back as she watched Leonard. She silently prayed for the safety of the members of the Noan River Sect, because now she was sure they were in danger.

The Abyss Sect members all slowly gathered, not saying a word. Richard retrieved a long and slender silver spear from his bottomless pouch. He grasped it with a firm flick of his wrist, facing Leonard with serious eyes.

By his side, an elder from the Abyss Sect inconspicuously broke a purple medallion.

Yes, call the protectors for help, Richard thought as he took a deep breath.

Even though Richard didn't want to fight, he knew there was no hope anymore. Leonard had been suspicious of them from the beginning, and now there was no room for explanations or negotiations.

❊ ❊ ❊

"What is going on!?" Amon shouted in surprise as wave after wave of rippled from his body. Even though he was shouting with all he had, his voice could barely be heard beyond the incessant roaring that had taken over the ears of all that were present.

"There is something in your shoulder causing this!" Lya shouted. "The distortions are too strong, I can't stop them!"

The shadows slithering from his body had completely encased the hall, imprisoning the fifty competitors in pure darkness.

"Who dares!" an enraged roar echoed directly in their minds as the guardian didn't hide his anger at all.

It was enough to make many of the competitors curl up in fear, trembling in the pitch-black hall as that savage roar made their consciousness tremble.

Another wave rippled, throwing the remaining disciples to the ground. Low grunts could be heard as most of them were caught by surprise, expelling the air from their lungs due to the unexpected impact.

"Use your divine sense to perceive your surroundings!"

Amon could faintly make up Jake's voice as silence took over the hall.

No other wave rippled, but the darkness still remained. Amon spread his divine sense, seeing himself standing alone. He carefully inspected his body, but couldn't feel anything wrong at all.

What the hell is going on?

"Jake, what is the meaning of this?" Reynard spat.

Reynard trudged toward the Abyss Sect disciples, his new light-blue crystalline sword in hand. "What are you people up to?"

"None of you move!" the guardian demanded as a silent pressure fell upon them, tightly holding them in place.

Amon could feel his bones creaking and he could barely breathe, much less speak—it was clear that Hati was extremely enraged.

Nevertheless, it was too late. Reynard had already spoken what he needed too. He smiled deviously for he knew that it was time for the seeds he had planted in the Trial of Heart to start germinating.

The guardian carefully scrutinized the bodies of each competitor, but he couldn't find anything abnormal. Not even Amon had anything strange within him. This made the guardian worried beyond reason.

As he tried probing their bodies again, he suddenly had a bad feeling. He extended his senses outwards, trying to peer past the hall. The shadows, however, blocked his divine sense. Still, the guardian could vaguely sense that the shadows in one of the walls were starting to churn.

A blinding light flashed in the hall, and a beam of silver light shot out into that wall, opening a hole in the shadows. The guardian could only observe in astonishment as something shone on Amon's shoulder, sending a beam of light into the wall.

It was a small medallion that was about the size of a toenail, and barely put any weight into Amon's shoulder. Both Amon and the guardian were taken by surprise because somehow neither of them could feel the medallion with their divine sense. To be precise, neither Lya nor the guardian could see the medallion. They were nothing but pure souls, and depended on their divine sense to perceive the world.

"It's the medallion!" Lya screamed in Amon's head.

While Amon could clearly see it with his eyes, Lya and the guardian could only faintly make its shape thanks to the light that covered it. The medallion to them was like a black hole in the middle of the light.

The guardian tried using his divine sense to crush it into powder, but his divine sense simply passed through it, as if it were an illusion.

"Kid, quickly destroy that thing!" the guardian ordered Amon, as he released the pressure. Amon ripped the medallion from his shoulders in a hurry. He threw it to the ground, drawing Windhowler and smashing the crude sword towards the medallion.

However, before the blade could reach the medallion it was forcefully deflected by something. No matter how much strength Amon put into his arms, the sword would not give way. There was some kind of shield in the medallion.

Lya could feel the strength of that shield, and that made her desperate. She knew that even if she used her full strength she wouldn't be able to breach it.

Dread rushed through Hati and Lya. Whoever had planned this was many steps ahead of them.

The medallion shuddered, letting out a loud hum as the beam brightened. At that moment, the wall hit by the light began to ripple.

Hati sensed something wrong. The Hellblaze Secret World itself started trembling. He could faintly feel that something was approaching, and the dimension itself was reacting. The Hellblaze Gateway had been activated, and it was opening a spatial tunnel directly into the hall.

For the first time in centuries, Hati felt fear. He was completely lost. The enemy had sealed all of his routes of escape, had blocked all of his methods. Hati was nothing more than a cornered beast, and he didn't know what the other party wanted.

It gave Reynard Stark a grave look. Somehow, that arrogant man knew of the Vermilion Token. He even knew that it had been taken out. He was the prime suspect, even if the medallion had been in Amon Kressler's body.

"Lya, help me breach this seal so I can send the kids away!" Hati bellowed, mustering all of its strength to rip space apart and unleash a blow on the shadows.

Lya didn't hesitate to show herself, holding Brightmoon in her hands. The blade shone with a divine light as a thick layer of qi formed around it, undulating until it distorted into the form of an extremely sharp edge.

The other disciples had their eyes open wide as they looked at the scene, not understanding in the least what was going on.

"Now!" the guardian shouted, releasing all of his strength.

The shadows waved violently as a black line perfectly divided them in half. Space turned still for a moment, and, as if it was nothing but a painting that had been torn, one of the halves that line divined started to fall down.

Looking at the scene made Amon feel dizzy. He felt that part of him was also falling down, just like the scene in front of him. The bending of the natural laws of space was too much for someone at his level to handle.

Lya struck and Brightmoon descended, and a wave of bright sword qi flew towards the line Hati drew in space, cutting through the wind with a piercing whistle.

BOOM!

The wave of sword qi made contact with the line, and the frozen space started to shatter. It fragmented into countless pieces; each containing a part of what was supposed to be the wall covered in shadows. The pieces flew about, turning upside down and rotating, like pieces of a glass mural. There was nothing between the pieces. They were surrounded by a black void. It was nothing but utter emptiness that surrounded the broken space.

Amon held his head, trying hard to hold back the urge to vomit. He was feeling as disoriented as when he first entered the spatial tunnel that led to the Hellblaze Secret World.

"It's working!" Lya sighed with contained relief.

"Again!" the guardian shouted, preparing another strike.

The hall quaked madly, and the shadows churned. The fragments of space seemed to have been swept by a gust of wind as they suddenly gathered together, being blown away by the guardian's attack.

Lya raised Brightmoon again, unleashing a second strike. The wave of sword qi was even stronger than before. Like the attack of the guardian, that wave of sword qi seemed to tear space apart, leaving a line of emptiness through its trajectory.

Suddenly, Lya turned her head with a surprised expression. Amon felt a wind blowing on his face. A very cold, heartless wind.

A thin wave of light whistled through the air, hitting Lya's sword qi at a blinding speed and deflecting it away. The wave of light dispersed, but Amon could feel an inherent, frightening sharpness from it.

Sword qi?

As Amon was dumbfounded, Lya's attack missed, hitting an undamaged wall and being absorbed by the shadows.

The medallion that had been emitting a beam of light shuddered once, exploding in a flash of silver light and disappearing. Its use was over.

"Who are you supposed to be?" a grave, cold voice echoed through the hall.

Amon felt a shiver running down his spine. That voice was slightly more aged, somewhat graver and somehow a lot colder than what he remembered. However, there was no way he would not recognize it.

With a pale face, he slowly turned around.

The wall that had been hit by the beam of light had disappeared, giving way to a wide circle filled with glowing silver light. It was the entrance, or exit, of a spatial tunnel.

Standing in front of it was a single man.

He had a hair as dark as the night reaching his shoulder. A pair of ravenous black eyes so cold that made one shiver could be seen in a pale face with sharp features.

Clad in black from head to toe, the man stood straight with a sword in hand. It had a straight blade that seemed to glow with a poisonous green light, and an intricate, curved guard made of gold. A single red gem was embedded in the pommel, giving off an eerie glow. Even though Amon couldn't recognize the sword, there was no way he couldn't recognize the man wielding it.

Standing in front of the newly opened spatial tunnel was the former-fifth protector of the Abyss.

Lloyd Kressler, the Dark Gale, had arrived.

Lya had Lloyd's undivided attention. His black robes were fluttering wildly as the air surrounding him seemed to move around his body at a dangerous speed.

"Lloyd!" the guardian growled.

His composure was long gone. Things were already getting out of hand and Hati would have to do everything in his power to salvage rectify the situation.

Ignoring Hati, Lloyd looked over Lya in disgust. To him, her presence was an unexpected variable in a plan that was running smoothly until then.

"Who are you?" he asked a second time.

With a flick of his wrist, the green sword in his hand moved, sending a sharp wave of sword qi in Lya's direction.

Lya didn't bother answering, nor dodging. The sword qi slashed through her, making her figure distort for a moment before stabilizing again.

"Indeed. Nothing more than a soul," Lloyd said, squinting his eyes as he carefully looked at Brightmoon in Lya's hands.

His eyes stopped at the red jewel embedded in the sword's guard, and a mocking smile made its way to his blank face. "It never ceases to surprise me how much soul cultivators enjoy having pets around."

Lya still didn't utter a word, but a faint light covered Brightmoon again. Her expression was solemn, and she made a great effort to not show her surprise. Lloyd had used sword qi twice and knew about soul cultivators. He clearly learned it from someone.

The thought worried her. Maybe Nemeus was right. If Dale was the one behind all of this, then the current situation was worse than what she previously thought. She didn't know how much Lloyd Kressler had learned, and whatever he wanted from the Hellblaze Secret World was even more difficult for her to guess.

"Well, it doesn't matter. You're in my way."

A fierce wind howled in the hall and the air surrounding Lloyd started moving faster, raising dust and gravel from the floor. A silent pressure crept up the competitors, adding up to the restraints the guardian had set on them before. Some couldn't take it, and immediately lost consciousness.

"Lya, hold him back! I need to send the children away!" the guardian said directly in her mind, with an alarmed voice. Without wasting time, he dragged all of the competitors closer to the breach he and Lya were opening in the wall, trying to keep them out of harm's way.

Lya didn't answer, but directly moved in Lloyd's direction as she raised Brightmoon. A thick vortex of qi formed around the blade, gathering and solidifying around it, turning so bright that Amon had to take his eyes away from it.

Lloyd still had the mocking smile on his face as he watched Lya coming in his direction, showing no fear at all. A layer of light formed around his green sword, albeit not as bright as the one on Brightmoon as he prepared to receive Lya's strike.

Brightmoon descended, aiming for Lloyd's head. He watched the sword coming for him with surprising detachment, as if the sword wasn't aiming at him at all. He didn't move an inch, calmly watching as the opposing sword came closer to him, splitting everything in its path to take his life.

Seeing this made Lya unnerved rather than pleased. She put even more strength in the strike, trying to suddenly accelerate the sword before Lloyd could do something. At that moment, however, her expression shifted into one of utter astonishment.

Swoosh!

Lloyd finally moved, stirring the wind with him. The air gathering around him had moved to his sword in a split-second, and before Lya could react, Lloyd had stabbed in her direction at a mind-numbing speed. The target of the stab, however, wasn't Lya's projection.

With an alarmed expression, Lya suddenly shifted Brightmoon's path, missing Lloyd.

Clang!

A wave of berserk sword qi shot out from Brightmoon, obliterating the tiles by Lloyd's feet and colliding with a wall, making the shadows squirm before dispersing. However, neither Amon nor Lya could be bothered with the sudden change of direction of the strike.

At that very moment, sparks were flying from Brightmoon's guard as Lloyd's sword scraped against it, making a hair-raising screech through the hall. That poisonous-green blade left a clear and long scratch on the iron sword, barely missing the red jewel embedded on the guard.

Lya's face paled as she watched him. Before she could say something, however, another stab came at her with blinding speed. Lya hurriedly retreated, creating distance between her and Lloyd.

"I'm surprised. I didn't expect you to be able to react so fast," Lloyd said, never wiping away the mocking smile from his face. "Still, I don't think close quarters combat will be the best choice for you. Even if it's the best way to try to hold me back, my hand might slip and you'll end up in pieces."

Lya's expression couldn't be more serious. Lloyd's attainments in swordsmanship had surprised her greatly. He was clearly at his peak condition and his ability was nothing to scoff at. Lya, on the other hand, had four hundred years of isolation slowly rusting her skills away. The biggest problem, however, was that he was directly aiming at the soulstone.

She looked at him for a moment, trying to scrutinize his expression. Her gaze slowly fell onto the sword in his hands, and at the inconspicuous red jewel embedded in the pommel.

A terrifying aura exploded from her, completely taking over all of the qi in their surroundings. Lloyd frowned when he sensed that, trying to fight back with his divine sense, but his struggles were useless. Lya's soul was much stronger than his.

He tried to protect himself as the elements crashed down on him, pressing his body from all sides, trying to crush his bones and stop his breathing. His movements turned sluggish, and before he could do anything, Brightmoon was pressing against his neck.

The polished iron blade had already penetrated his skin, making blood slowly seep down his neck before disappearing in the darkness of his clothes. He looked at Lya with unwavering eyes that glinted with hate.

"Who sent you?" Lya asked with a dark expression.

"Take a guess," Lloyd said in a mocking tone. He still had that annoying smile on his face, as if looking down on Lya's attempt to get information.

Brightmoon sank further into his neck, making even more blood flow. Lloyd didn't make a sound, still looking at Lya with those unyielding eyes. This made her greatly displeased.

"I find it strange that whoever sent you would even think that a weakling like you would be enough to defeat Hati," Lya whispered in a venomous voice.

She didn't bother with Lloyd as her gaze fell on the red jewel on his sword. She sent a wisp of her divine sense to probe into the red jewel, but to her surprise, something blocked her. As Lya tried forcing her way in, a terrifying force pushed her back, making her alarmed.

"Hati, be careful! Lloyd is not alone!" Lya shouted as she realized what was going on.

Hati was solely focused on forcefully creating a breach on the spatial seal that had locked the hall. Hearing Lya's words, he suddenly turned around, only to see specs of light gathering in front of Lloyd, eventually forming into the figure of a woman.

"Too bad, Lloyd, you lose. Although I can't say it was your fault," a beautiful voice suddenly echoed through the hall.

That melodious, coquettish voice gave Amon shivers, making him and the surrounding cultivators enter in a daze. That voice was far too charming. It gently tickled his ears, making its way into his mind, subtly calming him and making him relax.

A sudden warmth slowly spread through his body, making him feel very comfortable. He couldn't even feel the restraints the guardian had placed on him anymore. His body felt incredibly light and relaxed, almost as if he was floating.

He wanted to close his eyes and immerse himself in such sensations, but he somehow forced himself to look at the new figure that had appeared between Lya and Lloyd.

She had waist-length, green hair that sparkled with a faint light, like grass covered in morning dew. Her beautiful amber eyes glimmered with an intoxicating light, enough to entrap the minds of any man that dared to directly look at them.

"It really was you," the woman said with a charming smile, waving her hand dismissively as she looked at Lya.

A formless wave of divine sense swept through the hall, throwing all of the qi in disarray. The pressure on Lloyd suddenly disappeared, and Lya's face paled as her divine sense was forcefully pushed back.

Like Lloyd, she tried to struggle, but the foreign divine sense had taken over the entire hall. It was incredibly stable and incredibly resilient. As Lya desperately tried to fight back, it slowly enclosed around her, encroaching her soul and intercepting her attempts of regaining control. The difference was overwhelming.

As Lya froze in place, her figure started to crumble. Having lost control over qi, Lya couldn't maintain her projection anymore. The strange woman made sure to let Lya sense what was happening in the hall, but not be able to do a thing besides that.

Lloyd slowly rose from the ground, throwing Brigthmoon away as if it was trash. He absent-mindedly wiped the blood trickling down the wound on his neck and after a few moments, the long gash stopped bleeding and slowly started to close.

The competitors fell down as the restraints the guardian had placed on them were undone. Nevertheless, all they did was stay unmoving on the floor, still dazed by the woman's voice.

Amon's mind was trembling and his limbs were numb, but he somehow managed to raise his upper body and look worriedly at Brightmoon that had been thrown into the corner.

The green-haired woman scoffed, locking eyes with Amon and giving a bewitching smile. She started walking in his direction, never taking her intoxicating eyes from him. Her long legs peeked out of a green dress that clung tightly to her body, looking especially tight on her plentiful chest. Every move she made seemed natural, yet calculated and enchanting.

Amon shuddered. The numbness disappeared and his body felt limp as a strange prickling started affecting his mind. There was a strange buzz ringing in his ears, disrupting his thoughts and making him confused as the woman approached. He lost the little control he had over his body and fell powerlessly to the floor again.

Looking at the woman, Hati was taken aback. That woman was far stronger than even he was. He was as helpless as Lya in front of her soul's strength. He had lived for thousands of years, and had experienced more than a human could even imagine being possible, yet, somehow, that woman overpowered him.

Very few beings would be capable of such a feat. He focused his divine sense, carefully probing the red jewel in Lloyd's sword. Hati was sure he had never seen that woman before, but the aura she gave him was very familiar.

The woman smiled as she felt his intentions. Surprisingly, she didn't stop him at all.

As he carefully analyzed her aura, feeling incredibly anxious.

"Oura?" Hati asked in shock after a name finally appeared in his mind.

"Oh, you recognized me? I'm so happy, Hati!"

"It's you!?" Lya asked in astonishment. Oura, however, completely disregarded her, further enclosing Lya's soul with her divine sense.

Hati didn't waste time pondering what had happened with Oura or how she was there. Her presence meant she was an enemy, and that was all he had to know to act accordingly.

He ignored her, focusing again on the damaged wall beyond the broken space. He was trying to muster all of his strength in an attempt to wrestle away the control of a portion of qi.

"So rude. It has been so many centuries since we met and you can't even properly greet an old friend," Oura pouted with an exaggerated trace of betrayal.

She turned to the youths that had been gathered in a corner, still immobilized. She had a strange look in her eyes as she looked at them.

"I feel like maybe I should get to know those kids better if that is the case. After all, you do know how much I hate feeling lonely."

Hati stopped. His rage was starting to boil due to the veiled threat, but he ultimately gave up on his efforts. There wasn't much he could do against her, especially in the current situation where weak cultivators were involved.

"Now, that's better," Oura crooned. "This one in particular seems rather appealing," she continued, locking her excited eyes on Amon. She reached out a pale hand to him. "Maybe I'll make him my new toy."

She licked her red lips enticingly. Amon, however, felt a shiver running down his spine. Beyond his limp body and his muddy consciousness, his instincts were screaming at him that the woman was dangerous.

"Don't you dare, you old snake!" Lya shouted in Oura's mind, infuriated. Despite being completely helpless, she couldn't hold back her outburst.

"So he is indeed the one that you chose. Still as emotional as ever, Lya," Oura made a cunning smile, but her eyes expressed nothing but coldness as she looked at Brightmoon on the floor. "By the way, the next time you speak without permission I will rip you apart piece by piece, even if it incurs Master's rage."

Hati was silent. The events that took place showed that there were traitors within the trials. Certainly, the same could be applied to the cardinal sects themselves. It wasn't surprising that someone had gotten wind of Amon's sudden rise, even if it seemed insignificant at first.

The main point was that Lloyd was involved. His son's sudden change would certainly reach the ears of the one pulling the strings. They would know about him the best. If such a hopeless kid suddenly showed amazing progress, they would look into it, even if on a whim.

If that person heard about him returning from the Scavenging with a certain sword, and even selling a pair of danasian steel daggers to the sect to buy cultivation manuals and sword techniques... If that person knew about the events of the past, then it wouldn't be too hard to have certain suspicions, especially if that person was Dale Loray.

"What do you want Oura?" the guardian asked in a cautious voice.

Even if Amon and Lya were part of her objective, Lloyd had stolen the Hellblaze Gateway years before the last Scavenging, and abducting Amon and Lya would have been reasonably simple to do, considering their outcast condition and the spies infiltrated in the sect.

Their prime objective lay in the Hellblaze Secret World from the start. They had thoroughly prepared to act and had only waited for an opportunity. An opportunity that Nemeus, Lya, Borgin and Hati himself had provided when they decided to host the trials in a bid to get information about the enemy.

"I doubt you can guess, dear. But don't worry, you'll find out soon."

Oura ran her fingers through her hair as her divine sense carefully swept through every inch of the hall in search of something.

Hati had been thoroughly defeated. After centuries, he was finally feeling the bitter taste of defeat once again. The situation had escaped from his grasp, and he was incapable of changing it.

"Heh, a hidden layer in space. Arthur surely didn't play around when making this place," Oura's eyes shone with satisfaction as her divine sense locked on a particular location in the center of the hall.

"Wait, don't!" the guardian suddenly shouted in terror as he realized what Oura wanted. His words were cut short when Oura waved her hands and space broke in the middle of the hall.

However, instead of showing emptiness between the fragments of shattered space, the fragments revealed a small enclosure, as if they were hiding a box. Inside it, a red jewel the size of a fist glowed with a scarlet light.

"Found you!"

Oura giggled contagiously, and with a charming smile, she raised her hands. A boundless stream of divine sense enveloped the jewel, sealing the entity in it from the outside world.

Being contained in the endless void inside the soulstone, Hati's soul struggled fiercely. It struck wildly with its divine sense against Oura's consciousness, trying to break free like a caged animal.

"Hehe, you foolish dog. What in this place could possibly be more precious than you?" Oura transmitted her voice inside the jewel as a mocking smile made its way into her lips.

"Hati!" Lya screamed, desperate. She too, started struggling against Oura's domain with all her might, even if she knew it was useless.

"Shut up," Oura barked.

Waving her hand again, this time using her divine sense to silence Lya.

Amon squirmed on the ground, trying to regain control over his body. Sweat covered his back as he grunted due to the effort. He was finding it incredibly difficult to gather his thoughts. His futile efforts please Oura greatly.

"To manage to fight back against my charm, your will is really something, dear. I'm sure Master will be pleased with this." She tenderly looked at him, before turning to Lloyd. "Take the sword; I'll be taking the kid with us."

For the first time since he arrived, Lloyd looked at his son. His gaze was as cold and indifferent as Amon remembered. However, he noticed that Amon was different. There was no confusion, desperation, or pain in his eyes like before. His golden eyes were filled with hate and defiance—a look that made Lloyd greatly displeased, even somewhat angry.

"I don't remember Master ever mentioning this," Lloyd said to Oura.

"There was no need. Master wasn't sure and this doesn't really concern you."

She waved her hand dismissively and Lloyd didn't bother to refute. Oura's words meant that Oura's interest in Amon didn't stem from his relationship with Lloyd.

"Oh, since we're already here, we might as well take everything," Oura added.

She waved her hands again and another layer of space shattered. Beyond the broken space, walls covered in gold supported innumerable rows of bottles and scrolls of all colors and sizes that shone with a blinding light. Deeper into the trove, silver racks held various weapons.

Oura's eyes glinted with greed. This was an impressive collection, amassed with the efforts of all Five Cardinal sects. Even though most of the treasures were mediocre, a reasonable number of them were amazing. Leaving them behind would be a pity, but taking them away would serve another purpose.

Lloyd quietly sheathed his sword and reached into his clothes. He recovered a small metal bracelet, which he threw to Oura without ceremony. He walked to Brightmoon and grasped the iron sword haphazardly.

With a wicked smile, Oura made the bracelet float in front of her, extending her hands and projecting her divine sense into the trove. Strands of her divine sense coiled around the many treasures inside before retracting back to Oura.

The bracelet flickered with a silvery light as treasure after treasure touched it and disappeared. When the trove was completely emptied, Oura glanced at the fallen cultivators.

"Don't forget what you have to do," she said in a low voice as she offered her hand to Amon.

Boom!

The hall violently quaked from the deafening sound. The walls trembled, and the shadows covering them distorted. The wall Lya and Hati had damaged shook, and the spatial fragments surrounding it slowly stopped floating, being locked in place.

"It looks like those two did more damage to the seal than expected," Oura frowned.

Lloyd unsheathed the sparkling, green sword by his waist as running away wasn't an option. Lars Borgin and Nemeus couldn't be left alone with the competitors, or they would certainly spoil their plans. Their only chance was staying behind to hold Borgin and Nemeus back.

A wisp of divine sense coiled around the powerless Amon, dragging him closer to Lloyd alongside the bracelet and Hati's soulstone as Oura's figure dispersed.

BOOM!

Gravel and dust fell from the ceiling. Beyond his muddy consciousness, Amon could faintly hear an earth-shaking roar in the distance.

BOOM!

The damaged wall exploded into pieces, sending fragments of gold and scarlet crystal raining through the hall. An unexpected heat wave assaulted everyone, making breathing difficult. Amon felt as if he had been thrown into the Trial of Will again as fire blazed into the hall. Flames emerged from the newly made breach, swallowing the shadows that covered the hall.

A nauseating sizzle sounded as the shadows were burnt to a crisp by the hellish fire, and a small figure appeared amidst the flames.

His brown hair was a mess, and his clear eyes showed a rarely seen seriousness. His sheer presence caused an immense pressure to crash down on Amon, pressing him against the broken floor.

Every step the man took made the tiles of the floor crack and sink into the ground. His small figure looked impressively gigantic as he gazed at Lloyd with cold eyes, his back as straight as a javelin. In his right hand, he held a crimson sword covered in black flames. The blade appeared blurry as it vibrated and hummed in a low growl.

Lloyd smiled and waved his sword around. The silent pressure weighing down on the hall didn't affect him at all. A gentle wind spiraled around him, making his dark robes flutter and his black hair sway.

"It's been a while, Lars."

A hellish gloom faintly lit up the spacious room. The red walls squirmed strangely, as if a seething substance was seeping down along the wall's length. This made the lighting in the room uneven, making distorted shadows dance on the floor as the walls changed constantly.

Such shadows masked the expression of a small and frail boy that was kneeling on the floor. His brown hair was a mess, and his clothes were in disarray. The moving shadows covering his face almost hid his swollen right cheek and the bluish-green color that covered them, but in the end, even the shadows weren't enough to hide his injuries, nor could the shadows hide the glint in the boy's clear eyes. A deep fear and uneasiness could be seen in them but, far deeper, in the midst of those scared eyes, a spark of rebellion flickered.

In the middle of the room, a row of sparkling golden steps led to an incredibly ugly seat. It was a tall, wide wooden throne. Legend says that it had been white once, and incredibly appealing, but what the boy saw was a seat charred beyond recognition, twisted into a dark and deformed mess full of cracks. The little white that might have survived the ordeal of fire had been greyed out long ago by the river of time, or maybe its own ashes had tainted the throne.

The boy didn't know, and he didn't care. He dared not look up to the man sitting on the throne, lightly tapping on the armrest with his index finger in a rhythmic, but absent-minded manner. Every tap reverberated through the room, making the boy's heart skip a beat in fright.

Lying against the throne, a sword silently slept in its glossy blood-red sheath. The jet-black hilt in the shape of a cross seemed far too simple, far too unadorned for its wielder. The only thing that seemed luxurious at all about the sword, besides the color of the sheath, was a bright-red jewel embedded in the guard, glowing with a faint light.

"Why do you always do such things?" the man finally asked, breaking the uncomfortable silence. His tone was surprisingly gentle, his voice mild.

"I..." the boy cut himself short just as he was about to answer the question. He clenched his teeth and took a deep breath before speaking again in a forced voice. "I find Nolan Skoller annoying."

"Heh," the man on the throne scoffed lightly.

The boy suddenly felt constricted. The sheer thought of displeasing that man made him instinctively paralyzed in fear.

"Why lie to me?"

The boy closed his eyes and took a deep breath. He had been given a second chance. He couldn't lie again.

"Nolan said I was too small, and that I didn't deserve my position since I don't have an affinity to fire."

Though he tried to hide the nervousness in his voice, the result was rather strange, as his tone came out uneven. It was obvious he was holding back tears.

"What does an affinity to fire have to do with anything? We're not the Southern Flame Sect. The Abyss Sect does not have a ruling lineage, nor do we have any guardian beast to teach us the secrets of the elements," the man said. "What we have here is a place where all the elements are present, a place where everyone can cultivate in their field of talent. What we have here is freedom."

"But sir, sect master has an affinity with fire, and even close relations to the Vermilion Queen of the Southern Continent," the boy spoke in a hurried voice as he exposed his own doubts.

"So what?" the man asked in a dismissive tone, clearly displeased. "The one that will decide the next sect master of the Abyss Sect is me, and I don't care about affinities. My successor will be chosen according to his capacity and commitment in ruling the sect, not his mastery of the same element I have."

The boy didn't speak, and his body shuddered lightly. The man gave a sigh, shaking his head slightly.

"I don't care if Nolan has a good affinity with fire. His case is completely different," the man added, but his words didn't seem to affect the boy at all.

"Look up," the man suddenly ordered in a grave voice.

The boy almost jumped in fright, but slowly raised his head and looked up with big, teary eyes. The first thing the boy saw was his boots. They were simple, black boots made of leather. They covered a pair of long legs that were hidden behind a deep blood-red robe filled with golden embroideries. The man's chest was wide, and even the loose robe couldn't hide the muscles that covered it and the man's arms.

His features were sharp, giving his handsome face a heroic bearing. His eyes were of a bizarre bright red color, glowing like a pair of burning charcoals. The swept back hair that reached his shoulders was of the same color as his eyes, but the few streaks of gold amidst the red gave the man an even more exotic air.

The boy couldn't help but shudder once again when he met the man's gaze. Every part of his tiny body seemed to scream at him to run away, but the boy could barely move.

"It was a pity what happened to your grandparents. Geralt and Lara were close friends of mine, and I promised them that I would take care of their descendants and properly raise them into worthy cultivators," the man said, not hiding the sadness in his voice. "I did the same for Nolan's grandfather."

"Even though your parents won't reach far in the path of cultivation, they will enjoy the best resources we have and I will guarantee they will live a fulfilling life until the end," the man said, having some difficulty to choose words that would not upset the boy too much. "You are different from them. You have the talent, and I will do my best to make sure you tread this path as far as possible. It is my responsibility, even if I'm not your master."

The boy didn't speak. In truth, he couldn't fathom the thought of living longer than his parents. He was far too young to truly understand what the man's words meant.

"It is the same for Nolan, although, unfortunately, his parents are gone. So do not be too upset by what he says. This sect is all he has."

However, Nolan was probably trying to establish his dominance. He was already taking the competition for the sect master's seat very seriously. In that regard, he was already far above the competitors.

"But sir—"

"I don't care if you're too small," he interrupted, rolling his eyes.

In truth, he found it hard dealing with children. To his surprise, however, the boy didn't seem convinced.

"Who cares about height?" Arthur Royce asked, giving the boy a sharp look. Unconsciously, his expression slowly turned ferocious, making the boy pale. "The smaller you are, the more humiliating it will be for your opponent to lay at your feet after you're done with them."

"Remember this, Lars. It doesn't matter how tall you are if everyone has to kneel before you."

❊ ❊ ❊

CRACK!

The floor was smashed apart as two swords violently collided. They created a rain of sparks that were blown away by a violent gust of wind and wisps of black fire. Both Lars and Lloyd took a single step back to disperse the force of the collision before advancing again.

Lloyd's sword blurred as a fierce wind swirled around the green blade covered in light. His strikes were incredibly fast and precise, trying to slowly force Borgin's guard open with an unending torrent of attacks at different angles. His hair was whipping about and he had a savage look on his face as he swung his sword mercilessly.

Every strike he unleashed sent a blast of air towards Lars, and the speed of the attacks was slowly increasing, as well as the strength behind them.

Borgin, on the other hand, was surprisingly calm and an unprecedented focus could be seen in his expression. His movements were firm and stable, and he expertly parried Lloyd's attacks with Crimsonroar. Even though his movements were slower, the distance his sword had to cover was shorter, so Borgin managed to maintain the fight in a delicate balance.

A faint yellow aura covered Borgin, almost invisible amidst the flames coming from the sword in his hands. The blast of wind didn't affect his balance and concentration at all, being promptly dispersed by the yellow aura around him.

He and Lloyd were slowly sinking into the floor, as it couldn't hold their weight after being damaged repeatedly by their clash. The cracks on the floor were slowly spreading outwards, and tiles started to sink in by themselves as if their weight had suddenly multiplied.

To those looking from the outside, however, the figures of Borgin and Lloyd were almost indistinct. Colorless ripples were turning the air and space chaotic, as if the qi itself was struggling with something. It seemed to clash against itself around Lloyd and Borgin, raising the debris on the floor and launching them at dangerous speeds throughout the crumbling hall.

This was because Nemeus and Oura were engaged in their own fight.

345

They were trying to wrestle away the control of the qi in the area from one another and use it to attack the enemy. It was a battle of divine senses.

Both Borgin and Lloyd couldn't make use of the qi in the hall, and thus had to rely on their own reserves. They were stuck in a battle of attrition. It was at that moment that cultivation and experience would count the most —in a high-level fight, a single opening was all it took to decide its outcome.

"Borgin, we have to get the participants out of here," Nemeus warned directly in Borgin's mind.

"I know that!" Borgin snarled, trying to not take focus away from Lloyd.

If he went all out, more than a few of the cultivators would end up dead. He had to create an opening and buy enough time to evacuate them safely.

Swoosh!

Lloyd's glowing sword came whistling at Lar's head, rousing a gale in its wake. Borgin quickly parried, deflecting Lloyd's sword to the side. It was a small opening, just enough for Borgin to barely be able to counter, stabbing Crimsonroar toward Lloyd's chest.

The scarlet sword let out a sizzling sound as the dark flames covering it billowed toward Lloyd's chest. Lloyd grunted, taking a step back and swiping his free hand at the flames, dispersing them with a blast of wind.

Nevertheless, it was enough. In that fraction of a second where Lloyd had only one foot on the ground, Borgin acted.

The yellow aura surrounding Borgin flashed with a blinding light, and the floor in a radius of a dozen meters around him and Lloyd caved in.

His step back had cost him his balance. A violent gale swept at his back, holding his weight in the split-second he would need to recover, but Crimsonroar was already falling down over his head, splitting the air with sundering flames.

"Lloyd!" Oura shouted, diverting her attention just long enough to deflect Borgin's strike with a blast of condensed qi.

Just long enough for Nemeus to act.

With a thundering roar, he threw all of his focus at the bright soulstone floating near Lloyd, savagely ripping apart the divine sense that was restraining it.

A terrifying surge of power erupted from the soulstone as Hati finally freed himself, throwing the already chaotic qi of the hall into even more disarray.

To Amon, the world was being turned upside down. Sometimes his surroundings would become completely white, other times it was covered with an assortment of colors. The earth never stopped trembling, and the air itself seemed to be falling down alongside the badly damaged ceiling of the hall, as if the sky was crashing down from above.

Clouds of dust rose and fell as gusts of wind randomly swept through the place, throwing gravel at the competitors who were recovering from their daze. They desperately tried to protect themselves from the chaos, but what they were experiencing was too much for them to process.

Their despair didn't last long. They all felt an invisible force wrapping around them. Hati focused all of his strength on them. The breach on the wall surrounded by squirming shadows, broken space and emptiness shook. The spatial fragments froze in place once more.

They circled around the breach, slowly rearranging themselves. As they floated around, they were dyed a bright red before they finally gathered and formed a curtain of light.

Hati was utterly exhausted, but didn't dare lose focus. With a violent sweep of his divine sense, he dragged Brightmoon and Amon towards him, severing Oura's control. She was far too busy trying to regain the grounds she lost to Nemeus in the fight.

"Take the boy and run, Lya!" Hati cried out to the soulstone embedded in the iron sword.

"Wait!" Amon tried to say, but Hati didn't pay him any mind.

The Moonchaser Wolf took a look at the boy that had Skoll's Blessing with mixed emotions. He was far too young, inexperienced, and naïve. He wasn't ready for what was to come.

Hati transmitted his voice to Amon in a melancholic tone.

"I've already told you everything that I could. I wish you good luck. Hopefully, you'll do right by your lineage."

He threw the boy and the sword through the spatial passageway. Only when they were gone he bothered with the remaining cultivators.

Hati didn't bother being gentle or careful. He wasn't in a situation that allowed him such luxury. He was rather forceful and abrupt and, one by one, the cultivators were sent away. When he was about to send Reynard Stark away, however, he hesitated.

Although he was sure that Reynard was involved, he ultimately decided to send Reynard away. If he didn't send Reynard away and he ended up hurt, things would only worsen for the Abyss Sect.

When all was said and done, Hati faltered. He was completely exhausted, his power almost spent. It would take months of slumbering to recover his full strength, but it was worth it since he managed to salvage what he could.

"Finally," Borgin said with a ferocious smile. His aura abruptly surged, and the little that remained of the floor tiles sunk down. He looked at Lloyd with cold eyes, and his aura surged yet again.

Any normal human would have long been turned into nothing more than a bloody mess of torn flesh under the pressure, but Lloyd Kressler was completely unphased.

"Indeed. Took you long enough," he said with a mocking smile.

Borgin furrowed his brows, feeling something was wrong.

"It's a pity that Hati was smart enough to send the kid and the sword away first. We only allowed it to make sure he wouldn't take too long sending the others away too," Oura's taunted from Lloyd's sword; she was surprisingly calm and a bit regretful.

"Allow it? I don't think you two have a proper grasp of the situation," Borgin sneered, extending his left hand. The yellow light covering his body flickered before fading as his hand turned bright gold as he pointed downwards.

The floor of the hall, already compressed, suddenly caved in, becoming harder than metal as Lloyd lost his balance for a second time. A gust of wind hastily blew around him, pushing him upwards. Before his feet could even touch the ground, the unbearable pull coming from below subsided. For a moment, Lloyd felt like he was floating, before he suddenly shot up at breakneck speed towards the ceiling.

"Damn!"

He barely managed to twist his body midair, colliding heavily with the ceiling. Rare surprise showed in his eyes as he looked at an upside Lars Borgin, who calmly met his gaze.

"You—"

Before Lloyd could finish, he fell down again as Borgin brandished Crimsonroar.

Seeing the incoming strike, Lloyd raised his sword, preparing to parry. Just as they were about to clash, the pull on him shifted again, and he smashed sideways into a wall. Standing up on the squirming shadows of the spatial seal that covered the walls, a disheveled Lloyd grunted.

"Hoh, you delved far enough into the Natural Laws of Earth to touch upon the concept of gravity? Not bad at all for an elemental cultivator," Oura's voice echoed through the hall. "Reaching the peak in one of the elements might open up a cruel truth to you: all of the Natural Laws are one. If you only grasp a single facet of it, you will inevitably fall before someone that has grasped many."

As if to punctuate her words, Lloyd slowly slid down from the wall, safely landing on the ground in front of Borgin. Borgin waved his left hand, and the ceiling shook. To his surprise, however, Lloyd was completely unaffected, looking at him with a gaze that could kill. Borgin shot in his direction, Crimsonroar in hand.

"Need help, dear?" Oura offered, seeing Lloyd's bloodshot eyes and messy state.

"No need. I was just a bit surprised." Lloyd cracked his neck. "That aside, I don't think even you would have the leisure to waste time while wrestling with those two."

Oura gave a dismissive laugh. In truth, she didn't want to admit that Nemeus and Hati were giving her enough trouble to make her lose some of her control over the area. That standstill wouldn't last for too long, though.

Lloyd shook his head and sighed. The wind stirred, and Borgin suddenly felt the air surrounding him turning still before drifting away. He gasped for air, but his lungs could find nothing to suck in. As his eyes slowly reddened and his veins started bulging under his skin, Borgin extended his left hand, closing his fingers in a fist. The air that was floating away slowly started to approach him again, as if being reeled in. As he finally managed to take in a breath, Borgin's chest heaved up and down violently.

"I can't imagine how much energy you are wasting by trying to control the air using the Natural Laws of Earth," Lloyd mocked, seeing Borgin unsteady on his feet. "That left hand of yours though…"

Borgin couldn't deny Lloyd's words. He was already nearing his limit.

"The concept of gravity involves mainly attraction, but you can also reverse it to generate repulsion." Lloyd said with disdain, slowly approaching Borgin. "Those two concepts have a very big similarity with wind. Actually, if you look at the big picture, they are similar to many Natural Laws and concepts, for they entail movement. In other words, spatial displacement."

Borgin blinked, and Lloyd Kressler was suddenly upon him, covering the distance between them in a flash. The green sword in Lloyd's hands was already diggin on Borgin's left shoulder, ripping his red robe apart and tearing through his flesh.

"Grasping even the most basic form of the Natural Laws of Space will naturally give you a huge advantage in a fight." Lloyd pulled the green sword back.

Borgin's arm fell to the ground, still glowing gold. Lloyd looked at it with interest as the glow faded away and the solid arm, slowly morphed into a yellow stone before crumbling into dust. Lloyd raised his eyes, looking at Borgin's injury and, sure enough, no blood flowed from the gaping flesh.

"You stepped into the Transcendence Realm?" Lloyd was taken aback as he looked at the empty sleeve on the ground.

Borgin didn't answer, as the yellow glow covered his body again. The ground below him churned, and a tendril of earth rose, connecting to his shoulder and morphing into a new arm. Pulling his new fingers from the earth, Borgin faced Lloyd with a blank expression.

"You truly are impressive," Lloyd commended. "For an elemental cultivator to reach this far, despite it being only the left arm…"

"I don't need your praise. In truth, it disgusts me," Borgin spat.

If Lloyd had truly grasped even an inkling of the Natural Laws of Space, Borgin couldn't give himself the luxury of dispelling his gravity manipulation, for it was the only thing that would slow Lloyd down. Borgin raised Crimsonroar again, preparing to resume their fight, but suddenly froze in place.

Crack!

Borgin felt a light crack coming from something on his right wrist. His eyes widened in surprise as blood-red fragments slowly fell down from his sleeves. They hit the ground with a resonating boom, as if they weighed tons instead of grams.

"You…" Borgin's face paled ever so slightly, and for the first time, he showed a hint of confusion.

Crack! Crack!

More cracking sounds echoed from Borgin's sleeve, and his face slowly distorted in an unrecognizable mask of rage and bloodlust.

"It is too late now," Lloyd said in a scornful voice, still smiling as he waved his left hand. A green light glowed from him, gently enveloping his body.

Boom!

Borgin's aura was swept away as a raging wind blasted through the remains of the hall. Strands of light flickered through the wind, being swept away and hiding in the air. The shadows on the wall sent out ear-piercing shrills as deep gashes started appearing on them as the wind blew.

Borgin's face darkened. He could feel an inherent sharpness from the strands of light. It was as if the wind itself had turned into a weapon. His hair stood on end as an unprecedented sense of danger assaulted him.

"Lars, be careful!"

Nemeus was alarmed as he recognized the strands of light. He was at the same time amazed and horrified.

Lloyd's smile widened, and the winds converged to him, bringing with them the strands of light.

"Time to end this farce."

Reynard slowly opened his eyes when the strange feeling of the spatial transference disappeared. Nevertheless, he was completely aware of his surroundings, since he never retracted his divine sense in the first place.

Using his eyes would lead him to have nausea and dizziness while he traversed the spatial passageway, but using his divine sense would not. It was a somewhat bizarre feeling. The sense of movement was still there, but since he was completely aware of what was happening in a wide area around him, he didn't feel lost or confused at all by the changes occurring in his surroundings.

He was lying on his back and, above him, a multitude of pale leaves was glimmering with a dim silvery light in the gloom that covered Hell Keeper's City. They seemed to be gently swaying in a weak breeze, even though Reynard could feel nothing at all. Taking a closer look, it was more of a shuddering than a swaying, as if the tree itself was trembling.

Above the tree, Reynard could barely make the bloody light of the twilight through the leaves. The Hellblaze Secret World was certainly something else. Although he was sure he had spent at least a few days there, only a few hours had passed in the outside world.

Dismissing his thoughts, he promptly stood up and looked around. Dozens of cultivators were sprawled across the ground in the major plaza of Hell Keeper's City. Subtle groans could be heard as they held their heads, trying to get a hold of themselves.

Reynard looked closely, but he couldn't find Amon Kressler. The corner of his lips twitched slightly. The way Oura had given him special attention meant he was somewhat important, even if he wasn't the prime objective. Furthermore, there was a chance he had the Vermilion Token on him, even if it was only a gut feeling Reynard had. What displeased Reynard more was that they had returned to the Abyss Sect. Making a move would be harder now. He could only count on Leonard to hold the elders back for as long as he could.

"Jake, you owe us an explanation!" Reynard said, enraged.

His expression distorted into a mass of anger, and his aura shot up menacingly. The cultivators had started to get back on their feet, and many froze when they heard Reynard words.

"I owe you an explanation?" Jake faced Reynard with furrowed brows.

What was he supposed to say? Although his master had not explained to him anything regarding the sudden opening of the Hellblaze Secret World, he could figure out most of the situation. There was no way he could share the truth with them.

"I'm as lost as you are."

From the corner of his eyes, Jake could see a lot of brows furrowed at his words. Anna stayed silent and signaled for the disciples of the Noan River Sect to gather and keep quiet. She didn't know exactly how to feel. As much as she hated Reynard, she couldn't help but lean to his side regarding this matter. The recent happenings were far too strange and far too dangerous to be ignored.

The other sects gathered with their own as well, following the example of Anna and her team. There was no sense jumping to conclusions and they were all quite confused as to what was going on.

"Don't make me laugh!" Reynard scoffed. "Wasn't that man your fifth protector? Isn't that kid that brought in all those shadows a part of your sect?"

"You saw Amon's face as well as I did! We all saw it! He clearly didn't know what was going on!" Jake retorted without hesitation.

"Then have him explain himself!" Reynard said with a sneer. "Where is he?" Reynard asked in a serious tone, looking at each cultivator as if searching for Amon.

Slowly, the other cultivators too started looking around, searching for him.

Jake silently gritted his teeth without answering the question. The first thing he did when he came to himself was to confirm the state of all the members of the Abyss Sect. He naturally knew that Amon was missing, and Reynard certainly knew it too.

"Where is he, Jake?" Reynard asked again, in a louder voice.

"I don't know."

At that moment, Reynard knew he had already won. Still, it wasn't enough. He needed to completely convince the others, or at least plant doubt in their minds. Oura had certainly made his job easier, and even Amon had unknowingly helped Reynard with his mission after disappearing.

"Are you covering for him or did you let a potential traitor run away?"

Reynard asked in a grave voice. His dark eyes shone with ferocity, and his expression had an unprecedented seriousness. "I also don't see the Abyss Sect's spirit vessel."

"I..." Jake couldn't find words to defend himself or his sect from Reynard's questions.

There was no way Jake could find reasonable explanations for any of those questions, especially regarding Amon and the missing spirit vessel. Everything pointed out that he had run away.

He took a deep breath. He had to make a tough decision and try to salvage the Abyss Sect's reputation and solidify its position as an innocent party in this.

Taking a step forward, Jake fired back at Reynard.

"Covering for a traitor? You saw it with your own eyes. Our sect master got involved in that fight to protect us!"

Daniel's eyes widened. Jake had discarded any thoughts of defending Amon from that accusation. That was the same as calling Amon a traitor.

Daniel took a step forward, but Jake raised a hand to stop him. Daniel looked at his brother's eyes and saw nothing but decisiveness in them.

"Jake," Daniel called in low, but alarmed voice. He couldn't hide the disappointment in his eyes.

"Don't speak. This is for the sect," Jake said, avoiding Daniel's gaze. He couldn't bear the look his brother was giving him. "We can think on how to prove his innocence later."

"And how exactly are you going to do that?" Daniel growled.

If Jake was going to let the assumption of Amon being a traitor grow just so he could salvage the Abyss Sect's name, then proving his innocence later would be many times more difficult, as it would yet again put the Abyss Sect in a delicate position.

"If he was here in the first place this matter could've been solved already!" Jake retorted with a cold voice. "Not to mention that strange woman he had with him. Looks like he has his fair share of secrets, Daniel. We can't let our emotions take over right now. The first thing we need to do is hold our ground against Reynard and then slowly move forward in search of the truth. Even if he is indeed innocent, and I believe so too, he has a lot of explaining to do."

"Having fun discussing the excuses you're going to give?" Reynard interrupted their conversation with a sharp tone.

"What excuses do I need to give? Our sect master taking part in the fight should be proof enough the Abyss Sect is not responsible for this," Jake said with a cold voice.

His words made many of the cultivators exchange strange looks. It was indeed strange that Lars Borgin had appeared to fight against the invaders. Maybe the Abyss Sect truly wasn't the perpetrator.

"Do you truly think so? Yes, your sect master appeared to fight your former fifth protector, but I didn't see him landing a single blow, nor receiving one back! Not to mention that strange green-haired woman conveniently trying to put everyone in a daze so we couldn't see what was happening!

"There is also the fact that your sect simply decided to hold the trials out of the blue, after declaring they were canceled for a few decades," Reynard continued, taking a step forward in an incredibly aggressive manner. "Do you see yourselves as the owners of the Hellblaze Trials? Would the trials exist without the remaining cardinal sects?"

"What was the reason for canceling the trials in the first place? Did the Abyss Sect, by any chance, know that this could happen?" Reynard took a brief pause, letting his words sink in. "If that was the case, why reorganize them?"

Jake had a deep frown, unable to retort at all. He couldn't find suitable words to use. Mostly because, to make things worse, he knew Reynard was probably right. The thought alone made him secretly shiver.

"You either brought us into a trap or used us in a trap you set up for someone else!"

"Not only that, your sect either stole all of the treasures in the Hellblaze Secret World or you lost them through sheer incompetence!" Reynard laid down the final cards he had in his hands. It was time to give the finishing blow.

"Silence!" Joshua suddenly shouted, trying to jump forward.

His face was as red as his hair, and he couldn't hide his animosity in the least. Daniel promptly held him back. His expression was somewhat pale, and he had a deep frown on his face.

"What motive would we have for that? Do you think this was just an elaborate ruse to try and get everything inside the Hellblaze Secret World for us? Do you think we're in such a desperate situation?"

"Yes, I actually do! Not only is your sect waning, but you've also been robbing corpses to barely maintain yourselves over the years! If that does not reek of desperation, I don't know what does!" Reynard didn't hold back at all. "You are known as the Sect of Scraps, after all. Apparently, it's not for show!"

An uncomfortable silence took over the area. The cultivators exchanged awkward glances, but no one said a word. The Sect of Scraps. A name they all had heard, and most had used.

Although all the cardinal sects had been on the decline, the Abyss Sect's fall from grace had been too accentuated, and their stance regarding the Scavenging had been doubtful, to say the least. Reynard bringing this up, even if disrespectful, also made sense. If the Abyss Sect took over the Hellblaze Secret World's treasures, they would be able to recover at least part of the lost influence, and most likely stall their decline for a few decades.

"Not only that, your former fifth protector was involved!" Reynard pointed out again.

"Lloyd Kressler is a traitor! He left the sect six years ago!" Jake shouted, livid.

His hands were trembling in rage and his face was turning red. By his side, Karen quietly held his hand, trying to calm him down.

"If that is the case, then how did he get into the Hellblaze Secret World? Why didn't your sect keep an eye on his family? Why did his son take part in the trials? Wasn't his son the one that started all of this mess?"

"How do you know he is Lloyd's son?" Jake asked, squinting his eyes.

"Are you stupid? Didn't we all thoroughly study the information on our competitors?" Reynard promptly dismissed any doubts Jake might try to cast over him. "If you didn't, then you're even more of an idiot than I thought.

"Now tell me, what sect gives that kind of liberty to traitors or their families? This was either planned a long time ago or yet again it was your incompetence!"

Jake could feel every word of Reynard's hitting his face like a slap. Reynard's momentum was unstoppable, and he didn't seem to be done.

"Are you people stupid or do you think we all are?" Reynard had a disgusted look on his face as he looked at Jake.

His eyes, however, shone with a fierce glint behind that mask he was using in his act. It was a subtle glint, so subtle Jake couldn't catch it in his desperation to defend himself and his sect.

"How the hell do you want me to answer that?" Jake shouted. He had completely lost his composure.

"With the truth!" Reynard's demand was simple.

It was almost too simple. At that moment, he knew the conversation was already over. Reynard knew it had been decided even before it started, but that simple request had finally put an end to it. What came after didn't matter anymore.

That short sentence had sealed the Abyss Sect's fate as being completely at fault in the eyes of all present. Even if they meant it or not, they were responsible for the disaster that had occurred.

"I do not speak for the sect!" Jake shouted, exasperated.

What could he do? No matter what he said, Reynard had a retort. Worst of all, his questions and the picture he was painting started making a twisted kind of sense. The situation was turning graver at an alarming pace.

"Then what kind of inheriting disciple are you?" Reynard asked, not hiding the scorn in his eyes.

He then kept quiet, asking no more questions. There was no need to. This wasn't an attack to the Abyss Sect, to Lars Borgin or to Amon. This was a direct offense to Jake Meyer.

Indeed, what kind of inheriting disciple was he?

He had given up on a member of his own sect in order to try to protect the rest, but he had utterly failed. His master had barely told him anything at all about the situation regarding the Hellblaze Trials, and the end result was that Jake couldn't deflect any of Reynard's arguments.

Not only that, but Jake had tried to avoid responsibility in a bid to stop Reynard's unrelenting strikes. He had only worsened the situation. Reynard had full control from the very beginning, and Jake had unknowingly played along to his plan.

Karen's slender fingers tightened the grip around Jake's hand. He closed his eyes for a moment, feeling her warmth as he tried to accept his defeat and think of a way to remedy the situation.

Throughout the one-sided discussion, the expression on the cultivators present had slowly changed. From confusion and fear, the expressions of those outside of the Abyss Sect turned twisted with anger and incredulity.

The Abyss Sect member's expression shifted into a sheer rage for being suspected, but that rage soon numbed into a wordless shock. Even some of them had started thinking Reynard might be right. There was no doubt at all on who had won the argument, so naturally, the Abyss Sect was in a horrible position.

"Is silence all you have to give us?" a boy dressed in blue asked, taking a step forward and separating from the ranks of the Noan River Sect.

"Eli, that is enough," Anna said in a sharp, hostile voice.

"Enough?" Another voice broke the silence. It was a boy from the Roaring Mountain Sect, that looked at Anna with disdain. "Our inheritance is lost. Do you know how many artifacts we lost thanks to the Abyss Sect? How much of our rightful inheritance was taken away from us?"

"Not to mention the risks we were put through," the boy looked at Jake with hostile eyes and an expression full of despise. "You make us go through all of this and silence is all that we get?"

"Big words coming from a nobody like you," Joshua said, glaring at the boy and struggling against Daniel.

Daniel's hold over him tightened, but it was useless. Joshua was much stronger than he was.

"If you didn't notice, we were as endangered as any of you!" Joshua shouted, hitting his own chest wildly. "Our lives were at risk too! I refuse to take the blame for what a random kid plotted with his father!"

"Joshua!" Karen called with an alarmed voice.

She blinked in confusion, trying to understand what was going on. She had never seen him losing his cool like this. What had gotten into him?

"Well, that kid is nowhere to be seen, so I will demand an answer from you!" the boy from the Roaring Mountain Sect continued, almost shouting. His tone was extremely forceful as he pointed his finger at the Abyss Sect disciples. "As Reynard said, you were either plotting this from the start or are simply too incompetent to be a part of the cardinal sects!"

To Anna's surprise, Reynard simply stood by the side, his arms crossed as he silently watched.

"Say that again, Drace!" Joshua challenged the boy, patting his bottomless pouch and pulling his short spear from it.

"Or what? Are you going to strike me?" Drace asked, his tone as forceful as ever. He too patted his bottomless pouch, retrieving a silver sword that he held in his right hand. "I actually would want to see that. I want to see how you fare fighting instead of robbing corpses."

Something in Joshua's eyes changed at that moment. Jake didn't know what it was, but it alarmed him greatly. He jumped forward, trying to stand in front of him and hold him back. He should have had enough time. He had acted first, and he was faster than Joshua. He had always been.

Still, to his surprise, it wasn't what happened. Joshua seemed to turn into a blur, immediately shaking off Daniel and shooting forward at an unbelievable speed. It was far too fast. Faster than Jake could even imagine someone at their level could move. He desperately extended his hands, trying to grab Joshua before he was completely out of reach. Unfortunately, Jake failed. Joshua lightly brushed past him, leaving Jake grasping nothing but air

Drace looked at Joshua coming at him, spear in hand, with disdain in his eyes. He took a defensive stance, preparing to parry the incoming stab aimed at his chest.

Joshua's strike was incredibly fast, but also very straightforward. A normal disciple wouldn't be able to parry it, but Drace wasn't a normal disciple. He looked at Joshua with a bit of pity in his eyes.

It had been too easy taunting him into attacking. It had been too easy predicting the path of his spear. It would be too easy blocking it, deflecting the strike to his left and using the momentum to increase the speed of his sword, beheading Joshua with a fluid motion.

As Drace moved his right arm to seal Joshua's fate, his face suddenly paled—his arm wasn't moving.

He turned his head in surprise, looking in horror at his own arm. It was immobile, as if Drace hadn't even tried to move it yet. A disgusting numbness was spreading through it, and Drace could feel a slight pressure constricting his arm as he forcefully tried to move it, as if countless strands had been tangled around it, holding it in place.

He turned his head to Joshua in fright. The red-haired boy had a fierce smile on his face as he looked at Drace with scorn. The tip of his spear could barely be seen in the gloom of the major plaza, but it became increasingly clear in Drace's eyes as it came closer to his chest.

With a nauseating sound, the spear penetrated his skin, digging through his muscles and breaking his ribs as it made its way to his heart. Drace looked in horror as the spear sank into his flesh, completely burying the spearhead into his chest until the shaft hit his sternum, fracturing what was left of his ribs.

He opened his mouth, trying to speak, but only a torrent of blood came out, pouring from his mouth and spilling on the floor, dirtying his feet. Drace slowly turned his head to his right, looking at Reynard.

Reynard still had the same cold eyes as ever, and his expression was blank. His arms were still crossed, as if he couldn't react in the split second Joshua took to leave the Abyss Sect's ranks and strike him. Nevertheless, Reynard met his gaze, and Drace realized the truth. The numbness in his arm disappeared as the countless strands of qi that had bound it in place were released.

Clang!

Drace's sword fell on the floor, sounding like a bell. In the completely silent plaza, full of horrified cultivators that were trying to understand what had just happened, its sound was deafening. Drace's eyes lost all light as he still faced Reynard, incredulous at what had happened.

Puchi!

Joshua violently released his spear from Drace's chest, and his body fell violently to the floor. Blood gushed from the hole in his chest, tainting Drace's yellow robes and forming a pool beneath him.

The bloodied spear looked very sinister in Joshua's hands as he pointed it to the cultivators of the other sects with a savage expression on his face.

"Anyone else wants to speak nonsense?"

Blood slowly dripped down Joshua's spear as he spoke, looking menacingly to the other cultivators. Under the gloom of Hell Keeper's City, his red hair looked as dark as the blood that slowly fell to the ground. Drace's body was lying lifeless by his side, with the terrifying wound in his chest still gushing out blood.

"How dare you!" someone from the Roaring Mountain Sect's disciples screamed, stepping forward with a saber in hand.

Reynard finally uncrossed his arms, extending a hand and holding the disciple back. His face was expressionless, but his eyes were burning with sheer anger. He looked at Joshua with a glance that gave one shivers, and his brows furrowed.

"Is this the stance that the Abyss Sect will take?" he asked with a chilling tone, not hiding the murderous intention in his voice.

"No!" Jake shouted, desperate. His face was red and his eyes were wide open as he spoke, completely shocked. "Joshua, fall back right now!"

The situation was critical. A single misstep now would lead to a disaster. If Joshua retreated, he could still manage to buy time until the elders came. Even if the Abyss Sect had to somehow compensate the other sects and suffer heavy sanctions, there was still a very fine thread of hope to not worsen the situation.

Unfortunately, however, Joshua completely ignored Jake. Instead, he slowly turned to face Reynard, with his spear in hand and a murderous expression on his face.

"Yes," he said, completely indifferent.

He quietly sustained Reynard's gaze, not moving in the slightest.

"Damn traitors! All of you!" Eli shouted again.

Hearing his words, Anna's body slightly twitched. The whole situation had been strange from the start, but her instincts were screaming at her that something was particularly wrong now.

Her clothes slowly started to dampen, turning darker and clinging tightly to her body. Her hair started to stick to her neck and shoulders as a crystal-clear puddle of water started forming beneath her feet. Soon, the puddle had grown large enough to cover the area around all of the Noan River Sect's disciples, wetting their feet.

Reynard looked at Anna's actions and his lips twitched. It couldn't be helped, she was a competent leader. He didn't let his displeasure show in his expression, only feeling it was a pity that things would quite possibly not be as decisive as he had hoped for. Nevertheless, for the overall plan was more than enough. Even if things didn't fit perfectly, it was all in the realm of the acceptable.

Reynard momentarily looked at Joshua. In that brief moment, his eyes flashed with annoyance and disappointment, but those emotions were gone as fast as they had come. His furrowed brows relaxed, and the strange, tense smile made its way to his lips.

"Well then, this is your choice," Reynard said, turning his back to him and facing his fellow disciples. The crystalline sword Mirage was raised above his head as he took a deep breath.

Hearing Reynard's tone, Anna's meticulous movements became hasty. With another wave of her hand, the water beneath her blasted outwards, and the edges of what was now a shallow pool started to rise, soon forming a thick wall of water that enclosed all of the Noan River Sect's disciples. Crackling sounds started coming from the wall as a chilling cold spread from Anna and the water started to solidify into a robust wall of ice.

More water continued flowing from the wall, going higher and higher and slowly curving to Anna's direction before being frozen by the cold. When Anna finally stopped focusing, a thick dome made of pure ice had formed next to the Ashen Heart tree. With a flick of her wrist, a bright blue medallion slipped from her sleeve into her hand, which she promptly crushed before letting out a deep breath.

"Just standby until the high elder comes to our aid," she said in a tired voice before sitting down and crossing her legs to start recovering her stamina and qi.

"But senior sister, what about the others?" a small girl asked, looking deathly pale and clearly scared as she looked at Anna.

"They will have to deal with it by themselves. My job is to guarantee our safety, nothing more. All you have to do is stay put and not try anything funny," she said in a cold voice.

Beneath the misty veil, her eyes were locked on the disciple that had actually started the argument that led to all of this. Eli, shivered as he felt as if a cold wave had swept past him, but he didn't do anything out of the ordinary, looking as nervous as the other disciples. Anna closed her eyes to focus on her recovery, but still decided to remain attentive to his actions.

On the other side of the plaza, Alden called in an emotionless, bland voice. His usual enthusiasm was nowhere to be seen, and he suddenly looked abnormally distant.

"Joel..."

A boy by his side gave him a slight nod, squatting down and placing his hands on the ground. The earth quaked, and a loud rumble started echoing in the major plaza as cracks started spreading around the Southern Flame Sect's disciples. The cracks completely surrounded them before the earth beneath their feet distorted and rippled like water, slowly ascending a few meters above the ground.

Alden's powerful voice made its way to all of the present in the plaza as he reached inside his clothes and recovered a small triangular medallion that shone with a red color.

"Whoever tries to climb will be regarded as an enemy. Whoever tries to descend will be regarded as a traitor," he finished, decisively crushing the medallion in his hands and coldly watching how the situation would unfold from above.

The disciples of the Southern Flame Sect exchanged a few looks but ultimately said nothing. They knew better than anyone that when Alden dropped his act he meant every word he said, and he had the backing and the position to follow through with his threat without consequences.

The Storm Peak Sect members also started hastily retreating, and someone in their ranks broke a green medallion, not unlike what Anna and Alden did.

"Kill them all!" Reynard shouted, pointing the sword to the Abyss Sect members.

They had to end this before the elders came back. He knew Leonard wouldn't be able to hold them back for long after the inheriting disciples asked for aid.

In a heartbeat, the nine remaining Roaring Mountain Sect's members pushed forward, weapon in hand. Two of them surrounded Joshua, and the other seven directly threw themselves at the Abyss Sect's party.

"Reynard, stop this!" Jake shouted, hurriedly drawing his saber. Reynard didn't bother answering, instead, his pace seemed to quicken.

Reynard seemed to slide through the earth in a graceful, unpredictable manner. It was as if he was standing in a layer of ice rather than soil. The earth beneath his feet rippled as his body shot forward. He barely moved his legs as the earth itself pushed him forward. His eyes were set on Jake, and there was nothing but a murderous rage in them while a savage smile was stamped on his face.

"Spread out and don't let them surround us!" Jake ordered, trying to calm his mind.

The Roaring Mountain Sect had lost Drace, that was at body tempering, but they had left behind one member at elemental purification and one at body tempering to deal with Joshua. They still had four elemental purification and three body tempering members. The Abyss Sect had four of each remaining since Amon was gone and Joshua was stranded further away. Even though the difference in power was negligible, in the right circumstances it could make the difference between a victory and a loss.

"Face only someone on the same level as you! Daniel, you stay behind, use your swords to aid Karen, Skylar and Evan in taking care of the elemental purification members they will face!" Jake quickly ordered, and the Abyss Sect members soon fanned out with Daniel in the rearguard, ready to face the incoming attack.

Daniel's manipulation of swords would be valuable to guarantee the elemental purification members of the Abyss Sect had the upper hand in combat, or at least weren't overpowered by their opponents. It would be far too risky to leave even one of the elemental purification members on their side in a disadvantageous position.

There was a chasm in regards to destructive power between elemental purification and body tempering cultivators. If a single one of the elemental purification enemies managed to slip by, disaster might befall the weaker members of the Abyss Sect, and the remaining would soon be outnumbered and surrounded.

"Karen, you go to the right. Skylar, you go to the left. Both of you are wind cultivators. When they come, your job will be to make a pincer attack and try to blast back as many of them as possible," Jake ordered. "Evan, you're a fire cultivator like me. When the Roaring Mountain Sect tries to defend from the pincer attack, they will most likely raise earth walls to block the wind blasts. Even if they don't, they'll bundle up together to avoid as many attacks as possible. At that moment, we'll strike together."

Of the four elemental purification members of the Roaring Mountain Sect, three of them, Reynard included, were earth cultivators. The remaining one was a water cultivator. This guaranteed that at least two earth walls would be used in the upcoming clash, most likely to block the wind blasts, as water wouldn't be as effective and there was no feasible time to freeze it before the attack landed.

Jake also doubted that the water cultivator alone would be able to block the joint forces of him and Evan. This meant that Reynard, that was leading the charge, would most likely be forced to raise the third earth wall and momentarily pause to either change directions or wait for the attack to be over. Either way, their side would lose momentum.

"Do not let any of them break our ranks; we must stall until the elders come!" Jake's right hand trembled. The saber clanged as Jake tightened his grip on it, trying to make the trembling cease.

The first clash was already planned. After that, it would be chaos. He could only do his best to guarantee the best chances for his sect when both sides collided. Taking the initiative away from the attacking side was all he could do for now.

The best course of action would be to make sure no more blood was shed, but to do so Jake would have to order his members to avoid using lethal power. The problem was that the other side obviously had no such concerns. If his side held back, it would be hard to stall for time and guarantee that they would not lose anyone. He didn't want the blood of his fellow disciples on his hands because he had ordered them to hold back.

On the other hand, giving that order and making sure the other cardinal sects listened to it would be enough at some level to prove that he didn't want conflict and that Joshua had acted on his own. Jake had already said that the sect's stance wasn't the same as Joshua's, but Reynard Stark didn't bother one bit. He lost a member and he was out for blood. Joshua had given him the excuse to act.

If he said nothing, however, or even said to the Abyss Sect members to not hold back in order to properly defend themselves, it could be used later against him and the Sect. It would not fare well.

In other words, for the other cardinal sects, the Abyss Sect was already in the wrong. It was now a matter of trying to ease the situation but risking lives or doubling down on hostility to make sure they lost as little lives as possible and dealing with the consequences later.

Jake took a deep breath, making his decision. Time seemed to slow down as he closed his eyes trying to calm himself. What was but a split second felt like an eternity for him. What came after this moment would decide everything.

"No matter what, fight for your lives!" he shouted.

Even if it brought trouble for the Abyss Sect later, he would not allow any of them to hold back. He already made the mistake to try to mend the situation before, and the other side was abnormally eager to attack, not to mention Joshua's inexplicable actions. If they held back, he was afraid they would lose miserably.

Jake had a solemn expression on his face as he looked at the Roaring Mountain Sect members approaching with Reynard spearheading the charge. Jake couldn't help but notice Reynard's expression. His grip on the saber tightened even more, to the point where his hand started hurting.

"Now!" he suddenly shouted, taking a deep breath to focus and prepare for his attack.

From the right and left sides, Karen and Skylar dashed forward in a diagonal run, moving away from both parties in a bid to get some space. When the Roaring Mountain Sect members started passing by them, they both changed directions, facing each other with the enemies between them.

SWOOOSH!

The wind howled madly, and a cloud of dust rose from the ground as two violent gusts came crashing down on the Roaring Mountain Sect members from both sides. Jake's hair started whipping about as he spread his divine sense to depict what was happening in the cloud of dust, and he promptly signaled to Evan to follow his lead.

The ground beneath their feet started shaking and the soil on the sides of the attackers suddenly rose, forming two thick, crude walls that protected their sides. A deafening roar echoed as the gusts collided against the walls, throwing gravel and dirt everywhere before dispersing. Both walls trembled, but in the end, they managed to hold on.

As Karen and Skylar quickly retreated to the Abyss Sect's formation, Jake and Evan took a step forward. Scarlet flames danced on Jake's saber and Evan's sword as they focused. Stomping on the ground, they both roared as they struck with their weapons, sending a wave of scorching flames towards the now grouped Roaring Mountain Sect members.

Karen and Skylar then both waved their hands, sending a blast of air towards the flames, pushing them forward. The wave of flames suddenly turned wild and even hotter as the blast of air fanned them, leaving a trail of scorched earth and black smoke as it traveled towards the attackers.

At the moment the raging wave of fire was about to hit its target, the earth started rumbling again, and Jake almost let out a sigh of relief. Behind the searing flames, he could faintly sense another earth wall being erected, and he knew he had succeeded.

After that, however, the world came tumbling down.

"Commendable effort, but far too predictable."

A cold, ruthless voice made its way from behind the wall that separated the two opposing factions. Jake raised his eyes, looking at the wall directly in front of him. It was glowing with a bright red color, and parts of it were flowing down like some kind of viscous liquid. Pieces of burning dirt fell into the ground, looking like burning coals. The heat coming from the wall was terrifying, yet it was still standing.

Crack, crack, crack!

Innumerable cracks started spreading through the wall. The molten parts seemed to quickly cool down, firm enough just to crack like all the rest. Even though the surface of the wall was a malformed mess, it still had a dim glow. The heat in it hadn't been completely dispersed. Soon, the whole wall was covered in cracks of all sizes, looking like it was about to fall apart.

"Brace yourselves!" Jake shouted as his instincts warned him of the incoming danger.

He stood in front of Daniel as a thick barrier of qi appeared in front of him. Karen, Evan, and Skylar also covered the other members that were too weak to defend against the incoming counter. They quickly patted their bottomless pouches, producing shield talismans.

Jake reached inside his clothes, trying to find his own bottomless pouch... and he found nothing. His expression turned grave. When had it disappeared?

BOOM!

A horrendous force blasted out, hitting the wall and shattering it into thousands of pieces that whistled through the air. They flew towards the Abyss Sect members at blinding speed, burning with a threatening heat.

Jake's face paled. The fragments were coming at them with enough force and speed to blast a hole through a metal plate. He wasn't confident enough to face even one of them head-on, yet they would have to face thousands!

"Karen, Skylar, try to slow them down!" Jake ordered in a desperate bid.

Fire was immaterial, so there was no way he could use it to block the incoming rain of projectiles. The best he could do was use a rudimentary blast of qi to try to slow the projectiles down.

Karen promptly waved her hands, throwing a gust of wind outwards. Skylar was heartbeat late but did the same. The dust was blown away as the wind swept by, clashing with the projectiles. They didn't seem to slow down by any considerable margin, but some of them were thrown out of trajectory and stopped being a direct threat.

Still, deflecting a few droplets in a rainstorm made no difference at all. The deadly rain came pouring down on them, bringing nothing but pain and disgrace.

Bang! Bang! Bang!

The fragments of the wall struck the ground, opening holes a few times larger than their sizes, and digging meters deep into the earth. The burning projectiles ripped through Jake's protective qi as if it was paper, poking holes in it without the slightest difficulty.

Jake completely ignored the small fragments, but his arm moved at an inhuman speed to deflect the bigger ones that were coming directly in his direction. The impacts were enough to make the bones in his arm creak and the skin on his hand rupture, even if he was only skillfully deflecting the fragments away rather than directly slashing with his saber.

Nevertheless, it wasn't enough. Many of the fragments managed to get past his defenses, scraping against his limbs and taking away chunks of flesh. He was having the hardest time since he was directly in front of the wall, unlike Skylar and Karen, for example. Even so, Jake didn't move an inch. He knew that if he moved he would put his brother in mortal danger.

As such, he diverted his attention to defending his life rather than completely avoiding injury. When the deadly storm finally passed, he was left in a wretched state and on the brink of collapsing.

"You really couldn't see this coming? You are far too green, Jake." Reynard's mocking voice echoed through the plaza. With a wave of his hands, all of the dust in the air suddenly fell down, clearing up the view.

Jake cut out a sorry figure. His clothes were full of holes, and blood was covering his whole body. His hair was a mess and his face was full of scratches and bruises. His saber, a high-tier artifact, was covered in dents and cracks. His legs were trembling and his arms were motionlessly hanging from his shoulders; he couldn't even move them anymore.

Daniel was sprawled on the floor, and his right side was drenched in blood. He was slowly trying to stand, but he couldn't find the strength to do it. His black hair was glued to his face, and his eyes showed a hint of fear and dejection.

Evan lay motionless on the ground. His chest and legs were filled with countless holes spewing with blood. Not even his shield talisman managed to properly protect him. Even though he wasn't dead, he wasn't too far from it. The body tempering cultivator he tried to protect, on the other hand, had his arm directly blown off, and was in what seemed to be a daze as he silently gazed at his injury without blinking or moving.

Skylar seemed to have come out relatively unscathed, but a deep wound could be seen in her right leg. She was tying a piece of her own clothes around it. Malia, the body tempering cultivator she shielded, looked unharmed, despite her pale face frozen with shock.

Jake raised his head, looking at Karen's direction as his heart beat wildly. She was lying on the floor with a terrifying wound on her left shoulder. Blood didn't stop coming out from her injuries, but she didn't move to stop the bleeding. She had clearly lost consciousness. The boy she had protected had fallen to the ground, trembling in fright.

"Orson, get the fuck up and stop Karen's bleeding," Jake commanded in a weak voice, trying his best not to fall to his knees and pass out.

The frightened boy shuddered, but after a moment of hesitation, he tried to get on his feet, only to fall down. All of his body was shaking uncontrollably, but he managed to crawl over to Karen and put pressure on her shoulder.

The members of the Roaring Mountain Sect stood behind Reynard, still surrounded by the walls they had raised previously. However, they stood motionless with their weapons in hand, as if standing guard for their leader.

Looking at Reynard's mocking smile, Jake trembled with rage. He had probably predicted what he would do from the very start. Reynard had let his plan go on without a hitch only to make a brutal counter when he relaxed after the success. That mad charge he had instilled at the beginning was most likely only a way to pressure him into making a quick decision without thinking too much.

He had lost even before the battle started. Jake gritted his teeth, raising his eyes to look beyond Reynard. Joshua was still fighting the two cultivators from before, being pressured by them into a merely defensive role. He swung and spun his short spear wildly, masterfully blocking and deflecting all of the strikes coming at him.

Still, he didn't even spare a glance to the members of his own sect. He didn't seem flustered or affected at all by what had just happened. In fact, he looked completely absorbed in his own fight.

For the first time, Jake wished he actually failed at parrying and got struck down by the enemy. He had put them in this situation, and yet he didn't seem to bother one bit. Was this really the person that he had known for almost ten years? Was this really his best friend?

"This is it, Jake. It was fun while it lasted. Well, somewhat," Reynard said with a sigh.

He seemed incredibly disappointed. It was impossible to know if Reynard was disappointed with Jake or himself.

Reynard started slowly moving forward, unhurriedly waving his sword around. The crystal-blue blade refracted the faint light of Hell Keeper's City as if it was water, distorting it in dim wave patterns that spread through it.

The way Reynard swung it around made the effect seem almost hypnotic, and incredibly entrancing.

Jake used every ounce of his strength to stay on his feet, trying his utmost to raise his arm. Somehow, he still hadn't lost the grip over his saber. Fighting back against the burning pain coursing through his body and the crippling exhaustion he was feeling due to the blood loss, Jake slowly raised his saber, assuming a defensive stance.

"You are only trying to kill me, aren't you?" he suddenly asked in a low, weary voice.

His eyelids were becoming heavy, and he felt his consciousness was about to fade away.

"No," Reynard answered in an equally low voice, slightly raising a brow as he faced Jake.

"You damn liar," Jake rebutted and his body started swaying. "Leave the others alone. They aren't worth your attention. They are too weak, and even those with potential won't pose a threat to you in any way. What fun is there in killing such weak people?"

For once, a rare surprise showed in Reynard's face. His mocking smile completely disappeared, and his dark eyes widened for a split second before he regained control. He then threw his head back and gave a hearty laugh.

"Hahahaha!"

Many of the Roaring Mountain Sect members widened their eyes in surprise. They had never seen Reynard laughing like that, even more after what was clearly not a joke. Reynard, however, was oblivious to all of their thoughts. Rather, he didn't care.

When he stopped laughing, he looked at Jake with a solemn, even respectful expression. "Oh Jake, this is why I always saw you as an opponent, even if you are undeniably weaker than me."

"It was a nice try," Reynard said, shaking his head. "Too bad it won't work."

He then turned around, looking at the Roaring Mountain Sect members and thinking for a moment. Would risking the moral high ground to completely wipe out the Abyss Sect's disciples be worth it?

"Kill them all," he finally said in an enraged tone, repeating the previous order he had given. There would be no turning back and there would be no mercy for the Abyss Sect.

Even if it looked like an exaggeration, his side was still justified. The Abyss Sect had attacked first and he had lost his mind in the rightful anger that came from it. Yes, the after-effects would not be impossible to be reckoned with. Oura stealing everything in the Hellblaze Secret World would really make the difference when the cardinal sects weighted down the possible actions.

"You coward!" Jake shouted as the little bit of color left in his face disappeared. He looked utterly enraged, even somewhat disgusted.

"You talk too much for a traitor," Reynard promptly retorted, indifferent.

He raised Mirage, slashing down in a beautiful, deadly arc. Jake feebly raised his guard and changed his posture, barely deflecting the unexpected attack. The crystalline sword swept past his defenses, scraping against his chest and leaving a shallow, but long wound on it.

Part of Jake's clothes finally gave in, falling down to the ground like tree leaves in the autumn. His abdomen and chest were exposed, revealing not only the bloody line Reynard had drawn but also a multitude of minuscule holes.

Jake gasped for breath, losing his balance and falling forward onto one knee. The saber finally escaped from his grasp, falling to the floor with a clinging sound.

Reynard then raised his sword, looking at Jake with a surprisingly wistful expression on his face. Jake sustained his gaze without showing a hint of fear.

Swoosh!

A sword whistled through the air, passing by Jake's head. Reynard hastily retreated, being caught by surprise. The sword slashed at his neck at an unbelievable speed, making Reynard frown. He tilted his body to the side as the sword passed by, barely missing him.

It then suddenly changed its trajectory, spinning wildly in the air before shooting back at the back of Reynard's head. Reynard scoffed as he parried the sword without difficulty. It then flew away, stopping by the side of a man with black hair that could barely stand.

Somehow, however, the man seemed as stable as a rock as he faced Reynard with nothing but rage showing on his deadly pale face. Above his head, five swords danced through the air, in a complex and intricate movement. The blades were vibrating wildly, making a dangerous hum as they circled around him.

Reynard looked at him with an emotionless expression and cold eyes. He raised his arms and used the back of his hand to wipe a trickle of scarlet blood that was flowing down his cheek. There was a shallow wound in it, where the sword barely grazed in the surprise attack.

He looked at the back of his hand and the stain of blood in it, and his indifferent expression slowly changed into one of rage. He raised his dark eyes, meeting the gaze of the aggressor with nothing but murderous intent exuding from him.

Daniel Meyer sustained Reynard Stark's threatening look with a firm resolution.

"Get the fuck away from my brother."

Reynard didn't bother answering Daniel. He leaned his body to the front as he dashed in Jake's direction, sword in hand. Far behind him, the other six members of the Roaring Mountain Sect also moved, aiming for the injured Abyss Sect disciples.

Jake clenched his teeth as he tried to move, but his body refused to obey. No matter how much he tried or how desperate he was, his limbs didn't respond. Blood flowed freely from the wounds on his chest, and breathing was difficult and painful. It was impossible to describe his anger and unwillingness as Reynard closed in and he couldn't even defend himself. He had never been this helpless in his life. He refused to be taken down without being able to fight back, but there was nothing he could do.

Swoosh! Swoosh! Swoosh!

An ear-piercing whistle echoed in the plaza as five swords shuttled through the air at a blinding speed, aiming at the six members of the Roaring Mountain Sect that were charging forward. Daniel slapped his bottomless pouch, producing a round shield, which he held on his left arm as he rushed in front of Jake, blocking Reynard's path.

BAM!

With a deafening sound, Reynard mercilessly smashed his sword against Daniel's shield, sending him tumbling back. Daniel felt his left arm numbing as he did his best to maintain his balance while retreating. He could clearly see that a part of his shield had caved in, pressing against his arm and deforming the shield. Another impact of this level would certainly break his left arm.

"Do you think you can hold me back with just this?" Reynard asked, clearly annoyed.

He looked at Daniel's bloodstained clothes, and his gaze fell on Daniel's right arm which was bleeding profusely from a number of gashes and holes. Daniel had most likely used it to defend himself in the earlier onslaught.

"You can barely stand. Do you really think you can stop me?" Reynard sneered.

"Well, I just did, didn't I?" Daniel answered with a mocking tone, trying his best to keep his voice as even as possible. In truth, Daniel was inwardly shocked and deeply unsettled. Reynard's casual strike had almost broken his arm, and that was with him using a shield.

Reynard didn't answer and simply stomped the ground. Daniel's face paled as he felt the earth beneath his feet squirming. He quickly threw himself to the side, just in time to see a gigantic spike rising from the place where he had been standing just moments ago.

Daniel furrowed his brows as he patted the bottomless pouch yet again, producing another sword. These swords were all low-grade artifacts. Daniel could barely afford a set with six swords when he used all of his savings, but he felt it was worth it. The sword quietly hovered by his side as Daniel regained his composure and coldly watched Reynard.

Large beads of sweat were running down his face as Daniel focused. The movements of the five swords holding back the Roaring Mountain Sect members were somewhat strange, almost faltering. Nevertheless, they were still fast enough to give trouble to their targets. Even if they didn't truly land a hit, holding them back was enough.

The farther the swords were, the harder it was to have a proper grasp of the swords, not to mention Daniel was trying to control six at the same time while facing Reynard. Fighting two completely different fights at the same time and facing several opponents at once wasn't unlike him.

Reynard had a clear look of displeasure on his face as he sustained Daniel's gaze. He remembered what he needed to know about Daniel Meyer as, for the first time, he seriously analyzed him.

Daniel's stance was weak and slightly off, mostly due to his injuries. His right arm, that had already been crippled once, was now most likely truly useless, even when taken into account the method Daniel found to regain some of its functions. The new injuries Daniel had sustained would continue to bleed, the pain would disrupt his focus, and even if he forcefully moved his arm by controlling qi, what good would it bring him?

Still, Reynard knew he didn't need his right arm. Daniel's ability to manipulate qi with finesse gave him the capability to control multiple swords at the same time. If Reynard were at the Body Tempering stage and facing Daniel alone, it would certainly have been a thrilling fight.

Reynard, however, was at the elemental purification stage, and he wasn't alone. In truth, he almost pitied Daniel. He had no chance to win but was still struggling with all he could. Beyond that slumped stance, beyond that exhausted face and those burning eyes, behind too many lines, too many weaknesses to count, Reynard could feel an unbendable will, and that made him incredibly mad.

Reynard really wanted to face Daniel in a fair fight. He really wanted to suppress his cultivation, to deny himself the advantage of manipulating the elements and face Daniel with all he could. With only his sword, his body, and his wits. It was truly a pity for him, a maddening matter.

No matter what, Reynard couldn't indulge in his desires today. He had many missions to take care of, and the plan had already been thrown into disarray by the presence of the woman accompanying Amon Skoller. Reynard had found the need to improvise, and even if it had worked, the results would not be the best.

Reynard's face hardened for a moment as he clenched his teeth, and a rare unwillingness showed in his eyes for no more than a second. As if it had never changed, his expression returned to the usual coldness.

What was important was the mission. Fairness, honor, and the like had no right to be in his mind today. They were only excuses, chains to hold back the ones with strength.

Daniel shivered when he saw the changes on Reynard's expression. Even more than before he could feel a chilling killing intent wrapping around him as if the qi itself was becoming murderous.

What was this?

He had never experienced such a feeling before. It was a completely bizarre sensation that put Daniel on the edge. He felt that even the smallest of movements would make his muscles tear and his skin rupture. It was as if there was a primordial behemoth hiding in the air, setting its sights on Daniel, waiting for him to drop his guard to rip him into pieces.

Reynard suddenly moved, dashing towards Daniel. Daniel felt the earth beneath his feet rumble gently, making him jolt. It was different from the last time, this rumble was weak, and Daniel couldn't feel the earth moving beneath him other than that. His eyes widened as he realized what was happening.

He cursed inwardly, waving his arms desperately. The shield on his left arm shot out, flying through the air towards Jake. It violently bashed against him, knocking him away as a sharp spike shot out from the ground, scraping against Jake's left calf and leaving a deep gash.

Daniel knew he had no choice anymore. Reynard would not let him buy time until help came. The only way to stop Reynard from attacking Jake would be to directly face him and put him under enough pressure to stop him from attacking the others at a distance.

Both Reynard and Daniel knew that. If Daniel still tried to simply stall, Jake would be killed at the first opening Daniel showed. How long Daniel would last facing Reynard head-on?

The lonely sword hovering around Daniel shot out with a howl as it pierced the air, aiming for Reynard's head. Reynard didn't even bother dodging, instead, his pace quickened as he brandished Mirage.

Clang!

Daniel's sword went flying away as Reynard advanced. His eyes flashed with a cold glint, and the earth rippled again. Daniel suddenly felt his right foot sinking into the ground, throwing him off balance. He beckoned with his hand, and the sword Reynard had deflected changed course midair, aiming for Reynard yet again. The shield he had sent towards Jake trembled once before flying back to Daniel's direction.

Reynard didn't bat an eye as he continued to push forward. He lightly flicked his wrist, and the ground that had swallowed Daniel's foot slid to the side, breaking his poor stance and making him fall to the ground.

With a loud thud, Daniel heavily fell, bashing his head against the ground. The sword aiming for Reynard fell as Daniel's focus was broken and the qi wrapped around the sword dispersed.

Clang, clang, clang!

One by one, the other five swords Daniel was controlling fell to the ground. With a scoff, the Roaring Mountain Sect disciples pushed forward, spreading out as they relentlessly advanced towards the fallen Abyss Sect members.

The earth beneath Daniel rippled again, making his face pale. Blood was trickling down his head and his mind was blurred due to the headache and the impact, but he still managed to call out to him the shield that had fallen to the ground. He pushed his body up, and the shield slid behind his back.

CLANG!

With a heavy impact, another spike rose from the ground, aiming for

Daniel's back and hitting the shield. The force pushed Daniel back to his feet, but his right foot was still trapped in the ground. With a grunt, he punched the ground at his feet, giving himself enough space to pull his feet out.

His pale face was painted scarlet with blood, giving him a ghastly appearance as he waved his hand again. The six swords slowly rose back to the air, trembling and almost falling again. Daniel clenched his teeth, and the swords suddenly stabilized, spinning in the air as their tips pointed to the backs of the Roaring Mountain Sect disciples.

Swoosh, swoosh, swoosh!

The swords shot out at a blinding speed, and Daniel fell to one knee, grunting as a piercing pain coursed through his head. He barely managed to make the swords continue in a straight line.

"Can you give yourself the luxury to save everyone?" Reynard's voice suddenly sounded in front of him. Mirage was already falling towards Daniel's head.

Daniel grunted as he lifted his feet off the ground, and the shield at his back pushed him away. Reynard's strike barely missed Daniel, making him greatly displeased. With a cold look on his face, he stomped the ground.

Six small pillars of earth rose from the ground behind the unsuspecting Roaring Mountain Sect disciples, and the flying swords directly collided with the pillars. Instead of the expected impact, however, the pillars rippled like water, and rather than thrusting into the pillars, the swords seemed to sink into them, as if they were liquid rather than solid. With another stomp from Reynard, the pillars sunk to the ground, burying the swords along.

"Come on. It's easy to neutralize your trump card if you don't use those strange movements," Reynard said with a mocking smile. His voice, however, seemed surprisingly coarse.

Reynard's breathing was ragged, and a few beads of sweat rolled down his forehead. Even though elemental purification cultivators had obvious advantages over body tempering ones, their power was limited. Controlling the elements was exhausting, and they lacked the strength to do so repeatedly and for extended periods of time.

Fire and water cultivators had it the worst. If there was any source of fire and water near them, they could always use the elemental qi in their bodies to synchronize and take over those elements, as the expenditure would be lesser than having to spend elemental qi to channel and create the elements out of thin air. As such, earth and wind cultivators had an innate advantage.

Even so, there were drawbacks. Reynard's signature self-created movement technique, even if fast and unpredictable, required him to control a large amount of earth qi. He had to move the earth where he was stepping and the earth surrounding it, making it flow around his feet like water continuously to guarantee minimal effort and fluid movements.

Making earth spikes and walls, for instance, required a similar technique, otherwise, underneath them, a hollow space would be created, and the stability would be compromised. Ultimately, this meant that even if he didn't have to generate the element where it didn't exist, he had to manipulate much more of that element to achieve the desired effect. This had a drawback—the ground would rumble, signaling that Reynard was making a move.

Continuous use of elemental manipulation, even more so from a distance, was extremely taxing, not to mention doing it in many different places simultaneously. In other words, Reynard was starting to feel the burden of a surprisingly overdrawn fight. Even though only a few seconds had elapsed, it was still more than he had expected. Daniel was a surprisingly worthy opponent.

His choices had been almost instinctual and he clearly lacked experience fighting elemental purification cultivators, but all of his choices had been serviceable. If he had managed to step into elemental purification, he would have had the potential to stand up to Reynard on equal grounds. It was a pity that he lacked the talent.

Daniel looked at Reynard with a maddened look, patting his bottomless pouch and producing a seventh sword. This sword was a much higher grade than the others. Its scabbard was azure, and the hilt was of a spotless, pure-white. Daniel held the sword with his left hand, pointing it to the ground, allowing the scabbard to slide down.

It was a high-grade artifact. The first gift his father had ever given to him. A symbol of the hope his father had for his future. A symbol of his failure.

The round shield returned to his side, hovering around him. His bloodied right arm was swinging uselessly by his side as Daniel stood on guard.

Without a single word, Daniel shot forward, directly toward Reynard. He lost his swords because he was greedy. He did his best to try to save as many as possible, but maybe the right choice would have been to overwhelm Reynard with as many swords as possible. He could use the gaps Reynard would give to sneak attacks in the direction of the other Roaring Mountain Sect members and keep them in check. At the very least, he would have been able to protect his brother and he would take longer to get to his current disastrous state.

Now, however, it was too late for regrets.

He faced Reynard without fear in his eyes. He swung his sword from the right to the left, in an absurdly incompetent strike due to the openings he gave in the process. Still, he was far enough from Reynard to have an assurance of his strategy.

He took a step forward, and his sword moved. Reynard promptly took a single step back, letting the sword get past him before countering. Daniel's shield moved to intercept the attack, and Reynard's slash made the shield ram against Daniel's body. Daniel clenched his teeth and held his ground, raising his sword.

Aiming at Reynard's right shoulder, the sword came crashing down with surprising speed. Reynard leaned to his left, dodging the strike with ease. Seeing this, Daniel couldn't help but smile.

His shield came from the other side, slamming against Reynard's back, pushing him to his right. Daniel flicked his wrist, changing the direction of his strike. The downward slash turned into a slash from Daniel's left to his right.

Reynard was already too close to the sword to dodge. He could only face the strike head-on.

Clang!

Reynard raised his sword, blocking Daniel's slash. Daniel took a step forward, putting strength in his left arm, trying to push Reynard back as their swords interlocked in a struggle of power. It was a useless struggle that Daniel was fated to lose. He was originally weaker then Reynard, he was gravely injured, bleeding and was only using his left hand.

Reynard took a step forward, pushing Daniel back as he stomped the ground. The earth rumbled behind Daniel, but he didn't mind. He let himself be pushed back. As he took a step back, he let himself fall down. His previous useless right arm suddenly moved, wrapping around Reynard's nape like a snake. The round shield slammed Reynard's back, pushing him against Daniel before falling to the ground.

A single spike rose from the ground as Daniel fell down entangled with Reynard, aiming for his back. It was a thin, surprisingly sharp spike. It wasn't very large but looked incredibly solid, incredibly deadly as it mercilessly waited for its target to impale himself.

Puchi!

As Daniel fell, the spike sunk into his back. It pierced his skin, tore his muscles and ripped through his organs. With a light thud, Daniel's back hit the ground, and the spike's tip came out from his abdomen, as menacing as ever as Reynard fell in its direction, stuck in Daniel's embrace.

To Daniel's despair, however, Reynard's fall was cut short. He suddenly stopped moving, as if something had grabbed him. His chest hovered a few centimeters above the tip of the spike, and his dark eyes had nothing but coldness in them.

The earth rumbled again, and the spike retracted, painfully pulling out from Daniel's body. Daniel's right arm powerlessly slid away from Reynard's nape as the latter straightened his back. Both of his feet couldn't be seen, as they were buried deep into the ground.

"Nice try," Reynard said, patting his clothes and turning his back to Daniel. The earth squirmed below him, pushing him back up.

Daniel had a listless look on his face as he watched Reynard. He did all he could, he even tried to use Reynard's strike against him in an internecine outcome, but he had thoroughly lost. Blood started to seep from the open wound on his body, and a scarlet pool slowly formed beneath him, slowly expanding outwards like a blooming flower.

Reynard coldly watched his surroundings. Skylar, even if hurt, was somehow managing to push back an elemental purification cultivator and a body tempering cultivator with blasts of wind as she protected herself and Malia.

Evan was still unmoving, and Reynard was sure that even if he was alive, he couldn't be saved. A body tempering cultivator from the Roaring Mountain Sect was already facing the crippled boy that Evan had protected. It was a fight that would certainly end in a single exchange.

A bit further ahead, Orson was standing by an unconscious Karen, smashing one shield talisman after the other and trying to buy time as the remaining cultivators continuously broke past his defenses.

Joshua was still entangled with his enemies as if the fight had nothing to do with him. Reynard could only sneer. What a bastard.

He left Daniel behind without a second glance, running towards Jake. His face was slightly pale, but other than that he skillfully hid the signs of his exhaustion. Daniel Meyer was still a Meyer, in the end.

"You bastard! I will kill you!" Jake shouted with a weary and trembling voice as tears streamed down his pale face. He did his utmost to push himself up, but his arms were not moving.

"You won't," Reynard answered with a cold voice. "Dead people can't kill others."

He raised his arm, holding Mirage above Jake's head. He let out a long breath, and a white mist spewed out of his mouth. The sweat rolling down his face felt very cool and refreshing.

Reynard suddenly shivered. He gritted his teeth and slammed Mirage down with all of his strength, in a hurry. The light twinkled around the blade as it drew a straight path towards Jake's neck.

Clang!

The sword collided with something hard. Reynard's arm numbed due to the impact, and something slammed against his chest, throwing him back. He raised his eyes, and saw an ice dome in front of him, blocking his vision of Jake.

Reynard roared as if mad, raising the sword again. Thin lines of light slithered on the crystalline blade like snakes, covering it in a pale glow. Reynard's eyes were incredibly savage, and the air around him started to ripple, as the qi became restless. The layer of light on the blade turned incredibly bright and incredibly sharp as if it had turned into an edge.

He would shatter the ice wall apart, and blast Jake Meyer away with it if needed.

He pushed his arms down, putting all of his strength into it and... they didn't budge.

A terrifying pressure weighed down on the major plaza of the Hell Keeper's ity, locking all of the present in place. The ice dome Anna Hale had conjured fell apart, revealing the Noan River Sect members. The platform the Southern Flame Sect had summoned also started cracking, and they all fell down to the ground, motionless.

A woman could be seen hovering above the plaza, her silver clothes fluttering in the air as she slowly descended.

It was a woman with an abnormally pale face that gave her a strange appearance, even though her features were beautiful. Her eyes were hidden behind her dark-blue hair that contrasted strangely with her skin color and clothes.

Even though her eyes were hidden, it was clear that she was facing Reynard.

"Stand down," she ordered with a raspy voice.

DYING FIRE

I t was Selene, the first protector. Her voice thundered in everyone's ears, making some of the disciples squirm in pain. However, the woman didn't seem to mind one bit. She continued facing Reynard with her eyes hidden behind her dark-blue hair and her pale lips pursed together in a thin line.

Reynard's body trembled as he made an incredible effort to turn his head and meet her gaze. Mirage shook in his hands, making clanging noises as Reynard fought against the woman's suppression. With a ferocious look on his face, the crystalline sword moved a little bit in the direction of the ice barrier that protected Jake Meyer.

Boom!

With a deafening sound, something smashed at Reynard's chest like an invisible hammer, sending him flying back. His ferocious expression turned into one of pure animosity and defiance as he twisted his body mid-air and landed on his feet. The ground below him rippled wildly, as if he had fallen on a soft mattress, cushioning the impact of the landing and helping him keep his balance.

His eyes were blazing with a silent rage, and he was about to blow up. The moment that woman appeared he lost his chance to kill Jake Meyer. He had failed. He turned his head, looking at the wretched Daniel Meyer that lay on the floor, unmoving. That damn bastard had managed it in the end. The main reason for his success, however…

Reynard turned to look at the Noan River Sect members. Almost all of them were helpless under the pressure the woman was weighing on them, with only one exception. Anna Hale raised her head, facing Reynard.

They were very distant, but they could still clearly see each other. Reynard could see every single strand of Anna's luxurious black hair subtly moving alongside her breathing. He could see how her breathing was somewhat irregular, just like his own. A clear sign of exhaustion. Most of all, behind the billowing mist that covered her expression, he could feel it. He could feel the gaze she was giving him, he could feel the smile full of disdain she had on her face. He clenched his fist as his expression suddenly became blank.

His eyes also lost all form of emotion as he faced his fiancée.

Watching those changes this, Anna couldn't help but feel cold. A shiver ran down her back as Reynard looked at her with that blank expression. As she looked at his eyes, she felt as if she was being engulfed in an endless void, an infinite darkness permeated by a soul-chilling cold.

What she felt when looking at the young man in front of her wasn't the usual disdain, nor was it disgust over her fate or the begrudging respect she couldn't help but have for him. It was a more primal, instinctual emotion. For the first time, Reynard Stark scared her.

"I was very clear when I ordered you to stand down," Selene sneered.

Her pale lips twitched in displeasure as she saw the defiance in Reynard's gaze. It made her even more displeased when he refused to take the fall and landed on his feet after she threw him back.

"I don't remember ever being under your command," Reynard rebuked.

The woman's expression became grim as Reynard's words reached her. A sudden gust of wind wrapped around her, making her hair whip about and blowing it away from her face. For the first time, people could see the pair of eyes hiding behind her hair.

The world seemed to come to a sudden halt, and Reynard felt as if he was being sucked away into a different dimension, akin to when he traveled through a spatial tunnel. The color of his surroundings slowly drained away, and the only thing he could clearly make sense of was a glistening pair of eyes focused on him.

Looking at those eyes, he couldn't help but shiver. They were of a pale silver color and seemed to pulsate with a hypnotic light. What made his hair stand on end, however, was the fact that those eyes lacked pupils. They were like a pair of lifeless, ominous orbs that were slowly, inexorably, drawing him in.

Reynard gritted his teeth, struggling to maintain control over his thoughts. He closed his eyes, focusing solely on his divine sense as he fought back with everything he had. He felt his consciousness slowly slipping away into the illusion, even after all of his efforts to anchor himself to reality.

The first protector scoffed as Reynard finally went silent. That young man was still resisting her, even if he couldn't break free of her illusion by himself. She would have been pleasantly surprised by Reynard's resilience if the circumstances were different; after all, she had used enough strength to put people at the peak of elemental core into a trance. Nevertheless, she couldn't do much more to him, lest the situation turn even worse.

With a swipe of her hand, the Roaring Mountain Sect disciples were blasted away, being thrown in a corner of the plaza. The pressure weighing down on the disciples of the cardinal sects increased, holding them firmly in place, barely being able to make a sound.

The major plaza of Hell Keeper's City turned uncharacteristically silent, as if time had stopped when the woman made her move.

She slowly descended to the ground, looking at the disciples of the

Abyss Sect with a pained heart. Jake's body was filled with injuries of varying degrees. It looked like there wasn't a single inch of his body that didn't bear an injury. He was making hissing sounds as he breathed heavily, and more than likely one of his lungs had been punctured.

Treating him would take months at best, and even so, she wasn't sure if he could return to his previous condition, even with all of the resources the Abyss Sect had available. Just like that, it was very possible his future would be cut short.

The woman quietly landed by Jake's side, putting a hand on his shoulder and sending a gentle stream of qi into his body, suppressing his wounds. With her free hand, she took a white talisman that she promptly crushed, sending an emergency signal to the medical center and to Natasha Barnes.

Malia and Skylar were somewhat fine and a few weeks of treatment would let them return to top shape. Orson was completely unhurt, but the same couldn't be said about Karen. The wound on her shoulder was awful, and she had lost too much blood. Even with Natasha's skill, completely healing her would be hard.

She averted his gaze, and couldn't hide the pain in her eyes as she looked at the two stretched corpses near Jake. Evan had died an almost instantaneous death, lying motionless in a pool of his own blood, his body riddled with holes of all sizes. Abraham, on the other hand, had bled to death due to the injury that ripped his arm off. His expression was still full of shock and his intact hand was still firmly grasping what was left of his injured arm. His lifeless eyes were wide open and she could see the fear he showed in his final moments.

Seeing this, she couldn't help but send the still immobile Reynard a look full of killing intent.

The woman gently swiped a discrete white ring in her left hand, producing a blood-red pill. It was the highest grade of medicine she carried with her, and one of the few medicinal pills she possessed. Except for her sword and a few other possessions, she had long ago donated all she had to the sect, trying to keep it from falling further into an economic crisis.

All of the protectors had done the same, barely sustaining the sect for a few years. They could already barely sustain themselves selling the food rich in qi they raised in the sect. Soon enough they would have to start selling their services to the other sects, and maybe even mortal kingdoms in order to cover the Abyss Sect's expenses. When that day came, she wasn't sure how she would handle it.

Having to basically work as mercenaries to other sects and even mortals was the same as exposing themselves to danger. Their techniques and manuals would for sure leak on a scale they couldn't prevent, even if it took a very long time. By them, the sect would really have lost all hope of standing as one of the cardinal sects.

"My brother..." Jake croaked through gasps.

The woman didn't seem to mind the fact that Jake didn't greet or even thank her properly. He couldn't bother with formalities now, and neither could she.

The woman raised a brow as she finally looked at Daniel's direction. He was still alive, but she could tell with a glance that he was done for. He was agonizing on the floor with a huge hole on his abdomen, covered with dark blood. The spike that had impaled him had torn his stomach, liver, and parts of his intestines into shreds. Had he not tempered his body to the degree he had due to his father's backing at the time, he would have been dead long ago.

"There is no hope," the woman spoke in an emotionless voice, but she couldn't hide the pity in her eyes as she looked at Daniel.

"Please," Jake pleaded in a trembling voice.

The woman sighed gently, waving her hand, and Daniel was gently pulled to her side. She placed a hand on his chest, forcefully stopping his bleeding and buying him a few moments of life.

Jake tried to lift his upper body and sit down as he mumbled, "The pill."

The woman frowned. There was no way to heal Daniel's injuries. Medicine could only accelerate the healing speed of a person, not regenerate tissue. Her pill could stabilize Jake and prevent further complications, but it would have no effect on Daniel. She knew that, and so did Jake.

She lowered her gaze and saw Daniel's black eyes staring intently at her. No more words were necessary. She flicked her fingers, forcefully opening Jake's lips as the red pill flew directly into his mouth, melting into a bright liquid that soon went down his throat.

"I thank the first protector," Daniel gurgled with a genuine smile.

Selene gave Daniel a silent nod, not really knowing what to say. Realizing what had happened, Jake's expression transformed into one full of sorrow and misery as all that was left of his self-control finally crumbled and clear tears started falling from his eyes.

"Do you mind helping me a bit? There should be a silver wineskin here," Daniel requested, weakly motioning towards the bottomless pouch at his waist.

She hesitated for a moment, before sighing and reaching out to the bottomless pouch. She gently tapped it, producing a shiny silver wineskin that looked very expensive.

"Daniel..." Jake called weakly as even more tears streamed down his face.

Seeing his brother's sorrow, Daniel forced himself to smile, offering him the wineskin.

Jake grasped it as firmly as he could, but he couldn't help the shaking of his hands.

"I was saving it for your eighteenth birthday," Daniel said with difficulty.

Jake looked at him lethargically, his hands shaking uncontrollably.

"It cost me an arm and a leg, so don't drink it before then," Daniel joked as he saw his brother's eyes fill with tears.

Speaking was becoming harder and harder for him. He faltered. The warm stream of qi being injected in his meridians helped him compose himself, but he could feel a chilling cold slowly creeping up his body.

"Daniel, please, don't go," Jake pleaded to him desperately.

"It's alright," Daniel answered.

Death would come for all of those that failed to reach immortality. He couldn't be scared by it, because there was no way he would ever be able to escape it. He knew since long ago that, even if he was a cultivator, he was fated to die. If anything, he would choose how to go rather than when.

"I'm glad I managed to do something for you," he said with a warm smile. He would have turned to properly hug his brother, but he was already losing the sensitivity of his limbs.

Jake propped himself forward, leaning with difficulty and hugging his brother.

"The Abyss Sect shall remember your deeds today," Selene declared, finally breaking her silence.

Her tone was dull and stiff, almost as if she was following protocol. Her words might have sounded comforting for any other person, but not for Daniel.

"I don't give a fuck about the sect," he answered, slightly enraged.

He knew from the moment he attacked Reynard Stark that there was no way he would ever make it out alive. He had chosen this, and the Abyss Sect had never been on his mind.

He couldn't help but remember his conversation with the guardian when he was stuck during his climb of the mountain. The helplessness he felt then, and the choice he had made. In truth, Daniel's choice to face Reynard had been made there, when he decided he would die as a cultivator.

Still, could he truly say he had no regrets over it?

Maybe the guardian had been right, maybe Daniel truly could've been happy if he decided to give up cultivation and settle down on a peaceful life.

Daniel's eyes were wistful as he contemplated the choice he made. At the time, he had been under too much pressure, and his denial of the truth had blinded him. His despair had blinded him.

The truth was that there had always been someone like him, with whom he could share such fate; someone that could escape this miserable life. He had always known it, he simply never took the risk, afraid of what he could lose. Afraid of what he himself felt, because he knew deep down that maybe it was wrong, and that it wasn't reciprocal. He knew it was impossible, yet he couldn't help feeling that way. There was no way he could feel anything other than that for her.

In the end, there was simply no way someone like him could have what he wanted. He was a failure, and he always desired what was beyond his reach.

His vision started fading, and he felt his thoughts slipping away. He couldn't feel his body anymore, and a piercing chill was making its way to his very soul. Suddenly, in the middle of the darkness, he saw a flash of gold, and a beautiful pair of green eyes stared at him.

Yes, he had never been alone. The guardian had indeed seen right through him, he had been absolutely right. Daniel had been too scared to face the truth, too scared to look inwards and accept what drove him.

Unknowingly, Daniel smiled. A name made its way to his mind, piercing through the darkness of his consciousness like a beacon of light and giving him some clarity of mind before the darkness fully took over.

Becca...

Pak!

The wineskin fell, spilling dark wine on the ground. Its contents slowly flowed out, soaking the clothes that were already tainted with red. The man they belonged to didn't move anymore.

In the major plaza of Hell Keeper's City, the unabated silence was broken by Jake's sobs as he tightly hugged his brother's body.

Selene quietly took her hand off Daniel's back and lightly shook her head as she heard Jake sobbing. He was a cultivator and, more than that, an inheriting disciple. He should know better than anyone how things worked in their world.

Such a display was proof that he was human, but also proof of his immaturity. Death was unavoidable in the path they trod. If one didn't steel his heart to it, the suffering it brought would never stop. Being an immortal might mean that one would be far from death's reach, but the journey to immortality inevitably meant having death as a companion.

Selene had no idea how things had gotten to this point, but something made her restless. Sect Master Borgin was nowhere to be seen, and nor was any elder at all. There had been too many coincidences.

A spirit beast outbreak in the north that required two protectors and most of the high elders to act had dealt an almost crippling blow to the Abyss Sect's reaction time to any crisis. Even worse, had she not interrupted her reclusion due to the emergency signal an elder had sent, she would never have made it in time to save Jake's life.

Even so, she arrived too late to salvage the situation that led to this. As a result, the Abyss Sect had suffered enormous losses, and how the surviving disciples would fare from now on was unknown.

She raised her eyes to the midst of the Roaring Mountain Sect disciples. There, a red-haired boy was lying on the ground with a short spear by his side. Selene's brows furrowed as she swept her gaze through the battlefield carefully. From Drace's body to the unmoving Reynard that was covered in sweat due to his resistance to her illusion. A picture slowly started to form on her mind, but its implications were even above what she could deal with alone.

She suddenly heard the rustling of leaves and hurriedly turned her eyes to the Ashen Heart tree. There was no wind that would blow within the city, yet the branches of the tree were restless as if a fierce gale was blowing at them. The enormous silvery leaves waved nonstop, and the tree branches slowly started to darken.

The hellish red curtain of light in the trunk of the tree, the gateway to the Hellblaze Secret World, was flickering nonstop. The first protector's eyes widened as she saw this scene. The Ashen Heart tree was inexorably linked to the Hellblaze Secret World. If it was acting like that, maybe the secret world itself was becoming unstable.

She hastily stood up, leaving Jake's side and making her way to the Ashen Heart tree, trying to figure out what exactly was happening.

Boom!

The ground quaked violently. Gravel and debris flew everywhere as a huge hole appeared in the middle of the plaza, almost swallowing the Storm Peak Sect disciples that hastily retreated.

"Anna!" an aged voice shouted.

A woman dressed in blue with silver hair made her way from underground, followed closely by a man with a shaved head dressed in red. She looked on in horror at the scene and hastily moved to the remains of the ice dome near the Ashen Heart tree. The bald man rushed to the side of the Southern Flame disciples sprawled on the floor, and let out a breath of relief as he saw no one was hurt.

Next, a woman in green robes shot out of the hole, rushing to the side of the Storm Peak disciples. She wasted no time with formalities or assessing the situation. With a wave of her hand, the silver spirit vessel of the Storm Peak Sect flew over.

Following the faster high elders, the accompanying elders of the cardinal sects soon emerged, hastily approaching the members from their sects.

As the ten disciples and the elder climbed onboard, Veronica, the high elder of the Storm Peak Sect, turned her head and looked at the Abyss Sect's first protector for a moment. Without a word, she too jumped atop the spirit vessel. With a rumble, it rose from the ground in a sudden movement, blowing dust everywhere as it turned into a blur and sped off into the distance.

Sarah was left speechless, but couldn't waste time with trivialities. She lightly waved her hand, dispersing the pressure that was binding the Noan River disciples down with a deep frown on her aged face.

"What happened?" Sarah questioned after confirming that all of the Noan River disciples were safe.

Eli took a step forward as he started talking.

"Well, the Abyss Sect—"

A fierce coldness enveloped him. His face paled as he looked at the

381

source of the cold. Anna Hale had her head turned to his direction, and he didn't need to see her face to guess the expression she had. He promptly shut his mouth, taking a step back.

"Someone invaded the Hellblaze Secret World. They stole all of the contents of the vault and are currently engaged in a fight with the Abyss Sect's sect master," Anna said, trying to stay brief.

Sarah's expression darkened instantly as she heard Anna's report.

"What happened here?"

"The Roaring Mountain Sect and the Abyss Sect had a falling out. Joshua, from the Abyss Sect, made the first move," Anna replied, unphased by the unfortunate events.

"The details can wait. We are leaving."

Sarah closed her eyes for a moment. She half expected a situation like this when a disciple of the Roaring Mountain Sect died, but the situation was even worse than what she predicted. This matter would be completely out of her hands.

"Wait!" an angry voice suddenly interrupted her.

A man dressed in gold emerged from the gaping hole. His hair was a mess and he had a fierce expression on his face. On his right hand, a saber covered in blood gave him a terrifying appearance. From the gaps of the bloodstains in the saber, an eerie purple light shone, given the saber an even more horrendous appearance.

He gave a cursory glance through the plaza, and his eyes locked into the sorrowful Jake Meyer. His expression turned blank for a moment before he saw Reynard, who was still frozen in place, and a strange glint flashed in his eyes.

"Are you really going to leave just like that?" Leonard asked as his face distorted into a mask of hatred. "The Abyss Sect set us up, put all of the disciples we brought at risk and you're simply going to leave without demanding an explanation?"

"This is not a matter we can deal with, Leonard. It will be up for our sect masters to decide how to act." Baldwin answered.

His teeth were clenched and his muscles were tense. He was clearly unwilling to say those words.

"This is far from enough!" Leonard said as he turned into a blur, appearing in the midst of the Roaring Mountain Sect disciples.

"Who is responsible for this?" he asked in a sharp, authoritative voice.

A Roaring Mountain disciple quietly pointed to the ground by Leonard's feet. Leonard slowly lowered his gaze with a chilling look in his eyes. By his feet, Joshua was slowly trying to stand up. His clothes were in tatters and his body was full of bruises and lacerations. He was clearly not a member of the Roaring Mountain Sect.

"Here, I will help you," Leonard said with a murderous expression as he grabbed Joshua by the neck, raising him in the air with one hand.

Joshua started gasping for breath as his face slowly turned as red as his hair and he tried to pull away from the iron-like grip that was slowly crushing his neck. His feet dangled uselessly in the air as his hands powerlessly hit the arm holding him above the ground.

"Put the boy down," Selene demanded.

"Don't worry, I won't kill him. I will just make him pass out and take him to the Roaring Mountain Sect. We'll deal with him there," Leonard said with a strange smile on his face. "I'll be thorough with the punishment."

"This is your last warning. Put him down," she repeated.

Leonard didn't budge. A gentle breeze swept past the first protector, slowly ascending from the tip of her toes to her neck and making her clothes flutter. Seeing the veiled threat, Leonard's face turned grim. He had no real way to counter Selene's illusions if she went all out.

"Fine," Leonard said with clenched teeth. His eyes suddenly locked into the Ashen Heart tree, and a fierce light shone in his eyes. "Have it your way."

His arm moved like lighting, throwing the already helpless Joshua in the air as if he was nothing more than a doll. Selene promptly raised her hands, trying to stop Joshua's fall. As the qi gathered at her command, the air rippled. Just as the qi was about to reach Joshua, however, It suddenly froze in place.

The first protector's eyes widened as she realized someone had wrestled away her control over the qi. She could only helplessly watch as Joshua flew through the air in a precise arc, landing on the flickering curtain of light and disappearing from her sight.

"Let's go," Leonard said hurriedly, pointing a finger at Reynard and finally releasing him from his constraints.

As the illusion was suddenly broken, Reynard took a moment to recover. His legs almost gave in and he nearly lost his balance. His expression darkened as he fiercely stomped the ground, making the ground below him ripple and help him recover.

Leonard brought the Roaring Mountain Sect's spirit vessel to their side, carefully picking up Drace's body as he jumped on board. One by one, the disciples joined him.

Reynard was the last one to climb onboard. He slowly turned around as the spirit vessel rose, its pulsating purple glow casting ominous shadows on his face. He looked at the first protector's face with a ferocious expression. She quietly sustained his gaze with a blank face, not showing the anger nor the disdain she felt.

"I'll rip those eyes out of your face the next time we meet," Reynard said with a blank expression as the purple spirit vessel slowly turned away.

"The Abyss Sect can just wait for the outcome of this ridiculous stunt," Baldwin declared as he saw the Roaring Mountain Sect's spirit vessel disappearing from sight.

He looked at the Ashen Heart tree with a frown. It was unknown what was happening inside, but he wasn't willing to abandon the youths of his sect to try to retrieve the treasures. For starters, he didn't know if this was all an act and Lars Borgin was the mastermind behind it. Entering the Hellblaze Secret World would mean taking an unnecessary risk.

Baldwin looked at Sarah, and from her expression, he knew she had similar thoughts. This was no time to make a gamble, not when they were potentially in enemy territory. He gave a sigh, shaking his head.

"I hope you're ready for the consequences," Sarah sassed, glaring at Selene. "Considering its history, losing the Abyss Sect would be a tragedy. As shameful as it would be, let's hope the Abyss Sect will only lose its place among the cardinal sects."

With that, she turned around to leave, joining the Noan River Sect members in their glistening spirit vessel. The first protector couldn't find the words she needed to say. The Abyss Sect would face an unprecedented crisis.

Selene quietly watched as the remaining spirit vessels rose from the ground and left as she tried to stabilize the still uncared disciples of the Abyss Sect. She couldn't help but feel worried. She could only hope Lars Borgin would return soon so they could start taking the proper measures as soon as possible.

Her expression became grim. Borgin's status was unknown, and she couldn't enter the Hellblaze Secret World until the medical staff arrived to tend to the wounded. Worst of all, the second protector wasn't answering her voice transmissions and her emergency signals. Either Lawrence Meyer wasn't receiving them or he was willingly ignoring them.

Eh, ignoring his status as a protector...What could such a man consider more important than the son he was so proud of?

Shaking thought from her mind, Selene swept the major plaza with her divine sense, finally noticing a crucial detail: there were only eight disciples of the Abyss Sect present, including the dead. Joshua had been thrown into the Hellblaze Secret World, so that made nine.

There was still someone missing alongside the Abyss Sect's spirit vessel.

❃ ❃ ❃

The sun had already set, and a pale waxing moon hung in the night sky in a cruel grin. Rebecca Skoller had a terrible feeling as she contemplated the sky, and somehow she felt sorrowful. Something was weighing down her chest, and she felt a terrible sense of loss.

"Calm down," she said to herself as her chest heaved up and down and she started feeling nervous. "Everything is fine."

She tightly clenched the red necklace under the white sheets of her bed. That ominous premonition she had didn't go away, and her grip turned tighter, making the necklace almost break her skin.

Suddenly, something caught her attention, and she hurriedly turned to the door of her house. Her green eyes blazed with a strange fire and her nervous expression suddenly turned into one of sheer coldness as she probed outwards with her divine sense and realized what was happening outside.

The front door of the house creaked lightly as someone walked in, taking unhurried steps inside. The steps paused for a moment in the living room, as if the person had taken a small break to look closely at something. Rebecca's expression was grim as the temperature in the house became oddly cool.

A white mist started blowing out of her mouth with each breath the figure took, and Rebecca couldn't help but tremble due to the cold.

"How embarrassing. To think I wouldn't even be able to keep myself warm in front of you," she said in an emotionless voice, raising her eyes to the door of her room, that was now open.

"It is not surprising at all, considering you can't even circulate the qi in your body anymore if you don't want to die," a cold, scornful voice answered.

"It would still be better than having to stand you," she said, looking deeply into a pair of black eyes as dark as the night. Eyes awfully similar to the ones her husband had, but also very different.

"What do you want, Lawrence?"

A fierce gale blew in the night as a shadow streaked in the sky, blocking the bright stars that riddled it. Its speed was immeasurable, but for the boy atop the shadow, it was still not enough.

Amon was incredibly nervous as he rode the spirit vessel he had stolen from the Abyss Sect. He was confused, he was scared and, most of all, he was incredibly angry. After being thrown out of the Hellblaze Secret World, Lya had dragged him to the spirit vessel and quickly flew away.

He didn't need to ask where they were going or why—his life in the Abyss Sect was over. He could only hope they could escape fast enough.

Behind him, Lya carefully controlled the spirit vessel in complete silence. She could feel Amon's mood, and she didn't know exactly what to say. For now, she could only make haste for the Outer Ring of the Outer Sect, get Rebecca and leave the Abyss Sect as quickly as possible.

Hati, the guardian of the Hellblaze Secret World was right. The best she could do was stay away from the sect. There were traitors in their midst. Not only that, Lloyd Kressler and Oura knew of her presence, and Amon was now a target. Leaving and laying low was the best option.

Still, what could she say to him? What reasons could she give for hiding the truth? How could she explain to him what was truly happening?

How would she explain to him about Dale Loray? About Alexei? About Arthur Royce?

How could she explain to him what she had done?

Lya was confused. She didn't want to believe Dale Loray was alive and that he was behind everything that had happened. She didn't want to believe it because this meant that Dale Loray would certainly come after her.

She was scared. She was terrified of what would happen if Dale Loray ever managed to get his hands on her. Did he want to fulfill Alexei's obsession? Did he want to do something else entirely?

Anger filled her to the brim. She hated herself for failing to help Hati. She was angry at herself for not being able to stop Oura. She was angry at herself for having to run from the fight.

Nevertheless, there was hope. Hati had given Amon the Vermilion Token. With that, they could take refuge in the Southern Flame Sect and plead for help from the Vermilion Queen. She would certainly abide, as this matter was as related to her as it was to Lya. They could then contact the other cardinal sects and prepare countermeasures.

"Amon," Lya called for him with a soft voice, somewhat hesitant.

The boy slowly turned to face her, his ashen hair whipping about in the wind. Once Lya saw the gleam he had in his golden eyes, however, her heart trembled. What she saw in his eyes was unwillingness, and a fair share of conflicting emotions. What made her restless, however, was that, for the first time since their met, she could clearly see distrust in his eyes.

In a dry, emotionless tone he said, "Once we pick my mother up and leave the sect, we'll have a talk. Until then, don't speak."

He turned his back to her and tightly held Windhowler.

✽ ✽ ✽

"You want to know what I want, Rebecca?" Lawrence Meyer asked with a sneer. "I'm here to capture traitors of the Abyss Sect. I will patiently wait for your son to arrive to pick you up and try to escape. We can chat a bit until then."

Hearing his words, Rebecca stood in silence for a moment. Her weakened body trembled lightly due to the cold, but her eyes never wavered.

"Even if Lloyd did something, you have no proof."

She couldn't hide her uncertainty. The way Lawrence was acting gave her a bad feeling.

"Oh, I have proof. You see, we have plenty of witnesses that say your son was directly involved with Lloyd entering the Hellblaze Secret World."

Rebecca's sickly face lost all color. As she looked deep into Lawrence's eyes, she knew he was telling the truth, but that still didn't make any sense. Her son had no contact with Lloyd, and Lya was accompanying him. How could someone frame him under such conditions?

Lawrence approached the bed, leaning closer to Rebecca. He extended his hands to her, holding her head in place with his cold fingers as his eyes neared increasingly closer to hers. Rebecca was utterly disgusted. She knew that Lawrence would enjoy seeing that, but she still failed to keep her emotions in check.

"Truth be told, I would be here even without any proof, but who could guess that you were all traitors, Rebecca?" Lawrence spoke with a carefree tone. "I'm actually very satisfied. This way, no one can say I was in the wrong for killing you and your son. I could already have an excuse due to the suspicions I had, but having Jake being hurt and that trash being killed is more than enough to justify my actions."

"For that, I thank you from the bottom of my heart," he said, finally releasing her.

"D-Daniel... is dead?" Rebecca stammered, her eyes growing wide with shock.

Her face paled even more, and she grasped the sheets of her bed tightly. No matter what she did, she couldn't stop trembling. However this time, she wasn't trembling due to the cold.

"Yes, he is. My heart aches because of it," Lawrence said with an emotionless voice as he raised his right hand.

The scarlet sleeves of his robes slid down, revealing a silver chain with two blood-red beads attached to it. There was a single broken piece barely hanging on to it as well.

"As a father, I can't help but feel the pain of losing my firstborn."

His words made her sick. How could a human being fall so low? As much as she despised Lawrence, she never thought he would turn out even worse than Lloyd.

"What a pathetic man you are, Lawrence. Your firstborn is dead. Your second son, which you claim to be the pride of your life, is injured, and possibly just underwent the most terrifying and painful experience of his life yet here you are, speaking to me, without a care in the world," Rebecca fumed.

She couldn't bear it anymore. Her sadness was overwhelming her.

"Were you just lurking around my house, waiting for a signal? Do you truly hate Lloyd that much?" Rebecca asked with a wry smile.

Pearly tears were slowly streaming down her face as she spoke, and she couldn't hide the pain and the sorrow in her eyes.

"You would even recognize Daniel as your firstborn just so you can vent your hate for Lloyd?"

"Lloyd Kressler is the man I'll do anything in my power to kill. The humiliation he made me suffer and this hatred he planted deep into me... I will pay it back tenfold."

Rebecca felt a part of her die. This was what Daniel amounted to him, an excuse to throw a childish tantrum to seek revenge on the man that defeated him. She didn't want to believe that Daniel was truly dead, and she didn't want to accept that Lawrence would act like this.

Somehow, she still hoped deep down for Daniel to be accepted someday, even if she knew it would never happen. He deserved better, and now he is dead. Worst of all, his death will be the excuse the man that shunned him would use to kill the people Daniel wanted to protect.

"It's such a pity... You're far too emotional. You had everything you needed to become a legendary figure in this sect. You had a moniker even before you became a protector, but look at you. Becoming a cripple because of your failure of a son, and now crying because of my failure of a son," Lawrence said with a sneer. "I guess no matter how talented one is, the mindset is still primordial for a cultivator."

Rebecca's tears slowly stopped falling as she closed her eyes and controlled her breathing. Her hands stopped trembling, and she entered into a state of serenity.

Yes, Lawrence was right. He wasn't human anymore. He was a cultivator.

Rebecca focused. Lawrence felt a formless wave of divine sense washing over him and spreading its way out of the house.

"Hmm... Three elemental core elders surrounding the house from the north, east and west... I guess you're waiting to ambush my son as soon as he appears," Rebecca muttered to herself, opening her eyes and looking at Lawrence with disdain. "Were you really that enthusiastic in making sure we wouldn't somehow escape?"

"Even though I'm dealing with a cripple and a waste, someone else might barge in. I won't allow that to happen," Lawrence said, not bothered in the least by her words.

"Why do you think someone else needs to barge in?" Rebecca asked.

"You should remember very well how I paid back my grudges, shouldn't you?" Rebecca asked, giving Lawrence a cold smile. For the first time in years, he felt a shiver running down his spine.

Rebecca waved her shriveled hands, and a powerful blast of qi hit Lawrence's chest, sending him a few steps back.

"A pointless struggle," Lawrence said with an annoyed voice as he glared at Rebecca.

Cling!

A clear clinging sound rang from the living room, and something whistled through the air, rapidly reaching Rebecca's room. A black blur streaked through Lawrence's vision, and his face fell as he recognized what it was.

The blur halted as soon as it reached Rebecca, transforming into a pitch-black sword. Rebecca looked at it with sorrowful eyes before extending her right hand and unsheathing the curved sword. Looking at the scene, Lawrence's eyes gleamed.

"It is better that way," Lawrence professed as he looked at Rebecca. A fierce smile slowly made its way into his lips. "I was afraid the White Flame had truly gone out."

With a roar, white flames slithered along Raven's blade, exuding a terrifying heat. Lawrence's smile widened when he saw the intermingling shadows and light dancing in Rebecca's face as the flames on the blade flickered. The fire that blazed in her green eyes was even wilder than the flames dancing on the black blade.

Rebecca Skoller, the White Flame of the Abyss, raised Raven. Lawrence Meyer, the Scarlet Frost, extended his hands to the saber by his waist.

A deafening explosion rang out and splinters flew everywhere as the shabby house disappeared from sight.

In its place, a white flower furiously bloomed.

The throne room of the Abyss Sect was uncharacteristically silent. A man dressed in loose red robes covered with golden embroideries was sitting on the charred throne, and Lars was kneeling respectfully in the middle of the room.

The faint light that glowed from the walls was dancing without rhythm or form as the magma walls churned. A few decades had passed, but Lars Borgin was still incredibly nervous every time he had to stand in this room and speak with the man sitting on the throne. No matter how much stronger Lars became, that overwhelming pressure never ceased or weakened.

He could never grasp the strength of the Abyss's Sect founder and sect master when he was a kid, and he still couldn't now. It was as if the man sitting on the throne was an ocean of energy and power. The deeper Lars dove into it, the stronger the pressure wrapping around him became. No matter how much Lars probed, all he could find was unending power and increasingly horrifying darkness that hid the depths of the man in front of him.

"I honestly can't believe it," a gentle, sorrowful voice broke the silence. The man sitting in the throne gave a sight, and Lars, kneeling on the floor lowered his head even more.

"Explain to me what you're talking about. What happened?" Arthur Royce asked, gripping tightly the armrest of the throne. His voice was still as gentle as ever, but there was an uncharacteristic uneasiness in it as he spoke.

"I'm not too sure myself, sir sect master," Lars answered. His brown hair was covered in sweat due to his nervousness, and confusion could be seen in his clear eyes. "When I arrived it was already too late."

"The conditions of the body?" Arthur asked this as he moved a bit in his throne, somewhat restless.

"A single strike. Nolan died instantly," Lars reported with a bitter taste in his mouth. "Considering the direction he was facing, the fact that he had a sword in hand and that the trees behind him were destroyed, I don't think it was a sneak attack."

"Go on."

"Nolan knew someone was going to attack him and he even had the chance to draw his weapon. Not only that, he was clearly facing the attacker. Even with all that he couldn't even react when the attacker made his move," the kneeling Lars concluded with a calm voice. Nevertheless, he couldn't help shaking somewhat.

"Tell me something, Lars. In such conditions, would you have done something similar?" Arthur calmly asked as he coldly gazed at Lars Borgin from above.

"Sir, I would never—"

"This isn't what I'm asking."

"No, sir. Even if Nolan gave me the chance, I would never have been able to take him down in a single strike," Lars said honestly. He couldn't help but tremble as he remembered the scene he saw in the Western Continent.

Lars knew Nolan Skoller too well, and he also knew how inferior he was in comparison. If Nolan was taken down with an absurdly strong body and an even more ridiculous control over fire, he couldn't even imagine the strength of the murderer.

"How was the state of the trees behind him? You mentioned the after-effects of the attack destroying them," Arthur questioned in an increasingly cold voice, making Lars shiver.

"All of the trees affected seemed to have been cut in two. This phenomenon manifested from Nolan's location to about one hundred meters behind him," Lars answered with a frown. It was an utterly absurd scene.

"What is your take on that?" Arthur asked.

"It's very confusing, sir," he answered honestly. "I can't believe that the after-effect of an attack that could take down a fully prepared Nolan Skoller would only spread a hundred meters."

"Indeed. What would be the explanation for that, Lars?"

"Either a different attack hit the trees, or the murderer's control over the elements is on a level that I can't begin to grasp."

This was the best theory he managed to develop after analyzing the facts. In truth, he had no idea how such a scene came to be.

"Control over the elements, eh?" Arthur repeated in a low voice, almost as if he was scoffing at himself. "Such a pity. His child wasn't even born yet," he sighed.

Arthur shook his head and his red hair spilled over his shoulders, and the golden streaks gleamed momentarily.

Finally gathering the courage he needed, Lars spoke again. This time he had a question for the sect master.

"What was Nolan doing in the Western Continent?"

It was a question that had been bothering him ever since he heard the news. Given the condition of his family and his position, leaving them alone to live on another continent was a choice Lars couldn't understand.

"He was investigating something on my orders," Arthur answered dismissively.

"I see," Lars said in an emotionless voice. His disappointment, however, didn't go unnoticed.

"Raise your head, Lars," Arthur commanded with a sigh. He was truly very tired, and he was starting to become tense.

"Tell me, if you were sent on a mission that you knew might end up with your death, would you have done it for the sake of the sect?" Arthur asked, looking at Lars with his bright red eyes as if trying to peer into his very soul.

"Yes, sir," Lars answered without hesitation. "The Abyss Sect is all I have."

"Even though you had a family that relied on you? Even though you were about to have a daughter?" Arthur asked, his eyes sharpening as he leaned forward.

"Yes, sir."

"How can you say that if you have never even married? What if your mind changes once you become a father?" Arthur pressed on, still not satisfied.

"That will hardly happen, sir. After my parents died, I decided that nothing would stand between my cultivation and me. A family would only hold me back," Lars admitted.

"That was sixty years ago, Lars. Do you still feel that way?"

"Yes," Lars nodded his head, his expression serious. "The Abyss Sect is my everything, sir. My climb to the peak lies here and nowhere else. My grandparents died so this place could exist, and my parents died happily here. There is no way I would feel any other way."

"I see," Arthur closed his eyes. "This sense of belonging, this unwavering loyalty... a sect master's duty is to guarantee every single disciple has it. A sect master must know the disciples of his sect, and he must give them reasons to die without a doubt in the name of their sect.

"Cultivators value their lives more than anything, so achieving such a thing is quite hard. You need intelligence. You need to understand others. You need to be able to feel empathy."

Arthur gave Lars a piercing glance, carefully reading his reactions. Lars listened intently, not daring to move a muscle or give any sign of being uncomfortable or distracted.

"At least that is what people believe, and as such you must convince others that you have such qualities," Arthur added as a very discrete smile full of disdain made its way into his lips. "What is truly important is the strength to maintain your position and charisma to enthrall those around you," he continued, still using the same serious tone. His eyes shone with a strange light, and a hint of scorn appeared on his expression. "If you make good use of charisma, you can gather allies, and they can make up for the things you lack.

"A sect master is nothing but an illusion, Lars. What exists, in reality, is just a single man strong enough to protect his ideals. A man willing to make use of anyone and make any and all sacrifices in the name of such ideals. Nevertheless, he must learn to give back.

"This is what a sect truly is. A figure bearing the ideals and illusions of others as they help him accomplish his. This is why I will give Nolan's family all of the support I can. He died for the sect, and so I must repay him," he concluded, and his face went blank. "Do you understand?"

"I do, sir," Lars answered softly.

He already knew that. He had lived enough to understand how the world was.

"Very well. From this moment forward, you'll be the inheriting disciple of the Abyss Sect, and I will teach you everything you must know in order to become a proper sect master after I retire," Arthur said simply as if it was nothing much.

Lars lowered his head again, giving Arthur a deep bow and hiding the expression he was making. He felt both happy and conflicted. He knew that he had not been the first choice for the position, and now he would never be able to truly prove himself worthy. The blow that had taken Nolan Skoller's life had also taken away his chances of proving his value.

"Know this, Lars," Arthur said, slowly rising from the throne and descending the golden steps as he walked towards his successor. "Loyalty is absolutely necessary. Without it, the sect will fall apart because the illusion will be broken. If there ever comes a day when a disciple of your sect betrays you, then you failed."

* * *

Lars Borgin gasped for breath loudly as he supported his body with Crimsonroar. The ground below his feet was so compacted and dense that the sword's tip couldn't pierce it even after Borgin supported his full weight on it.

Still, the sword trembled nonstop. The shadows squirming in the walls were immensely agitated, and a loud rumble echoed. Without the guardian linked to the core array, the artificial dimension would start to fall apart. Hati was doing his best to try to stabilize the Hellblaze Secret World while pushing Oura back with Nemeus, but his energy was rapidly draining.

Deep gashes covered Lars' body, and bones poked through the gaps in his flesh. His blood flowed nonstop from the wounds. In front of him, Lloyd Kressler cocked his head, looking at Borgin with a dark interest in his cold eyes. He waved the green sword in his hand around, sending blasts of light with each strike and causing increasingly deeper gashes to appear on the ground below his feet.

Surrounding him, threads of flowing light floated freely, mixing with the dust and the gales that wrapped around his body.

"I expected more, Lars," Lloyd said with disdain.

Borgin didn't answer. He couldn't answer. His vision was slowly fading away, and he knew he was about to lose consciousness. He made an effort to maintain his expressionless face, but deep down he was shaken. He couldn't understand how Lloyd had attained such power in that short of a time.

Nemeus and Hati were still facing the strange entity, but Lars couldn't keep up with their fight anymore.

"Just give up already," Oura huffed through a muffled laugh. "Even though you both have a piece of Arthur's soul, you're a few millennia short of being able to hold your own against me."

As the voice finished speaking, the air in the hall suddenly became completely still, as if time had frozen. Borgin couldn't move anymore, nor could he spread his divine sense. A powerful force had overtaken control of the whole hall.

Her sudden outburst of divine sense had been enough to suppress Nemeus and Hati for a moment, allowing her to interact with the hidden core array, and what she sensed made her seethe.

"Well would you look at that... You thought you could fight me while holding this dimension together? Maybe you could have managed to do so if that bitch was still around. Too bad you sent her away."

"Oura, don't!" Hati bellowed, exhausted.

"Silence!" she ordered, and the world seemed to overturn.

Hati could feel each one of the smaller dimensions contained within the Hellblaze Secret World collapsing into themselves, creating a wild vortex of chaotic time and shattered space. One by one, the diverse areas used in the Trial of the Will, the peripheral parts of the Hellblaze Secret World, were destroyed in Oura's rage. Soon enough, the forest and the mountain range of the Trial of the Mind and Heart shattered and were lost into the infinite void.

Something lashed back against his soul, and Hati felt his divine sense breaking apart as his connection with the Hellblaze Secret World was finally lost.

"You dare show off your measly knowledge in the Natural Laws of Space in front of me? You think you would have any chance if I didn't feel like having a fight after such a long time? The four guardian beasts trembled when they heard my name—what can a vagrant godbeast like you do in front of me?" Oura's poisonous voice was the last thing Hati could hear before a boundless surge of divine sense wrapped around him. Hati's soulstone dimmed considerably as it flew towards Lloyd.

"End this already," Oura ordered, turning her attention to Nemeus.

"Very well," Lloyd said, slowly approaching Borgin.

His dark hair fluttered as he walked, and he was clearly unaffected by the power that was binding the hall. Lloyd slowly raised the sword in his hand, never taking his eyes away from Borgin, as if expecting to see his expression change.

"I've always hated the way you went about doing things," Borgin said in a weary voice. His expression was still completely blank, but he couldn't hide his exhaustion.

"Hah! Do you really have the right to say that?"

"Oh?"

Lloyd became motionless. He turned his head away and locked eyes with the flickering curtain of red light that shone in one of the walls of the hall.

The light started to churn and revolve, and soon enough a small figure

393

appeared from it, crashing loudly on the ground and rolling for a few meters before stopping.

"Ugh, damn Leonard. That bastard really took his acting seriously," the newcomer said, standing up with difficulty.

His clothes were in tatters, and his red hair was a mess. A deep mark could be seen around his neck as if someone had squeezed it tightly. He was in a sorry state.

"What are you doing here?" Lloyd questioned, raising a brow.

"A slight change of plans. The first protector appeared and Jake Meyer is still alive," the youth said, cracking his neck with a clearly annoyed expression.

"Huh, Reynard failed?" Lloyd asked in a surprisingly light tone as if he was really satisfied.

"Joshua!?" Borgin asked in shock as he realized who the youth was.

Joshua raised his head, looking at Borgin with surprise on his face as if he had just realized he was there. Then, he frowned.

"Why is he not dead?" Joshua asked, turning to face Lloyd. "I didn't think it would take that long."

"We were about to work on that, dear," Oura crooned.

Despite that, Joshua could still feel annoyance hidden in her tone as if someone had spoiled her usually playful mood.

Borgin couldn't find the words he wanted to say. No, he didn't want to say anything. There really wasn't anything to be said.

He gripped Crimsonroar tightly, and his body started trembling as he forced himself to move. Nemeus roared from somewhere, and Borgin could finally move. As if he was trying to walk on a swamp, he slowly forced his way forward, raising Crimsonroar.

All of the qi in his body slowly started gathering in his dantian. He would condense all of the energy he could and then detonate his elemental core, taking them all out with him on the ensuing explosion.

"As if I would let you."

A sweet, but poisonous voice made its way to Borgin's mind.Suddenly, he was frozen in place again. A foreign energy made its way into his body, slowly slithering through his meridians and reaching his dantian. To Borgin's horror, he felt his dantian being sealed away, and he could only watch in shock as the qi slowly dispersed from his body.

"Doing stuff like that is dangerous, you know?" Oura sneered, reveling in the despair and hopelessness showing in Borgin's face.

"Oura!" Nemeus roared, but he was ultimately helpless in front of her.

"This is ridiculous," Lloyd voice woke Borgin from his stupor. He raised his head, and saw Lloyd brandishing the green sword in his hand.

Time slowed down as Borgin faced the incoming blade. He watched helplessly as the sharp tip prickled the skin of his chest, slowly sinking into his muscles. He felt his flesh tearing as the sword sunk deeper hitting his ribs. He felt it grinding at his bones, finally carving its way through them and hitting his right lung. He felt is making its way out, in a process that seemed to be as slow as it was painful.

The green tip made its way out of Lars Borgin though his back, and he coughed. Dark blood seeped down his lips, through his chin and fell on his already bloodied clothes. A strange roaring blocked his hearing, and he could barely make out Nemeus shouting somewhere far away.

Before he realized it, he was facing the ceiling. He didn't even remember when he fell down. Nevertheless, he still wanted to fight. He raised his head with difficulty as the roaring in his ears became deafening. He realized his hands were empty. Crimsonroar was nowhere to be seen.

He moved his head, and saw the silver curtain of light on the other side of the room slowly decreasing in size, as if it was folding unto itself. It didn't take long for it to completely disappear.

The shadows that had covered the walls faded away, exposing the mix of red and gold that were their original colors. Borgin couldn't feel the quaking of the ground anymore, he could only faintly feel the world around him crumbling. The roaring in his ears was also starting to fade away.

Borgin finally realized he was hearing his own blood flowing through his body. Not that it mattered anyway.

As the world collapsed around him, he remembered his master's words. The words of the man whose shoes he never managed to fill. The words of the man he had strived to be, but failed.

Yes. He had utterly failed.

❉ ❉ ❉

In the major plaza, the tremors were becoming increasingly stronger.

The first protector and the newly arrived staff from the medical center watched in shock as the Ashen Heart tree started to tremble, and the curtain of light between its trunks started to fade away.

They hurriedly moved the Abyss Sect's disciples away as the silvery leaves that had hundreds of years old started to lose their luster and fall from the tree. They gently swayed as they fell, and the whole tree started to sway with them as huge cracks started to spread through it.

Branches that were dozens of meters long started to fall into the buildings they once covered, and the tree stopped to sway. It leaned to one side, and the curtain of red light completely faded. With a loud crack, a trunk snapped, and the tree started to break apart.

The first protector watched in horror as the gigantic tree slowly approached the ground, crushing the buildings beneath it as its humongous crown smashed against the floor.

White splinters flew in the air, reflecting the starlight that shone from above. They spread through the air, covering the heart of the city and gleaming brightly amidst a cloud of dust that rose.

A last terrifying tremor almost sent the first protector to her knees. A sepulchral silence took over Hell Keeper's City as the white splinters fell to the ground, making it seem to be covered in cinders.

The Ashen Heart tree had fallen.

A blinding light erupted and roaring, white flames bloomed like a hellish flower as the shabby house was torn apart by the explosion. The stars were obscured by the brightness, and the shadows in the area disappeared. For a moment, a white sun shone in the Outer Sect of the Abyss Sect, casting the night away.

As fast as the sun rose, however, it set. Rubble and dirt rained down on the remains of the house, leaving only fickle flames behind. Two figures were facing each other in what was once a small room. They were both kneeling, looking utterly exhausted.

A faint mist was spreading from one of the figures. A disturbing sizzle echoed as the reminiscent flames slowly died down and the mist expanded outwards. The scorching heat that had taken over the area was rapidly overwhelmed by a biting coldness.

Eventually, the mist thickened, and a faint drizzle started to fall from the sky, drenching the two figures. The pitter-pattering of the rain soon stopped, leaving only silence.

Lawrence slowly stood up, holding a saber in hand. His scarlet clothes were slowly covered in a layer of white frost as the water drenching them froze. With annoyance, he violently waved a hand. Glistening shards of ice fell onto the ground at his feet as the frost broke apart.

Rebecca followed suit, albeit with clear difficulty. Her white nightgown dried as steam formed around her. A thin streak of blood escaped through her lips, causing her to let out a raspy cough. Supporting her body with Raven, she straightened her back. Lawrence's eyes gleamed with a fierce light as he saw her managing to stay on her feet. Horrendously scarred shins could be seen beneath Rebecca's white gown. Not a single inch of skin was left unblemished on her thin legs.

"You can walk?" he asked in a chilling voice.

"Not really. This is the same technique that Daniel used for controlling his right arm," Rebecca said, wiping the blood on her lips with a shriveled hand, trying to find her balance. "At our level, it's not hard to pull off," Rebecca said dismissively. "Even though Natasha didn't get the chance to help me, the theory she came up with was more than enough."

Lawrence stood in silence for some time. A frown slowly appeared on his face as he looked at Rebecca.

"Since when?" he finally asked.

"Since the start," Rebecca answered, shaking her shoulders.

It wasn't a lie but was also not the truth. At most she could move for no more than a few minutes at a time, no matter what she tried. Horrible headaches would assault her after a while due to the straining. She had to support her upper body, and relearn how to walk by controlling every single strand of qi that remained in the broken meridians in her legs; it was in no way an easy feat.

A mind-numbing pain would course through her crippled legs at every step she took even if she was well rested, which only made the process even harder. Not only that, but a single mistake could stimulate her damaged elemental core, and her body would not be able to withstand the incoming energy.

After months of trying, Rebecca finally arrived at the conclusion that it was useless. She would never be able to properly walk again, at least not without Natasha's help, and Lars Borgin and Lawrence Meyer were making sure that such a thing would be impossible. Adding to that, even if she managed to regain her ability to walk by some miracle, she didn't know what measures the Abyss Sect would take to deal with her. She knew better than anyone the position she was in, and she knew what could happen if someone believed she was making a full recovery.

She could only accept the fact that the best for both her and Amon would be to give up, and that broke her heart day after day. A crippled Rebecca Skoller might be burdensome to her son, but one that could walk would be dangerous.

Lawrence's blank expression slowly morphed into one of rage, and Rebecca sneered inwardly. He had bought her bluff, and seeing him lose his cool was a small victory she would enjoy. Her satisfaction didn't last long, however.

She suddenly felt a surge of blazing energy coursing through her body. It spread from her dantian to all of her meridians, smoothly flowing through her arms and chest, but burning through the flesh when it reached her abdomen and legs. With damaged meridians, the energy couldn't circulate properly, and it would either accumulate and eventually explode or flow through her flesh and burn it.

Rebecca knew what the best option was, so she endured the pain and made her best efforts not to let her legs tremble. A metallic taste invaded her mouth as she felt blood surging through her throat. With a fierce expression on her face, she managed to avoid coughing blood and painfully forced herself to swallow it back.

"I knew we should have gotten rid of you and your son the moment you gave us a chance," Lawrence spoke as his expression darkened even more. His cold eyes were murderous as he spoke with pure hatred in his voice. "Lars Borgin was very hesitant in doing so for some reason, but I always knew that we should have killed you at the time."

"As if you could," Rebecca answered with a smile full of scorn. She made no effort to hide the derision in her eyes as she faced Lawrence. "If I remember well, at the time you had your tail between your legs, shivering in fear of my husband coming to finish what he started the day he left the sect."

As Rebecca slowly professed her words, Lawrence's face was completely blank. The tension he had shown before eased completely, his frown disappeared and his pursed lips relaxed. His eyes, however, grew increasingly sharper at each word that left Rebecca's mouth.

Once she was done, Lawrence simply waved his hand. The ground beneath his feet froze, and a layer of ice slowly covered everything around them within a radius of a hundred meters. Even though Lawrence could expand his influence more, he chose to condense the Frost qi he had in a smaller area, making it denser.

Rebecca took a deep breath, and let the energy leaking from her dantian freely move through her meridians in order to resist the cold. She could almost feel pity for the elemental core elders that were still lurking silently on the sidelines, trembling like leaves in a storm as the chilling cold assaulted them.

"Let's see how long you can last," Lawrence said as a forced smile broke his emotionless expression. "I wonder if you'll run out of energy or burn yourself to death first. It should be an interesting sight to watch."

Rebecca made an effort not to frown, but she knew Lawrence was right. With him covering the area in Frost qi, there was no way for her to properly replenish her own reserves. Even if she could, the strain would eventually destroy her body from the inside out.

She pulled Raven from the ground and looked at Lawrence with nothing but seriousness in her green eyes. Her body was still somewhat slanted as if she didn't find her balance yet, but somehow Lawrence couldn't help but feel a bit of awe seeing her.

That desire to fight to the end; that unwillingness to accept death... Those kinds of people were the ones he liked to fight with the most. The fire that blazed in their eyes; the energy and resolve they seemed to muster out of nowhere as they struggled...

Few things gave Lawrence more satisfaction than to put out such flames.

Rebecca stood silently as Lawrence slowly walked over. She held Raven tightly with her right hand, and the pitch-black sword was soon covered in torrid white flames. White stream billowed out from the sword as the heat clashed with the cold.

His smile slowly widened as he watched the scene. The saber in his hands started making *clanged* nonstop. It was only then that he realized his hands were trembling with excitement.

He would slowly enjoy driving Rebecca to a corner, and he would enjoy even more imagining how Lloyd Kressler would react when found out what had been done to his wife and son.

It would be an empty victory; nothing but a dull, childish move, but Lawrence didn't mind. A victory over Lloyd Kressler was a victory nonetheless. If this ruse could make Lloyd knit his brows for even a second, it would have been worth it, because Lawrence Meyer really hated Lloyd.

Amon was more and more nervous as the spirit vessel streaked through the air with its maximum speed. A terrible feeling was spreading through his chest, and he felt something slowly clenching at his heart.

The last time he felt like that was right before entering the Hellblaze Secret World, and he was afraid that his feelings would be proven right yet again. All he could do was hope he was wrong, and try to reach his mother as fast as possible.

Lya quietly watched Amon's restlessness, and she couldn't help but feel the same. Fear was slowly creeping up her mind, making her tense. If something happened to Rebecca, she wouldn't know how to react. She knew better than anyone that she would be at fault.

Boom!

Far to the north, a horrendous explosion rang. Amon's eyes widened as he saw that terrifying flash of white light pierce the skies. His expression darkened, and he turned to look at Lya.

No words were needed, for she knew what he wanted to say. She gritted her teeth, and her blue eyes shook with worry. She forced qi into the spirit vessel's core array, increasing the speed even more. The vessel would not last for long under such conditions, but she could only hope it was enough to reach Rebecca in time.

The spirit vessel swayed up and down, as it almost fell apart due to the energy overload. The sound of the wind howling at Amon's ears was almost deafening, but he somehow couldn't hear it. He felt his body numb and his senses fading. He could only hear the sounds of his increasingly fast heartbeats.

BOOM!

Another explosion rang, even fiercer than before. A second sun rose from the ground, much closer than the first one. Amon hurriedly raised his arms, protecting his face as a horrifying heat reached him. His hair stood on end, and he could feel his skin prickling as it turned red. Lya hurriedly waved her arms, casting a protective shield around him to ward off the heat.

A blast of air hit the spirit vessel, almost throwing it off course. The blazing sun was like a beacon in the north, and Amon was now sure of its location.

The world went silent again as the second sun was eventually swallowed by the darkness of the night, and the stars shone again in the sky.

Amon's golden eyes slowly went cold, and he reached to his back, unsheathing Windhowler. His hands were trembling, and the sword shook in his grip. Lya however, felt no fear coming from him. She could only feel nervousness and a rapidly increasing animosity.

"Come on, Rebecca," Lawrence complained, flicking his wrist and waving his saber.

The fresh blood that covered it flew to the ground, freezing as soon as it hit the layer of ice below Lawrence's feet. "If you were at your peak you might have given me some trouble, but this is just too disappointing."

Rebecca didn't bother answering him, trying to keep her calm despite being kneeling on the ground in clear defeat. A deep gash could be seen going from her left shoulder to her waist. Blood freely flowed from it as her chest heaved up and down. She was barely supporting herself with Raven, and her hands were starting to slip from the grip.

She clenched her teeth fiercely, forcing herself to stand up. She somehow managed to stand on her feet, but she was clearly about to fall down again.

"Guess that surprise blast was all you had in you, wasn't it?" Lawrence asked with a mocking smile on his face. "Is the pain really that much? I can't imagine how it would be to feel my insides being burned each time I used my qi. I think I would prefer death."

Rebecca couldn't help but frown with disgust. Lawrence was indeed very similar to Lloyd. It enervated her to no end.

"You're really annoying. Your tone, your stance, your attitude... You remind me too much of Lloyd," Rebecca said with a disgusted voice, turning her eyes away. Her left hand was closed tightly, and an explosive flow of qi was slowly coursing through her left arm from her dantian.

"Enough of this. You win, Rebecca. You will get what you want."

He approached her, letting the tip of his saber scrape against the ice covered ground. His steps were unhurried, and he started putting strength in his arm, making the ear-piercing sound the saber was making even louder.

Every step he took, Rebecca's grip tightened. Soon, her left hand was trembling due to the strength she was exerting, and she could feel the object she was holding digging deep inside her palm. The skin in her arm was slowly reddening, and the pain in her abdomen was unbearable. She held herself back from screaming as Lawrence stopped in front of her at arm's reach.

"You know, I will really enjoy showing your corpse to your son," Lawrence said, looking at her expression carefully, waiting to see her reaction. "I wonder what face he will make when he sees what will be left of you."

"Fuck you, Lawrence," Rebecca scoffed with a wicked smile.

She opened her left hand, revealing a small necklace with a scarlet jewel. A small dot of light floated at its center, flickering gently. It was the last gift her husband had given her, and now she was going to make full use of it.

Lawrence's eyes widened when he saw the necklace and Rebecca's smile. She felt her arm burning as she injected all of the remaining fire qi she had into the jewel at once. Not even her own body could withstand that amount of energy, even if it was flowing through intact meridians. Still, it was enough. The red light flickered, and the necklace suddenly heated up. A light crack echoed, and Rebecca closed her eyes.

The red light flashed, and the jewel exploded. A terrifying burst of energy was released at once, completely unrestrained. The accumulation of more than half a decade of fire qi that Rebecca had stored in that fire crystal had been suddenly released.

Lawrence watched in horror as that mass of energy suddenly expanded in front of his eyes, and he hastily raised his hand to protect himself. A bright light took over his vision, and for a moment, the world ceased to exist.

* * *

Lawrence coughed violently as he opened his eyes. It took him a moment to make sense of his surroundings. As soon as he recovered the least bit of consciousness, however, a fierce pain assaulted him, making him want to curl on the ground and scream.

He gritted his teeth, and slowly raised his head. His clothes were in shambles, and every inch of his body seemed to be bruised. Breathing hurt him tremendously, and he figured he had at least a few broken ribs.

He tried moving his arm to stand up, but an even fiercer pain made him gasp. He lowered his gaze, looking in shock at the right side of his body. His hand and arm were still whole, but his skin was mostly gone, and the flesh was charred to the bone. The few patches of skin that remained were either covered in horrifying blisters or shriveled beyond recognition. His fingers and legs were broken, twisted in unimaginable ways—they were in an even worse state than the rest of his arm.

Lawrence turned his head but felt his head spin. He felt the right side of his face throbbing, and a sharp pain almost made him pass out again. He slowly moved his left hand with the intention of touching his face, but ultimately hesitated. He wasn't sure if he wanted to know the real state his face was in.

If he had not hastily protected himself, the right half of his body would have been blown away, and he would certainly be dead.

He made an effort to sit down, looking around. He heard grunts coming from afar, and with a swipe of his divine sense, he confirmed the three elders he brought were still alive, even if injured.

He somehow managed to get up, supporting his body with his left leg and the saber that had fallen by his side. He was in a rather pitiful state, completely unbecoming of his status and the image he carefully cultivated over the years.

As he tried to start to move, a soft grunt caught his attention. He looked at the source of the noise, and a flash of gold caught his attention. The pain in his body immediately numbed, and his left hand started trembling with rage.

"Damn you!" Lawrence screamed with a hoarse voice, limping towards Rebecca's direction, dragging his saber with his left hand behind him.

At that moment, however, he stopped in place and hurriedly turned his head. From the skies, a black blur was streaking right into his direction.

Lawrence couldn't waste time thinking or trying to identify what it was, he could only follow his instincts and kick the ground with his left leg, jumping with all his might to the side. In the blink of an eye, the blur swept past him.

Time seemed to slow down as Lawrence recognized it as a spirit vessel. He watched in shock as the spirit vessel barely missed him, flying for a few more meters before crashing violently against the ground.

A blast of air hit him like a hammer, making him shiver in pain. A cloud of dust rose as the ground quaked due to the impact, and Lawrence nearly lost his balance.

His eyes turned cold as his instincts kicked in and he gathered his thoughts. A light breeze blew on his back, and he immediately twisted his body, avoiding a sneak attack. With a gust of wind, something brushed past him.

Lawrence raised his head, meeting a pair of golden eyes that glared at him with nothing but sheer hatred.

Following the golden eyes, a sword covered in a sharp edge of light howled through the air, making its way to his neck.

A crude sword made a simple, elegant arc as it crossed the air. The wind howled in protest as the wide blade spit it in two, covered in a layer of light so condensed it was almost solid. The blade followed its path with a terrible momentum, leaving a bright trail of starlight in its wake.

Holding the sword was a boy. His face was pale, his black clothes were in tatters and his ashen hair was a mess. Even so, his golden eyes shone with a fierce light as the boy brandished the sword.

Looking at the Amon, Lawrence Meyer felt a strange feeling welling deep inside of him. He paid the sword no mind as it made its way to his neck and, instead, looked straight at the boy's eyes. Deep in them, he saw cold hatred. He saw an unyielding fierceness. He saw primal, almost animalistic desire to kill.

His brows furrowed and dark lines creased his forehead. While facing those eyes full of emotions, his own eyes were nothing but emotionless.

Lawrence raised his saber with his left hand in a swift, fluid and precise movement. His form was surprisingly elegant as the saber in his hand seemed to come to life and tear through the air in a skyward strike.

Clang!

The saber collided with the sword with a dull, metallic sound. Sparks flew as the sword's blade rose, passing a few centimeters over Lawrence's head as his saber vibrated with a loud hum. Lawrence's frown deepened as he gripped the saber with more strength, making it stop humming. He coldly watched as Amon flew by him, eventually reaching the ground.

"Look at that, the little traitor indeed appeared to save his mother," Lawrence sneered.

Cracks spread beneath Amon's feet as he landed heavily on the charred ground. From Lawrence's words, he already could guess what had happened. Not that it would change anything. Amon would face whoever he needed to in order to get his mother out of that place safely.

He clenched his teeth, enduring the pain of the forced landing as he spun in place, sword in hand. He brandished Windhowler with all his might, aiming at Lawrence's head.

The light covering the sword flashed as the edge on it somehow turned even brighter and sharper, making one's eyes hurt. In the blink of an eye, Amon was upon Lawrence, and Windhowler appeared before his eyes.

Clang!

A saber fell from its wielder's hand with a metallic sound. It fell with its tip down, burying itself on the ground and humming as it vibrated gently.

However, neither Amon nor Lawrence bothered with it. Amon had a hard time hiding his shock, but Lawrence was still expressionless as he looked at Amon. A few centimeters away from Lawrence's head, Windhowler was still shining with sword qi, but couldn't move forward. It was stuck in place, being firmly held by a bare hand.

A soul-chilling cold started coursing through Amon's arms, coming from the sword he held. He desperately struggled to set the sword free from Lawrence's grasp, but it was in vain.

"I wonder how Daniel would feel, knowing that he died because of a traitor," Lawrence said, looking at Amon with a savage look in his eyes.

"Daniel... is dead?" Amon's eyes widened as he looked at Lawrence, and his mind went into shock.

"The stunt you pulled alongside your father in the Hellblaze Secret World was enough to make things spiral out of control," Lawrence said as his gaze grew fiercer. "Because of you, Daniel is dead, and Jake is gravely wounded."

Amon's eyes changed, and his face paled. There was no way this was the truth.

Yet... what reason was there for Lawrence to lie? Amon was already considered a traitor, and such a lie would not bring him any benefit.

Amon glanced at Lawrence's eyes intently, and his face became even paler as he realized it was very likely he spoke the truth.

Crackling sounds started echoing from Lawrence's body, and his broken fingers started twisting and turning before finally straightening as his bones fell back in place. It was a strange sight to look at, almost unbearably unnerving. Soon, even louder cracks came from his body as his right arm and leg started to move in an eerily similar way, making Amon frown.

The temperature suddenly dropped, and Lawrence's clothes dampened. He felt a refreshingly cool sensation as small droplets of water dripped down through his body before freezing in place, enclosing his charred limbs in a thin layer of ice. The layer of ice continued to grow, delicately covering the right side of his face and hiding it from view. The burning pain in his body gave way to a numbing prickling on his skin, and Lawrence gave a long sigh.

Natasha Barnes was indeed a genius. Controlling the qi inside one's body like this could serve to give movement back to crippled limbs and apply first aid care. As long as one had enough knowledge of anatomy and fine control over qi, the only real difficulty would be bearing the pain.

Indeed; at our level this is not hard, Lawrence thought.

He then looked at Amon again, who was still in place, glaring at him with those same eyes. Windhowler was still firmly grasped by Lawrence, and the temperature continued to fall steeply.

The sword started to make a disturbing sound and Amon's arms trembled as the blade was held in place. A layer of frost slowly formed on the blade, breaking apart and forming anew as the sword shook alongside Amon, and Lawrence poured more Frost qi on it. Eventually, the blade stopped trembling completely, and Amon couldn't exert more strength as his palms were already covered in frostbite.

Crack!

A thin, almost unnoticeable crack appeared on the layer of ice covering the blade, and Amon felt his heart almost stop. With a face full of hate, he let go of the sword and hastily retreated, creating a few meters of distance between him and Lawrence. Amon looked helplessly as the layer of light glowing beneath the ice slowly faded away, as if the sword was dying.

Lawrence continued to look at Amon with a blank expression as he violently closed his hand, alternating his grip on the blade into a fist. The cracks on the blade multiplied, eventually covering the whole extension of it.

CRACK!

Windhowler screamed for a moment as an ear-piercing screech echoed right before the blade finally gave in. Amon looked disgruntledly as the sword collapsed, shattering into hundreds of fragments in front of his eyes. Each piece glistened brightly, still covered in ice. Like snow, they fell on the ground at Lawrence's feet, who still didn't change his expression.

Lawrence looked at the pieces at his feet before discreetly opening his left hand. A deep gash, deep enough to reach the bone, was carved into his palm. The blood that was starting to flow through it slowly froze into red ice, sealing the wound.

Lawrence frowned as he looked at his hand. He didn't cause this wound by crushing the sword with his bare hands. He held the sword with his hand to hold it in place and give himself time to tend his wounds. He had enough experience with his body to know what it could or couldn't withstand. He almost couldn't believe it, but Amon Kressler had managed to hurt him.

Lawrence extended his hand downwards, reaching for his saber. Suddenly, he felt an overwhelming pressure bearing down on him. It wrapped around his body, crushing him. Lawrence's expression darkened as he felt the changes surrounding him. The bones in his body started to creak under the pressure, and the ice covering his wounds started to crack.

Lawrence was experienced enough to know what was happening. This was unlike Borgin's technique that increased the gravitational pull in a certain radius. This was sheer, unbridled control over qi, and Lawrence refused to give in to that. He fought back with all his might, and the pressure on him slowly started to ease, even if it was far from enough to give him back his freedom.

Amon Kressler couldn't do this. This meant there was someone else on that spirit vessel.

"Kill them!" Lawrence ordered, still fighting against the force bearing on him.

The three elemental core elders that were still recovering from the explosion grunted, but started moving. They were far from the blast and were hit mostly by the air pressure and the heat wave. Although they were injured, they could still move.

Amon snapped out of his trance, and started to move, running past Lawrence as fast as he could. His expression changed from one of animosity and hate to one full of worry as he left Lawrence and the crashed spirit vessel behind.

He couldn't let himself lose his focus. It was all that Lawrence wanted. He did his best to hold back his feelings, but his chest couldn't help but turn heavy. If this was the truth… then the fault was his for running away.

He could see it, a flash of gold far into the distance, and his focus returned. He shook his head as he accelerated further, trying to hold back the storm raging on his mind. The ground beneath his feet seemed to give in with each of his steps as he stomped the ground to try to go even faster.

The closer he got, the hotter it became. It felt as if he was approaching a wild fire rather than his collapsed mother. Each step he took seemed to make the temperature increase a dozen degrees. By the time he was by his mother's side, he was sweating profusely and his skin was red.

"Mom!" Amon called desperately as he approached the small figure lying on the ground.

She was lying on her side, with her back turned to Amon. What was left of her white gown was burnt black, and Amon could see terrible burns covering her exposed skin.

He gently approached her, putting a hand over her shoulder. The first thing Amon felt was how hot her skin was. Touching his mother was no different than putting his hand in fire. He endured the pain as he carefully rolled her onto her back.

His heart almost stopped.

Amon gasped, and his hands started trembling. Rebecca gave a muffled grunt, and barely managed to open her eyes to look at her son.

"LYA!" Amon shouted hastily as he took his mother in his arms. His eyes were open wide, and his lips were devoid of color as he tightly pursed them.

A rumble answered him as the spirit vessel crashed on the ground freed itself, raising another cloud of dust. The air rippled around it as it rose, hovering mid-air and turning.

"It's going to be fine, mom. It's going to be fine," Amon declared repeatedly, raising Rebecca in his small arms.

From the corner of his eyes, he managed to see three figures approaching at high speeds. Rebecca lightly shook in his arms, turning her head with difficulty. What remained of her golden hair fluttered gently, falling over her shoulder as she looked at something on the ground.

Amon followed her gaze, seeing a black hilt sticking out from the ground. He looked at his mother for a moment before giving a slight nod. The spirit vessel went over Lawrence's head, and the pressure on him increased again, crushing him against the ground.

The ice covering his wounds completely collapsed, breaking into pieces that were reduced to dust due to the pressure bearing around him. Lawrence grunted in pain as some of his broken bones were dislodged again and a crippling pain assaulted him.

He walked with careful, light steps, trying his best not to move his mother too much. Regardless, he tried to get her to the spirit vessel as fast as he could.

The three elders were quickly approaching, but a sudden blast of qi threw them away.

The spirit vessel was finally upon Amon. He felt a warm stream of qi gently wrapping around Rebecca and slowly lifting her from his arms with surprising care.

Seeing Rebecca's state, Lya drew in a sharp breath. She hurriedly sent qi inside her of the frail woman, trying to do her best to hold together her broken body.

Amon turned around, searching for a moment before finding Raven partially buried on the ground. He spread his divine sense, wrapping a line of qi around the sword and pulling it to his hands.

The curved sword spun through the air, whistling as it made its way to Amon's hand. Amon had a troubled look on his face as he held the black sword. He seemed to hesitate for a moment, before finally shaking his head and clearing his thoughts.

"Amon, hurry," Lya warned.

Amon turned around, holding the sword tightly.

"It's too late," a weary voice echoed from somewhere behind the spirit vessel. It was a cold, emotionless voice. Its owner was sprawled on the ground, covered in burns and wounds.

Amon stopped in place, slowly turning to look at Lawrence Meyer. There was no need for Amon to ask anything. He already knew all he needed to.

"Amon, wait!" Lya pleaded, but her voice fell on deaf ears.

Amon gazed at Lawrence with an indescribable look. His mother's state flashed in his mind as he gripped Raven tightly. He could still feel the absurd heat of her body in his arms; he could still see the overwhelming pain in her eyes.

Bright lines of qi shone on Raven's curved blade. A thin layer of light formed around the blade in the blink of an eye. Amon's hands started trembling, and the light grew brighter.

Amon remembered his first night on the Sword Abyss. The horrible feeling of being torn apart by thousands of blades, the pain of having his innards destroyed by sharp qi, the raw savagery, the overwhelming desire to murder and destroy imbued in the spiraling sword qi that remained in the Sword Abyss... That was a will strong enough to last four hundred years.

It wasn't enough.

"That look in your eyes... you're just like your father," Lawrence said in a hoarse voice full of hatred as he gazed at Amon from afar.

Yes, he knew those eyes very well. Those eyes gazed at him from above as Lawrence fell six years ago.

The light surrounding Raven suddenly churned, as if it was boiling water. It turned even more condensed, to the point of solidifying.

Shredding the body to pieces and grinding the innards to a paste wasn't enough.

Amon wanted nothing but complete annihilation. He wanted every inch of Lawrence's body to be pulverized, he wanted nothing to be left behind. He wanted to erase Lawrence Meyer's existence.

Simply killing would not be enough.

"Don't!" Lya shouted in horror as she peered into Amon's soul and saw the amount of nebula being produced.

Amon kicked the ground, and seemed to turn into a blur. A streak of light tore through the air at an unimaginable speed, like a shooting star tearing through the sky. It almost seemed to be cutting through space itself as it pushed forward with indomitable momentum.

Lawrence saw that streak of light coming to his direction, and his face changed. For the first time, he felt threatened. Still, that unbearable pressure was still holding him in place.

Suddenly, however, it disappeared. Lawrence couldn't even show confusion on his face before the ground beneath his feet rumbled and rippled like water. He looked to his side, and saw one of the elemental core elders not far from him with a hand on the ground.

As the flash of light arrived before Lawrence, the ground rippled again, and he was thrown away just as an ear-piercing trill echoed and something grazed past his body.

The flash of light suddenly stopped, revealing Amon holding Raven near the ground, having just missed his attack. He suddenly raised his eyes, looking at the elemental core elder with a chilling gaze.

He was involved. That was enough. Not only had the man saved Lawrence Meyer, he had been present when the fight broke out.

The elder looked at him with a confused, almost disbelieving expression.

Raven's sheath was nowhere to be seen. Nevertheless, Amon faced the elder and drew his sword.

The elder's hand rose and Raven descended.

Amon felt that Raven's grip was surprisingly comfortable. The blade was incredibly well balanced and incredibly sharp. The sword had no guard, but it had no need for one. It wasn't a sword made with clashes in mind. It was a sword made to be precise, swift and sharp.

It was a sword made to kill and nothing more.

A sword giving a strike would always be quicker than elemental qi. There was no need to interface with the dantian. There was no need to control the qi in the meridians. There was no need to harmonize with the elements. There was no need to overturn nature in some way.

There was no need to think, and there was no mistake to be made.

A sword strike just needed to be decisive.

The curved blade tore through the air.

It tore through qi.

It tore through fabric.

It tore through skin.

It tore through flesh.

It tore through bone.

It was surprisingly easy, surprisingly fast. Just like that, the sword was tearing through the air again.

Blood splattered on Amon as the elder fell. Amon turned to look at Lawrence, who was making an effort to stand up.

Amon separated his legs and slightly bent his knees. He pulled Raven next to his waist, never taking his eyes away from Lawrence. He drew his sword.

"Stop!" Lya shouted anxiously.

She waved her hands and countless threads of qi wrapped around Amon, dragging him to the spirit vessel.

Without giving him the chance to protest, Lya waved her hands again. The spirit vessel turned into a blur, shooting off into the distance.

"Why did you stop me!?" Amon asked, indignant, as he looked at Lya.

"I didn't want you to kill someone in such a condition," Lya answered in a hurt voice as she faced Amon.

"Bullshit! You saw what he did! YOU SAW IT!"

If the condition she referred to was his emotional state, or his use of the soulrousing technique to boost his will, it didn't matter. He knew he had every right to kill Lawrence Meyer, and she had denied him the right to do so.

He suddenly stopped in place, in shock.

He had killed a man. He had taken a life... and it had been surprisingly easy. One swing of his sword and it was over.

Amon felt nothing for killing a someone. It had been no different than what he felt during the Trial of the Heart, and that fact scared him.

His eyes widened and his hands started trembling. Why didn't he feel a thing?

A light sound interrupted his thoughts. He turned his head and faced a pair of green eyes looking at him.

"Mom!" Amon called, his voice filled with guilt.

From when Lawrence called for him to the moment Lya pulled him into the spirit vessel, only a few moments had passed. Still, Amon couldn't help but feel guilty. During those moments, he had abandoned his mother.

He hurriedly approached her, kneeling by her side. Somehow, the heat she was exuding was even stronger than before. Amon couldn't hide the worry on his face as he looked at him.

A burnt hand was extended to him, lightly touching his right hand. Amon looked at it, and suddenly realized he still had Raven in his hand.

Clang!

He dropped the sword on the floor without any regard, holding his mother's hand tenderly.

Rebecca opened her mouth, but no words came out. She started to shake on the floor of the spirit vessel. Her face distorted into one of pain, and she looked at Lya with a pleading gaze in her green eyes.

Lya's heart shook as he saw Rebecca's gaze, but she would never deny such a request. She extended a pale hand, lightly touching Rebecca's temple. Rebecca's expression eased somewhat as Lya alleviated her pain. The last thing she wanted was to suffer in front of her son.

"What is this heat?" Amon asked, confused and afraid as he held his mother's hand.

"Her elemental core is breaking apart," Lya said, hesitant. She was still trying to suppress Rebecca's injuries and she had a good grasp of what was happening.

Rebecca had overexerted herself during her clash with Lawrence. Her damaged elemental core was now collapsing, and her body was almost destroyed.

"What can we do?" Amon asked, almost shouting as he turned to face Lya.

Instead of meeting his gaze, Lya turned her face away, not knowing what to say.

"What can we do, Lya!?" Amon asked again, with an even louder voice.

His eyes were blurry, and Lya knew he was about to break down.

"I'm sorry Amon, but we can't do anything," Lya finally said with a sad voice.

"That can't be!" Amon said, holding his head in his hands. Suddenly, his face beamed. "The ring! I'm sure there must be some medicine in the inter-spatial ring to help her."

"It won't work," Lya said in a sad tone. She kept her head down, as if afraid to look Amon in the eye.

"But the medicine could help!" Amon insisted, almost bursting into tears. He was clinging desperately to anything that gave him even the slight-est hope. "The medicine could help stabilize her body. We need to find a way to stabilize the elemental core... Maybe if we slowly control the output of qi, it would run out of energy and the collapse would simply mean a loss of cultivation..."

"It won't work," Lya's voice trembled.

The elemental core itself was energy condensed in a stable, delicate structure. It couldn't run out, as it always would have itself. Even if someone spent all of the qi in their bodies, the elemental core remains unaffected. Letting it collapse would lead to an explosion of elemental qi. Trying to slowly undo the elemental core would lead to instability, and the result would still be the same.

"There must be a way! Please, we must find a way!"

Amon burst into tears as he fell into the depths of despair. The injured hand in his grasp gripped his hand tightly. Amon turned his head, looking at his mother as tears streamed down his face.

Rebecca opened her mouth, but, yet again, no words came out. She was clearly frustrated, and her eyes showed a hint of despair. Lya hurriedly closed her eyes, concentrating.

Amon lowered his head, sobbing desperately.

Rebecca's faint voice finally made its way to his ears.

"Don't worry."

Amon hurriedly raised his head, facing her again.

"Don't say that," Amon said desperately. "Please, don't say that."

"Don't cry," Rebecca said as her green eyes became blurry with tears too. "I never liked seeing you hurt."

"What should I do without you?" Amon asked between sobs, hugging her tightly. "What can I do?"

"You can do whatever you want. But there is something you need to always keep in mind," Rebecca said with a voice so weak it was almost a whisper.

"What?" Amon asked, trying to control his sobs.

"Never forget our promise," she said, giving him a smile full of warmth.

Silently nodding, Amon replied, "I won't," as he wiped a rush of tears from his face.

Amon tightly hugged his mother, ignoring the heat that was unbearable at this point.

"I love you, mom. I don't want you to go," Amon said, trying hard not to cry again.

"I love you too, son," Rebecca answered gently, ruffling his hair with her hand and closing her eyes. She also didn't want to go, but she couldn't say it.

Deep inside, she was feeling as much despair as Amon. She couldn't stand the thought of never watching him grow. She couldn't stand the thought of causing him pain. She couldn't stand the thought of leaving him alone.

Yet all she could do for his sake was to put up a brave front and try her best to not upset him even more. She really wanted to cry.

Amon didn't know how long it passed. It could've been seconds or minutes. For him, it seemed to be hours, and at least he was thankful for it.

Eventually, the ruffling of his hair stopped, and he closed his eyes, tightening his hug even more as he sobbed silently. The heat transformed into a roaring flame, but he still refused to open his arms.

His clothes were burned away, the frontal part of his body was covered in blisters and his skin was starting to rupture. Still, he didn't open his arms.

Only when he felt the weight on his arms lightening did he open them, looking desperately at the white ashes flying away from his arms. They slipped through his fingers, dancing in the wind and glistening like snow under the moonlight, already beyond his reach.

He looked at Hell Keeper's Mountain on the horizon and at the specs of ash fluttering away from his grasp.

There was nothing left.

He cried loudly. He couldn't hold it back anymore.

He cried for Daniel. He cried for his mother. He cried for himself. At some point, he didn't know for whom to cry anymore, yet the tears continued falling.

He eventually closed his eyes, wondering when it all had gone wrong.

Was his mistake in the Hellblaze Trials? Would things have turned out differently had he stayed behind?

Was it the Season of Rigor? Had he drawn too much attention to himself?

Was it the Scavenging?

He had forgotten it. He shouldn't have, but he did.

The excitement of finally finding hope in his path of cultivation, the drive to find the strength to protect himself and not put others in danger, the will to become strong enough just to be happy... It had blinded him. It had given him hope.

Now, he had paid the price for it.

Amon turned his head, looking at Lya.

For the first time, he felt regret in having met her. He felt regret in asking her for help.

Had he not started cultivating, had he accepted his fate, none of this would have happened.

Yet... It had happened.

The furious rage burning in his chest, the sorrow sinking on his mind... it wouldn't go away.

Nor would the people that cause all that.

"I WILL KILL ALL OF YOU!" Amon shouted to the skies as his tears fell once more. He punched the spirit vessel with all his strength, making it tremble.

Something broke.

In the night sky, a solitary star slowly rose, joining countless others in a river made of starlight that seemed to have no beginning and no end.

Lya didn't know what to say as she looked at Amon in such pain and misery. In truth, she didn't know if she had the right to say anything. Her eyes were filled with mixed emotions. She felt guilt, sorrow, and rage, but she felt regret the most.

If those emotions were aimed at Amon of herself, only she knew. She peered into his soul, and something she saw made another emotion show in her eyes.

It was fear.

Amon continued punching the spirit vessel, and his knuckles, already covered in blisters, ruptured. A small pool of blood was forming beneath Amon's fist as the spirit vessel's floor slowly caved in and his screams of rage and pain echoed through the night.

Above him, a waxing moon gave a devilish grin.

Yes, he had forgotten it, and he was a fool for that.

This world was hell.

In the Shadows, a Sword Rises

I t was a very cramped room, even somewhat shabby. Simple furniture adorned it, waiting for guests that usually never came. This day, however, there were two people in the room, both refusing to take a seat and quietly waiting next to a wide wooden door. Even though the room was well lit, one could still see the bright light shining through the door cracks.

One of the people quietly waiting in the room was a red-haired boy. His face was somewhat pale, his hair was disheveled, his clothes were messy and clear hand marks could be seen on his neck, already turning blue. Even though he was bored, he showed nothing but respect on his face as he silently waited for his chance to cross the doors.

By his side was a stern man. He was covered in black from head to toe, and his sharp features showed no expression at all. He stood completely still, like a statue, as he patiently waited to be called. His hands were behind his back, hidden inside a black cape that draped over his shoulders.

His right hand slowly rubbed a silver chain on his wrist, where a single blood-red bead could be seen hanging from. As the man's fingers rubbed against the chain, his cold eyes glinted with a strange light for a moment. His thoughts were inscrutable, but his hands never stopped rubbing the chain. It was as if something was bothering him, or something was missing.

Beside him, a bright green sword glowed faintly as it lay next to the door. A red gem fitted on the hilt shone ominously with a flickering, almost hypnotic light.

"I hope this doesn't take too long," the red-haired youth gave a sigh, somewhat agitated.

"I don't think it will. Master seemed to be quite mad at her," the man answered lightly.

"Well, from what I heard she did screw up big time," the youth commented. "I'm actually feeling a bit of pity for her."

The man returned to his usual silence. Somehow, his gaze seemed to waver for a moment. His hand never left the silver chain on his wrist.

"A pair of fools," a charming, melodious voice echoed in the room. "You don't understand Master at all."

* * *

The sun shone brightly in the azure sky. The vibrant blades of green grass that grew on a small garden gently swayed as a comfortable breeze blew. A small table had been set in the garden in front of a crystalline pond. A few koi carps swam peacefully in the pond, rousing small ripples on the glistening water. Above the table, the steam rising from a green teapot billowed with the breeze, quickly dispersing in the air.

It was a very refreshing day, one that anyone could enjoy. A refined man quietly sat with his back turned to the table as he gazed at the pond with a serene expression. His green robes fluttered, and he closed his brown eyes to enjoy the cool feeling on his skin as it was gently caressed by the breeze.

Eventually, the breeze stopped, and the man sighed. He ran his fingers through his brown hair, thinking as a tired expression showed on his face. He slowly turned his back to the pond, facing the other side of the table.

There, a young couple sat on the grass. One of them was a boy with blond hair and handsome features. He had a confused look on his face, and he didn't seem to know the situation. In truth, he didn't even know exactly where he was nor the identity of the man in front of him. He gave quick glances to his left side, but the girl he was trying to communicate with didn't seem to notice.

Her silky, black hair cascaded down her back, swaying nonstop as the girl trembled. Her beautiful face was tense, and her small hands were closed tightly on fists above her knees and hidden by the table. Her terror-filled eyes welled up with tears as she tried to remain quiet.

"You know, the tea is quite good," the man in green robes said with an amicable smile. He took the green teapot with both hands and served the green tea inside it on three porcelain cups that were lying on the table.

The boy opened his mouth to say something, but the girl promptly sent him a warning glance, making him even more confused. As he hesitated, he felt a warm current blowing past him, and the smile of the man sitting on the other side of the table became gentler. The boy couldn't help but smile too.

He politely extended his hands, accepting a cup. He carefully blew on the tea before taking a sip. His eyes immediately lit up and his expression eased. This was indeed quite a good tea.

Seeing this, the fear in the girl's eyes was clearer, but she found no choice other than to accept it. She slowly extended her trembling hands, carefully raising her eyes to look at the cup in front of her. The tea started churning as the cup shook in her hands, but she didn't dare spill a single drop. She slowly took a sip before putting the cup back on the table.

The boy continued to enjoy the tea as the girl lowered her gaze again. The man watched it all with a calm expression, holding his cup with his right hand and closing his eyes as he carefully drank the tea. After some time, he finally broke the silence.

"You know why you're here, don't you, Emma?" he asked with a calm voice as he slowly put his cup down.

The girl's body jolted and her fists tightened even more, but she still hesitantly nodded her head, never looking at the man's eyes.

"Good, that saves me the trouble," the man said, closing his eyes and massaging his temple with his left hand as if trying to ease a headache.

"What is your name?" he asked, looking at the blond boy with a gentle expression. His voice was somehow very charming and calming. Even so, the boy somehow couldn't look at the man in the eye.

"My name is Robert, sir," the blond boy said respectfully and giving a slight bow.

"That is a nice name," the man said, nodding slightly. "What do you think of Emma, Robert?"

"I think she is a wonderful girl," Robert answered immediately. "She is beautiful, smart and very gentle."

"I have to agree. I think she would make for a wonderful wife," the man said as a small smile crept up his face.

Hearing his words, Emma's body jolted again and her body started shaking even more. She closed her eyes tightly and pursed her lips.

"Well, Robert, you might not know this, but Emma already had a marriage arranged for her," the man said slowly as his expression became serious.

Hearing his words, Robert shuddered, before taking a deep breath. He opened his mouth to say something, but the taste of the tea suddenly strengthened, and his mind grew muddier.

"I didn't know of this, sir," he answered honestly.

"Even though you didn't know, you have to take responsibility, don't you?" the man asked, slowly standing up.

"Sir, I..." Robert's face paled as he looked over at Emma, and the taste of the tea resurfaced on his tongue. "There's no way I could have known."

"Ignorance is a sin, you know," the man spat, turning his back to the couple and looking at the pond again. "A very grave offense was made, and someone must be punished for it."

Robert's face paled even further, and he slowly started to back away. Something about the man seemed to change, and Robert's senses started screaming at him to run away as fast as he could. He felt cold all over, and somehow he felt his skin prickling, as if small needles were hitting it.

Emma bit her lip before finally standing up and raising her head. Her body was still shaking, and her eyes were still full of fear, but her hesitation seemed to vanish completely.

"If someone must be punished it should be me!" She said with no hesitation. "Robert didn't know, so he can't be blamed."

The man slowly turned around, facing Emma with a dark expression.

"Do you agree with that, Robert?" he asked with a complex look on his face.

Robert stopped in place. He was already scared out of his mind. Looking at the man made shivers run down his spine, despite the man having the same gentle demeanor as ever. Robert couldn't understand what was happening, and his mind raced.

The man's voice started echoing in his head, asking the same question again and again. Robert's mind muddied again, and he couldn't help but voice the truth.

"I... I think that is fair," he spoke, shaking like a leaf.

The man sighed, and sat down again, pouring himself more tea.

"Punishment will be dealt, then."

Emma lowered her head and closed her eyes. Shiny tears started streaming down her delicate face as she waited for the inevitable. Emma turned her head away while closing her eyes with all of her might. She hastily covered her ears, but she knew it wouldn't be enough.

Tap.

The man lightly tapped with a finger on the table. A swift wind brushed past Emma. Something fell loudly on the ground. Emma sobbed silently, and the man gave another sigh before drinking the tea in his cup.

He didn't bother Emma, quietly drinking his tea as he waited for her to calm down. When her tears finally dried out, he gave her a gaze filled with pity and empathy. He extended his hands, taking her cup and discarding the tea that had already cooled down.

"I'm sorry," he said, pouring another serving of tea into her cup and offering it to her. "I did give him a chance. Unfortunately, no one outside our Fallen Sword Sect might know of this place. To be clear, I have no problems with it. You can marry whoever you want—it's your right," the man said, clearly disappointed. "The heart of the matter is that you've already accepted the marriage I arranged on your own, and then you threw it out the window without telling me first. You have no idea how much trouble this has caused me, and the consequences that could have ensued.

"That was a betrayal, Emma," he continued with a stone cold expression. He leaned forward, slowly approaching his face to the girl's as he glared at her like a beast. "You know that, don't you?"

The girl felt her knees giving in, and she fell to the ground as her face became deathly pale.

"Even so, I still gave him a chance, because I understand what went through your mind," the man continued, looking very disappointed. "All I can do is to hope for you to choose better next time. I mean, look at him. He didn't step forward even once to defend you."

"You didn't give him the chance!" Emma cried out.

"I made sure he would speak what was truly on his mind, only that. The last thing I want is for you to be betrayed by someone you love."

His aura suddenly rose and his refined appearance gave way to overwhelming power, and he suddenly looked more like a primordial beast than a human.

"I will never let those I care about suffer such a fate, even if I have to break their hearts again and again.".

The ground rumbled and a violent gale swept through the garden, throwing the cups on the grass that swayed madly. The water in the pond churned wildly as if it was trying to burst out. The koi carps were nowhere to be found—they had been hiding in fear for a long time.

"I'm sorry, master," Emma finally said, breaking down in tears again.

The aura suddenly disappeared. The water in the pond calmed down, the gale quickly dispersed and the ground stopped rumbling. The man waved his hand, and the fallen cups and teapots promptly returned to the table.

"It is fine as long you understand," he said after calming himself. "Go on and tell Lloyd to come in."

Emma gave him a deep bow, with her face still covered in tears before turning away. She avoided looking in a specific direction, as if afraid of what might be there. The man waved his hands, and a raging flame crept up in a corner of the garden, on the place the girl refused to look at.

"Emma," the man called before the girl walked out of his view.

Emma stopped in place and slowly turned to face him.

"Never betray me again," the man said in a voice that made her soul tremble in fear.

She quickly gave him another bow, before running away. The flames died down, and with another wave of the man's hand, a sudden wind threw the remaining ashes away from his view.

He sat down again, pouring another cup of tea for himself. Yet, he didn't drink it. His mood had been spoilt, and his brows slowly started to furrow.

He heard light footsteps approaching and, without looking up, signaled for the newcomer to sit by the table.

Lloyd Kressler gave a deep bow before taking a seat. The green sword in his hands suddenly floated up before flying into the green-robed man's direction.

The man skillfully grabbed the sword with his left hand, and gently put its tip on the ground, letting the table support the hilt. A beautiful green-haired woman appeared out of thin air, also greeting the man with a deep bow.

"Master," she said respectfully without raising her head.

"Report," the man commanded.

"Our primary mission was a success. Well, more than that, to be honest," the woman said in her bewitching voice as she slowly met the man's gaze. "Still, most of the secondary objectives were a failure."

"Oh?"

"We successfully infiltrated the Hellblaze Secret World and stole the treasure vault. We also managed to capture the Moonchaser Wolf. The Hellblaze Secret World is no more," Oura explained.

"Nevertheless, we failed to secure the Vermilion Token. It was confirmed that one of the competitors has it, but we couldn't identify who. Not only that, Reynard failed in his mission of killing Jake Meyer and we can't say for sure how well we actually managed to rile up the cardinal sects against the Abyss Sect," she said with a regretful tone.

"What happened?" the man asked lightly.

"Lars Borgin and Nemeus managed to breach the spatial seal sooner than expected. We had to send the competitors away so Reynard and Joshua could continue the plan without being put at risk by the fight. We thought that letting the competitors see Lars being defeated would not fare well to the plan, so we could only let them go," Lloyd gave a second bow as he answered. There was no trace of scorn or disdain on his face, only respect.

"I assume that Reynard failed because he was interrupted," the man muttered to himself, pondering deeply. "How did Lars Borgin breach the seal before the expected time?"

"The Moonchaser Wolf had... help," Oura hesitated somewhat before answering. She knew how sensitive this topic was, even if Lloyd had no idea. "You were right. The sword reported being in Amon Kressler's possession was indeed Brightmoon."

"Furthermore, we had no choice but to let the boy escape with the sword. The Moonchaser Wolf decided that his escape was a priority, so we had to let them go in order to give Reynard and Joshua a chance," she concluded, showing uncertainty in her eyes.

"It doesn't matter. It was only personal interest, and wasn't related to the plan in any way."

Lloyd didn't seem to notice anything wrong, but the man's words made Oura sigh in relief.

"Still... I find it very likely that the Vermilion Token is in Amon Kressler's possession," the man said after thinking for a while. If Lya was involved, then the Moonchaser Wolf would have most likely given the Vermilion Token to her.

"I think so too. Joshua managed to get his hands into Jake Meyer's bottomless pouch, but the Vermilion Token wasn't there. Reynard as well thinks that the boy would be the second most likely to have received it after Jake, although I have no idea how he would reach such a conclusion," Oura nodded her head in agreement.

"Reynard is indeed very impressive. He can piece together a fleshed out conjecture with little to no information," the man assured with a satisfied smile. "Maybe this failure will help him grow. He's not very familiar with defeat, no matter how small it might be."

The man's eyes glinted with a fierce light. Sometimes, defeat was the best teacher one could have. It was a lesson he had been taught the hard way.

"Well, I assume you managed to get your hands on Crimsonroar?" the man asked as a cold smile appeared on his face.

Lloyd reached inside his clothes, retrieving a metallic bracelet. He carefully put it on the table in front of the man.

"Good. Very good indeed," the man complimented as a strange expression appeared on his face.

"I'll be leaving Emma in your care. I believe she needs to learn a thing or two about loyalty. Plus, her talent is quite exceptional, even though her mindset isn't quite satisfactory yet. I hope you can help her with that," the man requested as he looked back to the pond. "Tell Joshua that I will speak with him tomorrow."

The man stopped speaking, as if he suddenly remembered something.

"My condolences," he said in a soft tone.

"There is no need to worry, master," Lloyd assured. "I just feel it's a pity."

"I see," the man nodded. "You may go."

Lloyd gave the man a third bow and promptly turned to leave. His dark clothes swayed behind him as he made his way out of the garden.

The woman looked at the man with a slightly unsatisfied expression, and her amber eyes shone with disappointment.

Seeing this, the man gave a small laugh, before extending an arm to the woman.

"You did very well, Oura," he said with a smile.

An elated hissing sound was made, and the woman's figure distorted, transforming into a small snake. Its green scales glowed with a strange light, and its amber eyes hid immeasurable power, but the small snake happily coiled around the green-robed man's arm and rubbed its head against his shoulder. The man naturally felt no real weight on his arm or shoulder, it was as if an air current had wrapped around his arm rather than a snake.

"Now then, what to do," the man muttered to himself, looking at the pond.

"Are you thinking about the Storm Peak Sect?" Oura asked, tilting her triangular head.

"Indeed. Though, I'm quite surprised. I would've never guessed that the baby dragon would already have grown claws," the man said as his smile widened.

"I still can't believe that he managed to kill Thomas and Helen by himself," Oura lamented.

"That was just the result. What impressed me was that he actually managed to get information from us," the man said as a fierce fire burned in his eyes. "To think that Drace would betray us like that..."

"He had what was coming for him. I can't imagine what went through his mind at his last moments. He had no idea that Joshua was one of us," Oura said as if trying to comfort the man. "Having their death further our plans is how a traitor should be dealt with."

"It doesn't matter," the man said as his eyes flickered with madness. "Traitors will be crushed, the cardinal sects will fall into our hands and the Abyss Sect will be burnt to the ground."

"We are about to take control of the Noan River Sect. The Storm

Peak Sect will eventually fall too, even though that kid managed to cause some trouble," the man continued as the fire in his eyes grew brighter and brighter. "After that... all that will be left is the Southern Flame Sect."

"If there is someone that can make things interesting I will welcome them with open arms." His smile widened even more. "Derek Tyrell, was it... He will make a wonderful stepping stone for Reynard."

He closed his eyes for a moment. He completely emptied his mind as he started thinking. After a while, he opened his eyes again, and the fire in them was almost unbearable to look at.

"Oura, have Fafnir seize control of the Crystal Mines of the Southern Continent. It is about time we opened a rift between the guardian clans of the south and the east. Even if the Vermilion Queen and the Azure Monarch don't bite the bait, having doubts creeping up in their clans will be enough."

"What about the Vermilion Token?" Oura asked.

"Although it's not essential, it will speed things up in the Southern Flame Sect considerably. Even though I hate to admit that, that annoying bird is tough to deal with," the man pondered for a moment. "Have our people in the Southern Continent keep an eye out for the Vermilion Token. Reynard will return the detection amulet we gave him, make as many copies as necessary."

Oura gently nodded, but suddenly seemed to hesitate. She gave the man a gaze filled with uncertainty, unsure on how to proceed.

"You can ask me, Oura, even though I can guess what's on your mind," the man said, holding his hands behind his back. Even so, his expression darkened considerably.

"Why didn't you ask Lloyd about his son?" Oura finally asked. "I mean, if his son was talented enough to enter the Hellblaze Trials we could certainly make use of him."

"I didn't ask because I already knew the answer. I allowed it then, so I can't really bring it up now. If this turns out to be a mistake, then I can only do my best to fix it at a later time."

"So you won't go after them within the Southern Continent?"

"No," the man answered simply, seemingly very calm.

His hands trembled slightly as he exerted more force into them. After a moment, however, the trembling stopped.

"All in due time, Oura," he said after a while. "I already waited for four hundred years; I can wait for a few more."

"I can't let my emotions ruin my plans." Hell was let loose, and the man's face slowly distorted into a bizarre smile. "When the time is right, I'll go after them. Then you'll truly see how traitors should be dealt with," Dale Loray vowed, raising his eyes to the sky.

Far above him, way beyond reach, a starry river silently flowed. No one could tell where it began, nor where it ended. The old soul cultivators used to say that it was a river as old as time, and that, as long as there was life being created and death ending it, the river would continue to flow on.

For most, it would be forever impossible to do more than to quietly observe it from below.

For a few others, it was simply a matter of taking a leap of faith.

This story has been brought to you by

MoonQuill is a story-hosting platform home to original novels. Its stories can be found on its website, Moonquill.com.

Join our mailing list for free e-book codes, audiobook codes, and updates on new releases!
https://mailchi.mp/c615f2d70c73/moonquill

Made in the USA
Las Vegas, NV
28 April 2021

22142797R00245